JULIE SWIFT

Rara Avis

Rara Avis

Julie Swift

ISBN (Print Edition): 978-1-54395-536-1

ISBN (eBook Edition): 978-1-54395-537-8

© 2018. All rights reserved. No part of this publication may be reproduced, distributed, or transmitted in any form or by any means, including photocopying, recording, or other electronic or mechanical methods, without the prior written permission of the publisher, except in the case of brief quotations embodied in critical reviews and certain other noncommercial uses permitted by copyright law.

To Karen.

A thing of beauty is a joy forever. Its loveliness increases; it will never pass into nothingness...

—Keats

CHAPTER ONE

March 15, 1891

Michael Callahan stood on the deck of the steamship *City of New York*, a glass of champagne in his hand. He was watching New York distance itself from him, and in kind, he raised his glass to meet Lady Liberty's torch. "To the pursuit of happiness," he toasted, taking a rueful swig. "Funny how I have to go to England to find it." Then the young man stood and waited for the melancholy to set in, for his second thoughts on leaving. But after several minutes, all Michael felt was excitement about the voyage ahead. After all, nothing could be worse than what he was leaving behind—a life of falsehoods. Even Jeffrey seemed a hindrance of sorts, now. Michael smiled. *Nobody knows me in England. I can be someone else, even!* Then his smile became a grin. *I can be myself.*

March 22, 1891

Dear Jeffrey,

Well, I am in Merry Olde England! I arrived this morning and found a temporary residence until I get to know London a bit better. Guess what? I picked up a paper and you won't believe who is lecturing at Redwall in two *days: Henry Sewell! It is going to cost a small fortune to attend, but if I can meet him, I'm sure he'll give me a job. I shall write you all about it! I wish you were here to attend with me. Wish me luck.*

Sincerely,

Michael

Friday evening, Michael prepared for the evening lecture. He could hardly believe his luck. —Henry Sewell, the architect Michael admired most.! He had read everything he could about the man and coveted the drawings he had copied from books that illustrated some of Mr. Sewell's buildings. Henry Sewell was considered the most modern man in architecture, for more than anyone else, he detested the gothic revival and Queen Anne styles that were rapidly spreading through England. Some men placed Henry in the burgeoning Arts and Crafts movement at first for this reason, but the only thing he really had in common with the group was that they both found the current Victorian design repugnant. As a means of further separating himself from any established movement, Henry realized he ought to create his own, and he found it at the age of twenty-five, in a request from a friend to redecorate his home. Henry walked into the house, stripped it down to the bare walls, and painted everything white. He then used only three colors throughout the entire house: green, gold, and blue (though varied shades of each were permitted), and allowed no more than fifteen objects per room, including the furniture and decorations. Finally, one object in each room was designated superior to the rest, be it the oldest, the rarest, the most expensive, or the most treasured. This object was the *rara avis*, Latin for "rare bird." From this singular house, Henry created his design theory: In order to fully appreciate the truly remarkable objects man owns, he must strip the setting in which the objects are present. Therefore, every room shall be decorated sparsely, and all items in the room must be of supreme quality and design. Most importantly, there will be one item in every room that stands apart from all others: the Rara Avis. Henry quickly moved on from renovating interiors to creating exteriors that matched his aesthetics. His homes were absent the gingerbread trim, gables, turrets, clapboard siding, and mansard roofs so popular in the day. In their place were simple box shapes that featured floor-to-ceiling windows and arches inside and out. Henry, an enthusiastic early adherent of the new Portland cement-reinforced stucco, used the white material to cover the outside of the home, making it truly stand out from its neighbors, for better or for worse. This rebellious style was considered egregious by most people, yet for this show of defiance, Henry was rewarded. Like his contemporary in art, Claude Monet, Henry was declared heretical in his ideas but praised by his critics and, perhaps most importantly, eventually truly *loved* by the wealthy population, enough to make vast sums off their commissions. And yet it was a movement so severely limiting that even twenty years later no other professional architects subscribed to it. Michael was proud to think of himself as being the first. He was a fervent believer in the Rara Avis design although even he had trouble keeping faith to it utterly, particularly the three-color limitation. Still he identified with the movement and followed most all of the tenets in his designs. His professors predicted he would be pivotal in making the movement a credible one. Although Michael doubted Henry had heard of him yet, he knew he was still the one best placed to meet him that night at Redwall and ask for a job.

At 7:15 p.m. sharp, Michael left for the auditorium, carefully dressed and overly excited. While on the ship he had decided to shave off his mustache and was quite happy with his new look. Now, as he rode through the darkened London streets, he rehearsed his opening lines.

Michael arrived to find the expansive auditorium full of people. He was dismayed. Though he had paid good money for a seat seven rows from the stage, he realized meeting Mr. Sewell would prove more difficult than he thought. But when the man himself emerged, Michael's spirits rose. Henry Sewell was far more handsome than Michael could have hoped. The architect cut an imposing figure, and not just because of his tall stature. Henry's suit was made of fine black wool, with a charcoal-colored silk vest and black pearl buttons. His shoes were barely broken in, and they shone as the cuffs rested just so on them. His sandy brown hair was combed back yet tousled in a sort of playful way, and he tilted his chin up to affect a look of mild arrogance. He had heavy-lidded hazel eyes, and an assertive mouth that was currently forming a smug smile. He had just turned forty-one, and Michael marveled at how much experience the man must have, both professionally and otherwise. He began to relax as he realized that his plan to flirt his way into a job with Henry Sewell would come off very naturally indeed.

Quickly he found himself absorbed by the great architect's oratory skills and the content of his lecture, taking pages of notes. During the final part of the presentation, Michael reluctantly stole out of the hall, went around to the back doors, and waited.

Twenty minutes later, Henry emerged, and Michael prayed that his information about the man's "inclinations" was correct. "Isn't it ironic that a man of contemporary architecture should have to exit through such archaically monstrous doors?"

Henry turned his attention toward the American accent and saw a well-dressed young man leaning casually against the wall, hands in pockets. The boy gazed at him with a knowing smile. Henry looked at him, interested. "It is an irony indeed. Do I know you?"

Michael continued to smile. "You may select one of two choices: 'No, you don't, but someday my name will be next to yours in architectural history.'" He tipped his hat. "Good night. Or, 'No, you don't, but introductions can be arranged in the next hour.'" He removed his hat. "Good evening."

Henry stared. "You were at the lecture. Why, you're the boy who left!"

"Only to meet you," Michael replied, his tone laconic but his heart starting to race. Mr. Sewell had noticed him! He regarded the doors once more and sighed in disgust. "Gothic and Greek. An atrocity, I assure you."

Henry took a full look at the seducer before him: golden-fair skin, a slender nose, and a pair of imperious eyebrows framing amber eyes.

Michael's thick, burnished-blond hair was just barely tucked behind his ears, and it ended in soft waves at his nape. Henry had planned to attend his club tonight, where he'd no doubt find a boy to take home for the evening. But the young man standing before him offered a far more interesting, though admittedly dangerous, choice. "There's room," he said simply, and the steward opened the door. Michael coolly regarded the hansom as if it had been called for him, and stepped inside, Henry following.

As the carriage moved along, Michael said nothing, letting Henry take him in. Then he turned his head and gave Henry a penetrating look.

I can have you.

But Henry merely blinked. "Where are you staying, Mr....?"

"At the Sheffield."

Henry raised his eyebrows. "You're here temporarily?"

Michael smiled. "I'm at the Sheffield temporarily. Until I can locate a more permanent residence." Then he asked earnestly, "Mr. Sewell, where do you suppose is the ideal place to live in London?"

Henry chuckled. "You mean, besides my own house?"

Michael smiled. "I was thinking in terms of myself."

So was I, Henry almost replied, but he congratulated himself on his restraint. Then he frowned. "You're planning to permanently reside in London?"

"Yes." Michael turned his head back to the window and smiled. "Although I hear Paris is supposed to be more... forgiving." He stole a glance at Henry, who leaned on his cane.

"Have you any sisters?"

A shadow fell across Michael's face. "I have two," he said flatly.

"Ah. That would explain how you've perfected the art of coquetry."

Michael looked at him sharply. "Anything perfect about me, Mr. Sewell, is by my own design."

"Well then! I shall hand you full credit for your perfectly awful display of manners! Presumably it has to do with your being American, but you've breached even the most lax form of etiquette by engaging me in conversation without giving so much as your first name."

Michael tilted his head, amused. "I see it is a first for you."

Henry snorted. "Of course not! However, seeing as you claim to be an architect of some measure, it would be silly not to wonder about your identity. And it still makes you very rude."

Michael laughed. "Heaven forbid one should be rude in the hansom of Mr. Sewell." He extended his hand and locked eyes with Henry. It would be the first time he uttered his chosen new name for himself. "Colin Edwards."

Henry shook his head, knitting his brow. "Edwards? Edwards... I don't believe I've heard the name."

Colin smiled. "I'm sure few American names make it across the Atlantic."

Henry shook his head. "Well, I've heard of Burnham, Hunt, McKim, Callahan... that sort."

Colin's eyes widened. "You've heard of Michael Callahan?"

"Well, yes. He's that student who's supposedly the new me."

Colin nodded excitedly. "He is! I... I'm actually a contemporary of his!"

Henry studied him. "Really? You're a student at MIT?"

"I was. Not anymore. I'm here now."

Henry narrowed his eyes. "You dropped out of school to come here?"

Colin gave a wry smile. "My choice in that matter was decided for me, unfortunately."

Henry grew more curious. "If you were recently a student, then you must be nineteen? Twenty?"

"On the 30th of April I'll be exactly twenty years younger than you, Mr. Sewell."

"You know my age?"

"Of course," Colin smiled. "I know everything about you." He turned back to look out the window. "You may quiz me later, if you like."

"Not now?"

Colin continued to gaze outwards, his expression darkening. "No, Mr. Sewell. Not now."

By this time Henry was quite taken with this mysterious, impudent character. When they entered his home, Henry was pleased to see Colin utterly absorbed in the slightest details of decoration. After drinks were served, he sat down to appraise the appraiser.

Colin was a full head shorter than Henry, but he also held his head high in regal fashion, and he had excellent posture. Being an architect, Henry had an especially keen eye for proportion, and he had quickly deemed Colin's features perfect, from his smooth forehead (the very definition of *highbrow,* Henry mused) to his well-defined chin. He also admired Colin's lightly tanned complexion, so different from the pearlescent skin of the British. And then there was the boy's deliciously curvaceous mouth, which delivered forth words in a fascinating accent. Henry loved unique qualities in people, and he had never before met an American this young, this educated, and most importantly, this available. For unbeknownst to the new lad, Henry had been searching for someone like him for several months now. He hadn't told anyone yet, out of fear of appearing desperate, but Henry Sewell was looking for a mistress.

Mistresses were a mark of status in the society of the upper-crust regular fellows, and Henry believed the same would hold true in his own. It was a novel idea, spurred by the fact that Henry was finally getting tired of the routine that had been his for the past twenty years: take boys home, let them stay around a few days, and then get rid of them. It had suited him perfectly until now.

Lately Henry found himself craving possession, and he wondered if it was perhaps because he hadn't a wife or children to call his own. Never mind that he wasn't married; he didn't want a mistress in the truest sense of the word. He mainly desired a pretty young thing who belonged to only him and who he could show off to others. One could argue that all he was really in search of was a beau, a "sweetheart." But "mistress" had a much more thrilling sound to it, one that matched his reputation for being envied by his peers (a reputation Henry had steadily cultivated over the years). In fact, Henry thought the word "courtesan" was even better. For like a royal courtesan, his ideal boy would be smart, beautiful, and of course, sexually savvy. Unfortunately, such a young man was proving difficult to find. Henry already knew the boys at his club several times over; they were too familiar for him to make such an offer. Others he met appeared too louche: boys that eager to please were often from the street, a class Henry refused to touch. He wanted his boy well-bred and self-sufficient, yet dependent in some way on Henry. So, one can only imagine the opportunity that Mr. Colin Edwards was affording Henry this very moment.

At last, Henry found his voice. "Colin Edwards is a very Irish and British name. How did you come by it?"

Colin examined a painting on the wall. "My mother is Irish. My father is English. What painting is this?"

"It's a Bouguereau. *Evening Mood*. It was exhibited at the 1882 Salon."

"It's stunning."

"It is, isn't it? I'm glad you like it. Now do tell about your parents, Mr. Edwards."

Colin turned and faced Henry, smiling. "I would be happy to, if they were currently in favor with me."

"So you ran away," Henry deduced, somewhat condescendingly.

Colin sighed in minor irritation and fixed upon another objet d'art. "My parents no longer wanted me."

"They disowned you?"

Colin gave a laugh. "It was me who did the disowning."

"Well, what, did you break some sort of law? Have I unwittingly permitted a criminal to my quarters?"

Colin walked toward the sofa. "I don't think you do anything 'unwittingly,' Mr. Sewell." Then he sat down next to Henry and gazed at him. "The law I broke was a moral one, not a civil one."

"Is that so?" Henry murmured, tracing Colin's jawbone with the back of his hand.

Colin lowered his head so that his lips were on Henry's hand. "Yes," he whispered looking at his mentor.

Henry replaced his hand with his mouth, but in a few moments, Colin gently pushed him back. "I see we're both from the same school," he smiled. "And we could both do with some restraint."

Henry looked incredulous. "Restraint! Whatever for?"

Colin gazed at him. "Henry, everything I do is in deliberation. You won't have me in one night. Or two."

"Really!" Henry exclaimed. "And just how long a wait do you think you're worth, Mr. Edwards?"

Colin smiled. "A fortnight."

"A fortnight!" Henry stood up. "Mr. Edwards, I don't care if you're Prince Albert himself! Do you think you're the first amateur draftsman to try to cross my path and win a job out of me?"

Colin angrily leapt to his feet. "I'm not an amateur draftsman!"

"I've never even heard of you! Some supercilious dropout with the audacity to try and seduce me, then cry wolf when he succeeds? I don't know how you got the impression that I was in need of the likes of you, Mr. Edwards, but you are most mistaken! Most mistaken indeed!"

Colin glared at the clock and drew closer to Henry. "In twelve hours I'll return to show you my work." He brought his face within inches of Henry's. "And after you've seen it, you'll wait a thousand fortnights. Good night, Mr. Sewell."

Henry watched the young man exit, and then sighed. Really, his life would be so much easier without the difficult ones.

CHAPTER TWO

In keeping with his word, Colin climbed the steep stairway to Henry's door at eleven o'clock sharp Saturday. Before ringing the bell, he glanced around at the handsome brownstone. Henry had not built it, but he had certainly kept it up and it fit right in with the fashionable Mayfair neighborhood.

Instead of his servant answering, Henry opened the door to a surprised Colin. "I half-expected you to be on a boat back to America," Henry said dryly. "I see you've brought your precious plans. So do come in."

Colin was careful not to apologize for the outburst the night before, but it was difficult. He knew etiquette demanded his apology, but he sensed he'd lose respect from Henry if he did so. He clutched his designs and followed Henry into his study.

"Roll them out here," Henry directed, stifling a yawn. He placed weights on the corners and stepped back to view the first design.

"This is my finest work," Colin explained proudly as he unfurled the plans. "I call it The Helios House. It's not actually in progress, though, or even sold. Yet."

Henry said nothing but cast his eyes over the paper. Colin waited, and as time passed by, he became confused. Did he make an error in his calculations? Didn't Henry understand what he was seeing? Colin couldn't stand it any longer.

"Well?" he burst forth. "What do you think?"

Henry didn't look up, but said, "Yes, well, this is indeed amazing, Mr. Edwards, but I do have one question for you."

Colin leaned in expectantly.

"If this is your work, why does it have Michael Callahan's signature on it?" And he brought his finger from the top of the design to the bottom corner, where it rested under "Michael Callahan, 1889."

Colin was rendered speechless as he looked in horror at his own name. He'd forgotten to strike it from the print!

"You are aware, Mr. Edwards, that stealing is quite a serious offense," Henry spoke.

Colin appeared as if in a daze. "I... I didn't steal it," he said, shaking his head.

"No, I suppose Mr. Callahan's plans magically leapt into your hands!" Henry answered severely. "An explanation is in order now, Mr. Edwards, or I shall have you arrested!"

Colin stifled a laugh. "You can't arrest me, Henry."

"Oh, can't I? I can and I will!"

Colin cut in. "You can't arrest me because those *are* my plans."

Henry leaned on one palm. "Do you take me for a fool? It's all perfectly clear: you're some jealous colleague of Callahan's who took," he gestured at the topmost print, "apparently his greatest creation, and ran off to Europe hoping to pass them off as your own!"

Before Henry could react any further, Colin joyously clutched his arms. "It *is* my greatest creation! Henry! Permit me to tell you a bit about Mr. Michael Callahan." He smiled and lowered his voice. "Well, he happens to... *prefer the company of men,* and he was caught in a compromising position with one by his father. Are you following? Good. He refused to hide who he was any longer, and so he left his family and his country for London.

To start over. With a new name." He searched Henry's expression, which appeared completely at a loss. "Where do you think Michael Callahan is at this very moment, Henry?" Colin urged. *"Those are my plans."*

Henry blinked, incredulous. "You're... *you're* Michael Callahan?"

Colin smiled, shaking his head. "Not anymore. Not ever again." In a pause, his smile turned to a frown. "And I'll thank you to keep the confidence."

Henry's head spun. He stood back from Colin. "But, you already had a solid reputation on your real name. Why would you give that up? Now you're nobody."

Colin grimaced. "It was my parting gift to my father. I thought I would save his name from any further tarnish." He regarded his work. "But when I strike my name from

those plans and sign it as 'Colin Edwards'..." He looked at Henry and smiled. "Well then, Michael Callahan will become the nobody."

Henry was stunned with admiration. The boy truly was as captivating as he'd first thought. Or was he? Henry's forehead creased. "The young man I met last night... was that Michael Callahan or Colin Edwards?"

Colin tilted his head. "Why don't you invite me to dinner tonight and you can see for yourself?"

Henry nodded. "Very well then. Come back at seven. Do you wish to leave your plans here? I assure you they'd be safer than in that hotel."

Colin moved toward his plans. "Thank you for the offer, but the draft work comes with me." He rolled them up and bade Henry farewell.

Colin was so elated by the turn of events that it wasn't until he was in his hotel room that he thought of Jeffrey. Or rather, his betrayal of Jeffrey. As he sat at his desk to start a letter off to his lover, he wrestled with his conscience.

I will only be with Henry until he gives me a job. Then it is through. And I can by all means do that in a month's time, before Jeffrey arrives. After all, Henry is entirely infatuated with me already!

But Colin's heart sank as he realized he was becoming no less infatuated with the rather alluring Henry Sewell. With shame, Colin realized that he wasn't looking forward to seeing Jeffrey half as much as he was looking forward to this very evening and what

may happen with his hero. His hero, who wanted to see Colin again! With a sigh, Colin pushed forward with the letter.

March 25, 1891

Dear Jeffrey,

How I miss you! I must tell you the news—I have met Henry Sewell! You would have been proud—I waited for him outside the stage door while he was giving the lecture. I struck up a conversation with him and...

Then Colin stopped. How was he going to tell Jeffrey about his new name? Or that he showed Henry his blueprints already? Or that Henry discovered who he was? Colin decided none of that was necessary to share now. He would have to be vague.

...I will be having dinner with him tonight! I am certain he will hire me on; he seems very interested. I will let you know more details when I arrive back tonight. Your absence is a terrible void. I shall finish writing to you when I return...

Colin sighed and sat back in his chair, wondering how the letter really would end. He predicted that by this time tomorrow, everything could be very different, indeed.

This time it was 7:15 p.m. when Colin stood at Henry's doorstep once more. Henry welcomed him with a mixture of anxiety and anger. "You're late," he said, clipped.

Colin raised an eyebrow lazily. "Our line of work requires so much precision, Henry. I prefer to do nothing of the sort in my pursuit of leisure." He slowly led his eyes down to Henry's waist and then in a blink, met Henry's gaze.

Henry went slack-jawed and Colin admonished himself. *Too strong!* He gently pushed his way past Henry and looked about the room. "Are we dining alone, then?"

"Yes," replied Henry, faintly.

Colin turned and smiled broadly at him. "What are we having?"

Henry shook himself from his stupor. "Filet mignon, among other things. Allow me to escort you to the dining room."

Colin was struck by Henry's gallantry, and he let the man walk up to his side. But when Henry met him, Colin could only gaze at him, eyes shining. Feeling he had shortchanged Henry thus far, he drew close and kissed him deeply. Then he withdrew and studied Henry's face. "We truly are alone," he confirmed.

Henry kissed him back ardently. "Yes. Yes," he breathed, pressing against Colin.

With that knowledge, Colin began unbuttoning Henry's vest, then his shirt, pushing him toward the divan. After a few moments, he moved down to Henry's trousers.

Henry gasped. "I thought you wanted to wait a fortnight."

Colin lifted his head. "And I thought you wanted last night. So we shall compromise." Then he smiled. "Besides, I just thought of a perfect way to prove to you that I really am Michael Callahan."

Sometime later, Henry finally led Colin into the dining room. Colin stopped in the doorway, awestruck. Two objects dominated the whitewashed room. First was the dining table itself. Made to seat six on each side and two on the ends, the rough-hewn thick table was made of lightly stained oak, and its top was bare save for the very center, from which rose a majestic, life-size set of stag's antlers.

"It is all carved from a single piece of wood," Henry said proudly, as Colin fingered several of the dozen sharp tips in wonder. The polished curves gleamed in the candlelight. Into the sides of the table were carved ornate flora and fauna. Vines trailed down the legs, and deer leapt across the edges. The matching chairs had grapes and vines carved across their tops. The furniture would have stood out anywhere, but Henry made it the only detailed object in the otherwise sparse space, with the exception of the magnificent work of art that hung on the wall across from it. Spanning the length of the table was a stained-glass mural the likes of nothing Colin had ever seen. In the center of the piece stood a peacock in swirling cobalt and emerald hues. His glorious tail fanned behind him while along the top crept vines of purpled grapes. Flanking the bird were marble balustrades, and the sky behind it all pulsed in brilliant sunset colors.

"Oh! That is absolutely marvelous!" Colin exclaimed, moving closer to admire it.

"Isn't it? It was done by a compatriot of yours, a Mr. Louis Tiffany. Have you heard of him?"

Colin nodded. "Yes of course; he's an interior designer. I didn't know he created glassworks."

"Well, he's just starting to come into his own in that realm," Henry replied. "I commissioned it just over a year ago. Everyone else has Gallé; I wanted something different. You should have seen the thing when it arrived! It took hours to unpack."

"I can imagine," Colin murmured, studying the glass.

Henry ushered Colin to a chair. "You sit beneath it. Of course, normally I place guests opposite the piece, but this way," he went around the table and stood opposite Colin, "now I can see both of my beautiful American works of art at once!"

Colin laughed, and Henry pulled the cord to fetch the servants for their meal.

The two men conversed over three hours and as many bottles of wine. Finally, Henry gazed over his glass at Colin. "Stay the night."

Colin looked confused. "I beg your pardon?" He paused. "The night? You mean to say leave tomorrow morning?"

Henry smiled. "No, you must stay on tomorrow morning as well, so I can take you to breakfast."

Colin stared. "I can't stay here! My God, we'd be accused of being... well, you know!"

Henry stared, then laughed. "Mr. Edwards, until now you've given me no impression of the extent of your naivety. Well played!" Colin reddened, but Henry was thrilled to discover the boy was so callow. "Firstly, I assure you no one would even notice. Secondly, who is to say we didn't merely stay up all night engaging in a fierce discussion about architecture?" He smirked. "As I recall, a young man came here with the express purpose to stop hiding who he was."

Colin tsked Henry. "So are you saying we *won't* be up all night in fierce discussion?"

Henry looked at Colin's teasing pout while tracing the rim of his glass. "Fierce, yes. Discussion... no."

When Colin stirred from his sleep the next morning, he could barely believe where he was. *I have done it!* he thought triumphantly. *I have spent the entire night with a man, in his bed!* The shocking feat thrilled down his spine as he lay under the sheets. He felt smug. *And why shouldn't I have? After all, this is why I'm here.* He remembered how he and Jeffrey would lay together for several hours, dozing off while in bed, trying to imagine what it must be like to wake up with another person beside you. And here Henry was, lying beside Colin, who was sleepily realizing the effects of the wine shared at dinner. He got out of bed to get a drink of water. When he came back, he found Henry with his hands behind his head, looking contentedly at Colin.

"My pajamas are a bit large on you, but they fit well enough."

Colin laughed and sidled up to Henry in bed, who stroked his hair and then his shoulders.

"Do you know, you're positively warm to the touch, all the time!"

Colin shrugged, smiling. "I know. My family used to remark on that. I'm not sure why that is."

"Probably because of your lovely golden skin," Henry murmured. "I hate to think of how London will take away your American sunshine."

Colin drew back. "What do you think I am, a frontiersman? I've always looked this way."

"Amazing?" Henry smiled. "It makes me want to know how you're going to pay for breakfast."

Colin closed his eyes and laid his head on Henry's chest. "You'll have to start a tab, Henry. I've got a splitting headache and you've exhausted me from last night."

"I've a better idea. Work for me."

Colin raised his head. "At your firm? As one of your architects?"

"*Junior* architects to start, yes."

Colin jumped up. "I'd love nothing more than to work for you, Henry!"

Henry chuckled. "Wasn't it your plan all along?"

"Well yes," Colin admitted. "But I'm afraid my goal was temporarily sidetracked."

Henry smiled. "I'm glad to hear it. All right then, get dressed and we'll be off to Charlotte's." He watched as Colin rose from the bed, and dizzily, he realized it.

I have a mistress.

The smile slowly spread across Henry's face as the statement sunk in.

A mistress!

For Colin had proved to be heady stuff, and so far he was perfect for the job. But what was *so far*? A single night, that was all. Still, the added prize of finding out Colin was really Michael Callahan, who was truly a superb architect and in fact, *his protégé,* meant far more than Henry could have ever expected. Even if taken solely as an employee, Colin's potential would be invaluable. The amazing Helios House he designed proved his superiority already to any of the draftsmen in Henry's office. And when one added in Colin's charm, looks, and sexual eagerness, well, Henry wasn't a spiritual man, but he knew a sign when he saw it: Colin was meant for him. Now he would just have to wait and see if Mr. Edwards felt the same way.

When the two men arrived at the restaurant, Henry turned to Colin. "Let me do the talking," he told Colin. "You are not to say a word."

As soon as the maître d' saw Henry, he beamed. "Good morning Mr. Sewell!" He turned and smiled at Colin. "Good morning, sir!" Colin smiled and bowed his head.

"Good morning Arthur," Henry replied. "I'd like you to meet my new junior draftsman, Colin Edwards. He's come all the way from America!"

Arthur bowed to Colin. "Welcome to London, Mr. Edwards. It is a pleasure to make your acquaintance."

"As it is yours," Colin returned politely.

"We are positively famished, Arthur, so do please show us to our seats," Henry requested.

As Colin followed Henry into the restaurant, he was startled to see every head turn their way. After they were given their menus, Colin nodded to Henry, "You're quite the celebrity here."

Henry smiled. "Oh, no. *You're* the celebrity. You're the only one in the restaurant nobody has ever seen." Henry looked delighted with this apparent coup. He confided, "By now, I suspect word has just gotten around who you are. Any minute Kenneth will be—"

"Henry! You scoundrel!" A short, stout man magically appeared at the table. "The one new face in London and, naturally, he sits at your table!" He bowed to Colin. "And so elegantly, as well!"

Henry gestured, "Kenneth, this is Mr. Edwards. Mr. Edwards, Kenneth Fairchild."

Colin looked up to see a cheerful round face looking back at him, a face with two bright blue eyes, rosy cheeks, and a ring of fair hair around his head. Almost sixty, he reminded Colin of a small Saint Nick. The thought made Colin smile, and he exclaimed, "Mr. Fairchild, well, this is an honor! I've heard so much about you!"

Kenneth straightened. "Really?"

"Oh, yes. Your name came up more than once in the twenty-four hours that I've *known* Henry." Colin's face blossomed into a sly smile as he looked at Henry and back at a shocked Mr. Fairchild. Then Kenneth's face slowly bloomed into a smile, and he began shaking a stubby finger at Colin.

"You... *you* are not to be trifled with!" he chuckled admiringly.

Colin grinned and again glanced at Henry, who was as horrified by Colin's immediate use of his first name as he was by Colin's lie and his insinuation. Colin ignored him and pulled a chair back. "Won't you sit down, Mr. Fairchild?"

"Colin!" Henry barked. "Our waiter is here. Kenneth, if you'll excuse us."

As Colin broke his gaze from Kenneth, the man came to his senses. "Of course, of course!" he apologized. Before he left the table, he bowed down to Henry's ear. "Well done! He's quite the match for you!"

After the two had ordered, Henry muttered, "Your many admirable talents obviously do not include following directions."

Colin laughed. "Well certainly you don't expect me to play the part of a mute!"

Henry's mouth was a tight line. "Until you know who exactly my acquaintances are and their relationship with me, I do."

Colin looked down. "Right. Sorry." He realized he had assumed Kenneth was just like Henry and himself and that kind of carelessness could be dangerous, indeed. He snuck a glance at Kenneth's table. "Well, tell me about Mr. Fairchild, then. Who is he? How do you know him? And who's that woman he's with?"

Henry waved his fork. "His wife, of course. Anne."

Colin gasped. "His *wife*? Kenneth's married?"

"Do you see what I mean about assumptions?"

Colin was mortified. "Oh dear God, what do you suppose he thought of me?"

At this remark, Henry had to acquiesce into laughter. "All right, I give! Darling, it's a marriage of convenience. You read him exactly right!"

But Colin looked only more puzzled. "But... then, he married her... to hide who he is?"

Henry studied the face before him. *Dear God, he's so newly minted.* He sighed and said gently, "I'll explain another time, Colin. Put it out of your mind and enjoy your breakfast when it comes, hmm?"

They returned to the house, whereupon Colin asked for a proper tour. Even though Henry lived in the most expensive part of London, Colin still found his home to be quite undersized compared to what the man must be making financially. The house had three floors. The top floor was for the servants, as was the cellar, which was normal enough, but the first and second floor had only five rooms and four rooms respectively, ridiculous for a man of Henry's wealth. There was no ballroom, no music room, no children's rooms or nursery. Colin wondered if Henry didn't have a second home somewhere in the country. As if reading his mind, Henry quipped, "I'm sure you find it rather on the small side, but I wanted it this way. I've no need for a rambling home, what with just myself and the servants."

"But, surely you have a home that is purely in the Sewell style!" Colin blurted, and then gasped at his rudeness.

Henry laughed. "You would think so, wouldn't you? But I've been so busy that I haven't had the time or energy to consider creating for myself. You'll see how that works, my dear. For now, this has had to do."

"Fair enough," Colin smiled. "How many servants do you have?"

"Five," Henry replied. "Charlie is my valet and butler. Millie is the housemaid and scullery maid, and Nora's the cook. Then there's Daniel the coachman and Mikey the groom. No need for a chambermaid, headmistress, or lady in waiting, of course."

Colin smiled. "And I'd hazard a guess that Millie doesn't have to dust or beat rugs often either." For as he had observed thus far, there certainly weren't any of the usual Victorian trappings in Henry's house. Colin was delighted to realize the extent to which Henry applied his interior design theory to his own home. To begin with, every room on Henry's first and second floor was done in variations of only three colors: green, blue, and gold, and all the walls were white.

"The colors of Greece," Henry declared, and Colin beamed, for he knew it; he had read so in his books.

"The birth of true civilization," he asserted, causing Henry to look upon him in adoration. Like Henry, however, Colin disliked the mass perpetuation of Greek architecture into current times. "Now make no mistake Henry," he warned, "I'll have nothing to do with the pillars of Greece, but the tenets are all very good." The clever statement caused Henry to laugh, and he drew Colin near and kissed him dearly.

"You are precious and precocious all at once!"

"However," Colin said hesitantly. "One thing I've always wondered is, how on earth do you keep the walls so white, what with all of the coal dust?"

"I take my lunch and supper out most every day, so there's two less jobs for the stove," Henry replied, smiling. "But of course, I must admit that Millie's main job is to wash the walls. I have her do a room a day."

Colin gasped. "A room a day! Do you tell your clients that?"

Henry looked at him severely. "Of course not! They figure it out on their own. If they ask, then yes, I tell them. But it should be obvious to you that with my design there is little else in the house that does need cleaning."

Colin blushed. "Dear God, I forgot myself again, I apologize. You're absolutely right—what difference does it make whether she's cleaning the walls or beating all of the rugs and draperies?"

"Precisely." Henry eyed Colin. "Any more critiques from Master Edwards?"

"Oh no!" Colin insisted, chastened. "You know I think you're brilliant! Please, do let us press on."

On the first floor, Colin was presented with a formal sitting room on the right and a large library on the left. Colin had been in the sitting room last night, so it was the conservatory they entered next, in the southwest corner of the house. Four white wicker chairs were surrounded by numbers of fuchsias, abutilon, and citrus trees, with ferns and palms among them all. A beautiful bronze fountain burbled forth. Yet it was the aviary that caused Colin to exclaim in delight. Spread upon an entire wall was a large, gilded cage in which perched several birds. Two were yellow canaries, but the third bird was a kind Colin had never seen.

"That is a Greater Bird of Paradise," Henry said proudly. "My literal interpretation of the Rara Avis!" It was as large as a crow but its color was russet and its tail was a magnificent yellow plume twice as long as his body. "He's for looks," Henry nodded. "Then I have two canaries and two hermit thrushes for sound. The thrushes are shy. Perhaps when you're in here reading, you'll hear the male after a while; his song is like Pan's flute!"

Next was the dining room, previously visited, and then in the southeast corner was the smoking room. Again the same white walls, and again the scarcity of furniture save for four chairs and two sofas. By now Colin was onto Henry's scheme and looked around for the superlative on par with the Tiffany and the Bird of Paradise. He was disappointed not to find it straight away.

"Well, it's a very nice room, but..." he trailed off at a loss, and Henry brushed past him, chuckling. Colin watched as Henry pushed on the south wall and turned it ninety degrees. "Oh, no, Henry!" Colin gasped in disbelief. Beyond the false wall was a small second room! A settee, two chairs, and a table fit neatly inside.

"I use this when I have more company than usual," Henry nodded. "Isn't it something?"

Colin followed him inside. "It's amazing!" Henry swung the wall again so they were fully enclosed. And yet there was light! Colin looked up and above him the sky came streaming in through an oculus in the domed roof that stretched to the top of the house. He laughed and clapped his hands with glee. "Oh, I can barely stand it!" Henry looked upon Colin, his bright eyes shining in the dusky light, and was tempted to make use of the private moment.

But Colin was too excited and so instead Henry took his hand and said, "Now come to the library." He led him to a room full of whitewashed pine bookcases. Colin gawked. Only the very wealthy could afford so many books, for they were just beginning to be mass produced. In the middle of the library floor, two pairs of Biedermeier chairs faced each other, upholstered in gold-green velvet. But it was what lay between the chairs that caught Colin's eye, exactly as Henry intended.

"Is that an Aubusson rug?" Colin demanded.

"It is," Henry smiled. He knew it was doubtful an American would have ever seen one in person. But Colin was almost as interested in interior design as he was in exterior architecture, so he had at least read a little about histories of things like rugs. And now he rushed to examine this one. The weaving was so fine that the ribbons and flowers looked like oil paintings and the background like canvas. It was wonderfully soft yet delicately thin, for it was flatwoven. Colin couldn't imagine Henry letting anyone walk on it.

"There's a Savonnerie in the bedroom."

"No!" Colin gasped, scrambling to his feet. "But how did I miss it?" Henry winked and Colin laughed. "Of course." His eyes grew round again. "How on earth did you get one?"

"Never mind that. Just make sure to notice it when we go up."

"Oh, I will." Colin exhaled. To have both an Aubusson rug and a Savonnerie rug in one residence meant Henry had to practically be royalty. After all, Savonnerie rugs for many years couldn't be sold by anyone but the

King of France himself. There was little else in the library to see, save for the small tables between the chairs, the marble fireplace, several gasoliers, and a crystal chandelier, all very simple, expensive, and free of ornamentation.

Upstairs, they first came upon Henry's bedchamber, and Colin raced to see the famed rug and kneeled down beside it. This rug was much more colorful than the Aubusson carpet, although of course, it did have the colors green, blue, and gold in it as well. There were borders within borders within borders, all latticed with intricate designs: flowers, crests, ribbons, leaves. It was less fragile than the Aubusson, being piled and therefore thicker, but it obviously took much longer to weave, as it had five times the design and color. "It is truly a work of art!" Colin breathed. The rest of the room he knew well, particularly the generously sized bed that practically overtook the room. The feather mattress was so thick that when Colin stood next to the bed it came up to his chest.

The bed itself was canopied in dark blue silk with heavy gold tassels as tiebacks, and arrayed on the bed were a dozen blue, gold, and white velvet and silk pillows in different sizes and shapes. These fanciful details surprised Colin, but Henry shook his head and said, "It's the one place one *should* feel sumptuous." Even the connecting bathroom had a singular feature: a round sunken bathtub twice the size of the common claw-footed version.

"But surely you rarely bathe in it," Colin had commented when he had seen it the night before. After all, it had a showerhead installed as well.

"Of course," Henry replied. "But there are times I want to recall the heated baths of Rome." Colin already began thinking of when he could try it himself. Unlike many people, Colin trusted the hot water pipes and happily lived with the risk that they could explode under the wrong kind of pressure. Currently cold water was seen as healthiest for bathing, but Colin hated it once he had felt the effects of a hot shower after a hangover.

Next was another bathroom and then the would-be-lady-of-the-house's bedchamber. Both rooms were completely bare. "But why haven't you done anything with them?" Colin asked, incredulous.

Henry shrugged. "I haven't been inspired." He smiled. "Perhaps you can think of something." The idea was staggering to Colin: Henry Sewell allowing his protégé to design two rooms in his very own house! "Which leads me to ask," Henry mused, "if young Colin Edwards was to design this house, how would it differ?"

Colin walked slowly around the room, steadying his breathing. "I would keep everything the same, except I would install more windows. And I doubt I could master just three colors in the entire household the way you do, Henry. I love the entire palette and would have to use it, although in tasteful amounts."

"I challenge you to design this bedchamber and bathroom, then," Henry declared, testing Colin's commitment. "Only I'm afraid it *must* contain elements of only blue, green, and gold, seeing as the rest of the house is that way."

Colin broke into a grin. "Challenge accepted. When can I start?"

Henry smiled as relief overcame him—the boy seemed willing to stay! "Not for another month. I want you to get very used to the environment and have some time to think about it," he said. "But they are your rooms now, Colin, and I want you to surprise me, so you needn't bother getting my approval on anything. You shall be given blank cheques to purchase everything."

Colin swallowed, unbelieving. "Henry, I was only joking."

"I wasn't."

"Really? But that's... well, that's most generous of you. Are you quite certain of this?"

Henry moved toward him and tucked a lock of hair behind Colin's ear. "Yes. You see, I have this feeling you're a Rara Avis too, Collie, and I want proof."

CHAPTER THREE

That evening, Colin stood in Henry's library studying his collection. Henry sat and studied him. "Colin, I'm wondering, how did you know I was... who I was?"

Colin smiled. "I did a presentation on your work in one of my classes. At the end, our professor said, 'Well done, Callahan. Sewell is one of my favorite architects, and least favorite people.'" Colin cocked his head and narrowed his eyes. "And I said, 'Really? Why is that?' And he replied, 'He leads a wicked lifestyle.'" Colin's eyes widened. "And I asked, 'How do you mean, wicked?' And Professor Schuren smiled and said, 'Well, let me just say that he'd find someone like you very... *attractive*, Mr. Callahan. So you'd best take care if you ever meet him.'" The memory made Colin angry although Henry smiled at the comment. "Can you believe it? Then everyone laughed and I just stood there, not knowing what to think. I was half ecstatic about the possibility that you and I were alike, and half livid about being called 'wicked.'" Colin looked at the floor. "So finally I looked him in the eye and took a deep breath and I told him, 'The Greeks believed it to be the highest form of love.' And everyone fell silent and Schuren suggested that I sit down." Colin paused, catching his breath. He remembered Jeffrey looking at him in awe after the statement, and then smiling at him. It was when they had first guessed about each other. "After I sat down, I realized I *had* to know. I had to be sure. So after class, I asked him. He said he knew you were *that way* because of some acquaintance of his in England, whose friend had a nephew you supposedly consorted with."

Henry rolled his eyes. "That could be anyone," he said.

Colin shrugged. "It was enough for me to go on. I figured I'd cast the line about when I meet you and see if you would bite."

Henry rubbed his chin. "And I did," he chuckled.

Colin went over to him and kneeled down by the armrest. "And I'm so glad, Henry! You don't know what it means for me to know that someone like you, who is successful and influential and happy, is a person like myself."

Henry stroked Colin's cheekbone with his thumb. "You told a beautiful story, Colin. You are so brave, standing up to your professor like that. I wish I could have been there to see it."

Colin smiled. "I wish Schuren was here to see us! If I ever was to go back, I would walk up to him and say, 'I met Henry Sewell, Professor Schuren. And you were right about him... I have firsthand evidence!'"

Henry laughed and looked affectionately at the young man resting on his knees. "Colin, wasn't there anyone you were fond of while you were studying at MIT?"

Colin hesitated. "Well, yes. In fact, you could say we found each other thanks to Schuren. Jeffrey was in that class with me."

"Ah, he has a name," Henry smiled. "You two must have had a history."

Colin nodded. "It was all quite romantic, actually."

Henry raised his eyebrows. "Really? Then I want to hear all about it."

Colin sighed and remembered back to autumn of last year, when the glorious time began.

Jeffrey Adams was a third-year at Massachusetts Institute of Technology who shared classes with Michael. Michael had noticed the dark-haired young man right away, and to his dismay, Jeffrey had caught Michael gazing at him several times. It made it barely manageable for Michael to look Jeffrey in the eye, but whenever he did, Jeffrey always smiled, for he had admired Michael's talent early on; after all, Michael was promoted to third year halfway through his second, and with good reason. He had caught onto the theories and practices of architecture more quickly than any of the professors had anticipated. His ideas were full of innovations; some were unrealistic, while most were impossibly real. He won several student design awards each year. Some of the professors thought him too modern, but most encouraged his heresies. Jeffrey knew he was witnessing a legend in the making, and the legend was also the most handsome boy Jeffrey had ever seen. And because he also had an upper-class background, many ladies declared Michael the perfect catch. But as it turned out, pursuing a courtship with Mr. Callahan was akin to pursuing a puff of smoke. For once he found out a young woman had designs on him, Michael fell to such shyness and avoidance that a second attempt was futile for all but the most persistent. A certain number of ladies found his reticence an alluring challenge, but their boldness was met with a final brusque dismissal, a curt "No *thank* you, Miss X." His shocking behavior couldn't go on for long without comment. During one such social occasion, after Michael had excused himself from further conversation with one Miss Maurine Higgins—the most upper-crust young lady in the room—a peer asked him outright: "Callahan, are you mad? Do you realize how many of us fellows are falling all over each other to get to that one?" Michael turned to him and said severely, "Look here, Furlington. I'm going to be a Great Architect. I won't let a woman get in the way of that. Not even Miss Higgins. *You* may have her." Thus the self-sacrificial declaration spread, causing some men to call Michael "Narcissus" behind his back. He remained well liked but was decidedly eccentric. However, his eccentricity had more meaning to some men—including Jeffrey Adams—than others.

With only two weeks before the semester's end, Jeffrey summoned his nerve. After Michael had presented his latest project to the class to resounding applause, Jeffrey approached him outside. "Your design was absolutely amazing, Mr. Callahan!"

Michael tried not to blush. "Thank you, Mr. Adams. I... I think your work is quite good as well."

Jeffrey stood in front of him. "But you could sell those plans to a firm tomorrow—they're that extraordinary!"

Michael laughed. "Well, of course they are!" He paused. "But what I'm working on privately is even better."

Jeffrey frowned. "Really? Why?"

Michael looked at him thoughtfully. "I'll show you, if you're interested," he offered, his heart beating wildly.

Jeffrey grinned. "Absolutely! I'd be honored!"

Michael nodded. "I'm heading to my dormitory now, if you have the time."

Jeffrey fell in beside Michael. "Well then, we're off!" He tried to keep from bursting. He was finally speaking to Michael Callahan! After all this time spent with glances and smiles, his forwardness was paying off.

Michael was equally exhilarated. If Mr. Adams was like him—and Michael thought he was—then maybe something would happen once they were in his room. What exactly it would be Michael didn't dare let himself think, but his excitement showed in his nervous chatter as they walked.

When Jeffrey entered and saw Michael's surroundings, he gasped. He had heard Callahan paid extra money to secure a room without a roommate, another reason for the "Narcissus" moniker. But now he saw why: Michael had transformed it into his own creation. The wood-paneled walls were entirely whitewashed, as were the strung-up Venetian blinds on the windows. Even the floorboards had been turned white, with an earth-toned Turkish rug thrown down in the middle of them. Though the room was meant for two occupants, Michael had left most of the space bare. His furnishings consisted of a bed, a drafting desk, and a royal blue velvet reading chair by the fireplace.

The bed sported a velvet coverlet that matched the chair, and its edges were braided with expensive silver thread. The drafting desk was huge and made of oak. The walled bookshelves were loaded with valuable books, which must have been from Michael's private collection. Only a small space was left on one end for several bottles of liquor. Upon further study, Jeffrey noticed a row of well-tended tropical plants along the windowsill. Finally, a single print adorned the walls. It had been carefully framed and put under glass. Even from across the room, Jeffrey recognized it: a drawing of the Wyeth building, designed by the avant-garde British architect Henry Sewell. "I've never seen such a room as this," Jeffrey breathed.

Michael smiled. He felt a bit embarrassed that he had made such drastic changes and wondered if Jeffrey thought him pompous. "Yes, well, it was my first chance to experiment with the Rara Avis design. I assure you I've already caught massive trouble with the heads for doing it."

"It's spectacular," Jeffrey declared, and he meant it. He was a fan of Sewell's Rara Avis movement as well, although he didn't think it would ever be very fiscally successful in a broad sense. Most people would find this room barren, not freeing and focused, as was intended by its designer. But Jeffrey thought it perfect.

The late afternoon light was fading and Michael moved to lower the blinds and close them flat, hoping soon there might be a good reason to have done so. Then he poured two brandies and unrolled his drafts at the table where Jeffrey was seated. His hands trembled with excitement. "Well, then! This is what I call the Helios House. I want you to just look at the plans first, to see how clear I've made them. Then I'll explain the details," he said. He stepped back and sipped his drink, while he watched Jeffrey study the plans. Jeffrey's expression went from studious, to puzzled, to surprised, to ecstatic. He looked up at Michael.

"But, the entire house is circular! Do you think it can really be built the way you've designed it?"

Michael tossed his head. "Of course! It's not the first time such a structure has been created." An explanatory session ensued, and at the end, Michael crossed his arms. "You know, I'm really telling you too much," he teased. "You could steal my idea. I'm planning to use it as next year's final project."

Jeffrey shook his head. "I could have never fathomed this, nor could I remember it!"

Michael became emboldened and moved the large velvet chair next to his admirer.

"Well then, since I can trust you, let me show you the best part." He took a second, smaller rendering out of the tube and laid it on top of the first.

"This is a study of the grand ballroom. You see, the windows are floor-to-ceiling. The entire bank of them will face the west side. The top half of the windows will be installed as two hundred panes of beveled glass. Which follows that as the sun sets, millions of diverging, intersecting rays will be cast about the walls. The entire room will be a spectacular display of light, all in patterns, making the sun in the sky one with the sun on earth!" He threw an arm over his chair and looked at Jeffrey triumphantly.

Jeffrey stared at the drawing, and then murmured, "Its beauty is matched only by the artist who created it." He looked sidelong at Michael, who felt a numbing sensation course through him as he dared not believe what he wanted the words to mean.

Michael gave a small laugh. "I should only hope to be as attractive as two hundred panes of glass," he disdained.

Jeffrey seized the moment. "Oh come now, all the ladies are mad about you!"

Michael snorted, looking at his sketches. "I couldn't care less. They wouldn't appreciate a creation like this." Then he looked bravely at Jeffrey. "But you do." He paused, his stare penetrating. "You do, don't you, Mr. Adams?" Jeffrey fell speechless and could only look back into Michael's eyes. Michael waited, and then let his gaze drop. "Forgive me," he muttered, mortified. "I overestimated your professional admiration."

"No! Don't be sorry!" A hand landed gently on Michael's arm, and he looked back to see Jeffrey smiling faintly. "You're right." He enclosed Michael's slender hand with his own and guided it to the sketches.

"Look," he whispered. "Can you believe it?"

Michael's head swam. "What, the drawings?"

"No! I'm holding your hand, and you're letting me!"

Michael stared at the two hands. Jeffrey's warmth felt wonderful. He looked at Jeffrey, who burst into a grin. "We're the same!"

Michael smiled. "We're not the only ones in the world."

Jeffrey squeezed Michael's hand. "Yes, I know, but... my God, we're both... we're both even in the same school!" Then he froze and took his hand off of Michael's. "I don't even know if it's my place to be so forward with you. You've probably had a lot of lovers." He nodded solemnly. "Great men. With great minds."

Michael looked at him, incredulous, and burst out laughing. "What on earth would make you say that?"

Jeffrey gestured toward the prints. "Well, look. *You're* a genius architect and I'm..." he looked down, embarrassed. "I suppose I feel I would be a bit inferior now."

Michael rested his hand on Jeffrey's leg. "Jeffrey, I've never even met another boy like you... like us. I only know there must be a lot. We just all have to hide it so." Now he took Jeffrey's hand. "I *want* to hold your hand. And I *want* to... that is, I've been wanting to..." He leaned forward and gently kissed Jeffrey on his cheek.

Jeffrey closed his eyes, blushing. "I've been wanting that too."

"Really?" Michael was thrilled.

Jeffrey nodded and mustered the courage to kiss Michael back, only this time their lips met and Michael's eyes widened at the very sin of it, at the sweet taste of brandy and the softness yielding to him. They pulled apart hesitantly, but it was too late. Michael wanted to kiss Jeffrey again and again, and soon neither was barely able to breathe. After a few glorious moments, Michael confirmed his feelings with a whisper. "I knew it."

"Knew what?" Jeffrey murmured into Michael's neck.

"That it would feel like this."

"How?"

Michael sighed. "The way it's supposed to." He drew back and looked sadly at Jeffrey. "Wonderful."

Henry shook himself from his reverie once he realized Colin had ended his story. "But... what happened after that? You had the entire year together, didn't you?"

Colin, too, seemed to snap out of his storytelling, and now he felt depressed and guilt-ridden. "Yes, we did. Then several weeks ago my father caught us together, banned Jeffrey from our household, and I decided I had had enough with hiding and lying about who I was and who I loved. So I said to hell with MIT and to hell with my family and left it all behind to come here and start over."

"But that means you also said to hell with Jeffrey..." Henry ventured, rather scandalized by the turn of events.

"I didn't mean to. I told him when he graduated next year to come join me here. I'd have a proper job—with you, hopefully—and we'd live happily ever after and all that nonsense."

"Not nonsense, Colin."

Colin threw him a look. "Well, look at this! Look at me now! One night with you and I abandoned it all." Colin sighed. "I suppose I never fully believed that other story, and I don't think Jeffrey did either." He shrugged. "Anyway, who knows what's really to happen next. I don't intend to assume anything with you, Henry, as kind as you've been."

"I'd like to assume you're spending another night," Henry replied, his voice more unsteady than he intended.

Colin studied his earnest expression and a smile curled at his lips. "My tab must be frightful by now."

Henry paused to think. "Breakfast at Charlotte's... lunch at The Falconry... tea at Marzipan... and dinner at Ellison's. Plus lodging for a night. I daresay you haven't a choice, Collie."

Colin chuckled. "I *am* paying for my hotel room, whether I stay here or not." His words struck a reminder in his head. "I really ought to go back tonight." Before Henry could protest, Colin stood up and explained. "I have some items that are very valuable to me, Henry, and I'm already nervous about them being left unattended since yesterday evening."

"The Sheffield is perfectly safe," Henry waved a hand.

"Well, that's nice to know, but I'm afraid that until I find permanent lodging, I really can't spend any more nights away."

"But don't forget that you start work tomorrow."

"Precisely," Colin agreed. "And that means I need to get my own clothes, too, doesn't it?" He smiled apologetically. "I'll start looking for a place to live right after work tomorrow, if you'll help me."

Henry sighed. "All right. But come here." Colin obeyed, and Henry gently pulled him onto his lap. "At least let me have something to remember you by."

Colin smiled. "Yes." He kissed Henry and murmured, "You haven't a chance of forgetting."

CHAPTER FOUR

On Monday morning, Henry swept into his architecture firm with Colin beside him.

"Gentlemen! I found the most wonderful addition to our office over the weekend." He motioned to Colin. "I present to you, our newest *senior* draftsman, Mr. Colin Edwards."

A murmur ran though the room, and Colin tried not to react to the sudden promotion.

"Mr. Edwards will be using my office, but for today, I'd like him to just observe all of you and get a feel for the place. I expect you to answer any questions he has."

Raised eyebrows met knowing glances, and Colin felt a mixture of nervousness and resentment. They figured Colin to be nothing more than Henry's latest whimsy, and a temporary one at best. Colin wanted to fling his work into the center of the room and declare, "Behold! Unto you a great architect has been born!" But he had to settle for a polite nod and a brief smile, as Henry glided into his office. Colin realized he'd better act the part of a senior draftsman quickly or he'd be assisting their present beliefs.

"Well!" he shrugged. "Suppose you tell me exactly what projects you're working on." The draftsmen gasped: Mr. Edwards was American! They looked at each other with uncertainty, until one man spoke up.

"All right, sir. I am in the midst of working on a design for Lady Elston's home."

Colin smiled. "Really? Do please show it to me." And he walked over to the middle-aged man's table. As the draftsman explained his rendering, Colin studied the design. "Um-hmm... um-hmm," he nodded thoughtfully. "Very good." He moved on to the next table and then the next, until he had toured the entire room. He was excited about the projects he saw and wasn't able to resist showing off by often giving inputs. However, he made sure to compliment the men on their work and banter with them, as a means of ingratiating himself.

Eventually, one of the men spoke up. "Pardon me, Mr. Edwards. I know it's dreadfully bold of me to ask, but I cannot help wondering where you did your schooling."

Colin eyed the man. "You're quite right; it is dreadfully bold." The man reddened, and Colin broke into a grin. "But it's also a most intelligent question!" He paused dramatically. "I am a product of the Massachusetts Institute of Technology." The men nodded in recognition. Colin added, "But in my opinion, no amount of schooling can teach me more than Mr. Sewell himself, so that's why he has so very graciously thrust me upon you." He gave them all an affable smile that caused the men to laugh easily. They were eager to know more about this mysterious American boy, but protocol prevented any deeper questions, and Colin offered nothing further.

Over lunch, Henry gazed at Colin. "You understand all of my projects and you've won over my employees. I'm not certain I can say the same for myself, on either count."

Colin smiled modestly. "Yes, but by law no employee can love his boss one hundred percent."

Henry set his chin on his fist and murmured, "Then perhaps I shall have to fire you."

Colin blushed, and then grew solemn. "Why did you change my position from junior to senior?"

Henry smiled. "It came to me after studied observation last night."

"Of my work?"

"Of you."

Colin frowned. "Henry, what I've done with you... in the bedroom... well, you surely know it hasn't just been a means of getting what I want professionally."

Henry perused his newspaper. "All I know is I'm getting what I want, professionally *and* personally. And when I get what I want, I'm a happy man. And when I'm a happy man, I feel generous. And when I feel generous, you happen to benefit."

Colin laughed. "I see. Then am I really going to do my work in your own office?"

Henry sighed. "Well, I wasn't really planning on adding another senior draftsman. My offices are full." He drummed his fingers on the table. "I suppose I could let one of them go..."

"Don't be ridiculous!" Colin exclaimed. "I won't have you doing that! Working with you is perfectly fine. Actually, I think it will be wonderful, really, if you don't mind sharing your space."

"It's something I'd like to do more of," Henry smiled. "In fact, that is a beautiful segue to my next proposal: move out of the Sheffield today and move in with me."

Colin's stomach dropped. "Move in..." he stammered, "with you? You mean, until I can find a place of my own?"

Henry looked at Colin boldly. "No, darling. I am offering you permanent residence."

Colin's head swam. "Permanent residence! Are you serious?"

Henry leaned back and said, "I don't think there's anything 'serious' about it, do you?"

Colin gave a small laugh at the word's double meaning. "Henry, it's enough that you hired me on at your firm. You are my idol! But you can't possibly..."

"Be this enamored of you in only three days?" Henry suggested. Colin shrugged, and Henry took a sip of tea. "All right, so I'm your idol. That makes you my acolyte. Now, I've had a few acolytes over the years, Mr. Edwards, and I've had dozens of handsome young men. But you're the first to stand at the summit of *both* groups."

"I'll believe it about the acolytes," Colin muttered, but a pleased smile escaped from his lips.

Henry saw it and chuckled. "You believe it both ways."

Colin shook his head in wonder. "No, this is more than I could have ever dreamed of." Then he frowned. "When you thought I was trying to seduce my way into a job... I suppose it's true that I would have done anything to work under you. But..." Colin looked intently at Henry, "you ended up seducing the seducer. So much so that I ended up abandoning my foremost thoughts of business."

Now Henry looked pleased. "Then you *will* move in with me."

Colin smiled. "On one condition, that I make monthly payments to you as a sort of rent. You know, to pay for living expenses and such."

Henry sighed. "Absolutely not. Completely unnecessary and in fact, indecent." He tilted his head. "You do understand the extent of my wealth, Mr. Edwards, don't you?"

Colin humphed. "I have some frame of reference to go on."

Henry took his hand and stood up. "Well, then, speaking of frames, let us get yours fitted for a new wardrobe. You couldn't have packed more than two suits in your 'escape trunk,' I'm sure."

"Good afternoon, Mr. Sewell!" a chipper voice from behind the counter sailed forth.

"Good afternoon, Charles!" Henry replied. "Today is your lucky day, though not as lucky as mine." He looked at Colin, who folded his arms and smiled at Henry.

"I believe mine is the luckiest of all."

Henry laughed. "You just may be correct, Mr. Edwards. Charles, this is Mr. Edwards and we are in need of a complete wardrobe!"

Charles peered over his glasses at Colin. So it was true! Henry Sewell did have an American boy. Kenneth Fairchild had told him about the meeting at Charlotte's. And this Mr. Edwards must really be an architect, because Henry had brought many young men into his shop for a new coat or hat or gloves, but never a full wardrobe!. This one must have quite a bit more to offer than the others, Charles decided. His excitement was pierced with a sense of dread. The boys Henry brought in were often spoilt brats who made faces until about the tenth item was presented to them, and even then they would sigh and pout, "I *suppose* these will suffice." Henry would just shrug with a "What can you do?" look on his face and pay the obscene amount. Charles smiled widely at Colin and clapped his hands. "A complete wardrobe—what fun!" He took a deep breath. "Mr. Edwards, do you have a color preference to start with?"

Colin looked at Henry, who was clearly pleased to give his opinion. "I think Mr. Edwards would do well in grey, Charles," he stated, and looked at Colin for approval.

"Yes, grey. That's fine," Colin agreed, smiling.

Charles let out a sigh of relief. "Grey! Yes, very good, excellent choice! Let me see what we can do."

Twenty minutes later, Colin looked into the mirror in awe. He had never worn an entire outfit this well turned-out. Even Charles was impressed. "He wears grey very well!"

Henry nodded. "You look outstanding, Colin! You were absolutely meant to wear it! What do you think?"

Colin could only imagine what one outfit such as this could cost. It would use up the rest of his money, and Henry had decreed an entire wardrobe of this quality! What was he thinking? Colin thought he had better find out. He nodded to Henry, "It's wonderful." Then he glanced at Charles. "Charles, would you please excuse us for a moment?"

Charles strained to keep the smile on his face. "Of course," he bowed and left them alone. Colin turned to Henry, who looked worried.

"What is the matter? You don't like it?"

"It's not that!" Colin hissed. "I can barely afford this suit, let alone several more!" Then he added quickly, "It's just that... I didn't bring *all* of my money, you see. I left too suddenly."

Henry stepped onto the platform and planted a grateful kiss on a shocked Colin's lips. "Colin, it doesn't matter! Don't you understand? *I* am buying you your new wardrobe! You see, that is the beauty of being so wonderfully wealthy. I can buy anything I want, for whomever I choose."

Colin's eyes widened and he shook his head. "Henry, a new wardrobe will be an absolute fortune, and besides that, it would be offensive for me wear so many different suits!"

Henry put his hands on Colin's shoulders. "Colin, if you stay with me, you will someday be a partner in my firm. You need to dress the part." He looked upon him tenderly. "I'm going to make you my protégé, and I want you to look beautiful. Society women buy dresses that cost as much as their husband makes in one year! Well, you're my society woman and I'm still getting a bargain. If you have a difficult time accepting my generosity, just think of it as really a gift to myself."

"And I just happen to benefit?" Colin said faintly.

"Exactly!" Henry cried. "You clever, clever thing!" He turned to the front of the store. "Charles!"

Charles, who had been desperately trying to eavesdrop, dashed to Henry's side.

"We will take everything. Would you please show us another ensemble in fawn?"

This time Charles let a stunned gape appear on his face, and Henry chuckled. He walked with Charles back to the floor. "He's different, Charles. But then, I imagine you have already deduced that."

Charles nodded. "Are all American boys generally so easy to please?"

"Perhaps. But if Mr. Edwards is any indication, they are also impossible to satiate." He gave Charles shoulder a knowing nudge. Charles turned red at the indiscreet comment, and with a quick "I see," he began to put together a new outfit.

At the last of their stops, Henry picked out an evening cane for Colin. It was polished cherry with a gold tip, its knob encrusted with precious gemstones.

Colin gasped. "I don't quite think that's appropriate for someone my age."

Henry gave it back to the store owner and said casually, "Then pick out one you like."

Colin studied the collection. "That one, please."

The man smiled and gave the cane to Colin, and Henry slid it from his fingers to examine it.

"Twice the price yet half as showy," he commented wryly.

"But five times the quality!" the store owner exclaimed. "The cane is pure African ebony. It has a finial of mahogany set with three perfect diamonds. It is the finest in the entire store!"

Henry grazed Colin's jaw with the tip. "I should have known," he murmured, and still looking at Colin, handed the cane to the salesclerk. "We will take it."

As they exited the store, Henry briefly held Colin's hand. "And now, my dear boy, let us fetch your things so your new life may continue as planned."

Colin returned to his hotel room to pack up his belongings, and his shoulders sagged upon seeing the letter to Jeffrey still on the writing desk. He sat down and read what he had written. Then he picked up his pen, hoping the right words would appear on the paper as he wrote.

The dinner went well! Henry was impressed with my work and offered me a job starting tomorrow! Please write to me soon, at the address below. I have found a more permanent place to stay. Also, please note my signature. I hope you are doing well.

Sincerely Yours,
Colin Edwards

Colin stared at it. Before he could change anything, he quickly sealed it, left it with the hotel clerk, and got into Henry's carriage.

Henry watched Colin brood, and then he spoke with mild concern. "Was it that wonderful of a hotel?"

Colin kept his guilty expression turned outward. "I suppose I'm just realizing how astoundingly lucky I am," he lied. Then he looked at Henry and smiled at the truth of it. "Really, what are the chances!"

"You made sure your chances were favorable, indeed," Henry replied. "You determined to come to England, how to meet me, what to say to me, what to show me... you're very smart and very brave. I can't decide which part of you I like best."

Colin laughed. "I suppose I had a hand in it, but when you think about how well it's all worked out, why, it's really as if we were star-crossed, Henry!"

When they arrived at Henry's house, the valet helped them with Colin's luggage. "Charlie, I'd like to properly introduce you to Mr. Edwards. He'll be residing here permanently from this day forward." Henry turned to Colin. "Charlie is now your valet as much as he is mine. You are not to hesitate to ask him for anything."

Colin nodded, smiling at Charlie. "I'll try not to be an inconvenience."

"Oh, no sir," Charlie shook his head. "No trouble at all." He could hardly believe the scenario. Mr. Sewell had told him earlier that he had hired the American boy, gleeful about his "diamond in the rough." Charlie thought there was hardly anything rough about Mr. Edwards, with his fine features and sonorous voice. And he was suspicious of the young man's benevolent personality. He'd seen plenty of spoilt boys around this household, and surely Mr. Edwards wasn't any different. He had conned Mr. Sewell into letting him move in, after all! As Charlie lugged one of the suitcases up the staircase, he made a wager with himself when he'd be dragging the selfsame suitcase down to the front door.

Tuesday morning Colin sat in Henry's office, showing his work from school. By the third project, Henry was shaking his head in admiration. "By God, you really could be a senior draftsman." They discussed each other's work. Henry listened to Colin's suggestions about changes to his current project, and he even followed through on some of them. Colin began learning more about the business side of architecture.

"Your Helios House is a masterpiece, Colin, but to create it to the letter would cost an absolute fortune."

Colin shrugged. "There are plenty of men with fortunes."

"That doesn't mean they want to spend them all on a house. That's why every great architect knows to compromise some of his ideas."

"Every *successful* architect."

Henry frowned. "There's no room for impudence when you deal with clients, Colin. What works in the bedroom may fail in the boardroom. You'll soon find you must cater to the client. Or at least let them think you're catering to them. Now, I want you to tell me one thing you could change to your Helios House that would start making it a realistic project."

Colin glared. "The Helios House is perfect the way it is! Anything less would be an aberration and you know it."

Henry sighed. "I can think of several changes already that wouldn't affect its beauty or form at all."

Colin crossed his arms. "I don't want to hear them. Pick a different project."

"Why, for example, you could use granite instead of marble for the floor," Henry began.

Colin started. "What? Granite is nothing like marble! It has neither the feel nor the effect! It would ruin the floor plan!"

"It is half as expensive and much more durable."

"But it's not reflective in the same way! The idea is to have the floors appear to have captured the sun's rays, with the crystalline running through the marble. How do you expect granite to accomplish that?"

Henry casually pulled a granite tile from his desk. "Like so."

Colin regarded at the stone and gasped. It was ablaze in diamond sparkles. "That's granite?"

"Yes, it's granite specifically chosen for the amount of reflective flecks. It's fairly rare, but still far cheaper than marble. I think it would complement your design quite well, don't you? It looks like sun upon snow." He handed the tile to Colin, who tilted it in the light. Finally, he sat back in his chair sadly.

"It's even better than the marble."

Henry leaned over his desk. "Colin, I didn't mean to put down your marble floor, but you mustn't be so intransigent about your work. You must always think about your projects as ever-changing, always capable of evolving. By conceding that the granite works better than the marble, not only have you proved that you can be a successful architect, but a *good* one as well."

Colin looked morose. "You must have found dozens of flaws in the House."

Henry snorted. "Flaws! The marble floor wasn't a flaw. It would have looked beautiful. The idea, Colin, is not to change the end result, only the process of getting it there, and only if need be. We changed the entire floor of your house, but we didn't change the effect you wanted it to have, you see?"

Colin nodded, humiliated. "I'm sorry I was impudent."

Henry took Colin's hand. "And I'm sorry that you take things so personally," he murmured. "Though you're quite attractive when you're angry."

Colin smiled at the teasing. Henry stood up. "Anyway, do let's go for lunch. I need a break from the intensity of all this discussion."

While they waited for their food, Henry asked Colin, "I'm curious: were your professors at MIT graduates of the École de Beaux-Arts?"

Colin nodded. "Some of them were. A number of our really good American architects went to the École, of course, including Hunt, Richardson, and McKim. But I didn't have the patience for it. I know that MIT isn't the same; there's not even a degree for architecture there yet, but..." He looked intently at Henry. "You must understand Henry, my generation is very forward thinking, especially in America. We learned that one could be successful at something without going about it the usual way. Look at us: we ditched a monarchy and *voted* in a *president*!" His voice grew solemn. "A revolution is a very powerful thing, Henry. And I revolted against several things in my life, one of which was languishing at the École for twelve to fifteen years to learn some useless iotas of thought."

"You think that my education was useless?" Henry raised his eyebrows.

"Well, some of it was, wasn't it?" Colin challenged. "It had to be! My goodness Henry, for a modern architect like you, you surely had some revolutionary moments of your own while you were there!" Henry pursed his lips and Colin crossed his arms. "You said that I'm the newest incarnation of you. How do you suppose that's possible given my much more brief education?"

"*You're* a genius," Henry pointed out. "I can't imagine that a mere four years studying engineering, maths, and a few courses in actual architecture will do your peers any good at all."

Colin shook his head. "Mark my words, Henry, the legacy of the École will die soon." He looked apologetic. "I shouldn't have said that your education was useless. You were simply overeducated. I cringe to think of the amount of time you were required to study the Parthenon alone."

By now Henry was quite angry. "You must have a foundation, Colin!"

"I agree. And that foundation could have been taught in a handful of lectures." He gestured about. "It meant nothing to me, Henry! I skipped ahead an entire year because I had already taught myself the basic principles."

"You're joking."

"No," Colin replied proudly. "I was to graduate with only three years of attendance." Then he lent a soothing tone to his voice. "Education is a must, Henry, yes. But apprenticeship is ever so much more important. That's why working for you is far greater than a residency at the École, and you know it." He sat back and laced his hands behind his head. "A short formal education at University and a nice long one under the experts. What do you think?"

"I think you're impudent," Henry said tersely. "Whether you are right or wrong, you're being impudent and that is enough!"

Colin's shoulders slumped but even he had guessed his ideas would be too extreme for someone Henry's age. So he apologized again, and then quipped, "I suppose we shan't agree on everything." Henry, rather put off by the whole conversation, was thankful their lunch had arrived and told Colin he wished for some peace and quiet awhile.

Later on that night, in another attempted truce, Colin kneeled on the floor next to Henry's chair in the library, rested his chin on Henry's leg, and asked him, "Did you like studying at the École, Henry? Perhaps I should have gone there after all."

Henry sighed and ruffled Colin's hair. "Don't be silly. And no, I can't say I cared for it because I had to stifle my own ideas."

"But why?"

"Because they could have ruined me, that's why! There was an architect back in the twenties named Henri Labrouste—"

"The one who built the St. Genevieve Library," Colin nodded.

"Yes. Well, he spouted the selfsame theory that you and I have, that Greek architecture was all well and good for the Greeks, but that our own century needed to develop our own architecture. Architecture that met the needs of our modern age, with modern materials."

"Wonderful!" Colin grinned in delight.

"Not so," Henry frowned. "When the École heard his theories, they saw to it that he built *nothing* for the next ten years and that none of his students were ever eligible for the Prix de Rome."

Colin gasped. "Just because he had contrary ideas?"

"Oh, yes. It actually started after he insisted that the original Greek architecture was painted in bright colors. God forbid!" Henry smiled. "So now you can imagine why I played along to their tenets, got my education, and left to create my own style."

"But Henry, you could have tried out so many things while you were there if they had only let you!"

"Well, it turned out just fine. I hadn't a choice; no self-respecting architect back then would go without an École education." He sighed again. "But since then the place has rather gone downhill. It's just as well you didn't go there, I suppose."

"If it helps," Colin offered, "my architecture education did consist mostly of the École's principles. I was just lucky enough to be allowed to explain what I designed, and they liked what they saw."

"You're lucky indeed," Henry smiled. "And I like what *I* see. You've so much to offer, Collie."

"As do you, Henry," Colin replied, relieved that he had been forgiven. "And I promise you, the best is yet to come."

CHAPTER FIVE

The rest of the mornings that week were spent at the office, while afternoons consisted of Colin touring the city with Henry and meeting a number of important people along the way. Henry and Colin spent their evenings apart. One reason was that Henry wanted to officially present Colin on Saturday at his private club. For his part, Colin enjoyed having some time to himself and either dined alone at places he found while exploring or had a simple meal prepared for him at Henry's house, followed by some leisure reading and drafting. One thing Colin had not yet grown comfortable with was living amongst servants who knew his relationship with their employer. Henry apparently viewed them as trustworthy and having no interest in anything but a good paycheck. Still, Colin decided it best to avoid them as much as possible, and the tactic has been easy to manage thus far. Until Thursday evening.

As per usual, Henry left for his club at five o'clock, and shortly thereafter, a thunderstorm began brewing. Colin managed to eat his dinner as the sky grew dark, and he tried to read in the library amidst the rumbling outside. But soon the flashes and claps were right over his head, and he went off nervously in search of Charlie. He found the servant in his attic quarters writing a letter. "Charlie?"

Charlie jumped. "Mr. Edwards!"

"Sorry. I know I'm supposed to ring you. I forgot." Charlie glanced at Colin's paled visage. "Um, I don't particularly care for storms, you see, and I was wondering perhaps you could... come downstairs and keep me company." He gestured at the letter. "You could bring it with you."

Charlie struggled not to laugh out loud. A grown man, afraid of a thunderstorm! And worse, wanting a servant's company! He stood up and smiled. "Certainly, sir. This is most unusual for London—we hardly ever get storms. Do they have weather like this in America?"

"Oh, yes!" Colin exclaimed, wringing his hands. "They even have things like tornados and such. It's awful!"

"Tornados! My word," Charlie murmured. When they came to the library he sat at a desk while Colin retired to his chair and opened his book. But moments later, after a great thunderclap, Charlie saw that his new master was still on the first page, eyes glazed with fear. A pang of sympathy hit Charlie. *He's not so bad, is he? Hasn't done a thing against you since he's been here. Rather mild. It's so odd!* He stood up. "Why don't I fix us both a glass of warm milk with brandy, sir?"

Colin exhaled. "Yes, thank you. That's an excellent idea." When Charlie returned, Colin took the glass, and after a grateful swallow, he tilted his head and resolved to be friendlier to the valet. "Charlie, tell me: how did you come into Henry's employ?"

Charlie started. "I beg your pardon, sir?"

"How did Henry find you?"

"Er... he hasn't told you, sir?"

"No, but then, I never asked him."

"Oh. Well, I think you should ask him, sir."

"Why? Can't you just tell me?"

"I'd rather not, sir."

Colin's forehead creased. "Oh." Then he grinned. "But that means you should! You must have a story!"

"Well, it may be one that Mr. Sewell rather you not know."

"Really?" Colin was mystified, and Charlie was regretting following him downstairs.

"Yes. Well, with your permission, I'll be returning to my quarters, then, sir."

"Charlie," Colin stopped him. "Well really, what's the difference if you tell me or if Henry does? Either way I'll find out." He looked at his glass. "I know you've known Henry five years longer than me, but I've gathered that he's not the type to keep many secrets." Charlie was appalled. *Damn his American crassness!* Colin caught his expression and turned red. "Oh dear God, I'm sorry," he said contritely. "I didn't mean for this to be an issue of who you'll profess loyalty to. Obviously, it is to Mr. Sewell, as it should be, and it is none of my business." He looked up at the valet. "You are dismissed, Charlie. Thank you," he said and resumed reading his book.

Charlie was nonplussed. *He acts like a commoner! He doesn't seem to even know the proper role of master and servant. He's not supposed to retract a question; doesn't he know that?* And Charlie again felt a pang of compassion.

"I suppose you could at least know," he blurted. "That I am just as you and Mr. Sewell are, sir."

Colin turned toward him, agape. "You are? You mean you're..."

"Yes, sir. Mr. Sewell, well, he sort of rescued me, you might say." Then Charlie added hastily, "But I've always been a gentleman's valet, mind you. I come from a long line of them."

Colin shook his head. "I don't believe it! That's absolutely amazing!" He couldn't help laughing. "Well, thank you, Charlie! I feel much better now."

Charlie nodded and said, "Very good, sir." Then he wished him goodnight and fled for the safety of his room.

Colin forgot about the storm, and when Henry came home, he was greeted with an admiring embrace and a soft exclamation. "You're genius, Henry! Genius!" When Colin told Henry what he had discovered, Henry laughed.

"I forgot to tell you! Yes, it's funny, isn't it? And I too commend myself. I pulled him out of a scrape—his former employers found him out, but of course, that was perfect for me! So you needn't worry about him blackmailing us. And no worry, I've never done an improper thing with him either—he's far too valuable for that. And of course, he is ten years your senior." Henry stroked Colin's cheek. "The bloom's rather gone off him, I'm afraid."

On Saturday night, Henry prepared to take Colin to Porter's, a secret, upper-crust gentlemen's club in London that catered exclusively to men who preferred other men. Later Henry would introduce Colin to his *regular* businessmen's club, but he spent most of his time at Porter's and was keen to show Colin off. He had readied Colin earlier at the house. First, he spared no expense on Colin's outfit for the evening. "If it's formal, oughtn't I wear black?" Colin asked, eyeing the new slate-gray suit Henry held before him earlier that afternoon.

"Good heavens, no!" Henry exclaimed. "This is your official debut, after all. And everyone wears black there all the time. They don't spend their money on clothes like I do, darling. Hardly anyone does." Colin shrugged and went back to reading. Henry commenced to flit about anxiously. "Colin, some very, very important people are going to be there!"

Colin flapped shut his magazine. "Yes, I know, Henry. So why won't you have something to calm yourself? A glass of wine perhaps?" He sat up and grinned. "If they don't like Mr. Edwards, then you can just be through with me."

Henry regarded Colin with narrowed eyes. "Oh, your humor is in top form." He moved to rumple Colin's hair, and they began to tussle, laughing and then kissing.

"They will love you," Henry breathed. "Now go and get dressed."

And so Colin dressed into his bespoke suit. His vest was silver-threaded with a pastel blue and rose-hued flower pattern, and he was given a pale pink silk shirt to wear beneath it. He fastened his matching grey tie and sterling silver cufflinks and presented himself to Henry, wearing his charcoal silk hat and gloves for the full effect. "Oh," Henry sighed. "You look deadly. Better than anyone ever seen at that club. I cannot wait!" But the next step had to be addressed. "Now, Colin, I know this will be new for you, but I prefer you act as though you've been in dozens of clubs like this. Try not to react when I hold your hand or put my arm around your waist. And more importantly, don't stare when you see other men doing so."

Colin clasped his hands. "You can really do that?"

Henry smiled wryly. "As the evening wears on, you'll see even a bit more."

When he saw Colin go slack-jawed, he burst into laughter. "Perhaps we should run a rehearsal." He sat Colin on the couch, and after thirty seconds, Colin leapt up in shock.

"My God!" he squealed. "In front of other men?"

Henry frowned. "Good heavens. Maybe you shouldn't go just yet."

Colin grinned and kneeled before Henry. "No, no, you must take me! I'll be good, I promise!"

"Which is exactly why you shouldn't go," Henry chuckled.

Colin swam up between Henry's legs. "I'll be wickedly good."

"You'll do well enough just being wicked."

Colin rested his chin on Henry's knee. "And so, every man there is like you and me?"

"Yes. You cannot go there unless a member has invited you. And you cannot be invited until your identity is certain."

"Well then, how do they know I'm not a spy?"

"No spy would last this long with me if he kept his clothes on and his mouth shut," Henry teased.

"And who exactly are the men who are members?"

"Men of prestige. The price to join is as high as the most exclusive clubs, and men are only allowed to bring guests of good standing." Henry winked. "Which means it's a good thing you're not a renter."

"A renter?" Colin knitted his brows.

"Yes, a prostitute."

Colin gaped. "A *male* prostitute? There's such a thing?"

Henry laughed again. "You didn't know that? Oh, Collie, you never cease to amuse me! At least now I know that you've never used one."

"Have you?" Colin asked, fascinated.

"Ugh! Never!" Henry disdained. "They're all from the street and I daresay they're proud of it. Plus, who knows how many of them are blackmailers?" He paused. "Now I will say that many if not most of the men at Porter's use rent-boys, but they are not allowed to bring one to the club, no matter how comely or well mannered." Colin nodded. Secretly he thought it was quite wonderful that one *could* find a man to have sex with if he wanted to, just like regular men did with female whores. The thought struck a question in his mind.

"Are there even... male brothels, then?"

"Oh, yes," Henry nodded. "Just a few, mind you, and they're in the worst parts of town. I daresay I'd get robbed and beaten if I tried to make my way over to one; I don't pretend to know how to get by on the East End." He looked at Colin. "Porter's is the only *gentlemen's* club in London for men like you and me. The brothels are in themselves a kind of club for the rough type, and there are also some taverns that serve a certain population. But nobody of our caliber should be caught dead at any of those. They're all rather dangerous, actually."

The brief history lesson overwhelmed Colin. To think all of this had been happening while he was unaware of it! To think that it was happening at all—why, now he knew he wasn't just one of a few; men like him were all over the city of London and they came in every class. And if that were so in London, it must follow that such men lived all over the *world!*

Henry frowned. "I hope that smile doesn't mean you're thinking of courting danger."

"Oh no," Colin grinned at him. "I was only thinking of how truly callow I've been all along."

And soon they left for Porter's. Although it was a secret club, it wasn't in the East End at all but, to Colin's astonishment, just a short drive from where Henry lived. They exited their carriage and walked down a side alley, arriving at what appeared to be a door of an office building. Henry unlocked the door with a key he had, and they entered, making their way down the hall until they stopped at one of the doors. Colin thrilled with anticipation. Henry knocked on the lower right panel, and a small window at the top slid open. Henry leaned in. "How glorious it is, and also how painful, to be an exception." The door opened, and a handsome young man greeted them. "Good evening, Mr. Sewell! Good evening, sir!"

"Good evening, Thomas. How does it find you?" Henry replied jovially.

"Very well, sir, thank you."

"Thomas, this is Mr. Edwards. Mr. Edwards, Thomas."

"Hello, Thomas, how do you do?" Colin smiled, shaking his hand.

"It's an honor to finally meet you, Mr. Edwards! Enjoy your evening!" Henry held Colin's hand as Thomas unlocked a second door. The door opened, and Colin's heart raced at the sight.

The music was familiar. The bar looked like any other. The room was filled with men, like any other gentlemen's club. But Colin knew why it was different, and he cursed the Victorian proclivities that kept him from raising his arms triumphantly and shouting, "*This* is it! All I had ever wanted! It really is true! And it's here!" He turned toward the bar mirror to hide his emotions, and in doing so, he caught his own reflection. *You're here! It's real!* And now Henry was leading him by the hand down the carpeted runner, nodding to the well-dressed gentlemen seated and standing along the way. The club was long and narrow. On its left was the bar, a beautiful mahogany affair lit from above by crystal chandeliers. To the right were tables large enough to fit two chairs on one side and two men opposite, in a red velvet booth that ran the length of the club. Henry had told Colin earlier that for a certain price he and his friends had "bought" two tables, with room for six, and nobody was allowed to sit there but them. Only a few other men could afford to do such a thing; most of the members sat wherever they could or stood if they came too late. Henry's group had bought space in the middle of the club. The back was considered more prestigious and private, but they liked to watch who came into Porter's and not many boys made it all the way to the end.

When they were midway through, Henry and Colin stopped. Their spot was already flanked by two men, one of whom was Kenneth Fairchild. He and the other man stood up and warmly welcomed Henry and Colin.

"Kenneth! Howard!" Henry greeted back. "Colin, you've met Kenneth of course. And this fine fellow is Howard Durham."

"Hullo Mr. Edwards." Howard extended his hand. Colin shook it firmly. At forty years old, Mr. Durham cut an impressive figure. He and Henry were the same height, and he sported an immaculately groomed beard that matched his dark brown hair. He had black-brown eyes, yet they were warm and friendly and they crinkled in the corners. His russet-colored suit was expensive looking, set off by a gold-threaded vest and his broad shoulders. In his left hand he held an elaborately carved pipe. *He's as handsome as Henry*, Colin thought, smiling.

"Mr. Durham is one of the partners of the Bank of England," Henry said. "He's been an absolute godsend for my firm."

Howard chuckled. "Who's grateful for whom?" He looked at Colin. "Henry's always been one of our most reliable investors."

Henry sat down. "Yes, yes. Enough flattery. Colin knows well enough when something is to be appreciated." He beckoned a nearby waiter.

"Georgie, the usual for me." Henry turned to Colin and caressed his ear. "What do you want, lovely?"

Colin smiled at Henry and glanced at the waiter. "Gin and bitters, please."

Howard puffed on his pipe. "So, Mr. Edwards, Henry tells us you were a student at MIT in Boston. Are you from that city as well?"

"Yes, Mr. Durham, but you must call me Colin from now on."

"Very well then; I'll request the same from you," Howard chuckled. "You have a most intriguing accent. I hope you talk a lot."

"He's a regular chatterbox," Henry teased. "Do tell him to shut it sometimes."

"I'll do no such thing. What's your family background, Colin?"

Colin grinned. "Such astute questioning! Henry hasn't even asked that yet." He paused, keeping his eyes on Howard. "My father is the director of finance for the Archdiocese of Boston."

Henry's jaw dropped. "You're joking!"

Colin smiled proudly. "No, I'm not."

"But you're Catholic? I assumed you were Protestant!"

"No. Are you?"

"I'm hardly anything." Henry peered at Colin. "So do you follow the religion of your father?"

Colin glanced at him and then looked at his drink. "I'm a practicing Catholic, yes."

"Well, you're not practicing it very well right now, are you?" Henry teased.

"Love thy neighbor, Henry."

The three men blinked, and then laughed uproariously. Colin shook his head and laughed too. A thrill ran down Henry's spine. "Fiercely Catholic and yet with me." He kissed Colin. "Perfect."

"And your mother?" Howard queried.

Colin stared amiably at the man. "Now, I've already shared with you on account of your masculine good looks, Howard. I'm afraid you'll have to wait until the next time for that story." Then he nodded toward Howard and Kenneth. "Tell me something about yourselves that Henry doesn't know. That's only fair, isn't it?"

Howard grinned. Henry's boys usually were so self-absorbed they couldn't care less about engaging him and Kenneth in conversation.

Henry put a hand up. "Not tonight, men. He'll make you give away all your secrets if you're not careful. We'll just let him be an innocent bystander for the evening, hmm?"

Kenneth chuckled and Henry slid his hand from the top of the booth and rested it on Colin's thigh, massaging it. Colin tossed his head and took a breath. He had already finished his drink, which seemed stronger than usual, and he was starting to feel pulled under. Colin noticed Henry was smoking, so he dizzily reached inside his jacket for his own cigarettes. He had only recently taken up cigarette smoking himself, under Henry's recommendation. Colin took to them quite quickly. He had the tendency to inhale so deeply that the smoke would curl out of his nose the way his mouth curled when he smiled while talking. Howard watched him light his cigarette as Kenneth pressed on, "Oh, one more question, Henry! Colin, you know that London can be rather expensive. Have you found a place to stay yet?"

"He won't have to," Henry replied casually. "He's moved in with me."

"*Moved in* with you!" Kenneth cried.

Colin laughed. "Wouldn't you want to live with me, Kenneth?"

"That, unfortunately, is not my decision to make," Kenneth replied. "But Colin, you must be a master in the Dark Arts to have this kind of influence on Henry!"

"A confirmed bachelor if ever I knew one!" Howard gaped.

Colin smiled and nodded to Henry. "I believe they are up two questions to zero on us. Why don't I save ourselves by going to the bar and introducing myself to Mr. Colton?"

Henry commended his decision to meet the club's owner. "That's an excellent idea, my love."

Colin looked at the other two. "Gentlemen," he excused himself, and left the booth.

Howard leaned in, amazed. "Well, he must really be something!"

Henry grinned, ecstatic. "He is! I think I have finally done it; I've finally gone completely mad over a boy."

Howard shook his head. "Why this one, Henry? He's gorgeous, I'll grant you, but what's different about him?"

"He's brilliant. He does come from money." Henry leaned in close and said in a low voice, "His silk undergarments were monogrammed and from France!" He leaned back, thinking of Colin showing off his initials to Henry the second night of their acquaintance, in order to prove his identity. "And he's also very educated. He's an excellent conversationalist and he's independent as hell. My God, think of what it must have taken for him to leave everyone and everything he knew in America and come here! It's such a change from these spoilt, soft English boys. Nobody knows who he is. Nobody's had him on European soil but me. And he's absolutely a stunner! Christ, I keep thinking it's a dream. But gentlemen, perhaps best of all is that he's an absolutely extraordinary architect! I've already made him senior draftsman and he's proved entirely capable."

"But he can't be more than twenty years old!" Howard exclaimed.

"He turns twenty-one next month," Henry grinned. "He's got talents... I can vouch for those unrelated to business."

Kenneth chuckled. "But Henry, do you really think he feels the same about you?"

"I think he's a bit overwhelmed," Henry admitted. "For all his show of nonchalance, I'm sure that even he hadn't counted on all of this. He has a resistance in him. He doesn't want to rely on anyone. Which is why I love him!" Henry shrugged. "And I decided *I'm* ready for something new. I'm tired of the adulating boys. Colin is more my equal. He may be young, but he's at my level. It's been heaven having him around me. He's wonderful company. And I wake up next to a warm, lithe body every morning— what better way to begin a day?" He tapped his lips thoughtfully. "It's as if I finally can agree with that platonic ideal of love. Colin's soul is truly as beautiful as his body. He endears himself to you and... you feel as if you've known him for centuries."

Howard and Kenneth looked on in disbelief. "You are completely bewitched!" Howard exclaimed. "However, if he really is all of these things, I daresay I can't blame you." Then he smiled. "He certainly dresses beautifully."

"I bought him the outfit," Henry said proudly. "He wears clothes so well."

"He's absolutely striking," Kenneth agreed. "And he has a lovely voice too."

"Yes," Henry agreed. "His tenor complements my baritone, don't you think?" They laughed.

"I wonder if he's a pretty singer," Kenneth mused.

"He doesn't like to sing," Henry replied. "He's not castrato anyway; that's what everyone wants to hear."

"Yes, remember that one boy at the hall last weekend?" Kenneth asked. "He was excellent!" They continued their conversation.

Meanwhile, as Colin approached the bar, Jack Colton, the owner, approached him. "Ah! The infamous Mr. Edwards! It's an honor to finally meet you!"

"As it is you, Mr. Colton," Colin said graciously, extending his hand. "Although I'm afraid I haven't lived up to being infamous quite yet."

Jack cocked his head. "I beg to differ." He nodded toward Henry. "You're all Sewell's talked about for the past two weeks."

"Is it really so notable?"

"For Henry? Yes. I hear you're an architect too."

"Yes. He's hired me on."

"That's the story." Jack crossed his arms on the bar. "Sometime you and I will have to have a talk. I must have heard a hundred different rumors about you already."

Colin's eyes widened. "Goodness! I imagine they're all lurid." His voice was hopeful.

"They might be."

"Well then, in that case, I'd be the last one to set you straight, Mr. Colton!"

Jack laughed and poured Colin a glass of champagne. "Welcome to London, Mr. Edwards."

"Thank you." Colin lowered his gaze. "I hope in time you'll see for yourself which rumors are truths." He gave Jack a sly look. "Infamy loves company, you know."

Jack returned the look. "Well then, if you're ever lonely, let me know."

"I will." With that, Colin returned to his table. He sidled up to Henry and addressed Kenneth and Howard. "All right, let's hear it: did Henry manage to convince you? Or did you manage to convince Henry? In any case, *I'm* certainly convinced. Judging from your reactions, Henry *hasn't* ever had a boy live with him before."

Howard regarded Colin evenly. "Henry has never *felt* like this about a boy before."

Colin looked startled. "Henry, what did you tell them?"

"Only the truth," Henry smiled. "That I like you more than any boy I've ever been with." He gazed at Colin. "In fact, I've grown very fond of you in this short amount of time. It's... well if you must know, Collie, I think it's the closest I've ever come to being in love."

Colin's eyes widened, and as he took Henry's hands, his voice was an ecstatic whisper, "Honestly?"

Henry gave an embarrassed laugh. "Honestly—I do fear it."

Emboldened, Colin's whisper turned fierce. "Don't." He leaned over and gave Henry a grateful kiss, causing Howard and Kenneth to murmur in surprise.

Colin laughed and turned to the two men. "Is Henry the first among you to almost fall in love?"

Howard and Kenneth stared. "If you mean by a display like that... yes," Howard stammered.

Colin gazed at Henry with affection. "Well, I'll take your words lightly, however beautiful they were. After all, are you certain you know what love is?"

Henry raised his eyebrows and teased, "You question my feelings? I suppose it makes sense, what with that long list of lovers *you've* had."

Colin laughed. "Fair point. But I can say one thing, gentlemen." He turned to face Henry. "I am an architect, first and foremost. And Henry is the greatest architect of our time. His work—I put his work on a pedestal!" He turned to the two men. "So imagine how I feel about the man himself."

"But isn't that just hero worship, Colin?" Kenneth jested.

Colin returned his gaze to Henry. "Hero, yes. But the rest is tandem."

Henry took Colin's hand. "Yes. There is you, Colin. You and I on the precipice of a canyon. And at the bottom is the rest of the world." The two sat, engrossed with each other, and then Henry stood up. "Well, gentlemen, I'm sorry, but you'll have to excuse us. We will see you tomorrow, I promise."

Colin took Henry's hand and gave the two men a shy "Good night."

Howard watched them go. "Lucky bastard," he muttered.

"Oh, they're perfect for each other!" Kenneth marveled. "I can't believe it! What are the chances?"

"Yes, well, as convincing as Henry was tonight, I'll be interested to see if things remain the same a month from now," Howard groused.

"Even a week from now," Kenneth chuckled. Then he sighed. "But I do like him. I hope Henry keeps him on awhile."

Howard shrugged. "Well, with looks like his, if Henry ditches him, he'll have no trouble landing someone else."

Kenneth gave his friend a sidelong glance. Howard looked slightly troubled. *He's jealous. And who can blame him? Colin's the most beautiful boy Henry's ever found, and Henry—of all people—is making a commitment to him.*

Kenneth made his voice cheery. "Perhaps your turn is next, Howard. After all, if it could happen to Henry, it could happen to anybody!"

Howard rested his hand on his fist and said wryly, "I'm happy for Henry, of course. It's just strange seeing him so... lovestruck."

"I know," Kenneth nodded. "But like he said, maybe he's ready for something different, something deeper."

Howard tried not to show disdain. *'Something different!' When it's the same thing I've wanted all this time.* He drained his glass and shook his head decidedly. "Lucky bastard."

Back at home, in bed, Colin laid his head on Henry's chest. "What about your family, Henry?"

"What about them?"

"Well, you haven't told me anything yet, either."

Henry sighed. "I haven't told you anything because I prefer not to talk about it. Nor anything else in the past, actually. In short, my parents were both well-to-do and I have siblings, none of whom I'm in contact with."

Colin sat up. "Do they live in London?"

"Collie..."

"Well—"

"Well, nothing," Henry said brusquely. "Now that's all you're going to know about me and I don't care to know anything further about your history either. We both know enough, and I for one like living in the very present." He chucked Colin under the chin. "After all, surely this right here is much better than anything in your past, hmm?"

Colin was going to protest but he realized that Henry was right. He smiled widely.

"Yes. Better than anything."

Henry kissed him affectionately. "I'm glad. You see? You're taking after me more and more."

But when Colin tried to fall asleep, visions of his family filled his head. He hadn't thought about any of them since he had left, and now it hit him hard. He wondered if they were looking for him. His father probably hunted Jeffrey down in hopes of finding out where he was. Colin sighed. His mother surely cried, maybe even Papa did. Then he thought of the letter he had left behind and felt sick.

How could I do that to Papa? Poor Papa! Some son I've been to him.

But you're here to make him proud. Henry is going to help you.

Yes, Henry. If Papa saw me now he would—

Stop it. He doesn't know and he won't have to know.

But I miss him. I miss them all.

Maybe you could write a letter, just to let them know you're all right.

I can't. Papa would tell me to come back. He'd disown me if I didn't, that's what he'd likely say.

But then Colin realized he wouldn't have to tell his family where he was. Excitedly, he got out of bed.

"Where are you going?" Henry asked groggily.

"To write a letter. I want to tell my family I'm all right. Don't worry Henry, I'm not going to tell them where I am."

Henry groaned and turned over. Colin padded downstairs and went to Henry's desk in the library.

April 3, 1891

Dear Papa,

I'm writing to let you know that I am all right. I am in Europe and have a very good job. I'm sorry that I left so suddenly but things are better for everyone this way. I am really happy here and I wish you the same feeling. Please forgive me for that awful letter; I wish I had never written it the way I did. I miss you and Mama and the girls. Please give them my love. Someday I'll come back and see all of you again. For now, it is better for us to be apart. I promise to make you proud with my architecture, Papa. I owe you my life, and I intend to do the best I can with it.

Sincerely,
Michael

Feeling much better, Colin folded the letter and addressed the envelope. Tomorrow he would have to ask Henry for some money. In fact, tomorrow he would have to ask Henry about being put on the payroll, as he had yet to receive a single paycheck. But for now, he returned to bed, said a silent prayer for his family, and peacefully fell asleep.

CHAPTER SIX

The next morning, Colin stirred in bed. Henry was reading next to him. "Ah, you're awake!" he said, pulling a cord by his bed. In time, the French doors swung inward and Charlie entered, carrying a large tray with toast, juice, sausage, several hard-boiled eggs, and a pot of tea.

"Breakfast in bed today!" Henry said cheerily.

Colin sat up, smiling. "In bed? What happened to your Sundays at Charlotte's?"

Henry took the tray from Charlie. "Ah, yes. Well, not only do I think it will cause a wonderful scandal if we don't appear, but I wanted to talk to you about the whole marriage concept, before we see Kenneth and Anne again."

Colin stared at Henry. "Oh," he said and nodded. He picked up a piece of toast. "So, tell me, why *is* Kenneth married?"

Henry tapped an egg with his spoon. "Kenneth Fairchild is in the theatre business, and so while his performers couldn't care less what he is, his patrons certainly would. Kenneth relies on social contacts to make business deals. Therefore he must extend his social ties as far as he can. By having a wife, not only does his social circle double in size, but his reputation does as well. After all, Anne is very beautiful and desirable."

Colin munched his toast thoughtfully. "And she married him for his money and his social affluence," he guessed.

"Well, in so many words. It certainly occurs in regular marriages. Rest assured, Anne has had her own discreet encounters to make up for Kenneth's sexual avoidance of her."

Colin put down his toast. "She has?"

Henry waved a hand. "Yes, yes. Of course. You see, they have a mutual understanding. Anne and Kenneth take many trips to Paris and Rome, and once there, they find their own lovers."

"So it's a complete sham of a marriage!" Colin cried angrily.

Henry shrugged. "So what if it is? Really Colin, could you think of a better situation? They enjoy financial security, legal security, and social security, as well as a completely varied sex life with the other's permission."

"But that's not what marriage is!" Colin protested. "It's for people who enter into a covenant with God to devote their lives to each other." He shook his head. "It makes me ill to think Kenneth and Anne so easily and falsely entered into a union that is the highest form of regard for another person." He looked at Henry gravely. "Marriage is done in the eyes of God. It's sacrosanct, Henry."

Henry rolled his eyes. "Good lord, what a terrific romantic you are! The majority of marriages are borne of convenience and status, Colin, not commitment."

"Then it's wrong," Colin retorted. "And regardless of what some people do, God's pure definition of marriage remains."

"Well! You're one to care about marriage, considering people like you and I aren't allowed."

Colin looked down at his food. "I know," he said quietly. "And perhaps that is why I feel so strongly about it. It is the one thing that I know I will never be able to do. I will never be able to marry."

"Or have children."

Colin shot Henry a hurt look. Then he turned back and said grimly. "Yes, thank you for the reminder."

Henry put his arm around Colin. "I'm sorry, Collie. But you must be realistic about this."

Colin tilted his head. "Do any of your... non-Porter's acquaintances know who you are, Henry?"

"I imagine a few do, but most are still blissfully ignorant." He nudged Colin. "And so they shall remain."

Colin laughed. "Well, it seems very obvious to me. Why didn't you do what Kenneth did?"

"Marry a woman?"

Colin nodded, and Henry cut a piece of sausage. "Well, I didn't have to. I don't have to rely on anyone to bring business to me. I was successful early on, like you. So much so that nobody gave a damn what I did in the off-hours. It certainly wasn't going to affect their precious buildings I designed for them. I established a style that has yet to be surpassed, Colin. If anyone wants something in the design I created, they have to come to me."

"But what about all the offers of courtship from ladies?" Colin pressed.

Henry laughed. "I had no time for such things and that's what I told the young women back then. It was true; I didn't even have time for the gents, which is why I decided a long-term relationship was not my style." He picked up Colin's hand and kissed it. "I have plenty of time now, of course."

Colin laughed. "Good. Do you know, that's what I told everyone too, back in America? I told them that I was going to become a great architect and that no woman was going to get in the way of that!"

Henry rolled his eyes. "I can imagine what your peers thought."

"They thought I was a lunatic," Colin shrugged. "But I don't care."

"Well, the irony of it all is that you are *here*!" Henry quipped. "Your country lost its American version of Henry Sewell. Which means, perhaps, that I shall someday compete against *you*."

Colin sipped his tea uneasily. "I don't intend for that to happen," he replied. "I want to work with you, Henry, not against you."

Henry put down his cup. "You're a darling. We will work together, Colin. You and I."

They finished their morning repast in the sun-filled room with cheery conversation. Colin continued to show great interest in Henry's life and work, and Henry in turn enjoyed the attention. In the middle of his chatter, Colin stopped suddenly and laughed.

"What is it?" Henry asked, bemused.

Colin shook his head, smiling. "I've come to the conclusion that the risk I've taken is paying off quite nicely."

Henry looked pleased. "You're glad you're here?"

Colin regarded him warmly. "Yes, Henry." He tilted his head. "What about you?"

"I think you've spoilt me," Henry admitted. "I love having you around, Collie." He smiled. "I hope you don't mind me calling you that."

"No," Colin shook his head. He paused. "It's nice... to have a nickname."

Henry sensed Colin was thinking of his family. He put his arm around him and gave him a squeeze. "Yes, and if you've already earned yourself a pet name, that goes to show the effect you've had on me." He kissed Colin's head and Colin laughed.

"Then perhaps you shall soon have a name of your own. I'll begin thinking of one starting today."

The next evening Henry and Colin visited Porter's again, but this time, it was Henry who excused himself from their table to go to the bar. "I want to have a word with Jack," he winked.

Jack spotted Henry and walked over to him, shaking his head and rubbing his chin. "You'd best look out, Sewell," he chuckled.

"What do you think of him, Jack?" Henry asked earnestly.

"Can't say. Why don't you let me spend some time with him so I can get a better idea?"

"Not a chance." Henry gazed back at Colin. "He's a piece, isn't he?"

"Hell, if there was a trophy, I'd hand it to you. He's beautiful. And what a mellifluous voice!"

"Yes. I'm afraid I'm already in love with him."

Jack raised an eyebrow. "That superb in bed?"

Henry sighed. "Oh, it's more than that." He paused. "Although maybe not... Oh, yes, it is. It is. Well, thanks for your opinion, old chap."

"Now wait just a moment!" Jack protested. "I haven't even asked you all of the proper questions!"

Henry smiled. "He's twenty years young, the best architect I've seen, the prettiest mouth I've kissed, the nicest bottom I've laid my hands on," he paused, almost woozy. "He's smart as a whip, gentle as a lamb, independent as hell, and *mine*."

Jack eyed him, mildly alarmed. "Are you feeling all right, old fellow?"

Henry slowly shook his head. "No." He gave his friend a lopsided grin and chuckled, "God help you, Jack..." and he turned toward Colin and left.

On Colin's third visit to Porter's he got his first glimpse of Oscar Wilde. Someone had mentioned Wilde's name in his group that night and Colin inquired after him. "You don't know anything of the man?" Henry asked. "I can't stand the fellow myself. He is a pompous, egotistical windbag. And his new little consort is even worse. Bosie—that's the blond boy on his right."

Colin glanced at the young man who had caught his eye earlier that evening. Oscar's companion was one of the most intriguing boys Colin had ever seen, with flaxen hair and eyelashes to match. His skin was almost lily white, and his large eyes were pale blue. His slim frame was outfitted beautifully, and he had the most delicate features. He seemed to be in a constant state of agitation, his mouth showing only a smirk or a frown. "What does he do?" Colin murmured, fascinated.

"Nothing!" Henry exclaimed. "Or I should correct myself; he kills Oscar a little bit every day. Yes, that's his job." Henry lit another cigarette and Colin turned to him.

"What do you mean?"

"Oh, well, I have *heard* the boy is some kind of poet. He's being educated at Oxford—shows you how much that matters. He's actually the son of the Marquess of Queensbury; never mind that. Anyway, his real name is Lord Alfred Douglas—"

"*Lord* Alfred!"

"Collie, all it means is he's inbred. And spoilt. Oscar met him through a friend. They fight like cats and dogs, and I hear the boy's greatest talent is milking Oscar of all of his money. He's a lunatic. I shan't say another word."

Colin nodded and glanced back one more time at the pair. This time, Oscar was gazing at him, and Colin, horrified, turned quickly back around and tried to forget about them both. Henry had no intention of making introductions, but it happened eventually.

It was during a salon. Henry hated the things, but as a favor to Kenneth, who had decided to hold one, he attended with Colin. The group was comprised of only ten people, and Colin was delighted to find Oscar was one of the invitees. And as Oscar held forth (as Henry had said he would), Colin grew captivated while studying him. Oscar was very tall, taller than Henry, and quite large-boned. His droopy eyes seemed always amused, and his dark wavy hair fell below his ears. But best of all was the way he spoke. What a voice! What wit! He was defending some sort of movement that he called "aestheticism." From what Colin heard, he disagreed with the theory, but he could see why the others were falling for it, the way Mr. Wilde spoke. Whenever Oscar looked at him, Colin blushed and looked away, and Henry moved closer to him. After the salon however, Colin secretly bought Oscar's novel, *The Picture of Dorian Gray*, and was quite scandalized by it, just as was the rest of the public. He went on to read *Poems* and after reading *Requiescat*, written about Oscar's dead sister, he was sunk. *He truly has talent!* Shortly thereafter, a party was held by one of the social mavens. Henry was engrossed in conversation with one of the boys in their group, so Colin slipped away and went off to study the artwork of the house. Before long, he heard a lilting voice. "Pardon me, but I believe your chain has come undone."

Colin turned to see Oscar smiling at his shoulder. He broke into a grin. "Mr. Wilde!"

"Mr. Edwards, I believe. I hardly recognized you off your leash."

Colin laughed and shook his hand. "How do you do?"

"I don't do very well when there's a boy like you about." Colin's eyes shone and he was rendered speechless. Oscar wasn't deterred. "You're rather quiet for an American."

"More so for an Irishman," Colin laughed.

"Ah yes, Colin's a fine Irish name. How Irish are you?"

"Half."

"Ah, the better half. Mine's the worse, I'm afraid."

"Oh, no, Mr. Wilde, you've such beautiful talent! Your *Dorian Gray* was a masterpiece, and then I read that beautiful poem about your sister..." Oscar frowned. Most men would have known to avoid such a sensitive subject. But Colin breezed along. "... And it's the most lovely thing I've ever read! I think I shall assign *you* to carve my tombstone."

"Perish the thought!" Oscar exclaimed. "You've too many years left on your pretty bones." He tilted his head. "I heard a terrible rumor that you're Catholic."

"Aren't you?"

"Again, mine's the worse half."

"Protestant."

"Yes, but the gorgeous trappings of Catholicism suit me so much better. You *are* Catholic?"

Colin stopped smiling. "Very."

"Ah, I knew you suited me!"

Colin couldn't help but laugh. Oscar continued, "So you are a Catholic American in England, and one of *us* to boot... you're quite the suicidal little boy, aren't you?"

"I'm not a 'boy.'"

"Aren't you Henry Sewell's boy?"

"I'm nobody's boy." Colin's voice was now full of fierce disdain. "I can look well enough after myself, Mr. Wilde; take note. And while Henry may not care for you, I think... well, I think you're *talented*."

Oscar looked pleased. "How very kind of you. And yet, how cruel."

"Cruel?"

"Yes. Cruel that you've fallen into Henry's hands."

Colin shook his head. "Oh, you're two of a pair. Why isn't your Bosie here?"

"He's bored with these things."

"Bored of hearing you speak? That can't be true!"

"You flatter, Mr. Edwards. Do you know, your jawline is a parallel to my prose?"

Colin laughed, weakening again. "Your prose is a parallel to heaven," he told Oscar. Then he said in a low voice. "I place you second only to Whitman."

"Second!"

"Well, I'm American, first and foremost," Colin reminded staunchly.

"Pity. I was hoping we could forge a brotherhood," Oscar replied sadly. He studied the boy and cleared his throat.

"Er, Mr. Edwards, I'm having a salon myself next week. There will be ten dark heads to Bosie's blond. Won't you help?"

"I expect Henry wouldn't hear of it."

"I thought you weren't his boy."

"I'm *not* his boy. I'm his equal." Colin looked away shyly. "And I'm also loyal. I only wanted you to know, Mr. Wilde, that despite Henry, I find you quite remarkable."

Oscar smiled. "Well then, I shall be the better man for it."

"It was an honor to have met you."

"As it was you, Mr. Edwards. Back you go on your leash, now. Quick!"

Colin laughed and returned to Henry. Later on, he told Henry about the meeting. "Oh, he goes for all of the gutter boys, Collie!" Henry admonished him. "Don't let him turn your head for a minute! You're worth more than that."

"Henry, how can you dislike him so? It's true you and I aren't ardent fans of poets and writers, but you must admit to his talent."

"Talent! Hah! His talent is going to get him into trouble one of these days. Mark my words. The man is careless." Colin tried to inquire further, but Henry refused to speak any more on the subject.

And so a month passed before Colin saw Oscar again. They were attending yet another party. Colin had spotted Oscar earlier and was hoping to speak to him, but the man was constantly surrounded by his admirers, and Colin didn't dare join the group for fear Henry would catch him. He waited until he could catch Oscar's eye, and then he sailed outdoors to smoke. In five minutes, he had the pleasure of hearing the silky voice speak. "The loyal doggy has turned into a butterfly."

Colin turned and grinned. "I see you've been freed from *your* leash!"

"Oh no, Bosie merely lets the line out for me from time to time."

"To let you chase butterflies?"

"Sadly, he never gives me a net."

Colin smiled and drew closer to Oscar. "Foolishly," he corrected, batting his eyes. "Hasn't he realized your voice is the net?" Then he broke from their mutual gaze and crossed his arms. "I have some questions to ask you, Mr. Wilde. About your aesthetic movement."

"Do you? Your antennae must be burning!"

Colin laughed, and a question and answer session ensued. Suddenly, a blond figure burst through the doors to the porch. "Oscar! Where have you been? You can't just leave the party like that; it's rude!"

"I didn't leave the party, Bosie," Oscar said smoothly. "I merely left the house." He gestured between the two young men. "Mr. Edwards, Lord Alfred Douglas. Bosie, Mr. Edwards."

"Oh, pah!" Bosie spat. "Forget the useless introductions and get back inside!"

"I'm still in conversation with Mr. Wilde," Colin said, fully affronted.

"Are you? Then you can converse with him properly, inside, within his circle of friends!"

Oscar sighed. "Mr. Edwards is a friend as well, Bosie."

"Yes, *Bosie*," Colin purred. "Don't get so upset. I'm not going to steal Oscar from you." He gave Bosie a once-over, and then he winked to Oscar while walking away. "As if I ever could."

Bosie stared after him. "Who in hell does he think he is?"

"Why, he's an inquisitive American. Oh, I beg your pardon; that's redundant."

"Inquisitive in a private conference, I see!" Bosie fumed.

"I'm sure he doesn't want Henry to see me with him, darling."

"Well, *I* don't want to see you with him either! Really, if he's so stuck on Sewell, he's got some nerve flitting over to you."

"Perhaps, but Henry Sewell didn't write a book of poetry. Nor has he done anything to further the cause of art for art's sake. Mr. Edwards was asking me about it." Oscar saw the flash in Bosie's eyes and took his hand. "Bosie darling! That boy is a mere shadow. He's *American*, after all. For heaven's sake." He patted Bosie, and they went back inside.

But the truth was, Oscar had already gotten past Colin's Americanness. *True, Bosie is my Hyacinth, my perfect Greek boy statue. But for a taste of Mr. Sewell's honey...* For Oscar saw honey in Colin. Colin had honeyed eyes, honeyed hair, and honeyed skin. Even his lips, fuller than Bosie's, seemed honey-dewed. He was almost a *living* Bosie, Oscar mused. And although Colin was from America, Oscar was able to manage. *He hasn't been soiled by it. He is not of it; merely he has existed in it.* After all, who was Oscar to judge, himself currently trading favors with boys on the street? Arguments such as these allowed Oscar Wilde to think quite guiltlessly about Colin Sewell for a very long time indeed.

The next weekend Colin attended his first Continuation, held in honor of his twenty-first birthday. Henry had described it as an "after-hours soirée." Porter's stayed open only until nine o'clock on weeknights and midnight on Friday and Saturday. This was because so many men had to go home to their wives, and a good number also subscribed to the belief of the day that there were definite health benefits of getting enough sleep. Nonetheless, there were often enough men who wished to keep the spirited atmosphere going, and so usually someone planned to continue the party once Porter's closed. A Continuation was a small, private party, usually held at the nearby hotel, the Wickshire. Whoever was hosting the party reserved a suite of rooms, sometimes an entire floor. But if the man was a bachelor and lived within a reasonable distance, he always offered his home. Men went to Continuations for two reasons: to keep drinking and/or to have discreet sex.

Tonight's Continuation was at Kenneth's house. Colin had by now discovered that Kenneth Fairchild was the most popular fellow in every circle he traveled in. His power over London's theatre district combined with his affability endeared him to all, as did his and his wife's love of lavish entertaining. This only furthered Colin's sense of Henry and Howard's elite stature as the only two men Kenneth chose to be with every evening.

And now they were all assembled in Kenneth's ballroom. Colin sat on a couch with Henry and took it all in. One of the men sat at the piano, and to Colin's surprise, some of the men began to dance with each other! He nudged Henry. "How do they know who leads and who follows?"

"The ones who want to follow just pick it up somehow," Henry shrugged. "Probably by observing the ladies at formal balls and practicing on their own." Colin thought it was the most fascinating display between men that he'd seen yet. Of all the things! He watched them, mesmerized, when suddenly a hand took his.

"Would the guest of honor care to dance?" Colin looked up to see a very dashing Lord Alfred with a teasing look in his eye.

"Oh! Oh, I..." Colin stammered. "I don't know how to dance."

But Bosie had already pulled him to his feet. "You don't know how to dance at *all*?"

"No, of course I know how to dance. With a lady!"

Bosie took him to the floor. "Very well then," he sighed. "I'll follow. But with your looks, you'd be much better suited. Take off your coat."

Colin was dazed, and he realized that the other men had left the floor to encourage him and Bosie. "My coat?"

Bosie grew impatient. "Yes, Edwards. Here you don't wear your coat when you're dancing."

Colin guessed why. As he took off his coat the other men whistled and clapped. He blushed and didn't dare look at Henry, who had just told him that he didn't care for the business of dancing with other men. But Colin was transfixed. Bosie put him in position. "Ready?"

Of course, it was easy; all Colin had to do was dance like he had always done. It was Bosie who was doing all of the work. Once Colin overcame the novelty, he relaxed and began to thrill at the intimacy. His hand was on the small of Bosie's back, while Bosie rested his hand on Colin's shoulder. Their other hands clasped and their faces were only inches apart. Whenever Colin had danced with women, he felt nothing. But now he saw why regular fellows found dancing to be so marvelously nerve-wracking. He could smell the musk on Bosie's neck and was aware of every touch-point. "However did you learn?" he finally asked. "You're a natural!"

Bosie shrugged. "Oh, it's easy. You just reverse everything. See, when I'd normally go forward, I tell myself to go back."

"Have you ever forgotten yourself with a woman?"

"No," Bosie tsked. "You mustn't think me very clever, Mr. Edwards."

"Oh, it's not that!" Colin assured him. "It just seems so confusing. I could never do it."

"Of course you could. Here, let's have you try it." They stopped. "Mr. Edward's first dance lesson," Bosie announced to the small crowd, which responded by clapping and hollering. Colin muddled through it, laughing the entire time. He eventually got some of it down pat, and they ended in front of Oscar, who leapt to his feet. "Bravo, Bosie! Good show, Mr. Edwards!"

"Thank you," Colin said gratefully. "Bosie is a most excellent sport." He turned to Bosie. "Thank you, Lord Douglas. If you'll excuse me..." he bowed and turned to go back to Henry. They watched him cross the room, and then Bosie smiled triumphantly at Oscar.

"Shopping tomorrow, then!"

Oscar dragged on his cigarette. "It was well worth it." The image of the two boys dancing together would last him a lifetime.

Bosie rolled his eyes. "God, he's all show and no substance, Oscar! Everything is new to him! I'll bet you Henry's the first man to fuck him."

"Do you think so?" Oscar wondered, looking in Colin's direction. But Bosie was already talking to someone else in their group. Colin glanced over at Oscar, and they locked eyes. Oscar felt the pull, then Colin snapped his gaze away and rested his lips on the knuckle of his finger. He slowly kissed it, looking off into space. Then he tilted his head and smiled at Henry. As if he'd been stung, Oscar almost dropped his iced champagne.

At the next party, Oscar waited several hours before sidling up to Colin. "You've been quite the busy bee tonight, Mr. Edwards."

Colin held his gaze affectionately. "You've turned me from a dog into a butterfly, and now into a bee?" he laughed. "You're quite enterprising, Mr. Wilde."

"Thank you. I hope you like your next incarnation. I now see you as a fawn among fauns."

"And are the fauns licking their chops?" Colin looked about in pretended concern. When he turned back to Oscar with an impish tilt, Oscar unconsciously licked his lip. Colin tossed his head, not believing Oscar's flattery to be anything beyond entertainment. So he tested it. "I was told you and Bosie were joined at the hip."

"Mm. Speaking of lovely hips, just how loyal, exactly, are you still, Mr. Edwards?"

Colin eyed him, mildly alarmed. "As loyal as you and Bosie, I imagine."

"Well imagine something else then, would you? I know I have. I have imagined *you*, Mr. Edwards, in all of your exquisite forms. A beautiful boy like you and you're going to waste."

Colin stared. "I don't believe I follow..."

"Well, you're American, darling. But I forgive that." Oscar lowered his voice and said with passion, "Mr. Edwards, your honeysuckle beauty possesses every mind here! Leave Henry for a night and come away with me."

Colin narrowed his eyes. "A night?"

"To start with," Oscar crooned. He couldn't stop looking at Colin's mouth. "Please, won't you? I've got sonnets of lovely things to fill your pretty head with. And you do so admire me, don't you, Mr. Edwards?"

Colin felt starry-eyed. "You've written sonnets about me?"

Oscar hadn't, but who was he to correct the lad if it worked in his favor? "Why yes, of course! I've been waiting to ask you to pay me a visit, darling. You must hear them!"

And Colin, who was rather lightheaded from drink, tried to muster a reply. "But... but you're with Bosie," he said, confused.

Oscar paused, and then said with dramatic effect, "Because you are with Mr. Sewell."

Colin's eyes widened, and before he could answer, Henry appeared at his side. "Ah, Wilde, how is Constance doing these days?"

"She's doing excellently of course, as befits her nature," Oscar replied, straightening.

"Constance is Oscar's wife," Henry told Colin, whose mouth fell open slightly at the news, for neither Oscar nor Henry had told him such previously. But Oscar just smiled.

"Yes, you must meet her sometime, Mr. Edwards. She'd be ever so fond of you." He tried to escape, but Henry's words held him fast.

"Well, if she was fond of him as she is of Bosie, he'd be a lucky, lucky boy indeed, wouldn't he, Oscar?" He turned to Colin. "Oh, the trips he could take you on! With Constance's blessing, you see, because of course everyone knows Oscar is a *great writer* and *great writers* must have their solitude. So Oscar must leave his children behind—"

"Children!" Colin gasped.

"I have two fine sons," Oscar said. "Now Mr. Sewell, you're being quite rude intruding upon our conversation."

"The solitude," Henry continued. "The solitude... well, so far it's meant trips to Paris and Rome. And you'd drink and shop and have all sorts of fun with the local prostitutes, every night, Colin! Imagine it!"

"Mr. Sewell!"

"And best of all, it's all on Oscar's tab! Never mind his family at home; *you're* the star." He turned to Oscar. "Bravo darling, your wife has the most exquisitely appropriate name! Although perhaps 'Patience' would have done just as nicely—"

"That is quite enough, Mr. Sewell; that is quite enough!" Oscar drew himself up.

"What's going on here?" Bosie bellowed, cutting in on the group.

"Well, I would love to know," Henry countered. "Oh, I beg your pardon. I do know! It appears that your beloved Oscar was trying to trade you in, Lord Alfred."

"That's... disgusting!" Oscar stammered. "I most certainly was not!"

Colin turned to him in surprise. "Yes you were," he said, his tone a mixture of hurt and anger. "You were."

"Impossible!" Bosie exclaimed. "What would he want with an ugly little Yank whelp like you?"

Colin was too shocked to reply. The beautiful young man who had recently led him around on the dance floor now stood poised viper-like before him, and he tried not to shrink back. Oscar, meanwhile, just shifted uncomfortably. Henry put a hand on his shoulder. "That's right, Colin. Show them, would you? You see, he has *manners*, Bosie. He's *well bred*. He can control himself. As for you!" he glared at Oscar. "Keep your damned inscribed cigarette cases away from him. You've already got your Beautiful Boy—leave mine alone." And with that, Henry ushered Colin out of the party.

As they rode home, Henry looked severely at Colin. "You just can't help yourself, can you?"

"Well, I wouldn't have left you for him!" Colin replied, petulant.

Henry studied him, then shook his head. "I should be angrier, but I do believe you're the only boy Oscar's chosen over Bosie!"

Colin looked away, still hurt from Oscar's rejection. "Bah. I was just a... a stupid passing fancy."

"You weren't. I've seen the designs he's had on you." Henry smiled. "From what I've heard about that *Dorian Gray* book, I believe to Oscar you're Dorian before he was corrupted and Bosie is the Dorian after corruption." He frowned. "But then he'd corrupt you as well. Good riddance, I say."

Colin gave a small laugh. "Well all told, I suppose it was as much a compliment to you as it was to me." He lolled his head to the side. "He must have a touch of madness to like that Bosie."

"Mm. I think he's got a soft spot in his heart for the 'have-nots,'" Henry replied. "And in Bosie's case, it pertains to his brain."

"I can't believe Mr. Wilde is married, with children! Is that all really true, what you said back there about him?"

Henry sighed. "I'm afraid so. Wilde makes a poor husband and a worse father. Even he can't last forever the way he spends on that boy."

"But you treat me as well," Colin said generously.

"And I have three less mouths to feed," Henry reminded him. "I spend as much on you as he does on Bosie, but the man has a family to support! Meanwhile he traipses around handing extravagant gifts to half-class renters, most of whom probably hock them sooner or later." He looked at Colin. "He makes too little effort to hide who he is, and one day he'll be caught. It depresses me, Collie, to think about it. And that is why I don't like to talk about that man."

"Well, I won't have you keep me on a Bosie lifestyle," Colin crossed his arms.

"I'll just keep you on," Henry smiled tiredly. "For now, that's fine enough for both of us."

CHAPTER SEVEN

True to his word, Henry did keep Colin on. Over the next month they worked together, socialized together, shopped together, and made plans to travel together. Finally one morning the two were lying in bed when Colin brought up the topic of his salary. "Henry, I hate to bring this up now, but I was wondering..."

Henry propped himself up on one arm. "Good, you wonder so wonderfully! Go on."

Colin smiled. "Well, it's just that... we've been living so extravagantly, and you've been decent enough to pay for it all, but, I was wondering if I was going to be on the next payroll so I could start paying for myself."

Henry pulled Colin over and cradled him, despite Colin's laughing protestations. "I was wondering when you'd ask that." Then he paused, carefully considering his words. "I don't want you earning money," he said, nuzzling Colin's hair. "I want to buy *everything* for you. I can't bear the thought of you cashing a single paycheck."

Colin pulled away and sat up. "But you've bought me enough already, Henry! You've taken me in, for heaven's sake! And how am I supposed to pay for things if I haven't any money?"

Henry moved above Colin on the bed. "Colin, I don't want you to pay for 'things.'" He traced Colin's face. "I love your independence. I love that you want to be financially independent and that's why I *don't* want you to be. I knew you were going to ask about your first paycheck, but when I thought about it, I realized how horribly unromantic it would be to... to pay you wages. It spoils everything, Collie! Don't you find it so? Either way it will come out of my pocket, and I'd rather it not be in the form of a business transaction."

Colin mulled it over. "I suppose it could be awkward," he said finally. "But how can I make investments if I haven't any money at all?"

Henry raised his eyebrows. "Investments? What kind of investments?"

Colin blushed. "Well, I don't know... stocks, bonds, that sort of thing. And anyway, what about if I'm out somewhere without you, for example, eating a meal? How would I pay for that?"

Henry chuckled. "Colin, darling, of course you would have spending money. But I'm afraid I'm not making this very clear. You see," he ran a hand slowly down Colin's chest and lowered his voice, "I find it very exciting to buy you things." He looked into Colin's eyes. "I'm extremely aroused by the idea of you being 'kept.' Seeing you in the clothes I buy. Watching you smoke the cigarettes I pay for. Getting you drunk on the champagne I order. It's a thrill, because I know you've earned it." He began kissing Colin's neck and shoulders. "When I watch you work in the office. When you bring me to the brink of ecstasy in the bedroom." He moved further down Colin's body. "Can you understand that, Mr. Edwards?"

Colin crossed his arms behind his head, unsmiling. "Perfectly well—you want a mistress."

Henry brought himself back up to Colin's face and smiled. "I did at one time. But I thought of something better." He paused, and then said with a sparkle in his eye, "What do you think, Collie, about being adopted?"

Colin started. "Adopted! By you?"

Henry nodded, laughing. "Yes, I've been thinking about it." He sat up excitedly. "Of course, it sounds crazy at first, but Colin, think of this: If I were to adopt you as my *son*, why, you could live under my roof no questions asked! We'd naturally travel together, share hotel suites, spend all of our time together... It would be the explanation for the both of us! And if anyone happened to notice our *natural* affection for each other, why, once they found out we were *father and son* they'd nod and say, 'Of course!'"

Now Colin laughed, himself sitting up. "That might work if I was seven years old and not twenty-one. And how would you explain my accent?"

Henry shrugged. "I'll say you're an American boy who has long lost his family. I haven't any family of my own, either. So, I've taken you under my wing and you have grown on me, we shall say. You have *endeared* yourself to me. And since you *are* my professional protégé, why not take it a step further and make you the prodigal son I never had? It will be quite the story in the social circles!"

Colin grinned, but then he looked shyly at his lap. "I like the idea. In fact, I'll confess it's brilliant. But then, do you mean for me to keep my own name, or take yours?"

Henry chose his words carefully. "Since it's a legal procedure, Colin, I think you ought to take my last name."

The statement hung in the air as Colin tried to not make too much of what he thought to be the most extraordinary gesture he'd ever known.

It is as if we are marrying!

He held Henry's gaze and declared, "Well then, that means I shall be the second great Sewell!"

"That you shall! Colin, do you understand what this means? We will be a *dynasty!*"

"A dynasty," Colin murmured. *Dynasties last generations. Henry and I... forever.*

But when the actual day came to change his name, Colin grew morose. Henry noticed and tried to console him. "Collie, try not to think of it as a true change."

"But it is," Colin insisted. "It's going to be my legal name. I won't be a Callahan anymore."

Henry scoffed. "You haven't used it since you've been here, and given that your mother and father so disapprove of you, I would think that giving it up would be a relief."

Colin looked at the floor, setting his jaw. "They were good parents, Henry," he said quietly.

The comment softened Henry, and he put his hand on Colin's shoulder. "I know they were," he said tenderly. "I fell in love with their son."

Colin smiled up at him and sighed. "And I'm glad. All right, let us go."

The news was the scandal of the year at Porter's. Some men wondered if Colin was an heir to a family fortune. Others dismissed the move, believing it was merely a stunt to renew interest in the pair. They figured if Henry tired of Colin, he'd just disown the boy. But nobody could deny it was a dramatic action, and Henry reveled in the attention. However, Kenneth and Howard were worried. "Has he lost his mind?" Howard asked Kenneth at a dinner they scheduled shortly after hearing the news themselves. "That boy is now a legal heir to Henry's money!"

Kenneth shook his head. "I would have to think the attorneys would examine such a case, wouldn't they? Couldn't Henry just write a will excluding him?"

"Maybe he doesn't want to exclude him," Howard suggested. "He's in love with Colin; he said so himself. Personally, I'm not so sure there's a line drawn between Colin's appearance as son and lover."

"What?"

"Not in the incestuous sense, but Henry's a fool for the limelight. He's got to be intoxicated by the idea—it *is* brilliant. And with Colin being so much younger than him, and Henry is his tutor, his mentor..." Howard sighed. "I think it's bizarre."

"Well," Kenneth shrugged. "The only good thing so far is that Colin seems a nice enough fellow."

"We've known him for two months, Kenneth."

"But some of them you can't stand after three minutes."

"True. I suppose we'll just have to wait and see."

"And we can have fun with this!" Kenneth exclaimed. "Perhaps you can be Colin's godfather and I can be his nanny!" As Howard laughed, Kenneth put up a hand. "Wait a moment, what about his name?"

"What about his name?"

"Well, they're both going to be Mr. Sewell! How is anyone going to tell them apart?"

Howard frowned thoughtfully. "Hmm." Then he couldn't help it. "Perhaps Colin should go by '*Master* Sewell.'"

"Oh!" Kenneth clapped his hands. "Perfect! We shall call him that, yes! But we must find out what they're going to do at the office. That's where the confusion will be, you know."

"You don't think Colin will like being called 'Master Sewell' by his employees?"

"Well now, I don't see why not. He *is* younger than most of them after all!"

And so the two argued and laughed, agreeing by the end of the evening that even they couldn't really take the newly named Colin Sewell very seriously at all. And as it turned out, Colin and Henry had already solved the conundrum. From now on, anyone who knew Henry well would refer to Colin as "Mr. Colin." And that included Henry's employees.

A week later, Colin and Henry were visiting Paris as a belated birthday gift for Colin. He found the new Eiffel Tower a masterpiece of modernity, though his opinion was certainly in the minority at the time. "This!" Colin had shouted, jumping up and down underneath the spire. "This is what I meant! This is the future, Henry! The future I tell you!" He gazed up into the grid work, fully exhilarated and newly inspired. "Architects working with engineers... we can make anything possible!" His eyes blazed. "Your next building commission—I must have it! I'll work with engineers on it and together we can make an extraordinary structure; we can! Oh, it's absolutely astounding!" It took quite some time before Henry was able to calm him down, though he was pleased Colin found the tower as impressive as he did.

That night they visited an outdoor café with some of Henry's friends. Colin was so giddy from the Eiffel Tower visit, he inhaled his champagne and soon was as high as a fairy, his bright eyes darting to and fro. One young man named Alex, a junior editor at one of the city's newspapers, had spent the entire evening ardently flirting with Colin, trying to keep up with him. They were the youngest two there, and Henry relished watching the others gaze at Colin and Alex in their witty, giggly banter. Everyone finally started to leave and say their goodbyes when Henry decided to invite them all back to his and Colin's hotel room.

More liquor poured. After a half hour, Colin passed out next to Alex, who then looked so mournful that Henry called out to him from across the room, "Why don't you try waking your Sleeping Beauty with a kiss?" The others laughed, and Alex looked embarrassed. Henry found Alex very attractive and addressed him in an encouraging tone. "It's really the only way he'll wake up." But Alex looked doubtful, so Henry sighed. "For heaven's sake, Alex, I'm across the room in the middle of a card game. You are welcome to do it for me." With that, Alex laughed and lifted Colin's head to his. Colin stirred, but continued his slumber. Henry shrugged and nodded toward the bedroom. "His pajamas are in the closet. The blue ones, if you'd be so kind."

If Alex hadn't been so inebriated, he would have stared at Henry in disbelief. Instead, he stumbled into the bedroom and found the nightclothes. As Alex slowly undressed, then dressed Colin while the other men watched from behind their cards, Henry could hardly contain his thoughts. *Bravo, Colin! Beautiful Colin. Even when you're unconscious you're the center of attention.*

The next day Colin and Henry were in their Paris suite again, sitting together, reading. Henry put his arm across the back of the divan and massaged Colin's scalp.

"Colin, was that boy in Massachusetts your very first?"

Colin's eyes left the page and looked off across the room. "Yes. Jeffrey was my first everything."

Before Colin could dwell on the matter, Henry pressed on. "So it has only been Jeffrey and me. As far as your sexual experiences."

Colin winced. "'Only'! My goodness, Henry, women are chaste until their wedding night. I'm more than ahead of the game."

Henry gently but firmly turned Colin to face him. "Colin, the one thing I hold sacred about preferring men is that we don't have to follow the rules. If we can't marry, then there is no wedding night. And if there is no wedding night, there is no demand for chastity." He looked at Colin tenderly. "I love you, but you're only twenty-one years old. I want you to take advantage of the situation."

Colin recoiled. "You want me to have sex with other men?"

Henry looked away, sighed, and looked back. "I don't want you to go sneaking around and doing it, no. I want to be there with you. I want to show you who is safe. Who you can be with. Who you *should* be with."

Colin shook his head, hardly believing the words. "I mean no offense to you, Henry, but a man is a man." He looked into Henry's eyes darkly. "I'm very happy with you."

Henry tsked. "Oh, Colin. Are you telling me that every second of every minute you were with Jeffery was just as if you were with me?" Colin turned away, and Henry's voice was kind. "You see? It is different. Each time. It's all wonderful, yes, but the possibilities are endless!"

Now Colin turned back and eyed him. "How long have you been scheming this?"

Henry paused, and then decided it was best to lie. No need for Colin to know he never really *stopped* thinking about being with other boys. "Since I saw you and Alex last night."

Colin groaned. Henry leaned forward. "You're a natural seducer, Collie!"

"I was completely besotted!"

"That only served to lower your guard and show your skills for what they are." Henry pressed on. "Everyone was utterly absorbed in your game. They were positively green with envy! And you drove Alex absolutely wild!"

"Yes, I'm sure my passing out was the highlight of his evening," Colin muttered.

Henry smiled. "Oh, I think it was."

Colin whirled around. "What do you mean?"

Henry began to laugh. "Do you think in your condition you managed to change into your nightclothes by yourself? And that you could put yourself to bed?"

Colin stared, confused. "But, didn't you...?" Henry shook his head, and Colin's mouth dropped. "Alex?" He shut his eyes tightly. "Oh, Henry..." He stood up, sickened, and hurled his book at a table. "How could you do that? You made me the source of everyone's entertainment, with everyone except me knowing it!"

Henry leapt to his feet. "You were the *center* of everyone's *attention*, Collie! There's a difference!"

"Then I should like to know it!" Colin shouted.

"Colin, please, calm down!" Henry pleaded.

"You had some boy strip me of my clothes, in front of everyone, while I wasn't even conscious?" Colin seethed.

"You were never nude! Your underclothes were left on, remember?"

Colin threw his arms up. "Oh, right, then *that's* perfectly acceptable! Why didn't you just let Alex take everything off, Henry? Honestly, what would have been the difference?"

Henry stood helplessly in front of him. "The difference would have been that if you were nude, you *would* have been the source of entertainment." He shrugged. "Colin, it's not as if we all stood around while Alex lasciviously peeled off your clothes. You couldn't be roused, and the rest of us were in the middle of a card game. So I just asked Alex to change your clothes and put you to bed." Henry quieted his speech. "Now, I admit the fellows probably glanced up from their cards, but how could they help it? You were so beautiful lying there, Collie. You were my Sleeping Beauty. In fact, that's what I called you then. I just wanted all of them to see how beautiful you are." Colin stood silently, placated by Henry's voice, which remained soft and earnest. "I would have loved to have seen how you would have been with Alex, if you could have taken it further. There's nothing lovelier than two beautiful boys together, Colin. Especially when one of them is the most beautiful boy I've ever seen—you. And you deserve to be celebrated."

"If I had wanted to bed other boys, I wouldn't have committed to you," Colin said sourly.

"But you can have both!" Henry exclaimed.

"This is entirely too indecent of a subject to discuss further!" Colin said, reddening. "I refuse to talk of it any more. I am going for a walk." He stood up and left the suite, leaving Henry to smile at his opportunity seized.

As per Colin's wishes, the subject was not brought up again for the remainder of their trip. Back in London, Henry was sifting through his mail when he came across a personal letter. "Collie," he called out, "would that American lover of yours have possibly been 'Mr. Jeffrey Adams'?"

Colin jerked his head up from his desk and then stood from his seat. Henry was standing in the doorway, holding an envelope in his hand. Colin approached him with trepidation. "Is that... is that from him?"

Henry handed him the letter. "I'll leave the two of you alone," he smiled and left the room.

Colin stared at the envelope. He ran his fingers over the ink, read and reread the addresses. It had come all the way from America. Jeffrey had gotten his letter! He sat down again and carefully skimmed his letter opener across the top. Then he lifted the letter out, took a breath, and unfolded it.

Dear Colin,

Congratulations on your procurement of a position with Henry Sewell! I am not surprised in the least, of course. I have decided to remain in America upon graduation next year and look into jobs in New York, for various reasons, so there is no need to bother Mr. Sewell for a second position. Thank you all the same. I shall watch for your name to appear in the trade papers here. Best of luck.

Regards,
Jeffrey Adams

Colin read it and reread it. He turned it over. Surely that couldn't be all! Why would Jeffrey have written such a short letter? He was effectively ending their relationship. And he didn't even know that Colin was living with Henry! *My God, he doesn't even know I've done anything with Henry!* "I don't believe this," he said angrily.

Henry came to the doorway. "What did he say?"

"Listen to this." Colin read him the letter. At the end, he said, "I hadn't even yet told him about you and me! And what does he mean by 'I'm not surprised in the least'?"

Henry blinked. "He means that he's not surprised someone with your talent would be able to get a job with me."

Colin smacked his palm on the table. "No, he's accusing me of seducing my way into a job!"

Henry shook his head. "I don't think so, Colin. But even if he was... you did."

"But I didn't tell him that!" Colin cried. "He's not even upset about the whole thing! No argument, no fight, no effort whatsoever to win me back!"

Henry looked at Colin, incredulous. "But Collie, don't you remember what you told me? You said you didn't think he'd try to win you back. You said that by writing in your letter to him about meeting me would be enough information to tip him off. And apparently it was."

"But I expected him to accept it morosely," Colin insisted. "You know, 'I shall miss you terribly, and remember you always.' That sort of thing." He glared at the letter. "'Best of luck.' What garbage!"

Henry put his hand on Colin's shoulder. "Colin darling, I'm sure he's hurting. But he must preserve his dignity. I imagine he's thinking that if you wrote him such an emotionally detached letter, that he could do the same. You both got your point across in a civil manner."

Colin drooped. "I suppose you're right. It was really rotten of me to have written such a stupid letter." He brightened. "I'll write him one more letter, a nice one, to let him know what he meant to me."

"Colin," Henry warned. "Jeffrey doesn't want you to contact him. His way of saying that was the part about looking for your name in the trade papers. Preserve *your* dignity."

Colin looked indignant. "I am preserving my dignity. I want him to know that we can be gentlemen about this and that there are no hard feelings."

Henry sighed. "Colin, didn't you say that he's the kind of chap who knows more about you than you do yourself? He knows someday maybe he'll see you again, and that will be all right. Now don't be such a silly schoolgirl and keep writing letters for your own ego's sake."

Colin rested his chin on his fist. "All right," he conceded. "It's just that... it was the only correspondence from America I've had. It was the first, and now it will be the last." He stared at the letter. "Jeffrey is the only one who knows who and where I am."

Henry patted his arm. "Well, if there is ever a need to reach you, he knows to just find me, correct?"

Colin looked up at Henry and smiled. "Yes. I'd forgotten. You're very kind, Henry."

"And you're my little Romantic. Why don't we go out for a bit of fresh air?"

That night, they were at Porter's, regaling friends with tales of their trip. As a welcome-back gift, Kenneth supplied Colin and Henry with champagne the entire evening. When Colin returned from the men's room he saw his glass had been refilled for the fifth time. He dropped himself into Kenneth's lap and said woozily, "Kenneth, you're a darling! However shall I repay you for this superb champagne?"

"Oh! You may just stay right where you are; that will do," Kenneth teased.

"Well, why not? But this is entirely too formal," Colin shrugged off his jacket and threw it to Henry amid catcalls. Then he removed his pearl cufflinks and dropped one in his glass and one in Kenneth's. The men roared. Finally he attempted to unbutton his shirt, but after the fourth button he shook his head. "Too much trouble, those. It'll have to stay on, Kenneth." Everyone laughed, and Howard, in high spirits himself, caught the moment and comically put his fist on the table, announcing, "I'll be damned if Fairchild upstages me!" He caught Georgie's eye and said, "Bring out your oldest tawny, if you please."

Georgie stared, then reminded Howard, "That will be from Mr. Colton's private reserve, Mr. Durham." Howard smiled at Colin. "Yes, I know. Jack could use a week's vacation, and I'm giving it to him."

Colin's eyes widened, and Georgie bowed. "Very well, sir." When the dusty bottle was set upon the table, Colin gazed at it, then at Howard, and smiled. "Mr. Durham, I promised Kenneth I would drink only from his bottles this evening." He paused for effect. "May I extend an informal invitation to share this with you tomorrow night?" They locked eyes.

Finally, Howard narrowed his gaze, concerned he appeared too eager. "I think you and Henry should enjoy it," he said coolly, and glanced at Henry, who lazily blew smoke from his cigarette.

"I don't care for port. I'd much rather you and Collie drink it."

Howard looked back at Colin, who began to grin, and he laughed. "Very well then. I'd be delighted to introduce you to the pleasures a good port can offer, since even Henry apparently has his limitations." The group laughed at the double entendre, and Colin gave Howard a demure glance.

After Porter's closed for the evening, Henry and Colin got into their carriage to start home. Colin sat astride Henry on the seat and began kissing him madly.

"Colin," Henry breathed. "Any boy there, if you could have one, who would you choose?"

Colin was feverish on Henry's neck. "Henry..." he protested.

Henry pressed against him. "Tell me. One name. Just one, I dare you."

"No!"

"The Jennison boy, hmm? You find him handsome."

Colin gave a muffled laugh. "He's nice, but I wouldn't want a *boy* of course. I'd rather have an older *man*, like you."

"Is that so? Then name a *man* for me."

"Mr. Durham, then," Colin giggled into Henry's shoulder. "He bought me the port, after all."

Henry stopped Colin and looked at him ecstatically. "Really? Howard? Would you? Oh I think you should!"

Colin drunkenly tried to study Henry's face and then shook his head, embarrassed. "God no, Henry!"

Henry kissed him. "No, no, of course! He did buy you the port now, didn't he? Why, you'll have the perfect opportunity tomorrow night! Would you please, please just try it once for me? I promise if it's awful I will never ask you again." He slipped his hand into Colin's undone trousers and whispered, "I want to see Howard's expression after he realizes how worthy you are of his supremely expensive port."

"Don't be ridiculous," Colin said dizzily. "He'd do nothing of the sort."

"Don't be so sure," Henry smiled. "I've seen how he looks at you. And who can blame him?"

He worked on Colin, pleading all the while until passion overtook the latter. "All right then," Colin panted. "But I still think you'll have to convince Howard, you know. Good luck."

The next morning, as Colin bathed, Henry sent a messenger to Howard inviting him for breakfast at Charlotte's. When the two met, Howard looked surprised. "Where's Colin?"

Henry smiled. "At home. I wanted to speak with you in private."

Howard put up an apologetic hand. "Henry, about the port—"

"Yes, Howard, that was beautifully executed! I commend you!" He paused. "And yes, about the port... Actually, before I get to that, I must tell you what happened after we left Porter's!"

Howard folded his arms on the table. "Yes?"

Once their waiter left, Henry told Howard the story about Colin and Alex in Paris and the argument that had followed. "After we reconciled, I let the matter drop, although I knew he would be thinking about it," Henry concluded. "Well, last night when we were in the cab, I asked him, 'Colin, if you could have any boy there besides me, who would you choose?'" Then Henry burst into a grin. "And who do you think he said?"

"That Jennison boy you used to have your eye on?" Howard guessed, furious that Henry seemed he was going to have his cake and eat it too.

Henry looked around and leaned closer. "No. And I quote—mind you, this was without a moment's thought on his part—'I don't want a boy. I'd rather have a *man*. Like Mr. Durham.'"

Howard exhaled, not daring to believe it. He shook his head, feeling his face redden. "That was because of the port. He was drunk and he was impressed with the port, Henry. It doesn't mean anything. He probably doesn't even remember it."

Henry was clearly enjoying the effects of his delivery. "I thought of that. So this morning I asked him, 'Darling, do you remember what you said in the carriage last night?' And he gave me a wicked smile and said, very clearly, 'I think Howard ought to come at nine o'clock.'"

Howard sighed. "To drink the port, Henry."

Henry laughed. "Silly me, I forgot to tell you! After he named you in the cab, I told him I thought it was a wonderful idea, and I begged him to try it for me, just once. I told him I wanted to see your expression when you realized how worthy he is of your damned tawny port. And he said—most decisively, mind you—'Then you shall see it, the very look of envy!'" Henry looked at Howard triumphantly.

Howard stared hard at his friend across the table. "Henry, are you meaning to tell me that you want me to go on with the very boy you've professed to be completely in love with?"

Henry happily sipped his tea. "I am in love with him; there's no doubt about that. He's the most amazing young man I've ever known!" He paused, and then looked earnestly at Howard. "But Howard, I'm *used* to sharing my most beloved treasures; I'm an architect, after all! I *have* to give over my creations to other people. And think about it: If you had a prize thoroughbred, would you not enter him in any races? If you had a case of the finest vintage wine, would you consume it all yourself instead of sharing it amongst your friends? Well, I want people to have a taste of Colin. I want them to experience him and to fall in love with him. I want them to enjoy him immensely then know that at the end of the day he's mine."

"But you're accomplishing that now, Henry," Howard argued. "We're already envious of you."

Henry paused, and then chuckled. "Damn your cleverness, Howard. All right then, I do love Colin, but *I'm* not quite ready to give up enjoying other boys just yet. And Colin is young; he shouldn't limit himself either."

"You're going to... er... participate with him?" Howard asked uncertainly.

"Not in your case, but if he enjoys having you, then yes, after that, of course." Henry's eyes gleamed. "It's the perfect way to still get all of those lovely boys! And you see, Howard, he and I will always be together. That is the difference! It will be like we are team, of sorts."

Howard shook his head in disbelief. "Henry, I will come tonight at nine o'clock, and I will share the port with your beautiful American boy. But beyond that..."

Henry frowned. "Howard, I managed to get Colin this far. It was your name he mentioned. Please, as a friend, you must help me out."

Howard rested his hand under his chin and smiled. "It's a novel experiment, I'll give you that. I just don't know that I want to be the test subject." When he saw Henry's disappointed expression, he exclaimed, "You're one of my closest friends! It would be... awkward."

Henry sighed. "I won't mind in the least, and I promise to be out of the house for the evening."

Howard paused. *Do I dare...?* Then he made a face, pushing away from the table. "No. I couldn't. It's just repellent to me, Henry. I'm sorry."

Henry glared. "Repellent? Really! Then pray tell why on earth would you spend nearly a hundred pounds on a bottle of port if you didn't mean to go to bed with him?"

Howard looked away. "I was caught up in the moment," he said weakly.

Henry set his jaw. "Well, Colin didn't think so. He thought you found him attractive. So I suppose I'll just tell him that you don't."

"Henry," Howard protested, hurt.

Henry looked down for a moment, and then said quietly, "I apologize, Howard. I've thought about this for so long, I forget that it's new to you. You're too kind to say it, but your concern is that Colin may leave me for you, or anyone else he spends time with." He put up a hand. "I don't believe he will. And if I want you to be with him tonight, and Colin wants you to be with him tonight, then there's no argument." He smiled. "But, all right, we will leave it at the port, and we'll not discuss the topic further. Is that better?"

Howard sighed, relieved. "Yes, thank you. Yes." For while Howard felt odd enough imagining the thing himself, he wondered why on earth Colin would agree to it, causing Howard to fear that perhaps Henry was forcing him to.

But Henry was doing no such thing. At least, not directly. Colin had his own reasons for going along with the idea. It took only two weeks in London for him to grasp that he must stay in Henry's favor at any cost. The city was far larger than Colin imagined, and he knew not a soul in it. Henry proved invaluable with his knowledge of London and its inhabitants, with his clubs and his connections, all of which he shared with Colin, thankfully, for Colin had never felt so inexperienced in his life. As a recent incident illustrated, Colin still had a lot to learn.

The first time they had gone to the theatre in Leicester Square, Colin strayed off toward the statue of Shakespeare, where he was soon approached by a handsome boy offering to light his cigarette. Colin thanked him and began to chat. Within moments Henry rushed over and took him by the arm. "*Never* talk to the trade!" he chastised angrily, once they were further away.

"The what?" Colin had asked, perplexed.

"The trade! The prostitutes!" Henry cried.

Colin was shocked. "*He* was a prostitute?" And Henry had to stop for a moment and study Colin, to see if he was serious. Colin shrugged. "But... well, he was awfully well-dressed and good-looking, Henry."

Henry tsked him. "If you looked more closely you'd see his clothes were cheaply made. And that horrendous cockney accent! Well, I suppose you're not familiar with it yet. They're all over the Square at this hour, Collie; look at them!" Henry swept his arm aside causing Colin to cautiously regard the crowd by the fountain. The ladies did look awfully painted... and there was the boy who had chatted him up. He was laughing in Colin's direction and winking at him while elbowing his friends.

"Oh God," Colin muttered turning scarlet. "I thought they were just gents hanging about and taking in the people."

"Well then, it would have been a nice surprise for you when he asked if you have a room to go to," Henry smirked. Then his voice turned dark. "Collie, don't ever let them talk to you for even a moment. They'll pick up on your accent and realize you're game for a pickpocket or some other scheme."

It wasn't the first valuable bit of information and advice Henry had given Colin, and Colin was extremely grateful for the lessons.

Henry's guidance in social affairs was reason enough to stay on, but having the opportunity to work for him was Colin's real cause for commitment. Since Colin also had neither a degree nor a name of any import, he was no longer confident he could find a job, at least, certainly not with the status Henry had afforded him. And the very opportunity to work with his favorite genius was a coup to keep. So, he must stay on. And staying on meant keeping Henry happy. It would be sheer folly, then, to make the man sacrifice the very thing he enjoyed most. And of course, it was only after coming to this conclusion that Colin shamefully permitted another reason to factor into his decision: the idea of sex with so many well-connected men excited *him*. Unfortunately, Jeffrey had turned out to be rather conservative and guilt-laden about his and Colin's physical encounters. And while Henry was assuredly the opposite, Colin felt he now deserved to enjoy sex to the fullest, and what better way than this? For while it was amusing to flirt with men like Oscar and Jack, seduction was better, and now he could seduce a man as attractive as Mr. Durham!

But Colin knew it was easier making this sort of decision now, when he was only fond of Henry and not in love with him. Yet he was skeptical that Henry could really be anything more than fond of Colin as well, despite his daily devotionals. And so, Colin found a final, practical reason to take up with other men: if Henry did lose interest in him, perhaps one of his paramours might find him suitable. While Colin didn't wish for this to happen, he at least thought he could certainly do worse than a successful, handsome banker.

CHAPTER EIGHT

When Howard was ushered into Henry's house that evening, he spotted Colin leaning against the doorway of the den, arms folded and smiling. He was dressed in dark crimson and black, a ruby and jet brooch fastened at the collar of his cream-colored shirt. He had not changed from dinner, and now he walked into the room, beaming almost childishly. Suddenly Howard felt overwhelmingly depressed. Should he just drink the port and leave, or should he give in, share with Colin, and risk regret afterwards? Colin bounded to his side. "Well, enough stargazing, Howard. I am dying to try this superb port you bought!" He took him over to the divan and asked Charlie to do the honors of pouring.

Colin chattered the time away until he made a wry comment about arriving at work at ten o'clock the next day. He turned to Howard, "What time are you at work, Howard?"

Howard shrugged. "Oh, I'm usually there by seven o'clock."

Colin looked at him in horror. "Seven!" He glanced at the grandfather clock in the room. "But it is already eleven o'clock now!" Howard watched as Colin looked panic-stricken, and he burst into laughter. Colin tilted his head, amused. "What? What is so funny?"

"It's just... your expression!" Howard shook his head, chuckling, and Colin laughed too. Then he gave a sidelong glance at Howard.

"Henry told me you may not feel comfortable. I understand. It's perfectly—"

Howard waved a hand, teasing. "For heaven's sake, Colin, if you talk things out you'll never get very far. Aren't you supposed to be seducing me by now?" He winked at him.

Colin looked briefly affronted, then sized Howard up and threw an arm over the back of the divan. "I would very much like to. Did Henry tell you what I said in the carriage?"

Howard smiled nervously. "Er... yes, but I figured it was the port."

Colin narrowed his eyes. "I couldn't give a damn about the port." Then he remembered his manners. "Although it was an extraordinary gesture." He lowered his head, still looking at Howard. "I think you're very handsome, Howard. You're absolutely a man's man." He leaned forward and laid a hand on Howard's trousers. He paused as if to say more, but instead brushed Howard's hair with his fingers, then stroked his neck, resting his lips on Howard's mouth. After a fervent moment, Colin looked into Howard's eyes. "Follow me." Howard stared back, mesmerized, while Colin stood and extended his hand, smiling.

In the dimly lit bedroom upstairs, Howard kissed Colin ardently and while unfastening his ruby brooch murmured, "Are you going to show me what makes you so precious, then?"

"Oh yes," Colin breathed, undressing Howard in turn. "I *want* to show you, Howard." He finished undoing the last button and looked into Howard's eyes. "And then I want you to show me."

Three-quarters of the hour had passed when Howard lay down next to Colin on the bed for good. After their breathing slowed, Colin rolled over on top of Howard and smiled. "Next time, I shall be the one in control," he admonished. Howard closed his eyes and stroked Colin's arm. *Next time?* His eyes fluttered open as Colin kissed him tenderly and whispered,

"I hope you don't mind, but I'm about to drop. I'm sure Henry will show you out." He slid back down under the sheet and closed his eyes, a fevered flush blooming on his cheeks and a faint smile curling at the corners of his mouth. Howard rested his lips on the boy's glowing skin. He inhaled its glorious, spring-like scent and had to push out of his mind his desire to stay, to sleep next to him, to wake up looking at that lovely face. He struggled to get out of bed and get dressed. Before leaving, Howard walked quietly back, but Colin had already dozed off. Howard had hoped they could share a few last words, but he settled for watching Colin several moments before turning to go.

On the way out, he was startled to see Henry in the library. "I just got in, Howard; I hope you don't mind." He looked expectantly at his friend. "Well then, did you have a nice time?" Howard just stood, gazing at his friend.

"It was terrible," he deadpanned. "Absolutely terrible." Henry chuckled, knowing Howard meant the opposite. But really, Howard thought miserably as he rode home, it was terrible. It really was.

"Tell me more about Howard, Henry." Colin was drinking tea with Henry the next morning.

"And have you fall in love with him? Not a chance!" Henry chuckled.

"Don't be silly!" Colin scolded, sitting down. "How long have you two known each other?"

Henry stirred his tea thoughtfully. "Oh, about fifteen years, I'd say. Howard and I actually met through Kenneth. He was a rather quiet fellow then; he brooded a lot at the start. I thought of him as my pet assignment, and I took to coaxing out the butterfly in him. It took me almost a year—the boy would hardly come to the club! So it wasn't until I was designing one of Kenneth's theaters that I really got to know him. Howard was Kenneth's financial partner and he was in charge of financing that contract. We came to know each other throughout the project. He made me justify every change I wanted to make." Henry smiled. "He was a fierce defender of

Kenneth's money. But he also saw that I knew what I was doing. In fact, on several occasions, he persuaded Kenneth to agree to my insistences. And I realized then that he was the man I wanted to represent my own finances." Henry paused. "I told you how influential Kenneth is. Well, Howard is also very powerful, Colin."

A shiver coursed across Colin's skin as he thought of Howard commanding the banking world. He leaned in. "Did you and Howard ever...?"

Henry looked amazed. "No! Heavens, no. We actually became quite competitive in our pursuit of London's finest. A friendly competition of sorts. We compared notes quite often."

Colin's eyes widened. "Really! Howard doesn't seem the type to do that."

Henry put his teacup down. "Well, he *was* a bit socially awkward and, again, very reluctant that first year I met him. Kenneth and I think something awful must have happened to him before we knew him, but he's never told us. I think Howard followed my lead for a while because he didn't know what else to do. But he was always more of a romantic than me; what he really wanted to do was to find 'the great love of his life.'"

"He said that?" Colin asked, fascinated.

"No," Henry chuckled. "That's the phrase that Kenneth and I teased him with. Howard had good looks and money even then, but because he was so naïve, boys would treat him rather shabbily. He couldn't stand the idea of them bedding anyone else if they were doing so with him, and they often exacted gifts from him to remain loyal, which mind you, didn't really change anything. To add to that, he spent most of his time at work, and he really didn't know how to pay a boy proper attention. So, after so many unpleasant episodes, he turned bitter again and to be honest, I think he treated *them* quite meanly for a while. However, last year he met the 'love of his life' and, unfortunately, really got his heart broken. Since then, he's withdrawn from the game completely. A shame—he's passed on so many lovely boys."

"Who broke his heart?" Colin wanted to know.

Henry paused uncertainly. "It was a boy he met during a trip to Switzerland. A banker's son, ergo he was perfect. They were together the entire month that Howard was there. When Howard left, they promised each other they would write, and Howard planned to invite him to London shortly thereafter. He was going to ask the boy to stay, with him paying for everything! I know, Collie, it sounds familiar. So Howard sent off his first lovestruck letter, but the boy—Luca, I think his name was, yes—he never wrote back. Howard was devastated. Of course, he had told us all about him as soon as he returned, so it was humiliating for him. He even went back to Switzerland to find him. When he did, Luca just smiled and said something about a mutual assumption that their affair was just that—an affair."

Colin stared. "Poor Howard!"

Henry tsked. "I personally thought a month-long affair was perfect. But then again, I never met the boy." He smiled at Colin. "Perhaps he was somewhat like you."

A thought sprang to Colin's mind. "Do you think it must be painful then, for him to see you and I together?"

"Well, apparently not so painful that he declined last night's invitation," Henry said wryly. "That was some time ago, and anyway, Howard's a grown man. He needs to move on and get back into enjoying life once more. Perhaps seeing you and I will encourage him to try again." He frowned. "But Colin, don't tell Howard you know the story about Luca. I'm not certain he'd be pleased that I told you."

Colin sighed. "But it's such a romantic story."

"Yes, well, he doesn't need you reminding him that," Henry replied, draining the last of his tea before getting up to dress for work.

Later that morning, around 11:30, Henry's secretary appeared at his office door. "Mr. Sewell? Mr. Durham is outside. He's wondering if you could see him."

Henry glanced at Colin, who raised his eyebrows then quickly looked back down at his work, trying not to smile. "By all means, please show Mr. Durham in," Henry assented, standing up.

In a few moments, Howard appeared. "Good morning Henry! Colin!"

Henry leaned on his desk. "What brings you across town, Durham? Have you some insider advice?"

Howard chuckled. 'If only I did. I'm afraid all I've come with is an invitation to lunch. I'm in the mood for Ellison's, and since you're in the area, I thought I'd stop by."

Henry sighed. "That would be lovely, but I'm afraid I'm meeting a client for lunch. I daresay Colin could go with you."

Howard's expression froze. "Oh! Well, I... I hadn't planned on... I mean, I wanted to take both of you. Pay for your lunch, you know."

Henry laughed. "Well, if it's a lunch of gratitude, by all means, you must take Colin!" He winked at Howard, who turned bright red. "And you may buy me drinks tonight at Porter's."

Colin rose from his chair and rolled his eyes. "Howard is really getting the short end of the stick on that one!" He stood by Howard and crossed his arms.

"I think I shall pay for Howard's drinks, then!"

Henry grinned.

"And I shall pay for yours! It will be a lovely triangle of sorts!"

Howard was exasperated. "Or, we can just all three have lunch another day, instead."

Henry and Colin turned in unison and said, "No!" Colin took his jacket and hat and left with Howard.

Once they were on the sidewalk, Howard fumbled for words. "I... I tried to tell you good-night properly, but you had already fallen asleep."

Colin laughed. "I'm sorry. I suppose I'm not very familiar with the ways of port. America has yet to stand in its social graces." They walked on, not looking at each other. "I enjoyed the evening very much," Colin said pleasantly.

Howard stopped and turned to face him. "Did you?"

Colin looked at him and smiled. "Very much." Then he searched Howard's face uncertainly. "Did you not...?"

"No, no!" Howard shook his head. "I mean, yes, of course." He sighed. "I'm just glad that... I had hoped you enjoyed it as much as I did."

Colin gave a wry laugh and resumed walking. "Well, I should think it was rather obvious, Howard."

Howard shrugged. "At the time, yes, but sometimes one can have regrets afterwards." He glanced at Colin. "I suppose your youth has prevented you thus far from such experiences."

Colin grinned. "Perhaps. Or perhaps I'm just not the regretful type."

"Hmm," Howard mused. "That would certainly be in your favor."

Colin lifted his chin and took bolder strides. "Well, it must be true," he decided. "After all, I don't regret leaving my family, nor do I regret coming to London. I don't regret meeting Henry, or working for him." He looked at Howard. "And I certainly don't regret having been with you." He stopped short. "Isn't this Ellison's?" He looked at Howard, who felt rather lightheaded.

"Yes, it is."

Once they had settled into their table and ordered, Howard gave in to his curiosity. "So, Colin, if you found the evening's activities to be as wonderful as Henry had hoped, how exactly are you two going to go about the whole business?"

Colin regarded him excitedly. "Henry and I talked about that this morning. It's absolutely brilliant! It all makes perfect sense." Then he shrugged his shoulders. "All it is, really, is his current set of standards, of which you are probably aware."

Howard nodded. "Henry and I share similar views on that sort of thing, but tell me anyway."

Colin's eyes gleamed. "Well, to start with, Henry said neither of you use renters or brothels."

"That's correct," Howard agreed. "Did he tell you why?"

"No blackmailers or getting caught! He told me what happened two years ago, at that Cleveland Street place. My God, Howard, if you or Henry were there, you two would have been arrested!"

"Yes, it was very tragic for the men who were caught."

"Well avoiding such places is genius, Howard. I had no idea what trouble you can get into."

Howard looked surprised. "Really? I would think you'd have the same problem in your country."

Colin looked at him quizzically. "Well," he hedged, "I suppose we do. But to be honest with you—and I'd rather you not share this, although of course, Henry knows—I've been with only three men, two of whom currently live in London."

Howard pondered this information, then gaping at Colin, he whispered, "You're joking! You mean Henry and I?"

Colin looked down at the table and said shyly, "Yes. I hope you aren't disappointed to find you were with such a... a novice."

"Novice!" Howard exclaimed. "I certainly never would have guessed." Colin laughed and smiled gratefully. Howard shook his head. "Well, you fell into the right hands, then. Henry is a wise man."

Colin nodded. "Yes. He also said he never uses hotels, when he's taken up with someone, that is. He just uses his house."

"Henry is fortunate to be unmarried *and* live near Porter's," Howard chuckled.

"Yes." Colin grew excited. "And I have finally thought of a good use for his second bedroom—I am going to turn it into a grotto of sorts!"

Howard gasped. "You're joking!"

"No, it will be perfect for what we plan to do! It will have everything any man could want!"

"But all they'll want is you," Howard argued.

"That's kind of you Howard," Colin smiled. "But seduction requires all sorts of things if it's to be done properly. I ought to know."

"Yes, what with the extensive seducing experience you have."

"Well, I've *imagined* many things," Colin admitted, grinning.

Howard couldn't help it. "And what, pray tell, does Henry think of you turning part of his house into a bordello?"

"*Grotto,* Howard!" Colin reprimanded. "It will be an extremely tasteful *grotto* and I predict Henry will love it, because our own bed shall be kept to ourselves." Then he leaned in. "But I haven't told Henry what it will be yet, so don't tell him."

"I don't think I honestly could if I wanted to," Howard shook his head.

"Oh, for heaven's sake." Colin laughed. Then he looked pensive. "Oh yes, and the men we take home will only be those with everything to lose should they try to blackmail us." By now, Henry had instilled in Colin his own fear of getting caught. "Which means they will have to either be very wealthy, very famous, or be very involved in politics of some kind." Colin made a face, "As if I would care for any other sort."

Howard grinned. "That's another important tenet in our credo, yes."

"And to take it a step further," Colin added, "no more than two men at once. That way we either outnumber them or have our word against theirs."

Howard was taken aback. "You were going to engage in group... activities?"

Colin blushed. "Well, it just happened to come up in conversation. In Henry's defense, it was my idea." Howard felt his jaw drop, and Colin tsked him. "Don't tell me you've never thought about it, Howard!"

Howard rested his chin on his fist. "Do you know, I was worried about how you would manage Henry, but perhaps I should worry the reverse."

Colin laughed again. "Well, I would rather talk about something else, really."

"Very well then," Howard agreed. "Tell me how you decided to become an architect."

Colin's eyes lit up. "Oh! Well, it was actually due to my father. While I was growing up, he would tell me all about the great cathedrals of Italy—he had been there, you see—and we went on very many tours up the coast in America, studying the beautiful churches everywhere. It was then that I realized that to build a house of worship would be the greatest gift to God I could ever give. And to do that, I had to study to be an architect."

Howard was flabbergasted. *Wasn't the boy just talking about having group sex?* "Oh," he managed to reply. "But do you still have that desire today? To build a church?"

"Oh yes," Colin said gravely. "And someday I will. But since it shall be my greatest achievement, I must put other things to ground first. I want to learn everything I can. My cathedral has to be perfect."

It took every ounce of strength for Howard not to point out the irony, but he didn't dare, for he could see it all made perfect sense to Colin, and Howard didn't know him well enough to tease. "Well," he nodded, "That is certainly an admirable endeavor. I hope you see it through."

They were walking through Hyde Park on the way back when Colin stopped and gasped. "What on earth is that?"

Howard regarded the grand structure on the steps in front of them. "That's the Albert Memorial. Queen Victoria had it built to honor her husband."

"Good God it's atrocious!" Colin exclaimed. "And yet it's somehow glorious—just look at the gold leafing on the statue!" Colin whirled around to find a bench, and he grabbed Howard's arm. "Do you mind if I spend a minute to sketch it?"

"Not at all," Howard replied, interested, and sat down next to him. Colin whipped out a notepad from his jacket pocket and began to draw furiously. Howard was stunned by the boy's bold, scrolling lines and his eye for perspective. When Colin had finished, Howard exclaimed, "Colin, that is an absolute work of art in miniature!"

Colin looked skeptically from his drawing to the building and added a few more details. "Well, it will give me some idea, anyway," he shrugged.

"Some idea? Your reproduction is magnificent!"

Colin looked up. "That statue is magnificent." His expression was exuberant, his face flushed. Howard realized why it looked so attractively familiar. Colin grinned. "I imagine you get this excited when your accounts balance," he teased.

"I don't think I've ever gotten that excited over anything work-related," Howard admitted. He admired the drawing again. "It is just beautiful. I suppose if I drew like that, I'd be quite thrilled indeed."

Colin laughed and then gazed affectionately at Howard. With a flourish, he tore out the page and handed it over. "Here. You shall have it, then."

Howard put up his hands. "Don't be ridiculous! You just spent all that time committing it to paper!"

"I've committed two minutes," Colin admonished. "I can come back again. The building isn't going anywhere." He laid his sketch on Howard's lap, and Howard carefully picked it up.

"I'd be happy to wait while you draw one for yourself," he insisted.

"I can't! What if the second one is better than the first?"

"Then we will trade!" Howard exclaimed.

Colin shook his head, laughing. "Oh, very well." He began again, and Howard tried not to be obvious as he watched Colin's furious expression of study. He got caught up in the boy's manic pace, and suddenly Howard was overwhelmed with a desire to seize Colin and kiss him. Howard tore his gaze away, biting his lip. *Thank God we're in public,* he thought tensely, and he jumped when he felt Colin reach across his lap to snatch up the first drawing. After examining both works, Colin sighed. "I don't know. Which do you prefer?"

Howard's head swam as Colin leaned against him to show him both sketches. He could smell Colin's aftershave on his neck, the same neck he had kissed only a night ago. "Umm, I shall keep your first edition," he said faintly. "It has the soul of inspiration locked up in its lines."

Colin looked up in wonderment at Howard. "Did you just now create that? I love it!" He wrote it onto both sketches, then handed Howard's version back. He stood up. "Thank goodness Henry takes long lunches. I expect now we'll arrive back at the same time."

As they approached the office, Colin turned to his companion. "Thank you for the meal, Howard, and the pleasure of your company."

"The pleasure was greater mine," Howard smiled. And really, Howard thought happily as he hailed a cab back to the bank, it was greater. It really was.

Kenneth received a wire that afternoon to meet at Porter's a half-hour earlier than usual. When he sat down across from Howard, he was addressed thusly: "Kenneth, how would you like to accompany me on the next ship to America?" Kenneth searched his friend's face for an explanation. Howard shrugged. "Maybe we could find a Colin for ourselves."

Kenneth grinned. "Oh, no! Howard, whatever did he do to you?"

Howard sighed. "God, Kenneth, the boy is unbelievable. Henry's the damned luckiest man in the world."

Kenneth leaned in, rapt. "You must tell me details!" Howard looked as if he was uncertain where to begin. Then he started, slowly. He told Kenneth about Sunday, from the first glass of port to his last words with Colin. He ended with describing his onslaught of emotions after lunch. Kenneth was incredulous. "You had sex with him? On both his *and* Henry's insistence? Oh Howard, you lucky, lucky thing!"

"Well, don't be so sure, Kenneth."

"And he's designing a *bordello* in Henry's *house*?"

"I suppose he considers it an *earthly* house of worship," Howard chuckled. "He was extremely serious about building the cathedral."

"My word," Kenneth murmured. Then he looked up. "And I cannot believe you actually spent so much time alone with him today!"

"I'll kill Henry for that," Howard muttered. "He knew damn well what he was doing. I'll bet he didn't even have a client scheduled for lunch."

"Oh, nonsense," Kenneth pshawed. "I don't think Henry would have meant to cause you trouble. Remember, they weren't expecting you."

Howard shook his head. "That's true. But Henry is the craftiest person I know. And Colin's smart enough to see it; he respects it. I suppose I don't know what to think about Colin. He's too spontaneous to be the scheming sort. But he gets a sense of who you are so quickly." He frowned in thought, and then looked anxiously at his friend. "Kenneth, what will you do if they offer the same opportunity to you?"

Kenneth burst out laughing. "I can't imagine it! You know Henry's never shared his with me nor mine with his, at least not while we were with them." He sighed. "The truth is, I'm afraid I might not be able to walk away so easily as you did, Howard."

Howard was astonished. "What, are you already in love with the boy yourself?"

Kenneth blushed. "I won't give myself the chance. I know I'm no match for Henry, anyway. And I think Colin's going to need at least one friend who doesn't have designs on him. I know you can appreciate that."

Howard smiled. "Indeed I can. Very generous of you, my friend." They laughed, and Howard paused. "All right then, I shall join you in this noble venture, starting today. After all, we're going to be sitting with the two of them each night. If anyone's to be virtual eunuchs it'll have to be us."

Promptly at 8:00 p.m., Henry and Colin made their appearance. Colin sat down, and Henry followed, smiling at Howard. "Well, Durham, Colin informed me that you two had a delightful lunch."

Howard nodded. "Er... yes, I even got to see him in action. Did he tell you about the Albert Memorial?"

"Yes. Apparently you admired his charming little doodles of it."

Colin reddened and Howard sniffed, "Well, if you call those wonderful renderings 'doodles,' then I shall have to refer to Michelangelo's 'David' as a lump of clay." He looked at Colin. "They were marvelous."

Kenneth watched Colin smile gratefully. "Thank you, Howard." Then he regarded Howard, who had fallen into a gaze. *And whose heart must be nearly out of his chest*, Kenneth deduced. He stepped on Howard's foot. Howard glared, and Kenneth cleared his throat. "So, do tell, Colin, what do you think of the architecture in America?"

"Oh, well since you've been there once before, Kenneth, you know it's almost all a copy of what has been built here. But we have our own terminology for it. Before the Revolution, most homes were in the Georgian style, but we called it Colonial. Of course, after the Revolution, people wanted nothing to remind them of England, but instead of using the perfect opportunity to create something entirely original, they went back to the Greco-Roman style and called it Federalist." Colin crossed his arms. "Bah! Thank God Henry Richardson came along and finally enabled America to play its part in the world of architecture. We're finally making some headway."

"But you're not in America anymore," Howard quipped. "So, if you build all of your works here, will you be considered an English architect or an American one?"

Colin grew mystified. "Well, I'll always be called American, but as far as contributions to America itself..."

Henry caught Colin's uncertain gaze and quickly moved the conversation on. "It's of no consequence right now; he's working for me."

Colin grinned, and he had to laugh. "Yes, and it doesn't even feel like working at all!"

"Really?" Kenneth asked.

"Well," Colin shrugged, "all I do all day long is talk and learn and draw. With the master of contemporary architecture himself." He sighed. "I really get paid entirely too much."

He winked at Henry, who smiled and tilted Colin's chin with his fingers. "You know how talented you are. You're priceless."

Colin smiled broadly. When he looked at his glass before him, he remembered. "Oh Howard, I was supposed to buy your drinks this evening! Give over your tab!"

Howard waved a hand. "Don't be ridiculous. That was said only in jest."

Henry chuckled. "Well, *I* still intend to take you up on the offer, Howard. Luckily for you it will only be one drink, as you'll both be leaving. You should be glad we were so tardy."

Colin frowned. "Well then, I shall buy *your* last drink Howard." He looked off to the bar intently, and then he summoned Georgie. "A glass of Chateau Lafitte for Mr. Durham. And he is to take home the rest of the bottle."

Henry lit his cigarette and muttered, "Good lord, are we all buying bottles now?"

Howard frowned. "Colin, the glass will be enough. Don't be frivolous with your money."

"Spoken like a true banker!" Kenneth applauded.

Colin tossed his head. "The price of the bottle is what I earn in a few hours, Howard. In fact, I should really order two: one for you and one for Kenneth."

"And what about me?" Henry pouted in mock fashion.

Colin turned his head toward him but kept his eyes on the other two. "You shall be rewarded just as handsomely later."

When Georgie returned, Colin asked, "Do you have another bottle? Good. Please bring one to Mr. Fairchild." He looked into Kenneth's eyes, and Kenneth returned the smile weakly. *He really is kind. He cares for all three of us, doesn't he!* His brow furrowed as he tried to focus, but now it was Howard's foot upon his, and he was brought back to the conversation.

"Disgusting stuff. Promise me you won't make *that* your drink of choice, Colin."

"Why is it so terrible?"

"It's what those Bohemians in Montmartre drink. They think they're being such *artistes*, asserting their individuality, when all they do is sit around in absinthe cafes in their absinthe stupors."

"But then, why is it so popular?"

"Why is laudanum popular? It is the means to escape, Colin. And when one is a penniless, retched artist or poet, absinthe is the easiest method for losing one's mind. You are aware, Colin, that all geniuses are insane, so if you are not congenitally a genius, you must achieve that state artificially if you are to get any respect from your peers and patrons."

"But, Henry," Colin teased, "you then must be claiming that you and I are insane!"

Henry laughed. "Well of course! I'm not inferring that insanity is a bad thing, per se. And there are varying degrees. You and I are insane only in our perception of structural forms. We don't see them as other people do. Why, for example, take this afternoon: *You* practically climaxed upon seeing the Albert Memorial, whereas Howard here, well, to Durham it was just another statue, naturally. Perhaps he found it pleasing to look at, but Howard, being of more sound mind, found something else more pleasing to look at, I'm sure." He winked at his friend.

Colin scoffed. "Oh, Henry! I completely disagree, and I resent being called 'insane.'"

Howard spoke up. "Yes, Henry. Don't you think that if you were congenitally insane, you would be *more* inclined to partake in such vices, in order to blot out your unnatural urges?"

Henry sighed. "You two are both seeing insanity as only a negative thing. Forget the word. Colin, all I am saying is that you have a wonderful, natural genius that sets you apart from the other architects, and that drinking absinthe would only dull your brilliant mind."

Colin regarded Henry, intrigued. "Have *you* ever tried it?"

"Of course not! I wouldn't be caught dead with the stuff. Only those Decadents in France love it so."

"Yes, you're really not missing anything." It was Howard. Colin gaped at him. "*You've* tried it, Howard?"

Howard bit his tongue to keep from his horror at trumping Henry. "Er... yes, I did. But it's really a bit of nothing. Henry's right."

Colin was fascinated. "What was it like?"

Howard didn't dare look at Henry. He shrugged. "It was just a drink. Like your gin and bitters. It wasn't bad, and unless you've had quite a few, you don't feel anything. Really, it's the same as any other liquor. I think they just romanticize it by giving it a method, with the sugar cubes and slotted spoon."

"What are those for?

"Oh, well, you put the spoon over the glass, and a sugar cube on the spoon. You pour water over it, and when the sugar dissolves through the spoon and goes into the drink, the liquid turns a milky green."

"Really? That's amazing! How many did you drink?"

Howard laughed. "Only two or three. It tasted of licorice, and I didn't care for it. Too fussy, that whole method."

Colin was thrilled. "Have you been to Montmartre then, Howard?"

Henry cut in. "We all have, the three of us. Not together, though. It's a seedy, retched place."

"Yes, it's quite depressing," Howard agreed. Although he was tempted to add that when one is as young as Colin, it's a most exciting experience.

"Oh, it's positively lurid," Kenneth nodded. "Although I had *lots* of fun there, because I was too young to know any better."

Thank you, Kenneth. Howard smiled. Henry glared at Kenneth, who cleared his throat. "Er... but it was very dangerous."

"How so?" Colin was completely absorbed, and Henry was turning purple.

"Never mind that," Henry snapped. "I won't have you two filling his head with your stories. You're not going there, Colin, and that's final."

Colin crossed his arms. "Well, why not? *You* went. All three of you did! It couldn't be that terrible. And I'm sure it *must* be that fun."

Henry turned to Colin with a threatening look. "Are you telling me, Colin Sewell, that you are a boy who is interested in slumming the streets of depravity?"

"Well, no, but—"

"I'll take you to Whitechapel, then! That ought to suffice."

"Henry," Howard interjected. "Whitechapel is hardly Montmartre."

"It has every ounce of the rough and the exotic." Henry glanced evilly at Colin. "I could toss you in a tavern and see how you get out of it."

He sounded as if he meant it, which sufficiently cowed Colin to answer in a small voice, "No, thank you, then."

Howard couldn't help it. "Now, Henry, be fair. Montmartre is nowhere near as rough as Whitechapel—what with Jack the Ripper!"

"Jack the Ripper?" Colin turned his attention again to Howard.

"Yes, haven't you heard of him?" Kenneth asked. Colin shook his head, but before Kenneth or Howard continued, they looked at Henry. He glared at them.

"I'll do the honors." He narrowed his eyes at Colin. "Jack the Ripper is a serial murderer. He killed six women last year in Whitechapel. All prostitutes. And they haven't caught him yet." Colin's eyes grew large.

"Which is exactly why you can't compare Whitechapel with Montmartre," Howard insisted.

"They are both dens of iniquity!" Henry nearly shouted. He gestured at Colin. "Look at this boy—do you think he's seen a... a *hoodlum* once in his entire life?"

"I can fend for myself," Colin defended, slightly put off by the inference that he was helpless.

"You can't and you won't," Henry said. "The reason I adore you so, Colin, is because you haven't the taint of decadence on you. Not even a dot. I don't want you to be like Bosie, who's got a coat of slime on him so thick he'll never wash it off. Now I am finished with this story!"

"It's too bad Cremorne Gardens shut down." Howard teased.

"Shut it, Howard!" Henry roared.

"What's Cremorne—"

"Colin, one more word out of you about this and we are leaving!"

Colin raised his eyebrows, sighed, and took a drink.

Kenneth chuckled. "Forgive me for saying so, Henry, but if what you and Colin are about to do with other men doesn't qualify as decadent, what does?"

Henry snorted. "Hardly decadent at all. We won't be drinking absinthe or visiting opium dens. We won't be consorting with whores or street urchins, and we won't be in seedy parts of town." He sniffed. "We shall be discriminating and moderate in our affairs, in absolutely *fine* surroundings."

Howard shook his head resignedly. "Speaking of which, who will be your next conquest?"

"I'm sure we'll have a look around Porter's on Saturday," Henry said languidly. Colin stared off into the distance, resting his chin on his fist. "Whoever it is will have some difficult acts to follow."

CHAPTER NINE

Within a few weeks, word had spread among the subculture of Henry and Colin's modus operandi. Those who had chanced to spend an evening with them passed on to others the glorious experience, detailing with particular relish Colin's extraordinarily shocking singular skill. On a Saturday night at Porter's, one would see young men discussing it.

"Well, he puts his mouth on you—"

"His mouth? Where?"

The first boy leaned closer and pointed his eyes downward toward the other. "*There*."

"No! But that's like prostitution!"

"It sounds like it, yes, but he's not like any renter I've ever had."

"Why not?"

"Because he *enjoy*s it! Honest to God, it's like you've got a shrine down there." At this point the boy aimed his gaze heavenward and shuddered. "Christ, it's amazing, what he does!"

"Then does he expect you to do it to him?"

"Of course not!" He licked his lip. "But he's got a mouth on him, that one. It's always warm—his tongue is always warm and *he's* hot to the touch."

"In what way?"

"He radiates heat! He puts a hand on you and it's as if you've been..."

"Branded?"

"Well no, not quite. But... mm... he feels wonderful."

"What about Henry?"

"Oh, I didn't see much of him. He was *behind* me."

Another conversation went like this:

"The four of us were there for over two hours!"

"*Four* of you?"

"Well, yes. Henry and Colin, and Darcy and I."

"They took both of you home?"

"Well, here's the story: Sewell prefers boys—who doesn't? So if you're a young fellow, they'll take you alone, or two boys even. But if you're an older fellow like me, the only way you can get to Colin is to bring along a young companion."

"So you... pair up?"

"Sort of, but we were all in the same room."

"But then...?"

"Well, go on, Hastings. You can figure out the different ways on your own!"

Men quickly caught on to the ritual: Henry and Colin would enter Porter's Saturday night and spend the first two hours or so with Kenneth and Howard. Then they decided who would go home with them that evening by sending a drink to the boy they spotted earlier, or drinks to the couple, if there were two. If the intended were interested (and Colin and Henry had yet to be declined), they would join Henry and Colin at their table. Colin immediately took it upon himself to start conversation. It was a talent Henry admired more then he remembered to mention, for Colin seemed to know far more than was possible for a boy his age. He had the luck of memory on his side, and so besides talking of current events, he knew all kinds of folklore and fairy tales, jokes and limericks, childhood stories and American legends. He drew out more personal information than most others would dare to ask, and he shared quite a bit of his own, causing these new friends to consider themselves confidants to the highest degree. He kept up on the latest plays, poems, and literature, allowing much discussion and light-hearted arguing. If Colin came up short on anything, it was British history, but since many men knew that subject best, he eagerly pressed them for information, making them feel very important and smart indeed. All of this was done with sheer languidness, filled with significant pauses, long drags on cigarettes, flirtatious glances, and brief touches on the arms and legs.

And of course, once men were past the headiness of the club, they found Colin's *grotto* to be an experience completely unto itself. The entire room was done in dark blue, gold, and green silks and velvets against tobacco-colored wood frames and floor. The walls were painted navy, and the plush gold and blue carpeting extended to within a foot of the wall on all sides. The bed itself was the usual four-poster style, but it was twice the size of other beds and had a canopy of wood on top: two transverse beams forming an "X." The bed dressings were all silk, in watercolored shades of peridot and gold. There was much ado about the half-meter-thick featherbed mattress Henry imported from France, the same that was in his own bedchamber. Many men rushed to replace theirs after wading in Henry's (much to the delight of their wives). An armoire graced one wall; its purpose was to make the room look like it was truly a bedchamber. In reality, it simply hung two bathrobes for Henry and Colin.

In one corner of the room stood a graceful palm, and in another, a full-length dressing mirror that Colin had completely gilded. Next to the mirror was a wheeled chaise. Colin had slyly demonstrated for Henry that it was meant to be moved in front of the mirror if desired. And finally, in keeping with Henry's theme, Colin found a singular item to trump everything else: Himself.

Of course, he was already known for his fine looks and expensive dress, but Colin made himself worthy of worship down to every last detail.

On Saturdays he always bathed before going to Porter's. He followed his bath with smoothing lavender oil over his body and slipping into the finest silk underwear, so supple that men exclaimed upon it without fail. He brushed his hair often to make it shine, allowing him to usually dispense with the Macassar oil. He shaved twice each day: once in the morning and once after dinner, before going out to the club. Men were both delighted and scandalized to find he was groomed "in the private area," as well, which he trimmed with scissors on a weekly basis. He was a great fan of toothpaste, and though he left the liquor on his breath when coming home with guests—he didn't want to appear *too* antiseptic—he would sip Chartreuse as his final *degustif* of the evening. He ensured eternal softness of his lips by carrying a clandestine lip balm in his jacket pocket. Most men would disdain the entire ritual had they known about it, but remaining ignorant, they praised what they thought was Colin's natural loveliness. It was true that a number of men were excited more by the muscular body of a day-laborer than Colin's soft slimness, and by the smell of sweat instead of lavender, but even these men thought of Colin not as someone who might cloy their senses but more an acquired taste they were willing to accustom themselves to. After all, once a young man or pair was in the room, they were served the finest cordials and cheeses from a marble and glass serving cart. Although the lamps were turned low, the mood was always light and festive, for drinking had already gone on at the club for several hours. Colin and Henry kept the conversation friendly and unless one of the visitors made the first move, Colin made a point of doing it himself. In fact, Colin went first in everything out of pure selflessness. And once in bed with a man he never failed to murmur a compliment right away, usually referring to something he had noticed long before they became intimate. No matter how a man performed, Colin welcomed their embrace and guided them if need be. Such moves made every man feel quite loved, which endeared Colin to them ever more.

Of course, the whole thing was quite an education for Colin. He discovered new avenues of pleasure and obliged a variety of requests. And the privacy of being in someone's home as opposed to a hotel, and the singular attention paid to the guests, especially in the form of bedroom activity in luxurious surroundings, still caused stirring testimonies... and some awkward moments.

There was the time one young well-to-do man came back to their house the morning after his night with Colin and Henry. He presented Colin with a gigantic bouquet of hothouse flowers and a breathless speech. "Mr. Colin," he beamed, "if you would ever consider it, please! I would simply love to have you for all my own! I'll give you anything you want! Anything!" Henry had to pull the man inside before he made a spectacle, and Colin had to politely decline while surreptitiously passing the flowers off to Charlie. On another occasion, a gentleman at the club drew Colin aside and whispered in his ear, "Sit at my table tonight, Darling. Sit at my table *forever*. If you think you're happy with Henry, then let me show you what you're missing." And despite his vows, even Kenneth made an overture of sorts. During a rather drunken evening when Henry had teased Colin rather more than was acceptable, Kenneth reprimanded him. "Henry! The way you treat that boy! If I wasn't married I would take him from you so fast it would make your head spin!" Colin looked at him shyly. "Oh, Kenneth. He doesn't really mean it." Kenneth blazed his eyes at Colin. "Well I do!" And as Colin and Howard stared, Henry quit the antics on the spot. Colin made light of the situation by batting his eyes at his friend and asking, "Well then, Kenneth, whyever haven't you gotten a divorce?" The foursome erupted in laughter.

None of these declarations really troubled him, for Colin believed the only reason they happened at all was simply because he belonged to Henry, who had gone through more beautiful, desirable boys than any man his age in the club. *If Sewell is so committed to that American lad, then the boy must be something amazing indeed.* That's what Colin imagined was whispered between the members. Hence there was always a tiny nagging fear in the back of his mind of what would happen should Henry ever decide to drop him. It never occurred to him that his own actions alone were capable of proving his worth.

Henry had certainly grasped Colin's fever-pitched value. Every petition to steal the boy away thrilled him more, until Kenneth's outburst rained on the parade. Durham he had suspected all along of harboring an interest, but Kenneth... well, Kenneth's warning carried some weight, and Henry became a little more possessive from that night on.

Soon a kind of silent club formed among those who had kept company with Colin and Henry. They wore their acceptance as badges of honor, since it was well known that one couldn't be selected unless one already had a high-status position in society. This was the outcome Colin had hoped for, because he also believed that if he presented the experience as the *crème de la crème*, the reality of what he and Henry were doing would appear much less disreputable in everyone's eyes, including God's.

Eventually it became clear that one infamous couple remained snubbed. Oscar and Bosie were left to stare at the various paramours that left with Henry and Colin. Although Henry ensured that the four men rarely traveled in the same circles, Colin saw enough of Bosie's mercurial temper every time they were at the club, and he heard stories about Oscar's treatment of his friends, such as borrowing money that was never paid back, likely because of his commitment to keep Bosie in the lap of luxury. While Colin knew he should dislike Oscar, he could only feel sympathy for the older man and refused to say anything bad about him. He believed Mr. Wilde was just in the midst of an infatuation and soon enough would strike Bosie from his life. But for now, they were to be avoided. Bosie declared he wouldn't be caught dead trying to go home with Henry and Colin anyway, but Oscar... well, he was indeed the weaker of the two. Colin, after all, was still his living Bosie. So men saw his sad eyes grow sadder each time someone else was taken home, and finally one of his friends tried to intervene.

It was on a Thursday afternoon at a bookseller shop. Colin was studying a book on botany when a young man spotted him and approached. "Mr. Sewell."

Colin looked up and smiled. "Hello, Robbie." It was Robert Ross, an art critic who was also Oscar's close friend and legal advisor. Henry had told him, "That boy would do anything for Wilde. He's worth his weight in gold. But apparently he's too dull for our Oscar."

Robbie looked concerned. "Mr. Sewell—"

"Colin, please."

"Colin..." Robbie sighed. "Can't you take Oscar with you some night? It looks very bad that you're treating him so shabbily."

"*I'm* treating him shabbily? The whole reason we won't take him is because of that damned Bosie!"

"Well, I understand, but... couldn't you just take them one night, anyway?"

Colin made a face, then studied the plain-looking man. "We haven't taken you yet, Robbie. Why don't *you* come with us this Saturday?"

Robbie's eyes widened. "No, no, no. I mean Oscar and Bosie."

"And I mean you." Colin licked his lip. "You're as good as either of them. You shouldn't be dragged into this, I see that now." He smiled again. "Yes, we'll take you then."

"But that won't work—Oscar will never leave Bosie behind."

Colin drew in his breath and exhaled. "I don't care a whit about Oscar or Bosie. I mean for us to take you. Now you may tell Oscar of our intent and perhaps he can find something for Lord Douglas to do on Saturday night. If not..." And now Colin had to grin. "Well then, you will get what Bosie will never deserve. And he will see it." And because Oscar wasn't there and because Bosie was currently out of favor with Robbie, well, Robbie had to give in to a self-indulgent smile of his own. Colin winked. "Goodbye, Mr. Ross."

"Well then, goodbye, Mr. Sewell."

True to his plan, Colin arrived at the club that Saturday with Henry, glancing about for Robbie. Robbie was there, and so was Oscar... with Bosie. Colin threw Robbie a disappointed look, and Robbie shrugged apologetically. Henry, of course, didn't mind at all; he certainly had no desire for Oscar to join them. "I suppose it will just be Robbie tonight, then," he told Colin.

"If he's brave enough," Colin shrugged, for he realized this could be a perfect opportunity for Robbie to avenge Oscar's rejection, by declining Colin and Henry's offer in front of his friend. So the evening passed, and as closing time neared, Colin decided to send Robbie a note via the waitstaff.

May I approach you?

Robbie read the note and swallowed. If he went, Oscar would be very jealous, and Bosie would declare him no friend of Oscar's at all. But Oscar might also admire him... No, Oscar would think it was just Colin's way of angering Bosie further, which would in turn anger Oscar, who again, would disapprove of Robbie. Still, Robbie constantly struggled to keep the other men in the club from thinking him the fool, being so loyal to Oscar, who only wanted Bosie. And if Robbie went with Colin and Henry, it might put him in better stead with the rest of the population... He folded the note and looked at Colin with a slight smile and a nod. "Last call!" Jack shouted, and as the men all got up to leave, Colin came over to Robbie. "Come along, Robbie dear," he smiled and took Robbie's hand. Robbie didn't dare look back, praying Bosie wouldn't make a scene. Henry, though, did glance back and saw Oscar staring sadly after them, while Bosie laughed and muttered things.

True to their plan, Henry and Colin stayed together during every escapade with only a few exceptions. Henry had decreed that a select few men should have Colin to themselves, as an act of gratitude for their friendship and high ranking in the subculture. Howard was the first. Kenneth declined, which Henry enormously respected, but Colin disagreed with. The other three were Anders Ferguson, the owner of Charlotte's; D'oro

Fellipini, Henry and Colin's dresser in Italy; and Jack Colton. Colin hadn't been with Anders or D'oro yet; Henry chose Jack to go next.

"I think tonight's the night for Jack," Henry said one Saturday. Colin agreed and quickly became excited. He was fond of Jack and also quite intimidated by him, knowing how much power the man must have to run such an establishment for so long without being caught. It was said he had several connections with the police, which impressed Colin even further. Considering the substantial membership fee every man paid, Henry guessed a nice portion of it went to bribes, which was fine with him.

The bar announced its closing, and men got up to leave. Colin rose up and walked to the bar, smiling at Jack. "How much are you wanting to go to this party?"

Jack, who was wiping glasses, stopped his action and caught on instantly. "It depends if you'll be there," he replied, giving Colin a once-over.

Colin sighed. "Henry is. I'm not."

Jack put his glass down. "Really? Am I not to bring a boy, then?"

Colin smiled. "You can if you want. Or it can just be you and I." Then he looked down and demurred, "Henry wants to pay his respects to you. As do I."

Jack grinned in delight. "Well, that's certainly generous of both of you." He winked. "So infamy must finally want for company?"

Colin laughed. "Yes. May I wait while you close things down?

"Absolutely."

So Colin took a seat while Jack refreshed his drink, and when the men began to leave, Henry joined them with no hesitation.

The rest of the men gaped. Henry was leaving Colin behind, with Jack! They quickly grasped Henry's intentions, but they were still amazed and most of them thought the idea improper. "Really," one of them muttered, "for all he professes to love that boy, he certainly is free with him."

Back at Porter's, Jack finished cleaning up, and Colin apologized, "I suppose I should have encouraged you to bring another boy along, if you had wanted to."

Jack laughed. "That's most kind of you, darling, but I like this idea of the two of us." He walked around to the front of the bar with his coat, took Colin's hand, and went to turn down the last light. "Here, I'll guide you," Jack said in the dark. "We've got to go out the back way."

Colin squeezed Jack's hand. "Have you ever done it… in your bar?"

"Sorry, love. You wouldn't be the first."

"What about *on* the bar?"

Colin felt Jack stop. "On the bar!"

"Yes, why not? Imagine that—every time I walked in here I could look at the very spot and know that's where you had me!"

Jack laughed. "I'm sure it's not very comfortable."

"I'm sure it wouldn't take long." Colin drew Jack close. "Wouldn't that be a picture? You and me, on your bar, in this room that just minutes ago was full of men who would have had a perfect view?" He ran a hand down Jack's arm. "It'd be something to tide us over before going back to your place. After all, we've got all night."

"We do?"

"Well, yes. Henry and I insist."

Upon hearing it, Jack led Colin over to a booth and re-lit the lamps. "Well then, sit down." Colin obeyed, and Jack raised his hand to caress the back of Colin's neck. Colin put his hand on Jack's leg and leaned in to kiss him. He drew back and smiled shyly. "This is probably more exciting for me than it is for you."

"Why's that?"

"Because you're the most powerful man, in my book. Henry says you're the only one who gets better boys than he does, and he's right."

Jack smiled, stroking Colin's jaw. "Not in this case, Beautiful."

Colin gave him an earnest look. "But there's a reason why we waited as long as we did with you."

"Tell me. I'm dying to know." Jack languidly unbuttoned Colin's vest.

"We wanted you to believe that I could make it worth something to you. That this was a sure thing, you see."

Jack moved his hand downward and massaged Colin's thigh, kissing him deeply. Then he shook his head. "You were a sure thing when you walked that pretty little arse into my bar. Christ, I could have had you!" He gave a laugh. "Mister Colin Edwards."

Afterwards, Jack took Colin to his home. He led him inside, and Colin looked around. "What an amazing place!"

Jack chuckled. "I've had Henry's input on a few things. Can you tell?"

Colin smiled. "Of course. Have you any brandy?"

"In the smoking room. Come."

Once there, Jack noticed Colin wasn't playing shy anymore. He appeared more relaxed, confident. He even seemed several years older. He sat down next to Jack and lit a cigarette, offering Jack one as well. "No thank you," Jack declined, since he only smoked pipes, and then it was occasional.

Colin nodded, smiling. "It's a terrible habit, isn't it?"

"Not when you do it," Jack mused. Jack recalled a party where he had glimpsed Colin leaning back on a settee, his jacket open, stabbing his cigarette to make a point, while his glass of gin warmed on the table. *He actually makes it look masculine*, Jack had thought then. And now Jack, himself no slight drinker, was beginning to feel lightheaded, for he and Colin had shared a bottle of champagne after their foray on the bar. Colin noticed this and gave him a light kiss with a smirk.

"The brandy was a bad idea. Come on, then." He pulled Jack up and, holding his hand to his mouth, asked, "Where's your bedchamber, Mr. Colton?"

"That way." Jack stood behind Colin. "I'll tell you where to go. I want to watch you from behind. It's a lovely sight."

Colin smiled slyly, and as they walked he began undressing, cigarette dangling from his mouth. Jack caught up with him several times, and Colin let him. By the time they'd reached the bedroom door Colin hadn't an article of clothing left on him and Jack's mind was reeling. With a flourish, Colin flung back the duvet. "In you go," he demanded, feeling a bit woozy himself. He undressed Jack and then drew the duvet over them both. Jack fell back onto the pillows, his mind buzzing. And then he felt *that*. He drowned into a delicious kind of sobriety, and in a while he drifted off into bliss. Afterwards, it was Colin's turn, and Jack had become so smitten that he asked Colin if he'd like to do something Jack himself hadn't done in two decades.

Surprised by the request, Colin said, "Really? You've not been on your back since then?"

Jack laughed. "Of course not. I'm always the older one, you know. Why, has Henry?"

Colin gave him a look. "Well, just a few times. Although I'm guessing perhaps you're not to know that."

Jack studied Colin's face, which was currently above his. "It must be good, then. Please, do it."

Colin had a flash of Howard in his mind as he began to move on top of Jack: *"You know, I'll be damned if the first boy I've had in a year I take from behind. As pretty as this view is, darling, I want to see your gorgeous face more. Turn over."*

So Colin understood the power of the position, and tonight he was determined to pass on the appreciation to Jack.

The next morning they were brought tea and toast in bed. Colin didn't tell Jack that he had laced the tea with laudanum, and he turned his smile away once he saw the man drink it. Then he insisted Jack partake in a morning bath, and while Jack reclined in the hot, scented water, Colin perched on the edge of the tub nude, a towel on his head, the ends twisted behind him then falling in front of his shoulder in perfect imitation of Rosetti's Lady Lilith as he merrily inquired after Jack's life.

In the middle of this lighthearted conversation, it finally struck Jack. *That bastard Henry. I'm in love with his boy.* And he began to feel more and more foolish, as if he'd been tricked. So he tested Colin. "I say, Colin, are you really fond of Henry? Because after last night..." he sighed for effect, "if you were mine, I'd never share you."

Colin gave a shy smile and nodded—the coyness was back! "Yes, I care very much for him. Oddly enough, I do feel we're loyal to each other. I wouldn't leave him for anyone. I have every intention of making him my first, last, and only." He shrugged. "But I like sharing with men as much as he does. I admit it wasn't my idea, but it's wonderful fun! It's... it's almost like the perfect cordial that ends the entire evening!"

"A cordial?" Jack chuckled.

"Yes! And... well, I like doing it. Making men happy, that is." Colin's expression furrowed. "So many of them don't seem to get any kind of attention like that without a price. They either have to pay for it, and the act's done as quickly as possible, or they have to entice someone into it, with gifts or words. Either way's a false impression, and there's always the risk of being blackmailed." He looked at Jack proudly. "Men are happy when they leave me. The happiest they've been, some of them say."

"I've heard the same. And you?"

Colin laughed. "Surely you thought I was enjoying myself last night?"

Jack grinned. "I suppose you were. And I was too. But Colin, at my age, I know a few things. I just find it hard to believe you can keep going about like this, or that Henry lets you." He peered at Colin. "Surely some of the men you've been with have tried to persuade you away from him. Men who have just as much money or more."

Colin smiled. "They have. But then I tell them that Henry doesn't pay me anything, and they're at a loss!"

"Doesn't pay you?" Jack frowned. "But you're working for him."

Colin laughed. "Yes, and I do it all *gratis*. Henry buys me anything I want or need. How much he spends on me is representative of my work."

"But Colin, that means you haven't a shilling to your name!"

"Oh, I do; I just don't see it. Henry takes care of the banking matters. Now don't you worry a bit, Jack. I'm perfectly fine."

Jack shook his head. "I've never heard a stranger thing in my life! And I daren't say who's getting the better end of the deal. Although I think *I'm* getting a nice slice, what with having you all to myself for an evening."

Colin smiled once more, tracing the water with his fingers. "Yes, but nobody's had this kind of attention Jack, except you. You know this isn't the usual way, spending the whole night without Henry. I didn't even ask Henry what to do with you. It's just that..." He shook his head reverently. "*You've* made it possible for us to have such an extraordinary meeting place! I've never seen anything like it!"

"But New York has The Carlisle."

Colin's eyes widened. "It does?"

Jack looked upon him affably. "Yes, although I suppose you're too young to have known." He was even more pleased when Colin took offense to the comment.

"Well..." he sniffed.

"Never mind. Anyway, I can see how Henry's attached, now. You're wonderful. But I really wouldn't share you."

"Well," Colin teased, "you and I wouldn't have worked out then, would we?"

Jack couldn't have been happier with his response; it freed him from guilt. "No," he agreed. "I suppose we wouldn't."

Colin took Jack's hand out of the water and kissed it. "Thank you though, for looking out for me. I think it's very kind." And with that, he rose up to get dressed.

The next morning, Colin nuzzled up to Henry in bed as Henry rumpled his hair. "Good morning, Lovely. Do you know I have something for you?" He reached over to the nightstand and gave Colin a small, longish box. "S. Mordan & Co." was stamped in gold on the lid. Colin gingerly opened the box, and his face lit up as he lifted the treasure from its velvet-lined impression. It was an 18-karat gold magic pencil, embossed with a barley pattern and a single ruby insert on the end. The initials "CMS" were engraved on the barrel.

Colin looked at Henry. "'M'?"

Henry chuckled. "You never gave me a middle name. I thought the 'M' could be our little secret." He chucked Colin under the chin. "Michael."

Colin grinned, then ran his finger over the initials. "It's absolutely beautiful! May I take it to work?"

"Of course you may. It's really meant for you to carry around."

Colin held the pencil in drawing position. "It's perfect!" He leaned over to Henry and kissed him deeply. "I love it. Thank you."

That evening they dined at Poisson, a favorite restaurant of theirs. They had almost finished their meal when a couple approached them. "Henry Sewell!" the woman exclaimed.

Henry turned to look. "My word, Caroline!" He stood up and took her hand, and then shook her husband's hand and turned to Colin. "Ah, yes... er... Colin, this is *my sister Eleanor's* friend, Mrs. Caroline Hoopeston, and her husband Paul. I haven't seen them in ages."

"How do you do," Colin stood up, trying not to react.

"A pleasure to meet you, Mr...." Caroline smiled expectantly.

Unsure, Colin glanced at Henry, but Henry decided there was no use lying. "Sewell, Caroline. You're meeting my son, actually. I adopted him a month ago. He came to work for me and hadn't had the benefit of a family for years. The fatherly instinct finally happened to me and I took him under my wing."

It was the same line Henry had told everyone else, but he had intended to keep it from his own family as long as he could. Now he watched as Caroline was the one struggling to keep her composure.

"Oh! Eleanor hadn't told me!"

"That's because Eleanor doesn't know." Henry gave her a dagger-like smile. "But I'm sure I can count on you to tell her."

Colin's jaw dropped and Mr. Hoopeston studied him.

Caroline sniffed. "Well, if this is a private family matter, I'll leave it up to you."

"Oh, do tell her," Henry waved a hand. "I haven't the inclination and you'll enjoy it so much more than I."

Caroline barely hid her disgust for her friend's brother and curtsied. "Good evening then, Mr. Sewell." She looked at Colin. "*Mr. Sewell.*" Colin's face burned as he and Henry both sat down again.

"What will your sister do?" Colin asked worriedly.

"Who cares?" Henry shrugged. "They were bound to find out about you sometime."

"But they don't know about you, do they?"

"What they do know would still cause them to consider me a perfectly indecent influence on a nice boy like you." He winked at Colin, who laughed.

"Is Eleanor the oldest sister?" Colin inquired.

"Second oldest," Henry replied. "She's... Oh, I don't want to talk about her. Bah."

"Hmph." Colin slumped in his chair, disappointed. "I was just about to find out more."

Henry smiled at him. "And I was just about to have my dinner spoilt. Come, we'll go for a walk before heading home."

CHAPTER TEN

It was the last week of June when Kenneth told the other three men his plans for a July masquerade ball. Colin tilted his head at Howard. "Howard, whyever haven't *you* had a party yet?"

Howard started. "Oh. Er... well, I'm not really the entertaining sort. Neither is Henry, as you know."

"But I haven't even once seen your house," Colin reprimanded. "Which is unforgivable, considering that I'm an architect."

"Howard, it *is* summer," Henry chuckled. "Why don't you have us all over for a picnic on that sprawling lawn of yours?"

"A sprawling lawn?" Colin asked, fascinated already.

Howard smiled. "I suppose I do have a rather large lawn..."

"Rather large property," Kenneth shook his finger, smiling.

"Rather large *house*," Henry smirked. He nodded to Colin. "Howard's got a huge brick mansion on forty acres of land. He's the Country Mouse, you see."

"Country Mouse!" Colin laughed. "Oh Howard, have us this Saturday!"

"This Saturday!" Howard exclaimed. "But that's only four days away!"

Henry shrugged. "If it's only the four of us, we shouldn't be any trouble."

"But I... I haven't the proper things even for a small party," Howard insisted.

"We shall have a picnic, then!" Colin declared. "Henry and I will bring everything!"

"Oh, and I shall help too!" Kenneth clapped his hands.

"Hooray then, it's settled," Colin said gleefully.

Howard looked helplessly at Henry, who shook his head. "It really would be better to have a larger group of fellows," Henry decided.

"Of course it would!" Howard cried.

"Then we'll invite some." Colin grinned. "And Henry and I will arrive extra early to help you."

"What if it rains on Saturday?" Howard asked, defeated.

Colin shot him a look. "Then we'll picnic indoors. Now Howard, that's enough. We're coming to visit you, and that's the end of it."

Saturday came and the sun mixed with clouds all morning. "As close to sunny in this country as we'll ever get," Colin grumbled. But he was still excited to see Howard's estate. He and Henry arrived at two o'clock, two hours before the other guests, so that Colin could have a tour of the grounds. When their carriage drove up the lane, Colin gasped. "My God, it's larger than Kenneth's house!"

"Naturally," Henry replied. "He lives in the country. He's got the land."

"Oh, he has the land!" Colin gushed. "Look at it Henry!" Outside their window, rolling hills were bathed in the clearing sky of afternoon sun. Clusters of oak trees spread luxurious greenery atop while wildflowers carpeted the ground. A small pond lent itself to a flock of geese and several ducks. "I don't believe it," Colin whispered in awe.

"Well, the man had to spend his money on something," Henry said wryly, observing the expansive grounds. He saw Colin was falling in love with the place and he wasn't too keen about it. When they arrived at the house, Colin leapt down and rushed to Howard, who stood by the door to greet them. Colin clutched Howard's arms.

"Howard, it's the most beautiful place I've ever seen!"

Howard himself wasn't expecting Colin to have such a reaction. "Oh!" he managed. "Oh, I'm glad you like it."

"Like it? I *love* it!" Colin whirled around. "It's beautiful! It's absolutely beautiful! I can't believe Henry hasn't told me about it!"

"It's hardly your type," Henry said irritably.

"Well, the grounds may be rather wild," Colin skipped about on the gravel. "And Georgian never was my style. But the land! Howard, you have hills! You have trees! And a pond! And your house even faces southwest—it's perfect!"

Howard had to laugh. "Goodness, perhaps I should rent it out to you if you like it that much."

"Oh, Howard," Colin shook his head. "I wish I lived here. I can't wait to see the inside! Let us go!"

Howard gave an apologetic look at Henry, who rolled his eyes and sighed. The three went into the house.

"Oh my, it is rather like Kenneth's home," Colin tsked, regarding the formal interior. Then he laughed, looking at Howard. "Although I suppose it goes well with you, and the outside." He began to meander, fascinated by everything. "I'm going to have a look."

"*I'm* going to have a brandy," Henry muttered, heading for the decanter.

Howard grinned and joined him. "I can't say I blame you. He's already wearing me out."

"Well, he acted like this in my house too, when he first saw it." After Henry poured his drink, he jabbed Howard with his elbow. "Of course, then it was perfectly fine. It's not so fun seeing him absorbed in *your* things." They both chuckled.

Henry nodded toward Colin. "I should have known he'd love it here. I ought to have brought him 'round earlier."

"I thought he was a city-lover," Howard said, watching Colin explore.

"Well, for the most part," Henry agreed. "But he loves the idea of escaping to the country. I've thought about buying something outside of London. Just a small place for us to use."

"You could rent a cottage," Howard suggested.

"Yes," Henry agreed. "Perhaps we'll have a look around tomorrow. I'll surprise him."

Howard's cheer dissolved somewhat as envy crept in. "Oh. I shan't mention a word, then." They both headed in the direction Colin had gone moments earlier.

After Colin thoroughly looked over every room in the house and received a full history of the home from Howard, he pronounced himself satisfied and the three began to prepare for the guests. Colin demanded they picnic under a large oak tree on the hill nearest the back of the house, where they could look over the pond below. The servants spread several large blankets on the ground and began to carry out the baskets of food and wine that Henry and Colin brought. Kenneth came first, bringing the cheeses and desserts. Then the others followed. Six other men from the club had been invited: Jack and his current companion, Richie Dobbs, Charlie Stratton, and two young men Henry thought were nice to look at and good conversationalists. They all chatted under the tree.

"Howard, why *do* you have such untamed grounds?" Colin asked, looking about him.

"Well, I suppose I rather like the look," Howard shrugged. "It lends character to the house."

"Yes," Henry nodded. "Remember Collie, before William Kent came along, this *was* the English idea of groundskeeping. It was believed that man should not rule over nature."

"Hear hear!" Howard agreed.

"But," Colin refuted, "then the English began to see all of the beautiful formal gardens in Italy and France and they decided to copy them." He sighed. "They are ever so much more tranquil."

"Well then, I hope these grounds don't cause you any great distress," Howard teased.

Colin frowned. "Well Howard, they do, but the view is so lovely I'll just fix my eyes on that."

Now that architecture was the topic, one of the young men Henry invited, a musician, asked Henry and Colin a question. "What do you two think of Goethe referring to architecture as 'frozen music'?"

Colin knew the quote, but for amusement's sake decided on another interpretation. "I think it's ridiculous. What is frozen music but a sustained sound? And a sustained sound in any key or chord is excruciating to anyone's ears, is it not?"

"That's not what he meant—" the young man began, but Henry laughed.

"Yes Collie, Westminster Abbey is every bit as painful as a screaming loon!"

"Perfect, Henry!" Colin cried, joining in his laughter. "Oh, a screaming loon, yes!"

"He was referring to the structure of a composition taken as a whole," Albert, the poser of the question desperately argued. "The repeated elements, the proportional spans—"

"Wait just a moment!" Ritchie demanded. "Are you fellows saying you want to tear down Westminster Abbey?"

"No, no," Colin gasped, catching his breath. "Don't get me wrong, Ritchie. I don't want to tear down existing structures. After all, they reflect the very people who designed them as well as the people who inhabit them; they contain historical transactions. And Westminster Abbey is a perfect example—at least it's a structure whose design was revolutionary for its time, being Gothic and all that. But I say after ten or twenty years, design must change just as people and materials change. Inventions occur, after all. And the very fact that we are still using Doric columns sickens me to death!"

"It's a classic design," Howard refuted.

"And I *love* it," Colin insisted. "Mind you there is certainly something to be taken from each era of architecture, Howard, but those things should be used sparingly and toward creating something new. Those damn pillars are everywhere! They make a mockery of ancient Greece. And doesn't anyone see the folly of having *me* design my own structures inside a copy of the Parthenon? You would think men would realize the unstoppable human drive toward originality! After all, that man Darwin just proved that mankind evolves, so why can't our creations?"

"But don't you see your creations as timeless?" Charlie asked.

"Oh, yes," Colin nodded. "But in a decade or two even my designs will change. Nothing extremely drastic, I expect, but they will certainly incorporate the latest advances. Why, just look at the present: We've got steel now! And we can make gigantic sheets of glass! Imagine the possibilities! Mr. Eiffel has. Yet I worry that most men will simply use these new materials to build old buildings. It's just awful." He went on with his speech while Howard looked upon him with admiration. *Such intelligence! And so impassioned!* Eventually the conversation ended and the other young man, Stephen, tried cajoling the men into on-the-spot art lessons with the easel and watercolor paints he brought.

"Go on, Collie," Henry gave Colin a push. "You try."

Colin gamely took up a brush and followed Stephen's direction. After a few strokes he sighed. "Oh, I hate it already. I'm used to a pencil, not this giant, swishy thing!" But he managed to complete his picture of an oak tree and signed his name with a flourish.

Howard was surprised at Colin's lack of talent. "After those superb drawings of buildings, I thought you'd be a natural," he wondered.

Colin flopped onto the ground. "They're *drawings*, Howard, that's why. That brush is nothing like a pencil. *You* try it."

"No thank you," Howard demurred. "Henry, why don't you try it and see if Colin's right?"

Henry went forth and, after listening to Stephen's advice, painted quite an impressive picture of the very same tree Colin had tried to paint. "Henry," Colin squealed, "how dare you! That's practically frameable!"

Henry beamed. "It is quite good, isn't it? Well I never knew!"

The afternoon passed pleasantly with dinner, various lawn games, and conversation. After several glasses of wine, Colin fell asleep further down the hill. "It's the sun," Henry explained, amused. "He's like a cat. Whenever he finds a patch of sun in our house he lies right down in it and falls asleep."

"Oh, he doesn't," Jack pshawed, unable to picture Colin lying on the carpet fully clothed.

"He does!" Henry laughed. "He has every intention of reading there, mind you, but within minutes he's curled up and you can hear him purr." He winked at Howard. "But a patch on a rug in a house doesn't compare with being on the green grass in full sun and fresh air. Damn you and your 'property', Durham!" They all laughed, and while they continued conversing, Howard stole a look at Colin's dozing form.

" *I wish I lived here.*"

If you did, Howard thought. *You could sleep there every day.*

Then it was July, and all talk centered around Kenneth's masquerade ball. Of course, the talk had its limits, as nobody would reveal their costume choice. But they all chatted excitedly about what they had dressed as in the past. The only reluctant participant in these conversations was Howard, who dreaded the event. He hated balls, especially masquerade ones. He didn't like to dance, and he wasn't creative. Not only did Howard not know what to wear yet; he didn't want to wear it, whatever it was. Colin and Henry were the complete opposite: Henry was the one who asked

Kenneth to have the party, because he had an idea for himself and Colin months ago. And it was Colin's first masquerade ball. It was killing them to have to keep their secret, so proud of their costumes were they. *Bah and blah,* Howard thought while listening to their chatter. The next day he finally asked Kenneth for help in choosing a costume.

"Howard, you simply must be a pirate! It's *fitting*: you take people's money for a living, after all." But Howard did not want to be a pirate, so Kenneth tried again. "What about Louis the Fourteenth? You're rather king-like."

"Wait a moment!" Howard stopped him. "I have it! I shall be—"

"Howard, don't!" Kenneth put up his hands in fear. "If you *know* what you want to be, don't tell me!"

Howard laughed. "Right." Then his face fell. "Oh hell. I don't have the slightest idea how to look like the man. Kenneth, you must help me."

Kenneth sighed. "All right then. Tell me what you're thinking."

So Howard did, and he was glad to be able to share his own smug look thereafter when everyone talked about the ball. But he didn't look forward to it much more, and when the night came, he cursed himself for arriving to the party so dutifully on time. It would be a long evening. Howard donned his mask and remembered the main reason why he hated masquerade balls: he couldn't recognize anyone, forcing him to wander about awkwardly until someone else recognized him first. Fortunately, he was barely on the floor when Jack Colton came over to him and guessed his identity. Howard was relieved, and they stood together speculating on everyone else's identities. Around them flitted Cinderellas, queens, barmaids, can-can girls, harem girls, and dozens of prostitutes. Beside them strode Robin Hoods, kings, knights, pirates, and various members of the clergy. It amused Howard to notice that the masks made the pretty men and women even more fetching, and yet masks on ugly ones were no help at all. Eventually he strayed to the table of hors d'oeuvres and began to make a plate. A tinkling voice rose up to greet him. "Monsieur Durham, you look *magnifique!*" Howard turned and found a very striking Marie Antoinette batting her eyes at him.

"Oh! Why, thank you, *madame*. How did you know who I was?"

The girl gave a delicate laugh. "Why, Monsieur Durham, you're ze *handsomest* one here!" She opened her fan and hid behind it.

Howard smiled. It was Anne Fairchild. "If it's a compliment you're giving me, it's small wonder I didn't recognize you." He put a hand on his hip. "Your entrance was quite stunning." She had appeared at the top of the stairway alone, like all the rest, but billowing around her was a robin's-egg blue satin cape, lined with pink velvet. In a single flourish she threw the cape off, thrust open her fan, and descended the staircase in her matching blue satin and rhinestone mask. Now Howard winked at her. "You certainly picked the right costume. The men have been flocking around you all evening."

The faux-Marie peered at him coyly. "Yes, and for someone who *prefers* men, I see even you are taken with me, no?"

Howard tsked her. "Madame Fairchild!"

"Oh! But I am not Madame Fairchild, Monsieur Durham!"

Howard's stomach dropped. "You're not?"

Marie put a gloved hand on his arm and laughed again. "*Mais non!* Don't you recognize poor leetle me at all?"

Howard was at a complete loss and began backing away in confusion. "No, I'm sorry. I'm afraid I don't." Suddenly, the light touch on his arm became a grip, as Marie's shoulders slumped and her voice fell several octaves.

"Howard, you idiot. It's me!"

Now Howard was shocked even more than the first time. "Col—"

"Shht!" Colin put two fingers on Howard's mouth and drew back, laughing. "Oui, Monsieur. C'est moi!"

Howard couldn't believe it. Colin was dressed in full eighteenth century regalia, from his elaborate, towering powdered wig (complete with feather plumes and a small bird's nest) to his beribboned, high-heeled shoes. His dress was a massive affair of silk, satin, lace, and crinoline, all in that robin's-egg blue with touches of gold and punctuated with large silk pink roses. His face and neck were whitened, his cheeks were rouged, and his lips had been painted into a glossy, ruby bow. He even had a beauty mark by his mouth and a silver star on his cheek. His eyelashes were blackened and two strands of pearls circled his neck. And then there was his rather well-endowed chest, although none of it was bared. Howard shook his head. "How did you get *those?*"

Colin grinned. "Stuffing naturally. Loads of it. Of course, if I were a real woman, I'd be showing the tops of them, but nobody seems to notice!"

Why would they? Howard mused. *He looks exquisite.* Then he gasped. "Why you... you even danced with men!" He remembered earlier seeing Colin whirl elegantly around the floor with a number of gentlemen.

"Well of course I did!" Colin exclaimed. "You see? Learning to follow has its place. Even Henry had to admit that. It's genius!"

"Was this your idea, then?" Howard asked.

"No," Colin sighed. "*I* wanted to be a cattle rustler. Really, how much more American could I get? But Henry pleaded with me to be this instead, and I gave in." He swept an arm downward. "It's all authentic! I'm even wearing a woman's corset!" Then he made a face. "Which means I can hardly breathe. And then this bustle, and these skirts!" Colin lifted his dress slightly to show several layers of netting on top of a pair of pantaloons. "How the hell am I supposed to piss with these things on? It's ridiculous! I tell you Howard, the fact that women stand to wear these things shows how unbelievably stupid they are!"

Howard squinted. "Even your eyes look different. Why... they're black!"

Colin clapped his hands. "Are they still? I put Belladonna drops in my eyes before we left. Women in ancient times used them to make their eyes look prettier, you know."

"Is that safe?" Howard said, horrified.

"Oh, I'm sure," Colin waved his fan. "And it further disguises me! *Nobody* knows who I am yet, so don't tell. I've had eleven men make indecent passes at me already!" He laughed. "Wait until they find out whose neck and shoulders they were caressing." Then he ran his gloved hand lightly down Howard's chest. "And who are you supposed to be, Howard?"

"Hmph!" Howard smirked. "Who's the fool now?" With a gleam in his eye he seized Colin's wrist with one hand and brandished a knife with the other, holding it to Colin's neck. "Jack the Ripper!"

Colin froze, feeling the blade on his skin. Then he stared at Howard in admiration. "Jack the Ripper... that's brilliant!" He glanced downwards. "Er... is that a real knife?"

"It is, and a very sharp one too. So take care, madame. You should really save your neck for the guillotine."

Colin's heart raced as Howard pressed the sharp edge slightly in jest. "Vell then!" his voice rose. "I theenk zat..." Then he dropped his façade and said in his own voice, "Do you think it's cause for concern that I find you extremely dashing when you're holding a blade to my neck?" His smile disappeared as he gazed at Howard, who lowered his dagger and swallowed. Colin blinked, horrified at his admission, and made a curtsey. "Vell... er... farevell, Monsieur Jacque Ze Ripper. Please, stick to ze prostitutes, eh?" And he rustled off, only to be caught by a costumed Sir Lancelot who encircled Colin's waist in the name of protection and shook his finger at Howard.

Howard sighed, sheathed his knife, and picked up a canapé from his plate. It wasn't until later on that he finally met up with Henry, who praised his costume. "Jack the Ripper! Damn it, Durham, I wish I'd thought of that!" He stroked his chin. "It would allow me to rape Marie..."

"But then you'd have to kill her," Howard said tonelessly. "And anyway, who else but you could be the Marquis de Sade?"

"Ah yes!" Henry cried. "I love cracking this whip! Marvelous fun, you see?" And he dragged the whip back and snapped it, causing the surrounding guests to half-scream. "And look," Henry held up two leather cuffs attached to his waistcoat. The insides of them had small, sharp spikes. "You bind 'em with these," he said in a near whisper. It made Howard slightly uneasy. After Colin's comment about his knife and Henry marveling over his instruments of torture... well, it was just too horrid of a conclusion to draw.

He couldn't help it. "You're not actually going to use those things on him, are you?"

Henry gave him a funny look. "Who?"

"Colin!"

Henry gasped. "Good lord, no, Howard! That's disgusting!" But he read Howard's look of fear and he shook his head, laughing. "I don't *emulate* the Marquis de Sade. It's just because it's so lurid, you see. This stuff's an amazing conversation starter—that's the whole point of these kinds of parties, after all. And it's fun scaring people." He chuckled. "You ought to know, putting that knife on Collie's neck like you did. I saw that. Fun, no?" He took a drink while Howard smiled at his nonchalance. *Thank God he's such a good sport.*

"Fun, yes," he admitted. "But it's too bad Mr. Ripper didn't attack male prostitutes with equal gusto. This party could be so much more entertaining."

"Indeed," Henry agreed. Then he amiably offered his whip. "Here, you try it. It's a bit addicting."

As Howard handled the whip, Henry told him, "Oh, and I found the perfect country house for Collie and I last week, in the Cotswolds! We're going to rent it the second week of August, and if we like it, we'll go again in the fall."

"Marvelous," Howard muttered, dragging the whip behind him. He snapped it with a ferocious crack. He eyed the stunned crowd around them and handed back the whip to Henry with a forced smile. "Really marvelous!"

The night eventually drew to a close, and everyone took turns revealing his or her identities. As Howard and Henry had predicted, Colin surprised and delighted everyone the most upon tearing off his wig with the same abandon he did his cape. The effect it had on the audience made the entire act worthwhile, particularly the effect it had on the number of men who had to realize, in their besotted minds, that for one evening they had danced with, caressed, and lusted after someone who wasn't even a woman at all.

CHAPTER ELEVEN

With forays into society like these, Colin enjoyed the opportunities to entertain and be entertained. But he was still happiest at the drafting table. He felt that his honest work creating architecture balanced his decadent behavior otherwise. When he looked at his strong graphite lines on white paper, he couldn't help declaring, "*This* is purity! This is true beauty, laid bare."

Up until recently, he had only minimally contributed to Henry's projects, but now Colin was working on his first commission: The Lyon Steel Headquarters. He was designing just the offices, not the factory itself, but it excited him to no end. Steel was the future, and the chief executive officer knew his facility should reflect that, as did Colin, who couldn't have asked for a better opportunity. Granted, Lyon Steel didn't know that Colin was the chief architect, but Henry had presented the client's wishes to Colin and asked him to draw up the schematics. Henry was so impressed with Colin's proposal that he gave the project over to him.

"Of course, I will oversee you," he said, "and I'm afraid it will have to have my name on it, but it's a start."

Colin was ecstatic, and he immediately threw himself into the project. Henry refused to let him work after hours on it. "The client agreed to the deadline I gave him, Collie. If you finish early, it will set a precedent."

At the office, Henry often found himself gazing at his protégé across the room. *It is as if he is two different people. So serious, dedicated, and passionate here, he can barely contain his energy. And yet when he is entertaining, he's calm, sensual, deliberate. Here he works happily in rolled-up shirtsleeves; there he reclines languidly in opulent dress.* Henry smiled indulgently. *I have the best of both worlds.*

Howard visited the office on occasion, eventually noticing the very dichotomy that Henry observed. The boy's intensity was so inspiring that Howard found his visits becoming more frequent. After all, Colin seemed to enjoy his company just as much, often taking the time to explain things to Howard at such length that Henry had to remind him to get back to work. When Henry joked about this one evening at Porter's, Howard shrugged. "Well, you can hardly blame me for visiting. Who else among us has someone so delightful as Colin?"

Colin laughed. "We must find someone for you, Howard!"

Howard smiled. "Oh, I don't know. What you and Henry have is admirable, to be sure, but it's hardly realistic."

For the first time, Colin looked sharply at Howard. "Not realistic? What do you mean? You don't believe that two men can love each other?"

Howard stood his ground. "Love, yes. A lasting commitment?" He shrugged again. "Between two men, unfortunately it seems impossible, doesn't it? You and Henry are the only two I personally know who seem to have a successful relationship, and you've been together only a few months." He instantly regretted his words.

Colin's eyes flashed. "Only a few months! You think that it won't last?" he demanded.

"I didn't say that," Howard replied quickly. "I only meant that any other union between two men has ended unhappily. Violently, even. Look at Verlaine and Rimbaud. Look at how Bosie treats Wilde. It's appalling. It just doesn't leave me with the desire to attempt such a thing myself." He smiled at Colin. "I'm sure the luck Henry has had with you wouldn't strike again so close to home."

But the damage had been done. Colin glared at him, and then looked off and pouted.

Howard sighed. "Oh, Colin, I meant no offense—"

Colin whirled his head around. "Didn't you? It's quite clear you don't expect us to last. You've probably placed a bet on the day we're through. What is it? Tomorrow? The end of the week?"

"Colin..." Henry warned.

Colin turned on him, his voice rising. "What about you, Henry? Where's your bet placed?"

"Well, I may have to retract it if you're going to act like this to our friends," Henry replied irritably. "Howard didn't mean to hurt you, you know that."

Colin glanced at Howard, who agreed, "I didn't, Colin. I truly didn't."

Colin looked downwards. "Well, I don't want to talk about this anymore."

"Fine, then!" Henry exclaimed. "We won't! Kenneth, would you please tell us some gossip about your latest production? I'm begging you!"

Howard was tempted to excuse himself from the table, but he was afraid Henry would further berate Colin later. So he listened to Kenneth smooth things over with his wonderfully expressive voice. But Colin remained silent the entire time, moodily smoking. Finally, Henry sighed. "Master Sewell, do you wish to go home?"

Colin was startled. "What? No! No, I..." He looked at the three apologetically. "I was just thinking about some things, is all. I'm sorry. Go on, please."

And Howard realized that what he thought was a furious expression on Colin's face had all along been one of furious thought. Colin had surely been scouring his mind for an example other than him and Henry, someone who had lasted. Howard's heart sank.

And he's found none.

On Monday morning, one of the secretaries at the Bank of England appeared at Howard's office door. "I beg your pardon, Mr. Durham. There's a Mr. Colin here to see you?"

Howard half-stared in disbelief. "Mr. Colin? Are you sure?"

The secretary nodded. "He said you weren't expecting him, but he'd very much like to see you, if it wasn't too much trouble. He said he had an account to settle with you?"

Howard nodded. "Show him in, please." Then he stood up. "Wait. I will see Mr. Colin myself." He walked out from the parlors to find him.

Even though he was in his work clothes, Colin still appeared as a young man of wealth. Howard noticed the opal cufflinks, the fine sheen of his suit jacket, the tight weave of his hat, and his beautifully combed hair. He was studying the soaring interior: the lobby's ceiling was two stories high. The massive ribbed vaults gave way to skylit domes. Marble loomed from all walls and Colin seemed absorbed by the flurry of activity that was ceaseless around him. Eventually Colin's wandering gaze fell upon him, and Howard said kindly as he approached, "Perhaps your next project will be a bank!"

Colin regarded Howard amidst the backdrop of the stately cacophony, and Howard realized with surprise that he appeared to be intimidated, or was it impressed? "Oh," Colin replied awkwardly. "I don't know about that."

Howard made a motion with his hand. "Come. We'll talk in my office."

After he closed the door, Howard asked, "Does Henry know you're here?"

Colin smiled slightly. "Yes. He highly approved of my apology. That is..." he sighed, "I want to apologize for my behavior Saturday evening, Howard. I'm very sorry."

Howard was incredulous. "*You're* sorry? I was going to stop by your office later and apologize to you!"

Colin shook his head. "No, you were right. History has not been kind to us. You have every reason to doubt the permanence of my relationship with Henry."

"That is none of my business," Howard interjected. "And I've been thinking too, Colin. As you may have guessed, I couldn't admit Saturday evening that I'm purely envious of what you and Henry have together. We all are. So many of us have rather resigned ourselves to our fate of fleeting moments, you see. And I think those past histories have scared us from going any further. In any case, I felt terrible about hurting your feelings or mistakenly implying that you weren't worth keeping on. Nothing could be further from the truth."

Colin frowned. "You're too kind. Didn't you realize the irony? The way I acted that night was exactly the reason why one wouldn't want to bother keeping a boy on! Henry said I acted just like Bosie."

Howard smiled. "Well, Wilde is obsessed with him."

Colin tossed his head. "I should like to think I'm above that." He looked at Howard. "So I am sorry." Then he looked at the floor. "I suppose I reacted so awfully because you..." he looked up, "*you* of all of them, Howard! You seem to be the most idealistic of the group..." He blushed, realizing he couldn't mention his knowledge of Luca. "That is, because *I* am that way too, and to hear that you didn't believe that a lasting love between two men could exist..." He looked at Howard in earnest. "My goal in life is for a happy ending, like everyone else gets to have. Don't you think men like us deserve it too?"

Howard smiled. "That's rather Panglossian. But yes, of course I do, Colin. It just seems difficult when the rest of the world is dead set against you."

"But that's no reason not to try," Colin insisted.

"But why one man?" Howard asked. "Why do you want to be with only one for the rest of your life?"

Colin looked surprised. "Well, that's what true love is, Howard. That's the way we're paired off. If you love someone, then they ought to be enough, I think. When you have one, you don't have to look anymore. You have a partner in life, to weather the storms with and celebrate everything with, just like they say at a wedding." He paused. "You mean to say you wouldn't want one person for the rest of your life?"

Now it was Howard's turn to blush. "Well I... I just don't think it's realistic, that's all. I suppose it would be nice, though."

Colin nodded sadly. "Perhaps you're right. You've seen more than I have. I'll just have to be happy with what I've got, for now." He straightened. "Anyway, I apologize for my actions, as I apologize for coming here without a proper request."

Howard shook his head. "Colin, now hang on to your idealism; it's one of your best features. It's what put you on a ship headed for London, and look how far it's carried you!"

Colin gave a small shrug and looked around Howard's office. "Normally I don't care for this kind of design, but it's very fitting for a bank, isn't it?" He looked shyly at Howard. "Will we see you at Porter's tonight, then?"

Howard chuckled. "I hardly have a choice."

Colin looked relieved. "I can see myself out, thank you." He rose from his chair, and when he reached the door, he glanced back. "I'm glad I was able to see where you work. You're perfect for it."

After a minute, Howard got up and closed the door. He sat down heavily at his desk and rubbed his eyes. *Right then, no further visits to Henry's office.*

* * * *

December 1891

John Addington Symonds waited impatiently in his chair. The well-known poet and writer didn't often come to Latte Con Miele, but his friend David Morrow had insisted on his presence tonight. Henry and Colin Sewell were in Venice, and David had told John about them. "I'm sure you'll love them. They're supposed to be very educated and witty, and I've heard Colin is supposed to give any Italian boy a run for his money in looks!" Then lowering his voice, David said, "And the best part is, they've become infamous in London and Paris for taking the rich, well-connected, and well-bred home with them and doing wonderfully wicked things!"

The word "wicked" rankled John. "Wicked how?"

David's eyes lit up. "They take one or two boys and have their way with them. But Colin—he's American, by the way—he does... well, he supposedly does wonderful things with his mouth." And David fell into a blissful trance imagining it while John looked puzzled. "His mouth?"

David snapped back to attention. "You know." He looked at John's waist. "He's supposed to be *expert*."

John made a face of indifference. He'd never cared much for oral sex on his behalf. He preferred his lovers to be in power. "So am I supposed to come and watch as you're led off?" he asked, amused.

David's eyes widened. "John, *you're* the one who would want them! And you have as much a chance as I, if not better! I'm sure they've heard of you."

John waved a hand. "I'm not interested. I'm bringing Angelo, but they can't have him."

David frowned. "Oh, they wouldn't take Angelo. They've got to have a gentleman boy."

"That's ridiculous!" John sputtered. "I dislike them already, that they should pass up a near-godlike man like him!"

"John," David soothed, realizing his error, "just come anyway, will you? And bring Angelo; that's fine. I just want to see what you think of them."

So John assented, and now he was waiting here, entertaining Angelo, when Henry and Colin walked in. John was startled. Henry must have been the same age as himself, but he looked much younger. Colin looked like a typical wealthy young man, though John grudgingly admitted that he was very good-looking with his sensual mouth and refined profile. But he was extravagantly dressed and John guessed with disgust that he probably perfumed himself as well. How much better suited to a man's physique were simple work clothes! Although since Colin's clothes were perfectly tailored, there was no mistaking he had a fine form, albeit more slender than John preferred.

"Is that them, then?" Angelo asked in Italian.

"Yes," John sighed. He was already bored with them and wondered what David thought was so appealing. The boy was just another fop. But then John watched them make their way slowly through the room, and he noticed something intriguing. Colin appeared to be quite masculine. He didn't walk as much as he strode, and instead of tilting his chin up in the fashionable manner of high society, he kept his head slightly tucked, looking out from under his brow in a most intimate and powerful manner. And even though he was now in a more permissive environment, he still gave firm handshakes, direct, brief eye contact, a solid smile, and he crossed his arms genially when listening. He motioned a waiter with a curt nod and ordered drinks for himself and Henry, and John realized he was taking command of the room. As they drew closer, John could hear bits of their conversation, and he marveled at hearing the rare American accent.

Angelo was fascinated. "Oh, look at his dress! He's a true gentleman, isn't he, John?"

John chuckled. "I suppose you'd like me to buy you an outfit like young Mr. Sewell's, then?"

Angelo laughed and shook his head. "No. The one you bought me for tonight is fine enough." But John could see that Angelo was studying the boy, thinking in his mind what he might ask from John next. John didn't mind. He was glad to give Angelo things he couldn't afford. God knows he got back his own gifts tenfold.

Eventually the two were brought to their table and introduced, and John was face to face with the firm handshake, the warm smile, and the bold gaze. The sensual mouth. And the American accent. They met John first and then Angelo, and it was evident that they both found the young Venetian remarkable. "Would you mind terribly if we join you?" Henry asked. "I'm rather worn out from standing."

John motioned for Angelo to make room, but Angelo looked mortified. John leaned over. "I'm sorry; Mr. Fusato speaks only Italian."

"Oh!" Henry raised his eyebrows. He hadn't expected this. *What well-bred young man doesn't speak several languages?*

But Angelo's pride caused him to speak anyway. In Italian he said, "I'm sorry I don't speak English. Perhaps John can translate?" He glanced at John, who tried not to purse his lips.

Suddenly, David rushed over. "*I'll* translate for Angelo." He sat down next to Henry, and John could only hope that Mr. Sewell was polite enough not to recoil and leave once he found out that Angelo was lower-class. The mere thought made his blood boil, and he felt his anger rise.

Colin still stood, confused. *Doesn't he know about Henry and me? Does he think Henry's trying to steal Angelo from him?* "Would you rather we not stay, Mr. Symonds?" he asked quietly.

John turned his head to see Colin waiting there, looking utterly perplexed. Now John was horrified at his own appalling manners. "Oh my word!" he murmured, moving over. "Mr. Colin, I'm so sorry! I just... I can't imagine what's gotten into me! Please, please sit down."

Colin was still hesitant. "You're certain?"

"I beg of you; sit!" John cried.

Colin sat down next to him and looked at Angelo. John felt Colin's awkwardness and was touched by this surprise of sensitivity. He softened and said, "I've been admiring your accent whenever it drifted across the room."

Colin smiled at him. "But the British and romantic languages are so much more sonorous," he protested lightly.

"But the American accent is so pure," John insisted, admiring Colin's mouth. "It's absolutely symbolic of your country's history of freedom and bravery!"

Colin laughed. "You're very kind, Mr. Symonds." Then he looked at him intently. "Mr. Morrow said you're a writer. I confess I have not yet read your works. What do you write about?"

"Mostly essays, critiques on the Italian renaissance. I'm currently working on a biography about Michelangelo."

Colin raised his eyebrows. "You certainly are a man of letters, then! Were you educated at Oxford?"

"Yes. And you?"

"My schooling was done in America," Colin replied. "I'm an architect. I work with Henry."

"An architect, really? Then you must think quite highly of classical Italian architecture."

Colin shrugged as he drew out a cigarette. "I think very highly of it. I just don't see any reason to copy it, or borrow from it. It's been done." He looked stubbornly at the ashtray. "History hasn't done us any favors, Mr. Symonds. I'm not a fan of preserving things that remind me that there were times even worse than this." He looked back at John in earnest. "I want my structures to be progressive. To reflect my hopes for an advancing society."

John gazed at him. "That's very admirable. But then, why did you leave your country? It seems best groomed for such a transformation."

Colin rolled his eyes. "I came to England to escape the puritanical ways of America. Now we're in Italy to escape the oppressive ways of England." Then he looked around and shook his head, his voice dark as he lit his cigarette. "There is no place." He paused, and then gave an embarrassed laugh. "I'm sorry, Mr. Symonds. You must think me utterly melancholic."

"Fascinating," John corrected. He had already forgotten about how Angelo was holding up. "Do go on, Mr. Colin. It's a favorite topic of mine as well!"

Colin demurred. "Perhaps another time. I'm in no mood to argue theories. I'd rather hear more about you." So they discussed other topics. After a while, John realized it had been a long time since a young man had actually matched wits with him.

"Forgive me for saying so, Mr. Colin, but I didn't realize an American student of architecture would be so well-versed in the humanities."

Colin frowned. "Why would you say that? I was classically educated."

"But... isn't your Massachusetts Institute of Technology a... er... trade school?"

Colin looked offended. "God, no! It's a proper university, Mr. Symonds." Then he laughed at the older man's look of embarrassment. "And unfortunately, we're every bit as Victorian as you. Every man there grows up with a solid foundation of the humanities."

"Every man?" John asked. Colin nodded. John raised his eyebrows. "Even your working class?"

"Well no, I meant of course, gentlemen."

"Ah. Well then, it is, like you said, the same as here."

"Well of course it is. Why would a laborer have any need for the humanities?"

"Why would an architect?"

Colin stared at him. "Architecture is an art, Mr. Symonds—"

"I thought it was a trade."

"No, it isn't. It's part of the humanities and you must know it. And..." Colin sighed, smiling. "We're arguing theories. Do you live near here?"

John felt his heart beat faster. "Not too far. A twenty-minute carriage ride."

Colin smiled again. John was beginning to fall for those smiles. They always worked with the boy's eyes. *He must have dozens of expressions, with a mouth like that.* Colin spoke again. "I would be very interested in seeing the design."

"Tonight?"

"Why not?"

"Just you?"

"Oh, no. Henry would like to see it too."

John looked pensive. Slowly he said, "Angelo is coming, too."

Colin smiled once more. "Yes, I would hope so."

John sighed. How to say it? "Mr. Colin, from what I understand, you and Mr. Sewell have a rule..."

"A rule?"

"Regarding... selectivity."

Colin looked over at Angelo, and then it dawned on him. "Ah. You mean because Mr. Fusato is a man of more... modest means."

"Yes."

Colin smiled once more. "Mr. Symonds, that applies only to London and Paris. Henry has so many connections in those cities that it's just too risky. But here in Italy it's different, and besides, Mr. Fusato is with you." He gazed at Angelo. "I don't think Henry would forgive me if he was left behind." Still staring at the olive-skinned young man, he murmured, "And I don't think I'd forgive myself, either."

John studied Colin. "Do you find him attractive?" he asked, a trace of pride in his voice.

Colin cut short his gaze and haughtily tapped his cigarette. "He's absolutely beautiful. He's like a god." He drew in on his cigarette. "Such is Italy. If I was sober I'd be insanely jealous." He nodded in an aside to John, "As opposed to just jealous."

John chuckled. "That's very humorous. In this club the belief is that your looks give any Italian boy a run for his money."

Colin's eyes grew round and he looked at the well-built Angelo. "With *that*?" He gave a laugh and looked away. "I won't even dignify the idea with an argument."

John knew Colin was being coy, but he liked it anyway. "A beautiful boy is a beautiful boy, Mr. Sewell. And anyway, I was told you prefer older men."

Colin looked sharply at him. "And I was told you prefer common men. And here I've spent my hour with you discussing the rise and fall of the Roman Empire!" He sighed in exasperation.

"Your *hour*?" John asked, amused. "Is that your time limit, then? 'One hour to madness and joy'?"

Colin looked up in surprise. "That's Whitman!"

Now John was taken aback. "Yes, it is! I didn't think you would recognize that. But you're American, after all. And here I was hoping I could appear clever and appropriate it."

Colin grinned. "Not a chance. That's one of the best poems in the book!"

"*Leaves of Grass.*"

"Yes!" Colin stared at him. "You know it, then."

"I'd better. Whitman's a good friend of mine."

Colin's jaw dropped. "He is?" Then he shook his head. "Of course. You're both extremely democratic."

"Yes. So how on earth are you a fan?" John teased.

Colin laughed. "Whitman is American, and more importantly, he wrote for *us*." He looked fiercely at John. "Beautiful poems, of love between men." He gazed at his glass.

"*To be absolved from previous ties and conventions,*
I from mine and you from yours.
To have the feeling that to-day or any day
I am sufficient as I am."

He paused, and then murmured,

"To have the gag removed from one's mouth!"

John nodded.

"O to draw you to me,

To plant on you for the first time the lips of a determined man."

Colin nodded too.

"O to be yielded to you,

Whoever you are,

And you to be yielded to me..."

Colin's voice became forceful.

"In defiance of the world!"

He took on a determined look. "Every one of us should know Whitman." He glanced at Angelo and then back at John. "No matter what class."

John felt weak. Angelo was lust but Colin was love. He laid a hand on Colin's arm. "I'd like to show you my villa, Mr. Sewell." And this time, the new smile was his. He nodded toward the aisle, and Colin broke into a grin, obliging.

John wanted them to spend the night so that the next morning he could converse further with Colin. But they declined.

"It's all well and good for you," Henry told Colin on the way home. "But I'd be stuck with Angelo, and I certainly can't talk to him. He's fine for the bed, but the boy is simple! Of course, that may have more to do with the fact I can't understand a word he's saying and vice versa." He studied Colin. "You seemed to get on very well with Mr. Symonds at the club."

Colin nodded. "He's very interesting. But there's something tragic about him. I don't understand why he's attracted to lower-class men like Angelo. Beyond a sexual relationship, that is. After all, he comes from as well-bred a background as you and I."

"Poor Symonds," Henry agreed. "How awful to be in such conflict with your status in life."

Colin nodded. "His health is failing. He told me his lungs are damaged, and I actually was a bit concerned for him." He shrugged. "The man probably just wants to die at peace."

"Well then, good thing he didn't die tonight," Henry remarked.

"Yes," Colin laughed. "It's a good thing."

The next day, as they left for breakfast, the clerk gave a letter to Colin. "A post?" he asked. "For me?"

"A pound bet on who that's from," Henry smirked. Colin opened it and read the contents.

Dear Mr. Sewell,

I wondered if before you left Italy you would be interested in discussing a few of those theories you mentioned. I'm writing a book about the subject and would appreciate your thoughtful contribution. I was so impressed with your intelligence when we met! Please send a post round to the below address.

Yours,

J.A. Symonds

Colin excitedly read the letter to Henry. "What theories?" Henry asked.

"Oh, you know, 'Why we are the way we are,' 'Common traits amongst us,' that sort of thing."

"Colin, he's writing a book about it!" Henry cried. "You can't associate yourself with that!"

"Well, he's not going to put my name in it, I'm sure!"

"Hmph! Better find out for certain."

"Would you mind if I went, Henry?"

Henry sighed. "God knows I should stop you, but I can't deny you the opportunity to discuss at length the subject nearest to your heart."

"But we won't be discussing you, Henry!" Colin exclaimed with affection.

Henry laughed. "You're a dear."

Then Colin looked concerned. "What will you do while I'm gone?"

"Oh, have loads of fun myself, I imagine!" Henry grinned. He put a hand on Colin's arm. "Collie, we *are* in Italy. You must be tolerant. One can only resist so much here."

Colin's eyes widened. "You're going to... go on with someone?" he whispered.

Henry chuckled and then shook his head. "I'm just joshing, Colin. You know our rules. Now, there's some sightseeing I want to do, and this will be the perfect time." He smiled at Colin. "But before we breakfast, why don't you send Mr. Symonds a post?"

CHAPTER TWELVE

That afternoon, Colin was at John Symonds' door. He was ushered into the sunroom, where John rose to meet him. Colin spied a sheaf of paper on the table and relaxed. He had secretly been worried that the man's letter was a ruse to invite him for a second intimate encounter, but it appeared his intentions were honest after all. Angelo was nowhere in sight, and Colin chose to refrain from asking after him. The two men settled into their chairs. "Are you really writing a book?" Colin asked, fascinated.

John sighed. "I must. It is completely rational for us to be as we are, and the public must be educated to that end."

"But how will you publish it? They'll string you up on charges of indecency at the very least!"

"They can't if I'm dead," John smiled. "The book will be published posthumously, Mr. Sewell."

Colin frowned. "Then, will you name names?"

"Good heavens, no!" John replied in horror. He grew serious. "But what I *would* like, you see, is for men to reveal themselves after they die, as I am doing."

"You mean, leave a sort of letter only to be opened upon one's passing?"

John nodded. "Precisely. I'd never want anyone to put their lives at stake over such a thing, but if we continue to act as if we don't exist, we shall never escape this persecution." He leaned forward. "Think of it—hundreds of such letters opened over a course of years, from men of every class and distinction!" He sat back and said in an amazed voice, "'Well, imagine that! John Addington Symonds was one of them!' 'Yes, and that great architect Colin Sewell! *He* was too!'"

Colin beamed. "'And the poet Walt Whitman!'"

"'And the superb playwright Oscar Wilde!'"

Colin shook his head in wonder, and then a shadow fell across his face. "But then, what would concern me," he began slowly, "is that if people realize that so many men have this tendency, and they *still* choose to punish it, won't we actually be making it harder for those who come after us? The suspicion will be easier to come by. They'll have to go even further underground."

"How could they possibly do that?" John asked. "We're already marrying women we don't fully love and lying to our families."

"And that's why nobody accuses us," Colin argued. "They think, 'Of course Mr. Symonds can't be a sodomite. He's married, with children!' But once people see that most of these letters *are* from married, child-producing men, how can any man hide his identity believably? Because you see, then it will be, 'Of course Mr. Sewell can't be aberrant! He's married to a lovely wife and he has two children!' 'Oh yes, but look at Mr. Symonds! *He* was married, and *he* had a child. And Mr. Sewell even socialized with him on several occasions!'" He looked at John. "Once people have enough dots to connect, the suspicions will turn into accusations, and there will be no safe alibi."

John looked sternly at Colin. "The idea is to remove the alibi entirely. The idea is to move to a point where we won't need to hide behind false marriages and the like. Now, I never said it would be an easy transition." He leaned in and smiled. "That is why people like you and Henry are going to save us. If you eventually reveal that two men—yourselves—can lead successful, happy lives and make positive contributions to society without harming anyone, then you will prove this sort of lifestyle is anything but reprehensible."

"But the harm in society's eyes is that we are defying God's law and corrupting innocent boys," Colin reproved.

"God's law is open to interpretation, and as for the boys, they will have to step up and be brave," John argued. "They must tell the truth—they seek us out as much as we do them, and they remain this way into manhood."

"Well, not the prostitutes as much," Colin shrugged resignedly. "Most of them are regular boys who are too poor to do anything as lucrative."

John clucked his tongue. "I'm not certain that's true. They may be more diaphanous. I often wonder if there's not a third kind of person that enjoys both men and women equally."

"Oh, that *can't* be true!" Colin cried in disgust. "That would throw a wrench into everything! The only reason those fellows sleep with men is because women don't use prostitutes."

John looked evenly at Colin. "Angelo has a long-standing lady friend. And children. Now, do you think he prefers me or her?"

Colin sighed, surprised. "Well, he was with all of us."

"Only because I rewarded him handsomely for it, and he admired you."

Colin stared. "You paid him? Well then, there you have it! He's a regular fellow who's using you. He's using you for your wealth and your connections."

"Do you think *any* regular fellow would offer to be this kind of companion on a regular basis, Mr. Sewell?" John paused. "Would your father?"

Colin clenched his jaw. "How dare you! My father was never in desperate straits! Angelo is lower-class; he needs you."

"I disagree. And I didn't really want you to make a decision on Angelo's preference, Colin, because I think he's the example of a go-between. I do think perhaps Angelo wants a life with a woman, but he understands that sex is pleasurable with both genders." He saw the disbelief on Colin's face and added, "You studied the Greeks, of course?"

"Yes, yes," Colin grumbled. "But I don't really understand all of that. I think their culture was just completely different from ours. Most of those men stuck to platonic love anyway; that was the point of those relationships. After all, they had to bear children."

"Do you feel that need?"

Colin paused. "Sometimes I do, to be honest. But to lie with a woman?" He cocked his head. "I'd no sooner do it than my own sister would lay with her kind!"

John laughed. "There you have it! You're dyed in the wool, then, my boy." He frowned. "But for argument's sake, yes, I agree that probably most prostitutes are one way or the other. But look here, that's not the focus of our discussion, so let's return to it. I still think it's inherent that we expose ourselves. If people see that even great men, men who have made astounding contributions to society—strong, educated, successful men—that these men too lived such a lifestyle, then I am convinced that society will begin to realize it is not a sin."

"But they must be happy men," Colin insisted.

"I beg your pardon?"

Colin shook his head, thinking of Howard. "Rimbaud and Verlaine—passionately in love and then wretchedly miserable. And I've seen how Lord Alfred treats Oscar; it's the same thing. And you! You haven't found a happy ending yet either, have you John?"

John looked surprised. "But, haven't you found yours with Mr. Sewell?"

Colin shrugged. "Well, yes, but the odds are stacked against us, aren't they? I've not heard of any two men of our kind living happily ever after."

"That doesn't mean that such pairings can't exist," John assured him. "And if they don't, it's because society won't allow them to." Then he nodded in thought. "I imagine there are plenty of male couples who are managing to live happily to the end of their days. We just don't hear of them because they're not famous and they keep it secret."

Colin's face grew bright. "I hope you're right. Because I do think men can sustain a happy relationship. I think it's only so difficult because sexual relations are the only expression of love we can give each other in equal amounts." He went on, his pace becoming rapid. "Oh, I have thought about this. You see, the ability to be granted public displays of affection is not ours. A man and a woman may hold hands in a thoroughfare. A woman can be on a man's arm. They can tilt their heads together, hold each other's gaze with that look of love and affection everyone knows. The man can hold his misses' hand up to his lips. He can throw his coat over her when she's cold. They can huddle together in the rain. They can even give each other a kiss on the cheek, all in public!" He threw his arms up. "They take all of those things for granted, John! They walk around wearing their *regularity* on the outside without giving it a thought. And yet us! *We* must wear the equivalent of Hawthorne's scarlet letter on the inside. It's stitched upon our souls. Every day, all day, I'm reminded of who I am. And most of the time, I don't even know what that means!" He grasped for clarity. "A... a sodomite is someone who has sex with another man, and only in a certain way. It says nothing of being attracted to other men, it says nothing of loving another man. It doesn't explain *why*." His face fell into a disturbed frown. "So that is what I'm always thinking about. Why? How?"

John's eyebrows raised. "My goodness, your Henry must really favor intellectuals!"

Colin laughed. "No. He won't admit it, but he's as much an aesthete as Oscar Wilde. This topic is far too taxing for him. He'd rather just live as he lives and not concern himself with any sort of analysis." He smiled at John. "That's why he didn't mind me seeing you. This way I could 'get it out of my system', as it were."

John smiled in return. "It's a pity, isn't it? I suppose that being who we are depresses even many of our own kind. It's like thinking about death:

if you dwell on it for longer than a few seconds, you're overwhelmed." He straightened. "Well, the benefits of discussion are great indeed, but all progress occurs as a result of action. My proposal is the deathbed letter. What is yours?"

Colin shrugged. "All I've come up with is moving somewhere where you could live freely and openly. Sometimes I dream about living on the American Frontier. You know, taking a whole group of us and establishing our own sort of settlement. Gradually it'd be known as a town where men could go without fear of the law. In fact, we'd make our own law." He looked proudly at John. "And here is the best part: once we have a sort of town, people would have to acknowledge we are a segment of the general population. It would take a long time, grant you, but maybe people would 'get used to us', as it were, and accept us living anywhere, ultimately among *them*."

John grinned. "Don't you see that very thing happening in the major cities of the world right now?"

Colin paused. "I didn't think about that. I suppose it's true the larger cities are more accepting of any kind of... unusual trait. But we've yet to really be able to come out and reveal ourselves. We're still a hundred percent underground, and the goal, Mr. Symonds, should be for us to live *over ground*."

John clapped. "Admirable! And coming from such a young man like yourself—bravo!"

"Well, to take it a step further," Colin added, "by being an architect, I'm already leaving *my* mark on the world. Every structure I put to ground evinces my identity! When a building is completed, I can point to it and say, 'I was there. I made that. It exists because I exist.'" Colin smiled proudly. "I like to think of my creations as my soul. Long after I cease to exist physically, my memory will live on through all of the work I have done." He brightened. "And so, if the truth ever is found out about me, even posthumously, my work will still be out there! Colin Sewell will live on in the very streets and hills of England! People will be forced to acknowledge me just by walking through my structures."

John was pleased. "That's an extraordinary way of thinking. It is just like I am doing with my own writing—we are creating things to outlive us and carry on our work once we're gone."

"Yes!" Then Colin shook his head. "But I hate that I still have to go about it all surreptitiously. It's frustrating to think that a city for us to live freely in won't happen in my lifetime. I can understand why men are deciding to live as they live in secret." He raised his head. "But I'm tired of code words and of entering clubs through back-alley doors. I'm tired of using my eyes to communicate with other men, of politely refusing ladies' requests to arrange for me to meet their daughters. I'm tired of having to find excuses why I'm not married, and I'm tired of praying for the safety of a family I may never see again because I disowned myself from them." His voice grew in its bitterness. "I left home because I refused to *play the game* any longer. But it turns out I've been playing the game all along. I'm still playing it, and I'll play it to my death. And I'll never win it."

John looked tenderly at Colin. "Don't be too sure. Finding someone who loves you is no small victory."

Colin smiled weakly. "Perhaps." Then he looked at John in earnest. "But if you believe in lasting relationships, John, why haven't you found someone? Someone you can have permanently, and all to yourself?"

John looked at the table and paused before answering softly, "I would have loved to have been where you are now, Mr. Sewell. I did fall deeply in love—twice—to no avail. They were both chorister boys in England, at different times. I was young too back then. It was the first time I felt real love. Glorious! But I confessed my feelings to my father, who first thrust a range of therapies upon me, and when that failed, told me something far closer to the truth: we—the chorister boys and I—were of two very different classes and therefore would never be suitable." He smiled weakly at Colin. "I still argue that theory today. It's true, of course. Society doesn't allow the mixing of classes. But personally, I feel it is ridiculous."

"I told my father about myself, too!" Colin said, amazed. "But I left America before he could respond. I was afraid I'd be committed."

John patted his hand. "It's awful, isn't it?"

"But then, do you prefer lower-class men?" Colin asked, curious.

"I suppose so," John smiled. "You see, because many of them are laborers, they have the bodies so admired by the Greeks."

Colin's jaw dropped. "I... I never thought of that!" He recalled Angelo's physique, and with a twinge of shame, he realized how little he resembled a Greek statue.

John caught his crestfallen expression and hastily added, "But then again, well-bred boys have an allure for many men in their own lush, languorous way, with their flawless, unscathed bodies. If I dare say it, men like you, Mr. Sewell, resemble the lovely Greek youths whereas Angelo is more of the *elder*." John smiled. "And perhaps I'm really still trying to make amends with the choristers. Or perhaps it's because I don't feel as guilty being a man of wealth if I consort with less fortunate men. Perhaps it makes me happy that I can offer them something." He smiled at Colin. "I can't offer you anything. You're young, handsome, wealthy, educated, employed, and loved by another man."

Colin held his gaze and said bravely, "But if I wasn't with Henry, and I loved you, wouldn't that be perfection idealized? Then your offer would be *love*, because we would be equals."

"Mr. Sewell, you're as far removed from me as the gondoliers," John chuckled. "I don't mind being short on looks or health if I can compensate financially, which I can for Angelo. But men of your type can take their pick, and so they should."

"And I picked you last night."

"You picked Angelo."

"Henry did! I—"

"Yes, yes. Fine and very well then. Let me retreat to my earlier statement that I would love to be where you and Henry are now. But my life took a different course and I am quite at peace with it. My work leaves me little time for anything else, and my health the same. So it simply delighted me to have spent this heavenly afternoon with you, Mr. Sewell. If one can find for himself a few hours of bliss such as this every day, then his lifetime becomes no less a measure of perfection than that of any prince!"

Colin smiled. "The pleasure has truly been mine, and I thank you for the inspiring conversation, Mr. Symonds. I wish you the best with your book. We'll see whose dream is realized first. May the best man win!" He raised his teacup in a final toast.

"So that we may *all* win, Mr. Sewell. Good luck."

When Henry and Colin returned from Italy, it was just a week before Christmas. They went shopping and Colin mentioned gifts for the servants. "Oh, I don't bother with gifts," Henry told him. "I give them bonuses instead. They can always use money, and I'm sure they've come to rely on getting it."

"Well, do you mind then if I get them gifts?" Colin asked shyly.

Henry laughed. "Collie, you needn't buy them anything; they're my help."

"But they do everything for me as well," Colin argued. "I think it's important to show my appreciation too. It wouldn't hurt to have them on both of our sides."

Henry smiled. "I'm sure it wouldn't. But they seem to like you anyway." Before Colin could press further, Henry waved a hand. "All right, fine. If it's something you want to do, I won't stop you. Let's see what you come up with." So Colin chose a pair of cufflinks for Charlie, a vanity set for Millie, a necklace and bracelet for Nora, and a bottle of Madeira each for Daniel and Mikey. Henry frowned at the choices. "They border on improper, Colin. You really spent too much."

"I don't care," Colin sniffed, holding his gifts proudly. "I want them to like me. Considering what we do in that house and who we are, I feel I can hardly afford to fall out of favor with them."

Henry sighed. "Believe me, I pay them better wages than they'll get anywhere else, for that exact reason. But you're sweet, Collie. They'll love your presents."

They most certainly did, and they all agreed among each other that Mr. Colin was an asset to the household. Charlie was perhaps the fondest of the boy, since he was involved the most with the two men. He had seen others Henry could have ended up with, so he was grateful for Colin, who hadn't said a cross word to him yet. Charlie had even overheard Colin admonishing Henry on occasion for being *unreasonable* with the servants! So instead of expecting the day to come when he would pack Mr. Colin's things, Charlie now prayed the two would stay together as long as possible. He thought 1891 had come to a very favorable close, indeed.

But after the excitement of Christmas and New Year's, Colin fell ill with a bad cold and was laid up for two weeks. During that time, Kenneth and Howard paid him a visit to cheer his spirits. Henry welcomed them in, and Colin soon shuffled from the bedroom swaddled in a robe, a wan smile on his face. "It was nice of you to see me," he said to the men hoarsely as he settled onto a sofa. Howard was taken aback by Colin's sickly appearance, and he began to worry about catching illness himself.

"Well, we thought we'd break the monotony," Kenneth replied airily. "Now be a dear and tell us about Italy."

"Oh, the men there!" Colin exclaimed. "Kenneth, small wonder it's your favorite place to vacation! Howard, you must go! I've never seen so many beautiful males in my entire life!"

Then Henry came back into the room and sat down beside Colin. "And yet they were *so* impressed with you, darling!" He put his arm around Colin and kissed his cheek.

"Good heavens, Henry," Howard shuddered. "You'll catch it from him!"

Henry laughed. "I'd have caught it by now, I think, what with us sharing the same bed. And anyway, no matter. It's only a cold."

Colin looked up and smiled. "I promise not to breathe in your general direction, Howard."

"Oh," Howard said, embarrassed. "I'm sure I'll be all right. Er... so then, what did you think of the architecture there?"

Henry groaned. "You shouldn't have asked."

Colin elbowed him. "I liked *some* of the things there!" He looked at Kenneth and Howard. "The pantheon was quite amazing, what with that hole in the roof. If only it had rained that day. And the ruins of the Forum! At least they were original structures, so I adored them as well."

"But the Vatican City..." Henry sighed.

Colin made a face. "Oh, Saint Peter's Basilica was awful! I could barely breathe in there; it was so over-decorated. You never knew where to look, what the focus was. And it was bad enough that every centimeter was covered in gilt or painted plaster, but then that monstrous Bernini canopy debased it entirely!"

"You didn't like the Basilica?" Howard asked, astounded. "You're Catholic! That's practically heresy!"

"The one tenet I do not agree with in the Catholic faith," Colin said haughtily, "besides the obvious, is the belief that God's house be as ornate and overwrought as possible. It's possible to have grandeur without gaudiness. That is why I will build a proper cathedral and show everyone."

Kenneth laughed at Colin's impetuousness. "Surely you admired the Sistine Chapel."

Colin shrugged. "I don't know why people think painting ceilings is such a wonderful idea. I don't see anyone else continuing that tradition, and do you know why? Because it's the *ceiling!* I got a horrid neck ache after the first three panels of that vault! What a stupid idea on Michelangelo's behalf."

"Colin," Henry warned, turning to his friends. "He got me boiling mad with these comments the first time around. It's simply disrespectful!"

"But Henry, I still liked *seeing* everything!" Colin urged. "I'd read about them for so long in school; it was amazing to finally see them in person, even if I didn't like them very well. They certainly overwhelmed me."

"What did you think of the other cities?" Howard asked.

"Well, the sculptures of Michelangelo were very good in Florence," Colin said earnestly. "But again, I was put out by the odd style of their basilicas. I did not care for anything in Venice."

"Not even the gondoliers?" Kenneth winked.

Colin smiled. "Well, they were nice to look at. Again, the best part of Italy was the multitude of extraordinary men."

Henry smirked. "That's not what you originally said."

"Well, that's true," Colin conceded. His expression changed to one of bliss. "Despite my dislike of most of the architecture, nothing mattered more to me than being right there in one of the most Catholic countries in the world." He shook his head reverently. "It was absolutely amazing."

"Collie wanted to stay longer so that he could go to Mass in every cathedral," Henry teased.

"I did get to go to a few," Colin smiled. Then he looked fondly at Henry. "Thank you for taking me, Henry. I didn't mean to sound so ungrateful just then. It was lovely, really."

Henry drew Colin's head to his shoulder. "I know." He regarded his friends. "Collie had dreamt about visiting Italy for a long time. It was a sort of pilgrimage for him."

Colin snuggled into Henry and said softly, "Yes it was." He had grown tired. "Now you tell them about Italy, Hen-Ren."

So Henry did, stroking Colin's hair all the while, and when Colin dozed off, Henry took care to lower his voice to a near-whisper. Howard was transfixed. *What a picture of domesticity!* The image stuck with him the rest of the day and it made him morose. *Imagine Henry, of all people, more compassionate than me! What on earth must it feel like to have someone you love so much, you could give a fig about your own personal health?* Howard began to wonder if he could ever feel that way himself. After all, he was fond of Colin, and yet while visiting him, he had desperately wanted to cover his own face with a handkerchief. *Well for heaven's sake, it's just practicing cleanliness, after all! Common sense.* Howard shrugged off his concern and decided instead that he should really be glad that in some small way, Colin had managed to repel him after all.

But on Saturday afternoon, Howard was back at Henry's door. "Well, since the lad's still sick, I thought this might entertain him awhile," he explained to Henry, showing his gift.

Henry peered at it. "Well, I should think so! I've never seen anything like it." He took over from Charlie and led Howard to the sitting room, where a still-pajama--clad Colin greeted him cheerfully.

"You're being awfully brave, Howard," he teased, and then he leapt to his feet. "Oh! Whatever are those, blocks?"

"Yes," Howard nodded, embarrassed Colin remembered his prior fear of contamination. "I was passing by a toy shop and I thought you'd like something to do as you recover. We didn't think you'd be sick this long." He tried to sound casual, but in truth, he was proud of his gift, one that he had chosen after a long time looking.

"A toy shop," Colin clapped. "What an excellent idea! I haven't been to one in years! Oh, but look," he gratefully took the box from Howard, "these aren't just blocks..." He kneeled on the floor and began taking the smooth Maplewood objects out. "They're spheres! Prisms! Pyramids and cylinders and arches!"

"I figured you would have fun building with them," Howard chuckled. "Did you have such things as a child?"

"I had blocks, but nothing like this." He looked at Howard skeptically. "These are terribly fancy; did you really get them from a toy shop?"

"Robeson's!" Howard put his hand on his heart. "You can ask the man himself. They're designed by a man named Frobel in Germany."

Colin shook his head. "Well, they're wonderful." He smiled at Howard. "Thank you very much! That's very kind, Howard."

"Oh, it's nothing."

Colin stood up. "It's thoughtful, is what it is." He looked with affection at his friend, and Howard realized that Colin was minding not to come forth to even shake his hand, due to his cold. *And knowing him, he'd be more likely to give an embrace. Even a kiss on the cheek!*

Howard tried not to sigh. "Well, you're sounding better."

"I am better. I'm just still extremely tired. It's very inconvenient."

"Here, Collie. Let's put the blocks on the table so you may sit and play with them." Henry took the box of blocks and grinned at Howard. "A toy shop. Didn't know you had an imagination, Durham."

Howard laughed. "It was quite fun going in there, Henry. They still have some of the toys from when we were children."

"Do they? Perhaps we'll have to visit."

"Yes, well, I'll be on my way then. Enjoy."

"Goodbye Howard! I'll be sure to see you next week," Colin waved.

"Farewell, Colin. I'll see you tonight, Henry." Howard left, content to have decidedly resolved his so-called lack of caring.

CHAPTER THIRTEEN

Summer 1892

It was a warm, bright afternoon when Colin bounded into Porter's, with a more reserved Henry trailing. He alighted onto his seat opposite Kenneth and Howard. "The Lyon Steel Headquarters is finished!"

"Colin, that's magnificent!" Kenneth cried, as Henry settled into his seat.

Colin's eyes blazed. "Wait until you see it! It's absolutely stunning! Isn't it, Henry?"

Henry's face glowed with excitement, and he smiled proudly. "It is, it is. Colin has an eye for line the likes I've never seen. I'm afraid I'd be very jealous if he wasn't one of mine."

"When will it open?" Howard inquired.

"Not for several weeks," Colin replied breathlessly. "They have to move everything and everybody in. But they're having the ribbon-cutting ceremony tomorrow. Henry and I are both going to be there. Imagine, my very first design put to ground!"

Howard grinned. "Really? Henry's letting you take full credit?"

Colin looked a bit embarrassed. "Well, no. I can't really, yet. Remember that Henry was the one given this proposal. It's a huge project, too. You can't put a senior draftsman's signature on it."

"But after this one, we will be able to put *both* our names on projects," Henry chimed in. "We need to have Colin's name become recognized with mine, and then eventually he will be able to take sole credit for his work."

This decision wasn't made as easily as it now appeared. A week ago, Colin was at home with Henry, discussing the final plans. "Henry, isn't there any way you could somehow make it clear that I did most of the work on this building?"

Henry sighed irritably. "I really can't, Colin. I've already told you."

"But couldn't you, say, put my name above yours on the blueprint?"

Henry became furious. "Your name *above* mine! I can't even put your name *on* the print! Colin, you're not even a partner yet. And I can't make you one until people are used to seeing your name with mine and they understand that you are under my tutelage. No senior draftsman has taken on a project from design to creation!"

"Then why have you been keeping me a senior draftsman?" Colin protested angrily. He wasn't prepared for the cold glare that approached him.

"Listen, *Mr. Sewell.* Lest you forget, your identity is a complete fabrication! You have no credentials, you haven't even got a degree, and you're only twenty-one years of age! Nobody would believe you could be a partner yet, especially since I have never had a partner in my entire career! You don't seem to appreciate the risk I took with my own reputation when I made you *senior* draftsman. Certainly your "mysterious past" is all very alluring in the social sphere, but in the business world, nobody is going to place their entire investment in the hands of some unfledged architect they've never heard of! Now have some common sense!"

Colin hung his head and thought Henry's words over. Then he looked up with pleading eyes. "But Henry, *you* know who I am. My credentials are solid with you. You know you're not taking a risk."

Henry's expression softened. "I know, darling, but you must be patient. This has nothing to do with what I think of you. With only a few more projects, the rest of the world will be as ready to receive you as I have."

And so it was. Colin managed to find happiness in the fact that at least *he* would know who designed the Lyon Steel Headquarters. And he found out that it also hardly made a difference when, at the ribbon-cutting ceremony, the president of the company praised the building and led the audience to resounding applause. Henry took the opportunity to introduce Colin to the crowd, causing some to wonder if the younger Sewell had some part in this design. After all, as the chief architecture critic noted in his newspaper article, "The Lyon Steel Headquarters evince a departure for Henry Sewell. Never before has he used so many curving lines, never before has he used such tall windows, and never has he used any kind of metalwork. Could his senior draftsman and adopted son, Mr. Sewell the younger, have put forth any ideas into this effort? Is he perhaps, a true protégé?" But Henry refused to divulge how much, if any, of a role Colin played in the design. "That way," Henry had told Colin earlier, "those who hope *I* mainly designed it will believe that I did, and those who hope a star has been born unto their building will believe you did."

And the design certainly could be attributed to either architect. The Lyon Steel building was a two-story, flat-topped box of highly polished white granite. The edges of the box were rounded just slightly and the door was Palladian in style, with silver door handles. Two ribbons of floor-to-ceiling Palladian windows circled the entire building. Inside, everything was white and airy. In the future, employees would comment on how wonderful it was to work in such a welcoming, light-filled building. Colin rather envied them, as his and Henry's office was in the typical brick-and-mortar, older style and was very uninspiring.

After the Lyon achievement, Henry began to allow Colin to undersign his name on the succession of well-received projects. He allowed Colin to speak for himself and for his work, and it soon became clear in the architecture circles that Henry Sewell seemed to have found a great talent in the unknown younger Sewell after all. Henry watched his protégé develop with a sense of awe and pride. The boy was doing much better than Henry had ever expected, and he was touched by Colin's loyalty to him, considering he could have done like Henry and struck off on his own. But he seemed to like his position. Henry had basically let him take over the firm, and Colin still had Henry as a safety net if needed. It worked out well for both of them, and the fact they both still favored each other over anyone else in their private life was terribly good fortune too. The story of Colin's adoption had become well known by now in society circles, and everyone thought it was wonderful that such a beneficial relationship of teacher-student/father-son could happen. Everyone, that is, except for Henry's family. Henry himself was blissfully unaware of the commotion he was causing within his clan until the event of his father's death.

Henry was going through the mail on a Tuesday evening in August, while Colin went off to read a bit before dinner. He was absorbed in his book until he sensed a presence in the doorway. Henry stood there holding a letter, pale and expressionless. "My father passed."

"What?" Colin shut his book and stood up.

But Henry remained stock still. Finally he nodded slowly. "The funeral is Friday. We shall have to go."

"Oh, Henry. I'm so sorry." Colin embraced Henry, and then searched his face. "Are you all right?" For truth be told, he thought Henry might not make much of the thing; he had never mentioned his father to Colin once.

Henry walked past him toward the fireplace. "I... I am going to sit here awhile. I'm not hungry for dinner, Colin, but I want you to eat, of course. I'd like some time alone."

"Henry, you really should have something—"

"I will later. Go ahead, now." Colin went, albeit mildly concerned.

On Friday both men dressed in black, a color they only wore to the opera. As Colin pulled on his gloves, he regarded Henry. How darkly handsome he looked in his somber clothing. It was rare to see him in a state of brooding, and Colin understood why Henry liked the look on Colin. On Henry it commanded attention. With his height and his solid frame, he was the picture of seriousness, which had been enhanced by the simple, direct orders he gave to Colin that morning as they prepared to leave. Colin could just barely detect a hint of nervousness underneath Henry's austere features, and Colin realized with a shock that what Henry mostly resembled was a groom on his wedding day. *And this is the closest I shall get to seeing it.* And so while they rode in silence to the cemetery, both in formal dress, Colin pretended they were on the way to their wedding ceremony instead. He was quite pleased with himself for the idea and was enjoying it thoroughly, feeling rather sorry once they arrived and the door was opened for them.

The service was about to begin, and as they strode across the grass to the site, Colin assumed the dirty looks Henry's family gave them was because of their being late and the last to arrive. None of the dozen or so members acknowledged Henry, who ignored them in turn, bowing his head as the vicar began his speech.

"Just a moment, Reverend," Henry's brother Dwight interrupted. He glared at Henry and hissed, "Send him back to the carriage or I'll do it myself." He motioned toward Colin.

Henry lifted his chin but kept his voice low. "He's my son and he has every right to be here as much as the others."

"Son!" Dwight spat in contempt. "You may be able to fool others, brother, but you'll never fool us." He narrowed his eyes at Colin. "We've heard all about *you*. The way you and Henry carry on in your vulgar ways! How dare you show up here!"

Colin's cheeks flamed. "I haven't any idea of what you mean. Henry *is* my guardian, and I am only here to pay my respects."

"You're a bloody sodomite!" Dwight shouted, causing one of the ladies to cry out and faint. Dwight turned to her and then back to a white-faced Henry. "Well, bravo, Henry! Now look what you've done!"

As the vicar tried to restore peace, Colin backed away to head for the carriage. "Henry, I'll just go—"

"No!" Henry glowered at his brother. "Apologize to Colin for saying such an atrocious thing. Father hasn't even been laid to rest yet and you have to... desecrate his funeral with such a vile word!"

"Desecrate? I only said it! *You* actually are one! You both are!" Dwight retorted, clenching his fists. Then he approached Colin with a sneer. "You think you're some sort of *grand* architect, when all along everyone knows what you're really about." Drawing close, Dwight narrowed his eyes. "You're just one of Lucifer's hothouse flowers that Henry so loves to pluck." He paused in disgust. "But all you are is wilted rot!" Henry rushed forward to attack his brother and they tumbled to the ground. Several men tried to break up the scuffle. Finally Henry stood up and brushed himself off. By now all the men were threatening them and some of the women were too. The rest of the ladies were in tears and the vicar was vainly trying to bring everyone back to the matter at hand.

"Come, Collie," Henry said stiffly, escorting him back to the carriage. Then he quipped, "As you see, I have excellent relations with my family."

Once the carriage doors shut and the curtains were fully drawn, Colin looked at him desperately. "I thought they didn't know about you!" But Henry didn't reply. He held his head in his hands and began shaking. "Henry?" Colin moved to sit next to Henry and place a hand on his knee.

Henry broke down in tears. "Sixteen years! Sixteen years and the bastards won't let me even attend the funeral of my own father!"

"You haven't seen your family for sixteen years?" Colin guessed, shocked.

"No," Henry choked, fumbling for his handkerchief. "Oh God, Colin, I didn't want you to get involved with this. I shouldn't have brought you. How was I to know they'd see right through us?"

"But how *do* they know?" Colin asked, wringing his hands.

Henry shook his head. "Logical deduction, I suppose. And more likely, the travel of gossip." He tried to smile. "It looks like you'll finally get your story." Colin sat patiently, ready to hear it all. Henry took a deep breath.

"Well, I'm the oldest, you see, and so it was my reputation that set the bar for the rest of the siblings—my three sisters and brother. I didn't give them a very good one. From the time I graduated from the Ecole I was quite the reveler and caroused my way through my twenties, refusing to court any woman and declaring I'd never marry." He gave a harsh laugh. "And yet I managed to pay intense attention to any young men who were around me, which didn't help matters. I confess I loved the scandal it wreaked in my family. At the time it was thrilling and seemed very... *cosmopolitan*." Henry rolled his eyes. "But of course, it was my creative genius that did me in." He looked directly at Colin. "When I was twenty-five and first introduced the Rara Avis style, it was hailed as ludicrous, by almost everyone. My family was completely disgraced—thank goodness my mother had passed on by then—and my brother and sisters had had enough. They began reporting my *irregular* behavior to our father, who held our family name in such high regard that he decided his only course of action was to ostracize me, and suddenly I was shut out of all their lives. Not officially, but I knew when they didn't invite me home for Christmas that year." He looked out the window. "I haven't been back since."

"You mean you never denied what your brother and sisters said about you?" Colin asked, incredulous.

Henry shrugged. "I didn't know they were saying it. I'm sure my sisters couldn't believe it at all, and my brother should be damned for telling them such a thing and furthermore convincing them." His voice grew bitter. "But, they wanted to hear it. I had ruined their social seasons, after all, according to them. Any revenge they could exact, they would, especially once the Rara Avis style became lauded and I grew to be the most financially successful of the entire family. It was all jealousy after that and I was too proud to beg back into the family."

"They did inform you of your father's funeral," Colin reminded him.

"Well even they knew it was a sheer modicum of decency to do so," Henry disdained. "But then I showed up with you."

Colin shook his head. "After what you've just told me, how could you think they'd take me any other way?"

Henry sighed, gazing at the young man. "You're all I have, Colin. You see that now. They already think what they think of me. I'd be damned if I didn't show them that maybe they're right, but I have someone I love very much, too. And look how beautiful he is." He smiled, and then his voice grew sad. "But they didn't see it. They never will."

Colin reflected on this and said to Henry, "I suppose sacrificing one's family is a rite of passage in our world."

Henry looked up and ran his thumb along Colin's jaw. "Sacrifices are only made to achieve something greater, Colin. Never forget that." He paused, and then smiled. "It was worth it."

No more was ever said of the Sewell family, but Colin knew another bond had been forged between him and Henry, and he was happier for it. Henry felt the closeness too, and he was glad to soon have the opportunity to show how grateful he was that Colin was in his life. On a night in September, Kenneth told Colin and Henry about an upcoming gallery show. "That Singer Sargent fellow is showing his work," Kenneth said excitedly. "I've seen some of it and it's absolutely amazing. You two should really go."

Colin turned to Henry. "It'd be fun to see someone new."

Henry smirked. "He's hardly new. He caused a scandal in Paris several years ago with some lewd portrait."

"Lewd!" Colin exclaimed. "How so?"

"He painted a woman with a fallen shoulder strap on her dress. Horror of horrors!"

"Oh." Colin was disappointed. "Well, I've never heard of him."

"Because he travels in Oscar's circle," Henry disdained. "And Kenneth says he's extremely discreet in London, for whatever reason. That's why you never see him here."

"He's one of us?" Colin gasped.

"Yes, and to boot, he's actually American. Regardless of the fact that he's never lived there. His parents were American, so he's an *American artist*. That's France for you."

"Is he handsome?"

"He's rather nondescript," Henry shrugged. "He's been at parties we've attended, Colin. You just haven't noticed him."

"Oh!" Colin's curiosity was piqued. "Well I'd like to go, then. Perhaps I'll meet him."

"Wilde and Bosie should love that," Henry chuckled. "Perhaps he'll want you to sit for him as well."

And so that Saturday, they attended the reception. It took Colin only a few glances at the first pieces to fall in love with the work. "Henry, look at this!" Colin stepped an inch closer to the painting. "*Dr. Samuel Jean Pozzi at Home*," he murmured, reading the title. "Look at all of that red! It's stunning!"

Henry had to agree. "It is quite so."

"Oh, he's very handsome," Colin trilled. "And look at that—he's painted in a *robe*! Imagine!" Colin stood for quite some time just staring in awe. He was delighted with the next painting as well. "*Mrs. John J. Chapman*.... Henry, look at her! She's beautiful." He looked the entire painting up and down so intensely that Henry had to chuckle.

"I do believe you've fallen head over heels with paint on canvas." But he admitted, too, that the work was spectacular, and they spent a full hour gazing at the small collection.

"Henry, they are almost entirely portraits! I didn't know he was a portrait artist."

"Aren't they all? That's their bread and butter, Collie. Painting the rich and richer. But I like how he makes them look real yet attractive. Have you noticed that even the ugly people have a dignified look about them?"

Colin nodded. "Yes, and see how all of the colors he uses are warm, even the blues and blacks? Just a few swishes of the brush and he makes people look flawless. And everything looks so soft and vibrant; just look at the eyes!" Colin tilted his head while regarding a painting. "I wonder how much he charges."

"Do you want to be up on these walls?" Henry teased.

"Oh my, wouldn't that be something!" Colin marveled. Then he looked around. "Well in any case, where is he? I absolutely must meet him!"

"He's over there—the man with the brown beard and moustache talking to the lady in green."

Colin looked, and it was Oscar Wilde all over again. Mr. Singer Sargent was surrounded by people, and he would probably be in such a position all night. Although unlike Oscar, Mr. Singer Sargent appeared uncomfortable with the attention. Not far away, Oscar and Robbie were leading their own group around. Bosie was nowhere to be seen. "It's no use," Colin said sadly. "We'll never get to him. Especially in front of Oscar."

"Don't be silly," Henry argued. "He's his own man. Oscar can't stop you from making his acquaintance. Go on."

"I can't interrupt his party!"

"Well, try to catch his eye. He looks like he's dying for an escape."

But there was no need. John had been glancing in Colin's direction all evening, and now he saw the two men discussing something while looking his way. He summoned up his nerve and announced, "Ladies, gentlemen. Excuse me for a moment. I have a client I must talk to." He nervously made his way to Colin and Henry, to their surprise. "Er... Mr. Sewell and Mr. Sewell, I presume," he said, extending his hand.

Colin's jaw dropped. "Yes! How did you know us?"

"Well... um... Mr. Wilde had pointed you out. I've seen you both before, of course, at a few events."

"Oh, Mr. Singer Sargent," Colin enthused. "It's an honor to meet you! These paintings are amazing. I'm in complete love with them!"

John blushed. "Oh, I'm glad you like them. Which is your favorite?"

"Dr. Pozzi!" Colin declared. "I love that painting. All of that red—I wish *I* owned it!"

Henry shook his head, embarrassed at Colin's fervency. "Speaking of which," he said, "Colin, didn't you want to ask Mr. Singer Sargent something?"

Colin looked puzzled. "Hm? Oh! Oh, yes, well..." He began wringing his hands, hoping not to sound gauche. "We noticed that most of your paintings were portraits and I was... I was just wondering... um... what your commission fee is."

"Were you?" John asked, pleased. "You're interested in a portrait of yourself, Mr. Sewell?"

"Oh! Well..."

"Yes," Henry confirmed. "Mr. Sewell would like to have a portrait done of himself."

Colin turned to Henry and gaped, and Henry gave him a brief smile. It struck Colin: *Henry's going to commission it!* He quickly turned back to John. "Yes, well, you see I was really just... inquiring after your work..." he trailed off, not knowing what else to say. John wasn't much help, for he was shocked, too. *A man commissioning a portrait of his male lover!* But Henry was being discreet about it, so John followed suit.

"I see. I would be happy to paint your portrait, Mr. Sewell. Though I fear you've met me at a more fortunate part of my life. The current fee is five hundred guineas."

Colin's eyes fairly bulged from their sockets at the exorbitant price, but Henry just smiled. "My word, it's a shame you *didn't* find him sooner, Colin. Good thing you've been rather fortunate as well, eh?" Poor Colin wasn't quite sure what to make of this game, so Henry finally sighed and said, "I'll apologize for him, Mr. Singer Sargent. I've never seen him so taken with any artwork before. He'll grant the commission, I assure you. Just tell him a time and place."

Colin was mortified that Henry had to take charge. He drew in his breath and nodded. "Yes, I'm sorry. It's been so long since I've sat for a painting, what with all the photography about and such. Not that it's *any* comparison of course! No no!" He took out a small pad of paper and an elegant pencil. "When and where shall I call upon you?"

John couldn't help smiling at Colin's callowness. He had expected Mr. Sewell to be like Lord Douglas, after all. "My studio address is 33 Tite Street, in Chelsea. You may call on Monday if it is convenient for you. I prefer morning so that I may see you in the best light. Nine o'clock will do."

"All right." Colin grew excited again. "Oh, it's very thrilling! Thank you, Mr. Singer Sargent. I shall see you on Monday, then!"

Henry chuckled. "We'll be taking our leave now. It was a pleasure meeting you."

The two men left, and Oscar glided over to John. "Traitor," he sang.

"You're the one with the grudge, not me," John replied irritably.

"Hmm. And what did you think of our resident American?"

John was about to say, "He seems a bit dense," but he was already rather too fond of the boy to be cruel. So he said casually, "Well, he has good taste. He's commissioned a portrait."

Oscar gasped. "You can't be serious!"

"I am."

"But he can't possibly afford it! He—oh, surely *Henry* is paying for it." John shrugged, and then the actual price entered Oscar's head. It was still a shock. "Oh! Don't dare tell Bosie, please!" He wailed. "He'll demand the same! It's ridiculous." Then he quickly added, "Not that you're not worth it, but I certainly can't afford you on top of everything else I'm not able to afford the boy yet buying him." He gave a small laugh, and then narrowed his eyes at John. "Wait a moment. Did he actually say *how* he's paying you?"

John turned bright red, for Oscar had told him all about Colin's notoriety. "There was nothing mentioned of the sort!" he said stiffly.

Oscar laughed. "He probably thinks he's worth an entire portrait for his *services*." He began to guffaw. "Good heavens! He may offer you stroke for stroke! You'd best draw up a contract if it's money you want, John-John!"

"Is that so?" John huffed. "From what I hear about him, perhaps I should agree to his terms!" He stalked off, leaving Oscar staring in his wake.

Back in Henry's carriage, Colin wondered the same thing. "Surely he doesn't... he doesn't expect me to do anything with him, does he, Henry? Do you think he's going to make that part of the deal?"

Henry laughed at the thought. "He's far too timid to ask such a thing, and, I would hope, professional. *I* won't have it anyway. You're not going to whore yourself out for a portrait."

"But it's so much money!"

"It is. But he's worth it. You're absolutely beautiful and you of all people ought to have your portrait painted. Especially the way he can paint you."

Colin smiled. "You liked him that much, too?"

"I did."

Colin crossed over to sit by him. "Thank you, Henry." He rested his head on Henry's shoulder and snuggled into him. "You may choose the pose."

"Mm. I already know what I want you to wear."

"A robe?"

"Very funny. No, your caramel-colored suit. Put it on when you get home and we'll try different poses."

In two days Colin was greeted at the door of Sargent's studio by a manservant. When John saw him, he smiled again. Mr. Sewell was desperately trying to look reserved but his buoyant eyes gave him away. "Hullo Mr. Singer Sargent!" he said enthusiastically.

"Hullo Mr. Sewell," John chuckled. "Did Mr. Sewell Senior not join you?"

"Oh, no." Colin lowered his head shyly. "I suppose you've deduced he's actually the one commissioning the piece." He looked out at John from beneath his gaze.

"It's none of my business," John said curtly.

Colin nodded, surprised. "All right. You should know though, that he will be the one making payments to you. You only need tell me how you wish to receive them."

John waved a hand. "We can discuss that later. What kind of pose does he want? I mean to say, what kind of pose do *you* want?"

Colin laughed. "We spent a full hour discussing the very thing. I am to be standing, like this, but on a stair step." He walked to a pillar and struck a jaunty pose, his left fist on his hip, holding back his suit coat, and his right hand raised and resting on the top of the pillar.

John studied him. "Very scholarly," he observed. "And what color are you going to wear?"

"I have a light brown suit with an embroidered vest. I'm sorry; I ought to have brought it."

"Never mind. All right then, do you mind if I do a few sketches right now?"

"Oh! Er... certainly." Colin went to his pose.

John began sketching, and then shook his head. "You mustn't look so relaxed. This is an arrogant pose. Celebratory. Lift your chin. Straighten your shoulders. That's better."

After three minutes, Colin grew weary. "How much longer?"

"How much longer!" John finished his last stroke and stood up. "Mr. Sewell, you shall have to exhibit more patience than that."

"Well, I'm not used to this. How do people do it?"

"They need stand or sit still only for the first several sittings. After that I just need them for observation."

"But how *long* will I need to stand still?"

"An hour each sitting. But of course, I will give you time to rest in between."

"An hour! How trying!"

"Why do you think so many artists use prostitutes?" John chuckled. "They're readily available, cheap, and don't mind taking their clothes off." He winked at Colin, who in turn dropped his jaw. John thought he was offended by the crudeness of the remark, but Colin looked stung, and he drew himself up, indignant. John was horrified. "My God, Mr. Sewell, that comment had nothing to do with you!"

"Didn't it?" Colin's tone was sharp but hurt.

"It absolutely did not. I meant *female* prostitutes. Oh God, I meant... *you* are not one! At all!" Then he crossed his arms and became the accuser. "And why would you think I meant such a thing anyway?"

Colin's shoulders slumped at the growing argument. This was exactly why he and Henry did not associate with artists and poets. He looked away. "I imagine that is what Mr. Wilde has told you," he replied severely.

John was confused. Did Mr. Sewell not spend nights with men after all? Was Henry Sewell his only paramour? Finally, he said wearily, "I have told you that your affairs are none of my business. I am sorry if I offended you, Mr. Sewell. I honestly had no intention of doing so."

Colin tilted his head. "Well I'm not... *that*. I don't know what Oscar has told you but he's just bitter because we won't choose him and Bosie."

John was embarrassed by the intimate turn. He sighed. "Mr. Sewell, perhaps my painting you isn't a good idea after all. It seems there might be a conflict of interest."

The decision effectively chastised Colin. "Oh, no! There's no conflict of interest! I like Mr. Wilde, just not Bosie. But you can't separate the two, can you?"

"Mr. Sewell..."

"Right, then. I know; they're your friends. No more talk of either." Colin shook his head. "I'm dreadfully sorry, Mr. Singer Sargent. I suppose I'm overtired. I didn't get much sleep last night because I was so excited about my portrait!"

John sighed again. "Well, I suppose we can at least make an attempt. Come back tomorrow morning with your suit and we shall begin."

That first visit was the only rough patch the two men hit, for thereafter Colin minded himself and proved to be a very obedient subject. When he realized how worldly John was, he spent his sessions asking for stories, and John enjoyed the conversations. However, both carefully avoided asking after each other's personal histories. Midway through the project, when John was working on Colin's mouth, he commented, "You really ought to have a nude study done. You've a fine form."

Colin stared. John was working intensely on the canvas with nary a glance up. His tone was so detached that Colin decided it must have been a professional comment. So he replied calmly, "Never. I couldn't bear it."

John continued painting and after a few moments shrugged. "Ah, a shame." Then he quipped, "I suppose people will still be able to tell, even with the clothes on." Colin smiled, and then laughed.

Finally they were nearing the conclusion of the project, and at the end of Colin's most recent sitting, John showed him his progress. Colin was elated. "Oh John, it is amazing!" He gazed at the portrait. "I can't believe it's me! I can't believe you did it! It's just as wonderful as all the rest!" He slowly shook his head while staring. "I feel like Narcissus."

Colin's approval was all John needed. He summoned all of his courage and said quietly, "I'm glad you like it. I'm pleased with it too. In fact, while painting you, Colin, I decided to ask you something."

Colin saw John's seriousness and felt his stomach drop. "Yes?"

"Well, I was wondering if you'd... if you'd consider... doing something for me."

Colin felt his face burn crimson. "All right..." he hedged.

"I was wondering if you would sit for a second portrait."

Colin exhaled. "Oh! Er... in the nude...?"

John laughed. "No. I meant another formal portrait."

"A second portrait? Why?"

John smiled. "You've turned out to be an excellent sitter. You come off the canvas very well, as you see. I'd like to paint you again."

"Would you sell it, then?"

Now John tried not to blush. "No. I... I plan to keep it in my private collection."

Colin raised his eyebrows. "Really? Well, that's very flattering." Then he frowned. "But I've lost so much time at work as it is. I couldn't possibly sit again."

"If you sit for me I will charge Henry only half for his portrait."

"Half! Isn't it any good?"

"Of course it is!" John was exasperated. "Colin, I can't well expect you to sit for free; I understand that. So to be fair I will deduct some money from the fee."

Colin burst into a grin. "Ah! Well that's awfully generous of you. I'll discuss it with Henry and tell you tomorrow."

Henry, proud that Colin had become so attractive to Mr. Singer Sargent that he wanted his own portrait of the boy, agreed to the terms, and Colin showed up two days later.

"I have the suits you asked for," he said. John had asked him to bring a grey suit and a dark blue suit. Colin brought his dark crimson suit as well, in the highest of hopes. But alas, John decided on the blue. Colin had to withstand another hour's worth of posing and reposing, although these poses were quite different from before. For example, one pose had Colin sitting on a sofa, hunched over with a brooding look. In another, he laid on drowsily on a chaise without the suit jacket, his hair falling in his eyes.

But John couldn't find a pose that appealed to him, and he grew frustrated. "How do you look when you're at your club?" he finally asked.

Then Colin understood, and he grinned. "Why, I usually have a cigarette in one hand and a drink in the other."

So, arrangements were made and soon John had the problem of *which* pose to choose. "To be honest," he would tell a friend later, "I didn't quite see the allure of the boy when I first painted him, beyond his outward vibrant appearance. But when he is in full seductive stare, it's *quite* breathtaking." He finally chose an extremely unconventional pose: Colin was leaning back on the sofa, his right elbow thrown over the top edge with cigarette in hand. His semi-raised left hand held his drink. Suit coat shrugged off his shoulders, tie loosened. The top button on his dress shirt undone. But most evocative of all was his face. His head was tilted back and he looked up with a secret smile as if appraising someone in front of him. John painted a three-quarter profile, and it forever remained his favorite piece, even more so than the nudes he did finally paint a year later, of Venetian gondoliers.

Colin himself was chagrined at the result. "No good can come of this," he wailed to Henry, who upon seeing the second painting, privately wished he could trade portraits. For though Colin thought the picture technically fine and certainly a de-facto portrait of the Colin Sewell his closest friends knew, he knew it would appear to society as immoral as if he *had* been painted nude. With his loosened tie and undone button, the portrait was the male version of *Madame X*. *Who on earth is he looking at in that manner?* That's what the public would say. If it hadn't been meant for John's private collection, Colin would have likely protested. Fortunately, it never saw exhibition and the two men remained good friends as long as they were both in-country.

CHAPTER FOURTEEN

Spring 1893

The morning of Colin's twenty-third birthday arrived. It was a workday, and Colin was surprised to find Henry insisting they go to work, when for the past two years, they had taken the day off. Henry had pulled down the shades on the carriage windows, presumably so he could sit beside Colin in affection during the trip.

As they drew up to the firm, Henry squeezed Colin's hand. "Go on and pull up the shade, would you?"

Colin gave a quizzical glance at Henry and followed his request.

"Look up," Henry urged.

Colin's eyes landed on a new sign above their office door.

Sewell & Sewell
Architects

Colin's mouth dropped. "Henry!" he whispered. "What does it mean?"

"What do you think it means, darling? Your day has arrived!"

Colin turned to look at him. "I'm... am I a partner?"

Henry smiled. "Yes, Colin. If you'll accept."

Colin forgot the shade was up and made a mad dash to embrace Henry, who had to push him off. "Colin, we're visible!" he laughed.

Colin carefully opened the door and stepped out, his eyes fixed on the sign and all it meant.

"Happy birthday, Mr. Sewell!" an employee shouted as he opened the door.

Colin beamed. "Thank you, Peter!" Inside, Henry's employees greeted him with hearty congratulations. *His employees!* "Thank you!" he grinned at them. "Thank you so very much! I couldn't work at a better place than here, with finer men than you!" His co-workers had grown fond of Colin. They had noticed his work ethic and appreciated his frequent praise, encouragement, and guidance. They were relieved he'd be staying on, because as far as they were concerned, he could have easily started his own offices. He'd been doing most of the work lately, anyway.

That evening, Howard studied Colin surreptitiously across the table at Porter's. How far the boy had come! Here he was on his twenty-third birthday, holding court with Henry as always, surrounded by all of his admirers. Howard couldn't decide if it seemed like Colin's arrival was a long time ago or if it seemed just like yesterday. The way Colin looked was just like yesterday: striking. The way Colin acted was just like yesterday: magnetic. Howard's feelings for Colin were just like yesterday: deep. But Howard's interactions with Colin felt a very long time ago, indeed.

Howard gave up his hopes for another night with Colin when, a week after their affair, Colin confided to Howard that he and Henry had decided to take other men home before Colin would revisit him. After hearing this, Howard bitterly suspected that Henry was behind the idea more than Colin was. Still, Colin seemed to become rather cool toward Howard from that point on. Howard didn't mind, until he realized that it was false feelings on Colin's part. The act was most obvious after Colin had been drinking. Then he would often lapse back into his flirtatious ways with Howard. No matter whether Howard resisted or encouraged the repartee, Colin appeared smitten with him. Then—it would never fail—Colin would eventually realize what he was doing, look away, blink shyly, and change the subject, trying to engage someone else in conversation. Howard was ashamed to admit he lived for such moments. Little did Colin know that all of his couldn't-care-less treatment the rest of the time was negated with each eye-batting episode.

That is not to say Colin was rude to Howard. The four of them—Henry, Colin, Howard, and Kenneth—were all the closest of friends when they were together. But while Henry often met with Howard and Kenneth without Colin, the reverse never occurred, and again, Howard suspected it was Henry's doing.

For his part, Howard was a bit put off that Henry mistrusted his friends so. But he was also somewhat proud to think that perhaps Henry found him to be a real threat, and he began to fantasize about stealing Colin away. One night after imbibing too freely he told them both, "I'm going to find a boy just so I can see that damned *grotto* for myself! It's all I ever hear about."

Colin laughed and was about to encourage him when Henry replied, "Why Howard, just come visit us tomorrow afternoon! You may tour it all you want."

Colin had rolled his eyes and tsked, "It's not the same in the daytime, Henry."

And Henry replied, rather swiftly, Howard thought, "Oh, it's all the same to dear Howard. He doesn't notice subtleties unless they're mathematical." Thus, Howard's plan was defeated and he grew angry at Henry's refusal to let him join the very club he himself had practically started! In bitterness, Howard began to think Colin and Henry's relationship was a farce, and that it couldn't be long for this world.

Still, facts were facts, and here Colin was tonight, his arm draped over Henry. Here he was, kissing Henry and mouthing "I love you" into his ear. And, Howard's heart sank. Henry still loved Colin, too. You knew it from his toast, which was nothing short of a panegyric:

"To my darling Colin, the love of my life. The one who's proved himself as superlative a lover as he is an architect. Only you could become more beautiful as time passes." Colin winked at the crowd and jested, "Or as more wine is consumed!" "No, you are past mere beauty. You are mine. My alpha, and my omega. My beginning. My end. And I love you. Happy, happy birthday."

And here Colin was, eyes glistening. Here he was, whispering, "Oh, Henry." And there they were, exchanging a long kiss to the sound of applause.

And Howard couldn't understand why he was so unlucky. Really, it wasn't as if he hadn't tried to find someone for himself, but nothing had worked out. Most of the boys in Porter's were there because they were already attached to someone else; they certainly couldn't afford the membership on their own. Some of the independently wealthy ones did flirt with Howard, but after buying them a few drinks, he lost interest in their shallow chatter. They were either frivolous and vain, or dull and unattractive, and Howard admitted that his and Henry's elitist preferences were to blame. Young men who had everything to lose were bound to be egotistic and spoiled. They either had rich parents or powerful ones, though some were actually coming into their own prestige. Instead of pursuing Howard, they expected to be pursued themselves, which they readily were by every other fellow in the club. But Howard was tired of such games. At least when Colin played with someone, he was interesting to listen to and fascinating to watch. The way he would appraise a man with his eyes, the way he would show attention with that curvaceous smile that was only for his intended. The way he would ever so slightly tilt his head forward when he spoke and then draw back demurely upon hearing the reply. He had even mastered the art of glancing about him from time to time and then focusing back on his companion as if to say, "Ah yes, they are all still here, but it's *you* I'm interested in." Most curious of all was that Colin rarely laughed. Howard assumed men enjoyed others laughing at their witty sayings and their bawdy jokes, yet Colin would do no more than widen his eyes and tsk his partner with a batted eye and knowing smile. It took Howard some time before he realized that Colin's style was modeled completely upon women. And while Colin certainly wasn't the first fellow to posture in a feminine way, he may have been first to deny it vehemently. When Howard mentioned one evening how Colin was "Such a girl!" Colin glared daggers at him and said, "I most certainly am not! How could you say such a thing!" And then his expression turned to wounded.

"But your manners are completely feminine," Howard argued lightheartedly. "They're lovely; in fact, I commend you for such excellent delivery." Then he sighed, "It's funny, isn't it? *All* men must fall for womanly wiles." His look was so pensive that it caused Colin to laugh despite himself, and Howard got away with a mild chastising.

Yes, Colin was exceptional, and Howard knew he wasn't alone in appreciating him; there were other men holding out for the boy, or one like him. True, they still passed the time with other young bloods, but Howard was often party to their discussions about how perfect life would be if they only had Mr. Colin instead, and their stories about how some of them had tried to steal him from Henry had disturbed Howard more than amused him. But they made Howard feel not as pathetic as perhaps he should have, for he also hadn't a clue that his comrades were whispering behind *his* back as well. "How does Durham stand it, sitting at the boy's table every night and watching him, without one of his own?" "Because he's drawn a bead on Colin himself, that's how." "No! Do you think so?" "Of course! Being around that one has spoilt him so badly he won't even look at another! Good God, haven't you noticed? Thinks he's too good now for anyone but Colin Darling." "Really? Well, that's a trifle sad, don't you think? After all, Henry's not giving him up." "Indeed, but I think Durham's positively bewitched. It's just as well we're not at that table, I tell you! And truth be told, I think Mr. Colin may be rather bewitched by Mr. Durham, too..."

It was true that Colin made for a fascinating subject, and Howard did have the best view to observe him each night they sat in Porter's. Over time, he had gleaned bits of information about Colin that nobody else knew, such as the fact that Colin had severed ties with his family and had no existing contact with anyone back in America, and that Colin worked twice as much as Henry and was far more knowledgeable about current trends in architecture. Other men cared for him only as a coquette, which admittedly was a part Colin played willingly and very well.

Howard smiled when he watched the boy sit down across from him that night. Colin was beautiful again, this evening in a blue-black suit. His cufflinks were dark, brilliant-cut sapphires, a lovely contrast to the pearl buttons on his ivory silk shirt. Howard had seen Colin in his matching blue wool overcoat earlier, one with a raw silk collar and cuffs. He was impressed—D'oro knew how to dress the boy perfectly. He nodded in Colin's direction. "I say, Sewell, your hair is getting long." He was rewarded with a teasing smile.

"Yes. Since I haven't been able to find a decent barber, I thought I'd let it grow a bit."

Henry leaned back. "He has such marvelous hair. There are strands of gold spun in it, see?"

Colin's hair was indeed attractive. The length—by now just past his chin—had brought out a burnished hue previously unnoticed. He had developed a habit of tucking his hair behind his ears, which made the ends curl just slightly. His thick, softly waved hair was a beloved feature of the men he took home, for they could run their fingers through it, and the effect of seeing it go from carefully groomed to passionately mussed was akin to seeing a woman who has let her pinned-up, carefully coiffed hair fall down around her face. In fact, paired with his smooth-skinned, finely boned face, his longer hair completed a look of near-androgyny, but

Colin resented being referred to as feminine and, to compensate, had taken to striking masculine poses. Now he sat with both feet on the floor and slightly hunched, resting his arms on the table, one hand holding a drink. He had already taken up the thread of discussion Henry had started. "Most people would consider architecture to be an extension of the visual arts, perhaps, but I find it to be more a form of poetry. Some would even say, the better form."

One of the men in the group who had joined their table looked doubtful. "How so?"

Colin took a drink from his glass. "Written poetry engages the mind, Mr. Huffman, yes, but the body remains static. The only connection is from here," he tapped an imaginary book on the table, "to here," he tapped his head. Then he straightened. "But architecture involves the mind and the body. You are in a state of constant physical involvement." He looked around. "We're surrounded by it. My feet touch the floor, my body is in the chair, and because architecture is made for man, *we* are inextricably part of it. *We* are the poetry in motion, you see? Written poetry can inspire you to think things or think about doing things, but architecture forces you to interact. Written poetry may inspire action, but my poetry *is* action." He gestured about. "People converse in my art form. They laugh, work, sing, play. They're born, they make love, they give birth, and they die. All within this realm created out of the imagination of man."

Mr. Oswald puffed away thoughtfully. "I've never heard bricks, wood, and mortar receive such glorious attention. I suppose you feel the same way about water closets." The group laughed, including Colin.

"If the situation dictates, Mr. Oswald, I'll take a water closet over a fine book of poetry any day."

"Hear, hear!" Mr. Huffman said heartily.

Howard looked at Colin in admiration. "But Colin, when you finish a project, do you call it a work of art, or a work of poetry?"

Colin gave an amused shrug. "You are confusing the terminology, Howard. I doubt even poets look at their finished verses and declare them to be a work of poetry. No, they decide them to be a work of art." He looked down at his glass. "But I understand what you are saying, and in all honesty, I should say now that this idea is not my own. Étienne-Louis Boullée expressed it in the eighteenth century; in fact, he wrote a brilliant essay on it." He regarded Howard in earnest. "In any case Howard, I find architecture to be more like poetry because both involve construction. Poems have rhythm, rhyme, balance, juxtaposition, composition. There are rules with poetry. You know a poem when you see one." He directed his words at the group. "I see things in black and white. When you see a chair, you know it's a chair. One can't be as sure with visual art."

Henry cut in. "But Collie, suppose you had a long, four-footed, upholstered chaise, with no arms. Is it a bed, or a chair?"

"It is still a chair, Henry. An upholstered bench, isn't it? And if it was wide enough for a person to lie down upon... well, I've never seen such a thing! Unless it was a cot, but that's not upholstered. You see! Almost everything we have made, we have made for a purpose. And an invention such as an upholstered bed has no function, that we know of."

Huffman furrowed his brow. "Then Mr. Colin, can there be such a thing as architecture without function?"

Colin's eyes gleamed. "No. Then it is visual art. Sculpture, probably."

Howard motioned toward Colin. "So then, Colin, are *you* currently functioning as active or passive?"

Colin looked at him in surprise. "Howard, you are entirely too astute for a man of finance! And quite the aesthete with your comment! Perhaps you should be at Oscar's table." The men laughed. Colin paused, rubbing his chin. "All men are works of art, as are women. So, if you were to admire me from afar, then I would be passive. But since I am engaging *you* in conversation, since I am pulling you in physically, with my voice and my eyes, demanding your interaction, then I am functioning quite actively with you." *Not as actively as I'd like,* Howard thought wryly. "And after all," Colin finished with a flourish, "what else is man but the creation of God, the master architect of us all!" The men applauded as Howard shook his head and smiled. *Still as goddamn winsome.*

As each month passed, he was certain Colin would become bored and grow tiresome. Yet here they were celebrating Colin's birthday and Colin... Colin was just as kind and generous as ever. Why, even a month ago, Colin had given *Howard* birthday presents! "We've just been celebrating by buying you drinks," he told Howard on the special night. "Well, I think you ought to have some proper birthday presents for once!" Howard could only imagine how well the idea had gone over with Henry. But it was true: Henry and Colin exchanged birthday and Christmas gifts, as did Kenneth and Anne, but Howard didn't have anyone. Perhaps he ought to have taken offense at Colin's pity for him, but instead he found the move touching. Colin had picked out all three presents himself: a paperweight, a fountain pen, and a new pipe. Innocuous enough, but wonderful too. He thanked Colin warmly and gave Henry a look that could only be read one way: *I hope you know how lucky you are.* Henry smiled back. *I do.*

When Colin's birthday party had subsided, Kenneth and Howard walked out together.

"Howard, you're positively morose," Kenneth observed. "It's unsettling!"

Howard stopped and looked around before speaking. "Kenneth, I don't know how much longer I can stand it. I know I should be happy for Colin and Henry, but they sicken me just watching them."

"They make you sick?"

"With envy," Howard sighed. "And I suppose, I'm a bit indignant. Really, I'm every bit as good as Henry, aren't I? And yet all these years I've come nowhere near finding someone like Colin."

"Nowhere near!" Kenneth scoffed. "Howard, your problem hasn't been acquiring someone *like* Colin. Your problem has been not acquiring

Colin himself! And frankly, I'm disappointed in you. You have put the boy on a pedestal, and he's not perfect, Howard! If you can't find any flaws with him, I'd be obliged to tell you some."

Howard stopped, surprised. "What do you mean?"

"Oh for heaven's sakes, Howard. Don't you think he's completely fleecing Henry?"

Howard stared at Kenneth, and then noticed other men coming out of the club. "I'd like to argue that point. Let's discuss this further... I'll follow you to your house."

Later, when they were in his drawing room, Kenneth continued, "Colin is twenty-three. Practically a grown man! And yet, Henry still pays for everything for him!"

Howard tsked. "That's Henry's idea, remember? How much he spends on Colin is supposed to symbolize how valuable of an architect Colin is to Henry."

"And do you actually believe that?" Kenneth demanded.

"Well, yes. I've seen him work. He's very good, Kenneth."

"You're a banker, Durham. How on earth would you know if the boy's contributing?"

At this, Howard narrowed his eyes. "All right, then. If you so much as hint to Henry that you know this, I'll have your throat. This goes against everything I am as a banker." He paused as Kenneth, wide-eyed, sat down across from him. Then Howard carefully considered his words. "Henry has been depositing cheques of astronomical amounts, all from his clients. This started about a year after Colin began working for him."

Kenneth looked perplexed. "I don't understand..."

Howard gritted his teeth. "I think Colin has been doing all the work, Kenneth. Look at the number of contracts they've won since Colin has been on. And yet, Henry still manages to leave the office at noon every day? It's because Colin stays on! He is the sole architect, Kenneth! Henry must just finely tune things at the end and sign his name above Colin's." His voice fell to a whisper and he felt the shame of his breach of professional confidence. "Henry used to deposit money once a month, mind you. Now it's once a week! And it's always in his name, only." His face darkened. "And the cheques are for a lot of money, Kenneth, *a lot*."

Kenneth gaped. "But doesn't Colin have his own accounts with you?"

"None!" Howard cried. "He has no liquid assets whatsoever! It's truly like a medieval bartering system."

Kenneth looked hesitant. "And Colin isn't getting a fair trade?"

Howard's eyes flashed. "Let me put it in these terms, Kenneth: Henry can't buy the boy enough cufflinks and brooches to compensate him for his work. And if Henry decides to leave him, Colin hasn't a single shilling to his name." He sighed. "It's Henry who is fleecing Colin, *I* think. And Colin doesn't care. He loves Henry, so he doesn't care."

"But Henry does seem to love Colin too," Kenneth offered. "Look at how they acted together this evening. And Henry made Colin partner!"

Howard sighed. "Yes, I suppose. All the same, I can't help wondering how much of it is love for Colin's talent."

Kenneth swirled his brandy then said quietly, "Even if what you say is true, Howard, it is none of our business."

Howard nodded. "I know. But now perhaps, you can understand why I find all of this so frustrating."

"Here I thought Sewell was approaching the level of a scoundrel, and now you've changed him into a lamb!"

Howard chuckled. "I don't know about that. Colin isn't stupid. I just don't think he believes that Henry will ever leave him."

Kenneth furrowed his brow. "And you do?"

"Just wishful thinking, on my part," Howard joked. "No, sorry, that's awful. I take it back. I don't know... perhaps they shall go on forever, being a team. They do seem to have some kind of odd understanding towards each other."

Kenneth frowned. "Howard, the boy has laid down with every man in the club. Are you telling me that if he had met you instead of Henry you'd let him do the same thing?"

"Of course not. He would have never have thought of it; that was also Henry's idea."

"It's an idea Colin seems to certainly have embraced," Kenneth snorted. "I thought you would have found it repellent."

Howard swallowed. "I should. And for the most part I do. But I still think he would have been happy just with Henry." He sighed. "But you're right. I suppose it's just as well he's not with me; he can sow all of those oats."

Kenneth regarded his friend gravely. "And then what are we to do about you?"

Howard stared at his glass. "Talking to you has helped immensely, actually. I see I'm long overdue for a bit of fun." He looked across the rim at Kenneth. "I shall turn over a new leaf! And said leaf shall be on the table this weekend."

CHAPTER FIFTEEN

Henry and Colin were quite taken aback by Howard's sudden joie de vivre. Kenneth pretended surprise as well. The first night Howard took a boy home with him, Henry and Colin stared at each other in shock. The second night, they worried that perhaps Howard discovered he had a fatal illness. The third night, they asked him point blank.

"Goodness, Howard!" Colin exclaimed. "What's with you stealing our thunder?"

Howard smiled. "It's all your faults, really. Seeing the two of you last weekend made me realize that I've deprived myself for too long."

Colin grinned. "From deprivation to depravity? How very unlike you!"

Henry smirked. "Of course, we approve."

Colin looked about. "They're fawning all over you now. And what a lot you have to choose from!"

"Almost as many as you two," Howard replied modestly.

Colin laughed. "But they see *you* for your power, your manliness..."

Howard gave him a wry look. "My wealth..."

Colin's eyes gleamed. "Mm, that too." He gave Howard a once-over and then regarded the boys. "You're out of their league."

"Don't put on airs, Colin darling," Henry chided amusedly.

Colin's forehead creased as he looked at Henry, and then when he understood, he gave a small self-deprecating laugh as he sipped from his glass. "Maybe nobody's good enough for Howard!"

Howard smiled. He was relieved that he was finally finding pleasure in someone—or was it something—other than Colin. Surely a month of boys would cure him of any desire for *one* boy outright.

But it was not to be. Several weeks later on a warm evening in May, Howard's plans were destroyed. He was competing with Henry and Colin for the affections of a new boy at Porter's, a friend of someone's cousin. It was a game in good humor, but Colin had noticed, with a trace of concern, that Henry seemed unusually determined to win this boy over. And the boy, Nicholas, appeared to be more interested in the two older men than Colin. So Colin's attempts were halfhearted, and he drank heavily to tolerate Henry and Howard's foolish acts.

"If you think Howard will please you," Henry smiled. "By all means, go with him... if you don't want to feel anything, that is. Here, have my drink, darling."

"Oh-ho!" Howard challenged. "Henry has it wrong, sweetheart. It's *tomorrow* that you won't feel anything... below your waist." He took Henry's glass of champagne, drank it, and said "Georgie! We need the Grand Marnier!"

Colin winced. He inhaled so deeply on his cigarette that he felt faint by the time the curls of smoke left his nose.

"Nicholas, I grant you, Howard has an amazing mansion, but it's so far away, he'll take you in the carriage," Henry purred. "That's not right, now, is it? If you come with me—"

"*Us*," Colin muttered, rolling his eyes.

Henry waved a hand. "Yes, yes. If you come with *us*, why, we're right down the street, and you'll be in the most beautiful bed you've ever kneeled on!" At this, Nicholas laughed, and even Howard chuckled.

Colin leaned back and said in a bored tone, "I really don't see the point of this debate. We ought to just all leave together."

He let the impact of his statement hang in the air while he looked off, dragging on his cigarette. Henry glanced at Howard in a moment of panic, which Howard returned.

Nicholas looked at Colin in drunken admiration. "Splendid!" And the two men realized they had no choice but to go along with it.

Howard's heart raced. Clearly, Henry wanted Nicholas, so if they all went home together, he, Howard, would definitely get Colin, at some point. Really, he hadn't even given a damn about Nicholas; he just wanted to beat Henry. And now he would get something better. Then it struck him: *Why didn't I think of this sooner?*

Howard sent his brougham home and the four entered Henry's carriage. They resumed their drinking. Howard wasn't used to drinking up the boys like he had to lately, but when he saw that even Henry himself was absolutely besotted, he began to laugh. Henry teased Howard, and they kept at it until Colin and Nicholas both fell to the floor of the carriage in hysterics. Henry pulled Nicholas up beside him, which meant that Howard had to do the same with Colin. Henry began kissing Nicholas, who returned the passion eagerly. Howard turned to Colin, and apologized, "Oh, I am entirely too drunk."

Colin moved to straddle Howard and grinned. "Thank goodness. Then you won't remember this!" They laughed, and Howard found his hands on Colin's thighs. They moved further back, and Colin was leaning in, ardently kissing him. "It's been a while, Howard," he murmured good-naturedly.

Howard sighed. "Too long. We really ought to do this more often." He felt Colin's smile upon his skin.

Only minutes later, the carriage rocked to a halt. Everyone hastily prepared to exit. Once inside, Henry and Nicolas started upstairs. Howard took Colin's hand and nodded to the other two. "Right, then. I absolutely must see this grotto for myself. You two go on to your room, Henry. We'll all take care of unfinished business and you can meet us for a join-up."

Colin started. He and Henry had never gone to separate rooms, and didn't Howard want Nicholas anyway? Henry would surely refuse. He looked at Henry, who gave him only an amused shrug and a nod of assent. Colin could hardly believe it. Had he been with anyone but Howard, he would have been furious about Henry's decision. Instead, Colin was ashamed to admit finding himself thrilled to have Howard all to himself, once more.

Howard pulled Colin to the staircase. Halfway up, Colin stumbled, and they both burst out laughing. Howard scooped Colin up into his arms and carried him the rest of the way. "Are we married, then?" Colin giggled, as they crossed the threshold.

"Wishful thinking, Sewell." Howard tossed Colin onto the bed and stood before him. "Undress."

Colin locked his gaze with Howard's as he rose slightly to remove his jacket, and then lay back to breathlessly undo his trousers. By the time Colin had gotten as far as the fourth button on his shirt, he heard, "Stop." He looked up. Howard was transfixed. "Just, lie there. You look so nice, so beautiful."

Colin gave him a sly smile. "Ah, you tell all the boys that." Howard approached the bed and sat beside Colin. "And you hear it from all the men."

Colin bit his lip. "You. Your clothes..." But he made the mistake of reaching up to kiss Howard, who forgot about his own attire as he lost himself in Colin's face, his lips, his neck, his hair. He moved astride Colin, who tugged at Howard's trousers and then pulled him down, his head spinning as he smiled at Howard's whispers: "My little American architect! How I've missed you." And when Howard moved his mouth from Colin's face to his shoulders, he gave a cry of delight. "Oh, you still smell the same!"

Colin laughed. "You remember the lavender oil?"

"Mm, is that what it is?" Howard asked, kissing his skin. "Yes, it's wonderful. It reminds me of spring." Then he woozily sat up and ran one hand lightly down Colin's body, circling his hipbone with his thumb. "Look at you. You're extraordinary, do you know that?"

"Thank you," Colin smiled, running a hand down Howard's arm. "You're extraordinary too, Howard. You know I've always thought so." He sighed, gazing into Howard's eyes. "I've always liked you best, after Henry."

"Really? Even after all the others you've had?"

Colin laughed softly. "I didn't mean that. I like *you*." His voice turned shy. "We get on well, after all, don't we?"

"We do," Howard smiled. Then he sighed, brushing Colin's hair from his face. "How did Henry get so lucky?"

"I thought you didn't want a serious relationship," Colin teased.

"Mm. But having this every night would be nice."

"You *have* had it every night, for the last two weeks!"

Howard looked at Colin and smiled, shaking his head. Then he leaned over and resumed kissing him. Colin feverishly realized what Howard was thinking. He knew what the smile said because he had given the same smile back. But he shook the words from his mind and hugged Howard to him, closing his eyes and giving ardent encouragement.

Afterwards, Howard kissed Colin gratefully, moving his mouth down Colin's body. When he reached a certain point and stayed there, Colin froze. "What are you doing?" he panicked.

Howard continued his actions. "I want to taste you," he murmured.

"Howard, no! Please! You don't have to," Squirming, Colin's hands instinctively reached to block himself.

Howard stopped momentarily and looked into Colin's terrified face. "I want to." He gave him a reassuring kiss. "I've even thought about doing it to you."

"No, you probably won't like it! Really, I'd rather you not, Howard. I mean it!"

"I'll find out for myself. Now lay back." Howard moved to resume his activity, and then stopped in surprise.

"Oh, God," Colin moaned, turning on his side in shame. He had gone limp.

"Oh, Colin! Oh, I'm so sorry!"

Colin gave a small laugh. "Never mind. Just... well, just come here and lie next to me."

Howard obeyed and stroked Colin's outline as he faced him. "I'm sorry. I didn't know you didn't like it. I just assumed..."

"That's not it. I was only..." Colin looked away. "I didn't want you to be disgusted, is all."

Howard's brow furrowed. "How could anything about you be disgusting?"

Colin shrugged. "Most people think that is, even men. They love receiving it, but they aren't interested in giving it."

Howard traced Colin's jaw. *Henry must refuse to do it.* He spoke quietly. "Most people think our very nature of being is disgusting. Well, I don't. And I think you're absolutely beautiful. So why should putting my mouth there be any different than putting my mouth here?" He kissed Colin's lips and felt the boy's body tremble. Then Howard said gently, "We could have a go a different way. I wouldn't mind." He heard a deep sigh.

"No, it's all right. I'll save it for Henry and Nicholas." Colin got up from the bed, as did Howard, who felt lightheaded as he pulled on his trousers.

"Well then," Howard decided. "If it's all right with you, I think I shall go home." When he saw Colin whirl around, he smiled. "I already got what I wanted tonight. I don't really care about Nicholas."

Colin's shoulders sagged. "Surely you can't mean that! What with the way you and Henry were fighting over him!"

Howard shrugged. "Oh, it was more to beat Henry than anything. Nicholas is good-looking, but all the same, it'd be a bit of a disappointment."

"Well, it couldn't be any more disappointing than *that*!" Colin motioned toward the bed and then added, "I mean, what happened with me."

Howard stared at him. "You're too hard on yourself, Colin." He nodded toward the bed. "*That* is the ideal. *That* right there, what happened between you and me, is why a relationship is better than one meaningless night. You of all people should be able to understand that."

Colin looked at him foggily. "But, you and I aren't in a relationship."

Howard reddened as he threw on his coat and fastened it awkwardly. "No. No, I obviously wasn't referring to us." He gave a slight laugh. "You needn't show me out. Give Henry and Nicholas my regards."

"Howard, wait," Colin stumbled over to him and smiled. "Thank you. It *was* still lovely. Whoever ends up with you will be the lucky one."

Howard managed a nod in return, his voice thick. "Good night, Colin."

It wasn't until after he left that Colin realized Howard hadn't commented about the grotto at all. It was as if he never even knew he was there.

On Sunday, Colin resigned himself to the couch for the day, sipping tea and staring into space. It hurt too much to think, much less read, his hangover was so terrible. Henry felt out of sorts as well, and Colin was grateful for the paucity of conversation. At six o'clock that evening, Colin was still lying there. "Goodness, Collie, you've never been this badly off before!" Henry exclaimed.

"I don't think I can drink like that anymore," Colin groaned. "I don't know how you've done it all these years, Henry."

"Well, can I have Charlie bring you some supper? You haven't eaten all day." Henry had gone to Charlotte's that morning by himself, the first time since he and Colin had met.

"Maybe some soda crackers, thank you." Colin gave Henry a grateful smile, then felt overwhelmed with guilt.

All he'd done on the couch was think of Howard. He didn't have a choice, did he? He had nothing else to do to distract himself. And all day long while Colin thought of Howard, Henry doted on him, bringing him water, willow bark tea, blankets, and compresses. And with every visit, he gave Colin light kisses on his temple and forehead. So Colin tried to think of nothing, for Henry's sake, but his head pounded each time he tried to organize his thoughts. He gave up, and the thoughts of Howard rushed back in. Colin even began to worry he might say Howard's name in his sleep, so he told Henry he'd spend the night on the couch. Henry looked at him anxiously.

"Do you think we ought to call a doctor?"

"No, no. I'll be fine in the morning, I'm sure. Just wake me up in time to dress for work."

Monday was almost worse. Colin struggled all day to find the right balance between looking like he was working but not look like he was working too hard, because he was still sharing Henry's office. Whenever Henry left for a few minutes, Colin stopped moving and stared at the blotter on his desk, allowing his mind to relax.

This is different.

That's what Howard's smile had said. But why was it different?

Because I love you, Colin.

Colin doubted that. Howard was only attracted to him because he was Henry's boy. After all, didn't he and Henry have a game of rivalry over young men some time ago, and for that matter, even with Nicholas! Howard was surely jealous that his friend had someone and he did not. No, Colin decided, Howard didn't love Colin; he loved the idea of having *a* Colin. But it wasn't Howard's feelings that bothered him so much.

This is different.

Colin had thought it, too. For two reasons.

First, it was different with Howard because Howard had wanted to put his mouth on him.

And Henry did not. Colin tried not to think about this, but he never forgot how the conversation went that first month of his acquaintance with Henry:

"Mm, thank you, Collie. That was incredible."

"You know, Henry, if *you* would like to... I'd love it too."

"Oh, Collie. I wish I could, I do. But I just can't. I'm just too old-fashioned, I suppose. I'm sorry."

Colin, too afraid to argue so early in their relationship, just nodded and smiled. "It's all right."

And it had been all right. Hadn't it? Over the years, Colin found that everyone had certain sexual proclivities, and one of the most common was to be a receiver of the very personal aforementioned act, but rarely the giver. And so Henry hadn't seemed very odd after all. Still... Colin bit his lip.

It was different secondly because he admired Howard more than anyone else besides Henry. Stupid-smart Howard Durham, who had to know what he was doing to Colin, who drank in every drop of attention from the man at the club and then gave the same back, night after night. Colin knew Howard watched every nuance of his; he knew Howard was just waiting for him and Henry to fall out with each other, so that he might take over. Sometimes the thought flattered Colin; sometimes it disgusted him. Colin knew he should think less of Howard for harboring such thoughts against Henry, his best friend, after all! But as Colin had quickly found out, everyone was up for grabs in this underworld; boys and men alike broke each other's hearts over someone else all the time. And most of the time, they were forgiven for it. *It* was a given, it seemed. And granted, perhaps Howard's attention towards Colin wouldn't occur if it weren't so obvious that Colin liked Howard too. Immensely! But as Henry's friend, it was Howard's duty to recede, and yet instead, last night he took Colin's hand and marched him up to their own private room, where he proceeded to romance Colin and treat him like a... a lover.

But Howard was so kind. Colin closed his eyes and relived the night before. He was at the fourth button when he heard a voice.

"What was *that*?"

Colin jolted to attention. To his horror, Henry was standing in the doorway. "What was what?" Colin asked, trying to look confused.

"You gave some sort of shiver. I've never seen it. I say, Colin, are you all right?"

Colin blinked. "I... I must have fallen asleep. I still don't feel so well, Henry."

But this time, Henry kept his distance, eyeing Colin. "Is this about Saturday night?"

Colin was about to deny it was, but he realized an opportunity, and he sighed. "Well, maybe it is, a bit." He paused. "I didn't like being separated from you."

Henry smiled, with what looked like relief, and walked toward him. "Were you jealous?" he teased. Colin stared ahead. He was. Despite his feelings about Howard, he was angry with Henry.

"Why didn't you kick him out of our bed?" he asked in a tight voice.

Henry kissed the top of his head. "Colin, we had fallen asleep."

"You let him stay until morning! I had to sleep in the grotto!"

"You didn't wake us up! What was I supposed to do?"

Colin pouted, because Henry was right. "Did you like having him all to yourself, then?" he asked fiercely.

"Did you like having Howard all to yourself?"

Colin didn't miss a beat. "I'd preferred us all staying together."

Henry laughed. "Whatever for? You wanted Howard. Howard wanted you. I wanted Nicholas, and Nicholas... well, who cares what he wanted? He was so blasted he probably thought he had the three of us!"

"This is a stupid argument," Colin fumed.

Henry stepped away. "Oh, Colin! I don't give a whit about Nicholas, and you know it."

"All right, then." Colin tilted his head imperiously and began working, winding a lock of hair around his finger.

"Collie, are you still upset?"

"No!"

"Good. You're getting too old to be pitching fits anymore."

Colin glared at Henry and twirled his hair in defiance. Henry smiled. "Then again, old habits are hard to break."

"And if we choose this route, we may risk losing a percentage of our quarterly growth. What percentage was that, Mr. Durham? Mr. Durham?"

"Sorry?" Howard stopped twirling his pencil. "I beg your pardon, the percentage?"

"Yes, Mr. Durham."

"Ah. Yes, the percentage appears to be around five percent."

"Thank you. So the risk..."

That was it. Howard had to leave after this meeting and claim illness or people would wonder other reasons. He'd already been asked to repeat things several times today. He really wanted to be left alone and sort his thoughts.

An hour later, he was walking through Hyde Park.

I never actually said I loved him, right?

But he had to know.

We were drunk! Supremely. So maybe he won't remember the details.

You said something about Henry being lucky...

Oh God. Maybe he'll just think I meant it in a general sense.

But you didn't.

But this isn't about my feelings—I know what they are. But Colin... I swear he was about to say "I love you, too, Howard." He was! And wait... he said he thought I was extraordinary, remember? "I've always thought so." And... and "I've always liked you the best, after Henry... you and I get on so well, don't we?" What about all of that! I don't care if he was drunk or not.

Durham, you told him you thought he was beautiful. You made a complete arse of yourself.

But... I wouldn't have said all of those things if I didn't feel he was receptive to them. And he adored them! As if he hadn't heard such things in years.

But what if Colin was acting all along? Acting out your own fantasy?

No! That would be horrible! Well, that's how I can ask him. I could say, "Do you think it's really a good idea to play out men's fantasies like you do?" And if he plays dumb, I'll practically strangle him! I deserve an honest explanation. Because it's cruel to lead one on like that. After all, everything I said was true, and if...

"Howard?" Howard jumped at the sound. "What on earth are you doing here?"

Howard looked up ahead of him. "I don't believe it," he muttered rubbing his forehead. He had arrived at the Prince Albert Memorial, and there, as plain as day sitting across from it, was Colin.

Colin, taken aback by Howard's dismay, said stiffly, "Well, if you're wanting privacy, pardon me for intruding." He looked back down at his tablet.

"You followed me here, didn't you?"

Colin jerked his head up. "Followed you! I'm here to find specimens for Mrs. Dashworth's atrium!" He held up his drawings as proof. "If anything, you're the one without an alibi."

Howard gave Colin a cold look. "Why?"

Colin narrowed his eyes. "Because what would a banker be doing in Hyde Park at two o'clock on a Monday?" Then, horrified at his manners, Colin dropped his head. "It's none of my business. Forgive me, Howard. If you'll excuse me..." He took up his writing again.

"Colin..." Howard's voice fell like a hand on Colin's arm. He looked up. "I would love some company, actually. Care to join me?" Colin shrugged and stood up to walk beside Howard, who sighed. "To tell you the truth,

I'm here because I couldn't concentrate at work. I believe I'm still feeling the effects from Saturday night."

Colin looked at Howard, concerned. "Really? It was awful, wasn't it? I was on the divan all day yesterday. I told Henry, 'Never again!'"

Howard chuckled as they walked. "I'm sure he didn't care to hear that."

Colin shook his head. "After nursing me from dawn to dusk, I imagine he'll be agreeable, for a while."

"Hmm, and you probably don't remember a thing."

"I remember everything!" Colin defended, and then he looked at Howard anxiously. "Do you?"

Howard raised his eyebrows, and they walked in silence for several moments. "Colin, do you really think it's wise to act out men's fantasies the way you do?"

Colin stared hard at the path ahead of them. "Are we discussing Saturday night, then?"

"We are."

Colin lifted his chin. "In that case, I wasn't acting out anything, so it's not a question for you to ask."

"You were acting as if you were in love with me, Colin. Shall I ask the proper question now?"

Colin put a hand over his stomach, a pained look on his face. He paused. "It was different, that's all."

Howard turned and stopped. "Different for you? How?"

Colin took a deep breath in preparation to explain, and then sighed and shook his head. "Never mind." He looked at Howard. "I won't leave Henry for anyone, Howard. Not even you."

"I wasn't asking you that," Howard said, offended.

Colin tilted his head. "Weren't you? If I had answered your 'proper question', it would have followed." He lowered his gaze and resumed walking. They both trod silently, struggling to collect their thoughts. Finally Howard gave up. "So you still love Henry, then. Is that it?"

Colin smiled. "Yes. I love him very much." He stopped again and gazed upon Howard kindly. "Howard, some of the things that I love in you are different than the things that I love in Henry. That doesn't mean that they are better, or more important. Just different." He frowned. "But Henry was first, and we have been together for two years now. I really owe my life to him! So I won't destroy what I've worked so hard for, and what I believe so firmly in."

"But what we said to each other..." Howard began earnestly.

"We were drunk," Colin waved him off.

Howard stopped, angry at his flippancy. "Yes, you're always deep in cups, aren't you? Have you ever taken a boy home sober?"

"So what if I haven't?" Colin said hotly. "It's a social situation, Howard. And you certainly didn't seem to care about my state of mind when I was with you!"

"Then are you saying that you don't regret us being together Saturday night?" Howard challenged. "You don't regret the words you told me and the way you looked at me? You don't regret getting so drunk that you let yourself have me like that, and you don't regret that I made an arse of myself in front of you?"

Colin looked half chastened, but still angry. He said quietly, "You didn't make an ass of yourself."

"Really." Howard took a deep breath. "Well, telling someone you can't have that you love them is pretty foolish, Colin."

"You never said that," Colin said quickly.

"I didn't have to! You knew it when I looked at you. And you were saying it back to me!"

"Stop!" Colin crossed his arms and exhaled. "Howard, you're not the first one to get carried away. It happens lots of times with men I'm with."

"And you tell everyone you like them the most after Henry?" Howard demanded, incredulous.

"Well of course not! That was just you." Then Colin had to blush at his admission. He sighed. "All right, perhaps it was a mistake, Saturday night. And if so, I apologize because it was my idea." He tried once more. "You really ought to find someone else, Howard. Someone who can give you what you deserve, because I cannot."

"You cannot because you will not admit you've changed your mind about things," Howard said stubbornly. "You will not admit that perhaps there's another mistake you made." Colin gaped as Howard's expression became urgent. "I can give you everything Henry has given you! Without taking your money. Without... *loaning* you out. You never wanted that Colin; be honest! You told me you wanted *one* person to spend the rest of your life with. And you know I do too." He took a deep breath. "Well, I want it with you. And if you need proof by actually hearing me say it—"

"No, Howard, don't—"

"I've fallen in love with you."

Colin covered his mouth in shock, and then he squeezed his eyes shut and shook his head. "You've fallen in love with a fantasy, that's what you've done," he whispered. "I'm sorry. I can't."

Howard regrouped. He straightened and said evenly, "He will leave you. And you won't have a penny to your name. You will be struck from everything, Colin. Don't you see that?"

Colin backed away from him, sick to his stomach. "So now it comes out. The truth. You don't believe Henry and I will last. Well that's... that's handy to know, Howard." His voice grew weary. "Given all that you have just said to me, I won't hold anything against you. But me leaving Henry for his *supposed* best friend, who's so willing to steal me right out from under him *would* be a mistake, Howard. And fortunately for you, I won't make it. Good day!"

Colin's heart pounded its way through the park as he left. *He saw right through me! What if he tells Henry? He can't. He's the one who confessed he loves me. I can't believe he said it! How could he think it?* But Colin's gait faltered as he remembered the worst part of it. *"He will leave you."* Anger rose in Colin once more, and he shook off the words. He was walking so quickly that before he knew it he was in front of his church. He looked up at it and sighed. *If there was ever a time to ask for forgiveness, today's the day.* He ascended the steps and went inside.

The Church of the Immaculate Conception on Farm Street was a Jesuit church and simple compared to the great cathedrals of Europe. Still, it was built in the Gothic style and Colin loved gazing at the soaring ceiling as much as he loved to look upon the great stained-glass window above the altar. Unfortunately, he had just missed the 1:00 service; the next would be at 6:00. He considered requesting a confession, but thought better of it and, instead, found a pew and entered it to genuflect.

Forgive me Father, for I have sinned. I have led a man astray through my own misdeeds... Colin breathed, allowing himself to feel the silent warmth around him. Yes, that was better. *I know not what I do, at times, for I never meant to harm him, or anyone. Please grant us both the strength to consecrate our friendship and nothing more. I ask this through Jesus Christ our Lord, Amen.* Colin paused in silence before standing and slowly circling the church to visit each of the saints. They were so beautiful, in their carved robes of painted and gilded marble. He was especially fond of Saint Margaret of Scotland, because she was the prettiest statue. He toured all of them, and by the time he was back at the entrance, his step was lighter. *If only Henry and Howard attended church*, he thought sadly, *things would be ever so much easier; I'm sure of it.*

But church was the last thing on Howard's mind back in the park. "If I had answered your proper question, it would have followed." "I won't leave Henry for anyone, Howard. Not even you." "Some of the things I love in you, Howard... I love in you Howard... I love..." And Howard realized that what he had guessed was really true: Colin loved Howard, too. *But Henry was first.* Howard balled his fists.

Never mind that Henry is proving a piss-poor companion for Colin; he doesn't even appreciate what he has! I'd make Colin so happy he wouldn't even have known what happiness was before I came into his life! But now he's completely brainwashed!

Yes, Colin made his choice, Durham, and he made it quite clear: not you. You're the mistake.

Sadness overlapped anger as Howard concluded it was too much like his boyhood games of cricket, only this time with Colin as the captain: *I choose Henry Sewell!*

And just as quickly, anger overtook sadness once more. Howard turned on his heel and headed for his carriage. *To Hell with Colin Sewell, then. May he rot in his own misery! Goddamned brainless wretch!*

CHAPTER SIXTEEN

That June, Mrs. Dashworth's home had been completed. It was a city home, so Colin didn't have much room to work with. Therefore his love of nature had to be restricted to the atrium, which he made into the entire south-facing rear of the house; really, it was a greenhouse of sorts. Mrs. Dashworth was a bit worried about having such large glass walls on the first floor, but Colin assured her that it would be safe, wondering himself how many troublemaking youths passed through the alley in the back. He pointed out to the widowed Mrs. Dashworth that the room was even large enough to hold parties within it, and so she did, to great acclaim. Upon arriving, her guests marveled at the white interiors of the house and at each of her spare but priceless furnishings. They exclaimed over the lack of crown moldings and baseboards. They gawked at the modern paintings of unheard artists—how *did* one say 'Van Gogh' properly? But it was the atrium that took them to exotica and proved a romantic setting for those who were courting. Couples tossed coins into the sparkling copper fountain to mark their fortune. Finches darted freely between the fronds, cages of songbirds and Birds of Paradise were sprinkled throughout, and giant hibiscuses bent gracefully over the heads of visitors. For winter parties, Colin had built two fireplaces into the walls, and he had arranged waterfalls in two corners to run over hot stones, making the room as pleasant as the tropics. Yes, an invitation to one of Mrs. Dashworth's parties became one of the most sought after each season. And so, the ever-practical Mrs. Dashworth soon came to appreciate the ease with which her patrons could move about the spacious place after having one too many glasses of sherry, wine, or brandy.

Because he was the sole architect on this project, Colin demanded to sign his name above Henry's on the prints, and he alone gave interviews to the reporters.

"Gentlemen, welcome to another masterpiece in the Rara Avis portfolio," he told them. "Everything is revealed to show off its identity and to be appreciated for the fine work of art it is. No hiding behind heavy drapes and clutter—sunlight floods the room so that we may see true beauty laid bare."

After Mrs. Dashworth's home was profiled in the papers, Henry and Colin were invited by William Morris to a salon in order to discuss the Arts and Crafts movement, which Morris had founded. Henry declined and Colin attended out of curiosity, but he came away shrugging. "Well," he told Henry, "they've got some of the same ideas we do, principally the idea of the entire house, interior and exterior, being a total work of art designed by the architect. I really like that Charles Voysey fellow, and oh, I did like meeting Thomas Mawson! I must chat more with those two. But they're really unrealistic to expect all the goods made by hand! It would take me three times as long if I didn't use factories! The movement is positively Luddite, Henry, and as an American I was quite affronted by it."

"Are you going to go to France and join the Art Nouveau movement instead, then?" Henry teased.

"No," Colin laughed. "We may have some things in common but the Rara Avis style is yours and mine alone, and I intend to keep the name."

"That's wise," Henry agreed. "Remember Collie, buildings don't last forever—even the Forum is in ruins. If it's perpetuity you want, then what you must do is create an *idea* that singularly stands out on its own and is truly original. Then it can be preserved and replicated ad infinitum."

"Well, I certainly hope nobody tears down Mrs. Dashworth's home! Or the Lyon Steel building!"

"Be realistic, Colin," Henry warned. "It's your design that will live on. You must work towards that."

"So I shall," Colin nodded. "I just hope there are enough clients like Mrs. Dashworth to do so."

As Colin's fame as an architect grew, demand for him as a lover grew to equally unprecedented heights. Men now frequently came from other countries specifically to find him. It had lately become easier for Colin to take these men home in front of Howard, but it hadn't been so for some time. After their argument in Hyde Park, it took every bit of fakery they could muster at Porter's to act as if nothing had happened between them. However, Colin stopped flirting with Howard, and Howard took boys home early so he wouldn't have to face Colin any longer than possible. One evening, when Henry left the group temporarily, Colin quickly got Howard's attention with a fierce whisper. "Howard! Please let's just pretend that day never happened. Can we go just back to how it was with us, in a matter of speaking? Forgive and forget?"

Howard bristled at the last suggestion. He fixed his gaze on Colin and set his mouth in a grim line. "I will forgive. But I will *never* forget."

Colin was taken aback, but he nodded. "I... I understand."

And damned if Howard's anger evaporated upon seeing the boy's devastated countenance. Even though he was still angry with Colin and feeling the sting of rejection, he knew he had been less than kind with some of his words as well that day. So he sighed and agreed, "But all right then. Let's start over."

Colin lifted his head and exhaled. "Thank you." It was as close an apology they would get from each other, and they were both surprised to find how easy it was to return to their friendlier days. Howard began to wonder if their lives would ever change.

It would be only a month later, in late July, that he had his answer. The night began as usual, with the foursome sitting together and discussing the usual affairs, when Henry's voice called out, "Alfred's here!"

The group turned and grinned as their old friend Alfie Jones approached. Howard and Kenneth made room and Alfie settled in. The diplomat was in his late forties, with average looks and a thin-lipped smile. He had just become an attaché for the British Embassy in France, and tonight was his last night before being installed there permanently. He had been a generous patron of Kenneth's theatres for years, which allowed him to consort with some of the actors, who in turn were sworn to secrecy. He avoided any other boys, even Colin, so fearful was he of political ruin. It hardly mattered: Alfie was one of those types who found pleasure in giving pain, and that was a realm neither Colin nor Henry would entertain. But Colin liked the man because he seemed so worldly, and he always had good stories.

"Ah, and how does it feel to be moving to Paris?" Henry inquired, motioning for champagne.

Alfie shrugged. "With the amount of time I've been spending there the past five years, it's almost a relief to be *living* there."

"And how goes the politics?" Howard queried.

"Oh, perfectly crazy, but that's Paris for you." Alfie smiled at Colin. "Sewell's becoming quite well known over there."

Colin's eyes lit up. "Really?"

Alfie laughed. "Oh, yes! They call you the 'je ne sais quoi boy.'"

Colin furrowed his brow. "Je ne sais quoi...?"

"Yes, because you have a talent they just can't put their finger on!"

Colin laughed. "But I've only completed a few structures, all in England."

Alfie burst into laughter, while the other three looked on, embarrassed. Alfie coughed and sputtered. "Not your architectural work, dear boy, your *real* skill!" He leaned over the table and winked. "Your other nickname is 'Le prince avec la bouche d'or'—The Prince with the Golden Mouth!"

Colin gasped and turned scarlet. Henry nudged him, laughing. "It's a compliment, darling!"

Colin stared at the bar, his jaw set. "I didn't come all the way from America to go down in history as *that*."

Henry sighed. "Don't be so ungrateful, Collie. None of us have any such kind of title."

Colin lowered his eyes. "No." Then he looked at Kenneth. "You're a playhouse owner." He regarded the others in turn. "A diplomat. A banker. And an architect."

"You're an architect too," Henry assured.

"Ha! Who believes it, as long as I keep—"

"We can discuss it later," Henry cut in. "Let's enjoy Alfie for now, eh?"

"Yes, Colin, you silly thing!" Alfie exclaimed. "Only someone as brilliant as you could worry about such things. You need another drink, that's what the problem is!" He ordered the waiter over.

"No, Alfie. I'm fine," Colin protested. But soon a second glass was put before him.

Howard looked sadly at the liquor. *That's right. Get him drunk again. Get him so drunk that he'll forget he was ever upset about Alfie's comment. You'll be safe then, Henry. It's how you've always been safe. Don't drink it, Colin. I want you to think. I want you to stay angry.*

Colin sighed. "I suppose I've every reason to get drunk. It's Alfie's last night, and I've just learned I'm King of the Kiss in France." But he avoided looking at Howard.

Henry patted his leg. "Why then, it should be champagne for you too, sweetheart." He ordered another bottle. Howard didn't intend to catch

Henry's eye, but he did. And Howard realized he was still wearing a look of disgust on his face. Surprised, Henry opened his mouth as if to ask, but then he changed his mind and turned to Alfie and Kenneth. And as the night went on, Colin did get drunk. And as the night drew to a close, Alfie took Henry aside and discussed something with him. They appeared to be arguing. Finally, they returned.

"Colin, come along. We're giving Alfie a ride home." Henry's voice sounded forcedly cheerful.

Colin looked up, confused. "Alfie?"

Henry shifted nervously. "Yes, yes. Come, then." Alfie leered drunkenly at Colin.

Colin rose up, suspicious. "But... just Alfie?"

Henry yanked his arm. "Come!" he snapped. Colin gave a frantic look at Kenneth as he was dragged off.

Howard watched them go. "What's going on?"

Kenneth gazed at his drink. "I imagine Henry owes Alfie some favors."

"So he's using Colin to pay them back?" Howard's voice rose.

"Presumably."

"But that's horrible! Colin looked terrified!"

"I know. Howard, let's forget it; it's none of our business."

"But... but, surely we should do something about it, Kenneth!"

"We can't. Colin will be fine. He's drunk, as usual. I can't imagine Henry would let Alfie do what he wants with the boy, anyway. He'd mark him up!"

Howard hesitated. He knew Alfie was reportedly rough with boys, and the thought of someone manhandling Colin made him ill. Then it struck him: *Well, that's what he gets. If he's going to continue to go around like this, so be it. Maybe Alfie will teach him a lesson!* Howard smirked then took a guilty swig from his glass. *Shame on you, Durham. Just forget him. Perhaps you should find someone else to take your mind off things...* Earlier he had told the boys he just planned to be on his own tonight, but now... he looked around. "Kenneth, let's pick out a pair and go home."

"I thought you didn't want to!"

"I've changed my mind. I *really* want to." He kept picturing Colin pleading for help.

Kenneth sighed. "I'm not much in the mood anymore. You go on. I'll stay."

"What's gotten into you?"

"Nothing, I'm just tired. What's gotten into *you*?" He peered at Howard. "You're still hung up on Colin?"

"Yes I am, and I want to get my mind off of it." He beckoned a boy to him. "Cory, I'd actually love some company this evening, if you're still offering."

Kenneth watched them chat, drinking with a heavy heart. He had an idea of what Colin was in for.

Outside, Alfie entered the cab with Colin, and Henry shut the door on them. "Colin, you go on with Alfie. I'll see you at home later." His voice was unsteady.

Hearing this, Colin became hysterical. "What? Henry! What are you doing?" But the cab began to take off, and Henry turned away.

Inside, Colin sat across from Alfie, who reached over and put a hand on his knee. "Colin darling, Henry is being a very good friend to me tonight. I've done a lot of things for him, and I asked him if you and I could be alone tonight, that's all."

Colin, not quite in his senses, asked in trepidation, "Does Henry owe you money?"

Alfie laughed. "No, darling, don't worry about it. Here, if you're nervous, have some of this. It will relax you."

He held out a bottle of something. Colin didn't recognize the clear liquid, but he didn't care. He was shaking and sick to his stomach. He took it from Alfie's hand. "Thank you."

They sat there for a minute when Alfie's voice crashed in Colin's ears as he moved toward him. "Yes, that's better, isn't it? Now, come here and live up to your reputation."

An hour later, Henry was sitting in the library staring into the fireplace when he heard the door ring. He raced to answer it, but Charlie beat him. They stood in the open doorway, staring down at the threshold.

"Oh God, Colin!" Henry cried, picking him up. Charlie helped him.

"What *happened* to him, sir?"

"Never mind that, we must get him to bed." Henry stifled a sob as they carried his unconscious body to the bedroom.

"I'll call Dr. Langtry!" Charlie's voice was rising to a panic.

"No!" Henry put up a hand. "He'll be fine, Charlie, I promise you. I'll take care of him for now." They put him on the mattress. "Just leave him here," Henry instructed. "That will do. Thank you, Charlie." Charlie left hesitantly, closing the door, and Henry tried to see through his tears as he undressed Colin.

Flecks of vomit were on his lapels. There were bite marks and bruises from the neck down. Red handprints on his bottom. Fingernail marks. Welts. Dried blood. There was some sort of residue on his face and... his eyelashes. Henry gave a cry of anguish and went to soak his handkerchief. "Oh Collie... Collie..." he moaned, dabbing at Colin's eyelids. Colin's skin was cold and damp, and Henry bundled him in flannel pajamas before putting him in bed. "I'm so sorry, Lovey. I'm so sorry!" Henry whispered. He got into bed himself and pulled Colin close to him. Then Henry slept, fitfully, checking on Colin's shallow breathing each time he woke. Finally, around ten o'clock Sunday morning, Colin stirred. Henry stroked his forehead. "Collie?"

"Mm? Henry..." Colin swallowed, his eyes shut.

"Are you all right?"

"I'm... I'm thirsty."

"I'll fetch you a drink of water."

When Henry returned, he started. "Oh, Collie!"

"Hm? What?" Colin squinted, reaching for the water.

"Well, do you feel ill at all?"

Colin closed his eyes as he drank. "I feel like the devil. What happened last night?"

Henry sat gingerly on the bed. "What do you remember?"

"I... um... I went off with Alfie, didn't I?"

"Yes."

Colin nodded. "He gave me something. It was so odd. I felt amazing for a short while—we were really having a time! And then I must have passed out."

Henry wrung his hands. "Collie, you have got bruises all over you." They were worse now—yellow and blue, enlarged.

"Have I?" Colin looked at his arms. "Where?"

"Oh Collie, they're all over your neck..." Henry began to cry. "You look a fright!"

"I do? Hand me a mirror!"

"I'd rather you not..."

"Oh God..." Colin tried to get out of bed, and winced. He was sore. Down there? Front *and* back? His eyes widened, and he looked at Henry. Henry refused to return his gaze. It was then that Colin realized what had happened. He limped to the mirror in the bathroom and stood gaping before it. "Oh *Christ*, Henry!" He took off his nightshirt. "Jesus Christ! I'm bruised everywhere!" He leaned closer to inspect his skin. "*Bite marks?*" His voice grew desperate. "What in hell went on? What did you do, Henry? Why in hell did you leave me alone with him if you knew he'd do this?" Before Henry could reply, Colin slammed the door, and in a moment, there was a wail, and then sobbing. "Oh God! How could you do this to me? How? How?" Henry ran to the door and opened it. Colin was kneeling with his pajama bottoms down around his ankles, his face in his hands.

Henry rushed down beside him. "Collie, I am so sorry! I'm so, so sorry, love! I swear I didn't know he was going to do all of that to you! I told him not to! Please, please forgive me!"

By now Colin was in hysterics. "Oh my God, look what he did to me!" He cried, hiccupping. "It hurts! It *hurts,* Henry!"

Henry held him in his arms, crying himself. "I know it does, sweetheart! I am ever so sorry! I'll never ever let it happen again, I promise! I'll run you a hot bath, all right? And you'll feel better. I promise!"

"It hurts, it hurts," Colin moaned. "I'll fucking kill him!"

"Shh, forget Alfie, sweet. It's over, darling." Henry continued to cradle him as he began to run the bath.

Colin's voice was tinged with fright. "I don't feel well, Henry. Am... am I going to be all right?"

Henry kissed his hair, then his face. "Yes! Yes, you are, Collie. You are. You're not bleeding anywhere, anymore. You just had a bit of a rough go, that's all. You'll be all right. I promise."

Colin calmed down, mostly because he felt so sick. Sniffling, he nestled in Henry's warmth, waiting for the tub to fill.

An hour later, they were at the breakfast table. Colin was dressed, merely for the sake of a high collar so he could hide most of his bruises. Still, he declared he wouldn't go outdoors until they completely disappeared. Now he sat fiddling with his toast. "Tell me why you sent me off with him," he demanded quietly.

"Colin, I'd rather you not know. It's not for you to know."

"Henry, I can barely sit on this goddamned chair! It *is* for me to know!"

Henry shuddered. "Alfie did some things for me years back. As a favor. I didn't think he'd want it repaid with you."

"What things?"

Henry paused. "He managed to get some of my design bids won by the city."

Colin stared. "What?"

"Colin, it's the sort of thing that happens. Everyone does it. If you don't, you lose; you fall behind."

"You didn't win those bids on your own merit?"

Henry looked irritated. "Of course they were on my own merit. I don't build rubbish, Colin. But as you know, in architecture all the bids can be excellent designs, and it's just a matter of luck who wins them."

"Or connections."

"Yes. I suppose you should have learnt this sometime. It's not as dastardly as it sounds."

"Not if you've got a whipping boy at your disposal," Colin spat. "Literally."

"Stop it!" Henry shouted. He stood up, his tone desperate. "I told you I warned him not to hurt you, Collie! And I have told you I'm sorry—I am! I can't even begin to forgive myself! Do you really think I would have let him have you if I had known he was going to do all of that to you?" Colin stared at his plate. "*Do you?*"

Colin kept his eyes downcast and said softly, "You left me alone with him." Then he looked up at Henry in quiet fury. "You left me alone."

Henry gasped. Too horrified to speak, he turned and left the room.

And while Colin sat there trying hard not to wince with each breath, he quietly faced the fact that as the demimondes of London waxed poetic about young Colin Sewell and the Rara Avis Style, Henry Sewell... well, Henry's love for Colin seemed to be on the wane.

Howard would have never done this! Howard... Who's the fool now?

That night, after Colin went to bed early with no more than a few words exchanged, Henry decided to make his usual visit to Porter's. Kenneth and Howard looked fearful.

"No Colin?" Kenneth asked in trepidation.

Henry shook his head, avoiding their gaze. "He's not feeling well."

"Oh," Howard replied awkwardly. "That's too bad. Well, we'll have a drink for him, all right then?"

Henry just nodded, biting his lip. Then he began to tremble and gave a small sob. Kenneth, alarmed, put his hand on Henry's shoulder. "Henry? Are you all right?"

Henry's voice broke. "I sacrificed the boy, Kenneth! I positively sacrificed him, and he knows it!"

"What do you mean? Is he all right?"

Henry dabbed at his eyes. "No. That bloody Jones roughed him up!"

"Roughed him...?" Howard asked uneasily.

Henry's voice fell to a whisper. "Collie's covered with bruises. Everywhere! He was utterly beaten up, raped half to death, I tell you! I *told* Alfie he was not to lay a hand on him. Not a goddamned hand! And then he went and did it to him anyway!" Henry took a deep breath. "He looks awful, and it's all my fault!"

Howard closed his eyes, and Kenneth's shoulders slumped. "Oh my word," he murmured. "Is he very badly hurt?"

"He's in some pain, yes," Henry said miserably. "I finally got some medicine today from the doctor and that's helped. He's not bleeding anymore, but he's in a bad way." His voice was hushed. "He doesn't remember most of it. He said Alfie gave him something and he passed out. He looked *dead* when I next saw him! He was barely breathing, I tell you. He *could* have died! God knows what the man gave him!" Henry clutched his glass. "God help me! The boy could have died, and I was too lily to call the doctor! I thought we might be turned in, so I just watched him all night long when he should have had a doctor! It was me who was responsible!"

Never in their lives had Howard and Kenneth seen Henry so upset. Perhaps years ago, over a failed building bid, but never over another person. They sat silently, struggling to think of something else to say.

"But, he's all right, now?" Kenneth asked cautiously.

"Mostly." Henry stared into his drink. His tone was listless. "He looked dead."

"But he wasn't," Howard said firmly. "What does he think about everything that happened?"

For a moment, Henry didn't speak. Then shamefaced, he shut his eyes. "He hates me. He won't say so but oh, Howard! I can see it in his eyes—he hates me with all of his heart! And I can't blame him." Henry snatched his handkerchief and held it to his face. The men in the club were in full stare.

"He'll be all right, Henry," Howard reassured him, thinking of Colin lying in bed with a venomous look. "He knows it's all superficial. And he knows you didn't think Alfie was going to do that to him."

"Didn't I?" Henry's voice rose, quavering. "We all know what Alfie does to his boys! But even this, even this, gentlemen, was beyond what I would have ever expected, so help me God! The man is a monster!" He put his head into his hands again. "And so am I." Then he pleaded to Kenneth, "How can your actor-boys stand it? How could they let him do that to them?"

Kenneth shrugged. "Well, I don't think they were... treated quite the same way. I recall only a few marks on them, and they certainly never mentioned being drugged!"

"Then why would he do such a thing to Collie?" Henry cried. Neither man would answer. But they both knew. *Because Colin is the ultimate find, Henry. Nobody has ever mistreated him, and that along with his looks and reputation make him the grand prize for someone who delights in pain, no? Alfie's been waiting for perfection for a very, very long time.*

Howard shivered. He forced himself to sound lighthearted. "Well, at least he'll have some time off from work."

Henry nodded. "Yes. He's going to work at home this week. But what about here? Everyone here saw that he left with Alfie last night. If he's gone all week, people will know!"

Kenneth said in a low voice, "I can bring over some makeup from the theatre. It covers anything."

Henry looked gratefully at his friend. "Oh, that would be wonderful, Kenneth! Thank you."

Monday, Kenneth dropped by with the promised makeup, and after he left, Colin came out and sat down, examining the tins. Finally he said quietly, "I don't want to do this anymore."

Henry sipped his tea nervously. "Do what?"

Colin glared at the table. "Go on with other boys."

"Colin, Alfie wasn't a boy, and he was one in a million. It will never happen again, I swear it."

"Don't swear, Henry," Colin reprimanded. "It's not just Alfie, it's what he said. You heard him! I'm an *architect*, first and foremost. Yet my career is a joke to everyone, don't you see? I should be the Prince of Architecture, and instead I'm the Prince of Sucking Cock!"

"Colin!"

"*You* thought it was funny."

"I thought it was complimentary, and there was a time when you would have thought so, too."

"Back in the beginning." Colin eyes blazed. "Henry, we're on the verge of becoming a caricature! Look at all the other boys who are trying to be me, now. We're no longer unique; men will soon lose interest." He leaned forward. "If we decide to stop baiting boys and proclaim fidelity, imagine what a shock to the system that will be! We will be pillars of society anew! We must stay ahead of the curve, Henry!" Henry looked skeptical. Colin pushed on. "Think of it! Nobody else has done it! We will be the first committed male couple in the world!"

"Hardly."

"I mean truly. *Monogamous.*"

"But, then we won't have boys anymore."

"Oh, who needs them? Really, Henry, we've had them all, several times over! We're ready for something more prestigious, more difficult to attain—a committed relationship."

"But what would we tell everyone?" Henry asked anxiously.

Colin's eyes gleamed. "We will say we have become bored with it. Bored!" He crossed his arms and sat back. "And frankly, I am bored with it. I'm tired of the luring game. I think it'd be more fun to go 'round a bit and just flirt wildly with everyone and drive them mad with what they can't have."

Henry couldn't help smiling. "You already do that."

Colin lowered his gaze. "But now they won't be able to have me at all." He gave Henry a wicked smile. "And lest you think being with only me will be boring, I have a few things planned for you." His speech finished, he sighed and took out a packet of cigarettes.

"*Not* outside the smoking room, Colin."

Colin lit one and took a deep drag, leaning his head back on the chair. Then he studied a dubious Henry, letting the smoke curl out of his nose. "Bruises and welts take a long time to heal, Henry. Have you forgotten that I can't go 'round with anyone for at least a month? Have you a proposal as to how we're going to explain that? He spat the remainder of the smoke out his mouth and turned away. He pulled from his cigarette once more and watched the smoke drift upwards, nodding at Henry's resigned silence. "I thought not."

By the next Saturday night at Porter's, things were somewhat back to normal. Finally Colin looked at Henry and said, "Let's let Kenneth and Howard in on our plan." Henry looked a trifle embarrassed, but he let Colin launch into the details. Howard couldn't believe it. And yet, Henry seemed to be going along with it, although he appeared less than enthused. Howard wondered how Colin was going to follow through. He had actually managed to convince Henry to do something Howard never thought would happen, for a second time! *A Master in the Dark Arts indeed*. Of course, the Alfie incident surely played a part in all of this, for even Howard and Kenneth deduced it would take time for Colin's marks to disappear, although nobody else in the club was privy to those details. And if this newfound lifestyle was solely Colin's idea—which Colin wouldn't admit but Kenneth and Howard knew better—Howard was glad to realize that at least the horrific night with Alfie had a silver lining after all.

A month later Colin and Henry were still adamant about their monogamy despite numerous entreaties from the men to reconsider. Henry claimed the idea was his, as otherwise men would deduce Alfie had turned Colin sour on it. But one evening after a few rowdy hours, Henry leaned drunkenly onto Colin's shoulder and pleaded himself. "Oh Collie, couldn't we... couldn't we just have one last go? Please?"

Colin, who by now felt a bit guilty for forcing Henry into such a sudden withdrawal, laughed. "All right, Henry. It's only fair, after all."

Henry sat up. "But who?"

Colin's eyes were slits. "I know exactly who it should be." He summoned a waiter. "Would you please fill two glasses with Veuve Clicquot and present them, along with the bottle, to Mr. Wilde and Lord Douglas? And do tell them it's from Henry and me."

Henry gaped. "Bosie and Wilde? Are you out of your mind?"

Colin smiled at him. "No, darling, you are. You're out of your mind drunk, and I intend to show you a very good last time."

"But you hate them!" Kenneth exclaimed.

"Exactly," Colin replied. "Which is why they will provide us with the perfect proof that we are through with this lifestyle. They are to be our denouement!"

"Good lord," Howard rolled his eyes. Colin ignored him and looked to see if the two men were coming. They were.

"Are you moving back to America, then?" Bosie sneered as he approached.

Colin sized him up. "Oh, it's better than that. Won't you both have a seat?"

Bosie flounced down and took out a cigarette while Oscar sat down more quietly, next to him.

"Committing suicide, then?" Bosie puffed away.

Colin couldn't help grinning. He really did hate Bosie, but Bosie was like the devil. Colin was fascinated by him, and he was still a bit frightened of him. "I might be. I want you and Oscar to come home with us tonight."

Bosie's eyes popped out of his head. "Go home with you! Are you mad? All these years you've snubbed us, treated us like shit... we can't stand you! Why in the hell would we want to go home with you? We hate you! Both of you!"

Colin stopped smiling and locked eyes with the boy. "Then it'd be the fuck of your life, wouldn't it, Douglas?" He drilled his gaze into Bosie's eyes. *I hate you too. Let me show you how much I hate you, Bosie dear.* He was proud to see Bosie temporarily spellbound. Then Bosie shifted. "You still haven't said why you want to do this."

Colin leaned back and crossed his arms. "As you know, Henry and I don't take up with anyone anymore. But seeing how nobody is believing us, we thought we'd better make a statement." He tilted his head. "It'd be quite a statement for yourself, as well."

Bosie looked indignant. "Yes, a statement of utter humility! We've nothing to gain from it." He eyed Colin. "I've had my cock sucked more than you have."

"I daresay you have," Colin agreed. "Which is wonderful, because then you can truly appreciate how it ought to be done." He sighed restlessly and pushed a small piece of paper across the table. "We are leaving. Feel free to discuss the matter and decide as you like." He got up, as did Henry, and on their way out, he leaned down and whispered in Bosie's ear, "I'll admit it, I think you must be a spectacular ride."

Bosie glared thoughtfully, and after Henry and Colin left, he scanned the piece of paper. "Let us discuss this in the carriage," he told Oscar.

"Bosie, it would be humiliating!" Oscar wailed.

Bosie stood up crossly. "I didn't say we were going there. I want to talk to you privately." He didn't bother bidding Kenneth and Howard goodnight but instead stalked out the door with the champagne bottle in his hand. He let Oscar get into the cab first. "812 Westinghouse Avenue," he told the driver.

"Bosie!" Oscar protested, but Bosie was already inside, and the carriage took off.

Bosie took a swig from the bottle. "We should go," he decided, looking at Oscar. "Think of it! We can see their house—"

"Bosie, it's a terrible idea."

"Oh, quit being so milquetoast, Oscar! You've always been keen on Sewell, though God knows why, and he adores you. He just knew he had to get to you through me, you see?"

"I prefer you to him."

"Of course you do. As you should. And I'll bet Henry prefers me to him, too. All the same, I'd like to see what they can show us." He handed the bottle to Oscar. "Here, get drunker and you'll be fine."

Oscar hesitated, but since he knew they were already destined for the meeting, he decided he'd better calm his nerves. He took a long drink, and Bosie crossed over to sit beside him. "Do you know what he said to me on the way out? He said that he thought I'd be a 'spectacular ride'! Can you believe that? He's damn well right, too. I'll show him."

"Or he'll show you," Oscar murmured.

"Or you!" Bosie giggled, and Oscar suddenly felt giddy. He and Bosie hadn't been together sexually in months. Perhaps this was a good idea after all.

The cab stopped, and the two got out. Colin and Henry were just at the door and turned to see the two approach. Colin beamed as he watched

Bosie and Oscar walk stridently toward them. Without saying a word, Henry unlocked the door, and they all went inside.

"Very 'Sewell & Sewell,'" Bosie commented as he looked about the place. Colin poured brandy and they all sat down: Colin next to Bosie on the sofa, Henry and Oscar in armchairs.

"Oscar, tell Colin what you like about him," Bosie said lazily.

Colin raised an eyebrow while Oscar sat back in his chair. "Mr. Sewell knows I've always thought of him as a very lovely specimen indeed. Even the distance between us has not dimmed his luminescence."

Colin smiled. "That's very kind." Then he paused. "You generally watch, don't you, Oscar?"

"Not tonight!" Bosie cried. "I refuse to let him! You're to do your job on both of us."

Colin laughed. "Is that so? Well, I think he'd like to watch first, anyway."

Bosie held his cigarette with his teeth and began undoing his pants. "Right. Let's get on with it."

Colin looked at him and gave a long sigh. "Put your trousers back on, Douglas."

"What?"

"Put them back on." Bosie was about to fly off the handle, but Colin just rolled his eyes. "Bosie. You're not with a renter. If you think I'm just going to let you shove my face in your crotch… put them back on."

"*You* put them back on!"

Colin sighed, rolled his eyes again, and smiled at Oscar and Henry. "Very well. *I'll* put them back on." He stripped off his tie and shirt and then kneeled before Bosie to slowly button him back up. On the fourth button, he stopped. "These are very nice." He turned his head. "Did Oscar buy them for you?"

Bosie snorted. "Ha! Oscar's not a generous patron to me like Henry is to you. I had to beg these pants out of him."

Oscar is going to get his life's worth out of this night, Colin determined, focusing back on the buttoning. As he reached the top, he brought himself up to Bosie's face. "Now I'm going to undo my handiwork," he said slyly. He sat astride Bosie, taking the cigarette from his mouth. He dragged from it, and then began kissing Bosie deeply while Bosie inhaled the smoke. His breath was fiery on Colin's shoulders, and moments later, Colin slid back down and began to show Bosie what it could be like. Bosie, used to quick, violent exchanges, was hypnotized. He put his hands on Colin's head. "Mm, such marvelous hair," he murmured, running his fingers through it. He pulled Colin up and kissed him hard. Then he ran his thumb across Colin's lips. "And a gorgeous mouth. Christ, you've got a mouth on you, Sewell." He kissed him again and turned Colin's head toward the other two men. "Hasn't he got a lovely mouth, Oscar?"

"Yes, he has," Oscar replied faintly.

Bosie turned Colin's head to face his own. "A lovely mouth to do all sorts of nasty things with. Now, tell me what you like about me, Sewell."

Colin looked at him fuzzily, trying to think of a response. He blinked, and his voice was flat, but sincere. "I think you're the most beautiful boy I've ever seen." He smiled slightly. "And that's all that I like about you, Alfred Douglas."

Henry would later describe the long evening as "variations on a theme." When dawn arrived, Colin lay naked across Bosie's torso. Bosie was partially sitting up, his arms behind his head. "Now, aren't you glad I decided we should come here?" he said to Oscar.

Oscar looked at the two young men gazing back at him. "I've never seen a more handsome pair of panthers," he murmured. "Perhaps we could arrange a photograph session of that very pose..."

"Yes!" Bosie cried gleefully.

"No!" Colin groaned, as he rolled off Bosie and began undoing the bed sheets. "You see? That's the whole problem. You're too dangerous."

Bosie tsked him. "Oh, Sewell, you're so lily-livered! Nobody can find anything, as long as you hide it well."

Colin looked at him sharply. "You can't hide it from the photographer."

Bosie threw his hands up. "He takes photographs of that all the time! It's all he bloody does. He's not a proper photographer, you fool!"

"Exactly," Henry replied, coming back into the room. "Meaning if he's given the right amount of money, he'll talk."

"Or not talk," Oscar interjected. "It's all a matter of offers and counteroffers."

"I'm involved in enough bidding wars at work," Colin groused. He yanked on the blanket. "Are you getting out of bed, Douglas, or shall I throw you in with the laundry?"

"You don't want another go?" Bosie teased. Colin threw a pillow at him. "All right, all right, I'm getting out!" Bosie laughed. "Endurance is obviously not your strong point." He got another pillow in his face, which prompted him to lasso Colin with his arm and drag him onto the bed.

"Bosie! Stop it!" Colin yelped. They wrestled on the bed a moment, and then Colin was pinned. He eyed Bosie. "How did you get so strong on a diet of liquor and larder?"

Bosie looked into Colin's eyes and saw a glimmer of thrill behind them. "Physical recreation, darling," he panted. "Now, you're quite certain you don't want another go? You can stay right where you are..."

Suddenly, the thought made Colin's stomach turn. "Let up," he demanded. Bosie sighed and got off the bed. After showing them out, Colin leaned against Henry tiredly. "I'm ever so glad to have you to myself from now on."

Henry smiled, put his arm around Colin, and kissed his head. "As am I, sweet, as am I."

CHAPTER SEVENTEEN

To Colin's relief, Henry found great amusement in telling others they were "retired from the game," particularly since he was able to end it with the celebrity story of Oscar Wilde and Bosie Douglas. The telling was so often repeated amongst men at the club that one of them, a writer, was compelled to publish a short story about it, in pamphlet form. It was distributed within certain circles. Of course, all names and occupations were changed, but everyone knew who the four men were supposed to be, and Colin and Henry delighted in how much more obscene the story had become, although they were both a bit concerned about it ending up in the wrong hands.

By the winter of that year, men studied the couple for signs of an impending rift, but the two remained as affectionate as ever. Unfortunately, Colin now found his own evening entertainment wane as he watched his friends become inebriated while he stayed sober. He found that his hangovers had become worse and his work was suffering for it. Weekends especially were wasted, due to the heavier drinking that occurred. So several weeks ago, Colin had told Georgie privately that from now on he wanted only tonic water from the second round onwards, for he realized that, by drinking liquor early on, nobody seemed to notice what was in his glass later. Only Howard caught on, when one Saturday he himself felt too ill to drink more than a hot toddy. He noticed that Colin was on his seventh drink and should have been smashed, but he remained quite in control. "I say, Colin, you're certainly holding your liquor well tonight."

Colin sighed. "I'm afraid I'll have to give up gin. It doesn't quite have the same effect on me anymore."

"Do you care to switch?"

"No, no! I, er... I don't quite care for whiskey." Colin paused, and then smiled warmly at him. "But thank you, Howard. I hope that it makes you feel better." He shrugged toward Howard's drink. "Does it really work?"

Howard smiled wryly. "Not as well as taking to bed straight away, I'm sure."

"Then perhaps that's where you should be." Colin meant it to sound teasing, but it came out sounding firm. He didn't like Howard noticing his conduct and began wishing he'd leave.

Howard frowned slightly. "Are you calling yourself 'Nurse Sewell' now?" He also meant it lightly, but it sounded cold.

Colin looked down, chastened. "No. I'm sorry."

Howard got up from the table and threw on his coat. "Actually, your advice is spot on." He looked around them. "It's amazing how dull this can get when you're not actually drinking, eh, Sewell?" He looked directly at Colin and then at Colin's tonic water. Colin stared at his glass too, horrified, and Howard's heart sank. He caught Colin's eye. *You're very smart*, he mouthed, smiling, and then he left, gladdened by the fact that Colin was finally doing something right.

Eventually, Henry caught on too.

"Darling! You're already awake! How do you feel?" he asked Colin after the first Sunday of Colin's new plan.

"I feel quite good, Henry!" Colin grinned. "I think I figured out a way around the hangovers. Last night, Daniel told me to eat some biscuits and have a full glass of water before going to bed. It seems to have worked!"

"Thank God," Henry sighed. "I had about written you off." But after a month, Henry grew suspicious. "Why in hell are you getting up so damned early these days?" he asked. "You're driving me mad, the way you flit about!" Colin was rising only an hour earlier than Henry, but he had always been late getting up and was slow to get ready for work. Now, by the time Henry awoke, Colin was shaved and dressed. He was also alert, cheerful, and restless to go to the office.

"I don't know," Colin lied. "I suppose it's the biscuits and water!"

Henry frowned. "Well you're absolutely energetic. It's unsettling."

Colin laughed. "Well, why don't I go to work, then, and I'll meet you when you come in?"

Henry looked incredulous. "But... who will I breakfast with?"

Colin stopped and then sheepishly stuck his hands in his pockets. "Oh. Right. Sorry, Henry. Of course I'll breakfast with you." He brightened. "I'll just take work home with me, and I can work on it here in the morning!"

Henry eyed him. "You're daft. Why on earth would you want to work at seven o'clock?"

Colin pshawed him. "Oh Henry, I'm reading my architecture books here all the time! It's the same thing."

"It is not."

"It is!" Colin sat down on the bed next to Henry. "You see, I'll just do my work in the parlor, all quiet-like, and when you're ready for breakfast, there I'll be!"

If Colin had been his usual clever self, he would have gotten truly drunk that weekend, to quell any doubts. But he didn't, and when Henry stirred at ten o'clock Sunday morning and saw that Colin was nowhere to be found, he stomped into the library. "How long have you been up?" he demanded.

Colin cast about, puzzled. "I'm not sure; a couple of hours, perhaps."

"A couple of hours!" Henry was furious.

Colin shrank back. "Did I wake you up? I'm sorry, Henry! I tried to be quiet."

"You didn't wake me up! But you were supposed to be there in bed with me! It's Sunday!"

Colin regarded him guiltily. "I... I did lay in bed awhile. But I couldn't stand it any longer, and I didn't want to bother you."

Henry's expression became defeated, and he sat down next to Colin. "What is going on, Collie? First you don't want to be with other boys anymore. Then you're getting up at the crack of dawn. You no longer appear to enjoy yourself at Porter's. Yet you seem unnaturally cheerful otherwise." He gazed sadly at Colin. "I can hardly believe a few biscuits and water can change you this much. You must be in love with someone."

Colin stared at Henry, and then burst out laughing. Henry crossed his arms indignantly, and Colin pried one of them toward him. "Henry, I'm in love with *you*! That's why I'm so happy! I don't have to waste my time with those stupid boys anymore. I can give my full attention to you!" Then he looked down, embarrassed. "And as for the bit of getting up early and such..." he glanced at Henry, "I suppose I couldn't have kept it from you forever. I'm not really... drinking much anymore, Henry."

Henry squinted. "What do you mean? You've been drinking all along!"

Colin smiled. "It's just been tonic water, Henry. I've gotten so sick the last few times we've drank, that I can't stomach heavy drinking anymore. So I have two drinks early on and then switch over. I didn't want to disappoint you, or embarrass you, so I kept it a secret."

Henry looked incredulous. "What about the biscuits and water?"

"That was just a way to cover it up. I'm sorry."

"And you think not drinking is why you've been so jolly in the morning?"

Colin shrugged. "I'm not sure. I think so. It's quite nice waking up without a hangover. You can appreciate that, can't you?"

But Henry looked off, chagrined. *I don't believe it. My lover is changing. He's metamorphosing. But backwards! The butterfly reverting to a caterpillar.*

"So no more infidelity and no more drinking," he deduced in a small voice.

Colin sighed. "You make it sound as if it's a horrible thing. I still drink, Henry."

"Hardly! How are you going to have fun on Saturdays anymore?"

Colin brought Henry's hands to his lips. "I'll be fine," he assured him. "Anyway, aren't you getting a bit tired of spending *every* Saturday night at Porter's? I think we ought to do some different things once in a while."

Henry jerked his head up. "Like what?"

Colin shrugged. "Well, we could do more of what we already do: see some of Kenneth's productions, attend some salons. Even go to some different clubs, or stay in."

Henry considered Colin's words. When he spoke, his voice was tinged with anger. "I have gone along with your idea to give up boys. I suppose I'll go along with your newfound temperance. But I'll be damned if I give up the one thing I've done almost every Saturday for the past twenty-five years!"

Colin's jaw dropped. "Porter's has been open for twenty-five years?"

Henry narrowed his eyes at Colin. "Yes. It's a very *old* club, isn't it?"

"For that kind of club, yes!"

"And fancy that, you're getting to be just as old." Colin stared at Henry, who instantly regretted his retort. "I'm sorry, Collie..."

"That was very mean, Henry." Colin's voice was almost a whisper.

"Oh, for heaven's sake! I'm twenty years *older* than Porter's!"

Colin pushed away from the table. "Yes, but I'll never care how old you are, Henry. *I'll* still love you." He walked off.

Henry sighed. *Oh, Colin. Loyal, loyal Colin. He's afraid of getting old! He's actually starting to panic, and he still looks like a boy!* Henry stared out the window. *But one day he won't.*

As the thought turned over in his mind, Henry became uneasy. Finally he went to find Colin, who was tucked away in the corner of the solarium. The dappled sunlight fell across his face as he gazed out the window.

"Colin..." Henry began, soothingly, but Colin jumped anyway. Henry smiled at him. "You look beautiful, sitting there."

And Colin did. The morning sun haloed his profile, bleached his eyebrows and eyelashes, ambered his eyes, and flecked his hair with gold. He stared outside. "I've given up things for you, too, Henry," he said softly.

Henry approached. "I know, darling. And I love you for that. Let's just forget all this, please?" He stood behind Colin and crouched playfully by his ear. "*I* don't have to give up drinking, do I?" His face looked so mournful that Colin had to laugh.

"Of course not! I want you to be happy, Henry. As much as possible."

Henry studied Colin's features. "You make me happy, Collie Sewell."

Colin hugged him. "I'm glad I do. Thank you, Henry."

And so Henry adjusted to Colin's routine, and Colin in turn made some exceptions to his own rule, getting quite drunk on occasions such as New Year's Eve, to Henry's delight.

The next year passed without incident, and it wasn't until February of 1895 when Colin became witness to the most exciting event to occur since the infamous 1889 scandal involving the Cleveland Street brothel. He sensed the tension as soon as he and Henry entered Porter's. Kenneth and Howard jumped when they saw the two.

"My God Henry, Oscar's going to trial!" Kenneth cried.

"What?" Henry demanded, as Colin stood beside him, alarmed.

"That fool Bosie egged him into it! His father accused Oscar of being a sodomite and rather than ignoring it, *Oscar is suing him for libel!*"

"You mean he's going to say he's *not* one of us?" Colin gaped.

"Yes, yes!" Kenneth wrung his hands. "Oh, it's terrible! They're going to get witnesses against him, Henry. Renters, I'm sure."

Henry sat down heavily. "Well, that's why we never use them. Wilde's crazy." He motioned the waiter for drinks and nodded to Colin, "I told you his carelessness would get him into trouble one of these days."

"But just think of what could happen to all of us!" Kenneth cried.

"Let's not get in a panic just yet, Kenneth," Henry warned. "The trial might be dismissed."

"And if it isn't?" Howard challenged.

Henry blew smoke in his direction. "Then my dears, we're going to have quite a show."

The trial wasn't dismissed. It opened April 3rd, and despite the new risk, men still met every night at Porter's, fervently asking after any news. Several of Oscar's friends, including Robbie Ross, attended each day of the trial and reported back to the crowd. Everyone thought it might end up all right when Robbie said Oscar opened the trial with his witty repartee and he was met with resounding laughter and even some applause. But soon things took a turn for the worse.

"They brought in witnesses today," Robbie said in a near-whisper one evening a week after the trial began. He paused. "They have physical evidence—letters, cigarette cases—and they have eyewitness accounts."

"From whom?" one man pressed.

Robbie looked miserable. "Rent-boys. And hotel staff at the Savoy."

"What would the Savoy staff know?" another man asked dubiously.

"Well," Robbie hedged, "they did, after all, have to collect and wash the bed linens..."

Dead silence, and then moans of horror at the very thought of what the statement meant. Chatter quickly ensued: Who could believe those happy-to-oblige renters and the very staff at the hotel, who Oscar surely tipped generously, would do such a thing? The hypocrites! It made the men who used male prostitutes and rented rooms—the majority, after all—sick with fear. *Who would be next?*

And so Oscar Wilde had no choice but to drop the libel suit, and now that such damnable evidence existed against him, the court turned around and arrested Oscar, charging him with gross acts of indecency and crimes against humanity.

Everyone at Porter's was up in arms the night of his arrest. A few men announced they were leaving the country until the public furor quieted. In the middle of that announcement some attention was directed toward Colin and Henry.

"What are you looking at us for?" Henry asked.

Kenneth cleared his throat. "Henry, you and Colin ought to consider leaving the country too."

"I can't leave the country!" Colin cried. "I'm in the middle of all of my projects."

"You might be in the middle of a jail cell if you stick around," Kenneth retorted.

"Kenneth, calm down," Henry demanded. "You're scaring the boy."

Howard stared at him. "But you both committed the act with them! You might get dragged into this."

"How?" Colin demanded.

Kenneth took a deep breath. "It is common knowledge in this club what you did with them—there's even that pamphlet floating about!"

"Our names weren't printed," Henry waved a hand.

"But the witnesses against Oscar may have heard about it from either Oscar or Bosie, or some other man they've used in the past."

"But why would they want to bring us up?" Colin frowned.

"They'll get bribe money!" Kenneth slammed his hand into his fist. "You two are established members of society, not street urchins! Once they get you, they can get any of us. I tell you, this could be a witch hunt!"

Howard said severely, "You two are putting yourselves and, quite frankly, many of *us* in danger if you stay here."

"Are you *threatening* us to leave London, Durham?" Henry said, his tone tinged with anger.

Howard held Henry's glare. "*I'm* not, Henry." He gave a glance around, and then said quietly, "The fellows in the club think you ought to as well." Colin looked wildly about as Henry set his jaw.

"Henry," Kenneth pleaded. "Just one mention of your name and they'd find cause!"

Henry paused, and finally, it sank in. He looked at Colin. "Do you understand what could happen if we were put to trial?"

Colin looked worriedly at his drink and bit his lip. "Two years, hard labor."

"Yes, and mind you, it's not the death sentence per se, but it may as well be," Henry declared. "Hard labor for two years straight *is* death! They make you split rocks all day, walk the treadmill and the like; most men eventually die of exhaustion."

"Not to mention your reputation is ruined," Kenneth reminded. "If Oscar is convicted, he will never write a successful play again."

Colin looked as if he was about to cry. "But we can't leave London! What in hell would we tell our clients?"

Henry furrowed his brow and then said to Kenneth and Howard, "Yes, have any of you an answer for that?"

"Perhaps just you can leave, Henry," Kenneth suggested.

Suddenly Colin narrowed his gaze. "Wait a moment. Howard, you... and everyone in this club wouldn't care a fig if we stayed or not if we hadn't had sex with all of *you* as well." His voice began to rise, and the noise in the club fell to a hush. "Well it's your own faults for choosing us! I'm not going to prematurely sabotage my career just to put your minds at ease. You're all every bit as guilty as Henry and I. So, if you want to save yourselves, do it! You flee the country! I am staying here, where I will continue to do my job." He turned to Henry, who was beginning to smile at him. "And you won't leave either. All Jack has to do is shut down Porter's for some time. We can meet elsewhere if we want, or need to, such as our house, Kenneth's house, Howard's house!" He threw his hands up. "Even if our names were to be mentioned at some point, what of it? We've a perfectly clean record! Nobody we've been with would ever admit to it—it would be only secondhand."

"Secondhand is evidence enough, Colin," Howard refuted.

"Well then you leave, Howard!" Colin shot back, standing up. "You're all making this out to be our responsibility. We haven't done anything with anyone in over a year! And of all the men here in this club, Henry has been the most discreet man of all. We have been so careful! And that any of you would think we would just drop what we're doing? I'm not a damned poet or… or an artist! I can't just pick up and leave. I have a proper day job, and a proper reputation I'm *trying* to build, so if you please, I will stay in this very city. Place the blame where it properly belongs: on Oscar's head, which is now going to be served on a platter thanks to that damned Salome of his!"

Everyone in the club heard it, and they saw Colin's eyes blaze as he sought a waiter. "Would you be so kind! Bottles of champagne all around, Georgie, on our tab, so that we may toast with you our last night in this club until further notice." The men in the club gave a roar of admiration and Colin's voice grew to a shout. "As a strict Catholic, I ought to know what *decent* and *moral* men do!" The men cheered, and Colin threw down a final glare at Howard, who could only look up at the young man in utter amazement and note at that very moment, *He looks like Christ on the Mount himself.*

The second trial began April 26th, and to everyone's relief, it was dismissed for several reasons. The retrial was set for May 20th. Five days later, Oscar Wilde was found guilty of a crime second only to murder and sentenced: two years hard labor.

While men scrambled to find places to meet over the next several months, nightly get-togethers as an entire group were too difficult to arrange and feared dangerous. Renting a floor of rooms at a hotel was now out of the question because of what had occurred with Oscar at The Savoy. Therefore, men met in small groups during the week and Henry, Kenneth, and Jack opened their homes to everyone most Saturday nights. While Henry was mildly depressed by this change, Colin secretly preferred the new arrangement. He was tired of Porter's and of the same people night after night. Now he, Henry, Kenneth, and Howard met sporadically during the week just as a foursome, and usually just for an hour. It allowed Colin much more time to work and get a decent night's sleep. However, he still hadn't been given a major project to do on his own, and he began looking in his free time for such an opportunity.

The occasion arrived unexpectedly in August, while Colin read the newspaper at the office. He had just turned to the business section, and he could hardly believe what he saw. "Henry, Max Rademaker bought a giant parcel of land out in the country and intends to build an estate there!

Henry didn't look up from his mail. "Hmm. Pity the poor bastard who wins that bid."

Colin was confused. "But, we're going to draw up a proposal, aren't we?"

Henry perused his letters calmly. "Rademaker won't hire us, and I won't work for him."

Colin looked incredulous. "Why ever not? Did you have some kind of quarrel with each other?"

Henry sighed. "No, not really. In fact, he's a giant fan of contemporary architecture and knows everything about my work. He's probably my greatest admirer, reluctantly. But he's a bloody nightmare to work for. That, and he won't allow any extension of a deadline without a ridiculous penalty."

"What sort of penalty?"

"Usually ten percent docked off your bid."

"Ten percent!" Colin cried. "That's outrageous!"

Henry nodded. "Yes, I know. So forget Rademaker, Colin."

But Colin couldn't help looking at the photograph of the land to be developed. "But Henry," he murmured wistfully, "there's a forest, vistas, a rolling landscape..." Then he looked sharply at Henry. "And Rademaker's one of the richest of the lot. He'd pay a fortune to the winning firm!"

Henry became irritated. "We don't need his money, Colin. We can't do it, and we won't do it."

"But imagine the *everlasting acclaim* we'd get for this! And what if we did complete it on schedule?"

"Colin! The man is notorious for sabotaging deadlines! And even if we came in under deadline for Rademaker, we'd have to do the same for everyone else from now on! We're already the cream of the crop; we've no need for this man." Colin stared hard at the newspaper. After a moment, Henry said quietly, "And if you even dare to secretly put a proposal out to him, you're fired."

Colin started. "All right! I won't!" He eyed Henry. "I see my partnership in this firm doesn't allow me to have a say in much."

"Of course it does. You've had your say on the matter. But you're the junior partner, and if the senior partner opposes you, which I do in this case, you're overruled."

"Oh, what rot!" Colin threw the paper down. "I don't see why I can't take on this project independent of you if I want to. I've been doing it anyway for the past two years."

"Under my protocol," Henry said firmly. "If you took on the Rademaker project, you'd have to go outside my guidelines, which I won't allow."

"Why not?"

"Because you are still 'Sewell *&* Sewell,' Colin. The project will have both our names on it. I'm not about to set new precedents now."

Colin made one last attempt. "But Henry... haven't you ever, at least once, dreamed of having a Rademaker property designed by you?"

Henry snorted. "Absolutely not! Let the other hacks toil themselves to death for the sake of glory. It won't be me. Now Colin, I've had quite enough of this subject, and I'm warning you to leave it alone."

Several nights later, they were having a drink at an outdoor café. Henry was in an especially good mood because Jack had announced he would reopen Porter's next week. While he and Colin chatted, Bosie fell upon them with another friend in tow.

"Good, good! Still together, are you?" Bosie lighted upon a chair.

Colin looked at him irritably. "What on earth are you talking about?"

Bosie grinned. "I'm making fabulous amounts of money on you! Everyone's been predicting the day you two will quit each other."

Colin rolled his eyes and absently scratched his arm. "Oh, you're rich, you are, Douglas."

Bosie's eyes widened with glee. "It's absolutely true! You can ask Miltie over there. He placed a bet. Lost, mind you."

Miltie was their waiter, and Colin stared at him. Miltie's mouth dropped, and he scurried away, red-faced.

Colin grew pale. Henry spoke. "And just why would they think that we're going to quit each other?"

Bosie laughed, looking at Colin. "Well, everyone knows Henry prefers boys, and you won't really fit into *that* category much longer, and you don't fuck them anymore either, so what good are you, Sewell?" He tilted his chin. "Though I'm guessing Henry gets his cock sucked every night, which would explain the holdout." He licked his lip. "Maybe even I'd stay on for that."

Colin's mind reeled. *They're all betting against us! They think I'm worthless!* His voice dripped with disdain. "What Henry and I have is beyond that singular vulgarity that's been all you've known, Bosie. And... oh yes, unlike you, I've been delivering a paycheck besides."

Bosie guffawed. "What, for your work as an 'architect'? As if anyone believes that! Henry's been carrying your name out of sheer pity."

With that comment, Colin realized Bosie's truth. There was yet to be any firsthand evidence of Colin's own remarkable skills. *There's not been a single project with only my name on it. They think I'm a joke.* He cast about desperately for a response.

"Colin won the bid from Max Rademaker," Henry said severely. "He's designing his country manse. Completely independent from me."

Bosie stopped smiling. "I hadn't heard that."

Henry sniffed, "It's not been publicly announced, yet."

Bosie gave Colin a shifty look. "Is that true?"

Colin glared. "Yes. Put the word out, won't you?" He stood up. "Look at you, Bosie! You don't even care that Oscar's in jail! That you'll be the death of him! Well, it's completely clear that you're the product of everything wrong with this country: a spoiled, inbred son of a lunatic father who uses his title to make him believe he's important, that he's worth something, when all you've ever accomplished is the complete ruination of another human being!" Colin scoffed at him. "Small wonder we Yanks took your land from under your filthy, vile, piggish noses!"

Bosie flew from his chair, but his friend anticipated the move and held him back as Colin and Henry strode off.

Once in the cab, Henry patted Colin on the back. "Brilliantly done!"

Colin was shaking. Once his breathing slowed, he stared at Henry. His voice was faint. "You said I won the bid."

"Yes," Henry assented. "I suppose I did, didn't I?" Colin turned to face Henry, who was smiling slightly. "You'd better work on those plans tomorrow, don't you think?"

Colin's jaw dropped. "My God. You mean you're really going to let me do it?"

Henry shrugged. "I don't believe I have a choice, do I?" His expression hardened. "I'll be damned if that wretch is going to make fools of us, Colin. The more I think about it, the more perfect it is! Anyone who knows me knows I won't work with Rademaker, nor he with me, so it will quite obviously be you and you alone doing the work!" He looked sharply at Colin. "And I mean it, Colin. I refuse to lift a finger for this man. I can't help you with this."

Colin nodded. "That's fine, Henry! I can do it. I'll do it." He hugged him. "Thank you so much!"

Henry felt a sinking sensation. He wished he'd never said a word about Rademaker to Bosie. Damn him! He decided one thing: *Colin will have to suffer through this alone. If I help him in any way, he'll think he can do it again. He'll* want *to do it again. And then I'll lose him.* The irony struck him: *Then Bosie would be the death of us.*

The next morning when Henry awoke, he was startled. "Collie, you're still in bed!"

Colin snuggled up to him. "I know. It's the least I can do, considering how generous you were last night." After a half hour of nestling in each other's warmth, Colin sighed. "I'm sorry, Henry. I'd forgotten how nice this is."

Henry drowsily caressed Colin's hair. "I hadn't." He ran his hand over Colin's cheek. "I can't remember the last time I saw you with stubble!"

Colin laughed. "Well then, I promise I'll try and let you see it more often!"

Henry closed his eyes. "I suppose you'll want to be getting up so you can begin the plans for Rademaker. You really don't have much time."

Colin nodded. "I know. I thought about that. That's why I've decided to use plans I've already created."

Henry started. "You mean you did draw up plans behind my back?"

Colin smiled broadly. "No, Henry. I'm going to propose the Helios House!"

Henry's face fell. "Oh, no, Colin, don't."

"Henry, the house is perfect for it! You can't find a better piece of property than this!"

"But that's *your* house, Collie! You've been saving the plans to build it someday for yourself!"

Colin shrugged. "Well, I can always think of something better. I wouldn't be a great architect if I couldn't." He looked shyly at Henry. "And besides, I'm here in London with you. I don't know when I'd ever really have a chance to build it, so I don't mind."

"But that house is meant for sun worship," Henry argued.

Colin sighed. "I know. But I was thinking: if there's any place that's desperate for light, it's this country. Imagine how nice it would be to have your house flooded with daylight and what a difference it would make to your happiness!"

"And the climate *is* mild enough for all of that glass," Henry mused.

"Yes," Colin nodded. "I think it will be wonderful!"

Henry shook his head. "Are you certain?"

"Yes. But of course, there are a few things I'll need to adjust, so I really had better be getting up soon." He leaned over and kissed Henry. "But I think I'll take some time with you, first. Priorities, you know."

"Priorities," Henry breathed. "And how glorious yours are."

CHAPTER EIGHTEEN

At eight o'clock Monday morning, Colin appeared at Max Rademaker's office unannounced. Henry agreed it was the best plan, since Rademaker would likely reject any written request from Sewell & Sewell outright.

"May I help you?" the secretary asked.

Colin handed over his card. "Yes, I'd like to request a meeting with Mr. Rademaker regarding development of his property in the Cotswolds."

The secretary raised an eyebrow as he read the card. "But... you're from Sewell & Sewell, Mr. Sewell."

Colin couldn't help grinning. "That's correct. But if you'll notice, my card names only myself. I am here completely independent of my firm."

The secretary was confused. "I don't understand... You're freelancing, then?"

Colin smiled. "Yes, in so many words, if you like." He nodded at Rademaker's door. "Would you be so kind as to deliver that to him? I have to admit I'm as curious as you are to find his response."

The secretary obliged, and after a minute, he returned. "Mr. Rademaker will see you now."

Colin thanked him and followed him into the office.

Max Rademaker sat behind his desk. He was a stout man, with graying brown hair around his head and none on top. Colin had seen him at several social engagements and figured him to be no less intimidating than other men of his stature. However, Mr. Rademaker looked quite unfriendly now, and Colin hoped it wasn't entirely personal.

"By God, it is Mr. Sewell."

Colin stood before him, smiling. "You were expecting the devil, naturally."

"You might be one and the same. What's this about you wanting to develop my land?"

"I want to develop your land," Colin shrugged.

"Why?"

"Because it's the most amazing piece of property I've seen in my entire life."

"Your lifetime... that's all of what, twenty-three years?"

"Twenty-five."

"You've never had this much land to work with."

"Not yet."

"Some people say you've never had any land to work with."

Colin stepped forward. "I'd like to defend my honor seated, if you'd so oblige."

Rademaker consented, and Colin settled, leaning forward on the desk. "Some people believe you should seek the truth before heeding rumors."

"But the rumors remain the same, no matter which mouth speaks them. You're a very talked-about individual, Mr. Sewell."

Colin sighed. "Yes, for all the wrong reasons, I'm sure." He was surprised that Rademaker's circle knew of him so well. It made Colin wonder why Rademaker would even associate with him, then. Privacy of his own office, perhaps. He stared hard at the man. "See here: these rumors are part of the reason why I want you to contract me. Henry refuses to lift a finger if

I take on this project, so it will prove to everyone that I *was* the one behind the Lyon Steel building."

"You were, after all?"

"And the Walton Street Tea Rooms. And Lady Dashworth's residence."

"You designed all three of those yourself!"

"Yes, and many more are in progress." Colin sat back. "Now here's a question for you, Mr. Rademaker. Say you wanted to find out if that was all actually true. Who should you ask?"

Max clucked his tongue. "Henry Sewell could lie for you."

Colin laughed. "Of course, he could. Who else?"

Max narrowed his eyes. "I suppose it would have to be one of your employees. Draftsmen."

Colin nodded. "Yes..."

"But you could have paid them off."

Colin looked on in admiration. "Excellent, Mr. Rademaker! So you can't even trust my employees' opinions directly. What now?"

Max paused and regarded Colin's intensity. "I see you're not the devil after all, Mr. Sewell. You're the advocate."

Colin's smile faded. "It's important that you believe me, Mr. Rademaker. I won't have you taking me for a hack. Now, how will you find the truth?"

Max studied the young man before him. He had assumed Colin would be foppish and immature. Instead he appeared practiced and austere. His air was entirely masculine, from his straight posture to his serious black suit. Max frowned. "All right, Mr. Sewell. I would hire someone to find out from one of your employees about you."

Colin sighed, content. "Absolutely. Well played."

"And tell me why in blazes would I go through such trouble when I can hire someone else I already know about?"

Colin's tone was friendly, but firm. "You're a fan of contemporary architecture. And Henry Sewell is the best contemporary architect around.

Some people have said you've been searching for an architect who could mimic Henry's work." He paused, and his voice took on an edge. "A man of your wealth has to be very smart indeed. You know Henry. You know damn well he wouldn't have hired me, let alone make me partner, if I wasn't pulling my own weight." He took a breath. "I think you already knew I designed those buildings, Mr. Rademaker, because you know Henry's work so well. Tell me why *I* designed those buildings and not Henry Sewell."

Max was spellbound. "Because Henry Sewell uses only four colors per room and you use at least six. You use floor-to-ceiling windows and Henry never has. He rarely uses botanicals to decorate and you have them in every room. Henry prefers straight lines, you prefer curves..." As he listed other details, Colin drank it all in, exultant to be with someone who had truly studied him. When Max ended, Colin gazed at him.

"I believe you're the first man to have been so very observant about my work, Mr. Rademaker." He frowned. "So I suppose the question now is, do you like any of them?"

Now Max's eyes shone as he realized the full extent of this opportunity. "I think the Dashworth house is finer than anything Henry Sewell ever created."

Colin weakened. "Really?" His voice was a joyful whisper. "What do you like best about it?"

Max thought, and then crossed his arms. "The atrium. It's a masterpiece, Sewell, and you know it."

Colin beamed. "Your plans include an atrium!"

"My plans?"

"Yes! I already have your plans drawn up."

"You mean the proposal?" Max guessed uncertainly.

"Not the proposal. The entire plans, Mr. Rademaker!" Then Colin grew serious. "My proposal to you consists of the plans I designed for my own personal home someday. It is the best work I have ever done."

Max looked concerned. "But, aren't you still going to use them yourself?"

"No. I live in London. This house I've designed is meant as a country estate. I've come to terms with the fact that I may never build it if I keep it for myself. And your land is perfect for it!"

"I see," Max mused. "So, where are these extraordinary plans?"

Colin looked at him evenly. "They are at home. I can bring them to you at any time. However, there is a fifty-pound refundable deposit to view them."

"Fifty pounds!" Max exploded. "Are you out of your mind? Nobody charges a viewing fee!"

Colin remained calm. "I don't, either. But this is an exception, Mr. Rademaker." His voice went dark. "These are my finest plans, my most superior work. You can understand that I need to protect myself. While I would never expect you to do so, it would be very easy for someone to copy my plans and then hire someone else to build them. The deposit is merely a security measure."

"Has anyone else paid it?"

"No, because nobody else has seen the plans," Colin replied. "Except Henry." And now, the finale: "The Helios House was the basis on which he hired me."

"The Helios House..." Max murmured.

"If you see the plans, you'll understand the name," Colin said softly. He stood up. "I'll be at the office today until seven o'clock. Tomorrow the same, if you should decide to contact me."

Max stood up as well and shook Colin's hand. "Well, Mr. Sewell, I must say that you weren't at all what I expected."

Colin chuckled. "Ah. Well, Mr. Rademaker, one down, 999 to go. Good day."

Colin worked the rest of the day without hearing from Max Rademaker.

"Well, of course he doesn't want to appear overly eager," Henry reassured him. The next day, Colin tried to focus on his work as the morning progressed, and there was still no word. He hadn't told Henry about the fifty-pound deposit, and he was wondering if it had been a good idea. Finally, at one o'clock, Colin's assistant appeared.

"A message from Mr. Rademaker, sir."

Colin practically snatched the paper from the man's hands, and scanned it.

Mr. Sewell,

Please be at my office at 16:00 this afternoon with the plans we discussed. The fee shall be made available.

M. Rademaker

Colin was relieved, but annoyed. "Meet him in three hours! Doesn't he realize I have to go back home and get the plans? Does he think I have nothing else to do?"

"It's Rademaker," Henry said, in a singsong voice. "Get used to it." He tilted his head. "Or, of course, you can tell him that you'll meet him tomorrow."

Colin sighed. "That'd be suicide. Rademaker's busier than I am, or at least he thinks he is. I'll play it safe for now."

Henry himself was on his way out. "Well, don't worry about getting the other things done. Just concentrate on getting those plans to Rademaker. Good luck, Colin!"

"Thank you, Henry. I'll be at Porter's right afterwards." Colin tidied up and took a cab home to fetch the plans and change clothes. He went through his closet, deciding what to wear. He knew men like Rademaker disapproved of any ornamentation on men, such as velvet collars or jeweled brooches. That their only accepted clothing colors were black, dark blue, brown, or grey. He could only imagine what Rademaker thought of him at the few social occasions they had both attended and how different

Colin must have appeared at Rademaker's office! Today was no exception. This time, Colin chose a simple dark brown suit with a tan vest that complimented his eyes and hair. Colin laughed. *As if Rademaker would consciously notice that!* But he would realize the overall effect. Colin fastened sterling silver links onto his cuffs and finished the ensemble with a sober russet tie. "You weren't at all what I expected." Colin smiled as he regarded his figure in the mirror. *I disagree, Mr. Rademaker. I'm seducing you just like I seduced everyone else. What works in the bedroom* can *work in the boardroom... Take that, Henry Sewell!*

As he rode to Rademaker's office, he became increasingly excited. He had told the truth to the man: he hadn't shown anyone the plans for the Helios House since he met Henry. He recalled how Henry and Jeffrey had both marveled over them. He felt certain that Mr. Rademaker would have the same reaction, although he'd require a bit more interpretation, not being an architect. Still, Colin couldn't wait to share them with someone again. Every once in a while, he'd take them out and study them to make sure everything was still as perfect as he remembered it. Over the years, there were a few advancements in technology that Colin added, but otherwise, the Helios House was just as it had been five years ago. There was only a small thought that kept nagging at him: he was giving away his dream to someone else. But Colin pushed it out of his mind. He exited the cab and proceeded up the steps into the office building.

"Good afternoon, Mr. Sewell!" the receptionist said brightly. Colin was pleased at the friendly welcome; it was a good sign. "I'll tell Mr. Rademaker you're here."

"Thank you." Colin had worked himself up so much over his plans that when he was ushered into the office, he expected Rademaker to look equally jubilant. To his dismay, the old man looked as gruff as always. However, Colin noticed his desk had been cleared save for several leather weights.

"Mr. Sewell." A curt nod.

Colin smiled. "Good afternoon, Mr. Rademaker." The door closed behind him.

Max reached inside his coat pocket. "Here's your fifty pounds. Though I don't understand. If we are going to view it together today, the plans won't leave your sight, and you'll just be giving the money back to me in a few hours."

"I apologize for not being more specific, Mr. Rademaker. You may now keep these plans for a week. That way, you can take them home and study them at your leisure. Also, it gives you a chance to discuss them with others, if you wish." Colin was no fool; as soon as he began working for Henry he had made a full copy of the plans should something like this arise.

Max nodded. "Hmm, very good. Very smart, Sewell." He went to his liquor cabinet. "Care for a drink?"

"I'll take scotch, if you have it," Colin replied casually.

Max poured his own drink and handed Colin's to him. "Why don't you set out the first one," Max suggested, and Colin took out the exterior of the house and spread it on the desk. Max gave a low whistle.

"This is the front of the house," Colin began.

It was a quarter to seven when they completed the last sheet. Colin carefully rolled up the plans for Mr. Rademaker and handed the tube to him. As they both sat down across from each other, Max studied Colin while collecting his thoughts. Finally, he shook his head. "It's absolutely phenomenal, Mr. Sewell."

Colin smiled. "Thank you."

Max set his glass down. "I'd like to give you your opportunity to prove yourself, actually. But as you are aware, the reason I won't work with Henry Sewell is because he's lazy."

"You mean he takes too long with his projects," Colin clarified.

"Precisely." Max eyed Colin. "I want the house built in two years."

Colin's jaw dropped. "Two years! Mr. Rademaker, that house will take at least twice that, to complete it! Why, it's got—"

"Three, then."

Colin struggled to keep his temper from flaring. He stared at the carpet. Then he said, "Henry mentioned a penalty fee for not meeting the agreed-upon deadline." He looked up at Max. "Is that correct?"

"It is."

"What exactly is the penalty?"

Max gave him a steely gaze. "Two percent of the total cost for each day the project is late."

Colin exhaled. "I see." He put his fingers to his lips and thought, while Max watched him. *Come on, Sewell, prove your mettle. How much of a bastard can you be? Show me what you can come up with!*

Finally, Colin looked up. "Other architects have agreed to your terms because of the sheer prestige in designing a building for you. I didn't design a building for you; I designed one for myself. And therefore, it's better than anything else you'll get." He paused. "I have two counteroffers for you: Counteroffer A, a two-year completion date—three if you want me to design the interior, which I highly recommend, one percent of the total cost for each day behind schedule..." he sat back, "and no spending limit. Instead of a set price, I'll give you a bill every month of the expenditures. You'll pay it. At the time of completion, you shall be refunded any money totaled from any days late." Colin saw a glimmer of admiration in Max's eyes. He continued. "Counteroffer B, three-year completion date—four to design the interior, two percent of the total cost for each day behind schedule, and an exact cost, which will be relatively firm. I would estimate it to be around five million pounds, which includes the landscaping but not the interior."

Max smiled. "I think I'm going to like doing business with you, Mr. Sewell. Give me the week to consider it, and I'll get back with you next Tuesday."

"Fair enough," Colin agreed. They shook hands. "Thank you for your time, Mr. Rademaker."

Colin went straight to Porter's to tell Henry and the others how the meeting went. "He doesn't seem that horrible of a man, Henry."

"Oh, he's a perfectly fine gentleman before you actually begin the project."

Then Colin had an idea. "Oh, I should ask William Morris for advice!" Morris had designed the home Rademaker currently lived in.

"Colin, I hardly think he'll give you the time of day. What does he have to gain from it?"

Colin flounced himself back on his seat. "What do you mean? He'll love it! I'll bet he'd jump at the chance to share his war story!"

Henry gave a small laugh. "Collie, you'd discredit yourself. You'll look like a novice, asking for guidance from him."

Colin threw an arm back over the booth and looked at Henry. "And I suppose you have a better idea?"

Henry looked at Kenneth and Howard. "My idea was never to work with the man, but I suppose that's not an option for you."

Colin's voice began to rise. "No, it's not. Because Rademaker is going to buy my plans, Henry, and you may as well accept it. I know you don't like it, but since you're part of all of this, the least you can do is be supportive."

Howard shifted uncomfortably. He thought he'd feel a sense of guilty pleasure whenever Henry and Colin quarreled, but instead, he found the opposite to be true. It still tore at him anytime Colin's feelings were hurt. *I'd be supportive, Colin. Right now, I'd be embracing you, congratulating you on your success.* But of course, Howard said nothing. Ever since he had glared at Henry the night Alfie was in town, he'd been careful not to side with Colin, in a show of apology and loyalty to Henry. And Colin really hadn't done anything himself to win back Howard's favor, as far as Howard was concerned. Fortunately, Kenneth had always remained neutral. *Thank God for Kenneth. He has always kept things on an even keel.*

And now, Kenneth spoke. "Well, Colin, is it really for certain that Rademaker is buying your plans?"

Colin defused and sighed. "No, Kenneth, not really." He pretended nonchalance as he drew out another cigarette. "Nothing is certain until we actually sign a contract, of course."

"But they will," Henry affirmed. "Colin's right. Nobody in their right mind would refuse the chance at that house."

Colin smiled gratefully. "Thank you."

Henry continued. "This very house he's selling to Rademaker is the house that convinced me to hire him on the spot when I saw its plans."

Kenneth and Howard raised their eyebrows. "Well!" Kenneth exclaimed. "Tell us about it, Colin!"

Like anyone hesitant to reveal their most beloved idea, Colin demurred. "Oh! No. No, really, I'd probably go into too much detail and bore you beyond belief."

"Colin, don't be silly!" Henry urged. "It's absolutely miraculous! Tell them about it."

Colin appeared as surprised as Howard felt at Henry's encouragement. Then Colin did something that absolutely shocked Howard. Colin blushed. Blushed! Howard chuckled, "Since when is the great architect so humble about his work?"

Colin smiled. "I'm not humble. It's the greatest thing I have ever done. That's why it feels so... odd to be talking about it."

Artistspeak, Howard thought wryly. Sometimes the boy eluded him.

"But, all right," Colin agreed. "When you're looking at the front of the house..." As Colin's description unfolded, Henry would interrupt to proudly say things like, "Don't forget the atrium!" Or, "Colin, you must tell them what that's made of!" And with each interjection, Colin would look gratefully at Henry. And Howard realized he didn't like these exchanges any more than the quarreling. *Bah and blah*, he thought, though he was admittedly caught up in the description of the house. Still, he knew even Kenneth had to realize what this all meant: if this house was truly as amazing as it sounded, it really would hurtle Colin's name to the top of the list.

He would finally stand alone from Henry. Henry was losing more and more control; Colin was gaining it. *And Colin can't figure out that, by doing so, he's going to destroy the very thing he's worked so hard to build.*

When Howard told Kenneth this at a later date, Kenneth nodded sadly. "I know. Colin has come so far. He's no longer just a very clever plaything, is he?"

Howard agreed. "Perhaps Henry always knew Colin's potential but somehow never presaged he'd desire to use it, to the fullest extent, anyway."

Kenneth's tone was dark. "Howard, when Colin finishes this project he will be almost thirty years old. Imagine that—Henry has never been with anyone over twenty-five!" He shook his head and said slowly, "Colin won't look boyish anymore."

Howard looked at him sharply. "Do you mean to say you think that he won't be attractive?"

Kenneth shrugged. "He's still nice to look at now. But really, to think he's done *three* things Henry disapproves of... *and* he'll be so old—"

"So old!" Howard snapped. "He'll still always be twenty years younger than Henry, for God's sake!"

"But he won't always be *young*, Howard!" Kenneth replied irritably. "If things continue at this rate, it's going to end terribly; I know it."

Howard pshawed him. "Oh, come now. They're just like any married couple. They quarrel and make up. Look how moonfaced they became last Tuesday when Henry told him to describe his house to us."

Kenneth paused thoughtfully. "Colin pushes Henry, and then he begs him back. He pushes Henry too far, and then throws out a trick to reel him in at the last minute. Well, one day it's not going to work."

Now Howard felt depressed. It didn't help that they were both in Porter's, on their fifth drink. "Kenneth, please..."

Kenneth looked at his drink. "Have you ever thought about what we'll do if Henry becomes unfaithful?"

"Oh, God..."

"How will we face him? Colin, that is." They sat in silence, mulling over an answer. Then Kenneth spoke quietly, "I say, do *you* still fancy him, Howard?"

Howard's mind fuzzily spun but he tried to carefully choose his words. "I don't know anymore, Kenneth. I suppose that time has passed."

"Really? See? Even you think he's too old."

"He's not too *old*, Kenneth! Good God!" He looked accusingly at his friend. "You and Henry are really something; how stuck on *boys* you are."

Kenneth looked puzzled. "But so are you, Howard. You've always liked them."

Howard raised his eyebrows and then sighed. "You're right; I did. But they're too much work now, aren't they? They're so superficial and... and immature! Colin's already grown out of that, you see? Because he has ambition. And talent. He wants to take care of himself. He's not a spoilt brat like the lot, and he never really was. He could take or leave Henry's money. Remember how all those boys before him would just take advantage of Henry?"

Kenneth sighed. "But those boys... they were lithe. They were energetic. They were ephemeral. Howard, that is the essence of a boy." As if his mind suddenly cleared, Kenneth said definitively, "Colin is just like one of us, now! He's been here for *years*!"

"You say that as if it is a terrible thing!"

"I'm not, Howard. I'm only saying that this is perhaps the whole reason why their relationship has shifted. And perhaps Henry will adapt. So far, he has. I'm only saying it is quite amazing."

Howard brooded. Finally, he shrugged. "Well, I may not fancy Colin any longer, but I'm drawn into the drama of the whole thing. I've never known any men in an actual lasting relationship, and for better or for worse, I can't stop watching! It's played out here right in front of us, daily! It really is like some sort of theatre."

"But plays end, Howard," Kenneth reminded gently. "You could spend your entire life engrossed in this."

"The story of Henry and Colin will end, too, Kenneth," Howard mused. "Whether it ends in thirty years with Henry dying while Colin mourns over him, or it ends tomorrow with one leaving the other, it will end."

"You should concern yourself with your own ending."

"I am, Kenneth! I'm only living from day to day. What more do you want?" Howard put up his hands. "Honestly, I'm no different than before Colin came here, am I?"

Kenneth tapped his finger on his chin. "I suppose I never really considered it... You have always wanted someone for your own..."

Howard nodded. "Yes I have. And you're married, Kenneth. Even if it's to a woman, you've someone to come home to every night, like Henry."

Kenneth smiled. "Yes. But do you know, Howard, that sometimes, I too think about what it must be like to be Henry?"

"How do you mean?"

"Well, what if, instead of Anne, I had a *boy* to come home to every day? A *boy* to share my life with, like Henry has Colin?"

Howard frowned. "Kenneth, it just couldn't have been possible. You're in the public eye too much. And Anne's connections have been invaluable."

"I know," Kenneth assented. "I am glad for that. But every once in a while, I let myself imagine it..." He looked off, and after a moment, shook his head. "In any case, I do understand how you feel, Howard, because unlike me, for you, it's still possible."

"Yes, and look how successful I've been, given such opportunity!" Howard exclaimed good-humoredly. Then he smiled. "Perhaps when you retire, you can divorce Anne and live your life anew."

Kenneth laughed. "Yes! Then we'll both go looking for those elusive males to feather our nest with."

Howard's smile faded. "You know, Kenneth, it may not be what we want, anyway. Minutes ago, you were just saying how Colin has lost his boyishness. Well, what if you were the one with Colin, instead of Henry? Would you be happy?"

Kenneth thought for a moment. "I suppose not. Colin is quite extraordinary, but he's a grown man now. He wouldn't exactly race to the door and greet me slavishly upon my return each day, would he?"

Howard and Kenneth pictured the scene in their heads and laughed together. "I've discovered your problem, Kenneth," Howard chuckled. "What you really want is a dog!"

CHAPTER NINETEEN

A week after his last meeting with Max Rademaker, Colin presented himself to the man's receptionist for the third time. Today he wore a charcoal suit with a dark red tie and marcasite cufflinks. It was hard for Colin not to revel in the fact that his clothes were as fine as Rademaker's. Perhaps it was bordering on improper for a young man to be outfitted so expensively, but it was perfect for Rademaker: it was a sign of success.

Now Rademaker appeared as Colin had once expected. He greeted Colin jubilantly.

"Sewell! Come in, come in!" He patted Colin on the back. "Have a seat!" He poured Scotch for Colin and himself, and then he settled in his own chair, grinning. "I decided to go ahead and do some legwork."

Colin peered at him over the rim of his glass. "Really? And what did you find out?"

Max leaned back and gazed at him. "They absolutely adore you over there."

Colin's pride bloomed within. He had figured his employees respected him, but to hear someone else say it actually affirmed it. "That's very kind. They're excellent workers."

"I should say so. When my assistant told them he was doubtful that you designed all of the buildings you mentioned, they became fiercely defensive and said they'd go to court to prove it!"

Even Colin was surprised. "Is that so?" Then he checked himself. "Well, I suppose I don't see why they wouldn't."

Max continued. "Then my assistant asked what kind of work ethic you have."

Colin bristled with indignation at this. *But I suppose because of my affiliation with Henry, I can't blame the man.* "And...?"

Rademaker folded his hands across his stomach. "They said you were absolutely committed to your job. That you remain at the office long after Henry Sewell leaves." He narrowed his eyes. "They said you do practically all the work, Mr. Sewell."

Colin tried to keep from showing his embarrassment. "I've asked Henry to give me as much experience as possible," he hedged.

Max shrugged. "That's all very admirable, Mr. Sewell, but my concern is, how will you manage my house if you're juggling all of these other projects?"

Colin permitted a bit of anger to creep into his voice. "That is not to be your concern, Mr. Rademaker. Rest assured, the house will get top priority. And you have the one percent or two percent as a cushion."

Max took a deep breath. "I've decided to go with the two percent."

Colin smiled with relief. He didn't honestly know how he would have gotten the house completed in only two years. "Excellent! I'll have my attorney draw up a contract and I'll meet with you once it's completed."

Rademaker stood up and shook Colin's hand, beaming. "I feel like I've stumbled across a diamond mine! Such genius, and so hidden!"

Colin chuckled. "Thanks to you, Mr. Rademaker, it shouldn't remain hidden much longer."

"Yes, yes. Well, you'd best be off, now. I'll await your correspondence regarding the contract." Colin nodded, and they parted ways.

On the way to Porter's, Colin became increasingly nervous about sharing the news in public. He wasn't sure how Henry would react, because it was one thing for him to predict Colin's plans would sell but a whole other for him to find they actually did. Colin secretly believed Henry would warm up to the project as he had observed Colin working on it and might even help after all. But as for tonight... Colin would rather have told Henry in private, first, so he could see how Henry really felt. He'd doubtless act happy for Colin at Porter's, but later, when they were alone, who knew if his mood would change? Colin decided he'd lay on his charm thick tonight. Then he grinned. *As if I have to try! I'm building the* Helios House*!*

As for Henry, he had braced himself earlier. He knew Colin would win the bid. Still, he couldn't trust himself to react ideally when the announcement came, so he doubled his first few drinks. When Kenneth commented on it, Henry shook his head, smiling. "What can I say? It's like sending a son off to war, Kenneth. On the one hand, I'm terribly, terribly proud of him, but on the other hand, I'm absolutely anxious as hell." Howard watched Henry's cigarette tremble in his hand as he glanced toward the hallway. It was almost endearing. When Colin finally appeared, Henry leaned forward eagerly.

As far as Henry was concerned, the one good thing to come of Colin working late had been his delayed arrival at Porter's. Henry enjoyed watching him stride into the room in his stunning business attire. He loved watching Colin exchange friendly pleasantries with other members on the way to his table, and he especially took pleasure in the swooning stares of the new and visiting men left in his path.

Upon greeting Henry, Colin laughed. "I see you've begun the festivities without me, darling!" He sat down, an exultant expression on his face. "I shall gladly catch up!" He studied Henry's glass. "What are we having? Whisky sours!" He shot Howard an accusatory look, and then threw his hands up. "Oh, never mind! I could drink turpentine for all I care!" He called to the waiter, "Double that for me, thanks. But single for him, I beg you!"

Howard smiled. "You appear to have good news."

Colin didn't even bother taking out his cigarettes yet. He looked at all three of them as best he could. "Rademaker is buying the plans."

"Oh, bravo, Colin!" Kenneth clapped his hands.

"Well done!" Howard congratulated warmly.

Henry took Colin's hands into both of his. "I knew he would," he murmured, eyes shining.

Colin gazed back at him. "Yes, you did." He was so euphoric that he leaned over and kissed Henry, and only slightly withdrew. "I'm going to impress you, Hen-Ren. I'm going to make you so proud. I promise."

Henry nodded, his voice breaking as he spoke, "I know, Collie. I know."

"Oh ho! The old man's getting emotional!" Howard teased. Colin let go of Henry to let him recover and took out a cigarette. He excitedly told them all the story of how it came about. Howard would have given anything to have seen Colin negotiate with Max Rademaker. He realized that he'd watched Colin only in social settings, so he had difficulty picturing how Colin would broker a business deal. Henry had always taken care of that aspect in the past, and therefore Colin seemed to be too inexperienced and impassioned to go it on his own. Obviously, he was capable after all, to a great degree. Howard wondered if even Henry believed Colin would have done it so well. Then his thoughts were interrupted by a small black velvet box Henry had produced from his pocket.

"This is in honor of your achievement today," he said tenderly to Colin.

Colin stared at it. Henry placed it in his hands, and he stared at it some more. "Collie, go on!" Henry urged.

Colin smiled at him and opened the box. "Oh... !" He lifted it out—a pocketwatch, but unlike any he'd ever seen.

The cover was 18-k gold, like his other two, but it was entirely inlaid with diamonds and sapphires. Each concentric circle had a pattern: diamond after sapphire. "Open it up," Henry pressed. Colin shook his head. The glitter of the gemstones sparkled across his awestruck face. A small crowd of men had gathered to see the spectacular present. Henry guided Colin's hand to open the watch. The face was dark blue and bare, except for four diamonds to mark the quarter hours. "And look at the back," Henry whispered gleefully, basking in the attention of the club. Colin turned it over and read it silently.

"Read it, Colin!" one of the men said. The other men joined in. "Yes, read it! Come, come! Tell us what it says!"

Colin held it to his chest and laughed shyly. "No, I can't! It's personal." He got a load of ribbing for that. Colin Sewell, wanting privacy!

"Go on," Henry said affectionately. "I don't mind."

Colin gave up. "Well, you have to know French. I shan't translate it." More ribbing. Colin gazed at the engraving, his voice a murmur.

"Toujours amour.

Toujours grandeur.

Toujours nous.

1895"

The men were silent, nodding their appreciation. Then Henry spoke, "Today Colin found out he is in fact the official designer for Max Rademaker's country house."

The silence was broken with cries of surprise and hearty congratulation. Colin felt overwhelmed. He had planned to just tell Henry, Howard, and Kenneth today. After all, he hadn't signed the contract yet. And this pocketwatch! Colin hadn't expected any gift at all. A sincere congratulations would have sufficed, and Henry knew it. Then it struck him.

Bosie's bet.

The pocketwatch, by its very extravagance, was a symbol to everyone present. And the scripture!

Toujours amour.

Colin realized with a surge of triumph that he and Henry had just thumbed their noses at everyone who doubted their relationship.

Toujours nous.

He turned and flung his arms around a surprised Henry. "Thank you, Henry! I love you!"

Henry held him tightly and said, "Do you like it, then?"

Colin laughed. "Oh, it's the most beautiful thing I've ever seen!" Then he spoke sotto voce: "And you're just genius! It's the perfect foil to Bosie and every other rotter who bet against us."

Now Henry laughed. "I thought so, too. But I am so very proud of you, Collie. You deserve it regardless."

Colin beamed and kissed him again, and the rest of the evening passed very happily, indeed.

The day after Colin signed the contract with Max Rademaker, he approached Henry in trepidation while they were at the office. "Here, Henry. It's a check from Mr. Rademaker. I figured you could deposit it." He dropped the piece of paper from two fingers as if it were poisonous.

Henry stared at the check, and then looked up. "Colin, since this is entirely your project, I think you should open a savings account for this."

Colin bit his lip. 'But Henry, we've always done it this way."

"I know, darling," Henry smiled. "We still will for other purposes. But I think you should keep this money separate, for insurance purposes."

Confused, Colin panicked. 'What do you mean, 'insurance purposes'?"

Henry sighed. "I only mean that you can easily keep track of the money as you get it. Also, if you end up owing Rademaker at the end, you'll have this account to use."

Colin cast about desperately. "But it'll change everything."

"No, it won't. Colin, you're going to have to learn some financial skills if you're going to do this sort of thing."

"But I don't want to!"

"Collie, you're becoming hysterical. Now listen to me. When all is said and done, you can transfer what you have into my account. But for now, just keep it separate." He squeezed Colin's hand. "It won't change a thing between us. I still love you, silly boy."

Colin calmed down. "Are you sure you really want me to do this?"

Henry patted his hand. "Go pay a visit to Howard with this check. He doesn't actually open accounts himself, but he'll help you."

Colin looked mortified. "Oh God, Henry! It will be humiliating in front of Howard!"

"Howard knows how our system works, Colin. Just go to him and say, very businesslike, 'I need to open a separate account for Mr. Rademaker's checks.'"

"He'll probably ask, 'Does Henry know?'" Colin said wryly.

Henry laughed. "Then you tell him, 'Dammit, man, open the account and never mind what Henry does or doesn't know!'"

Colin laughed too and kissed Henry on his head. "Right, then. I'll go." He took his hat and the check, and left.

Colin had not been inside the Bank of England since he had come that day four years ago to apologize to Howard. There had never been a need, since Henry took care of all of the finances.

"Mr. Durham is in a meeting, but it shouldn't last much longer, if you'd like to wait," the secretary told him.

"Yes, thank you," Colin replied. He settled into one of the chairs and began studying the paperwork he brought with him from the office.

"Colin! I say, good morning! Whatever brings you here? Well, never mind that, come into my office!" Once they were inside, Howard asked, "How long have you been waiting?"

"Oh, not long at all," Colin smiled. "I brought work to do." He glanced down. "I'm actually here on a mission from Henry. He thinks I should open a savings account just for this project's earnings."

"Hmm," Howard mused. "And what do you think?"

Colin was taken aback. "What do you mean, what do I think? Henry said that's what should be done. He's the expert on this sort of thing. I haven't a clue."

"How much is the check for?"

Colin shifted uncomfortably. "Um... a thousand pounds."

Howard was surprised. He'd forgotten that Colin would feel awkward around monetary matters. After all, the boy hadn't ever had more than a few pounds in his pocket since he came here. And now he had a thousand to his name! Howard's voice was gentle. "I'm just wondering, Colin, if perhaps we should put your money in a more aggressive account that will make the most of your earnings."

Colin grew flustered. "Oh. Can you do that... with that?" Realizing how ignorant he must sound, he threw his hands up. "Oh, for heaven's sake, Howard, I don't care what you do with it. Just take it!"

Howard chuckled. "My! I wish all my clients were like you!" Then he became serious. "But Colin, see here: you're going to be dealt a lot of money on this project... It's wonderful! You should learn how to manage it. I'll explain it to you; it's really quite simple."

Colin looked dubious. "Let's just deposit it and be done with it."

"Colin," Howard reprimanded. "Give me five minutes. If you want to forget it after five minutes, fine. But at least give me that."

"Really, I have a lot of work to do..."

Howard banged his fist on his desk. "This is *one thousand pounds!* Don't you have any idea how much money that is?"

Colin, startled by Howard's tone, was momentarily speechless. Then he said defensively, "It's a lot of money, I know. And I don't care. Money has never meant anything to me."

At first, Howard mistook the words as pretentious, but when he saw Colin's perplexed expression, he understood that the boy was merely being honest. Colin further clarified himself. "I went from living out of my father's pocket to out of Henry's pocket, Howard."

Howard tried to soften his voice. "And don't you think now that you've earned your independence...?" He smiled at Colin, then sat down and looked him in the eye. "Five minutes. Please."

"My God, I don't think I have a choice." Colin said apprehensively. "You're absolutely passionate."

Howard motioned for him to bring his chair around. "Now," he began, "if it's of any comfort to you, I've done the same thing with Henry's money. I mean, really, Colin, how do you think the man has stayed so wealthy?"

Colin laughed. "All right, all right! I'm convinced. I just... I hate dealing with this sort of thing."

"I love it! So allow me..."

Forty-five minutes later, Howard put his pencil down with satisfaction. "There! You're a quick study, Colin."

"I think I have a headache," Colin muttered, rubbing his temples.

"Well, you certainly know your math."

Colin straightened. "I was the top student in my class, actually."

"At MIT?"

"Yes." Colin looked at him curiously. "Where else?"

Howard shrugged. "I'm not sure. It just seems odd for a top student to drop out of a top institution."

"Not really." Colin waved a hand. "The bottom students flunk out; the top students drop out. They taught me everything I needed to know. As far as I was concerned, they had nothing more to offer me."

Howard sat back in his chair. "With all due respect, Colin, I've known you for some time now. You don't seem the type to forgo a degree with top honors just because you were bored."

Colin glared at Howard. "Is that so? Well, I don't see what business it is of yours, or why you'd even care."

"I'm sorry," Howard apologized. "It was a transgression. Please forget I said anything."

"I will." Colin paused. "In any case, I was right. I'm Henry Sewell's partner, for heaven's sake! A damned degree wouldn't have rewarded me as well." He cocked his head. "And for that matter, if I hadn't left, I wouldn't have met you, either! So there!" As soon as he said the words, he turned scarlet. "Oh, God. Don't even dignify that with a response, I beg you."

Howard shook his head. "Fair enough." He looked at his desk. *And to think of all the misery I'd have been spared!*

"Howard, what do you do in meetings?"

"I beg your pardon?"

"Well, as I was sitting out there waiting, I couldn't help wondering what you discuss. Railroads? South American armies? Whether to buy more gold bullion?"

Howard laughed. "You have a very romantic idea of banking. Although yes, we certainly do make investment decisions about the kinds of things you mentioned."

Colin nodded. "It must be wonderful, having the power to change the world like that."

Howard's tone was amused. "The majority of our financial decisions are much more mundane."

Colin leaned on the desk. "But even then, Howard! You guide people's lives. Bankers build hopes and dreams! They give people carriages and homes. They help start businesses." He became starry eyed. "That's why you became a banker, isn't it?"

"Yes," Howard assented. "Although most people don't understand it quite as well as you do." He teased Colin. "You make my job sound almost as lofty as yours."

Colin's eyes widened. "Oh, but it is! Certainly, everyone needs architects, but I don't wield the kind of influence you do."

"That's not true. Look at the advent of the skyscraper in America. It's going to change architecture forever! You see, Colin, if architects had no influence, we'd all be perfectly happy living in mud huts!"

"Oh Howard!" They both laughed, and Colin noticed the time. "I've stayed far longer than I intended to. I'm sorry to have taken up your time, Howard, but thanks very much." He stood up and shook Howard's hand. "I shall see you later on?"

"Yes, of course."

After Colin left, Howard sat back down in his chair and stared at the tablet they had just worked on together.

* * * *

Several weeks later, Kenneth, Howard, and Henry were at Porter's one evening when Colin finally showed up and flopped upon his seat.

"Well, well!" Howard raised his eyebrows. "You're finally able to grace us with your presence!"

"I know, I'm terribly sorry. It's begun to get crazy." It was already Thursday, and yet it was Colin's first evening at the club.

"Goodness, Colin! How late have you been working?" Kenneth asked.

Colin smiled tiredly. "Until nine o'clock. I've been working on making the model for the house to show Mr. Rademaker. It's coming along swimmingly but what an effort! Because of all the courtyards, I have to—"

"Colin," Henry cut in. "You're not at work now. Just relax."

Colin grinned at Henry and shrugged. "Well, he wanted to know."

"Not in detail, I'm sure."

Colin sat back and exhaled, his eyes sparkling. "Anyway, it's been a hell of a week. I'm glad tomorrow is Friday. I can catch up on the weekend."

Henry frowned. "You're not going to work on the weekend."

Colin stared at him. "I have to! I'm already behind as it is!"

Henry was stern. "Colin, if you agree to work over the weekends, you'll never get a rest. I forbid you to bring work home."

Colin laughed. "Fine. The work has to be done at the office, anyway."

Henry glared at him, and Colin eyed him back. Then he shook his head. "Christ, Henry," he muttered, lighting his cigarette, "let's discuss the damned thing later."

Henry grimaced. "Colin, please. Your language." Colin tensed, nostrils flaring.

"Oh, it's jolly good!" Kenneth jumped in. "We can pretend we're all sailors." He slammed his fist onto the table. "All right, you bloody bastards! Where's the goddamned gold? I'll slit yer fucking necks if you don't tell me!"

Colin's mouth fell open, and then he burst out laughing while Howard chuckled, and Henry tsked him, smiling. Kenneth seemed surprised at his own words. "Well, I say! That was quite fun!"

Colin grinned. "Oh, Kenneth. You're a riot!" He looked down humbly at his drink. "All right, I'm sorry I was so crude just then, but I'm under a lot of pressure." He held up a hand. "Not that I didn't expect to be. Actually, things should quiet down again soon while I wait to hear from the surveyor. I get to go see the land next Tuesday!"

Colin's mood remained buoyant that evening, and it was evident that despite the rough week, he was ecstatic to be working on his very first solo project. But he didn't miss any more nights at Porter's, and Howard wondered if it was Colin's choice or Henry's insistence. Then he had his answer. He discovered Colin was now going to work at seven o'clock in the morning, staying late, and going in on Saturday afternoons when necessary.

They've compromised. Impressive.

But Colin's personality was compromised as well. A new routine took place. Colin would arrive at Porter's an hour after Henry, always straight from work, which meant he hadn't yet eaten even though it was eight o'clock. The excitement of his job had begun to wear thin, as Rademaker was already making daily demands that were difficult to meet and ate into time Colin had set aside for his other projects. At the club, Henry would tell his irritable lover to have a drink to calm his nerves, but Colin would refuse; the first time he drank on an empty stomach he became sick. Because Henry forbade him from discussing work, Colin became distracted sitting amongst them, trying to sort through his dilemmas, every so often catching himself and then bursting into cheerful repartee to make up for his withdrawal. It was all very clear to Howard.

All it would take is for one person to become a sympathetic ear to either of them, and they'd be through.

The only time Colin and Henry really appeared as their old selves was at weekend social gatherings, where they both wanted to leave the pressures of the week behind them. They always dressed magnificently, and they always drank plenty of alcohol. Colin actually looked forward to these occasions, even if they left him with the ever-worse hangovers. The bets Bosie had mentioned hounded him, and he was eager to prove things were still the same. And it was the one evening of the week Colin allowed himself to truly relax and shrug off his professional role.

Then the inevitable happened. It was December, and Colin and Henry were at a holiday party. Colin was in the middle of telling a rather risqué story when he looked up and paled. "Mr. Rademaker!" He hastily stood up and was momentarily relieved to find that his client seemed as inebriated as he was.

"Well I say, Sewell!" Max boomed. "I didn't know you were here! Come on then, I must introduce you to my friends."

Colin nodded. "Yes, of course." He bowed apologetically to the group and gave a frantic glance toward Henry.

The introductions were stiffly received; it was clear Max Rademaker's circle had their own ideas about Mr. Sewell's character. Colin stood miserably, wishing to God he hadn't worn his royal blue suit.

I look like a peacock among peahens, he thought. Mentally he sobered up quickly, though he knew his face was still flushed from drinking.

Max grabbed his wrist. "Look!" he crowed. "Sapphire and diamond cufflinks! You see, I know what I'm doing!" He grinned at Colin. "How much are those worth, Sewell?"

Colin sighed. "Sir, I'm certain that these gentlemen are all perfectly knowledgeable about the gemstone market."

Max nodded. "Three hundred pounds? Five hundred pounds?"

Colin raised an eyebrow at him. "If you must know, they are roughly the equivalent of one of the flagstone patios at the back of your house." The men guffawed, and he looked at them, bemused. "That's how I value all my purchases now, of course: 'Ah, a Rolls Royce Silver Cloud! Thank God for Rademaker's granite flooring.'" More laughter. Colin went on. "'The larger Ming vase, please. I convinced my client he *had* to have a fifth wing.'" The men continued to laugh and one of them said, "So, Sewell, you're saying Rademaker isn't a bear to work for?"

Colin shrugged. "He's a bear, I'm a bull—given the stock market right now I'm coming out ahead quite nicely."

"*Ha ha!*" Rademaker cried, clapping him on the back. "See, what did I tell you? Genius!" Colin was embarrassed; the joke was weak. But the men began to warm up to him and engaged him in conversation.

"Tell us, Sewell," one man said. "Is it true you're not putting a lick of wallpaper in Max's house?"

"It's true," Colin agreed. "Every wall in that house will be white, the only ornamentation being paintings on the wall and drapes on the windows."

"What a heretic!" another exclaimed. "But then, I suppose for you that's a compliment?"

"Not at all," Colin replied. "I would much rather that *everyone* thought the way I did, and then I wouldn't have to work so hard to change things. I wouldn't have to change things at all!"

"Then what's the challenge?" Max refuted.

"Every challenge ends in a goal, Mr. Rademaker. When the goal is reached, it allows one to pursue other matters."

"Such as?"

Colin paused, and then looked on darkly. "I can think of plenty of things that need reformation."

He tried to extricate himself from the group after such a comment, but one of them joined in. "So do tell us, Sewell: how is it that a man of your wealth and good looks has managed to fend off the ladies for so long, so successfully?" The man's voice was teasing but his eyes were accusing. The other men looked on curiously. Colin cocked his head.

"Well, well, Mr. Gardner. Do you know, I believe you're the first *man* to ask me that." His eyes lingered on him provocatively, and then he took on a pensive look. "Yes, it's always been the women who notice, or at least, care to ask. And of course, with women you have to be so cautious with how you word things and such." He looked brightly at the group. "But we're all men here, so I can tell you quite directly!" The men's jaws dropped. Colin savored the moment, and then looked severely at the man who had asked the question. "I'm already married, you see." Now their eyes bulged in dreaded anticipation. He paused again, and then smiled affably. "I'm married to my work." They exhaled with relieved chuckling, Colin joining them, laughing at their reaction. Then he addressed the group. "Well, gentlemen, I should hope Mr. Rademaker will invite all of you to see his house when it's completed." He regarded Mr. Gardner calmly. "It should prove that my marriage is unfailing." The men chuckled again, and Colin excused himself to return to his group.

"Damn, I wish he'd have stayed on a bit," one of the men said. "He's a clever one, Rademaker."

Max nodded. "That he is. I admit he's a bit... er... rakish, but I am telling you," he lowered his voice so that the men leaned in, "he's the best damn architect I've had yet!"

"Hmph!" one man replied. "Take care you're not confusing genius with disingenuous."

"Yes, Rademaker. How can you say that after you've had Morris?"

Max's eyes gleamed. "Morris didn't give me the keys to his own house, good man." He looked in the direction Colin had gone in, and then back at the group.

"Genius."

CHAPTER TWENTY

Spring 1896

Colin's long hours began to take a toll on him in a way he hadn't expected. It first appeared on the day he and Henry were walking down Brooke Avenue. Colin had to meet a glassmaker and invited Henry along. They were searching for the sign that the artisan said he had posted above his shop. "Oh, there it is," Henry pointed out.

"Where?" Colin squinted.

"Straight ahead, see? The yellow sign."

Colin saw a fuzzy patch of yellow with some black markings. "My goodness, you can see that far?"

Henry shrugged. "Of course. Can't you?"

"Not from this far away, no!" But they thought nothing of it until that Saturday when they were attending one of Kenneth's parties. Henry nudged Colin. "Look! It's John Tolhurst!"

Colin looked around. "Where?"

"There! By that hideous Oriental vase."

Colin peered in the direction Henry was looking. "Really? That's him?"

Henry looked at Colin and put a sharp elbow to his side. "God, stop squinting! You look like an old man! Can't you tell it's Tolhurst?"

"Well..."

Henry stared at Colin's furrowed brow and then said quietly, "My God, Collie. I think you've been working so hard that you've been straining your eyes."

Colin glared at him. "Don't be ridiculous! I just..." he glanced at Tolhurst. "I don't think I've ever had as good vision as you."

"Well, how far *can* you see, then?"

Colin shrugged, exasperated. "I don't know, Henry!"

"Hm. I think we should do an informal test at home and find out."

"That's a ridiculous idea. I hope you forget it."

But the next morning, Henry beckoned Colin into his study. He motioned toward a couch. "Now, you sit there, Collie, and I'm going to walk towards you with this card." He produced a large sheet of paper. "You tell me to stop when you can read what it says."

"Henry—"

"No protestations, Colin! Here we go, then..." Henry stood up in the doorway and held it up. Colin studied it. "No squinting!" Henry reprimanded.

"Well, I can't read it, Henry! Nobody can from that far!" Henry began walking toward Colin. When he was two meters from him, Colin scowled. "'I think you need spectacles.' You're a riot, Henry."

Henry went back to his desk and gave Colin a piece of paper. "Now, you write something and do the same to me."

Colin sighed and scribbled something as Henry seated himself. Colin walked over to the door and flipped over the card.

Henry looked up. "'It's not your decision to make.'" Colin tossed off the card in disgust. "Oh, Collie, of course I can't force you to visit the eye doctor, but aren't you worried about your vision getting worse?"

Colin threw his hands up. "Henry, what does it matter if my long-distance vision isn't very good? I'm an architect; I see things close-up."

"So it's perfectly acceptable to you that when you've completed your Helios House, you can see it from only two meters away?"

Colin laughed. "I'll see it fine. It's only small writing I have trouble with."

Henry eyed him. "And faces." He sighed. "Why are you so against the idea of eyeglasses anyway?"

"Because I don't need them, Henry! Now let it rest, please!"

But when Colin arrived at Porter's a week later, he had an announcement for Henry. "You'll be happy to know that I'm making an appointment with the eye doctor tomorrow."

Henry put his drink down. "Really? Whatever changed your mind?"

Colin gave a small cough. "Well, something happened with Rademaker, if you must know. But since I'm forbidden from speaking about work here, I'll just tell you later."

"Very funny," Henry smiled. "Now be a naughty boy and tell us the story."

Colin sighed. "It's too humiliating for words. In short, I mistook Mrs. Rademaker for Mr. Rademaker."

The three men burst out laughing. "You did what?" Henry cried. "Oh Collie! How?"

"Never mind," Colin said briskly. "It was God-awful and I apologized my guts out, as you can imagine, but once I explained to her about my increasingly poor vision she took it as well as one could. Though I'm certain she still did not appreciate having a hired man with degenerating eyesight. So I assured her I'd see the eye doctor at once."

"My goodness, Colin!" Kenneth exclaimed, after he caught his breath. "I wasn't even aware that your eyes were giving you problems!"

"That's because he's learnt to hide it," Henry replied. Then he chuckled. "Until now." The three men laughed again.

Colin made a face. "Well, I still don't think I need eyeglasses. In fact, you should come with me, Henry, because you probably won't believe me otherwise."

Henry patted his arm. "I'll be happy to escort you, darling."

Several days later, Colin was fidgeting inside Dr. Allston's office. Henry was hardly awake; it was only eight o'clock in the morning. But Colin had decided to see the house that day and he would need an early start—it was a one-hour ride each way. "Good morning, Mr. Sewell!" the doctor said brightly. Colin turned to introduce Henry.

"This is my father, Henry Sewell. He's here to bear witness to whatever diagnosis I'm unfortunate enough to receive."

Dr. Allston gave a confident smile. "Mr. Sewell, I'm sure we can help you. Step this way, please." The eye doctor asked a few questions and then had Colin face the eye chart. "Now, Mr. Sewell, you see before you a chart of seven lines of letters. If you would please read each line out loud as far down as you can go, starting with the top letter."

Colin began breezily. "E, C, B, D, L, N... P, T, E, R... F, Z, B, D, E..." He paused.

"You mustn't squint, Mr. Sewell."

Colin straightened. "O, F, L? C, T..." Colin faltered. "S?" Then the seventh line: "A... F? I? O..." He shook his head. "I can't read the rest."

"That's fine," the doctor reassured, as he took notes. Colin looked up at Henry and said anxiously, "Can you see it all?"

Henry looked at the chart. Even the bottom-most line was clear to him. He rested his hand on Colin's shoulder. "Yes."

Dr. Allston produced a pair of spectacles. "Try reading the chart with these, if you will."

Dubious, Colin took them and put them on while looking at the chart. "My word!" He removed them slightly, peering over them, and then pushed them back up his nose. Then he took them off and examined them. "Are these some sort of... what are these?"

Dr. Allston chuckled. "They're spectacles, of course! Can you see better with them on?"

Colin gingerly put them back on his face. He stared at the chart, bewildered. "Yes," he whispered, and then he shook his head and paused before murmuring, "I do need eyeglasses. I don't believe it." He took them off and turned to the doctor. "How could this have happened? Nobody in my family wears spectacles."

"Well, being an architect, you spend more time than most men looking at highly detailed documents. Your eyes were likely weak to begin with, and the added strain of your work may have contributed. Do you often work in low light?"

Colin shrugged. "Sometimes. I have to work late into the evening to finish things."

Dr. Allston nodded. "Well, then, just think: with a pair of spectacles, you needn't worry about such things ever again!"

But Colin looked worried. "I finish the project in a few years. Won't my eyes get better then, if I just give them a rest?"

The doctor gave him a sympathetic smile. "I'm afraid the change is permanent, Mr. Sewell. And if you choose not to wear the spectacles, you'll continue to strain your eyes and your vision may worsen."

"Well," Henry cut in lightly, "aren't we lucky to live in an age where such wondrous things have been invented?"

"Indeed," Dr. Allston nodded. "In the past, people have had to retire from their careers early because they could no longer see what they were doing." He spoke encouragingly to Colin. "Now, if you would be so kind as to put these back on and read the chart again. Then we'll determine exactly how strong of lenses you'll need."

Colin grudgingly put them on. Half of him filled with amazement that these pieces of glass could actually grant him perfect vision. The other half of him filled with dread about the change to his appearance that glasses would bring.

On the ride home, Colin stared out the window. "I can't believe my own career drove me to near blindness," he muttered.

"It's Rademaker who drove you to blindness," Henry retorted. "The man should pay for your spectacles! You didn't have this problem before you began working for him." Colin said nothing. Henry continued. "You're working these long hours, in low light... The doctor even said so! The project is taxing you, Colin."

Colin whirled around. "So what am I supposed to do, Henry? Drop it? Tell Rademaker I quit?" He turned back to the window. "You hate that I'm working this job. Why don't you just say it?"

Henry regarded him evenly. "I hate that you're working this job. I hate what it's done to you, what it's done to us..." he trailed off, deciding to cast his glance out the window as well.

Colin glared at him. "As if everything is my fault! When you've never helped at all—"

"I *told* you I wouldn't help, Colin!" Henry exploded. "You *knew* I wouldn't!"

"Well, it's very hard all the same," Colin replied bitterly. "I'd like to think that if you saw somewhere that you could possibly help out a little bit, you would, for both of our sakes!"

"Oh, I don't believe you!"

"Well, is it too much to ask, Henry?" Colin cried. "I'm drowning in work and you won't even stay an extra hour to help me!"

"*You* decided to get yourself into this," Henry railed. "I never falsely promised a thing!"

"Damn it, it's the principle, Henry!"

Henry set his jaw firmly and refused to say anymore. Colin's tone was desperate, now. "You don't even care what I'm doing anymore! You never ask about it—"

Henry snorted. "I don't have to. Because you're always whining about it! All you do when we come home from Porter's is talk about it. It's always 'I'm really sorry, Henry, I've had a really rough day, blah blah blah.' I don't even *care* if you've had a rough day anymore, Colin! You *always* have a rough day! And for that matter, you never ask after me or my day!"

"Because you do the same damned thing every day yourself!" Colin spat incredulously. "When, in the last ten years, have you ever not gotten up at ten o'clock, worked until five o'clock, gone home for dinner until seven o'clock, visited Porter's until ten o'clock, returned home, and gone to bed at eleven o'clock? What in *hell* am I supposed to ask you about that? And you don't think I wouldn't like that kind of schedule again?"

Henry looked at him hatefully. "No, I don't think you would."

Colin rolled his eyes. "You know something? You're right. I wouldn't. Because I'm an architect, Henry! *That* is my profession! Did you honestly think I'd want to just sit around and entertain you forever? That I wasn't going to actually ever put my talent to use? What were you expecting for Christ's sake?"

Henry had had it. "I certainly wasn't expecting to end up with *this!*" He gestured at Colin. "An obscenity-spewing, aging, overweight workaholic, who bores me to tears, who's become worthless in the bedroom, and who now is going to make fools of us both by wearing his stupid-looking spectacles!"

Colin's expression went from outraged to shocked to devastated. He looked down at his lap and then looked away, trying to say something. "Fair enough," he finally managed to whisper. "I asked."

Henry didn't respond. He knew he should apologize, that he should feel terrible for saying such atrocious things to Colin, but instead, he felt almost exhilarated. *Damn it, it is how I feel!* They said no more to each other. When they arrived back at the office, Colin grabbed a few items, and then he left for the estate.

Henry went to bed before Colin returned home. However, he woke up when he heard the front door shut. He looked at the clock: 2:30! Henry waited to hear Colin enter the room, deciding to feign sleep when he did. Instead, he heard a set of doors close. *The library? Whatever would he be doing in there?* Henry sat up in bed and listened. He heard nothing further. Now he was wide awake with curiosity. *Well, I'll never be able to go back to sleep until I find out.* So Henry crept out of bed and tread silently down to the first floor. He heard the heavy sound of the decanter clinking on the wood table. *He's having a drink. At 2:30 in the morning, he's having a drink!* Henry could picture Colin perfectly, drinking in all his moody angst. He wished Colin hadn't closed the doors to the library. He sidled up to them and tried to listen. Just sounds of a full glass being carried up and back down. *On the offhand chance he's planning to hurt himself...* Henry pulled the doors open slightly. "Collie?" No response. Henry opened the doors fully.

Colin was sitting at his desk, one hand holding a cigarette, the other resting on a glass of gin. His red, watery eyes stared at a framed picture. As Henry drew closer, he saw it was the photograph he had professionally taken of Colin the first month they'd met. In it, Colin was sitting in a chair, a three-quarter cross-legged pose toward the lens and a look of pure innocence on his face. He wore the grey suit Henry had just bought him, down to the gloves, though his hat had been removed. The photographer had remarked on Colin's handsomeness then: his narrow shoulders, his fresh face, his graceful posture, and his perfectly aligned features. Colin had blushed when the man asked to keep a print for himself, to add to his professional album.

When Henry approached Colin's shoulder, he heard a murmur. "I can hardly blame you." Colin gazed at his image, biting his lip. "I have changed."

Henry lay his hand on Colin's back. "Collie, it's late. Come to bed."

Colin shook his head as he stubbed out his cigarette. He stood up shakily, avoiding Henry's eyes. "Sorry about the cigarette. I... I just came to get some things." As he tried to maneuver around the chairs, Henry realized he was drunk.

"Why? Where on earth are you going?"

"Um... out. I'll go to the Sheffield."

"Colin, don't be ridiculous! It's almost three in the morning and you're very tired. Just come to bed."

"No, I can't." Tears began rolling down Colin's cheeks and he fussed for his handkerchief.

Henry sighed. "Collie, if you leave, how are we going to discuss what happened today?"

Colin froze. He stood there, contemplating the question. Then his shoulders sagged. "There's not much to discuss, Henry, unfortunately. You've made everything quite clear."

"Colin, I said those things in anger."

Colin turned to him, anguished. "It doesn't matter how you said them! The fact is, it's how you truly feel!"

"But it's not!" Henry protested.

"Then why would you say it?" Colin cried.

"Because I was angry."

Colin gave a harsh laugh. "Well, I imagine I'd be angry too, if I were living with an aging workaholic who bored me out of my skull, who was a horrible lover, and who was an embarrassment to your reputation. I've become all of those things and you've got every right to be angry, Henry. And I'm sorry. I'm sorry that I've done it."

And now. Now, Henry felt guilty. "Collie... Collie, listen, will you? Do you think you're the only one who's been thinking about this all day? I have something I want to tell you, Collie. I was going to wait until tomorrow but obviously I should tell you now, don't you think?"

Colin looked at him with a mixture of fear and hope. Henry held his breath. "But you must come to bed. Please."

Colin frowned, but he gave in. He followed Henry upstairs into the bedroom. When they were both in bed, Henry beckoned to him. "Come here."

"Henry..." Colin protested.

"Shh..." Henry soothed him, but Colin kept his distance. "Now," Henry began. "Do you know I thought about you all day? Well, I did. And I thought about the things I said to you. And I said to myself, 'Well, Colin's not stupid. He's going to ask me why I've stayed with him if I've felt this way, or if I'm planning on leaving him.'" He heard Colin's rasped breathing. "So then I decided, 'Well then, what if we *weren't* together anymore?' And I imagined what it would be like. I really did! And you do know, Colin, what I came up with?"

Colin shifted uneasily. "What?"

"Well, to start with, I'd be here in bed alone. And I like having you next to me, Collie." He drew Colin to him and this time Colin yielded, with a sigh. "And tomorrow, I'd have no one to breakfast with, or to have tea with. No one to talk to at the table. Then at work, I'd be partner-less. I'd have to tell everyone at the office that you've quit or whatever. And imagine Kenneth and Howard's reaction! They'd be crushed!" He gave Colin a small squeeze. "Although Howard would probably run right out and snatch you up." Colin gave a small laugh. "And everyone would stare at me at Porter's and think, 'Poor old devil. We knew it couldn't last.' Then I'd go home and go to bed knowing it was just me and the clock. And then the weekend would come. I'd be alone at Porter's, having to deal with the money-hungry boys. Now *they* would be tiresome, wouldn't they? And what if I saw you with another man? I thought about it, Collie. I never actually did before." He paused. "And it made me very sad, imagining you enjoying the company of a man other than myself. And, all right, Colin, I'll be honest with you. I didn't expect to end up having the feelings that I did. I believe I've been focusing so much on the negative that I never considered the positive." He kissed Colin's head yet again. "And there's so much positive, Collie. It's true what you said tonight. That you've changed. But I think of how long it has been since that day you met me outside the Redwall Theatre, and how we've been together ever since! There's a shared history between us, Colin. To lose someone who knows everything about you, who is always there as a companion to take walks with, to attend parties with, discuss life with..." Henry sighed. "I'll never have another Colin. I'll never have anyone who loves me like you do. And I love you, Colin."

Colin turned and propped himself on his elbow. "I took this project because I wanted to make you proud, Henry," he said softly.

Henry caressed Colin's cheek. "I know, darling. You are making me proud. And it's only a few more years; that's not so awful, is it?" He leaned over and kissed Colin. "Now, go to sleep. You can think about all these things in your dreams."

"Henry..."

"Colin, to bed."

Colin, exhausted, nodded his assent, and lay back on his pillow, falling promptly to sleep.

The next morning, Henry awoke to the sound of water splashing. He sat up and saw Colin shaving. "Colin, aren't you supposed to be at work by now?"

Colin continued looking in the mirror. "I'm taking the day off," he replied, his expression determined.

"Really?" Henry raised his eyebrows.

"Yes."

Henry propped himself on his pillow to watch Colin, who was dressed only in his pajama bottoms. His hair was already wet-combed and he was half done shaving. Henry admired Colin's slender fingers deftly handling the blade across his jaw and neck, and he gazed at Colin's naked torso. It was true that it had become a little softer, but Henry thought it hardly mattered when he considered what his own body looked like in the mirror. When Colin had finished, he strode out into the bedroom and was startled to see Henry's eyes on him. "The things I miss when I sleep in late," Henry smiled.

Colin glanced downwards and hurriedly threw on his pajama top. "I'll bring your breakfast to you, if you're ready."

Henry looked tenderly upon him, and then shook his head. "No, I'm not ready. Come here." Colin obeyed and perched on the edge of the bed. Henry sat up and put his palm upon Colin's newly smooth cheek, and then leaned in and kissed him. Colin returned the kiss fervently, but the rest of him held back. So Henry put his hands on Colin's shoulders and gently forced him downwards. Colin's eyes betrayed his surprise, and Henry's eyes smiled back. He knew he understood correctly when, afterwards, Colin tearfully kissed his skin in grateful repetition.

They were halfway through breakfast when Colin said quietly, "I'm telling Rademaker tomorrow that I'm off the project."

Henry stopped chewing. "Pardon?" But Colin didn't reply. Henry swallowed and put down his fork. "Collie, don't say that."

"Henry, it isn't worth it. Look at what almost happened to us!"

"But we have reconciled it! You cannot quit the job."

Colin crossed his arms. "It isn't worth it, I say! I'm not going to risk a living person over a nonliving thing."

Henry sighed. "Colin, a dream *is* a living thing. It has lived inside your head for years!"

"The house will still be built, Henry. Rademaker has the plans. He can find someone else to finish it."

"Rademaker will absolutely explode if he finds out you're quitting, Colin! You may see it as just a matter of gracefully bowing out, but your reputation will be ruined! It doesn't matter how good of an architect you are if you're going to abandon your projects when they aren't even half finished, you know that!" He rested his hand on Colin's arm. "Darling, I love that you're willing to make the sacrifice, but I told you, it's only a few more years. We've gone through one year already."

Colin looked at him hopefully. "Do you think you could make it through if I promise not to be so boring?"

Henry shook his head. "Sweetheart, you're not boring. I just want to hear your wonderful voice speak of things other than work sometimes. I think it would be good for you, too, hmm?"

Colin gave a small nod then looked away. "And... I didn't realize you were so... dissatisfied, in the bedroom."

Henry raised his eyes to the ceiling. "I shouldn't have said that. Collie, I only meant that it's so infrequent. Why, you're a superb lover, you know that! Can you blame me for wanting more?"

Colin still looked troubled. "Well, I promise I'll lose weight, Henry. I'm sorry."

"Colin, you're fine. Really you are. I'm sure you can keep your weight down."

Colin winced. "But I still have to wear spectacles."

Henry pointed his fork at Colin. "*That* was merely a mean shot taken at you and I apologize. The glasses don't bother me at all, but I knew they bothered you and I used it against you."

Colin stared at Henry. "That's horribly cruel!"

Henry glanced at him. "I was horribly upset. I'd rather not discuss anymore our exchange from yesterday. Can we think of some happier things?"

Colin smiled. "All right. I was thinking that after breakfast we could visit the museum for the latest exhibits, take a ride through Hyde Park, picnic there, then do some shopping."

Henry's face lit up. "Marvelous! Did you think of all of this just now?"

Colin shrugged. "I actually wanted to do those things *last* spring." He looked at his plate, shamefaced. "But I was always too busy to follow through on them."

Henry patted his leg. "Well, you know the saying: 'Better late than never.'"

"Yes, but better sooner than later," Colin reminded him, and he rose up to get dressed.

Several weeks later, Colin stopped by at Porter's. As he sat down, Henry asked, "Well? Where are they?"

Colin glanced at him, smiling. "In my pocket."

"Well, let us see them!"

Colin opened his breast pocket and withdrew a slim leather case. As he unfolded the gold earpieces, he said ceremoniously, "Ladies and gentlemen, I give you Colin Sewell, the Oxford scholar!" He put them on, and gasped. "Oh, I'd forgotten how everything becomes so clear! I can actually read the labels on the bottles of alcohol behind the bar!" He couldn't stop beaming as he looked around the room, seeing everything in sharp focus. "Even Kenneth and Howard are clearer!" he exclaimed gleefully.

The two men were amazed by Colin's new look. "Oh, Colin! You look so wise!" Kenneth cried.

He looks handsome, Howard thought. But he couldn't say that, so instead he nodded and said, "Yes, very distinguished."

Henry held Colin's hand. "You look supremely handsome, darling."

Colin smiled at the compliments, but in truth, his heart was beating furiously. He had almost skipped going to Porter's. He was thrilled to have perfect vision again, and in truth he wondered if his worsening vision had hindered his work. But he felt bizarre-looking wearing the spectacles. He was acutely aware of them on his face, and he still worried that everyone would find them unbecoming. He considered telling Henry that he had left them at home, that he didn't really need to wear them for social occasions. But he did, and he knew people would have to see him wearing them eventually. So, during the carriage ride from the eye doctor's office, Colin realized that if he pretended to be proud of his glasses and he actually showed them off, others might think they were the most wondrous things on earth. For the plan to work, though, he'd have to appear in them as soon as possible, and that, he admitted to himself, would have to be done at Porter's.

"Oh, they're very wicked, really, Colin!" Kenneth clapped. "They make you appear so innocent, like a good little schoolboy!"

"Who's naughty in the cloakroom?" Colin laughed.

"Now there's a thought," Henry mused.

Howard silently agreed. He imagined Colin in his glasses, standing against a brick wall of a schoolhouse... Then Howard would bring his hands up to Colin's face and gently take the spectacles off, lean in, and... Howard swallowed a long drink of whiskey. "Well, if anyone still has any trouble taking you seriously as an architect, they won't now," he smiled at Colin.

Colin's face lit up. "Really? Do you think so?"

"Yes, you look very mature."

Colin nodded faintly, and said, "Ah." Disappointment flickered in his eyes, and then he shrugged cheerfully. "Well, as long as they think I'm qualified!"

Howard wondered if his comment had somehow insulted Colin. Then it struck him.

He won't look boyish anymore.

And here they all were, using words like "wise," "distinguished," and "mature." Why, Kenneth was currently saying how Colin could easily pass as a banker, like Howard!

Howard rested his chin on his fist. "Yes, but you know, I almost think he looks younger now, actually."

Colin raised his eyebrows. "Younger?"

Howard gave a small shrug. "Well, you have such a young face. The glasses give you a boyish look. Like Kenneth said, a schoolboy." There was no denying Colin's pleased expression. He grinned at Howard. "So I'm 'boyishly mature'?"

Howard chuckled, looking into his glass as he drank. "I suppose that's what you are."

When Colin turned away, Howard realized it was true. That's why he just couldn't shake his interest in Colin. How could any eighteen-year-old compare to Colin, who at twenty-five was still amazingly young to be so successful and confident? 'Boyishly mature'. Perfect. He congratulated himself and relaxed, listening to the banter around the table.

CHAPTER TWENTY-ONE

May of 1899 had arrived, though Colin barely noticed. He hardly partook in the Queen's Diamond Jubilee celebrations in 1897. Oscar Wilde was freed from prison that year as well, but he was politely banned from Porter's, and most of his friends shunned him as well. Colin felt sorry for him, but he never got the chance to express his feelings. Henry insisted that to be seen with the man was to be marked as "Wildean," the phrase of the day for men like Oscar, and now that Colin was in full thrall to the Helios House, he wanted nothing left to chance.

1898 had passed with little excitement. There was the first fatality due to an automobile, and America began and ended their war with Spain. Colin bought the latest Henry James collection to read the widely talked about ghost story, *The Turn of the Screw*, but he had to set it aside. He and the house had been fastened to each other for four years now, and Colin would have even lost track of the seasons if it weren't for the gardens greening before his eyes. He had been told by Max to be at the house for certain on the second Sunday so he could take Mrs. and Miss Rademaker on their latest tour. He had shown the women the grounds twice before, but now that the house was nearing completion, as were the gardens, they were excited to see the newest additions and how the interior was coming along.

Mrs. Rademaker was likeable enough, but her voice when speaking to him held either a trace of disdain because of his youth or a trace of charm, for the same reason. Since Max was always with her, Colin was less liberal with his gallantry than usual, and so he didn't have Mrs. Rademaker quite under his spell. Like all wives of wealthy men, she acted as if she was the one in control of the finances and actually made many of the decisions about the house. However, Colin found her self-confidence more tolerable than if she were mousy. Margaret, the daughter, seemed to be a combination of her parents. Both times she came out to the house, she was extremely inquisitive about everything. As it turned out, Colin discovered that Max had taught her everything he knew about architecture, and Colin guessed that she was probably eager to show off her knowledge to an actual architect. She was very pleasant and smart, and Colin took to her immediately. She wasn't a natural beauty, but she played up what looks she had and, in her finery, looked attractive enough. Colin wondered why she hadn't been married off yet; she must be close to his own age. It was clear old Rademaker doted on her, especially as she was his only child.

Colin stood obediently at the entrance of the house, watching the Rademakers' carriage drive up. He was dressed in a modest navy-blue suit instead of work clothes. His cufflinks were brushed gold, as was his tie bar on his grey tie. He held his matching silk hat in his hands, smiling as they approached.

After the customary greetings, Colin showed them the house. On the second floor he announced, "And here is how Miss Rademaker's room is coming along."

Margaret looked around. "I should like to consult with Mr. Sewell as to the final decoration of the room."

Colin nodded. "Certainly." He looked at Max. "Her help would be greatly appreciated, for when it comes to young women's preferences, I fear that sometimes I'm at a loss."

Margaret put her hands on her hips. "Well, in that case, Mr. Sewell, I shall challenge you to decorate this room by yourself!"

Colin's jaw dropped. "What? I mean, I beg your pardon?"

"Do you think all women want frills and lace, and pink with gold? Do you think you couldn't possibly create a room for a young lady?"

"Margaret..." Max chided lightly.

Colin looked desperately from Mr. and Mrs. Rademaker to Margaret. "I... I meant no offense, Miss Rademaker," he stammered. "Really, I didn't."

"Then tell me how you would decorate it." It was a demand, but Colin caught a teasing look in Margaret's eyes.

Colin exhaled. "Well..." he studied her. "For you..." he looked about the room, "I would use violets and blues." He decided not to add "to tame your fiery spirit." "Silks, velvet. Fresh flowers, always, and the focus of your room would be... that corner. It is where you will do your reading and writing. And I shall put a mirror on the wall so you might see the fire in the fireplace." He smiled. "You seem to be a fire-gazer, Miss Rademaker."

Margaret frowned. "A 'fire-gazer'?"

Colin nodded. "Yes. You know, a thinking person. The fire helps you concentrate. Haven't you ever stared into a fire before? It's mesmerizing." Mrs. Rademaker raised an eyebrow but Max grinned, and so did Margaret.

"I like *your* way of thinking, Mr. Sewell. I like every idea. You see, you *are* capable!"

Colin gave an indignant look. "Well, of course!" Then he blushed and cleared his throat. "Well then, that's settled. Apparently I will surprise and delight Miss Rademaker with a theme of violet, blue, and fire. Moving along..."

When they were not too far into the gardens, Mr. Rademaker stopped short. "Mr. Sewell, you and Margie go on. I want to ask Mrs. Rademaker about the placement of the bowers."

"Are you sure?"

"Yes, yes. Go on. We'll catch up."

"Really, it's no trouble to wait."

But Margaret grabbed his arm. "Oh, come *on*, Mr. Sewell!" She laughed and off they went.

Max stood and watched them. "What do you think of our architect?" he asked his wife.

"Mr. Sewell? He seems very assured. A bright young man."

Max nodded. "Margie seems to be quite fond of him."

Mrs. Rademaker chuckled. "She can be as fond of him as she wants; she's not marrying him."

"Well, why not?" Max demanded. "What's wrong with him?"

Dana Rademaker threw him a look of disbelief. "Max, he's an *architect*, for heaven's sake!"

"An extremely successful one," Max defended. "I've told you that he's the best I've ever seen!"

"That may be, but Margie can do better," Dana argued.

"Oh she can, can she?" Max retorted. "Then pray tell why she's still cavorting around unmarried at age twenty-seven? Because she acts more like a man than a woman!"

"Well, if she didn't insist on challenging each and every suitor to describe his views of a woman's purpose in this world—"

"Exactly!" Max cried. "And I love her for it, I really do! But if we don't find her someone fast, she's going to become old and unattractive, and the only men who will want her will be those who just want her money."

"Darling, they want her money now."

"Yes, but she's still fair to boot. She can still bear children."

Dana sighed. "But an architect? That's practically a trade profession! And he's *American*, Max." She looked suspicious. "And why hasn't *he* married anyone yet?"

Max shrugged. "I'm sure he's been too busy carving out a career for himself."

"But we know nothing of his family! Henry Sewell *adopted* him! Heaven knows what ill repute he may have sprung from to be an... an *orphan*! Oh Max, I simply won't have it!"

Max rolled his eyes. "Dear, we are getting far too ahead of ourselves. I'm only saying that perhaps we should consider this." He became very grave. "More importantly than anything else, excepting our daughter's happiness, I trust Colin. I could, with every ounce of conviction, say that I'd die a peaceful death if he and Margie were to inherit our estate."

Dana stared at her husband, realizing that he must have been spending a great deal of time with the boy indeed. "Well then, perhaps we should invite him to dine with us this evening," she said faintly.

Max smiled and offered his arm as they walked down the path to find the couple. "That's a lovely idea. I want you to ask him."

Max thanked his stars that he never told his wife about his earlier suspicion that Colin Sewell cared only for men. He could see why the boy was tagged with the rumor, what with his fondness for flashy clothing, his scandalous adoption by that rogue Henry Sewell—who was also suspect—and his disinterest in women at parties. But since the first day Colin came into his office, Max realized he and his friends were wrong. Mr. Sewell was just a very ambitious, self-confident young man. He simply threw all his energy into his work; he was married to it, just like he had said. And Max had so been enjoying their partnership. Colin was always ready for conversation; he was polite, easy to talk to, and very professional. It was too hard to believe such a nice, normal young man could be anything deviant. And now he even seemed to like Margie, which made Max proud. Of course, Colin wouldn't just marry any woman—he wanted the best he could find, and wasn't that what Margie was? And so Max had decided there was no reason not to bring the two of them together, and if he could get his wife's approval, everything would fall into place.

"The house is thoroughly stunning so far," Margaret proclaimed as she walked with Colin.

"Thank you," Colin replied, pleased that she had given her approval. "I'm very glad that you like it, since after all, it will someday be yours."

Margaret smiled broadly. "You never know. I may commission you to build a house for me as well!"

"Hm!" Colin chuckled. "I couldn't possibly have that much luck."

Margaret gazed at the ground. "I can't believe you gave us your own house. Do you regret it at all?"

Colin shook his head. "If it weren't for your father, the house may have never been built."

"I know. I was told you intend to stay in the city. But you designed it for yourself, didn't you? So at one time you must have thought you would. Don't you plan to marry someday, and have children?"

Colin was taken aback by her boldness. Really, it was more rudeness, he thought, but he hid his offense. "Perhaps. But for now, I enjoy living on my own, and I've been so busy that there's been no time for anyone other than your father. If only I could court *him*!"

Margaret laughed. "I daresay you already have! He's extremely fond of you, you must know. I think perhaps he sees you as the son he's never had."

Now she was really out of bounds! Colin blushed at the compliment, and Margaret found it amusing. "Look at you! You're red, how darling!"

Colin drew himself up. "Miss Rademaker, my relationship with your father is purely one of business."

Margaret pshawed. "Oh, Mr. Sewell, don't be so silly! You know my father adores you!"

Colin gave her a reproachful look. "Your father is paying me a very handsome sum for this house. With all due respect, Miss Rademaker, I suggest you remain outside of your father's affairs."

Margaret's eyes grew wide, and Colin braced himself for her response: "Who do you think will handle my father's business affairs after he is gone, Mr. Sewell?"

"His attorney."

"My mother."

"All right."

"And when she has passed on?"

Colin sighed. He gave her a disarming smile. "You're going to be a very capable executor, Miss Rademaker."

"You're damn right I am."

Colin's jaw dropped, but Margaret stared ahead of her. "You're so lucky. Of course, you're still a bachelor. Why wouldn't you be? Nobody questions you about it."

"I beg the lady's pardon; you just did yourself moments ago."

"So I did. But everyone accepts your rationale. When a woman my age hasn't married yet, she's a spinster. There's no good reason she can give."

"You're hardly a spinster."

"I'm twenty-seven-years old!"

"Really!"

Margaret set her mouth in a line. "Yes, indeed. But I hate the whole idea of marriage. I despise sewing, cooking, the *art of conversation*, whatever *that* is. The *obedient, doting, loyal housewife*. Pah!" Colin grinned. Margaret glanced at him. "You find that droll?"

"I find it... surprising. Refreshing, even. I find it truthful, and honest." He paused. "But, most women aren't like you, are they?"

Margaret shook her head. "Many of us are. We just have to hide it so."

Colin stopped. He felt cold. Margaret stopped too. "Whatever is the matter, Mr. Sewell?"

"I... I said those exact words years ago. I can't believe you just said them yourself."

Margaret frowned. "But why would *you* say them? I don't understand."

Horrified, Colin shook his head. "I've forgotten. Never mind, it's only a case of déjà vu." Margaret studied him, and Colin peered back at her. "So, women *aren't* satisfied being *domestic doyennes*?"

"Oh, I'm sure many of them are! We've been brought up to believe we should be. It's a sort of repression of the spirit, you see."

"'A repression of the spirit'..."

Margaret nodded. "Yes. And when a woman thinks *inappropriate thoughts*, such as not wanting to marry, then she tends to feel guilt, and she thinks that nobody else must feel that way. So the thought must be wicked, and therefore must be banished."

Colin stared at her. "Is that your very own theory?"

Now Margaret blushed, and she bowed her head. "I have just thought that way for a long time."

"Well, it's positively brilliant!" Colin said, awed.

Margaret regarded him with shock. "Brilliant?" Then she laughed. "You're the only person to have ever even *heard* my theory, Mr. Sewell! None of the others have allowed me to get this far in explaining it."

"*Allowed* you?" Colin frowned. "Then that's the whole problem, isn't it? The matter of *allowance*?"

"What do you mean?" Now Margaret was fascinated.

"Well, it's horrible when people aren't allowed to speak as they wish, to tell what they believe, and who they are, so that they may educate others." He laughed ruefully. "As far as I'm concerned, we're not out of the Dark Ages yet."

"Do you mean in regards to women or society in general?"

"Society in general. Our society has so many manners in it, that it is as if without them we would revert to the basest of creatures. But instead of civilizing us, the formalities are oppressive. It's just as you said, a 'repression of the spirit.'"

Margaret clasped his arm joyfully. "Mr. Sewell! However did you come by this?"

Colin glanced at her, surprised by the emotion, and then cleared his throat. "Umm... I suppose that once again, I'll have to borrow your speech and say that I have 'just felt this way for a long time.'" He could feel

Margaret's eyes burning into him. But then she tossed her head and took her hands off his arm.

"Well, I'm glad to know someone else finds Victorian society so unbearable."

"I hate it." The fierceness of his voice made Margaret look his way again. He was wearing a grim expression, but it made him so handsome, she thought. And there was something thrilling about looking at a man from the side when he was wearing spectacles. As if she saw part of him that nobody else did. As if she were able to see him two ways, with and without adornment. The thought led to a slightly more indecent vision, and Margaret held her hand up to her mouth, mortified. But then a question came into her head. "But, Mr. Sewell, men have everything they want. Why would you—"

"You see? We caught up with you!" Max called out.

"Never mind," Margaret murmured.

When they finished touring the garden and were back at the house, Mrs. Rademaker said, "Mr. Sewell, you've been so kind to take your time for us. We'd be ever so delighted if you would join us for dinner."

"Dinner?" Colin glanced at Margaret, but she seemed just as surprised as he was. He smiled and shook his head. "Oh, no, that's very gracious of you, but I really had better stay here and finish some things."

"Nonsense, Sewell!" Max boomed. "Come with us. You have to eat supper anyway, don't you? I don't want my top man weakened by hunger!"

Margaret laughed. "Mr. Sewell, as you and I both know, it's no use arguing with my father, so you may as well come along!"

Colin gave her a sly look. "Miss Rademaker, I have a feeling you win quite a few arguments with your father. Perhaps I should accept so that I may learn your strategy." Max guffawed, and Margaret tsked Colin, smiling.

"So it's settled, then," Mrs. Rademaker announced. "Mr. Sewell will come with us in the carriage."

Margaret was thrilled. She could hardly believe her parents seemed to be so approving of Mr. Sewell. She wondered if they knew something she didn't. Of course, they'd already been through dozens of men with her, to no avail. So perhaps they were just giving up. Then she felt a pang of guilt. That wasn't fair to Mr. Sewell; he certainly wasn't a last resort. But he had no title of nobility, no known inherited wealth or highly reputable surname. And he was American, something she knew her mother would never permit. She checked herself—for heaven's sake, they were just inviting him to dinner! Her father enjoyed his company, and her mother had never spent any length of time with him. This event was probably more for their enjoyment than hers. *Well,* she decided, *I shall enjoy it too. It doesn't mean I can't use the opportunity to find out more about him for my own purposes.*

The carriage ride took them to Marseilles, a highly regarded establishment that Colin and Henry had eaten at several times.

"The usual for me, Jean," Margaret smiled at the waiter, who nodded and went on with everyone else's orders.

After he left, Colin raised his eyebrows. "'The usual'? Is there some dish here that is so sublime you order it off the menu every time?"

Margaret gave an apologetic shrug. "Oh, I'm a vegetarian."

"What?" Colin gaped. Then he remembered his manners. "That is, do you mean to say you don't eat *any* meat? At all?"

"Weren't you listening, Mr. Sewell?" Margaret teased.

"Margie!" Max scolded her. He seemed quite irritated, so she gave Colin a broad smile.

"Forgive me. No, I don't like the idea of killing animals and eating them." She could imagine her parents' response in their heads: *Must she start in so early and ruin a perfectly good meal?*

But Colin was fascinated. "You eat no beef, fowl, or game?"

"Or fish, if I can help it."

"But... but... how can you possibly still be alive?"

So far, Margaret noticed, his reaction was like everyone else's. "Oh, Mr. Sewell. There are fruits and vegetables, and cheese, butter, breads, eggs..."

Colin narrowed his eyes. "How long have you actually been on this regimen?"

"For five years!" Margaret couldn't help laughing.

Her mother cut in. "The ridiculous girl read a book some time ago about this entire subject, and she got it into her head to live like that herself!" She glared at her daughter. "It's unhealthy, I tell you!"

"It's unnatural," her father muttered.

"But it's quite par for the course, isn't it!" Colin grinned, looking at her. "But tell me, Miss Rademaker, don't you feel guilty, killing plants and eating them?"

She knew he was teasing her but answered him anyway. "Plants cannot feel pain. They have only mechanical reaction." Seeing him impressed, she fired upon him. "Do you hunt, Mr. Sewell?"

Colin was unfazed. "I attend hunting parties, yes."

"As any decent gentleman does," Max defended. "Now that is quite enough, Margie. I shan't have you interrogating our guest during his very first dinner with us."

"Oh, it's an intriguing subject," Colin reassured. "I'd be interested in hearing more, in fact. But your father is right; it's probably not the best of dinner topics. Think of something else." His tone was encouraging instead of patronizing, and Margaret was falling for him easily. He was being so attentive to *her*, whereas usually the men courting her—not that Colin was!—applied to her father instead.

Mrs. Rademaker noticed, too. *He either doesn't care for her at all and is just being friendly, or they are practically made for each other*, she decided. And she liked that he was strong toward, yet respectful of, Margie. Still, he *was* American...

"What do you think of women's suffrage, Mr. Sewell?"

Colin's mouth fell open. He looked at Max. "You don't take your daughter out to dinner very often, do you?" he deadpanned.

Max sighed. "You certainly can't blame me, can you?"

Colin smiled at Margaret, who was laughing. "Come now, Miss Rademaker. You couldn't possibly want to mire yourself in politics."

Margaret leaned forward. "But politics are fascinating! It should be every person's duty to learn more about them! Those people put word into law, Mr. Sewell." She began rattling off names of certain men, women, and organizations, as well as recent decisions made by the government and the effect they had on the public.

When she finished, Colin stared at her. "All right," he murmured. "You know more about Parliament than I do."

"Hmph! Than anyone!" Max snorted.

"Well, Mr. Sewell can't be expected to comprehend British law; he's American," Mrs. Rademaker said magnanimously.

"Yes, that's true," Margaret smiled. "I think America is wonderful! Tell us about it."

The conversation was light for the remainder of the evening. When Colin bade them goodnight, he held Margaret's hand and said, "Miss Rademaker, thank you for a most memorable evening. I look forward to learning more from you!"

At home, Max and Dana Rademaker prepared for bed. It was the first time they were alone since dinner.

"Well, that was certainly an interesting evening, wasn't it?" Max asked, following Dana into her dressing room.

Dana turned to face him. "Max, I have never seen her like that, have you? Halfway through dinner, she looked positively love-struck!"

Max chuckled. "I know. But I couldn't quite tell with Colin."

"Dear, I'm sure that the thought hasn't even entered his mind. After all, you're his boss, and I'm sure he expects us to press Margie into marriage with a man of nobility." Dana lowered her head and smiled. "So, somehow you must hint to him that it's all right for him to court our daughter."

Max looked at his wife in earnest. "You approve of him, then?"

Dana gave a small shrug. "I'm not entirely thrilled with the idea," she admitted. "But I think Mr. Sewell is going to be very successful and respected soon enough, and far be it from me to keep apart two people who are so obviously meant for each other."

Max kissed her gratefully. "One thing I like about Mr. Sewell: he respects a smart woman. And so do I."

Margaret lay in her bed, wide awake.

Should I? Oh, I don't dare! But... it's driving me mad!

Finally, she got out of bed and pulled out her diary. She had filled it with descriptions of her beliefs. It was her way of thinking them through and sharing them without anyone teasing or arguing with her. She also had written of her frustration with the men who had tried to court her, although she never mentioned any names and never went into detail about any particular man.

I'd be just like any other woman.

It was an admonition, but she decided to waive it. Really, she felt as passionate about this subject as the others she wrote pages about. She began by writing the date in trepidation. She gazed at it, and then boldly pushed her pencil across the paper.

18 June, 1898

I met a man tonight. Actually, I'd met him twice before, but tonight he became real to me.

Margaret kept looking back at the word "man," and a small shiver ran through her. The next line was decisively forward.

His name is Colin Sewell.

Again she looked. "*Man.*" "*Colin Sewell.*" "*Colin.*" "*Sewell.*"

She smiled in her embarrassment.

He is an architect for my father. He is wonderful! He has designed the most beautiful house for us. I shan't go into those details now. Suffice to say, he's genius, and he joined us for dinner this evening.

She paused, then continued writing.

I have never met any man so perfect. Yes, perfect! As love-stricken as that sounds. He's twenty-nine years old, tall, dark blond hair, lovely brown eyes...

Lovely? Oh please, Margie!

And he has such a handsome face. His smile... I struggle not to blush when he smiles at me! That is pathetic, isn't it? But he's so attractive! He wears wonderful gold-rimmed spectacles, and he dresses beautifully. And of course, none of this would matter if it weren't for the rest of him: Colin is exactly like me! Well, not to the fullest extent, but he finds me fascinating! He wants to hear me speak. He doesn't mock me or shrug me off, or humor me. He respects me! Respects and, if I have it right, admires *me.*

Margaret went on to describe the walk through the garden.

He called it brilliant! And then later, he said he hated Victorian society! But he's such a gentleman that I'm not sure I understand why. He did say that he believes everyone should be able to be themselves without question, and to speak as they like. It causes me to think that maybe he is hiding something. But perhaps it is just because he is American. Yes, he is American! I could listen to his accent for days. He's so very smart; he really theorizes! Can you believe it? It's so odd! I've never felt this way about a man before, and part of me wonders if it is because of my age, and part of me knows it's because Mr. Sewell is everything I have ever wanted.

Margaret rolled her eyes and gave a small laugh at that last line.

But I don't really know if he's interested in me at all. I couldn't tell, and of course, we were with my parents the entire time, my own father being his boss! I wish I could see him alone. I must see him again! I have to see if these feelings are really true. I'm not sure how to go about it though, since the man is supposed to make the first move. But I think Mr. Sewell wouldn't dream of doing such a thing with his boss's daughter.

Margaret stopped writing and thought awhile.

I have it! I'll bring refreshments to the house tomorrow afternoon on the premise that we were unable to discuss fully our conversation from today. Of course, I will have to tell Mother and Father, but their response will be a sign of what they think about Mr. Sewell. I will write here tomorrow and tell what happens!

She closed her book happily and climbed back into bed to fall asleep.

And Colin? When he came home, he went wearily to bed and fell promptly asleep. The next morning, he wrote a note for Henry.

I'm sorry I left early today. I lost half a day's work yesterday for reasons I'll explain later.

Don't worry Henry—it's a good story! I love you.

Fondly,

Collie

CHAPTER TWENTY-TWO

At around four o'clock the next afternoon, one of the workers interrupted Colin and the stonemason. "Pardon me, Mr. Sewell. Miss Rademaker is here to see you."

"*Miss* Rademaker?"

"Yes, sir. She said she knows you're busy and she apologizes for the short notice, but she has a note from her father."

Colin sighed. "Blast! Is she at the entrance?"

"Yes, sir."

"All right. I'll go see her." He pardoned himself from the mason and made his way to the front of the house. He couldn't help breaking into a grin when he saw her. Margaret was carrying a large picnic basket on one arm and a letter in her hand. She smiled happily when she saw him. Colin hadn't bothered putting on his jacket or hat, so when he came to her in just his white dress shirt and vest, she felt her cheeks begin to flame. But quickly, her expression turned apologetic.

"Mr. Sewell, I know you're extremely busy, but I managed it so my father couldn't possibly refuse you some time off." She handed him the letter, which Colin unfolded and read.

Beware the power of Margaret Rademaker, Colin! Once she finds an ally (as she has in you), she'll stop at nothing to take up further conversation. You may take this letter as a contractual adjustment in which I grant one week added to our previously agreed-upon deadline in exchange for keeping my daughter company this afternoon.

Yours Sincerely,
Max Rademaker
P.S. Good luck.

Colin stared at Margaret. "A week? For one afternoon?"

Margaret rolled her eyes. "Well, of course, he wanted an 'even exchange' of one afternoon added, but I told him nothing less than a week was acceptable."

Colin began to smile and then shook his head in disbelief. Margaret laughed. "Are you impressed?"

Colin stared at her. "I find everything about you to be impressive." He took on a slightly puzzled look. "I think you're the most amazing woman I've ever met, Miss Rademaker."

Margaret was speechless and caught in full blush by his directness. "Oh, for heaven's sake, Mr. Sewell!" She gazed at the ground. "Surely... well, in any case, would you mind very much?" She looked at the house. "I don't know how your schedule works... if you need to do something..." She turned to him excitedly. "I'd love to watch, really!"

Now Colin was temporarily speechless. He couldn't believe this was a *woman* he was talking to. She was so like a man! Although she certainly didn't look like one. She was dressed beautifully, in navy blue and white. Her gloves were also white, and she wore a blue silk scarf around her hat, which was accented with fresh flowers and a white ostrich plume.

He's looking at me! Margaret thought excitedly. And proudly. She'd spent a lot of time this morning choosing her dress.

"Mr. Sewell?"

"I... I was just thinking how the dust would get on your dress if we went inside."

Margaret reverted to her old self. "Oh goodness! It can be washed, Mr. Sewell. But if you're so concerned, we can start out in the garden. What do you think?"

"The amazing woman has an amazing idea!" Colin grinned, and he escorted her to the back of the house. As they settled at a table the workers ate at, Colin joked, "I'm sorry it isn't set properly. I hope it will do."

"It's perfect," Margaret assured, and she began unpacking the basket. "Now," she announced, "since I accomplished a full week's extension for you, I think I should choose the first topic of conversation."

"Oh, most definitely," Colin laughed, surprised at how little he minded being taken away from his work.

Margaret served them both cakes and tea and then sat down across from him. "I've been wondering and wondering why any *man* would dislike Victorian society, since everything is tipped in his favor."

Colin mulled this proposal over, and then sighed. "I suppose I don't like the moral code."

Margaret nearly dropped her cake. "But... but, you're not an immoral person!"

"You're right, I'm not. But I don't think laws should be made that define whether or not an action is moral or immoral, if it is done by the person's choosing and doesn't hurt anyone."

Margaret felt a bit uneasy. Mr. Sewell had seemed so straightforward. Why was he delving into the issue of depravity if it hadn't somehow affected him? She pursed her lips. "So you think that things like adultery and drunkenness should be condoned?"

Colin laughed. "Well, I suppose it would have been to *my* benefit if the temperance movement succeeded." His laughing eyes met Margaret's shocked ones, and he shook his head. "I see I've overplayed my hand." He reached for another cake. "Miss Rademaker, I'm afraid you've given me too much credit." He put his cake down and looked at her pleasantly. "With all due respect, I don't think you know men very well."

Margaret gritted her teeth. She wanted to yell at him, but she kept her voice even. "I most certainly do know men; I've had to get to know more men than I care to admit. And that is why I'm disappointed in you, Mr. Sewell. I thought you were above the foolishness of men."

Colin gave a small shrug. "We are what we are."

"That's not true! You're different from any other man I've met."

"And you're different from any other woman I've met, but you still have qualities about you that are universally feminine."

"And is that considered a strike against me?" Margaret challenged huffily.

"Only in *your* mind, I'm sure," Colin sighed. Then he looked at her intently. "What are you going to do if you don't marry anyone?"

Margaret was taken aback. "I never said I wasn't going to marry."

"You said you hated the idea of marriage!"

So she had. She thought quickly. "I meant that I hate the typical man's view of a woman's role in marriage. If I found a man who would let me freely express myself, then of course I would consider marrying him." Oh, she sounded so obvious! She resorted to blithely sipping her tea as Colin smiled.

"You haven't met *any* men like that?"

Margaret put her teacup down and addressed him directly. "Well, you see, I think I have, only they're so intimidated by my father that they're afraid to side with me." She waved her hand. "And they've all been men with highly regarded reputations, and they probably feel that that they'd suffer ridicule if they married a headstrong wife." She smiled. "I imagine that men aren't like that in America."

Colin shook his head. "No, we do still have a status-conscious society, but it's not as obsessive as it is here, I don't think. The lack of titles makes it easier to rise up in the ranks, class wise."

Margaret rested her chin on her hand. "Do you think you'll go back to America to find a wife?"

Colin snorted. "That's a perfect example of a ridiculous Victorian concept, isn't it? 'Find a wife.' I'm not going to do anything of the sort. If I happen to meet a woman I like, then that's fine. But I'm too busy anyway to be courting a lady now."

Margaret tsked him. "Mr. Sewell, if my father had used that excuse, I never would have been born!"

Colin paused to reflect on her words, and then he grinned at her. "You see? You're very smart, Miss Rademaker! A smart heiress. What could be better than that?" Margaret blushed and then looked down demurely. "And there!" Colin pointed out humorously. "That's a universally feminine response to a compliment!"

Margaret frowned. "Hmph." She looked at him appreciatively. "Well, what would you expect, when it comes from a man as handsome as you?"

Colin's eyes widened, and he looked away self-consciously. "A-ha!" Margaret laughed triumphantly. "You see, it's a universally *human* response, Mr. Sewell! So there!"

Colin looked at her, amused. "Touché. What about universally feminine roles, like charity work?"

Margaret folded her arms. "What do you take me for, some do-gooder?"

Colin laughed, shocked at her brazenness. "Aren't you supposed to be one? Isn't that the thing ladies like you do?"

Margaret made a face. "Would you hold it against me if I told you that I find charities tiresome, even though they *are* what is expected of me?" She smiled. "I'd rather talk about matters of the world. *You're* actually willing to discuss them with me." She batted her eyes at him. "Or so I thought."

Colin tilted his head. "All right, then. How does your vegetarianism fit into the world scheme?"

And so they picked up their conversation and went on to discuss politics, religion, Colin's early interest in architecture, and their mutual love for impressionist art. It was dusk when Colin realized that he was supposed to have shown her his work inside the house. "It's all right," Margaret assured him. "Do you know what I would really like to see? Your office downtown! Do you think that there's any way I could visit?"

Colin thought about it. "I'm not sure it would be appropriate," he said slowly.

"Why not?"

"Because it's full of men!"

"Mr. Sewell, don't be silly! What can they possibly do to me?" She laughed. "Some progressive thinker you are! And if you're escorting me, it doesn't matter at all, does it?"

Colin sighed. "I suppose you're right. Of course you're welcome to visit me, if your father allows it."

"He will. When are you there?"

"In the mornings. Usually between ten o'clock and one o'clock."

Margaret stood up and began to pack her basket. "That's wonderful!" She paused. "Mr. Sewell, you don't... would you think I'm being a pest?"

Colin grinned. "I think the looks on my employees' faces will be worth your visit alone!"

Margaret smiled with relief. "All right. Then I shall come tomorrow!"

Colin accompanied her to her carriage, which had been waiting for her the entire afternoon. He stood at her door, smiling. "I'll see you tomorrow, then! Good evening, Miss Rademaker." He watched her go and then got into his own cab to take him to Porter's. When he arrived at his table, he sat down excitedly.

"What's this 'story' you have to tell us?" Henry asked languidly.

"It's unbelievable!" Colin enthused. "Margaret Rademaker is the most amazing creature!" He told them at length about his walk in the garden with her, the dinner with her parents, and her picnic visit. When he finished, Howard gazed at him.

"I say, Colin. If we didn't know you better, I'd swear you were in love with the girl."

"And it certainly sounds like she's become quite smitten with you," Kenneth agreed.

Colin rolled his eyes and flounced back in his seat. "Don't be ridiculous! My God, she's Rademaker's daughter! They'd have nothing to do with me, thankfully." He paused. "That's why she's such good company, you see. For once I can talk to a woman without her thinking that I'm interested in courting her!" He smirked. "Not that I've met any women worth talking to at length anyway. Until now." He grinned at them. "She's just like a man!"

Henry gave a harsh laugh. "I certainly hope you didn't tell her *that*."

Colin chuckled. "She'd probably think it was a compliment."

"Does she look like a man?" Kenneth asked eagerly.

Colin tsked him. "Of course not, Kenneth. She's pretty enough. Today, she wore this beautiful dress of navy blue silk and white satin, with gloves and a hat to match. She even had fresh irises and a white plume in her hatband! She has brown hair and... and a smart expression on her face. She's quite a thing!"

Howard leaned forward. "Colin, do you know for certain she doesn't find you the least bit attractive?"

Colin shrugged irritably. "I don't know; she might. But she knows she could never marry me, so who cares? In fact, I think that's why she likes to talk to me—*I'm* safe with her as well."

Henry sighed. "Your naïveté is becoming infamous, Collie dear. From what you've told us about this woman, if she wanted to marry you, I daresay her parents couldn't stop her."

"She's an *heiress*, Henry!" Colin replied, exasperated. "She's not going to sacrifice her fortune, for God's sake! What has gotten into all of you?"

Henry clucked his tongue. "Rademaker himself has become quite fond of you, hasn't he?"

Colin threw his hands up. "So *what*? Do you honestly think that Rademaker would want me to *marry* his daughter?"

Henry raised an eyebrow. "Colin, he's not nobility. He's a German industrialist. They're in the same class as us. Margaret can marry whomever she likes. And judging from the situation, I'm only saying that you'd best be prepared should you be confronted by either of them, or the mother, for that matter."

Colin was furious. He glared at the three men. "I can't believe you!" he hissed, angry that his story was going sour. "The whole idea is asinine! Margaret just wants someone to talk to. You weren't there; you can't understand." He turned to Henry. "*You* can see for yourself tomorrow. I invited her to our office for a visit."

"What?" Henry cried. "I won't have it! No Rademaker is going to step foot in my office!"

"It's *our* office, Henry, and she is welcome if I desire it!"

Henry seethed at Colin. "You have become impossible. I wouldn't be surprised if you *were* in love with the girl. It would certainly explain a lot!" He stood up and stalked out, leaving Colin at the table, shocked. It was the first time Henry had ever left Porter's in a huff. Not even Colin himself had ever made such a rude gesture; instead, on such occasions he had forced himself to sit and sulk. Now he looked in panic at Kenneth and Howard.

"What was *that* all about?"

They shrugged, clearly as surprised as Colin. Howard sighed. "As odd as it may sound, Colin, I think perhaps he's jealous."

"Jealous!" Colin was incredulous. "Of *what*?"

Kenneth shook his head. "Well, she's a woman, Colin."

"Precisely! So what is he possibly worried about?"

"Well," Howard hedged, "you spent an awful amount of time talking about her."

"So?"

Kenneth leaned on the table. "Colin, don't you see? He can't compete with a *woman*."

Colin stared at him. "Who's asking him to compete? My God, that's not even possible!"

"Perhaps not in the physical sense," Kenneth agreed gently. "But it is possible that Henry's worried he'll have to compete with her for your time. And your attention."

The words pushed Colin slowly back against the booth. He thumbed the rim of his glass. "Oh. I didn't think of it like that. I thought Henry would be happy that I've made an acquaintance on my own." He stood up tiredly. "Well then, I suppose I'd better go find him."

Fortunately, Henry had decided to go home, and when Colin walked through the parlor, he heard him in the library. He walked into the room. "Henry, I'm sorry. I didn't mean to upset you like that."

Henry was agitated. "My word, Colin. I have never heard you talk like that about *anyone*."

Colin stepped closer to Henry. "Well, why would I? Everyone I knew up until now, I knew through you. I thought you would enjoy hearing about someone you've never met. I thought you'd be proud of me for making my own friend for once."

"*Friend*?" Henry snorted. "You were positively slavering over her."

Colin sighed, then smiled. "Listen to you. All these years you've never once been jealous of any of the boys we were with, and now you're going to be jealous over a girl?"

Henry's voice rose angrily. "She's not just any girl, Colin! She's Rademaker's daughter! Of all the people you had to pick!"

Colin clenched his fists. "I don't give a damn whose daughter she is!"

"I can see that. And it's clear you also don't give a damn that I do!"

"What? Why in hell do you care, Henry? I find it quite hard to believe that you hate Max Rademaker so much that you'd forbid my acquaintance with his daughter!"

Henry leapt to his feet. "Because first, that damn Rademaker robs you of your time with me, then he robs you of your sight, and now his precious daughter is robbing you of your senses! She will rob me of you entirely!"

Colin was confounded. "What are you talking about?"

"Good lord, don't you ever look into the future, Colin? Are you really that stupid to not see? You have before you the opportunity to marry Margaret Rademaker! You alone can marry into one of the richest families in London! She's the sole heiress—you'll inherit the entire estate, including your Helios House! Her parents will treat you like a son, which they don't currently have, and you'll have a family. And you can have children, Colin! And you'll have a wife who adores you and moreover a wife you apparently respect and actually enjoy spending time with!" He threw his arms up and looked at the ceiling. "My God, it can't get any better than that!"

Colin was agape. "You're mad," he whispered. "Henry, I don't want any of those things. If I did, I would have married years ago! You know I don't believe in sham marriages."

"You've never even once considered it!" Henry accused.

Colin was at a loss for words. "Well,... no," he stammered. "Have *you*?"

"What do you think? Of course not! But Colin, it's not what I want. I love the bachelor life."

"As do I!"

Henry laughed. "Do you! Why, you're every bit the devoted housewife, Colin. You frown upon excessive alcohol consumption, you've taken it upon yourself to be responsible for this entire household, you're absolutely faithful to your man, and you're happy as long as I'm happy."

Colin bristled. "First of all, I don't see why those things belong solely in a woman's character. Secondly, I didn't realize they were *negative* things, particularly the last two! And finally," he glared at Henry and his voice rose,

"I hardly think that *housewives* would permit themselves to be fucked anywhere outside of their cunt! I hardly think that *housewives* have ménages à trois and quatre for seven years straight! And I seriously doubt that *housewives* even suck their husbands' cocks, and if they do, I'm sure they don't do it with such... reckless abandon!"

Henry crossed his arms in disgust. "Well they certainly hold their language better, that's for certain!"

Colin furiously turned on his heel. "Oh! You're incorrigible!" He went to pour himself a drink.

Henry, impressed with Colin's defense, followed him. "Anyway Collie, you've lost your own family."

"I didn't lose them," Colin replied brusquely, liberally pouring the gin. "I know exactly where they are."

"Well, they've lost you, then. Now you're nobody's son. There are no parents for Colin Sewell. And I'm only saying that I think you'd enjoy being someone's son again."

Colin swallowed his drink and turned around. "Max Rademaker, a father figure? Oh, you are too much, Henry! One minute I'm too old for throwing tantrums; the next minute I'm young enough to qualify for parental guidance!" Colin's face was flushed with anger. "Apparently you've forgotten," he sneered, "*you're* my father now, remember? You know, Henry *Sewell*, Colin *Sewell*. Oh my, yes, what a coincidence! However did that happen?" With that he turned once more and poured himself another drink.

Henry advanced toward him. "All right, Colin, that's enough. Come to bed."

"I'll come to bed when I'm ready!"

Henry put a hand on Colin's tense shoulders. "No, you must come to bed now, because I can't help but adore you when you're like this." Colin turned and Henry looked into Colin's eyes with sensual urgency.

Colin glared back, and then leaned in and gave Henry a fierce, hard kiss. He pulled back and eyed Henry as he drained his glass. "I suppose this isn't very wifely behavior either," he scoffed.

"It's petulant behavior," Henry enthused. "And I want it. Come."

In the next hour, Colin was so forceful in giving Henry what he wanted that it never occurred to Colin that it was the opposite of what he wanted. He would have preferred being taken into Henry's arms and held lovingly, affectionately. Reassuringly. But Henry had been right about Colin's character. That night, Colin saw to it that Henry was very happy indeed.

Colin had his own victory the next morning: Margaret was at the front door of Sewell & Sewell. Colin greeted her warmly. "You look magnificent," he said approvingly. Although he was now conscious of the idea of Margaret being attracted to him, there was no way he could avoid commenting on her appearance, because she looked stunning.

She wore a deep violet dress with lavender touches, grey gloves, and a grey felt hat with purple velvet draped around it. She curtsied to him. "Why thank you, sir." Colin laughed. He introduced her to his staff, who were surprised into speechlessness. They didn't know which was more shocking: that a good-looking woman, who happened to be Max Rademaker's daughter, was in their midst, or that she was here to see Mr. Sewell. Colin began to feel awkward. He could already imagine the rumors amongst the men.

"Miss Rademaker and Mr. Sewell?"

"But he's American!"

"A *rich* American!"

"But I thought..."

"Lookit the two of 'em!"

"They're in love!"

"That sly devil."

"Always thought he was waiting for the right bird to come along."

"But... think her old man knows?"

Actually, Colin found that it was rather fun showing Margaret off to his employees. He escorted her to each drafting table and explained what was happening at each. The men had yet another surprise in the architectural knowledge Miss Rademaker possessed.

Finally, it was time to show her his own office and to present her to Henry. Colin pretended casualness as he opened the door with a sweep of his arm.

Henry stood up from his desk, smiled, and came forth. He reveled in Margaret's gasp. "Mr. Sewell!"

"Yes, I know, Miss Rademaker. I promise not to spoil you with a single touch. Colin insisted that I meet you—he's spoken very highly of you, you know."

Margaret tsked and held out her hand. "You will greet me properly and I shall tell my father you did so. If Mr. Sewell has spoken of me half as highly as he has you, I should be flattered indeed."

Henry was taken aback. Colin had mentioned him to her? He glanced at Colin who gave him an affectionate smile. "Is that so? Well then, by all means..." Henry held her hand, "it's a pleasure to meet you."

"As it is you," Margaret curtsied. "Mr. Sewell just goes *on* about you. And of course, my father greatly admires your work, even if he'll never admit it outright."

Henry grinned. All right. So Margaret Rademaker *was* endearing. "Well, that's extremely kind. I know your father is very conversant in the world of architecture. It's a pity there aren't more such knowledgeable men... or women! I hear you know quite a bit yourself, Miss Rademaker."

Margaret shrugged. "When you're an only child, you're the sole beneficiary of your parents' knowledge, whether you like it or not. Fortunately, I find architecture fascinating."

"Well then, I'll let Mr. Sewell finish his tour. I do hope you won't mind if I remain in the room."

"Not at all! I'm so glad I was able to meet you!"

He's very handsome, Margaret thought. *I never thought an older man could look so attractive. He and Mr. Sewell truly are a perfect father-son pair!* She laughed in her head and made a mental note to record her observation in her diary that evening.

Colin showed her around the room while Henry surreptitiously observed them. The couple constantly had their heads bent together, smiling all the while, with such wonderful banter. He saw Colin show a particular object and Margaret said, "Oh Mr. Sewell! It's just as you described! It is funny, isn't it, when we were talking in the garden about it…" Every so often they would both laugh about something, and by the time they got halfway around the room, Henry felt oddly depressed. When Margaret was even able to guess correctly that the art tile on his own desk was by William De Morgan (a gift from Colin), he stood up and took Margaret's hand. "Miss Rademaker, I have an appointment, so I must take your leave. Your lovely presence will permanently alter the mood of this room."

Margaret blushed, ecstatic that Henry Sewell made such a comment about her. Henry gave a curt nod to Colin, who looked puzzled as he watched Henry leave.

It was close enough to lunchtime that Henry could properly sit at Ellison's and drink for a while as he thought.

I don't know whom I feel more sorry for: Colin or Margaret. Colin, she's perfect for you. If you were a regular fellow, you'd have such an idyllic life. I can just picture both of you, with two beautiful children. You work so hard, Colin; she'd make you so happy. But Margaret, she'll be the one with the broken heart. For she sees everything that I do, and she believes it can happen. No, that it will *happen. Colin will be her dashing, ambitious husband who proudly supports her activities and beliefs. He'll treat her as an equal and be strong enough to give her what she wants, even in the bedroom.*

And while Henry didn't really believe that Colin was in denial about his sexual identity, he did worry that Colin had all along purposely refused to consider the benefits of a sham marriage. And then it finally struck him: *Why aren't I still considering how I'd feel if Colin did leave me for Margaret? Why, if I care for him so much, would I want this sort of thing to happen to him?* Frightened, Henry tried to fill his head with a million thoughts to thwart the answer from presenting itself. But it was no use.

Because perhaps I can live without him.

Henry stared at his drink. He would end up staying at Ellison's the rest of the afternoon.

Margaret left shortly after Henry, and not long after, Colin left to work on the Helios House for the rest of the day. He was in high spirits. It was clear that Henry was impressed with Margaret, though Colin still didn't understand Henry's abrupt exit. But since he never knew Henry's schedule anymore, it was possible the man really did have a meeting. Colin arrived at the house and cheerfully went to work. An hour later, a carriage drove up, and Max Rademaker jumped out. He appeared to be in high spirits himself, and he went about looking for Colin. "There you are!" he boomed.

Colin jumped, and then turned and laughed. "Two out of three, today! Is your wife coming up later, by any chance?"

Max smiled. "No, no. Actually, I'm only here briefly, to speak with you if you have a moment."

Colin resisted a sigh. This would be the thirtieth change in plans. "Of course," he said graciously.

"Good. Let us take a walk in the garden," Max suggested, and turned to lead the way outside.

Colin frowned. A walk in the garden? It was threatening to rain. And they always discussed things on the spot. Still, he thought little of it, and he went to fetch his coat and gloves.

CHAPTER TWENTY-THREE

At seven o'clock, Howard, Kenneth, and Henry were in Porter's when they looked up to see an absolutely miserable Colin slouch into his seat, smelling of damp. Sliding out his cigarette case, he muttered, "Congratulations, old fellow." He snuck a look at Henry. "You were right."

"You mean...?" Henry asked.

Colin shut his eyes and leaned his forehead on his hand. "Yes," he moaned. "God, I can't believe it!"

Howard's eyes widened. "You mean Margaret *does* want you to court her?"

Colin jerked his head up. "Her *father* asked me to *marry* her, Howard!" He turned to Kenneth. *"Marry* her!" Now he looked sadly at Henry. "I don't understand..." But Henry sat still, lips pressed tightly together. "Oh, God, I need a drink," Colin whispered.

Howard turned and beckoned a waiter. "Double gin, neat, please." He turned back and noticed that Colin was shaking. But stranger that that—Henry still hadn't said a word. He just sat there. *For God's sakes, Henry! Reassure him or... whatever!* Kenneth decided to fill in.

"Oh, Colin! That's positively outrageous! How could the man put you in a position like that? How did it happen?"

Colin shook his head and then smiled weakly at Kenneth. "First I'm going to have a drink. Three, if you please. And then I'm going to tell you."

The liquor was set before him and Howard ordered two more. After several large swallows of the first, Colin decided to begin the story.

"Rademaker started the conversation in the garden..."

"I want to thank you for taking so much time with my daughter, lately," Max said. "You've been a very good sport."

Colin shrugged. "Being a good sport has nothing to do with it. She's wonderful company."

Max nodded. "She finds you the same. Mrs. Rademaker and I just find it remarkable how well you two get on."

Colin turned his head. "Mr. Rademaker, it's amazing! She is a *real* woman! The kind all women should really be like!"

Max grinned. "So you do find her agreeable?"

Colin gave a laugh. "Well, absolutely! I think very highly of Miss Rademaker."

"Wonderful! You know, I do think very highly of you, Colin."

"Thank you, sir."

"And I couldn't help noticing..." he peered at Colin. "Do you—and I understand that this may appear improper to ask, considering we are architect and client—but... do you have... well... any *intentions* towards my daughter?" Colin stopped and stood facing Max in disbelief. Max sighed, admonishing himself. "I didn't mean for it to sound like that."

"Mr. Rademaker, I..."

"No, no, Colin, please! Listen." He paused and took a breath. "I have everything in life I could ever want, don't I?"

"Yes!"

"No! My daughter, my only child, is not yet married. I have two last wishes in life, Colin: one is for my daughter to have a husband, and the other is for me to have heirs." He smiled. "I'm completely powerless to make either of those things happen, for as you know, I've certainly tried."

He looked at Colin in earnest. "Margie is fond of you, Colin. She likes you more than any man she's ever met. I know this because she confessed it this morning after she returned from visiting you." Colin's jaw dropped, but Max went on, smiling. "Frankly, I have to agree with her, and that is why Mrs. Rademaker and I would like to encourage a courtship between you two," his smile became broader, "with the natural progression leading to marriage, of course."

Then Colin felt his body sway and fall to the side.

"You *fainted*?" Kenneth cried.

Colin glanced at him, humiliated. "Well, it wasn't so much fainting as my legs just... they gave way."

"Oh, God," Howard murmured. Henry stared at his drink, still silent.

"Rademaker *caught* me," Colin moaned softly. "He just laughed."

"Steady there, good man!"

"But, Mr. Rademaker..."

Max waited, but Colin just stood there helplessly. Max patted his arm and let go. "Colin, I know. That's why I wanted to talk to you and assure you that I know full well what you might wonder." He paused, and then leaned in conspiratorially. "The way things are going, I couldn't care less if you were a pirate on the Barbary Coast! She's in love with you, Colin. She's yours."

From somewhere came a strangled whisper. "But I can't marry her."

Max jerked back. "What? Why not?"

Colin slowly raised his gaze to meet Max's. "Mr. Rademaker, I've contracted consumption."

Max was horrified. "Consumption! For how long?"

Colin swallowed. "It's been three months. The doctor said I must have had it for years. My brother died of it back in America."

"But I haven't seen you cough once."

"I've been taking laudanum," Colin said guiltily. "I didn't want you to know. Nobody knows, Mr. Rademaker! Not even Mr. Sewell, and you mustn't tell him."

"But how are you sure that it's... terminal?"

Colin said nothing for a moment, and when he spoke, his voice was barely audible. "I've been coughing up blood. The doctor is only giving me laudanum because I have insisted on finishing this project." His own eyes widened at hearing it. Then he lent a desperate tone to his voice. "I'm so sorry I've given Miss Rademaker the wrong impression, sir! You see, I knew I wouldn't stand a chance with her, so I figured it wouldn't matter if I enjoyed her company." He raised his arms helplessly. "I never would have expected this, Mr. Rademaker. Honestly, I wouldn't." As he looked at Max, raindrops began to fall between them.

Max shook his head. "Good God, I had no idea." He peered at Colin. "My boy, if you don't mind my asking, how much longer do you have?"

Colin's voice was shaking. "I'm... I'm going to finish the house." It was all he could say. Max studied Colin's troubled expression. The boy looked absolutely devastated. He couldn't possibly be fabricating such a thing. Then Colin murmured, "Please give your daughter my most sincere apologies. I've never been so flattered in all my life, between you and she."

Max just looked at him dazedly. "Well, this is certainly an unexpected disclosure, Mr. Sewell! Please accept my sympathies."

Colin nodded, shivering. "Thank you. In... in my opinion, your daughter really deserves much better anyway." He felt as if he would be sick. "If you'll excuse me, sir, I think I'd best go home..."

"Of course," Max agreed, noticing the young man's sudden pallor in the drizzle. As he walked back to the house, Max didn't know whom to feel sorry for most: Colin, Margaret, or himself.

Now Colin sat slumped in his chair, having finished the story. Kenneth stared at him. "But... but, none of that is *true*, Colin, is it?"

Colin glanced at him. "Of course not. But it was the only thing I could think of!"

"But what are you going to do when a year goes by and Rademaker sees you're still as healthy as a horse?" Howard asked.

Colin shook his head miserably. "I suppose I could commit suicide."

"Oh, Colin!" Kenneth exclaimed. "It will turn out all right. I think it's a brilliant story! Oh, it's straight out of the theatre!"

Colin regarded him piteously. "But I lied to him, Kenneth! I lied eye to eye, a terrible lie! The man thinks I'm going to die! And so will Margaret!"

Howard spoke gently. "If people will persecute you for telling the truth, I see no reason for you to give it to them, Colin."

Colin turned to face him, distraught. "But it's all the same sin, isn't it? I've lost them, either way. Three good, honest people." He looked at himself in the mirror behind the bar. "Because of this."

Colin and Henry didn't speak at all in the carriage. Instead they stared at the rain streaming down the windows. They arrived back home and exited the cab. Finally, Henry spoke wearily. "Colin, you don't have to lose them."

Colin, ahead of Henry on the rain-slicked steps, turned his head. "What do you mean?"

"You're in love with the whole lot. Doesn't that mean anything to you?"

Colin whirled to face him. "Damn it, Henry!" he shouted. "Will you shut up about that stupid theory of yours?"

"It's not a theory, Colin!"

"It is!"

"I only want you to be happy."

"Bullshit! I *am* happy! I'm happy with you! That's why I did what I did today. I think you're the one who's not happy. You're the mopey one!"

Henry glanced about them. "Colin, keep quiet!"

But Colin was furious. "We've gone through this already, Henry, haven't we? I won't take on another project like this again; I've told you."

"That's not it!"

"Then what is it?" Colin narrowed his eyes toward Henry. "Wait a moment. Do you want me to marry Margaret so you can be done with *me*? Is that it?"

"Colin, shut it!" Henry hissed, hurrying past him on the stairs.

"Then tell me, damn it!"

Henry spun around in a rage. "Fine, then! Yes, Colin! We are done! Go back to Margaret!" But as he turned from Colin's shocked expression, he slipped and lost his footing. Colin tried to catch him, but he slipped as well and grabbed the railing as Henry tumbled to the bottom.

Colin stared in horror as Henry writhed on the ground. He raced down the steps and kneeled at Henry's side. "Oh my God! Henry, are you all right?"

Henry grimaced. "No, no... my leg!"

"Oh my God! I'll get help! Don't move!" Colin threw off his coat to cover Henry and ran inside. "Charlie! You must get Dr. Langtry! Henry fell on the steps and I think he broke his leg!"

"Oh no! I'll fetch him straight away!"

"Wait! Help me get him inside!"

"Should we move him, sir?"

"It's pouring out there! We can't keep him outside. We'll have to chance it."

"Right. Let's take him in." They carefully helped him inside and lay him on the floor. Then Charlie sped off to fetch the doctor.

Colin sat with Henry, stroking his arm. "You're going to be all right," he soothed. "Charlie's gone for Dr. Langtry." Henry broke into a sweat, gasping in pain. "I'll get some damp cloths," Colin said quickly and went to fetch some, along with a pillow and blanket. He sat with Henry until the doctor arrived, and then he leapt to his feet. He explained what had happened, leaving out the detail of the argument, and the doctor began setting Henry's leg. Later, when Henry was in bed and drowsy with morphine, the doctor told Colin, "Bed confinement will be three weeks."

"Three weeks!" Colin exclaimed, wringing his hands.

"Yes. He'll also need a nurse to help him during that time."

"Yes, all right; we'll take care of it," Colin agreed. A few minutes later, the doctor left and Colin walked back to the bed. As he sat watching Henry, he thought about their exchange outside. He remained sitting there for another twenty minutes. Finally he managed to rise from the bed and walk down to the dining room for supper.

Colin closed the office for the next two days as he cared for Henry and arranged for a nurse to come stay with him. He took notes of Henry's business affairs so he could manage them in Henry's absence. Neither of them spoke about the argument that had led to the incident. When Colin did go back to work, he returned for lunch each day and then went back out until five o'clock, whereupon he took over as the nurse for the rest of the evening. He even had his desk moved into the bedroom so he could be close at hand. He had insisted sleeping on the floor so that Henry could have the bed to himself without any risk of upset to his leg. On one of these nights, Colin, who was still dressed in his work clothes and had hardly touched the dinner brought to him, had fallen asleep on the carpet while reading up on downspouts, while Henry gazed at his exhausted companion.

I'm a monster. Oh Collie, how could you do this to us?

The next morning, Colin was going through his mail at the office when he came across a personal letter.

It was from Margaret. Colin sighed, opening it.

Dear Mr. Sewell,

My father told me several days ago about his meeting with you, and I forced myself to let some time pass before I wrote this letter.

I can scarcely believe the news. Mr. Sewell, if there is really another reason, I beg you to tell me. I can handle it—you know how strong I am.

Anything you tell me will be preferable to the thought of your life being cut short! I lay awake each night picturing you in coughing fits. Why didn't you tell me? I can't help thinking there is something you're hiding, and I can perfectly understand why you would keep it from my father. But you must tell me. Through my father, I have laid bare my feelings for you. I ask in all fairness that you do the same for me.

Yours Very Truly,
Miss Margaret Rademaker

Dear Miss Rademaker,
I regret to inform you that I do indeed have consumption.
I also regret to admit that I grew very fond of you.
I am very sorry.

Yours Ever in Truth,
Colin Sewell

The following morning, Henry called out to Colin, "Have you heard from Margaret at all?"

Colin entered the bedroom, looking down at his shirt as he buttoned it. "Yes, she wrote a letter."

"She did? When?"

"Yesterday."

"Yesterday! Why didn't you tell me?"

Colin looked up at Henry. "Because I don't want to talk about it."

"Then we had better talk about it."

"After work, Henry. I'm running late." He turned and walked out of the room.

"Colin..."

"You're done with me Henry, I know," he heard Colin's voice sail from the hall. "I'll take care of you and then I'll leave."

"I'm not done with you! Come back here!"

But instead he heard Colin's steps on the floorboards in the parlor, and then he heard a laugh. "Work on your speech, Henry." The door opened, then shut. Colin was gone. In the cab, Colin crossed his arms, a triumphant smile on his face. *He's not done with me. I knew it!*

When he came home that evening, he walked into the bedroom, began loosening his tie, and stated, "Fine, you're not done with me. I don't want a speech, Henry. I'm done with Margaret, and let's just move on. I can't stand the thought of another *discussion*." He walked into the dressing room, and Henry lifted his eyebrows.

"All right," he murmured. He was too tired to say much anyway, and he admired Colin's assertiveness. For the next few days, Colin was brisk with him and purposely ignored him for anything beyond necessity. It worked. Henry found himself pleading every night with Colin to keep him company, and by the fourth evening, Colin assented.

"Fine, I'll keep you company," he smirked. Straddling Henry upon the bed, he leaned over and began to aggressively work his way down Henry's body with his mouth. The only sign of tenderness was his minding Henry's leg. Afterwards, he left Henry without a word and retired to the library for the remainder of the evening. He left early the next morning, before Henry awoke. It wasn't really a game; Colin was truly angry with Henry for thinking of leaving him. Henry understood, and respected him for it, although he didn't like being ignored. But even Colin couldn't stay upset for long. The next evening, he came home exhausted and went straight to the bed, laying down next to Henry, closing his eyes, and resting his head near Henry's shoulder. Henry stroked his hair. "Oh, Collie. Stop working so hard."

"I can't," Colin sighed, his voice muffled by the pillow.

"Mm, you can. Why don't you go to Porter's?"

"Henry, I haven't any time."

"Colin, you must get out of the house. Please go to Porter's, for my sake! And bring me back some lovely stories."

"We'll see," Colin said drowsily. Henry kissed his head and watched him fall asleep.

As a form of truce, Colin returned to Porter's, and for the first time, Kenneth and Howard had him to themselves. Before he knew it, Colin was speaking to the two at length about his work, and since Henry had always forbidden the topic, Kenneth and Howard were fascinated to hear how much work Colin was actually doing.

"Henry must be very proud," Kenneth commented.

Colin just shrugged. "At least I haven't made any mistakes yet." Eventually, Kenneth and Howard delved deeper into Colin's personal life and were delighted to find he was a willing confidant. He began to tell stories about his earlier years: "Once, my father gave me a thrashing when he found me wearing Mama's paste bracelet! You can imagine his reaction as I sat in the window seat in my room, turning my wrist this way and that, mesmerized by the sunlight setting off all of those rays. Imagine—a cuff diamond bracelet on a *boy*!" And another: "My first real crush was on this particular dark-haired boy in my primary school. He had such bright eyes, such eyelashes. Anyway, we were on a class trip, and he had this gigantic, gloriously ripe peach for lunch. We were sitting under a tree, and halfway through eating his peach, he had its juice all over his face. He tried to suck on the fruit but the juice would always trickle down his arm, and then he'd suckle it from his arm. The teacher reprimanded him for his poor manners but he just laughed. He said to me, his red mouth all full of peach, 'She's full of envy, ain't she though?' About him having such an exotic fruit as a peach, of course. And I remember just staring at his red, red mouth, thinking, '*I'm* the envious one. Yes, I am.'" Colin's gaze drifted. "He was as exotic as the peach. The fruit of Eden himself." Then Colin grinned at his friends. "The apple that did me in." Suddenly, his face went dark, and he glanced downwards. "Sorry. I know Henry hates to hear anything about the past." Then he tossed his head and said, "So, really. Stop me if you prefer."

"Oh, we wouldn't think of it!" Kenneth cried. "Another! Please, tell us another one, Colin!"

And Howard, who had never known such intimacies about anyone in his entire life, could only feel closer to Colin with every revelation. But he had been wondering something for a long time, and now he seized the moment. "Yes, Colin! You've never told us about your family. What are your parents like?"

Colin paused, surprised at Howard's request. "Oh. Well, it's actually quite a story!" Then he looked angry. "Henry would never let me tell it, so I'm glad you asked, Howard!"

"We won't tell him," Kenneth winked.

Colin laughed, and then started. "My mother is American; I take after her in looks. Her family came over from England to do trading business in the port of Boston, before the American Revolution. Her great grandfather began a very successful textile business that continues to this day. Mama traveled extensively, and she met my father during a visit to Italy. She was touring Saint Peter's Basilica, and he was the one giving the tour. My mother originally fell for his looks and wit, but she actually became quite smitten with the Catholic religion as well, much to the chagrin of her parents."

"So your father isn't Irish?" Howard asked, perplexed.

Colin laughed again. "No he is. But he had long wanted to see the amazing churches of Rome, and when he visited there, he ended up staying, working for the Catholic church. My mother extended her stay in Italy while my father courted her, and my mother eventually converted to Catholicism! This was all against her parents' wishes, of course. But my father came from a wealthy family too—his was a line of landowners in Ireland. And so finally the compromise was that the two lovers could marry, but they would have to live in America." Colin smiled. "They did so; my father found a high-ranking administrative position for the Catholic Church in America, and the rest is history."

"Small wonder you wanted to visit Italy when you first met Henry!" Howard smiled. "The place your parents met and fell in love!"

Colin grinned. "Yes! It was amazing to walk around there for that reason. I didn't tell you when we went because, as I said, Henry doesn't like me talking about my past."

"But my goodness, Colin!" Kenneth exclaimed. "That is simply a tale of tales! And surely you've noticed the parallel between your mother and you!"

Colin's forehead creased. "In what way?"

"Well!" Kenneth practically squealed. "She had to fight her family's resistance towards something she felt was simply natural to her: loving your father. She fought against the odds to find her own happiness, just as you have had to come to terms with your own identity. Oh, it's a *wonderful* parallel! It's just perfect for a play!" He began to ponder the very thing, while Colin stared at Howard, who also looked surprised.

"Well, I never thought of it that way," Colin murmured. And then he became pensive, leaving Howard to grasp at straws as to how to bring his friends back.

"So then, Colin, have you ever kissed a woman?"

It worked. Colin broke from his reverie with a gasp. "What?"

"Have you?"

Colin frowned. "What a question to ask, Howard! Of course not! Why on earth would I?"

Now Kenneth raised his head. "You mean to say you've never kissed any girl? Not even a chaste schoolgirl kiss?"

Colin made a face. "God, no. Although they'd chase me and kiss me on the cheek." He shook his head. "No, I was seen as rather aloof early on. In fact, by secondary school I became known as sort of a snob, since it appeared I didn't think any girl was good enough for me." He frowned slightly. "If they only knew. It was funny, really, because I *was* drawn to the prettiest girls and their beautiful dress, but I couldn't care less about their personal affairs. It was easier when I was in college, since it was all men anyway and I could pretend I was too busy becoming a *serious architect* to care about ladies." Then he frowned a bit more. "I wonder what my parents thought. I suppose they weren't very concerned at that point." He looked up at Kenneth and Howard. "But I'm the only boy in my family, you see. And worse than that—I actually had *two* brothers, but they both died at a young age." Colin paused. "Patrick was my older brother. He drowned in a friend's pond when he was twelve. I was seven at the time and very fond of him. After I was born my two sisters came along, and then the youngest, our little brother Laurie. My mother nearly died giving birth to him so the doctor said she couldn't have any more children." Colin's voice grew soft. "Laurie died of TB when he was barely a year old."

"Colin, we're so sorry," Kenneth put his hand on Colin's arm.

"Does Henry not know any of this?" Howard asked, incredulous.

Colin looked up sharply. "God, no! He'd find it too depressing and then he'd be upset." He shook his head. "I shouldn't have even told you; I'm sorry." Then he shrugged. "But you see what a cruel joke it's been to my parents, that the only son who survived ended up being like this." He gave a rueful look around him, and then fell into a silent melancholy.

His words escaping before he could stop, Howard spoke up. "What, handsome? Talented? Successful? Wealthy beyond imagination?"

Colin jerked his head up and then blushed. "Oh, Howard. They just wanted... a real son."

Kenneth patted Colin's arm. "Why Colin, you are as real as they come. And, well, *I* think it makes the argument only stronger, doesn't it? That you obviously can't help being like this?"

Howard felt guilty for being the cause of this depressing conversation. He picked up his drink. "Hear hear! And to cheer you up, I shall tell you about one of *my* occasions kissing a girl."

Colin smiled gratefully. "Oh, I should love to hear *that*!"

"I was twenty-five years old..." Howard began, leaning back in his chair. Kenneth knew the story himself, so he nodded along. "I had just been hired at The Bank of England, and a few of my co-workers invited me out for the evening. Of course, being the new fellow, I had to accept." He paused for effect. "We ended up at a brothel. But I decided it would be the perfect opportunity to establish an identity with the men." He chuckled seeing Colin go slack-jawed. "So I took a room with a girl and that was that."

"You had sex with her?" Colin cried out.

Howard tsked. "I'm disappointed in your surprise, Colin. I thought you knew me better." Colin remained agog. Howard laughed. "Of course I didn't have sex with her."

Colin furrowed his brow. "So you just...?"

Howard chuckled. "I kissed her, yes. It was disgusting, but mainly because she was rough and not at all attractive." He made a face. "She had her whole face painted. How men can kiss lipstick and rouge and powder is beyond me." He drank from his glass. "Anyway, I suppose a light kiss would be the same, but in this case, it wasn't at all like a man. It was completely different."

Now Colin was thoughtful. "Hmm. That's interesting. I knew the body would be different, but I figured the kissing would be the same." Then he remembered the story. "How did you get out of the room?"

Howard shrugged. "I told her I felt sick from drinking and gave her the money and went home. The next day we all winked and nodded at each other. I was in."

Colin regarded him in admiration. "Well done!" He turned to Kenneth. "I know this may be too personal, Kenneth, but did Anne not want any children either?"

Kenneth waved an arm. "Good lord, no! It would mess up her traveling plans and her figure."

Howard cut in. "Kenneth was extremely deliberate in finding a wife, Colin. The entire club was stunned by his perfect choice. We couldn't believe it."

Colin nodded. "Henry told me how you met her, or I guess, *found* her." He looked at Howard. "And you decided not to marry at all."

Howard shook his head. "I didn't have to. Like Henry, my reputation didn't require a wife to solidify it with the partners of the bank. If I had been in a banking family, it may have been different. But since I was an outsider, my bosses didn't care if I 'continued the banking line', as it were. In fact, not having a family allowed me to work away the hours like no one else, and that pleased them quite a bit. Like Henry and Kenneth, I had no desire for children, so it all worked out quite nicely."

Kenneth said, "Well, I hope you don't intend to sire any yourself, Colin!"

Colin laughed. "No, no. Not now that I have Henry."

Howard raised his eyebrows. "But you wanted children before that?"

Colin paused, and then shrugged. "Well... I suppose I accepted a long time ago the fact that I wouldn't have children." He began to say more, hesitated, and then spoke shyly. "I did ask Henry once for a ring. He certainly didn't go for that!"

"You mean a wedding ring?" Kenneth asked, incredulous.

Colin reddened. "Well, not an official one, obviously." He looked at them in earnest. "But you know, I have always regretted not being able to marry, and it would just... it would just be nice to have something to mark your..." he looked down at his drink and said quietly, "your love for one another." He sighed. "But Henry's not keen on the idea of betrothal. I suppose nobody here is."

"Pish!" Kenneth tried to say cheerfully, "Look at Alfred Taylor—he's done it. But I think it depends on each man's personality, Colin. And you have to admit, having a boyfriend sounds much more fun than having a husband!"

Colin laughed, but Howard felt his spirits flag. *I think it's a romantic idea. Henry is a fool.* But he hid his feelings by seconding Kenneth's proclamation and adding, "Yes, I think most men just show it in less obvious ways, such as giving other kinds of jewelry and gifts."

Colin nodded. "I'm sure you're right." Then he leaned in conspiratorially. "Speaking of gifts, guess what I'm going to buy for Henry's birthday!"

The men were at a loss. Colin beamed. "Two tickets to America!"

"What?" Kenneth and Howard chorused in disbelief.

"Yes! I'm taking Henry as soon as I'm done with the Rademaker project! But he doesn't know yet, so don't tell him!" His tone became gleeful. "Of course, I'm not going to present it until I'm done with the house—it will have to be a belated present. But I've arranged for us to lodge in the finest hotels; we'll go to the best restaurants... everything!" Then his voice dropped down, and his smile was quiet. "But there's more to come. I'm designing a villa in Paris. For Henry and myself. But that's a secret too." He looked expectantly at his friends, but all they gave him were blank stares. He laughed. "All right. I know what you're thinking. But I've had both planned a long time ago. Particularly the villa."

"Henry's a lucky man." Howard said it honestly, and Kenneth nodded warmly.

"We're all lucky," Colin demurred, raising his drink. "Very, very lucky."

CHAPTER TWENTY-FOUR

The Thursday of the following week was Henry's forty-ninth birthday. Colin came home from work and dressed Henry in one of his best suits. They had dinner served to them in the dining room. Afterwards, Colin helped Henry use his crutches to get to the smoking room. "What is the point?" Henry complained. "I'm so tired of being an invalid! And on my birthday, of all times!"

"I know, darling," Colin soothed. "But I've brought you something that should cheer you up." He got up and went out of the room, closing the door behind him. Then he peeked his head back in. "Henry, since you can't go to Porter's for your birthday like you always do," he pushed the doors open in a grandiose sweep, "I brought Porter's to you!"

"Surprise!" a chorus of voices shouted, and some thirty men began streaming in, followed by a rolling bar, trays of cigars and glasses, and a baby grand piano, complete with a pianist. Velvet chairs followed, a roulette wheel, a billiards table, and Porter's own staff of bartenders and waiters, who went around the room dimming lights and filling champagne glasses. In no time, the room was transformed into a complete social club.

One after another, men wished Henry a happy birthday and told him how much he had been missed. After the last man had visited him, Henry searched the room for Colin. Colin's eyes met his, and smiling, he tilted his head and gave an innocent shrug. Henry motioned for him, and Colin crossed the room to sit on the edge of the sofa. "Happy birthday, Henry," he said, eyes sparkling.

Henry took Colin's hand into his. "There's not a man on this earth who deserves a boy like you," he said tenderly.

Colin blushed and gave a small laugh. He kissed Henry's forehead. "More than you." He smiled. "Now, drink up. To hell with the doctor's orders tonight." He patted Henry's lap and got up.

"I love you, Collie."

Colin stopped, and his expression softened. "I love you too, Henry. Very much."

Henry's voice was faint. "How are you paying for all of this?"

Colin tsked. "Never mind that. But it's here, isn't it, so you'd better enjoy it!" He winked at Henry, then went off.

The next morning, Henry woke fitfully. That was the damned problem with drinking too much: no matter what hour you got to bed, you'd wake up as early as if you were going to work. He looked over at Colin, who was dozing deeply. *At least he's not up yet, with his bloody morning energy.* In fact, this was the first time Henry woke before Colin in months. He propped himself on his elbow to look at his partner in the soft, sunlit room. At first, Henry was taken with the innocence that graced Colin's face while he slept, and he remembered what Colin had done for him last night. But then he couldn't help it; he noticed.

There were wrinkles around Colin's eyes. And lines etched in his forehead. Two rather deep ones from his nose to his mouth. When did all of these horrible lineaments appear? There was even a slight crevice between his eyes. Why, even Colin's skin looked duller, blotchy in places. Henry leaned closer and quietly gasped. There was grey stubble on the boy's chin! Henry's eyes followed Colin's features up into his hair. It didn't seem that his hairline was receding, no, but... *there*. Sure enough, there were some blond strands on his temples that looked—Henry's heart sunk—yes, grey.

Colin's thirtieth birthday is next year. Thirty! When did I allow the boy in my bed to become a man? Grey! He inched away from Colin, disgusted, and a pang of guilt ran through him. *I thought I was better than this. Does this mean lust was disguised as love all of this time?* Henry shook his head. That couldn't be. He did love Colin; he just said so last night. But if Colin looked like this at thirty, what would he look like at forty? Fifty? *Fifty!* Henry swallowed hard, and it was then that Colin sleepily opened his eyes and saw Henry staring at him. "However did you wake up before me?" He smiled, extending his hand to place on Henry's arm. But all Henry saw were the strands of grey hair, and he recoiled, struggling to leave the bed.

"I drank too damned much, that's how," he replied bitterly, annoyed that he had been caught.

Colin closed his eyes. *The mood's already worn off. But I must overcome it—I must!* "Henry, come back to bed."

"No, I've got a bloody headache."

Colin frowned. *That's never stopped him before.* But he threw off the covers and forced a merry tone. "Pity. Well, I guess it's off to Charlotte's for us, then."

It was Henry's first day to try walking using his cane for support. It was much slower going than he had hoped, and by the time he limped from the carriage to his seat at the restaurant, his mood had turned worse. He sullenly sat at the table while Colin made clever remarks about the menu to cheer him up. "Basted eggs," he quipped. "I wonder if that was originally *bastard* eggs. After all, they have no father!" But Henry made no comment, and soon their waiter appeared.

"Good morning sirs, what can I serve you today?"

Henry looked up at the young man while Colin recited off the menu. "I believe I'll have the hard-boiled eggs with corned beef hash. And tea. Henry?"

An elegant, charmed voice spoke up. "Dear boy, I would like your raspberry jelly with toast, lightly buttered. And two eggs, hard-boiled. And tea."

The waiter smiled. "Very well. Thank you."

Henry watched him walk away. "Remember when you were like that?" he said wistfully.

Colin was absorbed in the newspaper he had brought. "Hmm? What, young, naïve, and penniless? Yes, absolute fun." Then he added, "Thank God that's over."

"It should never be over," Henry murmured.

Colin rolled his eyes. "Oh come now, Henry! In ten years that boy will be an insurance salesman if he's lucky."

"Exactly!" Henry's eyes glittered. "But there will always be young waiters at Charlotte's."

"As long as Charlotte's stays open," Colin remarked wryly.

"But there will still always be boys," Henry said dreamily.

Colin frowned. "You sound like Oscar."

"I most certainly do not. The man restricted himself to a fifteen-year age difference."

Colin sighed. "I suppose you *would* find that implausible."

"Incorrigible!" Henry corrected. The two sat in silence the next few minutes, until the waiter brought their food. "Come my good boy, stay for a moment!" Henry commanded. Colin looked at the waiter and then at Henry. The waiter obliged. "Tell us, are you new here?" Henry crooned. "I don't recall seeing such a blond visage before."

The waiter laughed. "Yes, this is my first week. You're Mr. Sewell and Mr. Sewell, aren't you?"

"Why, yes!" Henry exclaimed delightedly. "And what is your name?"

"James, sir."

Henry gazed at the boy. "Taken from a king!" Colin shook his head and speared his hash.

James smiled. "This is just a temporary job, of course."

"Of course," Colin smirked. "Who makes a career out of being a waiter?"

James and Henry both frowned. James looked at the older man. "I'm really a poet. My brother is employing me here until I can get published." Colin had to stifle his laughter. He'd lost count of how many times he'd heard *that* story. He managed to limit his mirth to raising his eyebrows. But Henry was transfixed.

"Well James, how would you like me to personally introduce you to some of our city's established poets? Perhaps they could be of some assistance?"

Colin stopped chewing and shot a look at Henry. "You don't know any poets!" He glared at James. "He hates poets."

"*You* hate poets," Henry replied smoothly. "I've nothing against them. At long as they're not ugly, which unfortunately, many of them are."

"You hate poets, Mr. Sewell?" James quizzed, a derisive tone in his voice.

Colin quietly fumed. "I prefer waiters who know their place."

"Collie!" Henry cried. "You must forgive him, James. When you're going to be turning thirty, sometimes it makes you a bit petulant."

"Thirty! Really?" James slid his eyes over Colin, whose jaw clenched.

"Yes," Henry nodded. "How young are you, James?"

"I'm nineteen, sir," James smiled.

Henry broke into a grin. "Wonderful! What a wonderful age to be!"

"Oh yes, bully for you, James," Colin muttered.

James regarded him coolly but knew not to press further. "I'd best be back to work," he excused himself. "It was a pleasure meeting you, Mr. Sewell." He looked over at Colin. "And Mr. Sewell."

Colin glowered at his food while Henry munched happily on his toast. "What a fine young man!" he said brightly. Colin sat in furious silence and Henry sighed. "Oh, do eat your breakfast, Collie."

Colin pushed his food around his plate. "I believe you've effectively killed my appetite."

"Ridiculous." Henry waved his fork. "I understand if you're jealous, but—"

"Jealous of what?" Colin said hotly. "A stupid, talentless waiter?"

"Goodness, Collie! Don't get so upset!" Then Henry looked at him approvingly. "Though I must say it's most alluring."

Colin glanced up at Henry and was surprised to see him regarding Colin with attraction. He was so grateful for it that he sighed and said, "Well, I brought you here to cheer you up, so I suppose I should be happy that you were."

"That's excellent," Henry smiled. They ate their breakfast. When Henry finished, he said, "I believe I'll invite James to dine with us this evening."

Colin's head jerked up. "You must be joking!"

Henry shrugged. "He's a poet, and he's nice to look at. It would be amusing."

"Amusing!" Colin sputtered. "The fool probably doesn't even know a quatrain from a quatrefoil!"

"Colin—"

"We don't associate with his class and you know it!"

"Colin! Calm down! You must be more open minded."

"Open minded!" Colin slammed down his knife, angrily aware James was probably delighting in the entire scene.

"Hush, dear boy, you are most unsettled! Oh, but Colin, if you could just see yourself! You have the most passionate shade of red on your cheeks. Your nostrils flared, your eyes simply blazing embers!" Colin looked away, disgusted. Henry pointed at him with his fork. "Now you see, if you could remain that passionate, there would be no need for diversions such as our waiter."

Colin turned his head and hissed. "If it's diversions you want, you can meet me in the cab." He got up and stalked off, but not before throwing a knowing glance back at Henry. Henry stared, and then with some difficulty got up himself. He placed a pound note onto the table and began to follow Colin.

"Er... Mr. Sewell?" James hurried over to Henry. "Are you finished eating breakfast?"

"Hmm? Oh, yes," Henry replied absently, heading still for the door. "The money's there for you, James. Cheers, then."

And James watched Henry go, at quite a faster pace than when he came in, realizing perhaps Mr. Sewell the younger still had some power over the senior Mr. Sewell after all.

A few days later, Colin came into Porter's to find Howard sitting alone. "Where's Kenneth?" Colin asked, after greeting his friend.

"He's at a dress rehearsal, if you can believe that," Howard quipped.

"Really?" Colin ordered his drink. Henry hadn't returned to Porter's yet. After walking each day to help his leg heal, he was exhausted by six o'clock.

"Yes, and I have to apologize; I can be here for only a half hour myself."

"Oh. Well, you didn't have to come here just for me, Howard. I would have been all right on my own."

"I know," Howard chuckled. "But I thought it'd be novel. I don't think Kenneth and Henry have been absent together from Porter's since the day they were introduced!"

Colin laughed. "Well then, I'm glad you came. And what plans do you have this evening?"

"Well..." Howard smiled. "I'm actually having dinner... with someone."

Colin slightly lowered his glass. "With someone? Who?"

"Er... a young man I met at the Financial Club."

Colin's jaw dropped. "At the Financial Club! How?"

Howard gave an embarrassed laugh. "Well, we were introduced, completely innocently. But over the course of the evening he began flirting with me quite obviously. We had drinks, stood outside together for a cab, and, umm... and we're having dinner tonight."

Colin set his glass squarely down. "Howard! I can't believe it!" A ridiculous grin spread across his face. "Have you not told anyone about him yet?"

Howard smiled into his whiskey and shook his head. "No. You're the first." The revelation had the unintended effect of a moment realized between the two men.

We're friends. Of our own accord.

Colin was ecstatic. "That's wonderful, Howard! It really is!" He leaned forward eagerly. "So tell me then, what's his name?"

"Mark."

"And how old is Mark?"

"I don't know. I think he's about your age."

Colin practically squealed with delight. "Really? Oh Howard, and what does he do?"

"He works at the Stock Exchange."

"The Stock Exchange..." Colin repeated in awe. Then his eyes lit up. "He's perfect!"

"Well I don't know about that, Colin. Settle down."

The teasing comment set off a reminder in Colin's head. *Luca.* And so Colin sat back in the booth and calmed himself. "All right. But I still think it's amazing!"

"Hmm. And what did you do at work today?"

Colin sighed and began removing his cufflinks. He had commenced to do this in Henry's absence, and it became an after-work ritual, followed by him running his hands through his hair. Howard and Kenneth had marveled at the gaucheness of it all. "Well, I spent the bulk of the afternoon arguing with the bricklayer that the ballroom floor was supposed to be stained in *toffee* and he insisted it was in *coffee*. Honestly, what in God's name am I paying them for if they can't get the instructions correct?"

"You're paying for them to read English."

"Damn right! So, thank God I knew by now to make copies of all of the work orders." He grinned. "They're re-staining it free of charge."

Howard relit his pipe. "They should give you a damn discount on the whole thing."

"I know," Colin sighed. "But I've no room or time to get someone else. You can't make empty threats, Howard."

"Indeed."

Colin stretched and yawned. "And then Rademaker is insisting on wallpaper in at least one of the rooms, so I had to send off for samples from Zuber, damn it all."

"Zuber?"

"French wallpaper company. The best. Their hand painting is unrivaled, although I haven't a clue what theme I'll use. I suppose I'll put a foxhunting scene in the gun room. Very unlike me—it's disappointing."

"You're compromising?" Howard teased.

Colin sighed. "It's his house, Howard. I can only go so far; Henry taught me that early on." He clucked his tongue. "And you see, we can't move any of the furniture upstairs until the room's been papered; it's just ghastly." He rubbed his eyes.

"Colin, please tell me you're getting enough sleep," Howard said, concerned.

Colin smiled at him tiredly. "Enough to get by. Weren't you like this when you first started working?"

"Well, I suppose. But you've been working yourself to death! I just wish I could help in some way."

He said it without thinking, and Colin's eyes flashed. "Ha!" he cried. "Look at that! I couldn't even get help from Henry, who's an actual architect, and here *you* are, offering your assistance!" He rolled his eyes, took a drink, and muttered, "I shouldn't be surprised." And Howard saw that it satisfied Colin very much to say it. Colin put his glass down and tsked himself. "Sorry for that. But you're very kind, Howard. Believe me, if I could put you to work, I would. Now that's enough about me. How was your day?" Then he couldn't help it. "Who cares? You're having dinner with a Stock Exchanger!"

Howard laughed despite himself. "Colin..."

"Well, I'm glad for you, that's all." Colin took out a cigarette. "Really, Howard, you're the most eligible bachelor in all of Britain." He lit his cigarette, and then waved the smoke. "You'd better make him last awhile so we get to see the boy!"

"He's hardly a boy," Howard defended.

Colin paused in mid-inhale, and then looked down at the table. "Right," he nodded, blowing out a small puff of smoke. "He's hardly... that."

Howard cursed himself. But already Colin was looking up at him brightly. "Well, I wish you luck! Not that you'll need it, of course. Perhaps I should be wishing him luck!"

And Howard couldn't help it. *Of all the nights I have to leave early! Damn! Damn!* But he stood up and bowed. "You're too kind, Mr. Sewell. I wish *you* luck with your floor men and your Zuber wallpaper."

"Ugh," Colin grunted. "I'll need it." He drained his glass and rose from his seat. "Actually, I may as well be going myself. I can get some things done." Colin was far too tired to think of it, but Howard knew tongues were wagging at the sight of them leaving together. *Let them wag. All the better when I bring Mark in.* And as they walked out into the brisk air, Howard corrected himself.

If.

By July, Henry was fully recovered and well into his old routine. Colin had become so accustomed to being at Porter's that he continued to join Henry there. However, he had not gone to the club on Saturdays while Henry was bedridden, and after two recent weekend visits for Henry's sake, he declined going again, citing his desperately-behind schedule. Unfortunately, the excuse was valid. Colin had lost enormous amounts of time while Henry was laid up, and Henry, knowing he was the cause, allowed Colin to work longer hours. There were two months left to the deadline, and Colin still had five months of interior work to do. Henry decided to go to Paris for a few weeks to give Colin some peace of mind. He returned well rested and in high spirits, only to find Colin more frantic and distracted than ever. He had stopped visiting Porter's even during the week, so when Henry became seen without him on a nightly basis, the new boys and men at the club didn't think Henry was attached to anybody. By the end of August, the regulars began to think the same thing. Although Howard and Kenneth reassured anyone who asked that Colin and Henry were still together, the general feeling was that the two must have degenerated into mere work partners. Henry himself did little to amend this idea. He started off compensating for Colin's absence at the club by drinking more, but soon he also welcomed the offers of young male company while there, to the disgust of Kenneth and Howard. Yet they were equally disgusted with Colin's total absence, and after two weeks of watching Henry with his boys, they decided to call on Colin personally. The only way they could do it without Henry knowing was to see Colin at Helios House. They managed to find out from Henry the next time he was going there.

It was a Wednesday afternoon. Neither man had seen the estate until the day their carriage stopped at its front gates. A guard came to their window.

"May I help you, sirs?"

"Yes, please," Kenneth replied. "We're here to see Mr. Sewell." He produced his calling card. "We're friends of his, and we've come on urgent business."

The guard took the card and gave a nod. "I shall let Mr. Sewell know. Wait here, please."

Eventually he returned and ushered their driver through. Howard and Kenneth looked out from their brougham as they rode, marveling at the birdsong and dappled sunlight before them. Slender woods rose up on either side of the gently sloping macadam road, and dozens of wildflowers dotted the ground. They crossed over a stone bridge to find a burbling creek below. The drive was almost two kilometers long before the woods opened up to present, at last, the Helios House.

It rose majestically from a graded, lush lawn. The drive to the house was now cleared. The topiaries were in their infancy, and bold, colorful annuals bordered the thoroughfare. Just as Colin had described to them, the entire three-story house was circular. And if one were to look down from the sky, the structure would indeed appear as a sun, with a glass dome in the middle—the atrium—open-air courtyards encircling the atrium, and the rooms of the house around the courtyards. Six rays, the same height as the house, extended from the atrium to half a kilometer past the outer walls of the house. The inner rays created the walls for the triangular courtyards. The outer rays, from the outside of the house beyond, became arcades that ended in small round buildings, each with its own purpose. Every ray was six meters wide and had a peaked roof of terracotta tiles. The roof of the house was also covered in the red clay shingles. Both the rays and house were plastered in pale yellow stucco.

A large pair of burnished brown oak doors created the entrance, over which was a rising sun made of stained glass in hues of amber and gold. Centered above the sun was a white marble plaque engraved thus: "HELIOS HOUSE 1899." Twelve white shallow granite steps spilled from the porch, undulating like water ripples leading down to the gravel path.

Embracing the house on either side of the entrance were eighteen floor-to-ceiling windows, nine on each side, in a set of three per floor. The windows encircled the entire house, broken only by each space of the rays. They were framed in white, without shutters. The middle pane of glass in each bank of three windows was actually made up of two hundred small, beveled panes arranged into a diamond lattice pattern.

The entire effect of the house was as blinding and dazzling as the sun itself.

As the carriage neared its destination, Howard turned to Kenneth. "Only now, Kenneth. Only now am I realizing that he's truly an architect."

"Yes." Kenneth's voice was a hallowed whisper, and he gazed about in confusion. "He's done it! How could Henry..." he trailed off, gazing at the magnificent house.

Colin ran out to them in a panic. "What is it?" he said breathlessly. "Is Henry all right?" He searched their placid faces. "Either Henry's dead, or this is not an emergency," he said angrily.

"Henry's fine," Howard replied, stepping out of the carriage. "In a matter of speaking, anyway. And it is rather important." He glanced at Colin, who was sweat-damp in his dress shirt, which he had rolled up to the elbows. His hair was messily tucked behind his ears, and several tendrils managed to escape and lay against his cheeks.

"Rather important!" Colin exploded. "Well, what is it?" Then he realized that staff and crewmen were within earshot. He took a deep breath and lowered his voice. "Let us go around to the back."

He started off, and Kenneth couldn't help himself. "Colin, it's absolutely beautiful!" He choked, feeling tears smarting his eyes as he regarded the estate.

Colin stopped, turned, and dropped his shoulders almost defeatedly. Any other time he would have been ecstatic to have his friends here seeing his work. But he was exhausted and in no mood for whatever news they were going to hand him. "Thank you, Kenneth." The men didn't say another word until they reached the formal gardens, spectacularly laid out even in its infant stages, and Howard and Kenneth gasped. It was too much.

"Oh, God, Henry's being awful to you, Colin!" Howard cried, surveying the luxuriant surroundings.

Colin stopped again, this time, shocked. "What do you mean?"

"He's... well, we came here to sort of reprimand you for not coming to Porter's anymore, but this..." and Howard turned a full circle to view it all. Then he looked helplessly at Colin. "My God, if he only saw the place, he'd never mind your absence from the club."

Colin crossed his arms and glared. "You know he won't see it until it's finished. And what are you talking about anyway? What's going on?"

The two men looked at each other. Then Kenneth shook his head. "Henry has been having all sorts of boys with him at Porter's."

Colin's eyes widened. "Does he come in with them?"

"Oh! No! No, no, no. They come sit with him in the club."

Colin sighed. "Kenneth, I told Henry that I don't mind. Let him have some fun. It's not his fault that I can't be there." He shrugged. "It's just harmless flirtation."

"Yes, that's exactly what he said," Howard cut in. "But Colin, half the club doesn't think Henry's with anyone anymore, and the other half are convinced the two of you have fallen out."

Colin eyed them. "Surely at least two men there know the truth and have squelched those rumors."

"We've tried, but actions speak louder than words," Kenneth said desperately.

"What actions?" Colin demanded.

"Your absence," Howard answered. "And... and things that have happened with Henry."

Colin's heart skipped. "Such as?"

Again Kenneth and Howard glanced at each other. Howard looked at Colin with his mouth set in a sympathetic line.

"Well, there's been... sort of intimacies exchanged."

Colin's mouth fell open, and he tried to close it but he couldn't. Finally he shut his eyes and turned away, trying to breathe.

"Colin," Howard said quickly. "Really it was just a kiss, and only once. The boys have been positively swarming around him."

Colin whirled around. "And you just let them? Or do they swarm around you, too?" He gestured wildly. "After all, *you're* both available! Oh, excuse me, Howard. I'd forgotten *you* were taken! Did you?"

"We thought about trying to stop them," Howard said firmly. "But it's not our place. Henry is a grown man; we can't dictate to him."

"Yes," Kenneth nodded. "If you could just perhaps be there once in a while, it might stave those boys off."

Colin's eyes flashed as he looked at his house and then at his friends. "If I could *just be there once in a while*? Christ! Do you think I haven't been up until midnight every night since Henry's been laid up? I'm the one breaking my back over all of this! I'm the one paying our bills if you must know, and yet I'm the one at fault here? I'm the one who should be babysitting him?" He pointed to the two of them desperately. "*You* wouldn't do this to me, so don't tell me this is a normal consequence of my being *in absentia!*" The men were speechless, but Colin raged on. "Do you think it's too much to ask that the man I've been committed to for the past eight years exercise some damned self-control?"

Howard's shoulders slumped. "Well, he pushed the boy away."

Colin shook his head ruefully. "That doesn't matter. Henry never told me about this, and that says more than anything the both of you have revealed just now." He looked at the ground and exhaled. "Who was it?"

Howard and Kenneth couldn't bring themselves to reply, and by doing so, Colin had the answer. "Oh Christ, was it that waiter James?" His voice rose. "Was it?"

"Yes... of course," Kenneth said miserably.

Colin turned around and walked away in disgust. Then he came back. "You two are absolutely a piece of work, you know that? If I didn't know any better, I'd say you've let this go on as long as it has because you've been so damned bored, that this has actually been entertaining for you!"

"Colin, we told you—" Howard started.

"Oh, you told me, Howard! You've told me plenty! James! Of all people! I bet you really stood up to him, too! I'm sure you—"

"Colin, we *are* being loyal to you!" Kenneth cried out angrily. "We are *here*, telling you this! What else are we supposed to do?"

Colin wrung his hands. "Well, you could have told Henry you didn't want James sitting at the table!"

"We did!" Howard insisted. "We tried, but Henry told us to mind our own business." Then he sighed. "See here, Colin, we'd rather have it be you than anyone else, and Kenneth and I both understand that your work isn't making that possible. But we were hoping something could be done. We don't know what to do, either."

Colin glanced up at their gloomy expressions and sighed. "Oh God... I'm sorry to both of you. I don't know what's gotten into me." He took off his glasses and rubbed his face. "I've been so strung up lately. I hate that I barely get to see Henry anymore, you know. I'm sorry that you're both being put through this affair." He took a deep breath and nodded. "All right, then. What's this week's password?"

Kenneth and Howard straightened. "So sweet the sorrow," Kenneth answered quietly.

"'So sweet the sorrow,'" Colin repeated, and smiled bitterly. "All right." He looked at the two men and sighed. "Thank you. I know you're trying to help. If you didn't care, you would have let this go entirely, so I appreciate it." He didn't know what else to say, so he shrugged and said, "If you'll excuse me, I have work to do." And he turned and walked back into the house, while Kenneth and Howard trudged back to their carriage.

CHAPTER TWENTY-FIVE

Saturday night came, and Colin stood in front of his wardrobe, a tumbler of gin in his hand. Henry had left an hour ago, before Colin returned home from work. For the past month, Colin had been working from seven in the morning to between ten and twelve at night. Before that, he had managed to be home by eight o'clock. He had been ready to drop, but at least he was able to spend some time with Henry.

I haven't spent more than ten minutes at a time with him since. Small wonder things are happening the way they are.

Colin gazed at his clothes. He was to blame, Henry was to blame, and nobody was to blame. Yes, Colin took on this project, but he didn't know it would be so difficult, and he hadn't expected Henry to actually carry out his refusal to help him. And while Henry showed remarkable patience with Colin's hours, he couldn't have expected to be completely companionless month after month. But just three more months to go until the interior was done, and it would be all over. Colin would never fall into this kind of schedule again, and Henry would have him back.

But three months were still twelve weeks away, and Henry was being seriously tempted now. Colin tilted his chin upwards and narrowed his gaze toward the suit he drew out from the end of the armoire. He studied it, and a smile curled at his lips.

"So sweet the sorrow."

The door opened, and the boy guarding the entrance jumped back. "Mr. Colin!"

"Hello, Billy," Colin greeted him, stepping inside. "I'm sorry to give you a fright. I know I haven't been here for a while."

"I'll... umm... inform Mr. Sewell you're here," Billy said quickly.

"That won't be necessary," Colin replied casually. He took Billy's hand and palmed a ten-pound note in it. "In fact, I forbid you." He looked at the boy amicably. "I don't know which side you're professing loyalty to, so I thought I'd hedge my bets." Then he frowned. "I would like you to ask Jack if he'd see me, though."

"Yes, sir," Billy nodded. He looked down at the money and then pressed the note back into Colin's hand and looked him in the eye with respect. "I'm glad you're back, Mr. Colin." He turned and went to fetch Jack Colton.

Within a minute, Jack strode into the passageway. "Colin!" he grinned.

"Hullo, Jack," Colin said, relieved. But he saw the concern on Jack's face and sighed. "Look here, I know what's been going on and that's why I'm here, but I need your help."

"Of course, Colin." Jack looked guilty. "I wanted to do something about those vile boys," he shrugged. "But I couldn't. You understand..."

"Of course," Colin assured him. "I'd never expect you to do anything of the sort." He shook his head as he took out his cigarette case. "When the cat's away, the mice shall play."

"Well, I'd like to cut off the mice's balls!" Jack exclaimed. Colin laughed as he lit his cigarette. "The mice aren't entirely at fault. But here's what I need you to do: just act as if I'm the king of England for tonight, if you would." He winked. "Not that you don't anyway, but what I mean is, rather be nearby for the first half hour or so. Make the waiters appear to be at my beck and call. Send a bottle of your finest champagne to the table, on the house. I'll pay for it later, of course. And," he paused thoughtfully, "if I should need you to throw out a boy, just for the evening, could you do that?"

"Mr. Colin!" Jack raised his eyebrows.

Colin eyed him. "Is that party favor James here?"

Jack grinned. "I think I could manage to toss out one, then, and at the very least, force *him* to buy you a magnum of champagne. And everything *is* on the house tonight, Colin. I won't have it any other way."

Colin laughed and shook his hand. "Thank you, Jack. I don't know how I'll repay you." He rolled his eyes. "Well, a few years ago, *that* wouldn't have been a problem, would it? Perhaps I can find you someone or something that's worthy."

Jack, now at fifty-five, eight years older himself, tsked Colin. "You're still a catch, Colin. More than these boys, regardless of what you believe."

Colin laughed and began walking toward the club door. "You don't need to begin acting yet, Jack!"

He entered the club and smiled to see heads turning and then mouths dropping.

"Evening, Daniel," he greeted one man.

"Colin! Good to see you, finally!" Daniel thumped his back.

"Mr. Colin, get over here!"

Colin grinned and went over to Richie Dobbs. "Hello, Richie."

"Hoo-hoo-hoo! Look at you!" Richie yelped, the men in his group murmuring admiration.

Colin gave a curt nod and a wink. "Damage control. I'll be back shortly."

Richie chuckled, understanding. "Good luck, then. You won't need it, though."

So Colin made his way through the crowd, who saw by his determined stride and cigarette in his mouth—Colin never smoked until he was at his table—that he was on a mission. They parted for him deferentially.

"Who's that?" a brown-haired boy whispered to his companion.

"Colin Sewell. Henry Sewell's son and lover. Looks like he got wind of Henry's mischief." The man rose from his seat and took the confused boy's hand. "Come along. This should be quite a show!"

When Colin finally came upon his table at the end of the room, he was pleased to see Howard and Kenneth there; they could provide moral support. And because Colin expected it and thus prepared himself for it, his expression remained serene when he glimpsed the boy hanging on to Henry. The boy sitting in Colin's seat.

James.

Colin's stride never faltered, and he was soon at the table. He held his cigarette aloft as he tilted his head toward James, his tone laconic. "My, what an attractive seat warmer."

James jerked his head around indignantly, then his eyes widened when he realized who had said it. Henry looked up drunkenly. "Oh, look. It's my husband."

"Wife," Colin corrected, and then looked at James. "Really, don't get up, James. You look so very pretty sitting there. I'll sit over here by Howard."

James was too stunned to respond, but he also stayed put because, after all, he'd been in Colin's seat for weeks. Still, he saw that Colin was intending to crucify him and he felt trapped. Plus, he was taken aback by Colin's appearance: Mr. Sewell the younger looked like royalty. He was wearing a forest-green suit, the weave so fine and tight that there was a sheen to it. His vest was embroidered in a paisley pattern, gold and green. A thin braid of moss green edged it, and its buttons were 18-k gold, stamped with fleur-de-lis. Colin's silk shirt was a creamy white, its sleeves fastened at the end with gold cufflinks studded with diamonds and rubies. His tie was scarlet and gilded with metallic thread; it too was silk. The entire outfit would have cost James twenty years' worth of earnings. Colin's copper-gold hair shone in the low light of the candles, and there was a flush on his cheeks. James had forgotten what a fine profile Colin had, and he eyed him. *But I am younger than you.*

Colin ignored his glare and turned to his friends, smiling broadly. "Good evening, Kenneth. How are you, Howard?" He looked past his friend to the young man next to him. "And you must be Mr. Montague!" He extended his hand.

Mark shook it and laughed. "Yes. I hope *I'm* not anyone's seat warmer!"

Colin looked at him approvingly. "No, I've heard about you. Howard has always had superb taste; you appear to be no exception."

A gin and bitters was placed before Colin. "Your drink, Mr. Colin," the waiter said, and then melted back into the crowd.

"Where did you get that suit?" Henry murmured, gazing at it. Colin took a drink.

"Ah. I bought it to celebrate the upcoming completion of my project, but I decided to give it a trial run tonight."

"It looks Italian," Howard commented.

Colin silently applauded Howard for playing along. "Of course it's Italian. I only wear Italian suits and French shirts, Howard, remember?"

"It's lovely. You look absolutely stunning, darling," Henry said, and Colin smiled briefly at him.

Mark was spellbound by Colin's attire and forgot his manners. "Your cufflinks! They're amazing! Surely those aren't real gemstones?"

Colin smiled at him. Then he began removing the cufflinks and set them in front of Mark. "Mr. Montague, if you can't tell what real gemstones look like then you need these more than I do."

Mark's mouth dropped as he gazed at the cufflinks.

"Don't be ridiculous, Colin!" Howard reprimanded. "He can't take those!" He said in an aside to Mark, "They *are* real."

Mark shook his head. "Mr. Sewell..."

"If you give them back to me, I'll be insulted," Colin warned, taking off his jacket and rolling up his sleeves. He looked at Howard. "It makes a good story, Howard!" Then he gave him a sly smile. "Don't you think he's worth it? *I* think they'd suit him very well." He gave a mildly lascivious glance at Mark, who returned it rather fervently.

Howard shook his head but didn't argue further. He'd return them next week. "Fine," he replied, taking the cufflinks. "I'll hold onto them for safekeeping."

"Lord knows Collie has dozens more at home," Henry said. "He always picks out the best ones. Although at least half *are* from all his past admirers." He stroked Colin's hand.

Colin threw a look at James. *You are out of your league.* Then he leaned back and said casually, "Well, James, I hear you've been kind enough to keep Henry entertained in my absence." He looked at Henry. "He's no doubt shared his latest poetry with you?"

Henry was too drunk to care that he was caught. In fact, he found the whole scenario highly amusing, and he exclaimed, "Oh, yes! Yes, he has!" He turned to James. "Be a good boy and recite for Colin the one you told me tonight."

James looked smug. "The one in French?"

Henry nodded vigorously. "Yes, that one!" He looked at Colin. "He knows French," he explained proudly. Colin raised his eyebrows pleasantly and waited for James to begin.

When he finished, Henry said, "Now translate it for him."

"He doesn't have to translate it," Colin replied. He looked at James. "Ce n'est pas mauvais. Il est evident que vous admirez Jules Laforgue, n'est-ce pas? Votre poem est semblable."

James was taken aback. "Oui! Mais, comment est-ce que vous le savez? J'ai pensee que vous haissez la poesie."

Colin shrugged. "Non. J'adore la poesie. C'est les poetes qui je deteste." He winked, and James reddened.

Henry was gaping. "That's impossible! You hardly know any French!"

Colin drained his glass. "I took it at boarding school. Six years, actually."

"But all of those times we were in Paris..." Henry wondered.

Colin shrugged. "You spoke it. There was no need." He looked at James. "You see James, if you're going to be a proper seducer, you must never play all of your cards straight away."

"So I see," James replied coolly. "I would expect someone your age to be such a fount of wisdom."

Colin looked at Henry upon hearing this remark and gave a short laugh. He eyed James. "I'll take that as the compliment I'm sure you intended it to be." Then he frowned at Henry. "He's rather feisty."

Henry gazed back at him. "He rather reminds me of you."

Colin glared at him. "I'll forgive you for that!"

"Mr. Colin." A new waiter approached, placing a magnum of champagne on the table. "Mr. Colton asked to send this to you, Mr. Colin. Compliments of the house."

James took the hint. "I'd best be off, then," he said tersely. Henry turned to him. "Oh, darling, you can have a glass of champagne with us."

Colin looked at the table. "There are only five glasses." He looked triumphantly at the sullen boy. "Good night, James."

"Good night, Mr. Colin." James turned and smiled affectionately to Henry. "And good night, Mr. *Sewell.*" He leaned over and kissed Henry deeply. Now it was his turn to glare in triumph. Henry looked wildly at Colin, who had gone pale, his nostrils flaring.

When James rose up, Colin said stiffly, "Mr. Gilbert. Is Mr. Colton standing by the bar?" James glanced behind Colin. Jack was glaring at him, arms furiously crossed.

"Yes," James replied fearlessly, although he felt some dread begin to creep into him.

"Good. I'm sure he's waiting for you to bring another magnum of Moet & Chandon to the table with your compliments."

James stared and sat back down. "You can't force me to do that!" he hissed.

"No, but I *can* manage to have you permanently ejected from the club. Either way, I believe Mr. Colton would like a word with you. Immediately."

James looked again at the bar. "I can't afford a magnum of Moet!"

Colin was unfazed. "Oh, I think you can. Despite your paltry waiter's salary, you've managed to save over a month's worth of drinks, thanks to Henry. That's a start."

James looked again at the bar and sighed, walking toward it. Jack had the bottle waiting. "I don't have any cash on me, save a cab fare," James told him irritably.

"Then give over your pocketwatch."

"What? I'm not giving you my watch!"

"Collateral, James," Jack barked. "You can have it back when you've paid for the champagne." He looked sternly at the boy. "You couldn't have picked a worse man to insult than Colin Sewell, Gilbert, and you made him look like a fool. Everyone in this club just witnessed that. And everyone expects you to buy this bottle and pay your dues accordingly. I'm also asking you to leave the club for the evening." He paused. "It can be permanent, if you so desire."

James was trapped. He grudgingly took off his watch in full view of the crowd and placed it on the bar. Jack pushed the magnum toward him. "Now deliver it and leave, please."

James stalked over to the table, set the bottle down, and left the room. Colin, cigarette in mouth, got up and took a glass of champagne. He patted the men's backs. "Enjoy, gentlemen. I'll be right back."

"Collie..." Henry looked frightened.

"Drink your champagne, Henry. Nobody's going to get hurt." He disappeared into the crowd.

Howard shook his head. He was in shock over the entire chain of events, from Colin's stunning physical appearance to his conversational deftness—speaking French indeed—to his coup de grace of bringing down the full force of his influence in the club when it was called for. Howard grinned at Mark. "And *that*, Mr. Montague, is Mr. Colin Sewell."

Colin caught up with James in the vestibule. "Mr. Gilbert..."

James turned in surprise and then narrowed his eyes. "I don't want any trouble, Mr. Sewell. But once we walk through this door, it's just you and me."

Colin rolled his eyes. "Yes, I know." He looked at Billy. "Would you please keep anyone from leaving for a bit? I'd like to have a minute with Mr. Gilbert."

Billy gawked. "Yes, sir."

The two men went outside. Colin leaned with his back against the wall. He studied James and said quietly, "Look here, I know you're not the only one and I know it's not all your fault. But you may find yourself in this position someday, James, and it's a terrible way to be."

"If you care about him so much, where have you been for the last two months?" James asked defensively.

Colin sighed. "There's a stable's worth of asses in that club, and I'm one of them. So I've learned my lesson."

"You made a fool of me in there, getting me thrown out!"

"You made a greater fool of me and you know it!" Colin said angrily. "I'm not sure how to even go back in there and save face!"

"Hmph!" James replied sulkily. "They all love you. Who knows when I can go back without being treated like an outcast?"

"Jack's a fair man," Colin waved a hand. "This kind of drama plays out all the time in that place."

James looked at him, puzzled. "You're being awfully good about this... I expected you to be throwing punches right now."

Colin's mouth was a grim line. "I need my hands for work." Then he offered James his glass of champagne. "Here, take it for the ride home. You bought it; you may as well have some. Do you have cab fare?"

James was chastened. "Yes." He peered at Colin. "For what it's worth, I'm sorry, I suppose."

Colin crossed his arms. "Well, you're done with Henry. Good luck with your poetry, Mr. Gilbert." He turned to go back into the club.

"Is everything all right, Mr. Colin?" Billy asked anxiously.

Colin gave him a tired smile. "Yes, Billy, everything is fine. Thank you for your assistance." He took a deep breath and opened the club door.

The crowd was buzzing. They turned to see Colin returning and noticed that his glass of champagne was gone. He made a show of putting his hands in his pockets and smiled. "As you were, gentlemen."

The men burst into laughter, nodding their appreciation. They watched Colin pass by them, thankful for his absent jacket so that they could admire him from behind. "Will you look at that," one of the men murmured, focusing on Colin's lower half. "He's still lovely."

"Mm," another agreed. "Just as I remember."

A boy came up to Colin, proffering a cigarette case. "Here you are, Mr. Colin. Mr. Stratton noticed you're without." Colin looked over at his friend Charles Stratton and laughed. He gazed at the boy as he drew out a cigarette. "Charlie's a giant of a man. Are you with him tonight?"

The boy's heart raced as he lit Colin's cigarette. He found Mr. Colin dashing and wished he still took boys home. "Yes. He wanted me to invite you to our table."

Colin smiled. "I'd love to, but I must attend to my own, first. Perhaps you could both come by if I don't make it back here?"

The young man stared at him. "I'd love to!" he breathed. Then his eyes widened and he stammered, "I mean... I'll tell Mr. Stratton! Thank you!" He blushed, and Colin laughed. "Good. I'd like to commend Charlie on his excellent decision with you."

After a few more similar encounters, Colin was back at his own table. "If you don't mind, Howard, I'll sit here now." He took his place next to Henry, who sighed.

"Oh, Collie. I've missed you. You're so gorgeous."

Colin turned toward him. "Yes, well *you...*" he slapped Henry slightly on the wrist, "*you* behave." He pointed his cigarette at him. "I'm not leaving your side for the remainder of the evening, so settle on in."

The rest of the evening passed without incident. When Charles Stratton and his boy approached, they saw Colin's table uproarious with laughter. They were having a wonderful time with their champagne. Colin spotted them and motioned them over. "Charlie! You remembered!" He pointed to the boy. "Now *this* one, this one's good, Charlie. Don't let him get away."

Charlie chuckled. "Well, I'm glad you think of Stuart as highly as I do!"

"Stuart," Colin repeated, and then he looked at the boy in amusement. "I forgot to introduce myself properly to you earlier." He shook Stuart's hand. "I'm sorry. Colin Sewell."

Stuart, his own inhibitions shed from the alcohol, pshawed him. "I know who you are! You've no need for an introduction." He gave him a lopsided smile as he shook his hand. "Stuart Swift. I told Charles I wish I was born ten years earlier!"

Colin grinned. "Then you two have more in common than I thought!" They all laughed, and Colin beckoned them to sit down. The men chattered away, and as the club closed and everyone prepared to leave, Colin touched Howard and Kenneth's arms. *Thank you,* he mouthed, and they acknowledged him silently, smiling as they watched him and Henry enter a cab, close the door, and ride off.

Inside the cab, Henry gazed at Colin with a mixture of admiration and disbelief. "You speak French... I never should have doubted you, Collie."

"Never, Henry."

The next morning, Henry stumbled out of bed and into the dining room. Colin was already there, reading the newspaper. He had heard Henry awaken and had the servant bring in their breakfast.

"Good morning," he smiled, folding up his paper.

Henry sat down heavily and peered at him. "Don't you feel positively wrung out?"

Colin chuckled ruefully. "Oh, I've got a splitting headache, I assure you," he replied, and began to eat his eggs. He chewed slowly and realized Henry was staring at him. He frowned. "It'll get cold, Henry. Eat."

There was a long pause, and then a small anxious voice spoke up, "Aren't you upset?"

Colin sighed. "To be honest, I feel that things were taken care of last night. What happened was my fault as much it was yours. Let's just call it even and be done with it."

Henry studied Colin's placid expression. He wondered what it must have taken for Colin to come into the club last night, dressed like that. Cavalier like that. He was certain that Kenneth and Howard had informed Colin as to what was going on, and poor Collie had to decide what to do about it. He had put on a good show, but Henry knew that every minute must have terrified him. "I didn't realize just how popular you were at the club," he said lightly.

"I didn't either." Colin's tone became sardonic. "Apparently some greater good came out of being the club courtesan in that place."

"They do love you, Colin."

Colin smiled at Henry's heartfelt remark, and his expression turned expectant. But Henry stared at his plate and picked up a forkful of eggs. "Yes, you are certainly very much loved there." So Colin could only nod, and they ate their breakfast in silence until Colin could resist no longer.

"A waiter," he said derisively. "Worse yet a piss-poor poet. Some taste, Henry."

CHAPTER TWENTY-SIX

The date was December 30th, 1899, a Friday. It was seven o'clock in the morning, and Colin was at the Helios House. Max was due at eight o'clock for the final tour, whereupon Colin would hand over his own key and in effect the house itself. They would settle the contract and financial details there as well. Colin prayed it would all go smoothly, for if there was any difference of opinion, they'd have to bring in their lawyers and meet again.

Colin walked through the house feeling faint. Now that the last speck of plaster dust had been swept away, the house was truly complete, pristine. He could hardly believe it existed. *This came from me.* As he inspected each room, he brushed his fingers over the furniture in reverence and wondered if it was wrong to feel as if he was in a holy place. *It's my vanity talking. Pride.* But he couldn't call them sins. No, this was achievement. Man giving glory to God by showing Him what He made possible.

When he came to Margaret's room, Colin sat down on the bed and looked about. He hadn't seen her since the day she had visited the office seven months ago. He knew that yesterday the family had toured the house on their own so that any last changes could be arranged if necessary. Colin wondered what Margaret thought of her room. It was just what they had agreed upon: violets and blues. However, Colin decided that the palette was too cool for a lady's quarters, so he added gold as well. He had been tempted to leave a small gift under her pillow, but he knew she was supposed to 'mend her broken heart,' and such a romantic gesture would be inappropriate. Still, he did say he grew fond of her, and if he was truly going to die, wouldn't he give the woman he cared for something to remember him by?

So now, Colin took a small box out of his pocket and carefully tucked it under one of the pillows. He stood up and finished the rest of his tour. When Max arrived, he took Colin's hand and shook it warmly. "The day has come!"

Colin grinned, joyous. "Yes, it has!"

"I took a thorough tour yesterday and everything is perfect!" Max exulted.

"I couldn't agree more," Colin exhaled. "Do you want to go through one more time with me, then?"

Max waved a hand. "No, that won't be necessary, unless there's something you feel needs to be pointed out."

"Mr. Rademaker, we've worked so closely on this project that you know every centimeter as well as I do!" Max laughed. Then Colin had to know: "How did Mrs. Rademaker and Miss Rademaker find it?"

Max smiled. "They love it, Colin."

Colin nodded. "Miss Rademaker likes her room, then?"

"Yes." Max paused, trying to thwart his feelings of pity. "Colin, as you know, I'm having a party here tomorrow night to celebrate New Year's Eve—the real event will be in summer, of course, but I was wondering if you'd like to come to this one."

Colin was taken aback. "Really? Are you certain?"

Max sighed. "I'd planned to invite you in the summer, but..." his voice faded, and he awkwardly made a fist and hit his palm with it. "But by God, you deserve to be celebrated straight away! It's the least I can do! In fact, I insist you come as the guest of honor."

Colin stared at the floor, touched, and then he lifted his head to meet Max's gaze. "I'd be delighted, sir. It's very kind of you."

"Yes, well, you also may as well see Margaret one last time. The girl needs to get on with her life, and I ask you to make that happen."

Colin straightened. "What do you mean by that?"

"Just be firm with her, will you? Say your farewells at the party and such, and then agree that it's over."

"But it is over," Colin insisted. "I wrote her a letter saying so."

"You did? What did it say?"

"Mr. Rademaker, I can't tell you what I wrote in a personal letter!"

"Well, letters leave too much open to interpretation, apparently. I'm sorry to say she's still rather disconsolate. Talk to her at the party."

"She might avoid me."

"I'll tell her that she must speak with you."

"Very well." Suddenly, Colin remembered the gift he had left under her pillow. *Oh God! I didn't know I'd be seeing her again!*

"Well, that's settled," Max said. "Now, let's sit down in my new library and see if we can sign off on everything!"

When Colin returned to work, he ran into his and Henry's office, closed the door, and threw himself onto Henry in an ecstatic embrace. "He's accepted it, Henry! It is finished!"

Henry was surprised to find himself overcome with emotion as he hugged Colin back. "That's wonderful, Collie! Congratulations!"

"And he's invited me to appear at his party tomorrow night! It's at the house! Is that all right?"

"Of course."

"But I know we had plans to go to Kenneth's party. I wish you could come to Rademaker's."

"Oh," Henry managed. "Well, you can't really expect that now, can you?"

"No," Colin laughed. "I suppose not. Well, do you want to celebrate tonight, then? Let's, please! To Porter's!"

"No, we should wait until you've done your entertaining tomorrow night."

Colin's face fell. "Why?"

"Well, because I have a feeling you would be terribly hung-over tomorrow, and I want you to be fresh. It's important for you to fully enjoy such an extraordinary event." He smiled. "I'll never forget the first time I was feted. It will be just as wonderful for you, Colin."

Colin was still disappointed, but acquiesced. "All right. I suppose we can celebrate Sunday."

"Well, why don't we have a mini-celebration tonight with Kenneth and Howard at The Oak Room?" Henry suggested.

Colin brightened. "That would be nice! I'd like that, Henry."

"Good. I'll send a post to both."

Kenneth and Howard greeted the two men at the restaurant, and once at the table, Kenneth presented Colin with a gift. "This is from Howard and I, who are so proud of your accomplishment."

Beaming, Colin took the large, rectangular present and unwrapped it. He gasped. "A Monet! You bought a Monet?" He couldn't believe it—the two men certainly could afford it, but it was overly generous all the same.

"Well, we knew how much you like his work, and we also knew you hadn't bought any yet," Howard replied, truly thrilled that Colin loved the painting so much. He himself thought the whole Impressionism movement was ridiculous, but Colin proclaimed it the next step forward in great art.

"I was going to buy one with the money from the house!" Colin cried. "I really was, and now... now I have one! And it will remind me of you both whenever I look at it!" He turned to Henry, "Oh, we shall have to find a place for it tonight!"

Henry smiled. "Oh my. I'll let you be in charge of that. It's your painting."

The rest of the night found Colin in high spirits as he dominated the conversation and periodically turned to Henry, squeezing his arm and exclaiming, "I just can't believe it's finished!" Henry would smile affectionately and murmur, "I know. It's wonderful." Colin sensed his subdued attitude and garnered that perhaps Henry, too, was a bit overwhelmed. Maybe he was even a trifle jealous. Or was it envious? So Colin played up to him. "Imagine! All this inspiration I had... It came from you! *Your* work! Henry, the house is as much a product of you as it is me!"

This seemed to cheer Henry up. "You've learnt well, Colin. You've really learnt, and even surpassed me."

"Oh no, Henry..." Colin protested.

"No, no! It's true, you have! I take credit for most of *that*, of course, but I am proud of you."

"Yes, Colin," Howard said warmly. "Who would have guessed that eight years ago that the American boy Henry had picked would actually become the ambitious, successful young man sitting before us now?"

"*I* would have known it," Colin said, in mock haughtiness. Then he grinned as they laughed. "Now that I've finally accomplished something on my own, I finally feel that I'm one of you! That we are all a group of equals! Although," he added hastily, "I still haven't achieved as much as you three, yet."

"But you will," Henry nodded. "Sooner than all of us, Collie, you will."

At home, Henry claimed to feel sick and asked to go to bed. Colin was certain now that Henry was having difficulty adjusting to his success and decided to let him go, although he had planned to present Henry just then with the tickets to America. Surely after tomorrow evening, when Colin could officially lay the Helios House to rest, Henry would come back to his senses. Colin gave Henry a kiss goodnight, and since he himself was too wound up to sleep just yet stayed awake and sat in the library to reflect upon the fortunes that had brought him here.

To keep Henry's mood from affecting his own, Colin contemplated about the future.

What shall I do next?

Perhaps you ought to wait for a commission. Surely you'll get one the day after Rademaker opens his house to visitors!

Yes, but I ought to think of something new regardless. Another house. Or my cathedral...

It's not time yet for the cathedral.

Well, I can think about it. Anyway, Henry and I are really partners now! Partners in every sense of the word! I graduated! He's proud of me!

Yes! You can really begin to work with him now. He'll never leave you; you've truly become a team.

We are meshed as one, we are. I can tell he just can't believe it himself. I'll bet he can't believe he actually did find a diamond!

And the next project... the next project should be yours together! While on the trip to America you can dream it. You will be a united force the likes of none before seen!

Yes!

Colin leapt from his chair and then stifled his glee thinking of Henry trying to sleep. He felt as if he was radiating light from every direction. He stood in the library with his arms stretched out in glory.

We shall fly! Overground!

Saturday night was Rademaker's party. As Colin adjusted his tie, he glanced at Henry in the mirror and turned around. "Are you certain you're all right with me going?"

"Yes, yes," Henry scowled. He had been withdrawn all day, apparently a continuation from last night. He still used his excuse of feeling ill when he rebuffed Colin's excited overtures in bed this morning, and yet when Colin expressed concern, Henry softened and apologized for his behavior. But his distant mood lasted, and Colin's feelings were a mixture of sympathy and anger. It was possible that Henry was reminded of his younger days, when he had completed the Wyeth Building, his first solo commissioned project. Or perhaps Henry thought Colin would now leave Sewell & Sewell and start his own company. Or maybe Henry thought Colin would leave him entirely! And of course, they were spending New Year's apart. But Henry didn't give a reason for his melancholy, so Colin fell to resentment. My God! What an achievement! He had really done it—he had made his most esteemed project a reality, by the age of 29! His first solo commission, completed! And tonight he was being presented as one of the newest noteworthy architects of his time! Henry should be happy for Colin, ecstatic, really. Wasn't a spouse supposed to celebrate your achievements? Colin sighed. Well, it had been a four-year process. Perhaps Henry was just in a state of shock. Then Colin smiled. *Or reverence.*

He feigned cheerful casualness as he passed Henry on the way out. "Now, let Kenneth and Howard take care of you at Porter's," he winked. "You'll probably have a better time than I will."

"Colin..." Colin turned and looked expectantly at Henry. "Good luck." Henry's voice was strained but sincere.

Colin walked back to Henry and took his hands. "I wish you would tell me what's wrong," he pleaded softly.

Henry shook his head. "It's just a night full of emotion," he said blandly.

Colin frowned. Henry looked exhausted. "Yes, I know. But Henry, please go out and have a good time. We'll have our own midnight celebration when I get back, I promise."

As if the words were magical, Henry snapped into a bright grin. "All right, all right! Go! It's your night, Colin! I want you to enjoy it. Forget me—just go!" He pushed Colin out the door jovially.

Colin laughed, puzzled. "You're sure?"

Henry fell somber again and then smiled. "You will never have a night like this again, Colin. There's nothing like this first night. You must experience it to the fullest. I'm closing the door! Goodbye!"

Colin stared at the wooden panels suddenly before him. He was about to run late so he ran to the cab, but he still found the whole thing odd.

However, as the carriage drew up to the house, Colin pushed the thoughts from his mind. *Henry is right. I'm going to enjoy this evening! I'll thrash things out with him when I get back.*

Instead of being announced by the butler, Colin saw Max bound to his side and command everyone's attention. "Ladies and gentlemen, I present to you the newest architect to join the esteemed ranks of geniuses! A man I have had no greater pleasure in working with. A man whose vision is matched by his practicality. A man who has tamed his dream into my reality. The man solely responsible for this miraculous dwelling: Mr. Colin Sewell!" The crowd burst into applause as Max turned to him. "They demanded that you give them a grand tour. Would you be so gracious?"

Colin grinned. "Of course!" He bowed to the people before him and said, "Thank you all for coming this evening to Mr. Rademaker's new country house. This house was meant to be filled with people in celebratory fashion, and I'd be only too happy to show you why. Follow me!"

Halfway through the tour, Max said to Colin in a low aside, "Margie said she'll speak to you at the end of the evening." Colin nodded, wishing he could avoid the meeting. He had caught a glimpse of her earlier and noticed that she was not wearing the necklace, and he wondered if she had gotten it after all. He continued to lead the group of fifty people around the house, and at the end, everyone shouted "Bravo," accompanied by thunderous applause. Then they raised a toast to him and Colin felt giddy with joy. Afterwards he found himself talking with so many men and women that he scarcely noticed the time passing until the countdown to midnight began, and Colin tried to forget that this was the first New Year's midnight since he came to England that he wasn't kissing Henry. Soon after,

Margaret walked toward him, a smile barely on her lips. "Happy 1900, Mr. Sewell, and congratulations."

"Happy 1900, and thank you, Miss Rademaker." Colin took a deep breath. "Your father said you found your room acceptable. I hope that's true." Margaret dropped her gaze, and before she could reply, Colin murmured, "Universally feminine response."

Margaret jerked her head back up to see him smiling at her. She frowned, searching his face. "Why did you give me the necklace?"

Colin's smile faded. "I don't know," he replied guiltily. "I thought it could be something to remember me by. And... and because I have cared for you."

Margaret bit her lip. She looked at him, her voice a whisper. "I just can't believe you're going to die..."

Die. Any word but that and Colin could have managed, but not that one. Because tonight he had achieved fame as an architect. As Colin Sewell. He had finally struck the forge, and it would be a lasting blow. And he was not going to die in people's minds.

I've already died once.

Colin looked evenly at Margaret. "Get your coat."

Margaret blinked through her tears. "What?"

"Your coat. I must tell you something. Outside."

Margaret glanced about, and then took his arm. "Never mind that," she said. "I'll be fine."

And so they walked out into the chilled night air, and once they were away from the house, Colin threw his jacket over Margaret and said quietly, "I'm not going to die." Margaret stopped, and Colin turned to face her. "Margaret, I am fond of you, more than any woman I've ever known! But it will never be enough, you see, because..." he halted, looking askance for the words. Giving up, he sighed, "The truth is, I like men more than women."

Margaret shook her head, shivering from the cold and anxiety. "What do you mean?"

Colin grimaced. "I'm a..." and he looked around before leaning in and whispering, "I prefer men to women. I'm in love with another man."

Margaret's mind flew into a reeling snap, and she covered her mouth with her hand. "Oh my God!"

"I know! I'm sorry, Margaret! I never meant to lead you on!"

"You're a *sodomite*?"

Colin gasped. "No! No, I... I don't use that term and you shouldn't either. It's more than that. It's different."

Margaret shook her head. "I don't believe it. You're lying! Mr. Sewell, how could you say such a thing to me?"

"Margaret, I honestly had no idea that you harbored any feelings..."

"How could you not? It was so obvious! From both sides of us!"

"But I... well I've always kept my distance from women, you see, out of the very fear something like this would happen. But I thought I was safe with you. You're an heiress! How was I to know your father would entertain the idea of you and I together?"

"And you told my father you were dying?"

"I can't tell your father the truth! He could ruin my career! He could send me to prison! You saw what happened to Oscar Wilde!"

Margaret's eyes widened. "You're like Oscar Wilde...?"

Her voice was so full of hushed horror that Colin wished he could have disagreed, at least on several points, but instead he assented, "Essentially, yes." Then he shrugged. "To be perfectly honest, I thought your father sort of suspected me anyway, but he didn't mind because I was only doing business with him."

"And you kept me in the dark!"

"Well, it's not something to tell a lady! But I would have told you if I knew you felt this way. And I thought you regarded our friendship the same way I did, which is why it worked! You could be yourself around me because you knew I *wasn't* trying to court you."

"Oh, that is such a lie!"

Colin hung his head. "Well, that's what I thought. I am sorry." He met her eyes. "Margaret, you said you could handle the truth, and I thought you could as well. So I am telling you, and I am trusting you with my life because I cannot stand for you to think I would die."

"Yet my father still thinks you will."

Colin took a deep breath. "I know. I'll think of something, but you *cannot tell him.*" Colin's voice became threatening. "If you tell him what I said to you tonight, I'll deny everything." He looked desperately at Margaret. "I'll be ruined." But Margaret said nothing, so Colin went on. "See here: your father asked me to talk to you tonight so that you would 'get on with your life', as it were. Well, now you can, because you know this has nothing to do with you personally. Now, we'll have to walk back in there and pretend we have resolved to go on without each other. And if he asks me about it, I'll say that I told you that since I can't have a wife and children, it's my dying wish to see you find happiness in marriage and motherhood."

"You're joking."

"Please, Margaret, play along."

"Well! I haven't a choice, I suppose!"

Colin's spirits were plummeting. "Margaret, I do like you. I enjoyed spending time with you. I was hoping that perhaps we could at least write to each other...?"

"I can't even *think* properly right now, Mr. Sewell." Margaret began to head for the house.

"Right," Colin said miserably, following her. "We'll head back inside, then."

When they passed over the threshold, Mr. and Mrs. Rademaker were waiting. Colin bowed to Margaret, who made a small curtsey and went upstairs. Max saw Colin to the door. Colin told him his planned story, and Max gave him one final congratulatory slap on the back. Colin coughed, and he turned to face a wide-eyed Max. "Happy New Year, sir. Thank you for having me; it was a spectacular party. Enjoy the house."

When Colin returned home, he went tiredly to the library and poured himself a drink.

"Did you have a good time?"

Colin looked around him and saw Henry in the doorway, dressed in his robe. "What are you doing back already?" Colin said, his voice a mixture of amazement and irritation. He had hoped to unwind with a few drinks before Henry came home.

Henry was taken aback by Colin's demeanor. "What happened?" he asked, concerned.

Colin sighed. "Oh, nothing; it all went well. I don't want to talk about it right now." He strode past Henry with his drink. "But I haven't been entirely pleased with the way *you've* been acting lately, so I think I'll just go to bed. I'm exhausted."

"Colin, I must speak with you."

Colin turned, his eyes flashing at him, and he appeared so agitated that Henry was hesitant to continue. But it was too late now. He made his voice steady. "I don't think we should be together anymore."

For a moment, Colin cocked his head and narrowed his eyes. And then his entire body swelled up as he took a deep breath and uttered one word: "What?"

"I don't love you anymore, Colin. I'm sorry."

Colin slammed the glass onto the table and shook his head. "Oh, no, Henry. You're not going to pull this again. You've done this to me twice already!"

"This is final," Henry said quietly.

"I'll tell you what's final!" Colin shouted. "This conversation! I'll be damned if you're going to lay into me tonight!" Then he burst into tears. "How could you say this to me, on this night? 'It's your special night, Colin. I want you to enjoy it.' And then you do *this*?" He narrowed his eyes again, his voice coming in short breaths. "I don't even believe you. You're just jealous!" He raised his arms, incredulous. "I'm famous now, Henry! Don't you see? And it's thanks to you, so *your* reputation just went up tenfold!"

Henry sighed. "That's not it, Colin. I just don't love you; I haven't for years. You're not a boy any longer, and I don't want you anymore."

Colin reeled. Henry noticed he actually *fell back* several steps. "But I'm twenty years your junior!" Colin choked.

"You're almost thirty years old," Henry replied bitterly. "You know I've never been with anyone over twenty-five! How ridiculous will it sound that I have a thirty-year old lover! You're a *man*."

Colin put a hand out in front of him on the sofa. He couldn't feel his legs. "But, what about when you mentioned all of those things? Why we should stay together?"

Henry shrugged. "I'm afraid those feelings were temporary. I tried. For a while, I enjoyed being only with you, because it was under my terms, to an extent. And because you *did* show so much promise as an architect. But you can't stop time, Colin, and now, this isn't what I want at all."

Colin's chest was hicuppy, and his face was incredulous. "You... you want J-James?"

Henry shook his head. "Not James specifically, no. But the company of others, yes."

Colin almost didn't dare. "Have you been faithless?"

Henry sighed, pausing. "If there's one thing to convince you that it's over, I was faithful to you all those years Colin... until the trip to Paris."

"What?"

"I went to get away from all of this, to get away from you. I knew well my intentions when I left. So I met a charming boy there. Then I met another. I met loads of beautiful boys, every night. I already knew it was over between you and me, so I... I had the most wonderful time in my life. I'm sorry."

Colin crumpled to the floor. "You're sorry?" he whispered, sickness rising in his throat as he pictured the events.

Henry fell silent. He hadn't planned to tell Colin about Paris; he thought it would be unnecessarily cruel and now he saw he was right: Colin had his face in his hands, shaking violently. "No," he whispered. "Please, no..."

Henry pressed on, pretending not to notice. "Colin, I know how much importance you place on being in a relationship with another man. That is what's giving me the impetus to leave. You're so stuck on the idea of being with one person for the rest of your life that you refuse to consider whether or not you're happy about it. In fact, I think you'd prefer to be miserable rather than have your theory disproved."

Colin let out a cry as if he'd been pierced. "I wasn't miserable! I was never miserable!"

Henry made a face. "Perhaps in time, when you've found someone else, you'll realize how truly miserable you were."

Colin's jaw dropped. "So you're passing this off as if you're doing me a favor? I'll never let you! I would have never left you, Henry! As hard as it may be for you to believe, I still love you as much as ever! I love us! I love everything our life has become, for better or for worse! And you're going to chuck it all because you think starting over will make you happier?"

Henry frowned. "Colin, everything you are doing I have already done. In terms of work, what you are just beginning, I'm ready to end. And in terms of life, what you've ended, I want to begin again." He paused. "I never really wanted out, Colin. And now, I want back in."

Colin began running a hand through his hair, over and over. "Well... well..." he began but couldn't think of any words to follow.

Henry's voice remained calm. "Here is how we'll handle it: we'll tell everyone we've had a difference in creative directions, and you want to go off and set up your own offices."

Colin turned his head, aghast. "Wait a moment; you're *firing* me as well?"

"Colin, we can't possibly still work together."

"Henry, no!" Colin leapt to his feet. "Please! You can't do that! We're partners for God's sake! What am I going to do without you?"

"You'll manage fine," Henry said firmly. "You've practically taken over the office anyway, for which I was grateful. You know how to run a business."

"But I don't!" Colin protested, sick with fear. He slumped onto the floor in front of Henry. "I don't know how to do it at all! I can't! I don't want to, Henry! Oh God, please don't fire me! Please!"

"Colin, stop it!" Henry, uncomfortable with this groveling pose, backed away into a chair.

Colin desperately shifted the conversation. "Henry, it's only that this project has taken a toll on us, you see? I think if we... if we got away for a while, it'd make all the difference!"

"I'm afraid it won't."

"Please!" It was a near scream, and Colin began to sob. "Please, Henry! I love you! I bought us two tickets to America! I made reservations for us, at the best hotels! I was going to show you everything! I just knew we'd need to get away, Henry! That's all it is, don't you see?"

Henry stared at Colin. "Are you joking?"

"No! No, I was going to surprise you! The tickets are upstairs..."

"How could you do that?" Henry was incredulous. "How could you go and waste all of that money...?"

"It was only my money," Colin assured him quickly.

Henry closed his eyes and sighed. "Oh, dear God. I was planning on you having that money to live on for a while." He looked at Colin. "Can you get your money back?"

His eyes were met with a devastated gaze. "Won't you go, Henry? Please?"

Henry stood up briskly. "Colin, it's over. In one week I'm having the locks here changed. In that time, you are welcome to take anything from this house that you want. You'll need to clear your things out of the office as well. If I were you, I'd say you are taking a holiday before starting at your new place of business, wherever that may be. I'm going to bed. You're to stay at the Savoy tonight; I reserved a room for you. Charlie is there waiting on you."

Colin half-buried his face in the edge of the chair's cushion. "My God, you're even kicking me out?" He could hardly breathe. "Why are you being so cruel? Why?"

Henry paused his walk. "Because I don't want you to have any illusions about this. I'm sorry it turned out this way for you. It was wonderful those first few years, Colin. Let us just be glad for those times. I'm sure I won't find anyone like you again." And he turned, went upstairs, and with a click locked the bedroom door.

For a while, Colin sat there, his mind blank as the tears dried on his face and burned his skin. But eventually, waves of questions landed in his head, each one crashing in his ears until he had to get up and go upstairs. "Henry," he knocked. "Henry, please open the door. You have to tell me something." There was no reply. Colin banged his fist on the door. "Henry, please! You can't expect to do this to me and just... close the door on it all! I deserve to know!"

The door swung open and Henry shuffled out. "All right," he sighed, descending the staircase. "But I'm going to fix a drink first. Do you want one?"

Colin shook his head as they entered the library. Henry fixed a drink for him anyway and sat down opposite of Colin, who was wringing his hands. "Do Howard and Kenneth know?"

"No. Nobody knows yet. I wanted to wait until you had finished the Helios House. I figured I'd tell Howard and Kenneth on Monday."

"Did you tell them you were going to do this?"

"I never even told them I was thinking about doing this."

"But you were at Porter's tonight..."

"I didn't go. I sent a note around earlier saying I felt ill."

Suddenly it all made sense. Colin exhaled. "So you were waiting for me the entire time."

"Yes. I wanted to wait until after your party." Henry paused. "It's not as if we hadn't had our problems along the way, Colin."

"Most every couple has problems!" Colin insisted.

"Yes, and that's exactly why I don't want to be part of a couple anymore!"

Colin cast about in angry disbelief. "So it's all about sex? Sex with boys?"

Henry sighed. "You don't seem to understand that it's as much to do with *not* having *you* as it is with having them. I just want to be on my own again. A bachelor again."

"What, a rich, old, lecher bachelor?" Colin said bitterly.

Henry crossed his arms. "Is that how you see me?"

"No, but that's how you'll appear to them."

Henry pondered this, and then shrugged. "A rich, old, lecher bachelor. Yes, thank God! I don't care. I have more money than I have years of life, Colin. And that's why I intend to enjoy them to the fullest."

Colin narrowed his eyes. "Well, it's wonderful that you'll be indulging your twenty years left after having effectively destroyed the past twenty-nine of mine."

"Oh, quit the melodramatics."

"I meant to spend my life with you, Henry!"

"You have spent nine years of it, Colin. You're young enough to find someone else."

Colin shook his head. "I don't want anyone else! My God, we built a life together! You said so yourself!"

Henry threw his hands up and stood from his seat. "Yes, and when it comes down to it, you should be grateful for all you got! *I* took you in. *I* kept your secret. *I* adopted you and gave you *my* name! *I* taught you everything I could. *I* made you the youngest partner in architectural history. *I* introduced you to everybody. *I* adored you, worshipped you, and catered to your whims. And *I* let you change, and *I* changed for you. I gave you everything!" He stood up with a spiteful eye and a cold voice. "Every man should be so lucky as Michael Callahan." He stalked off to their bedroom, this time for good.

Colin remained in his chair, awed by Henry's outburst. It was all he could do to keep himself from shaking, and soon he began to fear that the longer he stayed there, the truer Henry's words would become. Forcing himself to remain calm, Colin made his way to the front door and left.

Henry heard the door shut and sat upon the bed. Lying down, he felt his heart beating wildly.

I've done it! I have done it!

He closed his eyes and sighed. Then he opened them and frowned. Oddly, he didn't quite feel free yet. He put his arms behind his head and, in doing so, brushed Colin's pillow with his elbow. He stared at the offending object and it struck him: there were reminders of Colin everywhere. Everywhere in the house, but especially here in this room. He moved to toss Colin's pillow ruefully off the bed but paused. "Poor fellow," he murmured, and gently placed the pillow onto the floor.

When Colin entered his hotel suite, he saw that the lamps were lit and the fireplaces were burning. "Mr. Colin?" Charlie's voice came forth, and soon the valet himself appeared.

"Hello, Charlie," Colin said hoarsely. "I suppose Henry has told you everything."

Charlie, unaccustomed to being privy to such matters, dropped his gaze awkwardly. "Yes, sir. I'm very sorry, sir. Mr. Sewell instructed me to be of service to you until you've found a valet for yourself."

'Found a valet for yourself.' Five pins in his heart. Colin couldn't look at Charlie but nodded. "I'm... I'm just going to go to bed," he said, heading for the room.

"Certainly, Mr. Colin. Let me know if you need anything."

"Thank you."

CHAPTER TWENTY-SEVEN

Sunday, January 1, 1900

The next morning, Henry debated whether or not to go to Charlotte's for brunch. He didn't really want to do so until people knew he was through with Colin. And before he told anyone, he wanted to tell Kenneth and Howard. He thought about inviting the two men to Charlotte's and seating them in Colin's place, but that would look crude, and it would also be rather inconsiderate to have their reactions to the news so publicly exposed. For while Henry never intended Colin to become a full-fledged fourth member of their group, that is what he had become, just as Colin himself had remarked. And so his permanent absence would be felt more strongly than his spotty presence. Which in Henry's case was a good thing, but for Kenneth and Howard... well, they would just have to get used to it. Anyway, Howard had been bringing Mark to Porter's for several months, about the same time Colin had stopped attending Porter's in order to finish the house. So actually, Henry reflected, they had been given a sort of transition period without even knowing it. Still, the affair was a delicate matter, and in the end, Henry decided to invite Kenneth and Howard over for tea that afternoon.

The two men, already wondering at the rarely issued Sunday invitation, were doubly surprised to see Henry open the door.

"Where's Charlie?" Howard asked as they stepped inside.

Henry gave an odd smile. "He's with Colin."

Kenneth raised his eyebrows. "Oh? And so where is Colin?"

"At the Savoy." Henry stood expectantly to take their coats. They removed them, Henry hung them up, and ushered them to the sitting room.

"And why is Colin at the Savoy?" Howard asked, completely perplexed.

Henry gestured for them to sit down opposite him, which they did, and he sighed, smiling weakly. "Well, gentlemen, as Colin has finished the Helios House, so I have finished with Colin."

"What?" the two men chorused, alarmed.

Henry nodded solemnly. "I ended it between us last night. I'm sorry. I know you were both fond of him."

"But..." Howard sputtered, "but, you're joking, aren't you?" *My God, we just feted him two nights ago!*

Henry put two cubes of sugar into his tea. "I'm afraid not. I would have done it sooner, but I didn't want it to affect his project, you see."

"But, what did you tell him?" Kenneth asked, incredulous.

"I told him that he was no longer a boy and I wasn't in love with him anymore." Then Henry's voice became anguished. "You both know the type of man I am! I thought maybe being with Colin was what I wanted. And for a time, it was. But we'd become a boring married couple, for God's sake! I'm almost fifty years old! I want to enjoy the time I have left. Surely you two can understand that."

Howard and Kenneth looked down into their teacups. "What did he say?" Howard asked quietly.

Henry sighed again. "He tried to argue with me. He took the news horribly, as I expected. But honestly, I didn't think it would be that much of a shock."

Kenneth looked up suddenly. "Oh, and he was going to take you to America!"

Henry was surprised. "He told you about that?"

"Yes," Howard admitted. "Just that he was going to surprise you with it, and..." he trailed off, about to add "and the villa in Paris," but figured perhaps Colin never got the chance to mention it himself.

Henry shook his head, disgusted. "Yes, well, that was a stupid thing to do. Romantic, maybe, but not practical in the least. I told him I had planned on him having that money to live on for a while once we separated. I hope to God he can get his money back. Or if I'm lucky, maybe he'll still take the trip, by himself. One way."

"That's being a little hard on him, Henry," Howard suggested softly.

"Perhaps, Howard, but I'm sick of him! All these years I've been stuck with him, tied to him, responsible for him! And I've been miserable; you know I have! Haven't you seen the change in us? I've become wholly resentful of the happiness that has been denied me. I can't even stand to look at him anymore; he's such a different person!"

"Because he's grown up," Kenneth concluded resolutely.

"Yes!" Henry exclaimed. "He has grown up! There you have it. It's not his fault, of course. Natural progression and all, but he's not the clever, young, beautiful tempter fresh off the boat. He's just one of us now. He's not the envy of anyone anymore." He gave a small laugh. "Even Howard is no longer interested in him!"

He glanced sidelong at Howard, who had winced at the comment, then quickly changed his expression and looked at Henry curiously. "Well, what are you going to do now?"

Henry put down his cup. "Really, nothing, for the time being. I just want to revel in the life of a bachelor again. I told him that he can come and get his things, and that he could take anything else here that he wants; I don't care. I think *that* in itself is extremely generous! Oh, and of course,

I also told him that he has to pack up his office, seeing as we certainly can't work together any longer."

"Oh God, that's true," Howard rubbed his face.

"And he went raving mad about that. As if we could actually still be partners! And obviously, I'm the one who stands to lose there, since Colin's been doing most of the work anyway." His voice dropped down. "But I'm thinking of closing shop."

"*What?*" Kenneth exclaimed.

"Well, I've got all the money I want," Henry smiled. "And I'm sure I could do some consulting jobs if I miss working, which frankly, I doubt I will." Then he was suddenly tired of talking to them. "Right. I know I've given you a lot to digest, and we can talk more about it tomorrow evening. But I wanted you to be the first to know, and I also want to ask you a favor." They looked at him expectantly. "I'm sure you'd do this anyway, but would you mind dropping by Colin's room sometime today and checking up on him? I have a feeling he's in quite a state and in need of some rationalism. You two mean the world to him." Henry regarded them gravely. "And it's very important that he understands it is over. Being the romantic that he is, I'm sure he's already imagined a hundred rendezvous, all with the same happy ending."

"And you're absolutely sure of this decision yourself?" Kenneth confirmed.

"Yes." Henry sighed. "I don't miss him one minute. I know it sounds cruel, but to me, it's only sheer proof that this was the right thing to do." He smiled childishly. "I can't tell both of you how *happy* I am! How *relieved* I am! It's wonderful! God, this should have been done long ago, really, for both of our sakes. I thought I was doing him a favor by letting him finish that house first, but oh, I wish I hadn't." As he sent them off, he said kindly, "Gentlemen, I am sorry about all of this. To be honest, it was partially due to both of you as well that I put off leaving him as long as I did. This feels rather like a divorce." He frowned slightly. "That said, I suppose I shouldn't expect you to profess loyalty either way. We'll sort this all out somehow."

The two men nodded, bade him farewell, and decided to go directly to see Colin.

Charlie gasped when he opened the door. "Mr. Durham! Mr. Fairchild! Thank God!" He stepped aside to let them enter.

"Henry sent us," Howard told him, and then added quickly, "but of course, we would have come, regardless."

Charlie was distraught. "Mr. Colin has fallen ill and I don't know what to do!" He paused, unsure as to how much information to give away. His voice turned into a whisper. "He cried all night long. It was awful! Wailing and sobbing! I don't think he inflicted injury, but I think he must have practically cried himself to death. This morning he went quiet and when I checked on him, he was just lying there, all weak like. I've tried to get him to eat something, but he won't, and yet he's already vomited twice!"

"Is he feverish?" Kenneth asked, mildly concerned.

"I don't know. Most of the time he just sleeps. When he is awake, all he does is cry."

"Well, let's have a look at him, then," Kenneth said briskly, and Charlie led them to Colin's room.

"God, he looks terrible," Howard murmured, filling with dread.

"Oh, Colin," Kenneth sighed.

Colin was sleeping, albeit uncomfortably, on half a dozen pillows. He was ashen, with an even grayer shadow on his face where he hadn't shaved. Stranger still were the two scarlet spots on his cheeks. His breathing was raspy, and the skin around his eyes was swollen and red. Handkerchiefs littered the floor. Colin's glasses were on the nightstand and Howard was touched by the vulnerability lent to his friend without them.

"He didn't come with a suitcase," Charlie explained desperately. "He needs pajamas, fresh clothes, and things, but I've been too afraid to leave him to fetch them myself." He looked angrily toward Colin. "Mr. Sewell should have known better! Seems to me if you're going to kick a gentleman out with no notice, you'd be obliged to make some arrangements."

"Well, he had this room reserved," Howard noted wryly.

"We'll go back to Henry's and get some clothes and toiletries," Kenneth nodded. "Charlie, you're a good man. You've done everything you could, and more."

"Thank you, sirs." Charlie looked at Colin again. "It's funny," he said, mystified, "I thought they'd always be together. I really did. And then it ends like it always does. It's a shame."

"Yes, well, these things happen," Howard replied swiftly. "We'll let him sleep. If he wakes up, tell him we've been here and we'll come back later with provisions."

"Thank you, sirs," Charlie replied. "I'll do that."

When they returned that evening, Charlie greeted them worriedly. "He doesn't want to see anyone. He was horrified to learn you were here. I had to lie and assure him that you didn't see him."

Howard shrugged. "Well, he can't avoid us forever, although I can understand his feelings."

Kenneth's voice fell to a hush. "Don't tell him we're here. We'll just go to his door."

Colin was asleep once again and looked the same as he did earlier. Howard stood in the doorway, unsure what to do. But Kenneth went over and sat on the bed, resting his hand on Colin's arm. "Colin?" he murmured. "Colin, how are you doing?"

Colin shifted, then opened his eyes. They widened, then closed as he sank deeper into the bed. "Kenneth..." he whispered. He realized why his friend was there and tears of humiliation squeezed from his eyes. "I told Charlie not to let anyone in!"

Kenneth put his palm on Colin's forehead and stroked his hair. "Feverish. You don't feel well, I know."

Colin turned away from him and shook his head. "No, I don't. I'd just like to rest, please."

"Do you want us to bring you a doctor?"

"No, no. It's just... I have to stay in bed awhile, you see. I've fallen very, very ill..." but he couldn't finish. He closed his eyes and breathed shallowly.

Kenneth stood up. "I think he's right. The poor dear is simply enervated; he's been working himself to death and he's no doubt caught something. His forehead is burning up." He turned to Charlie. "Has he eaten or drank anything at all today?"

"Just water. He's been thirsty," Charlie answered.

"Good. That's fine, then. I've had this sort of thing myself, if he is actually sick." He motioned to Howard. "We'll visit tomorrow. Charlie, please tell him we've brought clothes and things, and that we're coming tomorrow whether he likes it or not."

Outside, Howard smiled in wonder. "You were impressive back there, Kenneth. I didn't have a clue what to do."

Kenneth shrugged. "Well, I didn't do much. He's just got a fever and a sensitive stomach. But I think he'll be all right. Still, we ought to check on him every day." Kenneth paused. "I honestly can't believe this is happening, can you? The day we predicted in fear has finally arrived! What is Colin going to do?"

"I don't know," Howard said morosely. "Perhaps he'll tell us tomorrow."

On Monday they visited over their lunch hour. Colin was sitting up in bed, fairly alert and in pajamas. He still looked exhausted and sickly, the shadow on his face now definite stubble. He hadn't the energy to pick up even a razor, and he refused to let Charlie shave him. When Colin was told that his friends had arrived, he had desperately wanted to crawl under the covers, but he knew it would look rude, not to mention silly. Still, when they appeared at the door, he unconsciously slid down in his bed and put his hands over his eyes, thankful his glasses were already off.

"You're doing better," Kenneth approached affably.

"No," Colin muttered. "Please, this is absolutely humiliating. I know you're trying to help, and I appreciate that, but I just want to be alone. I've got to be alone for a while, Kenneth." But Kenneth sat down on the bed anyway, and Colin couldn't stand it. He turned on his side and hid under the sheets. "Please, for the love of God, leave me alone!" he begged.

"Colin, Howard and I feel simply terrible about what's happened."

"Oh, God! I can't talk about it! I can't!"

"Colin," Kenneth soothed. He rubbed the blanket on Colin's back, and slowly, Colin pushed the covers back and sat up, searching Kenneth's face.

"How could he do that to me, Kenneth? I... I just finished the most wonderful house in the world! Why would he...? How could he change so much? After all this time? I never... I tried... I didn't..." and then he broke down sobbing. Kenneth took him into his arms and held him. Colin cried only harder, and Howard stepped back, horrified at the sight. That the boy who had grown into a brave genius of a man was reduced to this... this display of histrionics in the presence of other men!

"He's gone!" Colin bawled. "He never wants to see me again! I didn't mean to do anything to make him not like me! I didn't! I really tried! And now I've got nowhere to go! I don't have anything anymore!" Kenneth made shushing sounds and caressed Colin's back and head. Colin became hiccupy. "But—I—love—him! I'm sorry, Henry—I'm so *sorry*!"

Howard was appalled. Colin was acting as if it was *his* fault! Why was he apologizing, for God's sake? Why wasn't he angry? Howard fell into a depressed mood. He wished he could leave the room, but he didn't want to hurt Colin's feelings. Kenneth was obviously the better friend, sitting there patiently.

After a while, Colin quieted down, blew his nose for the last time, and dried his face. "I'm feeling faint," he said wearily. "You should go." He took Kenneth's hand and thanked him.

"I'll stay on." Howard couldn't believe he said it, and from the looks of the other two men, neither could they. "Kenneth has an appointment," he nodded. "But I'm not due back for anything in particular." He looked at Colin. "I think someone ought to look after you for a bit longer."

Colin shook his head. "No, Howard..."

"Colin, I won't say a word to you if you don't want me to, but I am going to sit here and... er..." he looked around the room, "read a book. Kenneth, on your way out, would you have Charlie find me one?"

Kenneth smiled proudly. "Of course. Now you take care, Colin. I shall see you tomorrow."

For his part, Colin was secretly glad to have some company, even though he didn't want to talk. Kenneth left, and Colin slid down into bed again and pulled the covers over him. Howard tried to think of something to say, but soon he heard steady breathing and realized Colin had fallen asleep. Relieved, he settled into a chair and waited for his book.

Colin awoke later to find Howard still by his bed, staring at an opened text. "What time is it?" he asked fuzzily. If he had been more alert upon waking, he would have noticed that Howard had actually been gazing at him.

"It's almost half past four," Howard remarked, coming out of his own reverie.

"Oh, no! Howard, you didn't have to stay this long!"

"I wanted to wait until you woke up, to see how you felt."

"I'm all right. Relatively speaking." Colin moved to get out of bed. "I'm just going to get some water." He came back and suddenly stopped. He stood with the glass of water looking across the bed at the immaculately dressed, handsome Howard. Mr. Durham, who was looking intently at him: he in a smelly dressing gown and tangled hair and rough skin. Colin looked down and set the glass on the table. "This is pathetic. I'm going to draw a bath, shave, and get dressed."

"Colin, you're probably not well enough yet..."

"I don't care!" Colin cried, escaping to the water closet. "I can't stand that you're seeing me like this!" He began to cry.

Oh God, Howard thought. *And no Kenneth in sight.* "Colin, don't be ridiculous. You're still weak. You might cut yourself with the razor."

"But I look *disgusting*!" There was the sound of something light being thrown to the floor.

Howard was stunned into silence. That Colin would ever describe himself so lowly! "You don't look disgusting," he managed to call back. "You couldn't; it's impossible. And anyway, from what I've heard, people who are ill generally don't appear to be the picture of health."

After a few moments, Colin caught his breath and shuffled back into the room, a bleak smile on his face. "That's nice of you to say, Howard. But I... I'd best see you to the door. You must be starving."

The comment was true; Howard hadn't any lunch. But he was reluctant to leave Colin in such a state. "Why don't I bring us both something back to eat? Yes, I'll be back, then."

"Don't, Howard." Colin made his voice sharp. Then he softened. "You've been very kind. Any more and you'll be killing me with it, you see?" Forlorn, he walked past Howard to the door. "Besides, you've got Porter's tonight." His voice became bitter. "Where, no doubt, Henry will make his grand announcement, if he hasn't already."

I'd rather stay here with you. The response suddenly appeared in Howard's mind and it shocked him to the core. But Colin had made his wishes known.

"I'm sorry, Colin."

Colin nodded. "Good night, Howard. Thank you."

Colin closed the door. He went back into the bathroom, stood in front of the washbasin for a moment, and then turned around and sought refuge in the warm comfort of the bed.

I can't remember what a routine was. What my *routine was. What in hell was my routine? I can't think of anything for more than a second before it dissolves away. Without Henry... My God, without Henry, what am I going to do?*

On the ride back home, Howard struggled with his own thoughts. While he had watched Colin sleep earlier, he grew increasingly bitter. *Love! Is there really such a thing? When we know it's fact and not theory that all things must come to an end?*

You can love to the end.

Not in our world. God knows Colin tried, and even he's failed! The boy's only twenty-nine years old and now he considers himself dead! All of his accomplishments, all of the attention lavished upon him over the past nine years, and it's suddenly all forgotten.

Temporarily. He'll overcome it.

How do you overcome that? He always said "I am an architect." But I'll bet he really never got past "I am" before he thought of Henry.

But you never thought it was a sure thing anyway, he and Henry.

Then how could I have ever thought it could be a sure thing with anyone?

Because you always thought Colin would be a sure thing with you.

And that's where Howard's mind blanked.

Howard rode with Mark to Porter's that evening and told him the news of Henry's breakup with Colin. "Oh, no!" Mark exclaimed. "Poor Mr. Colin! But after that horrible episode at the club, I suppose it's not so surprising." He looked at Howard. "To be honest, Mr. Sewell doesn't seem the type to be beholden to one man." Howard smiled. It was an astute comment; however, Mark hadn't seen the near decade that Henry and Colin had spent together. "But, then again," Mark mused, "if he would pick one man, it'd certainly be Mr. Colin. What on earth he saw in that James boy over him is beyond me."

"He saw a boy," Howard replied. "And that's all he needs to see. I believe Henry is so afraid of his own mortality he feels spending time with youth will keep him young."

Mark raised an eyebrow. "Didn't I see that credo above the door at Porter's?"

Howard chuckled. "It's certainly not a phenomenon unique to Mr. Sewell. And admittedly, there's no denying the beauty in youth."

"I'll bet you've been with a boy or two yourself," Mark accused good-naturedly.

"Darling, at my age, everyone's a 'boy,'" Howard deflected. "But no, I don't prefer them singularly, the way Henry does." He smiled at his companion. "I place more value on experience, maturity, and wit."

Mark rolled his eyes and snorted, "Oh, you're full of it, you are! If that were true, you'd be with someone your own age and not a twenty-six-year-old!"

Howard shook his finger at him. "Wit! Very good!"

Henry was late to the club. "I told the office today," he explained to the group. "I had to spend the entire time answering stupid questions and the like." When his drink was set before him, he said to the waiter, "Oh, a glass of champagne next, if you would, Georgie."

"Certainly, Mr. Sewell. What's the occasion?"

Henry sat back and sighed. "My newfound freedom. Colin and I are no longer together."

"Oh!" Georgie was taken aback. "Er... my condolences, then."

"Ha! Only condolences on the past five years I've wasted. And you can offer me congratulations that I've finally done something about it."

Georgie nodded uncertainly and went off to fetch the champagne. Howard glared at his friend. "Really, Henry, you could be a bit more decent than that!"

Henry shrugged. "Well, I don't expect you three to celebrate with me. That's why I didn't order glasses for you. But I'm going to savor this triumph like the victory it is." Then he looked at Mark. "Howard did tell you, didn't he?"

"Yes, sir."

Then Henry looked at Kenneth and Howard. "Well, how is he, then?"

Howard looked at Kenneth and shrugged. "He's fallen quite ill, actually—feverish and vomiting. He's still a bit under the weather. He's been sleeping, mostly."

Henry frowned. "Well, I hope he's not going to confine himself to bed all week! I told him I was changing the locks to my house and the office, and so he has until Saturday to get his things!"

"Saturday!" Kenneth exclaimed. "Henry, the boy is truly ill! I don't think he'll have the strength to carry out such tasks so soon. Now be realistic!"

Henry smiled. "Well, in this case, I give Colin more credit than you do." He took his drink from Georgie's tray. "He'll do it. Colin's got more resolve than you know. How do you think he came across the Atlantic in the first place?"

By the end of the night the entire club knew, and Henry was glad for it. He certainly didn't want to have to tell everyone personally. However, he ended up having to confirm the rumor every five minutes, as each man dropped by and asked if it was true, acting terribly put out. Worst of all was Jack, who had waited until the club was closing to approach Henry, by then quite drunk on his champagne and quite tired of explaining.

"Sewell, what happened?"

"Age happened, Colton," Henry replied sourly. "Who could have predicted it?"

"But Colin can't be even thirty!"

"He will be this April. Remember your saying, Jack? 'Twenty-five, thirty-five, mortified'?"

Jack sighed. "Oh, yes. But he was exceptional."

Henry sat up. "He was shit! How dare you pretend to know everything that went on between us?"

Jack was aghast. "My apologies, Henry! It's just... hard to believe." He shook his head. "You two were the epitome of a couple."

"We certainly were, what with all those bets placed on our demise."

"Oh God, well, I'm sorry all the same. How's he taking it?"

"How's he taking it?" Henry was incredulous. "Christ, who cares? That's another reason I'm glad I'm through with him. He's like everyone's damn puppy dog around here. Throw him a bone if you care so much about him, Colton!" And Jack could only stare at Henry and go home that evening deeply depressed. Not that he was one to judge, but Colin Sewell! Colin just didn't deserve it. *'Puppy dog.' That's perfect, Henry. Because God knows, he was devoted to you.*

CHAPTER TWENTY-EIGHT

Colin was wondering about that devotion the next afternoon when Kenneth and Howard called. Charlie showed them to the suite's sitting room, where Colin, bathed, fully dressed, and clean-shaven, sat staring out the window. When Howard and Kenneth drew closer, they noticed a glass of gin on the table and alongside it the bottle, its liquor lowered by a third.

"I'm going to Henry's today," Colin announced, a notable slur in his tone.

Kenneth nodded. "To get your things."

Colin glanced up at him, surprised. "No, I'm going to ask him to take me back."

They stared at him. "Colin," Kenneth started. "I don't think you understand..."

"I have to at least try!" Colin pleaded. He looked out the window again. "If he wants to be with boys, fine. It isn't as if we haven't done *that* before." Then he turned toward them. "It's not the sex that is important, you see. It's more than that. We were a team. We worked together." He shifted his gaze back to outside, his breath frosting the glass. "He's all I have in this world."

"Colin," Kenneth began, "give yourself some dignity. You can't surely intend to go over there and let him bring boys home while you remain chaste and be some sort of *dutiful housewife*."

"But that's what I was," Colin insisted. "I took care of him."

Howard and Kenneth exchanged desperate glances, and then Howard tried. "Henry told the entire club last night, Colin. He doesn't want you anymore." He hoped the directness that drove Colin out of Henry's house could work again to keep him away.

But Colin stood up unsteadily and laid a hand on Howard. "And if *he* doesn't want me, nobody does. You understand that, Howard, don't you?" He pushed past their protestations and went to the bedroom to find his keys.

More frantic glances. When Colin returned to see them standing sentry at the door, he grew angry. "Oh for God's sake! This is between Henry and myself! Move out of the way."

"Colin," Kenneth soothed, "at least give yourself time to collect yourself. You know how drinking can cloud one's judgment."

Colin's voice became shrill. "I'm fine! What kind of friends are you? Do you think I don't have any chance at all? Do you find me that much of a lost cause yourselves?"

"No," Kenneth sighed. "Now don't be silly. But you're doing something you might well regret."

Colin gave him a venomous eye. "And what difference does that make? I've done plenty of things I've regretted, Kenneth." He gave a harsh laugh. "I've got one of them before me!"

At this, Howard's eyes widened and he grabbed Colin's arm. "Listen, you sodden little brat! We don't care if you do go to Henry, but I'll be damned if you're going to insult us! After everything we've done for you! Go on, then; make a fool of yourself!"

He shoved Colin toward the door, but Colin stumbled and fell down, and began to cry. "I'm sorry!" he whimpered. "I didn't mean it that way!"

But Howard had enough. "Come along, Kenneth, let's go."

Kenneth hesitated, confused. But Howard dragged him out. "They deserve each other," he said through gritted teeth, as they got into their carriage and rode off.

Back inside, Colin got up from the floor, feeling wretched.

You are a lost cause. Even Howard hates you. 'Sodden brat'. Drunken fool. Oaf. You stupid pile of shit, you're worthless.

Head throbbing, he tottered over to his desk and began to pen a letter.

Dear Henry,

By the time you read this, I will be on a ship headed to America. I can't stand the idea of seeing you anymore, so I am moving back permanently. I'm sorry if this causes any inconvenience on your behalf, but I imagine you will be glad. I will inform you of my whereabouts in a month, so you may pass on the information to anyone who asks (specifically, clients). Nobody knows of this departure yet except you, Howard, and Kenneth. I feel you should tell those outside of our circle that my aunt died and, as I'm the sole surviving relative, I had to leave the country to attend to estate matters. Once there, I would decide to remain, out of a desire to live back in my homeland, as it were. This is the only favor I ask of you.

I was working with our employees on some projects that I'm sure you can take over. I will arrange with Howard to transfer some money from my account to yours. Please divide that amount by 20 and add it to our employee's paychecks, as a gift of thanks from me for their work.

I am taking Charlie with me on your ticket. I hope you don't mind, but I will need a valet when I arrive, and Charlie is very excited to see America. He has left with Millie several names of valets who would be happy to be of service to you either temporarily or permanently.

I am leaving most everything else behind, because to have any reminders of you is torture. Do with them as you please.

I'm sorry for all that has happened. I'm sorry I disappointed you. I'm sorry about us.

Yours Ever,

Colin

With that, Colin folded the letter and sealed it in an envelope. He set it aside, as it wouldn't be sent out for another six days. He went to have a talk with Charlie.

On Wednesday morning, Colin entered his former office in trepidation. He had sent a post to Henry telling him he'd be coming to take his things and had requested Henry be absent until noon. He also brought Charlie along to help.

Colin burst into a wide smile when he saw that every single draftsman was there, waiting for him. "Oh, it's so good to see all of you," he exhaled. "I'm so sorry for everything that's happened."

The men nodded. "Mr. Colin, if you don't mind us asking, where are you going to go?" It was John, one of the senior draftsmen.

Colin ran a hand through his hair. "I haven't the slightest idea, John. But Henry is forcing me out by today, so I have to take everything now."

A clerk named Billy said quietly, "We didn't know you were so unhappy."

"Unhappy!" Colin stepped back. "I was perfectly happy! Mr. Sewell is the one who made this decision!"

Now the men looked puzzled. "But," John said, "Mr. Sewell told us *you* were choosing to leave. That you want to pursue projects on your own."

Colin's mouth dropped in horror. Henry had used the excuse he mentioned last Saturday, without Colin's approval. "Is that what he told you?" he demanded. The men shifted uncomfortably, and Colin, seeing that he couldn't use his aunt's death at this point, decided to tell the truth: "Gentlemen, Mr. Sewell *fired* me."

"Fired you! But why?" John asked.

This took Colin by surprise, and he realized now why Henry had lied to them. He shook his head. "Er... we had a falling-out. But I didn't expect the consequence to be having to leave this office! I swear it." Some of the men's expressions changed. *They know.* Colin felt his cheeks flame and he looked around, concerned. "Umm... did Mr. Sewell say that everything here would be taken care of? I know I was working on some projects with you. I'm assuming he took them over." Some of the men nodded and Colin sighed. "Good. Now look here, if I knew what I was going to do, if I knew I was going to need employees, I would ask you. All of you, to the man, to follow me! But, I have to take some time off, you see. Hopefully now you can understand why I'm a bit out of sorts about all of this. I hate this more than you do."

As the men regarded their former boss, they realized his sallow, sunken appearance backed up his words. "Of course, sir," John assured him. "If there's anything we can do..."

Colin smiled weakly. "It's all right. I should just be here an hour or so, packing. Please let me know while I'm here if you have any questions or need anything from me." He drew his breath and lifted his chin. "It's been an absolute honor working with such a fine group of men. I've arranged with Henry to put an additional sum in your next paycheck as a gift of my appreciation." He looked down toward the floor. "I'm extremely sorry to be leaving." He turned, and Charlie followed him into the office that Colin had shared with Henry since he had arrived in London.

Colin tried to work swiftly, knowing any pause over a single object might cause an emotional relapse. He'd be damned if his employees saw him break down. But one by one, the draftsmen and clerks came in to offer him good wishes and to tell him how much it had meant to work with him. By the fourth such visit, Colin was at the mercy of the crystal decanter full of brandy. And as Charlie stood quietly, listening to Mr. Colin's co-workers sing his praises, Colin put a glass in his hand as well. "Hell, I can't drink alone, Charlie. This is the least I can do for all of your help."

Charlie grinned, having admired the expensive liquor earlier. "Anything you say, sir!"

Colin looked at him, amused, and then broke into a laugh. *It's either laugh or cry. And that's about all I've done lately, isn't it?* Finally, he made his way out of the office, promising to keep them posted as to what his next step would be. He had a sinking feeling of guilt as he rode away, however. He already did know. And he was headed to the Bank of England to tell Howard.

The secretary was caught off-guard by Colin's humbled appearance and the smell of alcohol emanating from him. "Hallo," Colin greeted him, swallowing nervously. "I must apologize; I don't have an appointment with Mr. Durham, but I urgently need to see him, if he's here."

The man rose out of his chair. "Certainly, Mr. Colin. I'll let him know." Moments later, he came back, flustered. "I'm sorry, sir. Mr. Durham asked if you could come back another day." He decided not to tell him the rest of Howard's words: "Tell him to make a damned appointment like everyone else!"

Colin reddened, then sighed. "I'm going to write something. If you could give it to him..." He wrote a few sentences on a piece of paper, folded it twice, and handed it to the secretary. "Please."

The secretary took it, shocked at Colin's slightly slurred speech and bewildered as to how he had fallen out of favor with his boss. For while he had only seen Mr. Colin in the bank on a few occasions, Mr. Durham's reaction to his appearance had been so remarkable—such looks of affection for Mr. Colin—that he would never have guessed this outcome.

Howard grudgingly took the piece of paper and told his secretary to wait. He unfolded the note.

I beg you to accept my apologies, Howard. I'm moving back to America on Monday. I need to close my account.

Howard closed his eyes. *Oh God, Colin.* "All right, send him in," he muttered. Then, "Wait, I'll fetch him myself." He nodded the secretary to go and followed him out.

Colin was doing a magnificent job of looking chastened, Howard noticed wryly. He stopped, watched the secretary tell him, and when Colin turned, Howard motioned him back with a jerk of his head. He stood at his door with a disapproving look and let Colin enter first. The smell of brandy curled into Howard's nose and his disdain deepened. He closed the door while Colin stood cowed at his chair. Howard moved toward his own and crossed his arms.

"You're moving to America?"

Colin kept his gaze downwards. "Yes. But Howard..." he glanced up, a tortured look on his face, "I didn't mean what I said that day. I'm sorry. I only had the regret for your sake, and it was only because if it had never happened..."

Howard shrugged coldly. "It doesn't matter anymore. For God's sake, I haven't felt that way about you for years!"

Colin blushed furiously. He looked back down at the floor and gave a self-deprecating laugh. "No, of course not. I know." He took a deep breath. "Anyway, I'm moving back to America and so I need to close my account, but of course I need your assistance and I hope you can be of some help. I'm sorry to be such an inconvenience; really I am."

Howard dropped his arms upon hearing the words that Colin struggled to say. *He thought I still carried a torch for him! Rejected twice, in a matter of days...* His usual rush of forgiveness flooded him and he softened his tone. "Colin, sit down." Colin obeyed, and Howard followed suit. "Are you really moving to America, or just using the vacation time you had set aside?"

"I'm moving back."

"Colin, you know you don't have to do that."

Colin looked him squarely in the eye. "You know that I do. Every single person I know, I know through Henry. Every single establishment, I know through Henry. I'll never be able to go back to Porter's or Charlotte's, or anywhere else!"

"That's not true…"

"It is! I relied on Henry for everything, Howard! You and Kenneth are the only close friends I have and I…" Colin wanted to say "And I messed that up, too," but he couldn't. Instead, tears sprang to his eyes and he whispered, "I just want to get out."

Howard felt awful. Helpless, actually, because he found himself agreeing. Everywhere Colin went, there'd be a reminder of Henry. They had covered every meter of London together. "Oh, good heavens, Colin. Don't cry in my office. I'm getting quite tired of this lachrymose behavior, you know."

It was said lightheartedly, but Colin wiped his eyes, shamefaced, and took a deep breath. "I am, too." Then he straightened and said stiffly, "So, let us take care of business, please."

"But what about your work?"

"Henry fired me, remember? And I can't even think about work. I'm between projects anyway. I'll find work in America."

"Well, what about moving to France? Why, you even speak the language!"

Colin shook his head. "France is too close. You know me; I'd spend every day on the lookout for him."

"Oh." Howard reflected on this reply. "It must be difficult, to be so connected to a person," he wondered out loud.

Colin bit his lip. "It's the devil. Tennyson didn't know." He sighed. "Howard, I know I'm taking up your time. Really, if you could just please help me do this."

Howard nodded. "Right." He pulled out Colin's file. "Well, let's see… Henry transferred fifty percent of his money into your account—"

"Fifty percent!" Colin exclaimed. "I didn't ask for that! I didn't ask for anything!"

"Colin," Howard said patiently, "it's from your earnings as a partner. It's your money."

"No, no, no," Colin shook his head. "We didn't agree on that! That wasn't how it worked!" He grew angry. "It's pity money, that's what it is! He doesn't think I can make it on my own! Well I don't... I don't need it."

Howard frowned. "Perhaps not in the short term. But you had only a few hundred pounds left after the withdrawal for Mr. Rademaker's cut and the trip you're taking." Then he brightened. "Were you able to get a partial refund?"

Colin shook his head. "Only on my return ticket. I'm taking Charlie on Henry's ticket, so he can serve as my valet. Then he can use his return ticket if he wants."

"Oh," Howard paused. "Well then, I'm afraid if you don't take the fifty percent, you may fall quite short on funds in a few months."

Colin smiled bitterly. "I came here years ago with only twenty-five dollars in my pocket, and I managed to do quite well, with the exception of present events." He shrugged. "It's probably appropriate, actually, for me to be arriving yet again in another country, similarly short-changed."

Howard put down his pen. "Now see here, Colin. This is just like the argument we had some time ago. Don't be stupid! If this is a matter of pride, then you should take the money. Hell, you should have expected it; you've been doing most of the work in that office! Don't you see that if you refuse the money it will look like you don't believe your genius and effort to have been of any value? *That's* why Henry gave you the money. Despite everything, you must still believe he thinks highly of your talent." He paused, and then said softly, "It's not a crime to become a man, Colin. Henry may not be able to deal with it, but I think that you have turned out quite admirably. In fact, I like you even better now, because unlike most of those other boys, you've gone on to really make something of yourself." He hesitated, and then admitted, "To tell you the truth, I think you were out of Henry's league from the start. That's why he couldn't let go of you. But it was inevitable that you would outgrow him."

Colin gave a spiteful laugh. "Grow out of him? He grew out of me."

Howard shook his head. "Henry is much the same as when he was twenty years old. But you saw that time as the phase it rightfully is. You knew there was more to life than working four hours a day, getting drunk, and taking boys home. You knew your work was a passion unto itself and one that deserved pursuit. You made the right choices all along, but they were difficult ones, and for that, I admire you." Howard crossed his arms once more. "If *I* have to see you leave, then I ask that you do it with the dignity and grace that you've always possessed."

Colin felt his eyes water again. "Thank you, Howard." He gave him a grateful smile. "If anyone is a man of dignity, it's you. You've always been first rate about everything." He sighed. "All right, I'll take the money. But I want to set aside two hundred pounds to be divided amongst our employees."

Howard made the adjustment, then handed Colin the envelope. Colin stared at it, looked at Howard and laughed. "My first and last paycheck." Folding it, he stood up and shook Howard's hand. "Thank you."

"Colin..." Howard hesitated, "is there any possibility of you showing Kenneth and me the Helios House before you leave? We've been dying to see it."

Colin brightened. "I would love for you to see it. Actually, I'd most love Henry to see it, but he certainly wouldn't if I was with you... Tell you what: I'll write to Rademaker and ask if the three of you can see it this Friday. Rademaker won't need to be around; Henry will be able to show you everything—he knows it as well as I do. But Howard, Henry doesn't know yet that Charlie and I are leaving, so I ask you to keep the confidence. I'm going to visit Kenneth now to tell him. I have a letter set aside for Henry with all the details, but I won't send it out until Monday."

"Why don't you want to tell him?" Howard queried.

Colin looked sheepish. "Because I'll keep hoping that he'll show up at the dock to stop me." The he looked shyly at Howard. "I'll write as soon as I get there."

"What time *does* your ship leave, Colin?"

Colin shook his head sadly. "I can't tell you. I don't want anyone there, Howard. I couldn't stand it."

"But you must allow Kenneth and I to bid you farewell. If you won't, all I have to do is go to the dock and find out myself and we'd be there anyway."

Colin sighed. "It leaves at 10:02 in the morning."

Howard smiled. "All right. Good luck, Colin. We'll be there to see you off, and then I can congratulate you once more on your magnificent Helios House!"

The conversation with Kenneth ran along the same lines, with one exception. "Here is the address of a good friend of Jack's." Kenneth pressed a piece of paper into Colin's palm. "He runs a place in New York that's just like Porter's. Jack says he knows everyone there, and that you can look him up whenever you like and he'll take you under his wing. Jack has already sent a letter off to him explaining things, so he'll be expecting you."

Colin closed his palm tightly around the note. "Thank you, Kenneth. Tell Jack thank you, too, please. Say goodbye to Anne for me. I told Howard that I'll write to you both after I've crossed." Then he took Kenneth off guard and embraced him. "Everything! Thank you for everything, Kenneth! I hope I can find someone like you again, over there. I'll miss you so very much."

Kenneth hugged him back. "I'll miss you too, Colin! Oh, I can't believe this is happening!" He withdrew and patted Colin on the back. "Perhaps next year I can arrange a visit, if you like. I haven't been to America in ten years!"

"Oh, that would be wonderful!" Colin beamed. "Yes, please do! It would give me something to look forward to."

"Good! We'll plan on it, then."

The hardest task of all was yet to come. Several hours later, while Henry was at Porter's, Colin entered his house to pack his things. Not fifteen minutes passed when the front door opened and two voices could be heard. Colin was in the bathroom arranging his toiletries. He froze and listened. "Is that Henry?" he whispered to Charlie.

"I think so," Charlie whispered back.

Colin rushed to the parlor. He stood facing Henry, who appeared just as shocked. "Oh my God! I'd forgotten you'd be here!" Henry apologized. He gestured toward the young man next to him. "Umm... this is Mr...."

"Huntington," the boy replied uncomfortably.

"Right, Mr. Huntington. God, Colin, I'm sorry. I was just returning for a minute to get something, then going back to Porter's."

It took only a glance at the boy—young, slim, blond, English-Looking—to incite Colin to cold fury. "I know you don't love me anymore," he choked, glaring at Henry. "But do you hate me so much?"

"Colin, honestly, I forgot..."

"Oh, you're so full of shit!" Colin screamed, swiping a paperweight off the credenza and hurling it across the room. "You knew damn well I'd be here so you could show off the first little whore you've been fucking!"

"That's not true!" Henry insisted. Then he paused and shrugged. "He's the third."

They stared at each other, then Colin turned and ran toward the dining room. Henry blinked, and then he realized what Colin was about to do. He raced after him. "Colin, don't you dare! I'll have you arrested!"

Colin heaved the giant Tiffany off the wall, and as Henry threw his arms up to shield himself, Colin smashed the piece onto the magnificent oak antlers in the center of the table.

The crash was deafening. Henry gasped. Two hundred guineas' worth of artwork shattered to pieces. But he gave a cry of horror when he looked up at Colin.

Blood ran down Colin's face from the hundreds of glass splinters. Rivulets bloomed onto his collar as he seethed at Henry through his spattered spectacles.

"Now you're done with Americans, through and through."

He strode out of the room, and young Mr. Huntington, upon seeing Colin's bloodied visage, screamed and fled. Colin called out, "Come along, Charlie!"

"But sir, we've only got a few things..."

"I don't care! I don't want anything else!"

"But—My God! What happened to you?" Charlie rushed for some towels and hurriedly followed Colin outside. They left Henry to gaze at the scattered remnants on the floor, strewn amidst the blood and the dust.

Inside the carriage, Colin pressed a towel to his face. Charlie had instructed the coachman to drive to the nearest hospital, but Colin seemed unaware of any urgency. Instead, he addressed Charlie in a muffled voice, "Charlie, in the entire time I have been with Henry, have you ever once known him to come back home soon after arriving at Porter's?"

"No, sir."

Colin was silent, but Charlie noticed his breathing was labored, so upset he was. After a moment, Charlie said quietly, "So, you were right to break the Tiffany, Mr. Colin."

Colin slowly lifted his head. He kept the towel on his face, but the smile was in his voice. "Thank you."

When Colin, bandaged and sore, returned to the hotel several hours later, he poured a tumbler full of gin and threw his letter to Henry in the fireplace. Then he sat down and began anew.

Henry,

You'll no doubt be happy to know that, when you're reading this, I will be on my way to America—permanently. I will inform you of my whereabouts in a month so that you can pass on the address to anyone who asks. You can have everything. I am fully aware that I have left behind hundreds of pounds worth of jewelry and clothes. Take them. I'm sure your little rent-boys will be thrilled, not that they could even begin to appreciate such things. I did keep the pocketwatch. You remember: "Always us, always love" and that sort of bullshit. I intend to hurl it from the ship halfway through the journey and let it sink 200,000 fucking fathoms. And don't try to blame me for the Tiffany because you had it coming and you know it. I never guessed your cruelty knew no bounds like it did today. I hope you're ashamed of yourself.

You talked as if you gave me the world. What a load of shit! I would have been successful no matter what. Probably more *successful without you, since you happily usurped my talent without ever giving me proper credit or "proper" payment. You and those hideous boys deserve each other.*

With Utter Sincerity,
C.S.

Triumphant, Colin downed the last of his drink, folded the letter, and left the desk. He told Charlie not to answer the door from now on. He knew Kenneth and Howard would hear about what happened at Henry's and try to check on him, and Colin couldn't bear the thought of seeing them, particularly in this way. He sat in his room and continued drinking until his bitterness dissolved into melancholy. By the time he was in bed, he was hugging his pillow, pretending it to be Henry. "I loved you so much, I did," he whispered tearfully. "Oh Henry, God I miss you."

The next morning, he re-read his letter, head throbbing. Not very dignified, he surmised, but he liked the part about the pocketwatch. Really though, he should write a different letter. *Now that I've had it out with him, I can be a gentleman about this.* Still, he didn't know what to say. How to show that you hate and love, and won't forgive but can't forget? *I've got three days,* he realized gloomily. *I suppose I can manage a decent letter in that time.* So Colin decided that his final project in London would be to craft his farewell letter to Henry. It became an obsession—first finding the words to say and then the materials to use for the letter itself. Colin realized he had only the hotel's paper and India ink, so he sent Charlie off to buy heavy-weight ivory paper, gold ink for his signature, and a new pen. He practiced his calligraphic strokes and painstakingly wrote "Henry" and "Colin" half a dozen ways. He sent Charlie off again to buy gold wax and a seal. Having left his monogrammed one at Henry's, he had to settle for one with a simple "S." Finally satisfied, he set about to copy his final draft.

CHAPTER TWENTY-NINE

When Henry walked into Porter's the next evening, Kenneth and Howard were already seated and Howard was fidgeting in his seat with excitement. "Henry, Max Rademaker has invited the three of us to see the Helios House!"

Henry looked surprised. "How on earth did that happen?"

"Well, I asked Colin if Kenneth and I could see the house now that it's finished, and he said he'd ask Mr. Rademaker if it would be all right." Howard grew a little more serious. "Before yesterday happened, Colin wanted you to see it most of all, though even then, he knew you wouldn't go if he was there. I'm not sure how he feels currently, but of course, Rademaker doesn't know you're quits with Colin so he invited you anyway. I think he's relying on you to show us around. Would you be willing to go?"

Henry paused. "I have wanted to see it. I can separate the boy from the building. When are we to be there?"

Howard exhaled. He hadn't thought it would be so easy. "Er... tomorrow at four o'clock. The Rademaker family will be out, but there will be servants to permit us entry."

On Friday, it was hard to say who was more excited when the gates to the Helios House opened before them. Kenneth and Howard felt a renewed wonder at seeing the house again, but it was Henry who indulged in a broad smile upon seeing his protégé's paper house rise before him. "Good work!" he whispered, scanning the structure. It was flawless. Colin had really done it.

A servant met them at the bottom of the steps and ushered them inside. The three men immediately gasped. The house was flooded in light. "The foyer," Henry nodded, recognizing every detail. It was an open floor plan from where they stood. To their left was the music room; to their right, the parlor. Straight ahead of them the sparkling white granite floor led to a curving staircase of ivory marble. Behind the staircase was an entire wall of glass, showing one of the six courtyards beyond.

Howard grinned in delight as he went up two steps. "It's as if we're more outdoors than in!"

"Let's not get ahead of ourselves," Henry reminded them, studying the swirling silver matrices in the marble. "We'll go back and start on the right."

"There are so many trees!" Kenneth wondered, looking out.

"Yes, Colin's idea was to use sunlight in as many ways as possible," Henry replied. "Through the seasons the trees will cast different shadows into the rooms, as well as allow more light in winter and less in the summer. He picked the trees specifically for their dwarf size and flowers." They began to enter the parlor when their attention was immediately drawn to the hallway on their left. "It's one of the rays," Henry explained, smiling. "Look, it takes us to the atrium." They headed down the hall, wide enough for eight men abreast. As they walked forward, they saw the windows on both sides of the walls and doors leading out to the courtyards that made the pie-shaped wedges between each ray. "You can enter each courtyard, of course," Henry said. "And each one is different. This one is the arbor, with the trees and vines. Another is an aviary. One is a maze garden, another a fountain garden, then a music garden, and a reading garden."

"Henry, you've quite a memory," Kenneth remarked, impressed.

Henry shrugged. "This is an amazing house, Kenneth. When he first showed me the plans I must have pored over them for days!"

They entered the atrium and Howard peered up at the glass dome. "Oh, this is wonderful! No wonder he didn't care for my house; it's so terribly dark compared to this!"

The atrium was sunken, and they stepped down to look around. In the middle of the floor was a giant bronze fountain. The statue atop it was of Helios himself, holding up a multifaceted crystal torch that the water rose out of and cascaded down, making the crystal appear in flames when the sun shone down. A dazzling array of palms and flowering plants filled the space. "Look!" Henry pointed gleefully to the floor. "You see—there's a trap door here so that the servants can easily bring up plants from the storeroom below!" For the atrium was a year-round room, and Colin had built a greenhouse on the property to assure a substantial number of tropical plants could always decorate the house. They would be grown and tended in the greenhouse and then transported to the storeroom for pruning and arranging before being placed in the atrium.

After admiring the atrium, the men walked back to the parlor and began to work their way around. The parlor opened to the library. The library's walls had a revolving secret door just like Henry's, and it led into the gun room, which in turn led to the smoking room. As Colin had decreed, all of the floors thus far were in the same sparkling granite, and all of the walls were white. But his idea of making the floors and walls canvasses for everything else in the room was a success. The eye was immediately drawn to the rare oil paintings, the porcelain sculptures, and, in the case of the gun room, a stuffed stag leaping over a fallen tree. Even the furniture was eye-catching, for most of it had been designed by Colin himself. Every piece was curved, so not only could they fit perfectly against the outer walls of the house, but they would carry the entire circular theme throughout each room. He tried to avoid straight lines as much as possible, using scrollwork and curved wood for the backs and legs of chairs, tables, and beds. Colin had found circles to be too whimsical-looking if allowed in abundance, so he mostly used ovals instead: oval-backed chairs, oval-topped dining table, oval pillows on the beds. The effect was sensual and inviting. He did allow ninety-degree angles in a tea table here and a lamp and picture frame there, to balance the wedge-shaped rooms. And because the floors and walls were white, Colin had all the furniture stained in honey hues, so that they were still light-colored, but could also lend warmth to the room. The windows on the outer walls were so large they took up more space than the wall surface itself. "You see," Henry smiled, "Colin did use wallpaper—it's ever-changing: look at the view!"

Kenneth said excitedly, "And imagine the patterns of light that come in each morning through those beveled middle windows! Oh, I cannot wait to see the other side—the sun will be setting soon!" Although Colin had not wanted any draperies on the windows, Mrs. Rademaker insisted on the option of privacy, so he had installed wooden Venetian blinds, stained the same color as the furniture, on every window of the house. They were to be strung up at all times when company was present, though Colin admitted to himself they looked quite nice even when down. And they would keep the house warmer on winter nights. After the smoking room, the three men were at the back of the house, facing north. From here to the northwest was the dining room and then directly west was the ballroom, Colin's pièce de résistance.

The ballroom was the full three stories tall. The top six windows were beveled glass; the bottom three were plain. On either side of the windows, French doors were installed. Upon opening them, one could drift down into the Italian gardens, complete with a Tuscan fountain Colin had imported, that was three times a man's height. The floor was hardwood since it would be used for dancing. The opposite wall of the ballroom led to the music garden. Colin had designed this courtyard as an added venue for entertainment. There was a large concrete patio for a piano to be rolled out upon. He used wrought iron to create a set of twelve permanent outdoor chairs, with pillows for comfort. Wrought iron candle stands were affixed in the cement all around, as well as hanging candleholders on the walls. In the corner behind the three rows of four chairs stood a gleaming copper chiminea. Back inside the ballroom, the men admired a giant mural hanging on the wall. Colin had commissioned Maxfield Parrish to paint a landscape, done in three panels. He knew the artist was perfect, as his uncanny reproductions of evening clouds would perfectly complement the setting sun.

And the sun was crossing over to the west just now. Howard, Kenneth, and Henry waited for the first rays to hit the windows. In an instant, diamonds of light rained upon the room, causing the men to turn around and gawk. Soon they were surrounded by dancing prisms. Kenneth began to skip about with glee. "It's like a dream!" Howard walked enraptured within the snowstorm of light, and Henry stood back by the entrance to take it all in. He figured the show could last for an hour, for the sun was still quite high in the sky.

"It's beautiful," he murmured. And for the first time in years, a euphoric feeling overwhelmed him. He realized it was pride.

Howard looked and saw his friend grinning to himself. He walked over, looked at the patterns of light with Henry, and nodded. "You're thinking of taking him back."

Henry looked at him quizzically. "Who, Colin?" He laughed out loud. "God no! It's just that..." his voice broke a little, "you see, Durham, he made it. It's not that I ever doubted his talent, no, but this was the first project he ever did completely without me." He beamed. "I kicked him out of the nest and he flew!" He threw his arms up and shouted, "He flew! Oh Colin, you *flew!*" Kenneth and Howard exchanged glances, and then laughed along with him, remembering their own epiphany upon first seeing the house themselves.

And Henry would never admit to them that at that very moment, yes, he wished Colin were there. He would have liked to embrace his dear old Collie, who would have been so happy to have Henry's approval. He'd hear Colin's laugh and he'd rumple Colin's hair and they would kiss and it would be wonderful. But the moment would end, and reality would return with a vengeance. And so Henry allowed himself to indulge in the dream and then came to. "Right then, let's be on to the second floor. We mustn't overstay our welcome."

The second floor contained the family's bedrooms and bathrooms. That each bedroom had its own bathroom was a luxury most people at the time never knew; the lower middle class still used outdoor water closets, after all. And Max Rademaker was being very generous to allow the men to see the bedchambers, as these were always off limits to visitors. But he respected Henry's place as architect and Colin's mentor.

It was Howard who was perhaps the most grateful, for upon seeing Max's bedroom he cried out, "The Zuber wallpaper!" As Colin had told them, all of the bedrooms on the second floor were wallpapered. Henry pointed out that one thing Colin insisted on was consistency and flow; he couldn't bear the idea of just one room in the entire house having wallpaper. Instead of the hunting theme Colin had first guessed at, Max's wallpaper depicted landscape scenes from Europe, Asia, Africa, and America. Margaret's wallpaper was a floral landscape: a white background with violets and poppies and delicate bluebirds. "Colin said Margaret insisted on the American landscape when she saw it," Henry chuckled. "But Max threw a fit and even Colin told her it would ruin the theme of the room. The scene had steamboats, stagecoaches, slaves, Indians... Imagine!" In Mrs. Rademaker's room the wallpaper theme was Japanese gardens. "Oh," Henry sighed. "All this wallpaper must have killed Collie. But at least it's beautiful." And to compensate, Colin kept everything else very simple in the bedrooms. Elegant, but simple. The third floor had the guest bedrooms, but of course, these were without wallpaper. They too had their own bathrooms. Henry was quite proud again, thinking of all the plumbing Colin had to figure out in order to do such a thing. The basement was for the servants' quarters as well as the utility rooms such as the kitchen, laundry, and pantry.

They took a tour of the outdoors. "Colin said he had a horrible time trying to get the grounds stocked with game," Kenneth said, peering out into the woodlands.

"Yes," Henry recalled. "It's really quite something, when you think of it: the boy designed the entire landscape, the house, and every room within! But he had everything planned already for years; after all, a house like this can't entirely accommodate regular furniture." They could see that the landscape design had taken a great deal of work, too. True to Colin's beliefs, formal gardens surrounded the house, complete with topiaries, statuary, pools, terraces, and wisteria-covered arbors. Of course, much of the shrubbery was young and small; its full effect would take several years to witness.

"Now, what about those structures on the ends of the rays?" Howard wondered, regarding them.

"Well," Henry began. "One by the main entrance is the guardhouse. Then there is one that serves as the carriage house, one that serves as the stables, one is a tool shed, one is a greenhouse, and one is a gazebo."

"Can you imagine what it looks like from above?" Howard marveled. "A perfect sun!"

"Judging from what we've seen here," Kenneth said, standing back to admire the estate, "the boy's a celestial body himself. Why, he's Helios in the flesh! The world of architecture shall commence revolving around *him*!"

Henry and Howard chuckled at the man's melodramatics, but they had to agree. For Henry, the visit was sheer relief. *He's going to be just fine. He really doesn't need me anymore. Thank God.*

It was Saturday night when Colin heard the knock on his hotel door. He was in his dressing gown and in the middle of having Charlie change his bandages. They both jumped. The valet opened the door. "Mr. Durham!" Colin groaned.

"Yes, I'm sorry for showing up unannounced, but I simply had to tell Mr. Colin about his marvelous Helios House! Is he receiving guests?"

"Well, he's..." Charlie glanced at Colin.

Colin waved his hand and muttered, "Hell, let him in."

Howard quickly stepped inside. "Dear God!" he exclaimed upon seeing Colin's stitched-up face. The mixture of repulsion and concern felt familiar. He bravely took a seat opposite his friend. "You really did it!" he wondered aloud.

Colin shook his head as Charlie resumed his task. "Howard, honestly. You needn't see me like this. Look away, will you?"

"I just... I can't believe it." Howard gazed at Colin. "You're completely cut up."

"Sewn up," Colin corrected him glumly. "Yes, I really did it, all right. Scarring my own face just to spite the bastard."

"Now, now," Charlie countered, "Dr. Johnson used the finest thread, he said so himself. It will barely show when it's all healed. I'll just undo the last few wraps up here..."

And that was when all three men jumped upon hearing the pounding on the door. From the other side came a muffled shout. "Colin! Open up! Your house is on fire!"

Colin didn't know which to register first: Henry's voice or the message it spoke. Charlie raced to the door and threw open the lock. Henry burst in. "Helios House is on fire! You must come quick!" Beside him stood Margaret Rademaker in full terror.

Colin leapt to his feet, the last two bandages hanging down the side of his head.

Before he could utter a word, Henry yanked his hand and the three of them flew downstairs with Howard close behind. They all pushed into Henry's carriage as the horses went off in full gallop.

Colin turned his attention to Margaret. "What happened? How bad is it?"

Margaret regarded him desperately. "I don't know what happened! There were servants there today... Everyone got out but... but dear God, Colin! I think it is burning to the ground!"

"To the ground?" Colin shrieked. "That's impossible! It would take hours to burn so completely, days even! It can't be burning to the ground!" Suddenly, he went expressionless, and after a moment he spoke with beatific calm. "No. It won't burn to the ground..."

Nobody dared argue with a man in shock, but it didn't keep their own thoughts from running rampant.

What on earth happened to him? Margaret wondered, staring at Colin's torn-up face.

Good lord, Colin won't survive this! Oh, the timing! Henry despaired.

Heavenly Father, please let it be put out by the time we arrive, Howard prayed.

It won't burn down. It's not burning down. Impossible.

But as the carriage lurched up the drive, the glow was visible even above the trees. The road came to, and there it was: the Helios House engulfed in roaring flames, its fire grasping to the very top of the night sky.

Max and Dana Rademaker were on the lawn. Max shook his head. "It's too late. The fire department says there's nothing they can do but contain it. But of course we'll rebuild, Colin! The insurance will pay for it all! I'm so very sorry!"

Colin didn't reply but instead drifted apart from the group to take it all in. The sound was deafening: flames snapped, beams fell, wood split, glass shattered. The heat seared into his wounds.

His Helios House was burning to dirt.

Colin could barely hear the chatter of the group twenty yards away. He stood there, watching the fire obliterate his work. He blinked, and then he began to walk.

In the midst of conversation with the Rademakers, Howard's eye caught a blurred figure. He turned his head and nearly fell.

"Colin!"

Colin was halfway up the lawn, running full tilt at the inferno, his head bandages flapping in the wind. Howard sprinted toward the boy. "Stop, Colin! Don't! What are you doing?" But Colin ignored him, and Howard pushed himself harder, tasting metal in his mouth from the pain in his lungs. He fixed upon the ties of Colin's robe and lunged toward them. Finally, in three tries he had them, in his own hands.

Colin jerked back as Howard threw him to the ground, jamming his knees onto Colin's hips and pinning Colin's arms into the cold, wet grass.

Colin's eyes bulged. "Let me go, Howard! Please! It's everything I wanted!"

"You're mad!" Howard shouted. "Don't you see you'll kill yourself?"

"Don't *you* see?" Colin cried, struggling to escape. "I've nothing left! Nothing! It's a beautiful way to die, in my house..."

"No! I won't let you do it!"

"Howard..." Colin swallowed, gasping for breath and forcing his voice into steadiness. "Howard, you loved me once. If you have any of that love left, any of it at all, then prove it to me now by setting me free! Prove it!" His voice grew to a death-scream. "PROVE IT!"

Howard fell to silence, gazing at Colin's burning brown eyes and his tortured countenance as the flamelight licked their faces. Then he turned his head toward the group. "Help! For God's sake, help! He's gone out of his mind! I can't hold him much longer!"

Colin stared at Howard, and then saw the men coming to take him. He shut his eyes. "Damn you to hell, Howard, you son of a bitch!" Fury boiled within him.

Howard felt Colin rising like a leviathan. The men were still fifty yards away. He gritted his teeth. "Forgive me." His fist reared back and then hit Colin square in the jaw. In an instant, Colin went limp. Howard staggered to his feet, carrying the body past the men and putting it in the carriage, tears streaming down his cheeks.

Both Howard and Henry stood watch that night at the hotel, though the morphine would keep Colin assuredly asleep until morning. Exhausted, Howard's own eyes began to close. "He would have gone to hell," he murmured.

Henry looked up in surprise. "Hmm?"

Howard shook his head sleepily. "The Bible says if you commit suicide, you'll go to hell." He stared at the floor. "I couldn't let him do it, Henry."

Shocked, Henry could barely give an encouraging nod. "Of course you couldn't, Howard." He turned toward Colin's freshly bandaged face and the slow, steady rising of his chest. "If anyone will understand that, it's Colin. And he will thank you for that someday. I promise."

Howard had left by the time Colin woke. Henry had stayed, and moved to the bed as Colin sat up, still groggy. "Henry? What are you doing here? Oh... my house!" He looked at Henry, devastated. "Helios burned..."

"Yes, Colin. But it will be rebuilt. Everything is all right."

"I want to see it."

"You can't, Colin. It's still smoldering; it will for days. It's too dangerous. There won't be much to see anyway, I'm afraid."

"But maybe some things could be salvaged..."

"Colin." Henry grew firm.

Colin held his head in his hands. "Oh God, I can't rebuild that house, Henry. I couldn't bear to do it again. It would kill me!"

Henry nodded. "I know. Which is why I spoke to Rademaker and we agreed that I would take over the job for you."

Colin's head jerked up. "What?"

Henry regarded the boy solemnly. "See here. Howard told me about your plan to move back to America next week on that ship. And I think it's a fine idea, Colin."

"But I..."

"No, you need a fresh start, away from me, and away from all of this. And if you'll recall, Rademaker thinks you're to die any day now from your

TB—it's why he agreed to let me take over, so that you could return to your homeland and die in peace. Now, I know the Helios House almost as well as you. If I run into any problems I'll send a telegram, all right?"

Although at first glance it seemed an incredibly magnanimous gesture on Henry's part—he was actually willing to work with Max Rademaker—Colin knew what the real message was: *"We're not going to work on this as a team, you're not going to stay here, and there's not a chance in hell we will get back together."* So Colin nodded tiredly. "All right. Thank you, Henry."

Henry was surprised, as he had braced himself for another onslaught of emotional blackmail. "You're welcome. It's the least I can do, I suppose. You've been through enough." He peered at Colin. "Do you remember what you tried to do last night?"

"Kill myself," Colin muttered. "You can hardly blame me."

"You would have committed suicide!"

"What is it to you?"

"What was it to Howard? He saved you from yourself because he said you'd go to hell otherwise."

Colin stopped fiddling with the blanket. "He said what?"

"Self-immolation forfeits heaven, Colin. Remember? Believe me, I didn't think the man had religion either, but there you have it. *I* would have been satisfied with just saving your life, but Durham took it a step further, it seems." Henry stood up. "You ought to thank him." He regarded Colin sternly. "After all, you left things on rather harsh terms, hm?"

Colin rubbed his aching jaw. "Yes, well. I've yet to be convinced he made the right decision."

At seven o'clock in the morning the following Monday, Kenneth and Howard took a carriage together to Southampton to see Colin and Charlie off. But as they drew within sight of the place, Kenneth's eyes widened. "Howard..."

"Mm?"

"There's no ship..."

"What?" Howard leaned to look out Kenneth's side. They jumped out of the carriage and ran onto the planks. In the distance a steamship puffed northwards. Howard caught a steward. "Pardon me, sir. Wasn't that ship supposed to leave today at 10:02?"

The man looked at him in disbelief. "9:02, gentlemen! You weren't planning to board, I hope!"

"No," Howard sighed. "There was someone we were trying to catch."

The steward glanced at their expensive dress and authoritative manner and wondered if they were detectives. "He wasn't a criminal, was he?" he half-joked.

Howard and Kenneth looked at each other and then began to laugh. "Well, you could say that, couldn't you Kenneth?" Howard said.

"Oh, you certainly could!" Kenneth began to gasp. "Good thing he got away from... from the long arm of the law!" They guffawed and the steward shook his head and walked away. Kenneth peered at the ship. "Do you think he got on?"

"Of course he got on. He just tricked us. I should have known. But I suppose if he really couldn't manage saying goodbye that it's just as well." Howard waved to the ship. "Farewell, Colin! Godspeed!"

"Yes, Godspeed indeed, darling!" Kenneth waved. Then his shoulders slumped slightly. "There he goes. It's just absolutely hard to believe, Howard. I feel terrible. Do you think we should have tried to stop him?"

"It would have been impossible," Howard shook his head. "But it does feel so very odd. Like the end of an era." He clapped his friend's back. "Well, why don't we try and cheer ourselves with breakfast? I'll buy."

That afternoon, a visibly exhausted Henry arrived at Porter's. Kenneth looked at him expectantly. "So...?"

Henry shook his head. "What a day! I'd forgotten what pure slavery it is to work a full eight hours! Thank God it's only temporary." He took his drink directly from the waiter's tray. "One more for me, Georgie, then I've got to be off."

"Off where?" Howard asked.

Henry sighed. "I tell you, it's as if I've taken on the ghostly mantle of Colin Sewell. Now that I'm working on the Helios project I have to find time to fit everything else in. Tonight I need to finish up some things at home. But first..." he opened his suit coat, "I know Colin left today, and he left quite a few things behind, including these. So I thought you fellows would like to have them." He put the ruby and jet brooch in front of Howard and the pair of pearl cufflinks in front of Kenneth. The two men stared at their gifts. Then Howard, followed by Kenneth, picked up the jewelry and fingered it gingerly, each of them reliving their memories of the first time they had seen the pieces on Colin himself. "To my knowledge, he didn't give you anything himself, so there you are," Henry quipped.

"Henry, are you sure?" Howard asked.

"What am I going to do with them?" Henry shrugged.

"Well, did he give any reason for leaving so much behind?" Kenneth questioned.

"Oh, yes. He said that any reminder of his past would be torture. But also that he was afraid to take so many things onto the ship, where it could be stolen." Henry raised his hands. "But honestly, what is the difference if he leaves them with me? I haven't a clue what to do with them! They're far too extravagant to give away to any boys, and *I* can't wear them. I hate to sell them—so many are one of a kind pieces, and they'll wonder where on earth I got them."

"The jewelry?" Howard asked.

"Everything, actually!" Henry lowered his voice. "All the gifts given to him over the years from his... admirers: brooches, cufflinks, ties, scarves, coats, canes, clothing, liquor, *precious gems*—hundreds if not thousands of pounds worth—they were all left behind! My God, he could have lived off the sale of those for years!"

The two men were stunned. "My word," Howard murmured. "I had no idea the men were bestowing such lavish gifts on him!"

Henry lit a cigarette. "Yes, well, here's a revelation: most of the finest things you saw Colin wear never came from me, even though he said they did."

Kenneth was puzzled. "But why would he lie?"

"Oh, he felt embarrassed by them, you see, because they made him appear to be some sort of courtesan." Henry shrugged. "But really, let's face it, the boy *was* this club's courtesan, for a while, anyway."

"But he did stay loyal to you the entire time," Howard protested.

Henry smiled. "I was merely his number one client." He saw his friends' mouths gape and rolled his eyes. "Oh, all right. I do believe that he did it solely for enjoyment, and not for any financial or political gain. Still, I had to tell him, 'Colin, it's just their way of showing gratitude, you see? If you refuse a man's gift, he may think you thought he was awful in bed. By accepting, you're telling him 'Yes, this gift *is* worthy of our night together', isn't it? And that convinced him."

"So, he left all of those items with you," Kenneth confirmed.

"Two entire armoires full!" Henry replied grimly. "Once he gets his bearings in America, he'll realize he doesn't have the money to fund the lifestyle he's used to, even if he gets a job straight away." Then Henry sighed. "I didn't really help him, in that regard. He hasn't any concept of money at all. But, perhaps if he takes that realization a step further, he'll see that I certainly did intend, at the time, to keep him on always. Otherwise, I would have kept our finances separate from the beginning."

Howard kept his mouth shut on that comment and instead asked, "Did he remember to tie up any loose ends, business-wise?"

Henry puffed away. "Yes, yes. He did. For that, I give him credit. The story, should anyone outside our circle ask, is that he left for America because his aunt died, and being the sole relative, he had to take care of matters. Once there, he'll decide to remain in America permanently." He frowned. "Of course, the men here will know the truth, and they'll find it horribly romantic that he fled, so I expect Colin shall receive much sympathy." Henry rested his chin on his fist. "I'll say this only once, because I know I'll catch hell for it from both of you, but I never thought this would all be such a gigantic pain in the arse!"

Upon Henry's departure a half hour later, Howard allowed himself to muse. "Well, I suppose Henry is learning that he can't get away with this kind of thing easily."

Kenneth nodded. "Yes, but what was he expecting, lollipops and daffodils? I say he's damned lucky that Colin agreed to leave." He grew glum. "And he left us, too. The Grand Play is over. Really, what am I going to do without Colin's emotional travails for inspiration?"

"Retire?" Howard teased.

"No," Kenneth laughed. "I'll just have to see him again! I told him I'd visit him next year. I've been meaning to go back for some time, anyway."

"Really!" Howard wondered.

"Yes. Oh, and you should consider coming, too!" Kenneth exclaimed. "You could bring Mark and the three of us will have a wonderful time! Oh, the idea alone cheers me immensely!"

"Let's just wait to hear from Colin," Howard cautioned. "The last time we saw him he was rather beside himself and *I* was certainly out of favor with him."

"Oh Howard, you know he was just temporarily mad. He'll be right as rain once he gets to America, and he'll be sure to want to thank you personally."

Howard shrugged. "All the same, between now and next year, who knows what will happen?"

"Yes," Kenneth nodded. He fell to reverie. "I wonder if he *will* have any scars... I think they'd be so very dashing!"

The close of that evening found Howard back home gazing out of his window as he stood, a glass of sherry in his hand. He raised his arm and toasted the blackness before him. "Godspeed Colin. Wherever you are." As he lowered his glass his throat caught and he could not take the drink.

He's gone. I cannot believe he's gone. Colin! The love of my sorry life. And he's gone. I let him go. I let him go thinking I was done with him. And I shall never see him again. The reality finally hit Howard and his knees buckled. He grasped for a chair. *But it's over. It's really over.* Relief and despair flooded him and he held his face in his hands.

"Gone," he whispered aloud. "Oh, Colin. Where did you go?" He pictured Colin looking about in New York, a lost expression on his face... Howard grimaced. *Out of the fire into the frying pan. A lot of good my rescue did him.* What did Colin say Oscar Wilde once quipped about him? *"You're a fawn among fauns."* Howard pressed his fingertips to his lips in a final prayer. *God grant you the ability to be a wolf in sheep's clothing.*

CHAPTER THIRTY

Sympathy was soon forthcoming once Colin was on the ship. He used the excuse of his bandaged face to secure himself in his suite for the first few days. When the people at his dining table wondered about his absence, Colin directed Charlie to tell their servants that his wife had suddenly died and in a rage of sorrow he had smashed their giant glass-framed wedding picture and was cut up by its pieces. It also supplied a nice reason why he was returning to America: he could no longer stand any memories of their life spent together in England. Thereafter, once word got back to the wealthy passengers, there was an outpouring of feeling for the young man. Two unmarried sisters at the table found the story tragically romantic and grew even more curious to see him. Although they realized they stood little chance with a newly widowed man, they still found the idea of his brooding presence interesting, especially when they found out he was not only very wealthy, but rather young and supposedly handsome as well! They begged their servants to urge Charlie to convince Colin to join them for dinner so that they might lighten his mood.

But Colin's temperament was still unstable. He put on a good show during Charlie's visits each afternoon, enjoying his stories of the goings-on aboard the ship. But every night, Charlie lay in bed listening to Colin sobbing on the other side of the wall. After two such nights, Charlie moved his bed to another part of the room. Still, Colin's despondence was apparent. When Charlie stopped in, he'd find Colin in one of two places: in a chair near the balcony, staring at the sea, or lying on his bed, often asleep but other times pretending to read, though his eyes had a glazed-over look. He had dropped so much weight that his clothes now hung on him, and his face had turned sallow. It had been three weeks since Henry had severed ties with Colin, and Charlie thought it was an awfully long time to mourn a man who had inspired so much anger. He didn't realize that it wasn't just Henry that Colin despaired over. It was his entire loss of life as he knew it. As Colin lay about in his room, he wondered, *Is this how it's to be? To spend ten or twenty years fashioning happiness, then be robbed of it and flee the country to start all over again? To lose people you love every time? To fall behind in your career every time? To have to make up stories every time?*

To be rejected, every time.

I'll bet Jeffrey's fared better than I.

In the past, Colin disliked brooding longer than a few hours, but now he had no reason not to do so for days on end, since he was a prisoner on this ship for a week, with nothing to do. *I'm literally 'at sea'. I have both figuratively and literally lost my moorings.*

Colin hadn't even thought to shave, although it was partially owing to his cuts. On the day the ship doctor declared that Colin could go about bandage-free, Charlie exclaimed to Colin that evening, "My goodness! You look rather dashing with your moustache and beard, Mr. Colin!"

The word "beard" set off an alarm in Colin's head, and he examined himself in the mirror. "I don't care for it," he decided, and absently searched for his razor.

"Oh, Mr. Colin, how could you not!" Charlie argued. "Haven't you ever worn one before?"

Colin paused, then gave a rueful laugh. "Ironically, I had a moustache before I came to England." His gaze fixed on the razor and his voice fell to a hush. "I shaved it off on the way over."

"Well more's the pity, then!" Charlie quipped. "I think it's a wonderful way to have a new look, don't you?" Colin knew what Charlie meant, but before he could protest further, the valet had shoved a chair behind him. "Now let me just tidy you up a little and you see what you think. Sit here and I shall ring for some warm towels."

"Charlie..."

"Mr. Colin, I am going stir-crazy on this ship for want of something to do! I'm supposed to tend to you and now I have a proper job!"

Colin couldn't help being amused at Charlie's excitement, and so he replied, "Well, perhaps I'll keep the mustache, but I don't like the beard."

"Never mind, never mind. Just trust me." Charlie proceeded silently, and Colin relaxed, realizing the idea of being tended to was rather inviting. As Charlie worked, he wondered sadly when the last time was that someone held his employer's face so tenderly. He took his time. "There!" Charlie declared when finished. "I kept a bit of the beard around your mouth and chin. It looked too nice to get rid of entirely." He handed Colin his spectacles and Colin put them on and looked in the mirror. His eyes widened. "My word," he murmured.

"Oh, you look devastating!" Charlie cried gleefully. "Oh, how wonderful! Do you like it?"

Colin stared at himself, and then lowered his head. "Charlie, do you think I'll ever be attractive again?" he whispered fearfully.

Charlie knitted his brow. "Sir, surely you're joking. Far be it from me to step outside of my boundaries, but you're one of the most handsome men I've ever seen!"

Colin looked up at him anxiously. "Thank you, but I mean, do you think I can find another Henry?" He glanced at his reflection. "All anyone wants are boys."

Charlie shook his head. "I cannot believe you're saying that. You're still young by anyone's definition but Mr. Sewell's. Why, I'll bet every one of those men at your club would have killed to have had you." His tone became gentle. "You just happened to get the one who didn't."

Colin let the comment sink in and then gave an embarrassed laugh. "Oh, I'm sorry to make you say such things! You did a fine job of shaving, and an even better job putting up with me." He sighed. "I'll tell you what: you and I shall have a drink to celebrate my new appearance, and tomorrow I shall go and have dinner in the dining room."

Charlie grinned. "Bully for you, sir!"

Of course, it was more than one drink. Colin credited Charlie for his improved mood, and he didn't want him to leave. Charlie didn't mind too much, either; the brandy was Martell, after all. But it had been a long time since he had engaged in conversation with Mr. Colin. When he had first moved in with Henry, Colin frequently struck up long discussions with Charlie during Henry's absence. Charlie had attributed it to loneliness, but he grew to enjoy their conversations. However, as the years went on, Colin was home less and less, and when he was home, he attended solely to Henry. The last few years found Colin hardly home at all, and he was often tired and irritable. So Charlie felt awkward now, sitting with his new boss and being put in his old role as a sort of friend instead of a valet. But Colin didn't seem to notice. "Charlie, do you think any of us are truly happy men?"

Charlie swallowed his drink nervously. "Mr. Colin, this is why you're the gentleman and I'm the valet. I can't possibly savor this brandy and attempt to answer such a question at the same time."

Colin laughed. "I apologize." He looked out toward the sea.

"For what it's worth Mr. Colin," Charlie shrugged, "I think the term 'truly happy' would be difficult for anyone to affirm. You've had many happy days with Mr. Sewell, and other happy days as a child, I'm sure. And other days in between. So have other people. But everyone has low points in their lives, too."

Colin smiled warmly. "You're right. See, you're very smart. So I suppose the real question I wanted to ask is, do you think any of *us* are truly *glad* that we are who we are? Men who love other men?" He fell somber. "Do you think if any of us were given the choice to become a regular fellow, we wouldn't take it?"

Charlie stared at his glass. What a question! "But," he began, confused, "I thought we hadn't any choice."

Colin glanced at him and then back at the ocean, his mouth a grim line. "We don't." He paused. "I've been thinking that must be why so many of us do walk about posing as regular men." He sighed, shaking his head. "It must be so much easier. My life would have been a charm."

"Mr. Colin, you're wishing for something you can't have, and you know how those things turn out anyway. Even I grew up knowing that adage of the grass being greener on the other side of the fence."

Colin's brow furrowed. "But if that were true, Charlie, that would mean there'd have to be regular men who think it's better to be like us! And that's impossible!"

"No, I believe you're looking at it in the wrong way. Regular men envy you because they think you're just a bachelor, a playboy. You can have any woman you want, you've got loads of money that you don't have to spend on a wife and children, and you can come and go as you please. You can gamble as much as you like, drink as much as you like, smoke as much as you like, and live the life of a prince! Without any woman giving you any grief!"

Colin raised his eyebrows, slightly smiling. "I suppose..." Then he laughed. "What would I do without you, Charlie!" He poured the fifth drink for both of them and raised a toast to his valet.

An hour later, Charlie leaned back, smoking a cigarette. He snuck a look at Colin, who with his own cigarette looked more brooding and dashing to Charlie than ever. "So... er... Mr. Colin," he started, "seeing as it's just you and I, and seeing as it was so long ago, and seeing as we're on a ship hundreds of miles from London, and seeing as neither of us plan on seeing that fair city again, tell me, out of all of those paramours you had, who was the best?"

Despite the number of drinks, Colin managed to be shocked, and he gave a short laugh. "Charlie!"

"Oh, come now, Mr. Colin! Please?"

"Oh God, I couldn't even begin."

"Bullocks! There had to be one. Go on!"

Colin blushed and shook his head laughing. Charlie shrugged in pretended indignance, and Colin sighed. "All right. Does it have to be truthful?" Charlie gave him a sharp look. "All right, all right!" Colin took a deep breath. "Well, in second place, we have... Bosie Douglas."

"What! Good God!"

Colin was laughing. "I know! It's probably because we hated each other so. But he was so very handsome. And the very idea that we could do such a thing to each other... Well, anyway..."

Charlie leaned forward, rapt. "Number one?"

Colin finished off his glass and gave a small cry of embarrassment. "No, I can't! It's too personal!"

"Mr. Colin!"

Colin glanced at him sheepishly. "It's... it's one of Henry's friends. Well, it's his best friend. Mr. Durham."

"Mr. Durham!" Charlie was delighted. He thought Mr. Sewell's friend had done a fine job taking care of Mr. Colin once Henry had left him, and Charlie had suspected there was more than met the eye.

Colin turned scarlet. "Yes, well you see, out of all of those fellows, Mr. Durham was the only one who really... who really cared about me, through and through."

"Other than Mr. Sewell."

Colin winced and refilled his glass before replying bitterly, "Yes of course. But Howard... Well, we were sort of lovers too, you see. It was very dangerous."

"Really!" Charlie was fascinated. "Did Mr. Sewell find the two of you out?"

"Oh, no, it was nothing like that. We never had any sort of affair, but we saw each other every day at Porter's, of course, so we naturally grew quite close. Henry never knew it, but after our second time together, Howard suggested I leave Henry for him."

"He did!"

"Yes, but you could hardly blame him." Colin swirled his brandy. "He saw right through me. But I had to tell him, 'Howard, the things I like in you are different than the things I like in Henry. But Henry was first and I'm not leaving him for anyone.'"

"And what did Mr. Durham think about that?"

Colin's voice softened. "He was upset. Things were rather strained for a while between us. I believe we blamed each other." He sharply inhaled. "And I chose unwisely, clearly."

Charlie frowned. "But, Mr. Colin, you're not with Mr. Sewell anymore. So do you think that Mr. Durham would approach you again?"

Colin set his glass down firmly and stood up with a rueful laugh. "No. That was years ago. Howard has long since moved on." He walked over to the bar cabinet.

"But how do you know?" Charlie prodded. He'd never heard anything so romantic in his life.

Colin turned around and said acidly, "He told me himself. I was at the bank and I apologized for that horrid comment I made toward him at the hotel." Charlie nodded, and Colin continued. "Well, I was trying to tell him that I only regretted having been with him because of the pain I'd caused him, and he laughed at me and said, 'It doesn't matter! I don't find you attractive anymore! I haven't for years!'"

"Oh, he didn't!"

"He did!" Colin turned back toward the bar. He thought of the night of the fire and straightened. "But it's all right. I mean, dear God, the man would have been carrying a torch for me all this time, otherwise." After having cleaned up, Colin faced Charlie with a tired smile. "Well then, I think I'm going to retire, Charlie. Thank you for everything. I promise I will dine at the table tomorrow evening."

Charlie stood up. "I know you will, Mr. Colin. You've always been a man of your word."

In ten minutes Colin slipped into bed. In five minutes, he cursed himself for crying again, all over his pillow. The conversation with Charlie had brought to light something Colin had tried desperately to repress since Henry left him. Only three men had really mattered in Colin's life thus far: his father, Henry, and Howard. All three men had told him to his face that they loved him. And in their own instant, all three wanted nothing to do with him anymore. Ever.

In the next room, Charlie was coming to a similar conclusion, and he wondered. *How does a handsome young man with so much talent and loveliness fall to these depths? And what kind of men must* they *be to reject such a fellow?* And for the first time since he came onto the ship, Charlie knew for certain he had chosen the right man to work for. "I'm all you've got, Mr. Colin," he murmured in the darkness. "A poor substitute, I'm afraid, but hopefully better than none at all."

January 19, 1900

Dear Henry,

Now that I am in New York, I would like to request a letter of recommendation from you that I can present to potential employers. I am hoping to work with McKim, Mead, and White. I realize this request puts us both in an awkward position, but I am speaking strictly from a professional standpoint.

As you were my only employer, a letter from you would be invaluable. You may send it to the address below. Thank you.

Sincerely,
Colin

The same night Henry received his letter from Colin, Howard received one too. He was returning home from Porter's with Mark when his butler handed him the mail. As Mark walked into the dining room, Howard slowly followed him, examining the letters. He stopped.

A letter from Colin.

Howard stared at it then carefully placed it behind the other letters and flipped through the rest of the mail. He walked into the dining room. Mark was sitting at the table, having his wine poured. He smiled at Howard. "Anything interesting?"

"No, no. The usual. Bills and invitations."

"Have you heard from Mr. Colin yet?"

"Hmm? Oh, no. Not yet. I expect he'll write shortly. I've no idea how long mail takes to get from America to England."

Dinner was placed before them. They discussed other things. Sherry was followed by sharing each other. Mark left.

Howard poured himself another glass of sherry and sat in his robe, holding Colin's envelope. Henry hadn't exaggerated—Colin's calligraphic handwriting was impeccable. Howard admired the bold, flowing script describing his address. The envelope itself was disappointingly light. Only a single sheaf of paper could be enclosed. Howard sighed and ran his letter opener across the top.

January 19, 1900

Dear Howard and Kenneth,

As evidenced by this letter, we have arrived in America. We have begun our stay at the Waldorf-Astoria Hotel. I will remain here until I can find a permanent place to live. Should you desire to write, you may use the address below. I have also informed Henry of my whereabouts, for client purposes. Charlie has been a godsend, least of all for his English accent, which is the only one I hear now! I'm sorry if you tried to see me off. I honestly don't think I could have borne it. Please forgive me for that. Kenneth, I promise to contact Jack's friend soon; I'm not quite feeling sociable yet. I hope both of you are doing well. Your company is sorely missed. I'd love to hear what the two of you thought of the Helios House... may it rest in peace.

Regards,
Colin

Howard sat with the letter for ten minutes, staring at the exclamation mark.

The next day, he met Kenneth at Porter's earlier than usual to show him the letter.

"Well," Kenneth shrugged, "he seems to be doing all right."

"But the letter is so short!" Howard argued.

"Well, what else would you expect him to say?"

"It's just that... he's usually so verbose. I thought he'd tell us about the trip over, describe the hotel, that sort of thing."

"He's not 'feeling sociable,'" Kenneth reminded him. "I'm sure the Waldorf-Astoria could be a cell block for all he cares, given the tragedies he's suffered! I'm surprised he's already written us, and that he's mentioned the Helios House. Perhaps that's a sort of progress."

"Perhaps," Howard admitted. Then, in trepidation, "Shall we write him back, then?"

"Well, of course we'll write back. He's got to be positively lonely." Then Kenneth looked sympathetically at his friend. "But Howard, perhaps you shouldn't write to him. This is a real opportunity to rid him from your life, you know."

Howard bristled. "I don't need to *rid* him from my life. I told you ages ago that I was through with him." Kenneth rolled his eyes, which made Howard glare at him. "I've got Mark, for heaven's sake! I've been fine with Colin."

"Because you had no choice," Kenneth retorted. "You had to see him on a near daily basis! But you don't anymore. He's gone. Remember how long it took you, Howard?" Then, he couldn't help it. "Unless you want a go with him?"

"No, no," Howard replied quickly. "But Kenneth, I said something cruel to him before he left."

Kenneth's eyes widened. "What?"

"It was at the bank, before he went to see you. He apologized for his comment to me at the apartment, and I told him, just like this..." Howard looked condescendingly at Kenneth. "'It doesn't matter anymore. For God's sake, I haven't felt that way about you for years!'"

Kenneth sighed. "Oh, dear. Well, perhaps he needed to hear it."

"But not like that! You should have seen his face! He was absolutely crushed, Kenneth! I mean, really, the love of his life just kicked him out for good and then I turn around and back up Henry's claim that he's no longer attractive? And the worst of it is that it's not even true, you know that!"

"What did he say?"

"He tried to laugh it off and said, 'Well, of course not,' but his face was red and I felt like such an arse for that comment. I tried to smooth things over, but he could barely look at me after that." Howard looked at his friend in earnest. "That's why I'd like to write at least one letter to him, to leave things on good terms. He did send our letter to my address, after all."

Kenneth shook his head and smiled. "All right, then. Why don't you write him a letter and I'll write him a letter? That way he'll get twice the mail."

And that night, Howard came home and began to write.

2 February 1900

Dear Colin,

We received your letter today, and I must say I'm disappointed. Good God, man, you spent an entire week on a luxury liner, you've landed in a country you haven't seen for eight years, and all we get is one side of one piece of paper? Surely you can do better than that!

All right, I'm giving you a hard time. We miss you here. Everyone keeps asking when you're coming back. Is it possible that you may still use your return ticket? Maybe in two months you'll get so homesick for our accents that you'll leave!

Kenneth and I did try to see you off. No harm done. One of the stewards thought we were trying to catch a criminal! You can imagine the laugh we had over that!

Have you visited a New York bank yet? If so, please tell me about it. If not, please go so you can tell me about it. And what is New York like? The buildings must look so different compared to our ancient structures. Is there a lot of architecture for you to study?

Is the Waldorf-Astoria Hotel nice? Charlie must feel as if he's the most fortunate valet in the world! What does he think of America so far? I'm glad he is there to keep you company.

Everything is status quo here. Once again, you manage to do the most exciting thing out of all of us. You can imagine how Kenneth already misses the drama!

All right then, the Helios House. I confess I don't know where to begin; every detail was extraordinary! I fear I will be using only exclamation marks for the duration of the letter. Bear with me.

First, all three of us attended, Henry included. I know he was so very proud of you upon seeing it; it would surprise me if he didn't write to you about it as well. If he does not, know that he found the house to be absolutely perfect. I'll begin my reaction from the moment we drove past the gates.

Howard began to describe the experience he, Kenneth, and Henry had. He ended the letter with this:

Colin, I thought that I held you in high regard all along, but after seeing your House, I realize there is a facet on your diamond heretofore unseen! That you designed that incredible place... Well it only shows how brightly you must shine now! It's hard to believe that this year you will be a mere thirty years old! If I were you, I would be ecstatic to know I could die happy at such an early age, for the Helios House could easily stand as your greatest achievement! It makes my mind reel thinking what else is in store from you—you still have the majority of your career ahead of you!

I hope you're doing well. Please feel free to write back. It would be wonderful to hear your witty observations about all things American. And also the ship! Be sure to detail the ship, Colin. Kenneth will be sending his own letter. We thought you'd enjoy getting twice the mail.

All right then, carry on, and thank you for the letter, however brief it was!

Regards,
Howard

Colin was joyous when he finished reading the letter. Howard and Kenneth still thought of him as their friend, thank God. He read Howard's letter again, and with a laugh, took the pen from his desk and began his reply.

February 19, 1900

Dear Howard,

You can't begin to imagine the effect your letter had on me. I can't even remember when I last laughed, but I did today, every time I read your words. You come across so well on paper—it's extraordinary!

I thought I should be brief in that first letter. I didn't know if perhaps you'd prefer to end things and go on with your lives. You do have a foursome again with Mr. Montague, and I didn't want to be a hanger-on. And after this letter, you may change your mind about our correspondence. It's very lonely here and I've no one to talk to, although that is my fault. Poor Charlie has been extremely sporting, but I have pestered him enough. This coming weekend will be my first venture into the social realm. I don't anticipate any difference, but I will let you know. Truth be told, Howard, things are pretty awful. However, your letter was the first bright spot of my new existence, so I thank you for that.

I suppose I could be in a worse hell; the Waldorf-Astoria is gorgeous. Charlie is having a ball, I think. I'm playing the Mourning Cloak (that is a kind of butterfly, you know) and drinking Cointreau amongst the velvet drapery in my room.

Oh, the ship—it was also lovely, although I mostly stayed in my room the entire time. Please don't tell Henry any of this. He'll likely mock me and say I'm exaggerating my melancholy, but Howard, it is the truth. It is so horrid and wretched, that you should drop to your knees and thank God you never did have to suffer this sort of thing.

Well, enough of that! I don't intend this letter to have the opposite effect on you as your letter did on me! One last comment: I am *staying in America permanently*. As bad as this is, it can't be worse than going back and having to face everyone, even with you and Kenneth there to support me. Charlie has also decided to stay on, for which I am eternally grateful. I hope to find employment soon; I'm waiting to hear from Henry, who needs to provide me with a letter of reference so that I may present myself to employers. I am specifically hoping to join the firm of McKim, Mead, and White. They are whom I consider the top architects in America currently. Wish me luck!

Oh and I did go to a bank: The National City Bank of New York, which is the closest thing I can think of in comparison to the Bank of England. It is not quite as astounding-looking as the B.O.E. but an austere institution nonetheless. There are indeed several buildings in this city that I want to see which were constructed while I was in England. I have taken a few walking tours on my own. It is actually reassuring to be in a wholly unfamiliar setting.

The real building boom is in Chicago, as they are continuing to expand after the Great Fire of 1871. I sometimes think of heading out there because the opportunity is so great, and all the progressive architects are there: Burnham & Root, Adler & Sullivan, and Wright. But it seems too far away and too rough for my tastes. Still, I argue with myself that if I knew enough to pay my respects to the past by visiting Italy, I should now pay my respects to the future and see Chicago. It is something to think about.

I will be forever grateful for yours and Kenneth's extremely flattering reviews of the Helios House. Thank you, Howard; it meant the world to me. I can barely stand to write about it, but there's some comfort in knowing the three of you were able to see it the way it was intended, especially since Henry must bring the Phoenix up from the flames, as it were.

Dear God, I apologize for the constant relapses into pathos! I told you that you might regret encouraging me to write! I suppose I should end it here. Thank you, Howard, for giving me the opportunity to lighten my burden a bit by writing to you. I would love for you to write again, but if at any time you tire of it, that is all right.

Sincerely,
Colin

The day Colin sent his letter to Howard, he found an even more exciting letter awaiting him: Henry's. It shocked him to see the large envelope, for it wasn't until then that he realized he and Henry had never corresponded in the written word, not even when Henry was in Paris. And here was an entire letter...

5 February 1900

Dear Colin,
Please find enclosed several copies of your letter of recommendation. I should have written them for you before you left England; I apologise. Everything else is going smoothly. Preparations are in full swing for the new

Helios. But I would be remiss and even crueler than you already think me to be, if I did not give you my opinion of your House.

Well, Colin, I really must say to you, "Bravo." I think you did very well, and the granite floors turned out marvelous, didn't they? I was most impressed with the ballroom, although your courtyards came a close second. The furniture you designed is in a class of its own. The Rara Avis Style is here to stay! It would be tedious for me to give my impression of every feature, so I will just tell you that the House rivals none that I know of, even with the Zuber paper. In fact, I rather like the scenes you chose, and you did compromise, which is a difficult lesson to learn. Your landscape design skills are coming along very well—I would recommend you offer separate consulting services in that area should you tire of building projects. Give that Thomas Mawson a run for his money.

Now I will admit that I was reluctant to write all this to you, but as your mentor, I feel an obligation to congratulate you formally on your finest hour. As I have chosen to soon taper off my own work, I would take no greater pleasure in knowing you will carry the great mantle of modernity in architecture. Unlike that Solness character in Ibsen's play, I have no qualms about you succeeding me. In fact, I expect you to. So, best of luck to you in your career, Colin. You have done very, very well so far. I am proud of you.

Do let me know if you need anything else. I have no doubt that you will find employment with McKim, Mead, & White. You're a prodigy of them as much as you are of me.

Regards,

Henry

Colin seized one of the letters of recommendation from the envelope.

To Whom It May Concern:

I present this letter as a recommendation to hire Mr. Colin Sewell. Mr. Sewell has been in my employ for eight and a half years. For five of those years, he has been partner of the firm and proved himself entirely capable.

Gentlemen, I say without a doubt that you will find no greater architect of contemporary style than Mr. Sewell, and you would deeply regret passing him up. In the time he worked with me, he designed forty structures and managed a staff of twenty employees. His practicality is flawless; his vision, matchless. His last completed structure in England was the Helios House: a masterpiece that surpasses anything I have seen of the Art Nouveau movement. He is one hundred percent dedicated to his work; a more loyal man you won't find. Any architectural firm of importance must consider Mr. Sewell if they are interested in their reputation growing tenfold. For it is not a matter of Mr. Sewell being fortunate if you hire him. It is a matter of you being fortunate if Mr. Sewell chooses to work for you. I would be happy to provide specific details on any of Mr. Sewell's projects upon further request.

Sincerely Yours,
Henry Sewell
Sewell Architecture

And so the next morning, Colin visited McKim, Mead, and White. Only Charles McKim was in the office when the receptionist read from Colin's card: "There's a Mr. Colin Sewell in front to see you, sir."

The name caused Charles to start. *Colin Sewell? Isn't he in England?* The curiosity was enough to force him to leave his desk and see for himself.

"Mr. Sewell?" he said uncertainly, and Colin extended his hand.

"Yes, Mr. McKim! It's nice to see you again."

Charles squinted. The boy did look very familiar, but before he could ask, Colin gave an apologetic smile. "I'm afraid you know me better under my first name, Michael Callahan. You offered me employment upon my graduation ten years ago."

Flabbergasted, Charles spent a moment comprehending the situation. "Michael Callahan... *you're* Michael Callahan?"

"Yes," Colin nodded. "I'm very sorry for the confusion. You see, I was forced to go to London at the last minute and I ended up staying there for eight years. While in England I took the name Colin Sewell."

Charles' mind reeled. "But you're... *you're* Henry Sewell's adopted son?"

Colin suppressed his panic. He didn't expect Charles to have knowledge of the more personal details of his life. "Er... yes. That's a rather long story. I'd be happy to tell you at a more convenient time for you. The reason I'm here now is to apply for work."

"You're here in America now?" The whole thing was too hard to believe.

"Yes," Colin sighed. "I'm afraid so. I don't want to trouble you with the details, Mr. McKim..."

"Well," Charles began, "I... we really aren't looking for someone of your caliber, Mr. er... Sewell."

Colin nodded. "I understand. But I'd like to work for your firm most of all. I need employment with an American firm so that I can study the latest codes and whatnot. Would you please take this letter of recommendation from Henry and a copy of my curriculum vitae to look over? And here is my card where you may reach me."

Charles took the documents and was sorely tempted to ask Mr. Sewell to stay and tell him all that had happened. But he had work to do, and it would be a waste of time if he had to retell William and Stanford later. "Yes, all right then." He gave Colin a final look-over. "We were wondering whatever happened to you."

Colin reddened. "I sincerely apologize, Mr. McKim. I hope to make it up to you. I'm worth much more now than I was back then anyway; I can prove it."

"No, no, I've heard about you," Charles murmured. "Your name came to our shores many years ago. Well then, what do you say the four of us meet for dinner sometime next week, eh?"

Colin grinned. "Yes! I'd be very grateful, and honored."

"All right then, Mr. Sewell. We'll be in touch."

"Thank you, sir!"

Charles watched him go, shaking his head and looking forward to his partners' return from out of town.

CHAPTER THIRTY-ONE

"Gentlemen, I have a wonderful surprise for you tomorrow night." Harold Dearborn sat back and puffed his cigar as he watched the expectant looks on his friends' faces. "You're going to meet someone new."

It was the last Friday of February at The Carlisle, and Harold was sitting at a table surrounded by five men. He smiled at them. "His name is Colin Sewell. He's an architect. Twenty-nine years old. Just came from London last month, but he's an American. He's spent the last eight years in England involved with a man named Henry Sewell. Yes, that's right, they both have the same last name. Apparently, Mr. Sewell the elder was so taken with Colin that he adopted him just a month after meeting him!" Murmurs flowed among the group as Harold paused. "Henry Sewell is a well-known architect, twenty years Colin's senior. But he dropped Colin two months ago because Colin apparently lost his *youthful charm*. And now this very bright young man is back on American soil, and I daresay you'll enjoy his company as much as I did earlier this week when I met him myself."

"Is he good looking?" Jonathan asked eagerly.

Harold slightly frowned. "Well, he's a bit short on the looks, but none of you should be thinking of putting advances on him anyway. I think it's going to take a long time for him to recover from having his heart broken.

Still, he's got a sharp wit and is clearly well bred. My friend knew him through Henry and grew quite fond of him."

"Oh, so he's to be our pet, then?" Adam teased.

"Now, be nice, Mr. Meredith!" Harold reprimanded. "I have absolute faith in all of you to welcome him into the fold. I shall bring him tomorrow night and leave him with you."

"Oh well, who cares if he's homely?" Toby sighed, as Harold left. "At least he'll be interesting. He can tell us all kinds of stories about London!"

The others agreed, and Friday turned into Saturday. Harold's friends were grouped around their table, keeping an eye on the staircase. Finally, Harold appeared.

"*That's* him?" Adam wondered, watching the pair descend.

"My God..." Daniel murmured.

"I don't believe it," Alex muttered.

"But he's—" Toby began.

Adam leaned over and retrieved his cigarette. "Right. He's mine." He got up to make his way toward Colin and Harold.

Colin was trying to look relaxed. Harold hadn't told him there'd be a damn center staircase! It would have been perfect in the old days, but tonight the last thing Colin wanted to do was draw attention to himself. He should have known better. This club, like Porter's, didn't receive many new men, secretive as it was. And so, whenever someone did bring in a new companion, it was imperative for everyone to be able to see him and for the member of the club to show him off. Fortunately, Harold seemed to approve when he picked Colin up earlier that evening. "You look spectacular!" he crowed, as if, Colin thought, he had dressed Colin himself.

"It's all right, then?" Colin asked, looking down at his suit.

Harold laughed. "Oh, darling! I told them you were rather a disappointment in the looks department, just for fun! They'll absolutely thrill!"

Anger rose up in Colin's chest. "They may agree with you yet," he muttered, taking his hat and feeling suddenly conscious of his glasses.

Harold saw his error and took Colin's arm. "Mr. Sewell..." he said kindly.

Colin stopped. Harold gave him a knowing nod, and kept nodding until finally Colin laughed. "What?"

Harold gave him a squeeze. "That Henry of yours was a *fool*."

Colin blushed, looked away, and shook his head. "Mr. Dearborn, I'm going to have what you're drinking tonight."

Harold clapped his hands. "Oh, yes, splendid!" And he led the way to the carriage out front.

So when Adam approached that evening, he was heading toward a blond-haired, amber-eyed, slender young man with gold-rimmed spectacles who was wearing a dark blue suitcoat, powder-blue and gold vest, ivory shirt, and navy silk ascot. Adam extended his hand. "Mr. Sewell, you should have this man arrested for fraud!"

Harold hmphed. "And *you* should be arrested for committing acts of desperation!"

Adam grinned and looked at Colin. "Adam Meredith. Isn't he awful? When he introduced me, he told everyone I had syphilis so that nobody would 'take advantage of me straight off.'" He mock-glared at Harold. "My benefactor."

Colin laughed, shocked at the story and at Adam's bold appearance. He could believe the tale. Adam was very handsome, although quite a contrast to Colin. He wore his black hair short, parted on the side, and heavily pomaded. His fair-skinned face sported a dashing moustache, and he appeared to be in his twenties. His black irises had a hint of malevolence to them, and he had a teasing flush to his cheeks. *Naughty schoolboy*, Colin thought wryly, and he wasn't sure he liked being paired off with someone who reminded him so much of his former self.

"Come, Mr. Sewell. I'll navigate you through the waters from here." He winked at Harold, who raised his eyebrows.

"Well, I'm not sure I would have chosen *you*, but..." Harold warned, but he smiled at Colin. "Go on. I'll see you in a bit."

Colin had little choice; Adam had taken his arm and brought him to his side as they walked. "Harold doesn't trust me," he confided. "He thinks I'm the best looking of the bunch and so I'll be jealous of you. But the irony is, I'll be absolutely relieved to have someone else be the object of affection for a while!"

"But I don't want that, either," Colin protested.

Adam gave him a sidelong glance and smirked. "Too late."

Colin tsked. "Is your group such a den of lions, then?"

Adam stopped and sighed. "Well really, you'd *think* they'd have named the club that, don't you?" He held up his hands, framing the words. "Den of Lions."

Colin laughed. Perhaps he'd get along all right with Mr. Meredith after all.

"Here we are, then!" Adam swept him forward to the oval table, where four other men sat. They quickly stood up and greeted him warmly as Adam made introductions. Colin was relieved. They looked to be an amiable set of men.

"After suffering Harold *and* Adam, I'm surprised you're still here," Alex quipped.

Colin seized the moment. "Honestly!" he agreed. "One lies about me; the other lies to me!" Pausing as Adam gaped, Colin sighed and looked at him. "You *said* you were the best looking of the bunch." The men guffawed as Adam turned bright red and put a hand on his hip. "I did not! I said *Harold* thought I was the best looking of the bunch!" The men laughed even harder and Colin grinned at Adam, who rolled his eyes.

"Marvelous. I have a sparring partner." He pulled Colin down to a seat as he put out his cigarette. "What are you drinking, Sewell?"

"Umm... what does Mr. Dearborn drink?"

"Why do you want to know that?"

"Well, he was so beside himself this evening—apparently thanks to his little joke—that I told him I'd have to drink what he was having."

"You can't afford what he's having," Adam teased.

"Why, yes I can!" Colin said haughtily. He was about to say, "Order it!" But he backed off, apologizing, "I suppose that's gauche. Gin and bitters, please."

One of the men in the group chuckled. "Actually, Harold only drinks bourbon. Would you prefer that?"

Colin laughed, thinking of Howard. "No, no." He made a face. "I can't stand the stuff. But thank you all the same."

"So," Adam said, once he ordered for Colin, "Harold said you're an architect."

"Yes, that's true," Colin nodded. He looked at everyone sitting with him. "I suppose Mr. Dearborn has filled you in as to why I'm here."

The men shifted uncomfortably. "Yes, terrible luck, old boy," Adam replied. "Cigarette?"

Colin smiled gratefully. "God, yes, thank you. I left mine at home. I wasn't sure what the protocol here was."

"Protocol!" Adam laughed. "Half the men here are smoking hashish-laced cigarettes, I'm sure."

Colin chuckled. "And are they carrying flasks of laudanum to woo the boys with, as well?"

"Well," Adam declared with mock incredulity, "I wouldn't know, Mr. Sewell! That's never happened to me. *Jonathan* might know something about that..."

But Jonathan just laughed, causing Colin to raise his eyebrows and drag on his cigarette and remark, "Well, anyway, so, here I am, and there you are. How do the rest of you fellows bide your time?" The men took turns stating their own professions. Jonathan was a pharmacist—now it made sense—Toby's family owned several hotels, Alex was a milliner, and both Daniel and Adam came from wealthy industrialist families.

"So, Mr. Sewell," Adam leaned in eagerly, "what did you tell Harold that made him choose to put you in our group?"

Colin thought about this, and then smiled. "Well, you all work for a living—that's a start. I can't stand the poet-layabout type, I'm afraid, as pretty as some of them are."

"*All* of them," Alex sighed.

"Hmph!" Colin snorted. "And you all appear to be around my own age—"

"I'm nowhere near thirty!" Adam protested.

Colin narrowed his eyes at him. "Yes, you're the virginal vessel, I'm sure." Then he pleaded with the rest of the men, "Please tell me he's the youngest."

They laughed. "He is," Thomas replied. "He's twenty-five. I'm twenty-nine, Alex is, too. Daniel is...?"

"Thirty-one," Daniel said.

"And Jonathan is thirty-five."

"Oh, hell, it's all the same after twenty-five, anyway," Colin groused.

"I'll drink to that!" Jonathan raised his glass. He, Colin, and Daniel clinked each other's glasses.

"*I* know the real reason why Mr. Sewell is with us," Jonathan proclaimed.

"Oh yes?" Adam teased. "Do tell, Blackwell."

"Because he'd outshine anywhere else. But here, with Meredith, who has finally met his match—o-ho! Why, it's like the melody and harmony of the group!"

"Or oil and water," Colin offered, and then laughed when Adam elbowed him. "I'm sorry," he turned to him. "You're just such a good sport!"

"Hmph. Good target is more like it. Buy me a drink."

Colin's eyes caught a waiter. "Another gin and bitters please. Oh, and a glass of seltzer."

Adam punched him in the shoulder, causing Colin to nearly fall over as he laughed. "I can't help it!" Then he held up his hand. "No, the glass of seltzer is for me, you see."

"Oh, really? I hate gin and bitters!"

"Fine!" Colin said, and when the waiter returned, he gave his order. "Three bottles of Renaudin Bollinger, please."

The group fell silent. The waiter looked perplexed. "*Three*, sir?"

"Yes. Oh, and six glasses, of course."

The waiter looked uncertain, but he nodded and was off.

"Mr. Sewell, that's not necessary!" Adam whispered.

Colin sighed. "Mr. Meredith, I'm onto you. This is exactly how you get everything you want, isn't it? And you're very good at it. Don't you think your skill should be rewarded?"

Adam turned scarlet as the men laughed at Colin's insight. "I didn't intend to put you out like that," he murmured.

"You're not putting me out," Colin said airily. "I believe now I was also placed in this group because it appreciates luxury; that much I can tell. And I'm in the mood for appreciating the ability of a fine champagne to make one forget one's past for a bit, you see?" With those words, Colin suddenly felt much older than anyone in the group, who he realized probably did not share the experience Colin had lived while in London. He was surprised to feel almost fatherly to the men, yet not minding how he sounded at all. Adam leaned on his fist and said dreamily, "Oh Mr. Sewell, don't forget the past. Tell us about England."

And as they waited for their drinks, Colin began to tell them all about the club he had visited so often, leaving out the details of his own reputation there.

When the Carlisle prepared to close for the evening, Adam stood up, giving a sharp look to Jonathan, who was about to open his mouth, but shut it. Adam turned to Colin. "I'll share a cab with you, Sewell, to make sure you get home safely."

"Oh, that's all right, I came with Mr. Dearborn."

Adam smiled. "Yes, I know. I think he expects one of us to take you back, though. He generally stays awhile after closing."

"Oh," Colin said again. A small race of panic flew through him. "Well... if you're certain it'd be no trouble..."

Adam gave him a friendly look. "I'm certain." He put on his coat. "Come along, then."

The group walked out together and Colin's cheeks began to burn. Everyone thought he and Adam were going to... "Really, Mr. Meredith, I'm sure I'll be fine on my own."

Adam crossed his arms indignantly. "Am I not good enough to share a ride with you then, Mr. Sewell?"

Colin's shoulders fell. "That's not it and you know it," he muttered. "Thank you for your kindness, then." He followed Adam to the carriage.

Once they were inside, Adam smiled at a somewhat forlorn Colin. "They don't think you and I are going home *together*, you know," he quipped.

Colin jerked his head up. "Oh! Um... I didn't know..."

"It's all right. I can see how you would think it. I just thought I should look out for you. And you're perfectly safe, because I don't... do that... with anyone, anymore."

Colin's eyes widened, and he was about to ask why not when he remembered his manners. "Well, that's your business," he shrugged, feeling slightly depressed. "I certainly don't expect to be doing anything of the sort myself, anytime soon."

"Yes, well, I figured as much, which is why I thought you and I made a good pair." Colin knitted his brow, and Adam continued. "You see, I'm married, with three children."

"You?" Colin asked, incredulous. "But you're so young!"

Adam smiled. "I'm only five years younger than you. My father wouldn't let me inherit the business until I got married and 'sired a few' before he died. So now, I have a beautiful wife and three wonderful little ones."

Colin tilted his head. "Well, with all due respect, Mr. Meredith, the married men I knew in London had no trouble enjoying the company of other men."

Adam cast his eyes downward. "I know," he nodded. "But two years ago, I was careless at home, and my oldest son came barreling into the room. The other fellow and I were just... kissing, fully clothed and all, but he saw us. He was only five years old at the time, and I don't know if it registered in his head. I hope to God not. But for weeks I couldn't sleep or think. I kept worrying he would tell my wife about what he saw. For a long time I was too scared to repeat anything like that. Then, one night I did try it again, but my son's image of his discovery actually came into my mind, and I just couldn't go through with it." He looked up at Colin. "I don't want to resort to hotel rooms, alleys, and cabs. Now that I'm a family man I feel a sort of obligation, you see."

Colin smiled sympathetically. "I understand, but don't be so hard on yourself. My own father caught me, and there was a lot more going on than just kissing."

Adam's mouth fell open. "Really?"

Colin nodded. "That's why I went to England, actually. I was tired of sneaking around, so I said, 'Sorry Papa. I'm a sodomite!' Then I left."

"You didn't!" Adam cried. "You *told* your father that?"

"Well, not really," Colin admitted. "I tried to tell him but he refused to believe me, so I told him in the letter I left behind."

"And you haven't seen him since?"

"Well, no," Colin shrugged. "I haven't seen any of my family. I've been in England all this time."

"So then, they don't know if you're alive or dead?"

"And vice versa."

"But, wouldn't they have been able to track you down?"

Colin looked sheepish. "I changed my name. It was a way of saying to my father, 'I *am* going to live like this, but I won't drag the family name into it.'"

"You changed your name! So your name isn't really Colin Sewell?" Adam's voice was rising with excitement.

"Never mind that," Colin said brusquely. "It is now, and it has been, for years. And anyway, I didn't tell them where I was headed, so it would have been impossible for them to find me."

"Yes." Adam wondered. "Are you their only child?"

"I have two younger sisters." Adam fell silent at this comment, and Colin knew what he was thinking. "I didn't have a family business to inherit, like you," he explained.

"I know." Adam grew pensive. "But your father... it must be hard on him, to have lost his only son."

"Hard on *him*!" Colin exclaimed. Then he bowed his head. "All right, yes. I'm sure it has been hard on him. I hate that, you know. I wish I wasn't the only son. But it's not as if I had a choice."

"I know," Adam nodded quietly.

Colin eyed him. "No, you don't. It's obvious that you're in the group who believes the child has a duty to his family, and I am in the other group."

Adam looked up. "It's none of my business, Mr. Sewell. For what it's worth, I think you're very brave. But don't you ever miss your family?"

Colin bit his lip, angry now at Adam's cheek. He looked out the window and Adam saw his nostrils flare. "No," he replied flatly. "I don't miss them at all." But Adam caught Colin's eyes beginning to blink. *You stupid idiot!* Adam cursed himself. He struggled to think of something to say. "Sorry Sewell," he said cheerily. "With a friend like Meredith, who needs enemies, eh?"

It worked. Colin turned and gave a laugh, exhaling. "I think you'd be a wonderful friend. Nobody else wants to talk about it."

"About what?"

"About the melancholic side. The darker side of being this way. Nobody wants to go beyond, 'Well, we're just this way, tra-la-la.' Do you know that in all my years in London not a single man asked me if I missed my family?"

"Not even that fellow you were with all that time?"

"Well, yes, he did. Once. And my reaction was the same as what you just saw, so he didn't ask again. But he hated any discussion about the past, I discovered. It turns out he had a difficult time of it, himself." Then Colin looked at his lap. "But I think of my family every day."

"Then Mr. Sewell, you should see them," Adam urged gently. "I know it would be hard to see your father, but your mother... They don't even know you're back in America!"

Colin shook his head. "I think it's better this way. I don't think I could face my father. He'd tell me what a poor excuse for a son I was. That I was selfish, and that he regrets the day I was born because I amounted to nothing, as far as he was concerned. Because I'm a... an aberration."

Adam shook his head sympathetically. "Fathers are supposed to be pricks. I hate mine."

Colin looked up, surprised. "Oh, my father's not like that. He's the kindest man you'd have ever met."

They stared at each other. Then Colin sighed and looked out the window in silence. When the carriage rolled to a stop, he turned to Adam. "Thank you, Mr. Meredith. Do you think we could please keep this conversation just to ourselves?"

"Oh, yes! Of course," Adam assured him. "I wouldn't think otherwise." He smiled. "Will we see you again tomorrow night?"

"Well," Colin hesitated, "I really only attend clubs Saturday nights, if that's all right."

"As you like. Then we'll see you in a week?"

Colin smiled. "Yes. May I sit with your group again?"

Adam tsked him. "You haven't any choice—you were assigned to us, remember? And if you weren't, I'd have words with Harold!"

Colin laughed and bade him goodnight.

The next evening, Colin was reading at his desk when someone knocked at the door. He crept toward it and then turned the knob.

"Hullo, Mr. Sewell!"

"Mr. Meredith!"

"I should have sent 'round a post, but I wanted to get out for a bit and I thought I'd call on you."

"Come in!"

Adam looked around the room and flopped into a chair. "Not a bad place. I've never stayed at the Waldorf."

Colin brought over drinks and handed one to Adam. "I wish I wasn't. It's costing me a fortune! But I'm—" he stopped and stared at Adam. "Wait a moment! This is perfect! I'm looking for a permanent residence, but I don't know New York very well at all. Can you make some recommendations?"

Adam grinned. "Of course. What kind of place are you looking for?"

"Something in the city, definitely. This area is wonderful, in fact."

Adam laughed. "This is Park Avenue!"

Colin looked at him blankly. "What does that mean?"

"That this area is outrageously expensive!"

Colin shrugged. "I'm sure it won't be any problem."

Adam sat up. "You must really be a successful architect."

Colin smiled. "I'm getting there. I had a lot of money saved back in London. Really, the price of housing doesn't affect me." *All right, thank you Henry.*

"Well, then," Adam started eagerly. "Here's an idea: My official reason for this visit was to invite you to lunch at my house next Saturday. That offer still stands, of course. But how about after lunch, I take you around here as well Fifth Avenue, which is where I live, and we'll see what we can find?"

Colin looked pleased. "That's very grand of you!"

Adam jumped to his feet. "Wonderful! I'll have my carriage pick you up here at eleven o'clock."

Colin nodded. "Will there be a group of people lunching with you, then?"

Adam laughed. "Oh, no. It's completely informal, just my wife and me. And you."

"Oh, so your wife really exists?" Colin teased.

Adam pretended offense. "Mr. Sewell, everything I say to a handsome stranger when we're alone and I'm drunk is absolutely true!"

Colin laughed. "Well then, I look forward to meeting her, as well as those supposed three children you have."

Saturday came and Colin was escorted into the Merediths' library, where Adam and his wife were playing a game of checkers. They both rose upon Colin's appearance.

"Glad you made it, Sewell!" Adam came forth and gestured toward him for his wife. "Tressa, the venerable Mr. Sewell!"

His wife laughed. "So you *do* exist, Mr. Sewell! I had feared Adam had become delirious!"

Colin stood, transfixed. Adam's wife was a classic beauty—all high forehead, blue eyes, blond hair, and shapely body. "Sorry?" he said weakly.

"Well, he's gone on and on about you since *last* Saturday! I told him he'd simply have to invite you over so I could be certain you weren't a figment of his imagination!"

Colin glanced at Adam, who grinned and said, "Oh yes, I told her all about you being a famed architect and your wittiness and such. How you were *almost* as handsome as me—"

"Oh, Adam!" Tressa admonished. "For that, I'll have Mr. Sewell escort me to the dining room!"

She offered her arm and Colin took it, smiling. "I'd be honored."

Lunch was a playful repartee between the three of them, and Tressa shook her head at the ease of conversation. "It's as if you were long-lost brothers," she murmured.

"But it's you and Mr. Sewell who look like siblings," Adam teased.

"Nonsense!" Colin argued. "I have brown eyes; she has blue. She's much more refined than me. I couldn't possibly pass for one so becoming as Mrs. Meredith."

But they are like brothers, Tressa thought, smiling at the compliment. As impressed as Mr. Sewell was with her, it was clear he had a greater affinity for her husband. *More like two lost souls, perhaps.*

Lunch was over and Adam called in the children. Within minutes, two boys and a girl stood in the doorway with their governess. "Mr. Sewell," Adam declared, "these are our children: Oliver, seven; Catherine, six; and Nicholas, three." The boys bowed and Catherine curtsied. "How do you do, Mr. Sewell?" they chorused.

Colin smiled. He walked over and shook Oliver's hand—Oliver! The one who saw Adam with another man! "Oliver Meredith, a pleasure." Oliver beamed at the adult formality. "Miss Meredith," he held her hand close to his bowed head, causing her to giggle. "And Master Meredith." When Colin bent down on one knee to shake his hand, Nicholas simply threw his arms around Colin's neck and Colin instinctively picked him up. It wasn't until the boy buried his face into Colin's collar that Colin realized he hadn't held a child since he was... thirteen years old? "Oh, you're a wee one, there," he crooned, delighting in the child's affection and warm scent.

"Boy, you've really got the Irish in you," Adam rolled his eyes, grinning.

Tressa stared in shock. "Mr. Sewell! You're an absolute natural!"

Colin blushed. "I haven't held a child in years." Nicholas thrust his head back. "Play horsie with me!"

"All right, then!" Colin sat on a chair and put Nicholas on his knee. "First, the horsie takes a nice walk." He bumped the child slowly and smoothly. "Then the horsie trots." He bumped Nicholas harder, making him giggle and then laugh. "Then the horsie... gallops!" And Nicholas screamed with glee as Adam fell to his own knees in hysterics. Tressa held her hand to her mouth, her heart filling with tenderness.

"Why on earth hasn't he married, yet?" These were Tressa's first words to Adam when he returned from showing Colin some real estate in the city.

Adam poured himself a drink. "Do you like him, then?" he teased.

"Like him? Adam darling, if you weren't in this world, I'd be bidding on Mr. Sewell!" Adam burst into laughter while Tressa shook her head. "Really, Adam, look at him! He's handsome, bright, talented, and he's just a gift with children."

Adam nodded. "I know. But he was married at one time. Back in London." At this his expression became somber; his voice, quiet. "Then something tragic happened. I'd rather not tell you."

"Oh Adam, you must! Or else I'll imagine terrible things."

Adam paused, and then looked at the floor. "His wife was killed in a robbery attempt. Colin was with her, and she... she was wearing diamond jewelry he had just bought for her. He told her to give it over but she wouldn't. Before they knew it, the thieves slashed both of them and ripped her jewelry from her." Adam was having difficulty talking at this point. He turned to look at his wife. "She bled to death, Tress. And... and she was pregnant with their first child."

Tears welled in Tressa's eyes. "My God!" she whispered. "That's horrible!"

Adam gazed at his drink. "Yes. He just told me tonight himself, because I thought the same way you did, and I asked if he hadn't been considering marriage very seriously. Then he told me. I furiously apologized, of course—my God, I was mortified! But he seemed relieved. He said he didn't know how to go about bringing it up, but he was glad he told me because he said he doesn't feel like marrying anyone now, maybe ever." He sighed. "I'm sure he has a horrible feeling of guilt, even though he's not at fault. And that's the real reason why he came back to America. He couldn't bear being there anymore."

"Oh, how awful," Tressa cried. "Oh, poor Mr. Sewell! I'm so glad I didn't know that story when he was here today. I probably would have just broken down when he picked up Nicholas." And as that very scene replayed in her head, her eyes began to water anew. "Oh, what a lovely man! I'm glad he has you, Adam! You must be a good friend to him."

Adam went over to his wife and encircled her waist. "I will. I like him a lot. And he likes our company—he thought you were wonderful." Adam tried to quell his feelings of disgust at the monstrous lie he had just told her. But he had to admit it was a good one. Especially since he had helped Colin conceive it just hours ago when they were talking in the carriage right after leaving Adam's house.

"Your family is wonderful," Colin said wistfully.

"Thank you. *You* certainly got on well with everyone!"

"Impossible not to. You've got a beautiful wife, in every sense of the word, and all three of your children are impeccably mannered."

Adam laughed. "I'll agree with you on most points, but believe me, the children can be absolute terrors!"

"But they're just being children," Colin smiled.

"Yes, which means they argue, throw tantrums, cry, disobey, get sick, vomit, and destroy things!"

Colin laughed. "Oh, I can't picture any of them doing that!"

"Well then, you're very naïve," Adam sniffed. But he gazed affably at his new friend. "I have to say, I didn't think you were such a family man, Sewell."

Colin averted his eyes. "I didn't, either. Perhaps it's just your family—who wouldn't want a life like that? And I suppose I've been lonely, as of late."

Adam nodded. "You know, if you're considering marriage yourself, I'm sure Tressa could find some very nice ladies for you."

Colin's expression froze. "Oh, no, no. No, I don't plan to do anything like that." Then he sighed. "At least, not for a long time, if at all."

"But Tressa is going to ask. I know she is, and then what do I tell her?"

"Well, why can't you just tell her that I enjoy being a bachelor?"

"Sewell, in all due respect, if you plan on spending the rest of your life here, and being *my* friend all that time as well, you'd better think of something that will shut people up." He grinned. "You are entirely too marriageable for anyone to believe you'd rather be alone."

"Well... what should I tell them, then?"

And so they hatched the story together. Colin was still doubtful by the time they worked out the details. "That's a horrid lie to tell people. What a horrible thing to make them think!"

Adam clucked his tongue. "You're the one who doesn't want to marry. Can you think of a better reason why not to, with this story?"

"Well, at least we decided not to have the thieves rape her."

"Yes, that was far too gruesome. You couldn't have divulged that anyway."

"And at least it really *didn't* happen. What a tragic story!" And then they couldn't help it; they had to laugh at their own serious expressions.

Adam's words sank into Colin's mind all day Sunday. *Family man...* Colin chuckled when he said the words to himself. Family man! Hardly. But when he took Adam out of the portrait and put himself in his place, Colin found he could picture it quite easily. And a sense of dread suffused him. *I can't possibly get married. I don't want to. I don't have to, after all, like Adam did. I could never live that ultimate lie. But Tressa seems happy. Well of course she is; she's married to a future millionaire. Even Henry thought I should have considered marriage. Why in hell did he say that? Oh yes, because unlike him, I needed a companion. So what? I was with Henry. And I'd rather have a male companion than a female one.* He glimpsed the idea of himself and Margaret Rademaker together with their children. *I would love the children. And I would love Margaret for being their mother. But,*

God! The lie would eat away at me. If it was me and I was with a man for the rest of my life who was actually a regular fellow... Oh God, that's horrible. I couldn't do that to a woman. And I'd be terrified of going out to the club—I'd be so guilt-ridden. How do those men do it? Meredith, Kenneth... Well, Kenneth's wife knows, and Meredith doesn't even do anything with men anymore. Could I do that? After all, I've screwed enough men to last a lifetime! Colin paused, and then realized a new problem. *But which is worse: to marry a woman falsely in the Catholic church, or to not marry one at all but continue going on with men? To procreate as we are supposed to or to let a woman marry a man with true intentions, so that a real Covenant occurs between them and God?*

Colin then decided swiftly that entering into a false union in God's very own house, under His eye, had to be the worse of the sins. *I cannot do it. I will not do it.*

CHAPTER THIRTY-TWO

February 25, 1900

Dear Henry,

Thank you for the letter of recommendation. It was above and beyond what I expected, and it could not have come from anyone I admired more. Therefore, it meant a great deal to me.

I am now employed at McKim, Mead, and White, much thanks to you. Something I hadn't told you was that they had offered me a position with their firm eight years ago, when I was about to graduate. So they knew me by my real name and you can imagine the stories I had to tell them. I daresay they enjoyed them, especially White; he seems quite the gadabout. They have already told me they are not looking for a fourth partner, so when the time comes, I will strike out on my own.

From a personal standpoint, I am enclosing what I hope to be appropriate payment for shipment of any belongings of mine you have left. As you probably already deduced, I am going to eventually fall short on funds, and liquidating many of those items would be the practical thing to do. Thank you in advance. I will admit that I hadn't the nerve to throw the timepiece overboard whilst on the ship. I am certain that doesn't surprise you. I am glad things are going smoothly in terms of work. You were right, Henry—I was lucky. For eight years I worked alongside the greatest architect of our time. Thank you for that opportunity. I think when everything is all said and done, I will say it was worth it.

Sincerely,

Colin

P.S. Please note my new address:
900 Fifth Avenue, New York, New York 10016

A week after writing to Henry, Colin was delighted to hear again from Howard.

7 March 1900

Hullo Colin!

I hope this letter finds you in better spirits. It sounds like you got through the worst, and although I have had some concern about you, I know that you've overcome too many trials to ever be vanquished. I am certain that your next letter will tell me how much better you're doing and that you've come up from your Stygian depths.

I was sorry to read that you and Charlie are staying in America permanently, though who am I to judge? I can understand your reasons. Kenneth mentioned visiting you next year. If your letters are not sufficient enough in detail between now and then, I may have to join him and see that country for myself. So let that be a warning to you!

Honestly, what is New York like compared to London? I've always pictured America as an open frontier with cattle rustlers and lots of fringed buckskin. Ha! Is that your Chicago, then? Actually, I'm just curious about New York's climate, the shops, and the population. When you were here you certainly surprised a lot of us. I admit we think of Americans as a rather rough, feisty lot, posing desperately as upper-class Europeans, yet falling short. We tend to think more of the hardscrabble revolutionaries than their leaders (Washington, Franklin, and Jefferson). Hmm... as you can see, we're still more than one hundred years off on the history of American civilization.

Speaking of which, do you feel you've changed after spending so many years in England? Does America now feel foreign to you? Has anyone noticed a trace of an accent in your voice?

You might be pleased to know that your absence is causing quite a stir. A lot of people were hoping to scoop you up once they found out; you know what I mean. And it's just far too romantic for them that you fled back to America in "passionate anguish," especially with Henry's valet! You can imagine. How did your reintroduction into society go? Do you plan to take in some theater and musical performances anytime soon? Mark and I just saw Beerbohm-Tree's production of A Midsummer Night's Dream. It was very funny. There were even live rabbits on the stage! I wonder if it will come to New York. A week before that, we viewed La Boheme, my favorite tragic opera.

Well, that's enough from me. I hope you're not still soaking in Cointreau! You should probably try something more salubrious, such as a hot toddy.

Sincerely,
Howard

March 23, 1900

Dear Howard,
I have found New York to be quite salubrious.
Yours,
Colin

March 24, 1900

Dear Howard,
I am still laughing! I laughed all the way to the post office yesterday, over my reply to you. I am praying you got the joke, because it did require you

to remember what you said toward the beginning of your last letter. Can you blame a man for wanting as much British company as possible?

Oh Howard, there are many things I would like to tell you. Ask you. It's difficult for me to write. You do it so naturally. I should clarify: writing to you is a joy. Refraining *is* the difficult part. As much as these letters serve as a bridge across the great Atlantic, there's a deluge of words dammed until they can be spoken in person. That said, it would be wonderful if you and Kenneth could visit America sometime. And of course, Mark is welcome too! I have even finally purchased a home! It's a nice place on Fifth Avenue. It's a bit beyond my means at the moment in terms of size and money, but it's the incentive for me to work and have the confidence that I'm good enough of an architect to afford it! I'll write the address below. I was hopelessly ignorant on how to go about hiring help. With assistance from a friend who lives nearby, I managed to secure an excellent cook and a housemaid. I think Charlie is happy to be in a more settled environment, as am I.

Speaking of projects, I landed a position with McKim, Mead, and White! Unfortunately, as they do not need a fourth partner, I am back to being a senior draftsman, which is admittedly a sting. Really, after being a partner with the greatest contemporary architect of our time, it's an insult! I entertained the idea of opening up my own office, but the thought rather overwhelms me. This way I can establish some connections and review the American building codes and whatnot.

New York is similar to London by way of the arts and shopping. The climate is very different, though. Winter is much colder and they get quite a bit of snow here. Summers are very hot and humid. I'm beginning to think there's a pattern of torturing myself, actually. London was perfect. It was so perfect. I hope you realize that and appreciate it.

It's funny that I exceeded the expectations of you Brits! I suppose as long as you have your refined accents though, we'll always come up short. America does feel foreign to me, as you wondered, but it's foreign in a good way. You know my fondness for leaving past lives behind and starting over—ha! I feel

English enough that New York feels like a completely novel experience, and it is a relief. I have made some friends at the club Kenneth told me about, and they seem to be a nice group of fellows. I don't have a trio like you three, but one can hardly expect to have that kind of luck again! Still, a nice bunch of men, around my own age. I don't know how much of me they really know (I suspect they know nothing at all), but they do know why I am here, so everyone has been fairly easy on me. Of course, I just met them a week ago, so who can tell? I admit it gets me out of the house and keeps up my conversation skills.

In the few brief conversations I've had with people, they have asked where I am from. I can't tell any difference myself, although one young lady teased me about saying "Sorry?" instead of "I beg your pardon?" And apparently, I have gained some kind of inflection in my voice.

It was interesting to hear that certain people miss me, however dubious some of their intentions and reasons. It really is just as well that I left as suddenly as I did, or else I'd still be there finishing my goodbyes. I have thought often of the people I do miss. Speaking of which, if you'd rather not tell people you're corresponding with me, I understand, because it could end up being a burden on you. Just do keep writing! By now I fear I've become attached to your letters, Howard. As I said, a pattern of self-torture... But better paper than drink, although I did have a hot toddy last night. It was absolutely disgusting! You can keep your filthy whiskey!

I'll end here. This letter is ridiculously long and a grotesque measure of my leisure time. Don't feel you need to respond to all that I've written, as you are busier than I.

Sincerely,

Colin

My new address:
900 Fifth Avenue, New York, New York 10016

10 April 1900

Dear Colin,

I had a hell of a laugh when I got your first letter. I knew exactly what you meant. Mind you, I was glad that wasn't your sole correspondence. But a good joke, lad. And what a letter that followed! That's more like the Colin Sewell I know. Before I go any further, I must congratulate you on your new job! Colin, that is absolutely wonderful that you landed a position in the most prestigious firm in New York (as per Henry's description)! I'd expect nothing less, of course, but I am happy for you all the same. I think it is wise to join a firm, at least in the beginning. You're correct that you will make a lot of contacts this way. And you can start making payments on that mansion you own! It must be impressive—what are you going to do with the interior? Will you use ideas from your Helios House?

I can see absence does make the heart grow fonder: have you forgotten how cloudy and rainy London is? And the fog! I think it would be exciting to have snow every year. The few times we've had it, it was so pretty to see everything coated in white. But I do love London and can barely imagine living anywhere else. I'm not the intrepid traveler you are—that's one of the things I've admired about you: Colin the Fearless!

I about fell off my chair picturing you trying a hot toddy! Did you even finish it, Fearless? Actually, the hot water, sugar, and lemon should have made the whiskey barely noticeable, so perhaps whoever made your drink was an amateur. Or perhaps you felt cheated at not being able to taste the liquor! Now, Hot Buttered Rum—that is disgusting. Why don't you inventory all of the hot drinks and rate them for me, Fearless? Ho, ho, now I'm having a time of it! All right, back to serious topics.

I agree—writing letters provides only the veneer of confidence, but it is better than nothing. I hope you have found a friend in that new group at the club, one who can help you sort things out. It is frustrating that I can't help you as much as I'd like to, but given our history, perhaps it's better that way. To just be friends from afar.

Everyone knows Kenneth and I keep abreast of your progress. We don't mind. It would look worse if we treated it as some sort of secret.

Well, this letter comes up a bit short. I'll have to think of some more interesting things to share for next time, or just become a more interesting person! Take care, Colin.

Sincerely,
Howard

April 26, 1900

Dear Howard,

What your letter lacks in length, it makes up for in quality, despite the ribbing I had to take!

Work has been going well. In fact, I landed a giant project! It started when McKim gave me my first project: the lavatories of a department store! I said to him, "You have got to be joking. What other offers have come across the table?" I finally got him to admit to a few large-scale projects and would you believe it—one of them was a bank! I snatched the outlines from him and said, "Give me two weeks. If you don't like my proposal, fine. I'll design the damned lavatories. But let me try." Of course, by this time, I was so insulted that if he didn't accept my proposal, I was going to present them to the bank president myself and freelance. A stupid thing to do, perhaps, and fortunately, I didn't need to do it. For my work sufficiently amazed all three men. Howard, what a thrill it was to see them at last realize on their own that I was good. Long story short: the bank approved my design over four other firms and I started work on it today. Can you believe that? I still remember the time I visited you at your bank and you suggested perhaps a bank was in my own future. I didn't think so at the time, but perhaps America is a bit more open to interpretation, as this bank is not going to resemble the Bank of England in any way, shape, or form (as much as I like it on you)! I'm not going to tell you much more about it, though, because some things will probably change, and if you do ever come here, it can be sort of a surprise! I have to say I'm back to working long hours, but after the hell of working for Rademaker, this is a walk in the park! And nobody minds if I work late, which is refreshing.

You mentioned in your prior letter that La Boheme is your favorite tragic opera? I myself prefer Aida. At least at the end they die together, at the same time, and of their own free will, not due to some stupid mistake such as what occurs in Romeo and Juliet. And The White Plague is far too depressing—it occurs enough in real life; who needs it in an opera? All right, I'm teasing you. I enjoy La Boheme as well—the singing is amazing. But if you visit me we will see Aida. Of course, all told, give me The Mikado any day!

Here, I've put together a list for you:

Hot Drinks (With Liquor)

Rated in Order

1) Blue Blazer (My word, this drink is amazing! Admittedly, it has whiskey in it, but the show in making it—see if Jack can make it at the club for you!)
2) Brandy Blazer (same idea, less thrilling to watch)
3) Brandy Toddy
4) Café Brûlot (this is a coffee drink—how I have missed coffee! You must have this if you visit)
5) Bull's Milk (it has maple syrup in it—truly an American drink)
6) Irish Coffee
7) Whiskey Toddy (on the 2nd serving, not bad)
8) Rum Toddy (I now know I am no fan of rum)
9) Gin Toddy (what a disappointment! Gin should never be served hot!)
10) Hot Buttered Rum (most disgusting of all—you were right!)

I'm sure you can imagine what trouble it was to do this research. I hope you appreciate it, as it was a difficult task. Well, I am now drinking #3 and have become quite drowsy, so I'm going to end this letter. If a Howard can do it, I should be so entitled as well!

Sincerely,

Fearless

(I like it, but I must think of one for you!)

CHAPTER THIRTY-THREE

April 30—the accursed day had finally arrived. But while Colin was shaving, it struck him: *Wait a moment—nobody here knows it! Why, as far as anyone else is concerned, it's just another day!* Colin's spirits lifted. There was something wonderful in realizing that everyone back in London knew it was Colin's thirtieth birthday, but he, the guest of honor himself, was a thousand miles away, where they couldn't reach him. Even Charlie hadn't said anything, obviously thrown off by the complete change in schedule since they'd arrived.

Colin worked at the office in a better mood than usual. At five o'clock he got into a carriage to return home. *I'll just have dinner, do some reading, and go to bed. When I wake up tomorrow, it will be all over!*

Charlie opened the door to him with a flourish.

"Happy birthday, Mr. Colin!" Charlie cried, a tray of caviar pastries in his hand. He stepped aside to reveal a standing ice bucket of champagne.

Colin gaped at him. "Charlie! What on earth...?"

Charlie grinned, shaking a finger at him. "You thought I'd forgotten."

Colin stared at the ice bucket. "I *wished* you'd forgotten."

Charlie tsked him, heading for the champagne. "Now, Mr. Colin. Your birthday comes only once a year. That in itself is cause for celebration.

But your *golden* birthday! That..." he popped the cork, "*that* is once in a lifetime!" He poured the bubbly. "I realize this isn't how you intended to spend this day, in more ways than one. But I'll be damned if you're not going to spend it at all!"

Colin smiled, taking the champagne. "That doesn't even make sense, Charlie."

"Well, you know what I mean." Charlie raised his glass. "To golden opportunities from here on in!"

Colin clinked his glass to Charlie's, sighed, and drank.

Charlie motioned him to the dining room. "Now come along! Dinner is waiting!"

Colin followed him to the dining room and gasped. Floor-length candelabras flickered in each corner. A massive floral centerpiece graced the table. The table was set for one with Colin's fine china and crystal. Charlie held the chair out for Colin and lifted the lid of the first course: "Duck consommé, sir."

Colin shook his head as he was seated. "Since I paid for this, I suppose it's all right."

"Mr. Colin!" Charlie looked hurt. "I didn't use a cent of your money! It's a gift from me, in honor of you."

"But—"

"Not another word!" Charlie bit his lip to keep from laughing and took a small box from the table. "Here. You must have a present on your birthday, too!"

Colin stared at the pale blue box. *Tiffany.* "You didn't..." he whispered.

"Open it, Mr. Colin! It's in honor of the first Christmas present you gave me."

Colin gingerly lifted the lid, peeked inside, and then shut it in disgust. "I can't accept it." He held it out to Charlie, who appeared devastated.

"Don't you like them?"

"Charlie, they're 18-k gold! Don't be ridiculous!"

Charlie turned scarlet. "I'm sorry. I couldn't afford gemstones..."

Colin dropped his hand. "It's not that! They're beautiful cufflinks! And they are far too extravagant!"

Charlie lifted his head. "Extravagant? After how well you treated me while you were living with Mr. Sewell? And now? Inviting me to America, paying my passage? Allowing me to use Mr. Sewell's first-class ticket when you could have put me in third and saved your money? And the same with the hotel, Mr. Colin! And all the meals in those expensive restaurants!" He shook his head. "I could have never afforded a trip like this in my entire lifetime! And you think a pair of cufflinks is too extravagant?"

"But you cannot be spending your money on me," Colin insisted.

"Mr. Colin, you've been paying me full salary since we left London for practically none of the work! In fact," he reached for an envelope on the table and pushed it toward Colin, "this is the other gift I wanted to give you. I refuse to keep it."

Colin looked at the envelope that clearly held dollar bills inside. His voice grew dark. "That I won't take."

"You must."

"Charlie," Colin frowned, "you are insulting my position as your employer. A good valet—an excellent valet—often goes above and beyond his duties. Your usual services have been replaced with more important ones, specifically, your companionship. You're practically the only person I know in this entire country! If you chose to leave me and find work elsewhere, I'd be left alone."

"That's not true, Mr. Colin. You have your co-workers, and your friends at the club."

"Yes, but..."

"You need gentlemen friends again, Mr. Colin," Charlie urged gently. "I can only offer you so much." He crossed his arms and smiled. "Now, you should start eating before it grows cold."

Colin was at a loss. "Well, it's all very wonderful, Charlie. It really is." Then he looked up at him. "In fact, why don't you join me?"

Charlie was taken aback. "Oh! No, I... I thought perhaps you've had enough company for now and you'd like to eat in peace."

"Nonsense!" Colin admonished. "Call for another place setting."

"Mr. Colin, really... This is exactly what I mean. Having dinner with your valet... It's improper."

Colin popped a caviar pastry in his mouth. "Well, you certainly didn't mind sharing the champagne with me."

"That was a birthday toast. I just wanted to make sure someone raised a glass to you."

Colin grinned and sat back. "All right then, let's make a deal like we did on the ship: if you'll have dinner with me now, I promise this will be the last night I require your companionship. From here on in it will be with gentlemen friends only."

Charlie's shoulders sagged. "It's not that I don't enjoy your company, Mr. Colin..."

"I know, Charlie. And you're right, as always. After all, I'm the one who just clarified our relationship. It's only that the thought of me spending the rest of the evening by myself while Henry's no doubt throwing some kind of *Thank-God-He's-Gone-Because-Today-He's-Thirty* party..." He looked at Charlie. "Please?"

Charlie understood, and smiled. "All right. I'd be honored."

Colin laughed. "Wonderful! And I'm going to put on your cufflinks."

They had finished off the champagne when Charlie's meal arrived, and then they opened a bottle of wine. Then another. And still a third. "To hell with it," Colin decided ruefully. "I'm going to get out of my mind drunk!"

"*Going* to?" Charlie laughed. Then he said nobly, "As your loyal companion, I shall try to keep up with you."

Two hours and a few cordials later, Colin stumbled from his chair and beamed at Charlie. "Thank you, Charlie-boy! It was wonderful!"

Charlie took a good look at Colin's drunken appearance and giggled. "Are you sure you can find your way upstairs?"

Colin pretended he was lost, looking around the room. "I dunno. The carpet is looking pretty suitable."

"Oh, no, Mr. Colin!" Charlie cried. Before he knew what he was doing, he took Colin's hand. "Come along," he said, leading him into the bedroom.

"Oh, right. Here we are," Colin replied. He flopped on the bed and curled up on his side. "G'night, Charlie."

"Mr. Colin, you can't sleep in your clothes."

"Mmph."

Charlie sighed and went over to the bed, where he rolled Colin onto his back. "Thank goodness this *is* my last night as your 'companion,'" he muttered, fumbling with Colin's vest buttons.

The motion was too familiar. Colin looked up at him. "Want to end it with a bang?"

Charlie raised an eyebrow. "What do you mean?"

Colin smiled evilly. "I dare you... to stay on a bit."

Charlie stared at him, and then shook his head with a nervous laugh. "I thought *dining* with you was improper. Sit up."

Colin groggily complied. "Oh, come now. Men sleep with their servants all the time. Although in most cases, you'd be a chambermaid or something of that sort. Wait! My cufflinks..." He removed them and then studied them. He looked up at Charlie with great tenderness. "Well they really are beautiful, Charlie. Thank you."

His affection weakened Charlie. "Oh, well, you're beautiful, Mr. Colin. You oughtn't to let Mr. Sewell make you think otherwise. He's a proper fool!"

"D'you think so?"

"I know so, sir."

Colin laughed. "'Sir.'"

"It's true. You were loyal to him!"

Colin shrugged, smiling. "You've been the loyal one, Charlie. To me."

It was then deemed proper for Colin to lean in and give a grateful kiss to Charlie. And when Charlie couldn't help kissing him back, it was deemed proper for Colin to continue. As they pursued each other further, Charlie murmured, "You won't fire me for this, will you?" Drunk as he was, he knew he was crossing the line and thought it at least a perfunctory courtesy to ask.

"I'll fire you if you don't," Colin reprimanded giddily. "I've never done it with a... I mean a..."

"A servant," Charlie smiled. "Nor I with, er..."

"An architect?" Colin giggled.

Charlie's expression grew serious. "No. With anyone as handsome as you."

Colin sighed. "Oh Charlie..." It suddenly struck Colin that although the idea of having sex with a servant was titillating enough, it was also the perfect counterattack to Henry's dismissal of Charlie. *"The bloom's rather gone off him."* Henry had said it when Charlie was thirty—why didn't Colin take notice then? And even though Charlie hadn't the good looks Colin did, he wasn't ugly by any means. Just average, and he had managed to keep his shape well. Colin ran his hands down Charlie's sides, where they came to rest at his hips. "You've a fine form," Colin smiled.

Charlie's head spun with the impropriety of it all. He would finally get to see Mr. Colin completely undressed! "You've a fine *everything*, Mr. Colin," he said admiringly, helping Colin out of his shirt. "I mean, sir! I mean... er..."

"I like the formal address," Colin replied woozily, undoing his trousers. "It sounds so proper. Let's have it be the only proper thing done this evening!"

In the middle of the night, Colin woke up to get a drink of water. He lurched out of bed, staggeringly ill. But when he returned, he saw Charlie, sleeping next to his spot, and he joyfully got back under the covers and with a long blissful sigh, nestled himself into Charlie's dozing form. Though Colin had been drunk at other times since leaving England, he had managed to resist begging his valet to grant him what he really wanted: someone to fill the yawning space beside him in bed. He knew Charlie wouldn't understand, believe, or comply with his real desire for just a sleeping partner. Fortunately, his valet ended up being a decent lover, and Colin's secret wish was granted: Charlie stayed on. For Colin, the absence of another warm body next to his had become unbearable.

He was almost reluctant to go back to sleep and lose consciousness of the man beside him. He wondered if Henry was missing the same thing. Then a rush of guilt came over him: Henry had gone to sleep and woken up in Colin's absence for years. *And now I'm being punished for it.* Colin mourned for Henry, but then forced himself to stop. *Well, I've made the transition easier for him, anyway.* He pressed himself closer to Charlie, who stirred slightly, and then he fell asleep.

The room had lightened when Charlie awoke. He turned over and felt a knee. When he opened his eyes, he saw his employer sleeping inches away from him. Horrified, Charlie slunk out of bed and went to his own room. His head throbbed and his mouth was dry. He eased himself onto the edge of his bed and held his head in his hands. *My God, what did I do? What kind of a valet am I?*

He wanted you to sleep with him.

It doesn't matter! It's my job to use good judgment and then I went and did this? It was my idea to celebrate his birthday, after all. He'll kill me.

He won't.

Maybe he won't remember.

Do you?

Oh God, what should I do? Do I act as if it never happened? Do I apologize?

Just wait and see what he does.

What if he fires me? Not because he's angry with me, but because things might be too awkward? I don't know anyone here. Who's going to hire me? And what are the chances I'd find a third gentleman like Mr. Sewell and Mr. Colin?

Anger began to swell up inside of Charlie. *He's never slept with men beneath his class! He's always known his place!*

He was drunk.

He's always drunk when it comes to the bedroom!

Charlie!

Well... I know he's been lonely, but honestly, his valet? Really, doesn't he have any respect for himself?

Not anymore. Mr. Sewell saw to that.

Yes, he did...

And maybe he did it as a gift for you!

I never hinted at such a thing!

You told him he was beautiful. You spent twenty-five dollars on cufflinks for him! You've been stroking his ego since the day Mr. Sewell left him.

Only to cheer him up! And anyhow, it's the truth. So what? That doesn't mean I was trying to have relations with him.

So, never mind that fantasy of yours you used to have? Seems like Mr. Colin had it, too...

I used *to have it, and that was just when I first met him. He never knew about it! This has all gone to pieces...*

Charlie didn't want to think anymore. He got up, splashed cold water onto his face, brushed his teeth, shaved, got dressed, and went to see if Colin had awoken. His nervous expression softened when he returned to Colin's bedroom.

Colin was still asleep but he had moved partly into Charlie's space, his face buried in Charlie's pillow, which he hugged with one arm. The scene struck Charlie as familiar. He recalled the many times he had entered Henry and Colin's bedroom in the early hours of the morning to deliver breakfast at his appointed time. The two men were sometimes still asleep, facing each other, Colin's arm over Henry's, Henry's leg over Colin's. And when they were awake they'd be cuddling and drowsing, with little short kisses and hugs. Charlie had been envious. He remembered once hearing Henry say, as Colin got up for a drink of water, "Mm... your pillow smells like you."

Charlie sighed, watching Colin unconsciously nuzzle the pillow. That was it then; Mr. Colin was lonely. He almost felt guilty for having left the bed. Still, *they* wouldn't be cuddling, so it was just as well. God, he felt like hell. He went downstairs, and the cook gave him tea. Then he sat and waited for Colin to rise. Finally, he heard the bell pulled.

Charlie walked into Colin's room, a sympathetic smile on his face. "Good morning, Mr. Colin. You'd probably like some tea." He produced a cup, hardly believing that last night he had his hands on the bare chest now before him.

"You're already dressed?" Colin squinted.

"Yes, sir."

Colin looked ashen as he took the tea. "Thank you," he whispered. He took a long drink, and then groaned. "Oh, God. I feel positively ill, don't you?"

"The price of entertainment," Charlie quipped. "And yes, my head is about to burst."

Colin rubbed his eyes and put on his glasses. He blinked, glancing at Charlie, and then he fiddled with his blanket, not sure what to say. If he wasn't so hung-over, he could have leapt out of bed and greeted Charlie with a cheery pat on his back on the way to breakfast. *No harm done, old boy! We had a good time!* But the bile in his throat and the thick fog in his head reminded him that he had really done something questionable. What if Charlie was so disgusted that he decided to find employment elsewhere? "It was nice," he finally murmured, cradling his cup and smiling wanly. "You've got a kind heart, Charlie."

Charlie rolled his eyes. "That's very generous of you, Mr. Colin, but I think my heart was the last thing on my mind last night, hmm?"

Colin gave a short laugh, and then winced. "Ow. I think I'll have breakfast in bed, Charlie. Then I'll let you do the honors of shaving."

"Excellent, sir." Charlie got up and went to the door. Both men sighed a deep breath of relief. They were still together.

Colin continued to throw himself into his work on the bank. It was easy to forget his worries; the project was exciting. He thought he'd never tell Howard, but he pictured his friend between the charcoal lines in each frame. *Howard is a tall man. I must make the doorways loom. Howard strides. I'll add wide hallways. No carpeting—this is a place of business. The sound of money must be heard! No, no... the offices must have carpeting, to match the hush of fiscal decision-making. What would Howard say about all of the windows? And no pillars!* Colin became manic at times, appearing to scribble furiously, only to produce a perfectly detailed, smooth-stroked tableau of a particular feature of the building.

The junior draftsmen often stopped and watched him. Charles, William, and Stanford did, too. They began arguing on whether or not they should make him partner, for it was clear if they didn't, he would freelance and compete for their commissions. An accord was reached to give him until the end of the year to prove himself. "If he doesn't leave us before then," Charles sighed.

On the first Saturday of May, Colin stopped by the Carlisle for a few early drinks. Adam hadn't arrived yet, and it wasn't until Colin was about to leave that he appeared. "Sewell!" He plopped himself down next to Colin. "Seen your father yet?"

Colin frowned. "No. Why?"

Adam lit a cigarette. "Sewell, it's been four months! Don't you think you should call on him?"

"Call on him!"

"Yes! Look, I'm a father, and I've been thinking. If that was Ollie or Nicholas, I'd about die if they dropped out of my life like that."

"Even if they led a universal boycott against your company?" Colin said wryly.

"Absolutely! As their father I have a right to know their whereabouts."

"Fathers have no such *rights*."

"Fine. A privilege, then. I am entitled to the privilege—"

"You can't be entitled to a privilege."

"Colin! Listen to me: I helped bring my sons into this world and if I raised them right, they should at the very least have the common decency to give their father the opportunity to react to what they've done."

"Well, I'm sure my father *has* reacted. I'm sure he's struck me out of his will!"

"I'll bet he hasn't."

"Oh, to hell with you, Meredith." Adam fell silent, and then he got up and took his drink. Colin looked up at him irritably. "You don't even know my father."

Adam glared at him. "I know he was the kindest man you'd have ever met. Or so I heard. I'd like to think my own sons would say that about me someday. And I certainly hope I'd be treated more fairly." With that, he stalked off. Colin was too tired to persuade him back; they'd caused a scene enough as it was. He rose up, bade the others goodnight, and left.

Three days later, Adam received a telegram at work.

SORRY. MEETING FATHER THIS SATURDAY GOD WILLING. CS

Saturday morning arrived and Colin was too nervous to eat breakfast. He drank two tumblers of gin the night before to force him asleep, and now his stomach turned. He was already bathed and dressed and had nothing to do until ten o'clock, the time his father said he would arrive.

It was a rather devious plot. Colin had sent a telegram to his father that read: IMPORTANT BUSINESS REGARDING YOUR SON MICHAEL CALLAHAN PLEASE CONFIRM OR DENY DATE OF MEETING AT TEN AM AT 900 FIFTH AVENUE SEND REPLY TO THIS ADDRESS

Colin knew his father would think someone found Colin dead or in jail and they were trying to find him, but he didn't know what else to write. It somehow seemed gentler than his first planned words: FATHER PLEASE MEET ME AT 10 AM AT 900 FIFTH AVENUE REPLY EITHER WAY YOUR SON MICHAEL

Also, he was afraid that his father would realize that 900 Fifth Avenue was Colin's home address and show up immediately, unexpectedly.

So Colin was now pacing about in his light grey suit. He had sat Charlie down the night before to tell him the entire story so that he would understand the gravity of the meeting and not interrupt. "Of course, if you hear a gun go off, by all means come and intervene," he had joked. Now as he paced, he fiddled with his glasses and kept brushing imaginary dust from his coat. He began his habit of wringing his hands. With thirty minutes to go, Charlie peeked around the corner. "Mr. Colin, please have some biscuits."

"No, Charlie, thank you." Colin had already brushed his teeth, and it'd be his luck to be brushing them when the doorbell rang. When it was five minutes to ten, he felt as if he would throw up. He regretted not having the biscuits. He took a deep breath and wished he could peer through the glass windows flanking the front door so that he could see his father before his father saw him. But he forced himself to walk back to the parlor and sit down.

The doorbell rang. Colin went pale. He heard Charlie open the door. "Mr. Callahan?"

"Yes. I'm here in regards to my son, Michael," a nervous voice replied.

"Yes, sir. Please follow me."

Colin stood up. He waited. He watched the doorway. His father emerged. Mr. Callahan's mouth fell open. "Michael!" He strode over to him and took his son's face into his hands. "You're alive!" The shock of his father's touch and the light in his father's eyes struck Colin mute. Then his father embraced him. "Oh, God, where have you been?"

"In London, Papa." Colin's voice was strained. He began shaking.

His father stood back. "London! All this time?"

Colin nodded. "Yes."

"Well, are you all right? You look well. You're not in any trouble, are you? What have you been doing? Is this your home?"

His father's earnest concern and lack of anger were almost unbearable. Colin motioned to a chair. "I think I'd better sit down, first, if you don't mind. Yes, I live here. I just moved in last week."

His father nodded. "Yes, of course." He too sat down, across from Colin. "Did you just come back to America, then?"

"Four months ago."

"Four months? Michael, why didn't you call on me earlier? Why didn't you ever write? We didn't know where you were, if you were safe. How could you..." Then his father stopped and bowed his head. "I know why you left. But Michael, to vanish without a trace? What if your mother had passed away, or we all perished somehow? And we've been sick thinking about you. Every day I hoped to God you were still alive. And then when I got this telegram, I was certain that it was a notification from the authorities!"

Colin's cheeks flamed with shame. He put his head in his hands. "I'm sorry, Papa. I just... I knew you wouldn't consider me your son anymore."

Mr. Callahan looked around and leaned forward. "Michael, we could have gotten help for you. You aren't still... um... are you?"

Colin looked up at his father and then looked away. "Yes." He started wringing his hands.

Mr. Callahan grimaced and then peered at his son. "But you seem unhappy about it."

Colin glanced back in surprise. "No! No, I... I've been fine. I was one of London's premier architects, Papa. There are forty designs in England that I have done!"

"Forty!"

"Yes! And I'm designing the Bank of Manhattan right now!"

"Is that why you're here?"

Colin's excited expression fell flat. He looked down at his hands. "No. I decided to move back here."

Mr. Callahan frowned, his voice filled with dread. "Did something happen in London?"

"I... I had a falling-out with the man I worked for."

"And did it have something to do with your... activities?"

Colin stared into space as he considered his father's words. Then he couldn't help it—he laughed. "You could say that. I was *with him* for eight years, after all."

The sly look in his son's eye and the intonation in his voice made Mr. Callahan ill. He felt his mouth fill up and stood quickly. Colin, alarmed, took him by the elbow and raced him into the bathroom. He apologized in anguish while his father heaved. And then Mr. Callahan's anger came. "You selfish, horrible brat! Prancing along with your disgusting paramours while we've prayed for you! Nine *years* of praying, and then you laugh in my face? You're not the son I raised!"

Colin began to choke up. "I'm sorry, Papa! I didn't mean to upset you! I'm sorry!"

But his father raged on. "Your mother was devastated, Michael! I had to lie to her face! And to your sisters' faces as well! To the entire family! While my only son, the only one who could carry on the Callahan name, delved into sodomy and depravity without a second thought!" And now the very sight of his son caused him to swing the back of his hand

and strike Colin, who fell back in pain. "God help me!" his father cried, stalking over to Colin and gripping his shoulders. "What is *wrong* with you, Michael? Why haven't you tried to *fix* it? Surely you've got enough brains to realize that you're sick! You know it's filthy and it's vile! You will go to hell, Michael!"

"I don't believe that," Colin replied, steadfastly holding his jaw. "God created me this way, Papa, and He'll explain it to me when I see Him."

"Is that what you believe?" Mr. Callahan stood, incredulous. "Michael, it's Satanic temptation! You're being tested, don't you understand? And... and God is waiting for you to triumph over the devil's work!"

Colin's eyes smarted as he regarded his father's words with suspicion. "What? Who told you *that*?"

"Father John. Michael—"

Colin was aghast. "You told *Father*?"

"I had no choice! I had to turn to someone. Michael, you're not alone; you know that. But Father John said you have to realize that you're abusing the glorious body that God gave you. You were made to create life, Michael. Don't you want to have any children?"

Colin fell quiet. "I don't know," he muttered.

"Michael, you can't just go spilling your seed all over town!"

"Papa, I'm not!" Colin paced, mortified.

"You've been wasting it!" He grabbed his son once more. "Don't you miss your family at all?"

Colin stared back into his father's hopeful eyes. "Yes, of course I do," he replied fiercely.

"Then talk to Father John. Please. You've always liked him, haven't you? He can help you, Michael; I promise. Please just say you'll consider it."

Colin sighed. He felt so guilty already. "I'll consider it. But Papa, does Mama know you're here?"

Mr. Callahan shook his head. "No. I figured I'd wait until I discovered what this meeting was about." He straightened up. "And given the present circumstances, I'd rather have her continue to imagine you married to some contessa in Italy with four beautiful children, rather than the reality."

"A contessa! Is that what you told her?"

"It's what I told everyone. But eventually—just a week after you'd left home—I told your mother the truth. But we have lived this lie for so long, we began feeling as if it might be real."

Colin gave a small laugh. "Well then, this *is* a letdown."

Mr. Callahan frowned. "It doesn't have to be, Michael. Your sisters miss you—if they knew they could see you again! And your cousins..."

"Well, they *can* see me. I'm back here, now."

His father drew in his breath. "Michael, until you've reconciled yourself, I forbid you to see them."

Colin glared. "I'm thirty years old, Papa! You can't keep me from visiting anyone!"

"I could turn you over to the police."

"On what grounds?"

"I'm sure I could find the grounds!" Mr. Callahan warned, and then sighed. "Michael, I don't want to do such a thing, but you must understand. You said you'd speak to Father John..."

"I said I'd consider it! Are you threatening me? With blackmail?" Colin shook his head. "My own father! All these years I've been so careful! And to think *you* of all people!"

"Michael..."

"Papa, haven't you ever realized the irony of all of this?" Mr. Callahan looked puzzled. Colin looked at him in disgust. "*You* let Mama leave her religion to join you. Mama denounced the Episcopal Church! And how do you think her parents felt? Well you *know* how her parents felt, but you wanted her to do it anyway! It was against everything her parents wanted, Papa! Don't you think it made them sick?"

"She did it because it was the right religion, Michael! That's how she saw it!"

"Exactly!" Colin exhaled, triumphant. "She *knew*, Papa! And her parents saw that, and *they accepted it!* This is the exact same thing!"

Mr. Callahan drew himself up. "It is most certainly not! Michael, that's blasphemous! Your mother still believes in God and Christ, just as her parents did. It wasn't that different."

Colin looked at him in disbelief. "It wasn't that different? I know it's different." His voice was steady. "Catholicism is the one true religion and all others are false. But I have never turned my back on anyone who believed differently. For we are to love the sinner and not the sin, aren't we Papa? And mind you, I am not a sinner; I don't believe it!"

Mr. Callahan's voice broke. "Then how can you ever believe in the Catholic Church?"

Colin's shoulders sagged. "I think that God hasn't explained everything just yet," he whispered.

His father closed his eyes. "Oh Michael."

The fight now felt familiar, and Colin couldn't manage any more. "Papa, I... I think you'd best go, for now. I don't feel very well and I want you to think about what I've said. Please."

Mr. Callahan nodded. "I'll be at the Fairfax Hotel until tomorrow morning. If you'd like, you could return home with me for a few days, to see Father John."

Colin walked him to the door. "I'll think about it." Shaking, he watched his father make his way down the steps into the carriage he had waiting for him. And then Colin Sewell softly closed the door.

CHAPTER THIRTY-FOUR

Two weeks later, Howard was arriving home with Mark, who was in a cranky mood due to a bad day at work. As per usual, Howard's butler handed him the mail. Mark was trailing behind him. "What is *that*?" he asked. Howard knew what he was referring to: the bulging envelope covered in stamps.

"I don't know," he lied, glancing at the envelope. *Damn.*

"Well, who's it from?" Mark pressed.

Howard felt like telling Mark that it was none of his business to pry, but he had always shared his mail with him before. "Oh, it's from Colin," he replied absently, putting a touch of surprise in his voice.

"Mr. Sewell! Why in hell is he still writing to you?"

"Mark, your language!" Howard reprimanded.

"Well, honestly! Do you two *correspond* regularly, or what? Does he always send you such massive envelopes?"

Howard turned and glared at him. "What Mr. Sewell writes about is none of your business. For God's sake, go into the dining room and have a drink."

"So you can read your love letter?"

Howard thrust the letter at him. "*You* can read it. I won't have this turn into something it's not."

Mark snatched the letter and stalked off to the dining room. Howard followed, wondering what on earth Colin had to say. He dreaded hearing Colin's clever prose read in Mark's irritable tone. They sat down at the table, and Mark took a swig of wine. "'Dear Howard,'" he began, and then he muttered, "Well, I suppose that's innocuous enough." He squinted. "God, you can hardly read his writing! 'How are you? I am afraid I have felt better than I do now. My father just left. I hadn't seen him in nine years. Since I left America. Our meeting didn't go well.'" Mark smirked. "He's certainly got a way with words."

Howard uncrossed his arms, concerned. "I don't think you should read any more."

But Mark continued, "'I know it didn't go well, because I actually made him get sick to his stomach, Howard! And after that, he struck me. Not that I could blame him, God knows—'"

"Give me that!" Howard shouted, taking the letter from Mark's hands.

Mark stared at the letter, surprised. "Well! He's in a bad way."

Howard anxiously read a few more lines, and then put the letter down. "Yes, he is. I'm sorry, Mark, but I'm afraid I must finish this letter. In private. You're welcome to stay for dinner yourself." He rose up and left.

Mark rested his hand on his chin and thumbed the stem of his wine glass. "No, thank you," he said flatly, rising himself. "I can see where your priorities are. He's not even *here*, in the *room* with you!"

But Howard ignored him, closing the door to his study. When the front door slammed, he exhaled, fingering the letter.

Colin.

He read the letter from the beginning.

I know it didn't go well, because I actually made him get sick to his stomach, Howard! And after that, he struck me. Not that I could blame him, God knows. I realize that you don't know the entire story about my family, or for that matter, me, and for you to understand this letter, I'll have to explain some things. I wish I could tell you in person, Howard. I'd much prefer to, but since I'm not sure if you'll ever be here, much less when, I'm going to take the risk and tell you in writing. I pray it falls only in your hands.

Suddenly the script became smoother, clearer, more legible. Howard pictured Colin walking away, collecting himself, and then coming back with a gin and tonic. Or more likely, a gin straight, Howard mused. The idea of anyone hitting Colin made him queasy. He pushed his eyes along.

I never told you or Kenneth about someone I left behind in America (Henry knows this story). Well, the day before I left for England, my father caught the two of us together. Picture the worst-case scenario, Howard. So naturally, he demanded an explanation, which was futile because he already had one made up for me. Nonetheless, I actually implied that I might well be the person I am, and he still refused to accept it! He insisted that such a "disgusting, vile" person never came from homes such as ours. That did it. I decided I was tired of lying, and of course, I knew that the person I was with would never be allowed near the house again. So the next day, I left a letter for my father. In it, I told him that such boys can come from homes like ours, and I am living proof! I told him I was going away and not to try to look for me because I would be changing my name. I told him that by doing so, I wouldn't besmirch his own name and reputation, but in truth, I was worried I would be found and locked up in a sanitarium or such. Then I went and told Said Person that I was going to move to London and I wanted S.P. to come with me. S.P. refused. Tempestuous Colin went anyway, with the full intention of S.P. following him to England in another year. The rest you know.

So therefore, my father, and for that matter, my entire family, never knew where I was, if I was dead or alive, for almost ten years. Until today. You may be wondering why I even bothered contacting my father. Since I left that long time ago, I have thought of my family every day, Howard, particularly my father, for whom I have always held a deep affection. As you know, I am his only son, and a great deal of guilt has burdened me for what I have become. One of my friends from the club urged me to see him, and so I did. Now I wish I hadn't, for my father's sake. Really, can you imagine finding your son again after all these years, only for him to tell you he's still doing something you believe is fundamentally evil and that he probably won't marry or produce any progeny? My father actually told everyone that I ran off to Italy, married a contessa, and had a brood of children! I have to laugh as I write it. Some disillusionment! Worst of all, he and my mother, who also knows the truth, came to somewhat believe the story themselves! Grand disillusion!

So here I stood before him, today. Unmarried. Unsaved. He wants me to see the family priest. I don't know. I feel it's the least I can do for him, even though I can't imagine any success with that. My father has forbidden me to see any of my relatives until I have "changed my ways" so to speak. He threatened to expose me if I attempted to see them anyway. I don't honestly think he'd do that, but it's enough to give me pause.

I have never told anyone this, but I do sometimes think of marrying, Howard. I know! I'm literally wincing now at the thought of your reaction! I wouldn't do it any time soon. Maybe in a year. My friend is married, and he's very happy. He has a beautiful wife as his lifelong companion, he's got three darling children, his family accepts him, and nobody suspects him. I have none of those things, and admittedly, I've been left bitter and none too keen to try anything like what I had anytime soon, even though it is what I want most. Really, out of the four of us, Kenneth seemed the most content, don't you think? I used to think men who entered into false marriages were horrible, but now I feel differently. Some of those marriages are just as satisfactory as "true" ones. Kenneth has a wonderful life, as does this friend of mine. I sometimes wonder if perhaps that's what we are supposed to do. People are meant to be paired off in life, and as you so wisely pointed out, pairs of one particular kind don't seem to be very successful in the long run. I suppose there were a couple of others like myself who, as far as I know, are still together. But let us face the facts: it is not a very realistic option.

So, the question I pose to you, Howard, is this: how is it that you have lived so long and still refused to marry? What are your reasons, other than that you didn't have to?

In going over my letter thus far, I realized that I forgot to expand on something: You were right. I would never drop out of university simply because I was "bored." It was only to escape my family. I hated having you think all of these years that it was a matter of irresponsibility on my part that I did not complete my studies. Although the decision to leave was impractical, at the time I couldn't bear any other option. And now you can see why I was indebted to Henry: I came to him without a degree and I changed my name, which meant any recognition I had gained as a student (which was considerable) was lost once I was in England. Fortunately, Henry had already heard of me, and I was able to convince him that I was really me!

The bank project is coming along splendidly. I admit to using you as the person to base my design on. While this bank is markedly a contrast to the Bank of England, I am trying to picture you working there, because you are what I think of when I think "banker." How is work going for you?

Well, my jaw is absolutely throbbing, so I'm going to have to go. At least the beard will cover the bruise somewhat. Either that or draw more attention to it! I'm sorry to have made you read such a ponderous tome. Just writing everything has made me feel much improved. I hope you are doing well, and I anxiously await your reply.

Regards,
Colin

P.S. I'm sorry I haven't told you my real name yet. It seems too vulgar to do in a letter, even though I know I said I no longer care who knows it. I will tell you in person if I get that opportunity. You've always known me as Colin Sewell and that is who I feel I am, and that is how I wish you to know me.

Colin did end up going to see Father John, although he declined to return with his father. Instead he wrote a letter to the priest and arranged a visit on his own. While half of Colin chafed at the idea of entertaining religious dogmatism, the other half figured it would be one more person's insight into why he was who he was. Colin had always liked Father John because he had been a younger priest, in his thirties when Colin was growing up. He had been humorous, patient, and surprisingly realistic about life's events. When Colin began to experience attraction to other men, he often considered talking to Father, but he was too embarrassed and ashamed. By the time Colin felt more confident about it, he was in college and questioning some of the Church's teachings anyway, although he still saw Father whenever he was home.

As Colin rode in the carriage, he wondered if Father John was surprised when his father told him. Had Father seen the signs early on? Or was he shocked and disappointed? Disgusted. Colin gazed out the window. It was a beautiful spring day. He began to think of what the Helios House would have looked like now. His landscaping would have been in full flower.

When the carriage arrived at the church, Colin felt his face flushing hot. *I can't believe I'm going to step out of this carriage and walk into a priest's home, to look him in the eye. I'm a sodomite. Sodom and Gomorrah. Sodomy.* The words made him angry. *I am not a criminal.* He took a deep breath and began walking toward the door.

"Michael Callahan!" Father John emerged and headed toward him. Startled, Colin felt all of ten years old again. He stepped back and bowed his head.

"Father John, hello." They shook hands.

"It's wonderful to see you!" Father John exclaimed as he turned and walked with Colin up the path.

"It was kind of you to see me, Father."

"Don't be ridiculous! It's rather my job, don't you think? My goodness, you're the age I was when I first came here, aren't you?"

"I suppose so. I'm thirty years old."

"I was thirty-two! And as I found my success then, so are you, now. I heard you have made quite a name for yourself as an architect!"

They were inside now. The maid took Colin's hat. Colin managed a smile. "Yes. My father told you?"

"He did, he did." Lemonade and pastries were brought out, and they sat down. Colin didn't know what else to say. Father John sat back. "I thought it very impressive, Michael, that you came here on your own. Not on the trip back with your father, to please him, but for your own interests."

Colin looked at the priest. "I am doing this for my father, but also for myself." Father John nodded, smiling. Colin looked down at his lemonade and asked quietly, "Well, what is your explanation for it, Father? My father has given me the short of it. I'd like to hear the long."

Father John took a sip of his drink. "Well, Michael, I'd be glad to. But first, I'd like you to tell me what *you* think the church believes."

Colin sighed. "All right. God created Adam. Adam asked for a companion. God created Eve out of Adam's rib. The church believes Man and Woman were meant to pair together to propagate the earth. And of course, Christians must produce children to help spread Christianity, the one true religion."

Father John chuckled. "Very good! A bit didactic, but you've got it. And what is your interpretation on the Christian attitude toward... sodomy?"

Shame swept over Colin, and he frowned in disgust with his feelings. Father John watched Colin bite his lip as he tried to reply. Seconds passed. Colin took several breaths. But he knew Father John was patient, and finally he said, "Sodomy is not condoned. It is considered a sin. It's considered to be contrary to what God intended." He turned to face the priest. "My father said I'd go to hell. I told him only God can decide that, and when I got to heaven, He'd explain it to me. Don't you think so?"

Father John patted Colin's knee. "You're both right. If a man commits a sin and is not given the opportunity to be saved, he is then given the chance in purgatory." He paused. "However, if he is shown the path to redemption and he still rejects the opportunity for salvation, his punishment would be given in hell."

The words slammed into Colin's face. He looked on, horrified, and shook his head. "No! I don't believe that!"

Father John nodded gently. "I understand. Michael, you're a good man. A wise man. You're not evil, not a criminal, or anything like that, no matter what people tell you. God created you, and God never makes a man He doesn't love." He paused, looking frustrated. "For whatever reason, God gives some men challenges. Obstacles to overcome. I believe he chooses the strongest ones. These men are the role models for the rest of the world. He truly believes in them, Michael. You were one of the ones he chose. And every other man you know who is like you, all those friends, men you likely admire..." he sighed. "I can't explain everything, but this much is true: you represent weakness in Man's spirit and being. And God wants you to show that *any* man can overcome his weakness, be it abuse of drink, theft, violence, and such, if *you* can overcome yours. For the temptation that you face is just as strong as that faced by a thief or murderer. I'm sorry you were given this burden to bear, Michael, but God wouldn't have done it if He didn't think you were capable. Do you see?"

"You told my father it was Satanic temptation."

"Yes, it is that, in a way. After all, the devil is pleased any time God is disobeyed. Every time you give into sin, Satan is winning his game, for ultimately, he will gain a soul in hell."

Colin considered this, and then asked, "Father, don't you think it's possible that we're supposed to be, sort of eunuchs, so to speak? That men of my kind serve society with their professions, but just aren't supposed to bear children?"

Father John smiled. "If that were true, you wouldn't be able to procreate. But of course, many men like you have done that."

Colin nodded glumly. "Well, what if a man who was like me *did* marry and have children, but on occasion... was with another man?"

"Adultery, to say the least."

"Ah. Yes, that's true. Well then, what if he never spent time with a man again, but still frequented men's clubs to socialize with them?"

"Michael, a man must give up any and all trappings of an errant lifestyle to become fully redeemed and welcomed into the house of our Lord." He patted Colin's knee again. "Tell me, are you going to church regularly?"

"Yes, every Sunday and holidays."

"And how do you feel when you are in the house of God?"

Colin paused, and his voice grew soft. "Safe. Sheltered. Awe-inspired." He looked at Father John. "I intend to build a cathedral someday."

Father John smiled. "I don't doubt you will, then." He leaned forward. "Michael, you see, you have other passions in life: your architecture, your family, and your love of God. Turn your unhealthy desire toward these and you will be *saved*."

Colin frowned. "But when I'm in church, I feel saved, Father. I feel that God loves me unconditionally."

"You *are* feeling God's love, Michael. And you're feeling his prayer. His prayer for you to ask for salvation. He is trying to show you, my son." He sat back. "Now, the very fact you're here shows that deep in your heart, that is what you want."

Colin looked troubled. "I was really just looking for your explanation. Are you saying that even though I've been doing this for the past ten-odd years, God will forgive all of that if I ask for salvation now?"

"Yes. If you confess and repent, God will forgive you, Michael."

"But what if I continue on for another ten years and then repent? Or for that matter, since I'm baptized, isn't it true that I could live my entire life this way and then repent on my deathbed? Isn't that the point of last rites?"

Father John frowned. "I'd hardly consider it an authentic repentance to knowingly embark on a life of sin and then 'play your card' at the very end. Furthermore, that's not the kind of behavior I'd expect in the Michael Callahan I know."

Colin reddened. He knew he ought to be offended, but what Father John said was true. He wouldn't really do such a thing, would he? Still, he felt a secret victory. He was right: baptism meant you could repent any time you wished. Father John stood up. "Michael, I don't want you to make a decision here. You have a lot to think about. I want you to go home and spend time on this. After all, it is a very serious undertaking. But it is a challenge I know you are up to facing."

Colin nodded and stood up as well. "Thank you Father, for explaining the Catholic viewpoint." He smiled weakly. "It wasn't quite what I wanted to hear, but I will take every word you said into careful consideration."

"I know you will, Michael. I'll send word to your father that we met."

"Thank you. Good day."

CHAPTER THIRTY-FIVE

18 May 1900

Dear Colin,

I don't even know where to begin with this letter, but I feel I must write now, as per your request.

Everything you told me threw me for a bit of a loop, I confess. I am a little concerned for you: should you be so personal in your correspondence? Perhaps I just want to believe that everything is all right with you and live in blissful ignorance. I can't believe I thought I knew you so well, only to find out how much more there is to know! That's not to say I wish you hadn't told me the things you did, but I'm afraid I'm not very good when it comes to dealing with affairs anything other than financial.

I can hardly stand to see in print the things I want to tell you, but if Fearless can be so brave and strong, Howard should be able to manage (Note: Time for a whiskey highball)!

First, the thought of you enduring any kind of physical abuse makes me sick to my stomach. If I had been there, I would have wrung your father's neck, even though we've all taken licks from our fathers. I understand, yes, how he must have felt, and I suppose I should feel grateful that he didn't kill you, correct? I see your smile now, Fearless!

All the same, I hate the very thought. I will admit that the only thing that would ever have caused Kenneth and I to step between you and You Know Who is if we found out you were being harmed. I don't believe it happened, but I'm merely trying to demonstrate the extent of emotion brought about here, you see.

How on earth you and Y.K.W. kept your amazing story secret for so long is beyond me! I understand about not sharing your other name yet. That is a very personal matter, and I am happy enough with the daring you evince having a pseudonym! You must tell Kenneth, because he'll like as to fall off his chair when he hears it! Speaking of Kenneth, I'll take this opportunity to tell you that yes, we both intend to visit you! We were thinking of coming over next year, for a month. Of course, we don't expect you to take off from work, but we wondered which month is best for you. Please let us know as soon as you can, as we are quite excited! Kenneth, you'll recall, has been to New York once, and I have never been. I figure I'm long past due to try a few new things. But enough of that. Colin, you know your father can't forbid you to see other family members. And if he exposed you, he'd be exposing himself! Like you, I don't believe he'd do that—he is merely trying anything he can to save you. Nevertheless, if you want to see your mother and sisters, you should do that, immediately. As for visiting your priest, I hope to God you can make it through that. I'm sure that he will do and say everything in his power to convince you to mend your evil, ill-begotten ways. It's his duty, after all. Colin, stay Fearless! God will have the final say, and I can't shake the feeling that we'll be all right. He is just and loving, and we can't go to hell for loving someone, Colin. You may be told (and perhaps, believe) that you are harming people who love you: family and friends. But I believe God wants us to find our own way in life and obey no one completely but Him. While I'm not so naïve to think God approves of my whiskey highballs and a few other sins, I do believe that He gives us a somewhat loose rein, for heaven's sake! So, please let me know if you do visit your priest, and if so, how it went.

Now for the weighty subject of marriage (2nd highball). Yes, of course I have considered it. I think almost every man has. Some perhaps for only ten seconds, others a bit longer, and then there are those who go and actually tie the knot. I was in the very first group, as you have probably deduced. I will say that after having seen Henry's experience over the last eight years, added to the fact that I no longer live that earlier, wilder bachelor lifestyle, I have come to believe that my heart's desire all these years was unfailing: to have someone to spend the rest of one's days with. But for me to find a suitable woman at my age is ridiculous. I'd be pursued strictly for my money. I also don't want any children, and since my intended would lack some things from me, it would be a rather cold and perhaps even bitter marriage. Even the other choice—what Henry had—is unlikely to happen to me, for some of the same reasons. Fortunately, I have three close companions I enjoy spending my time with (I wish it were still four!), and so I am quite content.

But mind, this isn't about me; it's about you! And if you want children, and you want back into the family fold, and you want to live by God's law of Man and Woman, and you want someone legally bound to you as your loving and faithful companion, then Colin, you must consider marriage. Kenneth thinks you are far too young to do such a thing (never mind that he married when he was 26) and that you should just focus on your work for a bit longer. Easy for him to say, I know. I can't really go into any further details about this subject. Why don't you at least hold off on any nuptials until we see you, and we'll have a wonderfully drawn-out discussion about it!

I have to admit, I was taken aback by your allusion towards having children. Is that something you've always wanted, or only just recently? I remember one time you had thought of the very thing, but after having met Y.K.W., all that changed.

Well, you certainly have a lot of important decisions facing you, Fearless (I don't honestly know why that nickname keeps cropping up)! Since each one will truly impact your life one way or another, I only urge you to take your time considering them. As far as your work life, congratulations on landing the bank commission! I can only imagine how you are going to turn banking architecture on its head! It's very exciting, and I look forward to hearing all about everything you are doing, as I have a very personal interest in this particular project, as you can imagine.

I hope by the time you receive this, your jaw will be back to normal and you are a happier man. And by the way, Kenneth and I raised a glass in your honor on the 30th. Happy Golden Birthday, Colin! I'm only sorry we couldn't have celebrated with you in person. Here's to your best year yet!

Encouragingly,
Howard

P.S. My word! I just reviewed your letter and you mentioned having a "beard"! When on earth did you grow one? I am certain that it looks positively dashing on you!

P.P.S. Leave it to me to get as excited over your beard as you being hit in the jaw. Sigh.

June 17, 1900

Dear Howard,

I received your letter today! You were so funny about the beard! I can't blame you, though—I completely forgot to tell you that I grew one, and since you've never seen me with one, I can imagine it would be quite a surprise. On the ship ride back to America, I had to go the entire first week without shaving, and Charlie convinced me I should try a beard. It's not a full beard though, just the moustache and around the chin. I figured it could be a new look to go with my new life. Y.K.W. always preferred smooth skin, of course, but I suppose that person's opinion isn't worth much anymore. In truth, I don't know how long I'll actually have it. It's easier just to shave your entire face. I have always admired your *immaculately groomed* beard though, Howard, and I hope you never get rid of it.

Well, I had to address the most important issue first! Now onto the rest of the letter.

Howard, at the risk of sounding emotionally weak, your letters have meant the world to me—the absolute world! To be able to lay myself open like I did in my last letter... Well, I couldn't have done that with anyone else. I'm sorry that I made even you uncomfortable with some of the statements, but I was so grateful to be able to tell you, because I didn't know what else to do. And then I was afraid that I might not hear from you after all of that soul baring. I tend to fear that with each letter, actually, because I must appear so histrionic. Anyway, Howard, thank you for all of your help so far. I am badly in need of some levelheaded insight and you are just the thing.

Right then, on we go. First off (well, by now I guess it's "Third off..."), you're right. Y.K.W. never laid a finger on me. You and I both know that if anyone would have, it would have been me, and I'm glad to say I did not either, although I destroyed a few things at the end of it. Someday I know I'll be ashamed of those acts, but I'm still at the stage where I believe every damn bit of it was deserved.

I did end up seeing our family priest. I was actually very fond of the man while growing up. He was a younger priest back then, and very kind. I suppose our meeting went better than I expected, although he told me exactly what I thought he would. Essentially, he said God chose us to serve as examples to others on how to overcome "extremely immoral behavior" and stand strong in the eyes of God. Ergo, the sooner I repent, the better. I reminded him that Catholics could repent on their deathbeds. He replied that if that was my plan, that it wouldn't be a very authentic repentance and that I should essentially be ashamed of myself if I intended to attempt such a stunt. I had to concur. But I still feel that I am not an immoral person! I completely agree with your thoughts and was so glad to see them. They helped me immensely, Howard! So fear not—Fearless is still his old self, for the time being. At the very least, I've resigned myself to the fact that religion is something I shall struggle with throughout the rest of my life. Of course, I had to relay my decision to Father John. I didn't see the need to ride all the way back down to Boston to tell him, though, so I wrote him a letter. I made a copy of it so I could re-write it here. It went this way:

'Dear Father John,

Thank you again for spending time with me last week. It was very important to me that I know where the church stands on this issue. I have thought things through and have decided that I am no more immoral than any other person, and therefore won't be sent to hell. I understand that the church disagrees, as do you and as does my father. I truly apologize for disappointing you. You were a wonderful guide for me in my early years and I do take your words to heart. But other words in my heart ring truer, louder, and those are the words I have chosen to listen to. Would you please share the contents of this letter with my father? Tell him that I am sorry I wasn't the son he hoped I'd be. I wish I could have been. But then again, tell him that perhaps he ought to get past that aspect and see me for everything good that I have become.'

I heard from my father several weeks later. I am sorry to say that his idea of correspondence was a copy of a legal document disowning me from the family. My father circled where he had signed it. I could hardly believe it, Howard! It is really killing me. I suppose I have not been going by my family name for years anyway, but I am devastated by this turn of events. I am now no longer a part of their family any more than I would be part of yours. The only thing it helped me with is the decision to see my mother and sisters. I will. I have to figure out when my father will be gone so I can see them safely. The only way I can imagine is to ask my father to come here for a visit, and then I will go down there! He'll be duped, but that is what he gets for trying to prevent my seeing them and for disowning his only son! I'll let you know how things go.

All right then, onto marriage. You are correct—I never gave it any thought when I was with Y.K.W. But since then, I have had a lot of time to think about it. I don't have any intentions of doing it currently, especially *when things have been so busy (part of the downfall of my first 'marriage'). However, I think if I met someone like Margaret again, I would consider it. The point of the matter is this: I don't really have many opportunities to meet marriageable women, and I'm not sure that I would even know how to properly court one anyway! I suppose my family would be of some help, since if I went this route, I'd be taken back into the fold. Still, as I write this and see it in print, I can hardly believe it is me. There is a large part of me who still refuses to live that ultimate lie of being falsely married in the church. I suppose that if in the next few years I haven't any luck with 'being true to myself,' then I really will go that route. Because if I can't have the one thing that I want most, I'll get all of those other things that I want secondary. Which leads to my next answer to you: yes, I would like to have children. Very much. I have always wanted them, but once I met Y.K.W., I just decided to give that thought up. It was all right, because I was so happy and not really at the age yet to want children. But just the other day, I was reading in the park and a ball came by my feet. A little boy about five years old came running up to fetch it. "Oh, I'm ever so sorry, sir!" he said, in his little out-of-breath voice. He picked his ball up and again, "I do beg your pardon!" I laughed and told him it was no trouble at all, and I complimented him on his fine manners. I looked for his parents, and they waved and called out an apology. I watched him run back. A darling boy. And I found myself staring at the picnicking trio, wishing I was the father. And I began wondering what my own son or daughter would look like. It about killed me, Howard. But, like the idea of marriage, reality sank in eventually. As I have said, I've been hugely busy, and a child requires time. Grant you, I'd have a nanny and a wife, but I would want to spend as much time with my children as possible, every day. But one other very important thing to consider is that I would be putting a wife and children at risk should anything happen to me. I hope you can guess what I am referring to, there. Of course, I still would trade having a child for having a life-long companion, who (given my past experience) can be very much like having a child anyway!*

Finally, I am going out tonight to celebrate the fact that you and Kenneth will *be visiting here next year! Howard, that is absolutely wonderful news! I cannot wait! Is Mark coming too? For he is invited, of course! If you really want me to pick a month, then I would suggest June, for it is the nicest weather then. If you can't make a trip in June, then September or October are the next best choices. Every other month is either sweltering hot, freezing cold, or rainy. Welcome to America! Yes, it's a bit different than the one long year of mild weather you have there. I've just now remembered how supremely limited I'll be in the choice of suitable landscaping plants. Oh, those beautiful English gardens!*

I think this letter is even longer than my last one! So I had better finish it and give your eyes a rest. Thank you for always replying so quickly. Please don't feel that you must write immediately, the way you do. As much as I enjoy it, I don't want to pressure you. Please tell me in your next letter about your work. I never really did get a full explanation of what you *do, Howard. What is the Bank of England all about, anyway? And I will share some like-minded things in my next letter, too. Now that I know you'll be here in a year, I feel that I can more easily wait until then to discuss the more personal matters with you. I hope you are doing well, and I look forward to hearing from you again.*

Sincerely,

Colin

P.S. Please feel free to tell Kenneth everything I have written in my letters, if you haven't already been doing so. It is rather difficult to write a letter like this all over again, and of course, the poor man can't be expected to write back at length like you do. Thank you, Howard!

The next day, Colin sent off an invitation to his father to visit him in New York. His father confirmed, and the morning that his father started off, Colin left for Boston. He had told Charlie to say that he had been called off to an emergency on a project and that his father was to be given a check for expenses incurred in his trip up.

Two days later, Colin's rented carriage drew up in front of his family's house. He had no idea if his mother would be home, but it was Sunday, so his odds were good.

Instead of the sick, nervous feeling he'd experienced with his father, he was almost overcome with excitement to see his mother and sisters again.

The butler had seen the cab approach and called Mrs. Callahan to the door. Both of their mouths dropped when Colin jumped down from the carriage.

"Mama!" he cried and jogged up to her.

Sarah Callahan gaped at her son and then burst into tears as he embraced her. Colin gently took her arms and pushed her back so she could look at him. "Oh, Michael! I barely recognized you!" she said amidst sobs. "Your beard, and… and your spectacles!"

Colin smiled. "I know, Mama. I'm sorry I didn't tell you I was coming."

His mother just stared at him as if an apparition was before her. Then she hugged him tightly again and sobbed harder. "Don't go, Michael! You can't leave us ever again! Oh, don't go, don't go, don't go!"

"Mama, I won't…" But his mother heaved even greater, gasping sobs, and Colin began to fear that she would hyperventilate. He stroked her back awkwardly and reassured her with Shh's. Then he turned her toward the entrance of the house. "Come along, Mama," he gently urged. "Let's go inside, all right?"

Mrs. Callahan nodded, and Colin felt like telling Franks to bring some tea, but since he was no longer part of the household, he didn't feel it was his place.

"I'll bring some tea, a damp cloth, and some handkerchiefs," Franks said.

"Thank you, Franks," Colin sighed.

Mrs. Callahan wrung her hands. "Oh, Michael, your father's gone on a trip! He won't be back for several days! You must stay until he returns!"

"I've already seen him, Mama."

"What? You have? When? How?"

Colin took a deep breath. "Mama, I'll tell you the whole story. About where I've been and all that. Papa didn't tell you?"

"No! What are you talking about?"

Franks returned with the tea. "Perhaps you'd best bring some sherry," Colin nodded at him. "And a glass for me as well, please." Then he turned back to find his mother shaking her head. "You've turned into such a fine, handsome young man," she choked, and then began to wail.

"Mama, please!"

"Mother! What on earth...?"

Colin turned to see a young woman stop dead in her tracks at the sight of him. He rose to his feet. "Elizabeth?"

They faced each other, blinking at their changes in appearance. Elizabeth was ten when Colin had left home. Colin only recognized her by the large freckle on her nose and by her presence in the house. She squinted at Colin. "Michael?"

"You're all grown up," Colin whispered, awed.

Elizabeth drew up to him and took his hand. "Where have you been?"

Colin, still staring at her, felt feverish. "I, um... I... where's Mary?" He searched the room for his older sister.

"Mary's married, Michael," Elizabeth replied faintly. "Have you been in Italy this entire time?"

Colin jerked his head back. "Italy!" Then he remembered. "No, I was... I was in London." He wanted to sit. "Elsie, please sit down with us."

Elizabeth softened at hearing her nickname. Ever since her brother had left, she had felt hurt and rancor toward him because of the trouble he caused Mama and Papa. Some days she worried about his safety, but most of the time she couldn't care less if he was dead, so bitter was she about his disappearance. Now here he stood, a very well-dressed, dashing young man, but a man who also looked positively exhausted, and she had a sinking feeling he was going to share some terrible news.

"Would you like something to drink?" Colin asked her as he took his glass from Franks. She shook her head, dazed at the change in his voice.

"You've an accent," she murmured.

Colin blushed. "It's... oh... it's just from being abroad," he stammered, and then he sighed. "Elsie, you don't know the real story, so I am here to tell you. I left ten years ago because—"

"Michael, no! Please!" his mother begged.

He looked grimly at her. "Mama, she's an adult now. She can handle the truth, can't you Elsie?"

"Yes, of course," Elizabeth nodded, looking at him expectantly as visions of theft, rape, murder, and illegitimate children raced through her mind.

"Well, I ran off to England because I didn't want to disgrace the family, you see."

"Michael!" his mother wept.

"You committed a crime, then?" Elizabeth guessed, slightly alarmed.

Colin frowned and then looked her in the eyes. "I suppose some people would think so, yes." His voice fell to a hush. "I prefer men to women, you see." And Elizabeth saw her brother's eyes fill with pain and apology. He looked down at his drink while his mother dropped her head into her hands, crying further.

Elizabeth felt her jaw fall open, but she was confused. "Oh. Oh, I thought... you had killed a man or something of that sort."

Colin smiled at her weakly. "No." He looked back at his glass. "I told Papa. I left a letter behind for him, and eventually he told Mama. But they never told you or Mary, for your protection. I'm sorry, Elizabeth. I know it was a terrible thing to do."

"But, I don't really understand," Elizabeth said. "What do you mean, you 'prefer men'?"

Colin was taken aback. He didn't expect Elizabeth to be so naïve. He took a deep breath. "I'm what you would call a, umm... well, to the church, I'm a..." But he couldn't say it. "Well, you see, I can't marry a woman, because I don't want to. I prefer men to women—I would rather marry a man, as it were. But of course, I can't." Colin had lived with his identity for so long now that he didn't realize how shocking his words were to his sister or his mother.

Elizabeth stared in horror. "I don't believe it! Surely you're just... perhaps you're sick, somehow, aren't you, then? Like you aren't feeling right. Haven't you seen a doctor for this?"

Colin felt defensiveness rise up inside him. "A doctor can't do anything, Elsie."

"How do you know?"

"Because he can't! Elizabeth, I don't expect you to understand this, or even accept it, but I wanted to tell you the truth because I can't change, and I'm not... I'm not ashamed of it."

"How could you do this to us?" his mother cried out, leaping to her feet. Colin's insides pinned unto themselves. "How could you come back here and slap us in the face like this? We've prayed for you all of this time! We have missed you and we have mourned you! And Michael, you gave back nothing! You left without a single glance back toward us!"

"That's not true, Mama!" Colin stood up desperately. "I prayed for all of you, too! Every night since I've left, I swear! I wanted to see you again! I'm sorry that I left the way I did, but I didn't want to keep lying about myself, and I was afraid of Papa."

That last comment jogged Sarah Callahan's memory. "You said you've seen your father. When?"

"Last month. I sent him a telegram from New York City. That's where I'm living, now. We met and he asked me to see Father John. I did, but it didn't make any difference." He paused, and his voice fell to a whisper. "So I told Papa, and he has legally disowned me from the family."

Mrs. Callahan reeled. "He's... he's disowned you? Oh, Michael, no! That can't be! He wouldn't do that—he would have told me!"

Colin couldn't look at her. "I'm sure he wanted to protect you, Mama. I'm sorry I had to tell you." He raised his head. "And Papa said that if I didn't reform myself, I was forbidden to see any of you. But I had to see you again, at least once! So I tricked him into going to New York to see me while I came down here to see you." Then he grew frightened. "Papa said if I tried to see you, he'd turn me over to the police! So you mustn't tell him I was here! You won't, Mama, will you?"

Mrs. Callahan could hardly believe her husband would do something so scandalous. She could hardly believe anything Michael said his father had done. But she shook her head. "I won't tell him." She approached her son. "So despite all of these terrible things happening, you're choosing to stay this way. You're choosing to do this to your family."

Colin's shoulders slumped. "I'm only choosing not to live a lie, Mama."

Anxiety filled his mother's voice. "Then I suppose your father is right. You should not visit here anymore."

"Mama!"

"Michael, you understand, your father makes that decision. And I can't condone your behavior in the eyes of God."

"But I'm your son!"

"Not like that." She didn't look at him anymore. He turned to his sister in desperation.

"And you, Elsie?"

Elizabeth bit her lip. She wanted to yell at him and second the banishment. It would have been satisfying. But she felt confused, and her brother was clearly distraught. She took her Colin's arm and ushered him to the door. "I'll see you to your carriage," she replied quietly. When they were outside, she asked him, "Are you really living in New York City?"

Colin's spirits rose. "Yes. I've been in London until a few months ago. Look here." He pulled a card from inside his coat pocket. "Don't show this to Mama or Papa, although I imagine they could find me if they wanted to, all the same."

"'Colin Sewell'?"

"Yes, that's the name I've taken. If anything happened to me, I didn't want our family name involved."

"So you've been going by this name all of these years?"

"Yes. Elsie, please, if you ever need anything, you can contact me here. And Mary as well, for that matter. I wish I could see you both again. I'm very sorry about all of this."

Elizabeth gazed at the card. "You're still an architect."

Colin nodded. "Yes. And I've done extremely well. But Papa doesn't care about that." His voice was resigned and he opened the cab door. "I'd best go. Goodbye, Elizabeth."

She stared up at the humiliated eyes of her brother. "Goodbye Michael." Then she glanced at the card. "Or should I say, 'Colin.'"

Colin shook his head. "No, I don't want you to call me that." She nodded.

Inside, Mrs. Callahan sat listening to the cab door open.

Your son is leaving. He's leaving.

There's nothing I can do.

Ten years—he's come back to you, and now you'll never see him again? Michael... Michael...

"Michael!" she screamed and ran for the door. The cab had started to pull away, but Colin had heard his mother's shout. He looked out and saw her running after the cab. He motioned for it to stop and he rushed out.

"Mama!"

Again she threw her arms around him. "I just wanted to say goodbye!" she cried. "I just wanted to say goodbye!" She clung to his coat, her face in his shirt, shaking silently.

"Mama, please don't do this," Colin begged, tears filling his eyes. "Please let me see you again!"

"I can't, Michael," Mrs. Callahan shook her head. "But I do love you. You'll always be my son and I wanted you to know that."

Colin felt sick to his stomach. He tried to breathe. "I'll be all right, Mama. Papa can find me if he needs to, all right?"

She nodded into his chest. "Yes. I'll still pray for you."

"I know you will, Mama. Thank you. I have to go."

She pulled herself free and held one hand to her mouth as she watched him leave.

After a few minutes inside the cab, Colin collapsed onto the seat, his damp cheek pressed against the velvet.

I'm so tired. I'm so tired of this.

CHAPTER THIRTY-SIX

A week later, a clerk in the office brought a letter to Colin. "For you, sir." Colin took it and turned over the envelope. On the back, he read the return address.

Miss Elizabeth Callahan

143 Canton Way

Boston, Massachusetts

My God! It's from Elsie! Colin cursed at not having his own office yet, for he had nowhere private to go. It was an hour until closing time. He'd have to wait until then.

As soon as he got home, he sat on the nearest chair and tore open the envelope.

Dear Michael,

I pray this letter finds you well. It has been several days since we last saw each other and you can imagine all of the thoughts that have filled my head since. I have told Mary about you (to the best of my limited knowledge), and she and I would like to see you again. Unfortunately, it is not possible for the two of us to come to New York, unescorted and without reason. Would you be willing and able to come to Boston again? I know you were just here and you must have a very busy schedule. Therefore, you may name the date and we will keep it open. Mary is offering her house to us for the visit. She will arrange for her children to be in bed or elsewhere during the visit, and her husband as well. So it will just be the three of us. Please consider this invitation with thought and care.

Your Youngest Sister,
Elizabeth

P.S. Please post your reply to Mary:
Mrs. Mary Hawkes
439 Fulton Avenue
Boston, Massachusetts

Colin was ecstatic. He started reading the letter again, but really his eyes only scanned until he came to the point he was looking for.

She will arrange for her children to be in bed or elsewhere...

Colin burst into a grin. *Mary has children! She has continued the line!* His eyes welled up. It was almost as good as having children himself. He sprang out of the chair and told Charlie to keep his supper warm. He went to his study to pen a response. It took him three tries.

Dear Mary,

I have received Elsie's letter just today, and I am praying that it is all still true. I wouldn't mind at all making the trip to Boston, especially to see both of you! I would come this very Saturday if I could, but I must give you time to make arrangements. So I hope that Saturday, June 29th, will be a good date. However, I'd be happy to arrive on a weekday, if that would make things easier. Mary, only name the day and I will be there. I owe you and Elsie (the entire family, really) so much; I'd like to make amends. Please reply to the below address.

Your Loving Brother,
Michael

When Mary replied, she commended Colin on his idea of meeting on a weekday, and the three decided to meet on Friday, June 28, at one o'clock.

That day, Colin rode up to Mary's house and was impressed. She lived in a stately, old, brick Georgian that was covered with ivy, the very idea of Boston architecture. As he stepped out of the carriage, he saw both sisters appear in the doorway. Elsie was smiling, but Mary's face looked like Elsie's did the first time she had seen him. And so he greeted Mary first, with an embrace. "Mary! You've done well for yourself!"

"I've heard the same about you," she replied, shaking her head in wonder. "I can't believe you're really here. Is it really you?"

Colin laughed. "Yes, yes! And you and Elsie are so grown up!" He embraced his younger sister. "I scarcely recognized Elsie when I first saw her, in fact."

"Well, come inside," Mary beckoned, and the three went into the house.

Colin looked around, and then smiled at Mary. "It's a beautiful house."

"You could probably tell me everything that's wrong with it," she laughed.

"No, no, it's wonderful. Given the way you've decorated it, I apparently didn't inherit all of the talent."

Mary called for tea and cakes, and they sat down. Colin couldn't hide his excitement from his voice. "Mary, Elsie mentioned your children in her letter. How many?"

Mary smiled. "Four. Joseph is six, Jonathan is four, Andrew is three, and Matthew just turned one a month ago!"

"Four boys!" Colin wondered.

"Yes! They're a handful, but they're darling, really."

"That's wonderful," Colin repeated. "Mama and Papa must be very proud."

"They are," Mary agreed, and then she motioned to Elsie. "Now, if they can just get *this* one married off..."

Colin grinned at Elsie, who rolled her eyes. "Oh..."

But Mary suddenly became mortified. "Oh, Michael, I'm sorry! I meant no offense!"

Colin glanced at her. "It's all right," he reassured. "So Elsie, *are* you being courted by anyone as of late?"

Elsie hmphed. "I may not have seen you for ten years, but you're still my brother, and if you think I'm telling you, forget it!"

Colin raised his eyebrows and pretended offense. "I couldn't possibly care less," he sniffed, using words from when they were children. He and Elsie laughed, but when they looked at Mary, she began to tear up. "Mary?" Colin said uncertainly.

Mary burst into tears. "I'm sorry!" She tried to exhale. "But look at the three of us! We're suddenly back together again! As if you never left! We thought you were gone forever, Michael."

Colin hung his head. "No. I thought of you every day. Every Sunday, I'd go to church and pray for all of you. I've asked God for forgiveness. And every night I prayed for you again, I swear it. Right before going to bed." He looked at both of them. "I never forgot you. I'd never do that."

"But all of these years and not a single word..." Mary insisted.

Colin winced. "I know. I would have written a letter, but you were both still living at home at the time, and I was afraid Papa would find me and commit me to a... a sanitarium!" He regretted the word as soon as it left his lips. Mary's eyes flickered with fear, and Elsie swallowed uncomfortably. *They think I am mad.* Colin shook his head. "I suppose too, at that age, I thought I didn't need anyone; that it would be a very dashing thing to do, to run off to Europe."

Mary lifted her eyes to meet his, and said slowly, "Michael, why *did* you tell Papa that you were... what you were?"

Colin hesitated. "Papa..." he began, and then he sighed. "I was tired of hiding it all of the time." Then it struck him. "Remember how aloof I had become around women? And they thought I was stuck up, a snob." His sisters nodded. "But you see, I *couldn't* pretend any interest in them because that might have led to courtship, and then what?" He recalled now how he had wanted to explain it. "Elsie, Mary, it would be like the world telling *you* to court *women*! Think of how that would feel to you! What if the way the world worked, was that women married women and men married men? And yet here you two would be, preferring men, even though you're not supposed to... Mary, think about if instead of your husband, you had a *wife*. A woman for a spouse, not a man. And you were supposed to hold her hand and kiss her and have children with her... and love her. Could you? Could you live a lie like that, even though every fiber of your being is resisting it?"

"But your way is against God," Mary protested, disgusted at the scenario.

"That's only according to the Bible," Colin argued, disappointed that his explanation didn't have the intended effect. "I don't believe God would really be so cruel as to make men like me, if he thought it a sin." He put up a hand. "I'm not saying the Bible is false. I'm only saying that perhaps... perhaps there was some misinterpretation along the way, as it were."

His sisters gasped. "Misinterpretation!" Mary exclaimed. "Of the Bible! Michael, surely you can see that if we all chose to believe in only parts of the Bible, then we'd have no Bible at all."

"And you can't believe some of it is true and not others," Elsie chimed in. "That's blasphemous."

Colin took a deep breath. At least they were still talking to him. "All right, all right," he conceded. "I cannot possibly argue religion with you. After all, I've been examining it my entire life, and I'm still trying to sort it all out." He looked at them hopefully. "I'm still Catholic. I still go to Mass every Sunday. I pray nightly. I observe all the rituals."

"Do you go to Confession?" It was Elsie, and her tone was abrupt.

Colin fiddled with his tea. "No," he admitted quietly. "I have stopped going to Confession."

"Oh, Michael..."

Colin was at a loss. Normally with a comment like this he could shoot back that, comparatively speaking, he didn't live any worse a decadent or sinful lifestyle as the person arguing against him. But his sisters were matchless. It was impossible that they could have even imagined the things Colin had done in his life, let alone lived them. *They certainly didn't study Greek history.* He swirled his drink. "I suppose this would be the appropriate time to ask why you wanted to see me again." He glanced at Elsie. "Since you did already know this about me."

Mary sighed apologetically. "I'm sorry Michael. We didn't mean to argue. We wanted to see you because you're our brother. Our only brother. And because we haven't seen you for ten years. Because I wanted to know what you look like. Because we wanted to hear your story."

Colin looked up. "My story?"

Mary nodded. "About what you've been doing all of this time. Please, why don't you tell us about London? From the start."

So Colin gave them a rather condensed version of his history in England, including his relationship with Henry. Even though he left out all of the sensual parts, his tale still took up an hour's worth of time. When he finished, Elsie spoke slowly, "Michael, do you mean to say that if you hadn't had a falling-out with your boss, that we may have not *ever* heard from you?" Her voice was incredulous. And her guess was correct.

Colin hadn't planned on being caught in this trap, and when he realized he couldn't get out of it, he dropped his face into his hands and began to cry in spite of himself. "Elsie, I'm sorry! I didn't mean to lose both of you forever!" He looked at her incredulously. "I never thought I had a choice! I figured that at some point you'd find out the truth from Papa, and you'd want no part of me! And I told you earlier that I was afraid he'd find me if I wrote to you."

Elsie and Mary were rendered momentarily speechless upon seeing their brother cry. Colin dried his eyes, embarrassed. "You wouldn't know it now, but I've led such a happy life ever since I left Boston. And that is what I'm trying to tell you: not even keeping my family could have balanced out the suffering I'd have had if I had stayed here and pretended my whole life to be someone else. Was it a worthy expenditure of time to be apart from both of you for a decade? Absolutely. *That's* how miserable I was. You couldn't have saved me."

"Well, you're back now," Mary said hopefully.

"Yes." Colin lowered his eyes. "And I am paying the price. Willingly, but with regrets, to be sure."

"Aren't you afraid of getting caught?" Elsie asked timidly.

Colin sighed. "Not anymore. I used to be terrified of it, but the chances of such a thing happening turned out to be low." He paused. "Although I still think Papa could turn me in if he finds out I'm seeing you."

"We won't tell him," Mary promised. "But I can't imagine Papa doing that. After all, then he'd have to suffer everyone knowing it!"

Colin smiled. "That's true."

Elsie tilted her head. "So Michael, do you have a... er... oh, well, I guess you'd still call it a... 'sweetheart'?"

Colin reddened. Really, it was improper, coming from his youngest sister, but her bravery rather cheered him. "No. You have to remember, being with one man for eight years was like being married." He sighed. "I suppose it's nice to be alone now, in some ways."

"And there's no children," Mary surmised.

"No, that's one surprise you'll be spared."

"I suppose you wouldn't want any," Elise commented.

Colin's gaze dropped to his lap. "Actually, I would like to have children. Very much." He looked at his sisters. "It's the one thing that still really tears at me, in fact. I know it doesn't make sense. But there are even times when I think I might still marry yet, so that I may have them."

"But you can't!" Elsie exclaimed.

Colin looked surprised. "Of course I can. Most of the men like me *are* married, Elsie. You can understand why after seeing what happened between Papa and myself."

"They enter into false marriages?" Mary asked, incredulous.

"Yes. Of course, the marriage is legal, and they never tell their wives. They just go about their business living as regular fellows, but they still prefer men." He paused. "I never thought I could do such a thing. I always thought of you two and how horrible it would be if something like that happened to you! But then I think how some of those marriages are. The wives seem happy; I've met them. They're on good terms with their husbands. I'd give my wife anything she wanted. I'd treat her well." Then Colin stopped short, realizing that perhaps he had revealed too much. His sisters were surely displeased at his transgression... but no, they seemed to just be studying him. He sighed. "But at the moment, I remain on my own, and plan to for some time." He looked at his sisters and smiled. "Well, I certainly think that's enough talk about me for a while. I want to hear more about both of you! Please, tell me what has happened in your lives since I've left." His sisters obliged, and their stories took up another hour and a half. When they finished, the three sat quietly for a moment. Then Colin took several items from inside his jacket pocket. "I do have something for both of you." He handed each woman an envelope and a small box. He nodded at Mary. "The envelope is a belated wedding present, and also in celebration of your children. The other is just an attempt to make up for all of your birthdays that I've missed. And Elsie, your envelope is for living expenses, and the box serves the same purpose as Mary's. You needn't open them now, if you'd rather not."

"Oh, Michael," Mary looked at him tenderly. Then she declared gaily, "Well, I want to open the box!" She untied the ribbon and lifted the lid. Her eyes widened. In her hand was a starburst brooch, radiating flawless stones of peridot, citrine, aquamarine, and diamonds.

"I thought it might go with your summer occasionals," Colin offered.

"It's beautiful!" Mary breathed. "It's absolutely beautiful. Michael, it's far too extravagant of a gift."

"Hardly," Colin shook his head. He smiled at his younger sister. "Do you want to open yours, Elsie?"

Elsie blushed. "All right." She pulled gently at the ribbons, and then gave a gasp of delight. Her gift was a bracelet of gold mesh, centered with a large opal rimmed with diamonds. "Oh Michael! It's breathtaking!"

Colin bit his lip. He felt the happiest he'd been since he left London. "I'm glad you like it," he managed to reply.

"I love it," Elsie affirmed. Then she began to cry, and Colin stood up.

"I've overtaxed you both. I'm sorry. I should take my leave for now."

Mary stood up too and gave her brother a tight embrace. "You're at the Metropole Hotel, aren't you?"

"Yes," Colin replied. "Through tomorrow."

Mary nodded, walking him to the door. "I'll send a post around tomorrow morning, all right?"

"That would be fine, Mary." Colin gave her one more hug and then bade her farewell.

Back at Mary's house, the sisters began to talk about what they should do next.

"Well, what did you think?" Elsie asked Mary.

Mary flopped down on the settee. "Oh, I could almost faint! I don't really know what to think! He seems perfectly normal, doesn't he? And yet, he's..."

Elsie sighed. "I know. But Mary, he hasn't got anyone else. I just don't know that we should kick him out of our lives like Mama and Papa did."

"I know. But by associating with him, does that mean we're giving approval to what he does?"

"No! I think we should tell him that we still want to see him, but that he should keep that part of his life private from us."

"Yes. That's a good compromise. Anyway, the Lord said we must love one another. And 'Let he who is without sin cast the first stone.'"

"When you say that, it does seem awfully cruel to shut him out," Elsie said softly.

Mary nodded. "It does. He came back to us, after all. He seemed to be dying on the inside, didn't he? It breaks my heart."

"What are you going to tell Daniel?" Daniel was Mary's husband.

"Well, I certainly am *not* going to tell him *that* part about Michael! He'd throw him out himself!" Mary paused. "Perhaps Michael can help us. I have a feeling he's had to lie a lot, anyway. We may as well use the same story he's been telling people."

"Can you imagine? Having to go about your life living a lie like that?" Elsie wondered.

"I know. It's funny when you think about it: he's still living a lie, but this one's of his own choosing. It's a wonder he told us the truth." Mary sat up. "And look at how handsome he is! He must have had to turn down dozens of women in England! I wonder how he did it?"

"Maybe he'll tell us," Elsie suggested. "I have to say I still don't understand most of this."

"I don't either. I wonder what happened to make him like that." Mary's voice fell to a whisper. "I wonder if Papa thinks it's his fault."

"Oh, that would be horrible!" Elise cried. Her face grew very sad. "He and Michael were so close. Michael was so fond of him! Remember all the time they spent together, Mary?"

Mary's expression was mournful as well. "Yes. I wouldn't dare say whom this is harder on. But poor Papa! His only son! And he doesn't even have any children!"

"Well, let's call on Michael tomorrow, at the hotel," Elsie decided. "I don't see why we can't. We'll just say we're going into town shopping."

Mary shrugged. "Why not? I'll send the post tomorrow morning. I said I would." Her face brightened. "You know, nothing says we have to make any kind of decision at this point, anyway. We ought to get to know him a bit better."

The next day, Colin anxiously waited for the post to arrive. It came at half past ten. He was overjoyed to find out his sisters would be visiting him later on that day. When Mary and Elsie received their brother's ecstatic welcome, they were glad they had decided to see him again. Eventually, the three sat down to discuss how to go about things. Colin crossed his arms. "Well, I agree we cannot tell Mary's husband the truth, but how about this? We'll say that I told our parents the Italy story but I was actually in London. I really was working as an architect but living the life of a playboy on the side. Recently I realized the 'error of my ways' in severing ties with you, and so I came back to America to make amends. However, my insistence on remaining a layabout bachelor has caused our parents to disown me, and I'll appear to Daniel as very callous that way, but I'll have to accept that. This way, though, he can understand that he is not to tell our parents that I am in contact with you." Colin's heart grew heavy as he regarded Mary. "And I didn't know if... if you wanted to keep me apart from your children. I wish I could see them, but that is up to you. Of course, I would never tell them anything either." He waited for Mary to reply.

She looked surprised. "Well, of course you must meet them! They're your nephews!"

Colin looked as if he was about to cry. "Oh, that's wonderful! Thank you, Mary, for being so kind! I can't wait to see them! It's all I've thought about!" He sighed a breath of relief. "But I can't be introduced as their uncle, because they'll ask why I'm not with you at Christmas and the like. Instead, I'll have to be known as a 'family friend' to them, and I'll have to go by a different name, too. You can choose one for me, if you like. But Mama and Papa already know 'Colin Sewell', so even if one of your boys said, 'We saw Mr. Sewell yesterday,' Papa would know." He noticed his sister's overwhelmed expressions. "I know this is awful, and it's asking a lot of you. I understand if you just want to chuck it all."

"No, no," Mary shook her head slowly. "I just can't believe how you can think of all of this so quickly. I would have never guessed the problems that could arise."

Colin sighed. "Yes, I've gotten to be very good at lying, I'm afraid."

"Speaking of that," Elise began, "Mary and I were wondering: what have you told women who are interested in you? There must have been so many!"

"Not really," Colin smiled. "I stayed out of parties and social occasions as much as I could, for that reason. However, I couldn't avoid all of them, and so I had some friends spread rumors that I was a rake and a threat to women's decency."

Mary and Elsie laughed in shock. "Oh, no!" Mary cried. "I can only imagine that such an idea would attract even more women to you!"

Colin laughed too. "Sometimes. But then either their mothers or friends would yank them away, or I would eventually find a way out." He decided not to tell them about Margaret Rademaker. "Oh, but I forgot to tell you the story that is being told in New York." He revealed his and Adam's story, and at the end he hung his head. "I know it's positively horrible to say such a thing, but now that I'm getting older, and I clearly *don't* live the life of a playboy, I had to make something up to stave off any suspicion."

"Goodness, Michael," Elise murmured, "you could write a book of tales!"

"Yes, well, I hope I don't have to tell any more," Colin said, regret in his voice. "I'm ashamed to have to tell you these things and that you have to do the same." He lifted his eyes. "And for what it's worth, I don't ever want you to have the burden on your conscience. If I am doing something wrong, it will be for God to concern Himself with, not you. You're both completely innocent."

Mary and Elsie smiled at their brother. "I think you're doing the best you can, Michael," Mary said. "We won't ask any more from you."

Meanwhile, on that same Saturday, Howard showed up at Porter's without Mark. "Well, gentlemen," he remarked to Henry and Kenneth as he sat down, "looks like we're back to a threesome."

Henry raised his eyebrows while Kenneth leaned in. "What happened with Mark?"

Howard lit his pipe. "Apparently, he's quite the jealous type. He's jealous of people who aren't even here."

"He found out about your past with Colin?" Henry guessed.

"No, he was upset that I was still writing to him."

"But didn't he know you were?" Kenneth asked.

"Well, I haven't exactly been mentioning it, and Colin's last letter was rather long. Meaning it came in a rather thick envelope. Meaning Mark spied it and when he found out it was from Colin, he had a fit. I made the mistake of letting him read it to calm him down. It turned out to be quite a... personal letter. After he read the first few lines, I seized it from him and, I confess, I chose to leave him at the dinner table and finish the letter myself in my study."

"Well, no wonder he got upset!" Kenneth exclaimed.

Henry frowned. "What do you mean by 'personal'?"

Howard glanced at him and then continued, "Anyway, I never apologized for my behavior. I admit I'm to blame, but I'm too old to be making concessions like that—I'll write to whomever I please." He shrugged. "So, he's gone." Then he looked back at Henry. "Colin saw his father for the first time since he left America, and it didn't go well. He told his father that he hadn't changed, and his father got so upset that he got sick to his stomach, and then he struck him!"

Henry stared at him. "He told you all of that?"

Howard felt a secret surge of triumph but shrugged. "He hasn't anyone else, Henry." Then he added, "He's told us the whole story, of his family and how he met you. His past. It's extraordinary!"

Henry groaned. "He's a regular dramatist, I'm sure."

"It's absolutely fascinating!" Howard defended. "I can't believe the two of you kept his identity secret all this time!"

Henry made a face. "It was rather silly for him to have changed his name, although I admit to being impressed at the first."

"But you knew all along what a great architect he was, and yet you couldn't reveal it!" Howard said.

"Oh, who would have known who Michael Callahan was anyway, in these circles?"

Howard went pale. "My God, is that his real name?"

Henry looked up to see his friend's horrified expression. "Didn't he tell you?" he wondered.

"No! He wanted to tell us in person! Oh God, Henry, I should have told you that!"

But Henry found the unexpected revelation amusing. "Oh, dear. Well, there you have it. Cat's out of the bag, I'm afraid."

But Howard felt as if he had been punched in the stomach. And worse, his eyes began to water. He got up from his seat. "Excuse me for a minute."

"Howard?" Kenneth rose up, concerned.

"Never mind me—I don't know why I feel like this." Howard laughed shakily. "I'm just going to get some fresh air. I'll be right back."

"Goodness, Howard, I'm sorry!" Henry apologized. But Howard waved him off and left the club.

He walked along the avenue in the cool night air. *Michael Callahan. Michael. Callahan. It's so Irish!* He immediately pictured himself face to face with him. "Michael," he whispered, looking into Colin's eyes. He shook his head. "Oh God, it's too strange." He filled with remorse at the thought of telling Colin that his privacy had been prematurely violated. *I suppose he won't mind. Really, it's not that extraordinary—why am I so upset? And Henry! What a ridiculous scene I made! He must know now! But it was such a personal revelation, and it was supposed to be a private matter between Colin and myself!* He thought about the letter in his suit jacket pocket. Crossing the street, he headed back toward the club.

As soon as he sat down, Henry leaned forward, "Howard, I do apologize. I didn't mean to upset you so!"

"Well, how could you have known?" Howard said, unable to look at him. "I haven't the faintest why it set me off so. It just came as a shock." He nodded to the waiter for another drink.

Henry narrowed his eyes. "Just how often are you writing to Colin?"

Howard forced himself to sound casual. "Oh, I don't know. Once a month, I suppose."

"Hmm! And when you get his letters, how many days pass before you write back?" Henry challenged. "Or should I say, 'minutes'?"

Howard turned red and rolled his eyes. "Oh, Henry!"

"He's always been fond of you, Howard," Henry smiled. "In fact, those last five years I kept hoping he'd leave me for you so I'd be spared the trouble!"

"That's terrible!" Howard gasped.

Henry shrugged. "You were such the better suitor for him by then. But I do commend you for staying loyal to me."

Howard turned a darker shade of red. "This is a ridiculous discussion!"

Henry frowned. "Howard, I know how much you liked him, too. And here's your chance! Keep writing to him! I beg you—the boy obviously needs someone to pour his heart out to."

"Yes, I'm doing that, Henry. I'm being a friend to him."

"Really?" Henry tilted his head. "Just a friend? Because if that is truly the case, you ought to stop writing entirely." He grew serious. "He admired you greatly, Howard, and if he's writing these kinds of personal letters to you, and you're responding in kind, *and* you're going to see him next year, which Kenneth just told me, then you can't possibly think he's not going to expect something to happen between you two! Otherwise you're being a selfish tease and even I think that he doesn't deserve that."

"I'm not teasing him!" Howard insisted, hurt. "I just don't know how you can say such things, looking into the future the way you are."

"I've known the boy for nearly a decade," Henry sighed. "He'll become attached to anyone who gives him half the chance. He can't stand the thought of being alone. That's why he stuck it out with me so long. In fact," he said gravely to Howard, "if you *are* interested in him, dear Howard, then you'd better make your intentions a little clearer, and soon. He's too biddable to stay single for long."

Howard's eyes widened at the accurate description, and he took Colin's last letter from his breast pocket. "All right, you've got me," he sighed. "So I'll ask you: would you both please read this letter and tell me what you think?" He handed it to Kenneth first.

Kenneth began reading. "A beard! Henry, Colin's grown a beard!" Then he continued reading. "He saw a priest?" And then, "Marriage!"

"Kenneth!" Henry reprimanded. "Will you please shut it until I have a chance to read it myself?"

Kenneth obliged, and when he was finished, he turned to Howard, slightly angry. "This is positively romantic! I should have known! I told you to write one letter and you fell right into the deep end of the pond again!" Howard blushed, and Kenneth gave the envelope to Henry. "I don't know that you should read it, Henry," he warned.

Henry unfolded the letter. "Well, that's about the last thing you should say. Now I must read it!" He began perusing its contents. "I see I've been reduced to 'Y.K.W.'?"

Howard gave a nervous smile. "Well, it's to protect you—he can't refer to you by your name, considering your past together."

"What's this mention of 'laying a finger' on him?"

"Er... I think in my letter I mentioned something about hating the fact he was hit by his father, and that the only reason Kenneth and I would have ever intervened between him and you were if you had actually physically abused him." Howard was embarrassed. "Of course, I also told him we certainly never thought you did. You see, he says in the letter, 'You're right—Henry never laid a finger on me.'" He grew increasingly anxious about Henry's reactions. *Laying one's self bare, indeed!*

Henry nodded and read on. A few moments later, he looked up again. "'Fearless'? Is that your nickname for him?" Howard wanted to crawl under the table. He settled for covering his eyes, unable to reply. Henry waved a hand, "Never mind. It's charming, quite." He read the rest of the letter silently, various expressions crossing his face until he reached the end. He handed the correspondence back to Howard. "Lord!" He sighed. "If you can put up with that drivel, you are meant for him! He's as tiresome as I remember. Interesting comment about Margaret Rademaker and having children, though. And I do pity him for being disowned. He was obsessed with his father."

Howard stared at him. "How could you say he's tiresome, after all of those things he wrote?"

Henry took a drink. "Oh, he was always that damned... introspective. The boy could never be concise, which was odd considering his design work was so stripped down. When I was in the mood to listen to him, it was fine, but most of the time it drove me mad. I just wanted to enjoy life, but with him it was always, 'Why are we this way? Do you think we'll go to hell? Do you believe in God, Henry? Don't you miss your family?' Blah, blah, blah." Henry leaned back and leered at a group of boys nearby. "Hell, give me a vacuous young buck any day." Then he turned his gaze to Howard. "However, you seem to love the stuff, and you've been alone too damned long, Durham." He nodded at the letter. "There's your Luca for you. I say you should pursue things!"

Howard was mortified. "Henry, I just don't know if I could, after all those years you were with him! It would still feel like I was taking him from you."

"Howard, I fell out of love with him years ago. I couldn't possibly care less. In fact, as I said, he's always been your secret admirer, and that's because you and I are so much alike. Why, I'll even go so far as to say I'd actually feel better about having gotten rid of him if I knew you and he could end up together!"

Howard stared into his glass. "But do you really think that's possible? Or even advisable?"

Henry shrugged. "Well for starters, you must stop being so cautious. Grant you, a lot can happen between now and next June. I suppose the difficult part will be deciding if you actually want Colin for *keeps*, and not just for one night alone with him. You know, finally achieving the long-suffered, unattainable goal." He frowned. "I don't mean to discourage you after all I've said, but Colin's quite complicated. The boy has a few... demons, if you will, that he never was able to vanquish. But I'm sure you'll be of some help to him, if you want to be."

Howard frowned. "What kinds of demons?"

"Oh, as I said, he was always brooding about his family, particularly his father. Apparently they were very close. He felt enormously guilty about being the only son... Oh, you know about that? Well then, of course there was his Catholicism. Always the religion." Henry snorted. "Although given what *he* did, I'm hardly surprised." Then he sighed. "He was homesick, he was lonely, he had frequent nightmares. He wrote ghost letters to his family, he'd get drunk while reading his Bible, and he'd have crying jags for no reason..." He saw Kenneth and Howard's shocked expressions and nodded. "Now you see? It wasn't all peaches and cream. The boy was maudlin. I know you think I'm an ogre for leaving him, but I put up with a lot."

"We never said that," Howard replied evenly, but on the inside, he was overwhelmed. *Henry really knew him. So much more than we did.*

"Well," Henry shrugged, "maybe I think I'm an ogre because I finally got what I wanted and he didn't." He smiled at Howard. "But you could change that." Then he cocked his head. "One more thing though, Howard. Colin is truly coming into his own as an architect, and I can't imagine that things are going to slow down for him at all. Which may mean one of two possibilities: You'll relive this Rademaker project over and over again, for most of your life, or he'll force himself to slow down and limit his potential just to cater to you." Henry sighed. "I don't mean that to sound so negative, but when we had a row about him working so much, *his* solution was to quit working for Rademaker, the very next day! Mind you, he was only midway through the project, but he was going to do it. I had to convince him such a rash move would ruin him."

"So I'm damned if I do and damned if I don't?" Howard bristled.

"Well..." Henry trailed off. "I can't say. But remember how *you* were at his age, Durham. We barely saw you, and your own love life suffered a bit, didn't it?"

Howard ruminated on the point and then declared, "Yes, and *I've* been completely alone for forty-nine years." He smiled. "Which means even ten minutes a night with someone is an improvement."

Henry burst into laughter. "Well then, that's the spirit, old man! I'd say you have made your case!"

But Howard himself wasn't actually convinced. That night, he lay in bed thinking. He had to admit that now that he had told Henry and Kenneth the truth, it felt as if things could truly start to happen.

Do you really know Colin?

Perhaps not as well as I'd thought, but he's been with us for nine years—ten if you count my correspondence with him!

And what about those demons?

Well, that was a bit shocking. But they're nothing extraordinary. Nothing I wouldn't expect considering his past. I'm actually jealous that he never showed me *that side of him. I could help him feel better, and anyway things might have improved for him now, since he's back in America.*

Yes, he's in America. And let's say you go over there and have personal relations with him. Then what? He's there; you're here. He probably won't move back. Would you move there?

Howard took several moments to consider this option.

Well, it depends on whether I could tolerate living in America.

So if Colin was in, say, Africa, you wouldn't follow him there?

Colin would never live in Africa!

But if you really love someone, you'd go wherever they were, wouldn't you?

Not true. Anyway, Colin's not just in America; he's in New York City, which seems to be quite similar to London. And I've been thinking it might be nice for a change.

You'd leave Kenneth and Henry? All your friends at Porter's? Your family? Your job? Everything you love about London?

I've spent over half my life in England, with everything except someone to share it with. I surely think I could spend the rest of my life elsewhere. I'd miss Henry and Kenneth and the rest, but I haven't much family left, and there has got to be more to life than this! That's exactly why I commended Colin for leaving it behind!

And your house?

It's empty, anyway.

Howard started to cheer up. Perhaps he really was still fond of Colin. He had been afraid and ashamed to ever ask himself these questions before, and he was relieved with his answers.

What about your job?

I'll ask for a transfer. Or I'll find a new job in New York. And if worse comes to worst, I just won't work at all.

Colin shall love *that.*

That was the catch. Colin would still be working regular, if not long, hours, and he wouldn't entertain the idea of Howard being home all day with nothing to do. It would be too similar to his problem with Henry.

Fine, I could be a private financial consultant. He grinned in the dark. *All right then, what else?*

Colin is nineteen years younger than you.

So?

You'll widow him.

Howard's mind went blank. He struggled.

Well, does that mean I shouldn't enjoy the years I have left, with him? And anyway, I may live very long and he very short. You can't predict death. And that only matters if it matters to Colin. After all, who's to say that if he doesn't fall for me, he won't fall for some other chap my age?

Howard thought of Henry. Henry had no problem with Colin's age, and he also had no problem with starting over at age fifty, so why couldn't Howard do the same thing?

Fair enough, then. What if Colin isn't *attracted to you?*

That was the one thought Howard had pushed from his mind, always. He refused to let even the first word of the sentence form in his brain. But of course, he had an answer already.

I suppose I shall return to England and start over.

But Howard couldn't stand the idea. Wasn't that what he'd been trying to do since he met Colin ten years ago? And if it didn't work with Mark, or any of the other young men he met, could it work with anyone else?

So if Colin has been this much of an obsession with you, could actually having him, spending the rest of your life with him, possibly measure up to the fantasy?

My dream all along has been to make the fantasy a reality!

And you'll still like him when he's forty? Fifty? Sixty?

Good God, I'll be seventy-nine *when he's sixty, if I'm lucky enough to live that long!*

So he'll be with you when you're truly an old man?

Absolutely. Colin is loyal. And I'd never make him work for it like he had to with Henry.

But what if he finds someone else before you tell him?

Well, I can become more ardent in my letters. I'll put the idea in his head. I'll make him want to wait.

Howard waited for a retort, but there was none. Silence. He sighed. *Right then, that's it, isn't it? I'm going to try. One last time.* The widest smile of all spread across his face, and he turned over and set to sleep.

CHAPTER THIRTY-SEVEN

14 July 1900

Dear Colin,

I just spoke with Kenneth and we plan to book passage to America for June 1901! Like you, we are very excited. Perhaps you could keep that beard awhile longer and we'll see if we can recognize you from the ship! I can't wait to hear all of your stories, new and old. I am keeping a running list of questions in my head about things to ask you when I see you, as well as some things to tell you. Speaking of stories, I was fascinated by your account of the visit to the priest. Colin, you could write a book, honestly. How you stood up to your father and your priest, not to mention venturing back to see your family, is beyond my comprehension. You are quite simply the bravest person I have ever met. When I look back to your beginnings in London, I've long since deduced you're a pioneer of new.

Fearless has managed to stun me again—this time with the picture of you married, with children. On the one hand, I can picture it absolutely perfectly, Colin, because you're the most loyal person I know, and you'd make a lovely father. But then, as you said, you were always the staunchest defender of living the truth. I've really no doubt you'd be exemplary in either role.

What sort of qualities are you looking for in your ideal companion? Surely if they number less than five, you'll find someone within your one-year deadline. Goodness, when you reach my age, the only qualifier is that the person be breathing!

I suppose that's a bit of a stretch, as I've recently ended relations with my former choice. Meaning yes, it will just be Kenneth and I coming to visit you. Those details will have to wait until I see you. I can't complain, really, because it was my decision. But it has become a little disheartening. Have you any advice? I don't see why the benevolent assistance can't go both ways. Thank you in advance!

Well, now I'd say "Enough about me," but you asked after my work. We haven't had any kind of excitement since the Baring Crisis ten years ago (that happened right before you came to England), but essentially, the role of the Bank of England is to provide financial stability. Simple enough, eh? But there are many ways we go about this:

Surveillance (monitoring current developments both in England and abroad to identify key risks to the financial system)

Risk reduction (reducing vulnerabilities and increasing the financial system's ability to absorb unexpected events)

Oversight of payment systems (oversight of the main payment and settlement systems that are used for many types of financial transactions)

Crisis management (developing and coordinating information-sharing within and outside of the bank to ensure future financial crises are handled and managed effectively)

Did you get all of that, Fearless? I could certainly go on but I think this is probably enough for you in one sitting!

I've read several good works of literature as of late: The Strange Case of Dr. Jekyll and Mr. Hyde, by Robert Louis Stevenson; Middlemarch, by George Eliot; and The Light That Failed, by Rudyard Kipling. Have you heard of or read any of these? Let me know of any recommendations you might have.

Kenneth and I just saw a new opera by Puccini called Tosca. Since he also did La Boheme you know I enjoyed it. And yes, it's a tragic opera.

I've decided I need a hobby. Since I don't care for hunting or botany, I'm rather at a loss. I don't consider reading a hobby, or the casual outings to the theaters and museums. I suppose writing to you is a hobby, but then I have to wait to hear from you before I can write again. It will be better in June, when I can see you daily! Until then, what is a gentleman to do? Ah good, more solicitations for advice! Let's see if I can beg you once more before this letter is through!

I'm glad to hear you like my letters as much as I do yours. I don't know if you'll believe me, but things just aren't the same here without you. Henry would kill me if I told you, but here's a tale about an occurrence a few weeks ago: Henry was chatting a boy up, who was quite witty. The next evening, Kenneth and I commented on his liveliness, whereas Henry sighed and said, "Yes, but he's no Colin. That boy was one of a kind." And then we spent the remainder of the evening recounting things that you said and did during your tenure here. Your mannerisms, your style. I think by the time the club closed, the three of us were crying into our drinks. All right, figuratively speaking, but nevertheless, you made your impression on us, Fearless. I wonder if you're doing the same to the gentlemen of America.

I suppose I should go to bed. Remember, you promised to detail your architect's way of life as of late! I look forward to hearing about that, as well as everything else you write about. If anyone should give a man space, it's me to you. You're the one who is caught up in the hustle and bustle of New York City, whereas things here remain the same for me. If it ever becomes a chore to write, then don't—I beg you. We'll visit soon enough, and I'd understand completely.

Sincerely,

Howard

P.S. What sort of a nickname have you thought for me? Ha! You thought I'd fail in my goal!

When Colin finished reading the above letter, he felt his usual surge of affection for his friend, but something disturbed him. He re-read the letter, frowning in thought. He still couldn't figure it out, so he opened a drawer in his desk and took out all of Howard's letters. Colin began to read each one, from the first to this very latest. When he finished, he knew.

Howard lied. He lied! He said he was over me but look at these letters. Certainly, the first few may have been written out of pity, but he continues to write. Three-page letters! And they're all full of blandishments, humility, and teasing. He just ended things with Mark. 'Do you have any advice?' How could he ask me that, after his rejection of me?

Colin paused in thought, and his mind sank into the memory of that day in Howard's office, Howard's words. "God, I haven't felt that way about you in years!"

His look. *You must be joking!*

The hurt, confusion, and anger began to depress Colin. *Howard is either writing these letters unaware of how intimate they sound, or he's writing them fully intending the intimacy. Perhaps, though, he's just lonely.*

Colin snatched a tablet of paper and went through the letters again. He began to make a list:

I was sorry to read that you are staying in America permanently.

I'm not the intrepid traveler you are—that's one of the things I've admired about you. Colin the Fearless!

If Fearless can be so brave and strong, Howard should be able to manage!

The thought of you enduring any kind of physical abuse makes me sick to my stomach.

I have come to think that it would be nice to have someone to spend the rest of my days with.

Fortunately, I have three close companions to spend my time with (I wish it were still four!).

I am certain that your beard looks positively dashing on you!

I can't wait to hear all of your stories.

You are the bravest person I have ever met.

You are the most loyal person I know.

I've really no doubt you'd be exemplary in either role.

I'm glad to hear you like my letters as much as I do yours.

Things just aren't the same without you.

You made your impression on us, Fearless.

Colin read the list and then looked out the window. After a moment, he turned back to the paper.

16. I'm still in love with you, Colin Sewell.

Isn't that what Howard is saying in numbers 1–15?

Then, why isn't he admitting it?

Well, he can't possibly, in a letter! Perhaps he's going to say it when he sees me in June!

Oh, come off it, Sewell! You're a thirty-year old architect, not some playboy socialite eager to romp around in bed.

Well, maybe not romp...

But when Colin tried to picture himself as the object of Howard's desire, his hands flew to his face. *God, what a joke! That was too long ago! After all, Henry probably told him all of my faults.* Colin could just imagine. "Believe me, Howard, living with Colin wasn't what you'd think it to be..."

But Colin wasn't with Henry anymore, and yet here Howard was, still pursuing him. And Howard had made that observation about him: "You saw that time as the phase it rightfully is." Howard said he wasn't like Henry, anyway. But Howard was in London.

I don't want to move back there. I can't.

Come on man, be realistic. Are you saying you're in love with Howard Durham?

Well... Howard is wonderful. He's always been. I fell in love with him once.

And that was years ago.

But I've cared for him ever since, haven't I?

Colin sat back and thought about the possibility. He relived the memory of their second night with each other. *"Colin, you're extraordinary. God, how did Henry get so lucky?"*

Colin sighed. *To have someone who has known me for so long... that would be magnificent. If I gave him a chance, we'd get on famously.*

Do you miss him?

Well, yes! Of course I do. Look at my letters to him, after all! Why, if he were to make a list like I did today...

Right. So you're both still fond of each other. Then why are both of you writing such letters if things can't work out?

Would Howard move to America? Colin could hardly believe he would. *The man will be fifty next year. He's one of the heads of the largest bank in London. And he's hardly been outside England. He said he couldn't imagine living anywhere else. But... he's excited about visiting America.*

Colin went back through his letters. *Yes! Here it is! 'I'm long past due to try a few new things.'* Still, it would be a large step. Colin sighed, rubbing his eyes. *Well, let's see what happens during our correspondence. I'll like seeing his response to* this *letter!*

August 4, 1900

Dear Howard,

Damn it! I can't think of a single good nickname for you! How's that for an opening to a letter? Alas, it's true. I assure you I've tried, and I've come up with all sorts of words that describe you, but none translate well into anything familiar. So "Howard" you shall remain, and I'm quite fond of your name, anyway.

You really must stop turning me into more and more of a legend with your letters. A man is only brave if he has to make a choice. I had no choice back in London; Y.K.W. made the decision, and I had to live with it. As for the priest and my family, in fact, as for everything I've done living here, well, I don't feel very brave at all. I'm just here. And I'm certainly not the conqueror you make me out to be. It's not like the old days, Howard. It's difficult trying to start all over again, when you're older and more afraid. When you realize that consequences mean something. I still like being Fearless to you, because it gives me courage. But believe me, I've become much more the observer than the observed.

My ideal companion? Where? Honestly, it seems like everyone is so concerned with appearances and making an impression. Not that it's any different from London. It's just that I wish I could meet someone outside of that atmosphere. All that matters at the club is that I'm wealthy and well dressed. Then there's the fact that the older ones like those in their twenties, men my age like those in their twenties, and the ones who are in their twenties prefer each other, unless there's money to be spent, or a professional gain. So, advice from me on what you can do? You can see why I'm not going to be much help. The only thing I can think to say is that you've lived alone for so long, Howard, that it may take some time to find someone you are willing to share your life with. I'm sorry to hear your last prospect didn't work out, but you should be proud that it lasted as long as it did. For future reference, just make sure to avoid the ones with eyes only for your pocketbook—you deserve far better than that. Find someone with the same qualities you have. That means, of course, you have to find someone who is handsome, humorous, intelligent, refined, generous, kind, and, dare I say, vulnerable—but just enough to allow a person's confidence. With this in mind, I'd advise you to choose someone who is more established, shall we say. Someone who will value those qualities that I listed, above that incredible amount of wealth you have!

Now you see why advice is bitter medicine. As for hobbies, I have thoroughly enjoyed playing billiards lately. I'm afraid that's a dirty secret on my behalf. Y.K.W. absolutely disapproved of it, of course, and forbade me to admit even knowing how to play! Now that I'm free of that silly restraint, I've been playing with a vengeance. Of course, I never saw you or Kenneth have any affinity for it, so perhaps that's not a good option for you. I think hobbies are fine, but you shouldn't feel as though you must have one. Between your literature, theater, and museum visits, you hardly have time left for a hobby. But, let me know if you begin one. I don't suppose aquariums catch your fancy? Or you could consider getting a dog.

Well! I'm certainly a fount of advice today, aren't I? I've struck out on all counts! Moving on, then...

Yes! Happy news! If I had a calendar for next year, I'd circle the entire month of June in red! Would you believe it—I've just thought of a hobby for myself: I shall scour the city for places to take you and Kenneth during your stay! We are going to have a grand time, I promise you!

And I loved hearing your bank story! I barely understood it, but I got drunk on the language. I must have read that passage aloud ten times! I don't really have any architect news that would interest you—the day-to-day work life is really mundane, I'm afraid. So I will tell you the latest about my sisters and my mother instead. In short, I did visit them. I saw my mother and youngest sister first, then I met again with both my sisters. My mother has decided to side with my father, which disappoints me to no end. I am trying to forgive my father, since I would like him to forgive me. The good news is, my sisters have allowed me back into their family! I will tell you the details when I see you, but my oldest sister, Mary, has four sons, Howard! Isn't that wonderful? I will be meeting them next month, when I return to Boston for a visit. I am so excited I can hardly concentrate on anything else. I am so happy that I can share this news with you!

Finally, I've read all of those books you mentioned. My favorite was *The Strange Case of Dr. Jekyll and Mr. Hyde*. Extremely fascinating! And how amazing that Mr. Stevenson portrayed the idea of the good and evil in all of us! I found *Middlemarch* rather dull, particularly the character of Dorothea. Really, I couldn't have cared less what happened to her. *The Light That Failed* was good, but so devastating. I'm beginning to dislike all of these stories with tragic themes. There's enough tragedy in real life, I say. Give me the triumph of the human spirit any day! Oh, and yes, I do have one book recommendation to you: READ WHITMAN. And you can't write back until *you have, and then you'll have to tell me about it, so I will know for certain that you have read it!*

Well, that was this letter. I'm off to enjoy that "hustle and bustle" of New York City that you mentioned. In short, I'm getting a cup of tea and going to bed.

Good Night,
Colin

20 August 1900

Dear Colin,

I don't know how I can stand to write you another letter, nor do I know how you've suffered through my writing all this time. Yes, I have read Whitman. Specifically, Leaves of Grass. I read the entire book last night, and now I understand why you refused to recite any lines to me—the poetry is very intimate, isn't it? I could hardly believe there was a poem titled Pioneers! O Pioneers! It should have been Fearless! O Fearless! And Give Me the Splendid Silent Sun spoke of Manhattan! Which poem is your favorite? I admit to two: I Heard You and One Hour to Madness and Joy. I think the former is preferable to the latter. I've never been much one for poems longer than two stanzas. Obviously, I have never read The Faerie Queen! In any case, I've read your favorite poet and am a better man for it. Just please don't read his work before reading any of my letters. Inferior prose, indeed!

I agree, for the most part, on your observations regarding the three books we both read. However, I don't mind tragic endings at all. It must have been all of those Greek courses at Oxford. Perhaps it's because tragedy is such a prevalent theme in the great works of literature that it's what I'm most familiar with. It's either that or comedy, which is all right in small doses. Comedic endings seem so insipid, and I find comedies as a whole to be rather unsatisfying. Tragedies run so deep.

Although certainly, I don't wish for the Story of Howard to be a tragedy! At this point, it may indeed be more of a Comedy of Errors. But I took heart with your kind words. The only thing I take issue with is your idea that I only want "twenty-somethings," as you called them. I'll grant you the last one was twenty-six, but I'd hardly consider that the same as twenty. Furthermore, men my age *have* to use our money and influence, because darling, those other qualities you mentioned, however nice they are, mean little more than a hill of beans. Thank you all the same. Most men don't mind buying *their* companionship in one form or another, since it's so temporary. I can't help but take umbrage most of the time, since I'm not interested in that sort of thing. I haven't exactly returned to sainthood, mind you, but all the same... All right, I'll be patient and look around. As Henry said, you were one of a kind, and we really need more Colins here! I completely agree with your observation that it's all a display of artifice. It takes our sort such a long time to really know one another, and everyone is so afraid of showing any weakness. I suppose I'm glad, then, that you found a spot of vulnerability in me, although I have a feeling you didn't discover it until after we began writing to each other. I didn't see yours until things went sour with Y.K.W. I admit I was a bit shocked, but I saw how you conquered it—yes, conquered—I have a right to choose my words! And your openness has allowed me to write so freely to you. For all I know, you're dismayed to find that I'm not a rock of utter strength, either. If so, at least you hide it well!

Anyway, you were so overflowing with compliments that I feel I must return the favor. Colin, I know for certain that you are leaving out at least a dozen who have shown interest in you since you landed in the States. Y.K.W. was an absolutely magnetic personality, and you're going to have some fairly high standards. This nearly fifty-year-old finds it hard to believe that all those who are my age prefer the younger ones, as you grouchily pointed out (and by the way, Fearless, you *are* still one of the younger ones). And don't you remember my earlier letter about those people who were dying to snatch you up when they found out you were a bachelor again? Yes, they were assorted ages—all the more compliment to you. Regardless, you and I both know that you don't get attention just by your dress and wealth alone. Your good looks and charm count for as much, and your accomplishments even more. I have a feeling those others are just chafing at the bit over you! All you have to do to drive them mad is to open your coat, slide out your cigarette case, flip it open, draw out a cigarette, light it, and exhale. You made an art of it, Sewell, didn't you know?

Well, to flatter you any further would be gilding the lily. I about dropped your letter when I read that you play billiards! While I'm by no means an expert player, I enjoy the game when I'm at the Financial Club. Yes, Y.K.W. held sway over both of us, it seems! Since I knew he frowned upon it, and I never heard you mention it, I figured I'd keep my mouth shut. Bully! We can team up once we're in New York! Or I shall play against you for ridiculous sums of cash! I had better hone my skills before then. Viola! A new hobby!

I found one comment of yours to particularly stand out: "It's difficult trying to start all over again, when you're older and more afraid. When you realize consequences mean something."

While I can see how you could utter such a belief, I find it interesting that I feel just the opposite, and if it helps explain things, I imagine Y.K.W. feels as I do, too. When you've lived the majority of your years, you look at the ones you have left and say, "To hell with risks and consequences. 'X' would make me happy, and I'm going to do it!" It's a sort of giddy fatalism, if you will. That's why you see so many men my age acting like the twenty-year-olds we wished we were. I do agree that we now realize that consequences mean something. But whereas you see it as meaning "Throwing caution to the wind has its downside," I see it as "Taking a risk may give me the ultimate happiness I've been seeking." Isn't that funny? You are far more the melancholic Gibson Girl than I, and may that be to your advantage! You're right, too, that I do have "an incredible amount of wealth," and I fully intend to start depleting it. I suppose the visit to see you will be a good start.

Well then, I'll send this off. I pray this letter finds you well, and write back when you can.

As Ever,

(Apparently, since you can't think of a nickname)
Howard

The night after Howard mailed off his letter, he went over to the Financial Club. "Roger," he hailed a fellow businessman, "do you think you can teach an old man how to play billiards?"

"Billiards! Who's the old man?"

"Me. I'm afraid I spoke too soon and I'm to play a game in a few weeks."

"Not a problem, Durham. Come along; there's no better time than the present!"

CHAPTER THIRTY-EIGHT

September and October passed, with Colin and Howard delighting in their exchange of ever-more-fervent letters. Then two weeks before Thanksgiving, something occurred that would disrupt the balance.

Colin was sitting with Adam at the club. "Sewell, isn't there anyone here you could entertain spending an evening with?"

Colin shook out his match. "Nobody I could spend a life with," he muttered, his cigarette between his teeth.

Adam threw his hands up. "God, how could you possibly know? You're putting the cart before the horse!" Colin laughed. He hadn't told Adam about Howard and didn't plan to, but it would have made things easier. "Really, Sewell, how long's it been?"

Colin narrowed his eyes. "Since what?"

"Since you've been to bed with someone!"

"Well, not as long as it's been for you!"

"Au contraire! I'm regular."

"With your *wife*?"

"Well, it's better than nothing, which is what you've got."

Colin hmphed and then paused uncertainly. Adam eyed him. "What? What were you going to say?"

Colin shrugged. "Well, actually..." He leaned closer to his friend. "What's it like, being with a woman?"

Adam gasped. "Mr. Sewell! That is beyond the line of decency, even in a place like this!"

"Really," Colin insisted. "How's it different? Or, how different is it, exactly?"

"It's night and day different if you must know," Adam sniffed. "And that's all I'm going to say about it."

"'Night and day,'" Colin wondered aloud. "Then how can you possibly stand it?"

"Colin!"

"Well, I'm curious!" Colin defended. Then he whispered, "Is it all mushy and squishy?"

Now Adam couldn't help laughing. "'Mushy and squishy'! All right, er... yes, they are a lot softer everywhere, if that's what you mean."

"Do they like it?"

"Well..." Adam hedged, trying to determine a limit on the topic. "Oh really, Colin!" But Colin wouldn't give in, and Adam sighed. "Well, at first... that first time of course, she didn't. She was scared—as if I wasn't! And you see, I thought I was smart. I went to a brothel beforehand so I could at least figure out where to put it."

Colin's jaw dropped. "Oh, that would be true! I wouldn't have the faintest!"

"But when I tried to do the same thing to Tressa, the damned thing wouldn't go in! I had to really... er... push to do it, and the poor girl cried."

Colin reeled. "That's ghastly!"

"Well, I think they know it's going to hurt," Adam shifted. He decided not to mention the blood. "And then, after that, she was fine."

"She likes it now, then?"

"Yes, Colin. She likes it."

"But you can only do it that one way..."

"Well, she'd be a prostitute otherwise! She's a lady, Sewell; she's not going to do anything like that!"

Colin nodded. "Yes, yes. Of course."

But then Adam waved a hand. "Well, sometimes, if we've been to a party and she's had a bit to drink... she uh... she'll be a little more frisky."

"Frisky?"

"Well, she... um... Oh, never mind! The point is, it's not all that bad, and we're always in the dark anyway. Modesty you know."

"Modesty," Colin repeated. "That's fascinating. You know, I always wondered, but—"

"Excuse me, Mr. Sewell? Hello, Mr. Meredith."

Adam and Colin both looked up. "Oh... er... hello Jim," Adam replied, horrified to be caught in such conversation.

Jim smiled. "Yes, sorry to interrupt. I wanted to tell Mr. Sewell that I just came back from London and I thought he might like to indulge in a bit of reminiscing."

"Well, I can't imagine he wouldn't," Adam replied. "Please, take my seat."

"Glad to," Jim grinned, making his way in and sitting on Colin's left. "Jim Pullman, by the way." He extended his hand. Colin smiled. He had seen the man often at the club, in a group of similarly older men. They looked to be Henry's age, although Jim had dark silver hair with some black in it and an olive complexion. He was medium built, and he dressed more conservatively than Henry had. He seemed to enjoy talking up the younger men, and Colin had noticed how relaxed and confident he always was in doing so. Adam had told Colin that Jim was married, so Colin had admired him from afar. In fact, he found Jim Pullman rather intimidating, and now he prayed he wouldn't start shaking.

"Colin Sewell. So Mr. Pullman, why were you in London?" Colin inquired.

"Family trip. We went as a large group of friends and relatives. Spent the month of July there."

"Oh, how very nice!"

"Mm, it was. I'd been there many years ago, when I was in my twenties. It was very interesting to go back."

"How so?" And before long, Colin was on his third drink in less than thirty minutes and feeling giddy. Jim had ordered the fourth even before Colin finished his third, and Colin suspected he was trying to get him drunk. But Colin found it flattering. *He actually wants me!* When Colin was halfway through with one of his own stories, Jim interrupted him with a smile.

"Your cheeks are flushed."

Colin stopped talking, then rolled his eyes. "Well, considering you've been ordering drinks for me at a rate of one per ten minutes!"

"And you've been drinking them."

Colin laughed. "Well, they're very decent drinks!"

Jim leaned over and with his thumb stroked the red on Colin's face. "I like it on you."

Colin's eyes widened and his mouth hung open. *Oh God, I haven't any decorum left.* "Well," he tried to sigh, "if I'm boring you..."

"No, Mr. Sewell, I love the story! I just couldn't help but notice. Do carry on."

Colin finished the story, and Jim leaned back in admiration. "I knew there had to be something fascinating about you."

"Besides the fact that I'm more than you expected?" Colin challenged, and then he thought in horror, *Christ, where did that come from?*

Jim raised his eyebrows. "You're exactly what I expected. What I'd hoped to expect, anyway. I —"

"Last call!" the bartender rang out.

Colin gazed at his glass. "Oh. Pity."

"Indeed it is." Jim paused. "Do you live very far from here?"

Colin shrugged. "Only about twenty minutes." He peered at Jim over his drink. "Why?"

"Well, I thought we could continue our conversation at your place. I'd love to see it."

Colin laughed. "I didn't build it."

"The inside!"

Colin looked skeptical. "You want to see how I decorated it?"

"Mr. Sewell, from what I've heard you're some kind of famous designer. Yes, I want to see how you decorated it!"

"I'll hold you to that, then," Colin teased. Disappointment flashed across Jim's face, and Colin panicked. *He thinks I'm serious! He's angry, I'm sure!* He put a hand on Jim's arm and smiled. "No! I'd love to show you! It's just that it will be sort of a letdown... I haven't had any time to do anything because I'm mostly at the office."

But Jim thought he had received his cue. "Well, really, if you don't think there's anything to see..." he said detachedly.

Damn it! "No, look here! I'd love to show you..." *Desperate! Desperate! God, I've really lost it!* "Really, I would. Let's take a cab and go."

"You're sure?"

Colin took a breath and settled into the game. He sat up straight, tilted his head, and then leaned forward gravely. "Well, Mr. Pullman, frankly... Yes. I'm sure."

Jim's frown turned slowly into a smile, and then a grin. "Come on, then." He took Colin's hand.

"Wait!" Colin grabbed his cigarette case and waved goodbye to Adam, who laughed and bade him goodnight.

Colin gave directions to the driver while Jim waited. "Jim, go in!" he urged.

"Beauty before age," Jim bowed.

Colin finished with the driver and got into the cab. "Hmph. In that case, we should enter together."

"Really? You're hardly my age."

"I'm forty-two."

He watched Jim's mouth drop, and he burst out laughing. "I'm sorry! I'm not really. I'm, um... well, never mind, anyway." They sat next to each other in the cab.

"You're thirty," Jim smiled.

"Oh. You know."

"Do you know my age?"

"Thirty-eight?"

"Oh, come off it, Sewell!"

"You bought me drinks! I'll stay at thirty-eight."

"Forty-seven. Anyway, you *are* beautiful."

"You're very handsome."

"Thank you."

"In fact, I've always thought you were sort of, intimidating, actually."

"What? Why's that?"

"Well, just... well, you're handsome, and you're self-assured. The way you get on with the fellows and the way you dress..."

"The way *you* dress," Jim took Colin's hand, "you're the best dressed in the entire club. And you've got the prettiest eyes. When I finally got to see them up close tonight, I could barely breathe."

Colin looked at his lap and blushed. "Thank you."

"And the way you're so shy. I love it." Jim squeezed Colin's hand. "Mr. Sewell, may I kiss you?"

Colin's eyes flew open, and then he looked down again with a small laugh.

"What?" Jim smiled.

"I've never been *formally* asked that."

"Well, maybe I'm finding *you* to be a bit intimidating."

Colin rolled his eyes at the idea and then turned his head and gave Jim one slow, soft kiss.

"That's lovely," Jim murmured, taking both of Colin's hands into his own. The comment and the motion reminded Colin of another age. He shed his inhibitions and fell into his formerly seductive self. Jim was taken aback by Colin's suddenly ardent emotion, but he was also delighted. As Colin pressed against him and kissed into his neck, Jim sighed, "God, you're making this difficult."

Colin pulled away from Jim slightly and looked at him in wonderment. "And you're making it so easy."

Jim leaned in and began to kiss him again. After a few more minutes, he whispered, "I don't want to do it in the cab, Colin. Are we almost there?"

"Yes, I think so."

Finally the cab stopped and they went into Colin's house. Later, as they lay in bed, Jim rested an arm on Colin's side as they faced each other. "I can't stay the night, you understand."

"I understand. Your wife."

"I wish I could, though. I'll bet you look lovely in the morning, with your hair all tousled."

"Well, you oughtn't have gone and gotten married," Colin teased.

Jim sighed. "I hadn't any choice, you know that."

Colin raised his head, curious. "How do you mean?"

"Well, like so many other fellows, I truly felt I had to get married. It was never even a question. Remaining single, like you, was as much a fantasy for me as an orgy with twenty boys!" Colin laughed. "And perhaps because I was prepared for marriage, I never minded it. It's an inconvenience of sorts, certainly, but overall, the benefits have outweighed the downsides."

Colin nodded. "I sometimes still think of marrying, myself."

"You seem to be doing just fine without it."

"But I don't have those benefits you just mentioned."

"Yes, but you have everything I don't. Colin, unless you feel that not being married is preventing career or social promotion, don't bother with it."

Jim's friendly advice warmed Colin up to him. "Well, it's all right that you have to leave. I'll show you out."

When they reached the door, Jim turned and cupped Colin's cheek. "Sleep well. I'll see you next Saturday?"

Colin, thankful he was too tired to show his disappointment, nodded. "Yes, of course." He shut the door, shuffled back to bed, and fell soundly asleep.

The next afternoon, Adam appeared for his usual Sunday visit. "How'd it go?" he inquired merrily. Colin sighed. "I'm not sure. It was nice, I guess. But he..." Then Colin stopped, embarrassed that he was about to act like a schoolgirl.

"But he what?"

"Oh, he just said he'd see me next Saturday." He paused and then said slowly, "I didn't think I was going to be a charity project."

"Who says you are?"

"Well if *I* was interested in a fellow, I'd call on him the very next day."

"He's got a family, Colin, and work. Next Saturday probably *is* the first time he could see you again, and remember, you only attend the club on Saturdays. Did you two...?"

"Yes, and I don't know why it was so easy with him. I wonder if he just thought I was interested in one night."

"You weren't?"

"Well, no! I wouldn't have done something like that. I liked him. A lot. Say, what do you know about him?"

"Well, he was interested in you when you first came here. When I made my rounds back then, he motioned me over and asked me about you, but I told him you weren't available for a while. I hope you don't mind. I told everyone that, back then."

"No, I don't mind. It was true."

"I don't really know much else about him. But he's good looking, isn't he? For an older gentleman? He's always gotten any boy he wanted." Adam's expression froze. "Whoops!"

Colin looked glum. "Well, I'm hardly a 'boy'. And it serves me right. Going on with him like that right away and falling into flattery."

"Sewell, if you had a good time, that's all that matters."

"I know. It's just that now I'll have to save face the next time I'm at the club. And what if other men think now that it's open season on me for pity fucks?"

"'Pity fucks'! Where on earth did you get that expression!"

"I made it up. You do that kind of thing when you're bitter, see?"

"Oh, go on. I'll be at the club too. Surely between today and then you can think of some nice phrases to decline invitations from the 'pity fuckers'."

Colin laughed. "Oh, that's even worse! I'm sure I can think of something. You help me!"

The following Saturday was Thanksgiving weekend, however, and the Carlisle was closed for the holiday. By the time Colin visited the Carlisle in December, it had been two weeks since he had seen Jim. He and Adam had no sooner reached the floor of the club when Colin saw Jim coming toward him. He put on a brave smile. "Hullo, Jim!"

"Colin! I'm so glad you're here! I've been watching for you all evening! I was wondering if I could talk to you for a moment."

Colin struggled to keep his smile, feeling that everyone was watching them. "Certainly." He motioned Adam to go ahead without him.

Jim beamed. "Good!" He ushered him over to the bar.

"Oh!" Colin laughed with relief. "I'm buying tonight, aren't I?"

"What?" Jim asked. "Oh, no, really, that's not necessary."

He ordered his drink, and when it arrived, Jim glanced at Colin, who said tonelessly, "Gin and tonic, please." His mood was utterly deflated. He sat and waited for Jim to begin.

"Colin, I want to apologize. I didn't mean to go an entire two weeks without seeing you again."

"It's all right."

"No, honestly! I woke up that Sunday after seeing you and thought of inviting you to dinner, but then I realized I don't have anywhere to post you."

"You forgot my address?"

"Honey, I never even looked at your address that night, and can you blame me? I tried to remember what you told the coachman, but I had more to drink than I thought. And I didn't know the name of your workplace. I contemplated going to the club and asking Meredith, but I was afraid he'd give me a hard time."

"Adam? He's a good man."

"Well, anyway, I can see I'm not convincing you..."

Colin smiled weakly. *I'm convinced you want another fun go!* "I believe you, Mr. Pullman. But really, one evening was fine."

"*Mr. Pullman!*" Jim was hurt. "Well, I gather you must not be interested in dinner, then." Colin was surprised, but he hesitated. *What about Howard?* Jim said quickly, "Colin, it seems you've already talked with Meredith, and granted, I haven't exactly a record of spending more than an evening with someone. But I didn't mean for you to fall into that category. You weren't that at all."

Colin couldn't resist the hope of being flattered. "No?"

Jim sighed. "No. I'd actually been interested in you for some time. Who hasn't? But the story at the time was that you weren't ready to date anyone yet."

"Right..."

"Then I had the wonderful fortune to go to London and realize that would be my way in." Jim paused, and then sighed. "In any case, I've been doing all of this talking of my admiration for you, and yet I haven't heard if you feel anything of the same, so..."

"I'm sorry Jim," Colin apologized. "You're extremely complimentary. I suppose... it's been a long time since I've heard such nice things." He looked up at Jim. "I would love to have dinner with you." Then a thought came into his head. "Actually, since we both work in the city, why don't we meet for lunch instead?"

Now Jim was disappointed. It was clear to him that Colin wanted to keep things informal, whereas he was hoping to impress the young man with a more elegant evening affair. But perhaps if lunch went well... "That could certainly be arranged. Juno's at twelve noon?"

Colin laughed. "What day?"

"Oh, right. Well, what about Monday?"

Colin grinned. "I like your thinking. Yes, Monday is fine."

"Good!"

Colin glanced at his table. "I should go and see my friends. Would you mind if I joined up with you a little bit later?"

Jim looked pleased. "I was hoping you would. Please do."

"All right." Colin parted from Jim and walked toward Adam's group. When he told them what had happened, Adam laughed. "See? You were all worried for nothing!" Then he cocked his head. "So you turned down a dinner invitation for lunch?"

"Well, lunch is less formal. I thought it'd be easier for us to talk. I haven't really found out much about him yet."

"Except that he's married and has a family."

"Yes, I know. But really, who isn't?"

"Lots of them aren't."

"Over the age of thirty?"

"You're stuck on the age?"

"I already act older than I am. I don't want to have to keep up with some twenty-year-old."

"You're funny, Sewell."

"Well, what's your opinion?"

Adam regarded his drink. "Well, the night you met him, you talked about wanting to 'spend a life' with someone. You can't do that with a married man, Colin."

"Well, obviously not in the strictest sense. But I could feasibly see him on a frequent basis for the rest of my life."

"But what about holidays and such? You'll be alone on Thanksgiving, alone on Christmas, New Year's Eve, his birthday..."

"I spent Thanksgiving with you."

"Right. But once you're in love with someone, you'd rather be with him, and he'll *have* to be with his family."

Colin nodded, sighing. "And I can't very well spend every holiday with your family."

Adam smiled. "You could. But do you see what I'm saying?"

"Yes, but those are only a few days out of the entire year."

"Well, how often do you think you'd be able to see Jim?"

Colin shrugged. "Well, we're having lunch on Monday, then maybe dinner after that, and I'll see him on Saturday."

"So three days a week. And he can't spend the night with you."

"We might take a vacation together," Colin offered. "But all right. I see your point. And I agree—it's not ideal. But it's better than being alone *all* the time."

"Now that is true," Adam agreed.

"But there is one other problem," Colin said slowly. He finally told him about Howard. "So I'm not sure what to do."

"My goodness! You're saying you think that this man, Howard, has carried a torch for you for ten years, and you've always been attracted to him, and now you're going to see each other next June?"

"But I don't know if he actually still feels anything for me."

"But if you knew Howard was coming in June to 'propose' to you, for lack of a better term, would you see Jim on Monday?"

"Of course not! But that's the whole problem. I don't know."

"So, you could either ask Howard in your next letter or you could see Jim until Howard visits and then decide."

"How could I possibly ask him in a letter? You can't put things like that in print!"

"Sure you could. You could write something like, 'Dear Howard, I have recently met someone I am attracted to. However, I think perhaps you may have something to tell me that would keep me from pursuing this...'"

"Oh, that's good!"

"And then you could write, 'I myself have been wanting to tell you something, but I haven't yet, out of fear and uncertainty regarding your possible response.'"

"Keep going."

"'So in your next letter, would you please tell me if I should go ahead with this person, or if I should wait?' And then you end the letter with, 'I would prefer to wait.'"

"That's brilliant, Adam!" Colin paused. "But then, what should I do about Jim?"

"Oh, I say, have lunch with him on Monday. Have dinner with him, even. You've already started something with him, and you can't do anything until you hear from Howard, so you may as well enjoy yourself. You'd kick yourself if you ended things with Jim tonight only to find out Howard isn't interested."

Colin looked skeptical. "I don't know. It seems duplicitous."

"Look, Jim can either be disappointed now, or you can give him some attention and disappoint him later. At least you'll be giving him something with the latter."

Colin grinned. "Adam, you're the best friend! Thanks ever so much!"

A half hour later, Colin made his way over to Jim. It wasn't before he was within several feet from him that he realized Jim was within a group of men. *Oh God, this is going to be awkward. What if he doesn't introduce me?* For it was a general rule that anyone intended for just a night's worth of enjoyment needn't be introduced to the man's friends. Jim's face lit up when he saw Colin. "Colin! Wonderful!" And much to Colin's relief, he was introduced formally to Jim's circle, without any winks or sly comments. If anything, Colin thought he detected a few impressed glances at Jim. After a few minutes, Jim steered Colin into their own private conversation, and the other men took up where they had left off amongst themselves. "Thank you for coming over," Jim said, his tone grateful.

"I said I would."

"I know, and I'm glad."

Colin was glad, too. Jim was friendly, and Colin relaxed easily around him. Still, he knew better than anyone how charisma could be mistaken for honest feelings, so his guard was still up. "I believe our conversation left off at how you found your calling to be in the printing business," he quipped.

Jim laughed. "Is that so? You've a better memory than me. All right then, I'll tell you."

They talked over the next hour, when yet again they were stopped by the bartender shouting out the last call. "Pity," Jim smiled, winking.

Colin grinned. "Indeed it is." He began to blush, but went ahead with what he was going to say. "If you like, I could take you back to my house and actually show you the whole thing, this time."

"Will you hold me to it?" Jim teased.

Colin flickered his eyes over him. "I'll do half that."

Jim stared at him. "Do you want to go now?" He almost apologized for the lust in his voice.

"Why not?" They put their glasses onto the bar and left the club together, engrossed in each other as they walked out.

Colin did take Jim on an actual tour of his home, even though it was still rather bare. As they began to undress each other in the bedroom, Jim murmured in Colin's shoulder, "I missed you."

"You did?"

"Mm. This. I missed this." Jim sighed, reaching his hand around. "Mm, lovely. And your face, your eyes, your mouth, your skin. You. You talented, talented creature." Jim nuzzled into Colin's neck, and Colin was smitten. He worked his way down Jim's body, lowering himself with a smile. *"Talented." I know something about it.*

Parting was easier this time, as they reminded each other of their lunch together on Monday. But while Colin lay alone in bed, he couldn't help feeling odd about the whole situation. Tomorrow he had to write to Howard. He had to write *the* letter. Drifting off to sleep, Colin wondered if he would still want to ask the question when he woke up.

CHAPTER THIRTY-NINE

December 5, 1900

Dear Howard,

Merry Christmas and Happy New Year! Your gift is enclosed in this box. I wish it were a drawing of one of my own buildings, but those have to belong to the owners. I sketched the Bank of England to include in my bank architecture portfolio. Yes, I have such a thing! Therefore I was able to use my miniature to recreate a larger picture for you. I thought it would be a fitting gift, for it reminds me of that first day we were in Hyde Park, at the Prince Albert Memorial. That day is burned into my memory, as is every day I've spent with you.

Howard, there is something I must tell you. I know I owe you a full response to your last letter, but I can't just tack on what I'm about to say at the end of such a letter when I'll have been thinking about it from the start.

I recently met someone I may be interested in. However, I think perhaps you may have something to tell me, something that would keep me from pursuing this. Perhaps I have been getting the wrong impression from your letters. I read them all the time and I can't help but think... I have been wanting to tell you something, too, but I haven't yet, out of fear and uncertainty about your response. After your comment in the bank the day before I left. Also, I didn't quite know how to put it in print. But this latest turn of events is forcing me to put the question before you, for one cannot treat too lightly a friendship of ten years, and I must confess some things have not changed, in my heart. In your next letter, could you please tell me if I should go ahead with this person or should I wait (I would prefer to wait)?

Yours Truly,
Colin

Colin sent the package and letter the next day, before he went to have lunch with Jim. He reached Juno's a bit early and was already seated when Jim arrived. "How wonderful to see you by the light of day!" Jim exclaimed as he sat down.

"It's strange!" Colin laughed. The waiter came by, and Jim gazed at Colin while he ordered from his menu. There was something about Colin's businesslike tone toward the waiter. About his simple, elegant workday suit. About his thirty-year-old face lit by the sun streaming in the window. Jim placed his own order, and once the waiter left, he chuckled. Colin raised his eyebrows. "What?"

"It's just... we look like two business partners out to lunch."

Colin smiled. "Well, we are."

"I know, but I've never done this before."

"You haven't?"

Jim shook his head. "It's so different for me than it is for you. What was it like, being with that man you were with?"

Colin sighed. "Henry and I had meals together every day. I suppose I took it for granted. Something like this was nothing at all."

"I've never taken anyone to lunch."

Colin leaned in. "Who says you're taking me? It's high time I paid for something. I don't like being the sole beneficiary."

"Who says you're the only one benefiting from this relationship?"

"I mean it should be even fiscally, Jim. I insist."

"Oh, well all right, if you insist. That's funny. I'm so used to patronizing that the idea of equality never crossed my mind. Sorry."

Colin sat back in his chair. "So all of these years, there's never been one particular person you wanted to spend more than a night with?"

"Oh, there were a few I spent many nights with," Jim winked. "But no, I was too busy to entertain the idea of having anything long term. My wife was enough of a 'kept woman' that I certainly didn't need two!"

Colin hesitated. "Is it because I'm so much older that this is different for you?"

Jim frowned. "You're not 'so much older'. I think it's more of a maturity issue. I'll bet you've changed very little from when you were twenty. You're a serious fellow, Colin. I like that. And I like that you don't laugh at my musings, that you don't look at other men when you're with me, that we're able to talk about the stock market and such after finishing in bed. You're a good listener, and you're so smart." He paused. "My sons are grown and it's nice to have someone to talk to about these things, and to have someone to be intimate with at the same time." Then he stopped, and his face reddened. "Goodness," he muttered. "Pillow talk at twelve noon!"

"I like it," Colin remarked, smiling.

Jim sipped his drink. "Oh? Suppose you tell me why you're still here."

Colin lowered his eyes. "Because you still want me here. Because you're easy to talk to. You're self-assured, good looking. You're ahead in the game enough to appreciate what I've done." Then he glanced about and lowered his voice. "And moreover, you've been an exceptional lover."

Jim's eyes widened. "Really?"

"Um-hmm." The first course arrived, leaving an awkward pause that kept Jim from asking further on the topic. "So," Colin said, picking up his silverware, "tell me about your children."

"Hardly children anymore. Neddy's the oldest. He runs the firm with me. He's married, has two children. He's a good boy. Christopher's the other one. He's rather worthless. Sides with his mother on everything. Thinks I'm negligent. Doesn't refuse the money I give him, though."

"What's he do?"

"He runs a photography business." Jim snorted. "After all that college, the boy goes into photography. He's got a wife too, and a rather bratty son. Then Christina's the youngest. Spoiled, just like her mother. I wish she'd find someone and move out of the house."

"Oh my. I'm sorry to hear that."

"Well, you know, children are like that. They go through periods where you couldn't love them more, then periods when you can hardly stand them. Then they become loveable again. On and off."

Colin was mildly shocked. "I've never heard it described like that!"

"Well, that's how I see it."

"You regret having them, then."

"What a thing to say! Of course not. If I was going to marry, I damn sure was going to have children."

"Oh."

"You see, Colin, even if they aren't always what you want them to be, they're *yours*, and they're your lineage."

"That's very British."

"It's very human." Then Jim put down his fork. "Forgive me. That's not to say you should have them. Don't marry a girl just so you can have children, Colin. It's not worth that."

Colin gave a half smile. "That's easy for you to say."

"Colin, I'd give anything to trade places with you. Look at you—you spent almost ten years with a man! It's staggering! It's something I'll never have. Even if he did end up leaving you, you have the chance to do it again, with someone else."

Colin reflected on Jim's words. "Well, we can enjoy each other, anyway. For now."

Jim smiled, and felt slightly uneasy. He *was* enjoying Colin, and if things continued like this, what was he going to do? They continued their conversation until they finished lunch. Colin paid the bill, and they walked outside.

"I suppose you don't take a two-hour lunch," Jim said wistfully.

Colin, looking ahead, smiled. "No. But I can manage another half hour." Jim stopped. Colin kept walking a few feet, and then turned around, his eyes laughing. "What?"

Jim shook his head and walked up to Colin. "How did I get so lucky?" he murmured.

Colin stared at Jim's mouth. "I don't actually know where we can go," he admitted.

"I do. Come." Jim almost took Colin's hand, but quickly remembered where he was and forced his fists into his pockets. As he walked, he struggled with his thoughts. *This is crazy. It's the cold light of day and I'm going to a hotel? Good lord.* But the thought of himself and Colin in bed, in sunlight rather than candlelight, overruled any fears. They arrived at the lobby of the Brigand Hotel. "I'd like a room please," Jim told the receptionist. He turned to Colin and said in a low voice, "I figure that's a safe enough place to discuss the new plans."

Colin nodded solemnly, glad for Jim's excuse. He himself had never procured a hotel room for this purpose, and played along, standing with his arms crossed like a bored business partner.

They shut and locked the door and became giddy upon their success. "This is a day of firsts," Jim wondered. "Having lunch with a lover, bedding him in the daytime, and doing so while completely sober!"

"I feel a little drunk myself," Colin admitted.

Jim stepped closer and put his hands on Colin's shoulders. "Mm, is that so? On one drink?"

Colin's breathing became shallow. He nodded and kissed Jim, who whispered, "Now that we're here, let's take our time. I want to really see you."

An hour later they prepared to leave. "Did you pay for a night's stay?" Colin asked.

Jim shrugged. "I think so, yes. No matter."

Colin's smile grew into a sly grin. "Well then, we may as well put it to good use. Why don't we meet again after work?"

Jim chuckled. "In three hours? I love your thinking."

"Yes, well, it's your room. Be here at 5:45 and I'll come up."

Jim kissed him gratefully. "You're irresistible."

"*This* is irresistible," Colin smiled, and bade him goodbye.

That evening, as they drowsed under the sheets, Jim said softly to Colin. "Have dinner with me tomorrow night."

"What will you tell your wife?"

"I'm working late, and one of my associates is celebrating something at the club."

"What club?"

"One of the *other* clubs, of course."

"Won't Neddy tag along?"

"God, no. I made sure to join a club he can't get into yet, for that very reason."

"I'd love to have dinner with you."

"Good. But it's *my* evening. I want to take you out."

"But what if someone your wife knows sees us? Or anyone you know, for that matter."

"On a Tuesday night? Highly unlikely. Anyway, I'm taking you to Aria and we'll have a private booth."

"Aria!" Colin propped himself on his elbow and stroked Jim's hairline. "Are you sure of all of this?"

Jim slowly shook his head. "No. And yes. It will be a businessmen's dinner!"

Colin laughed, laying his head on Jim's chest. "Yes! There you have it, then!" He crossed his arms over Jim's body. "All right, tell me what time to be there."

Jim kissed him. "Seven sharp. And wear that green suit you have."

Colin smiled. "All right. You wear something dark blue."

"Dark blue?"

"Um-hmm. I like that color on you. Now, we really had better get going."

Jim sighed. He wondered if he would be able to leave Colin for longer than twenty-four hours, for it felt like they already spent too much time apart. When they were ready to leave, Colin said, "I should probably go out first, and then you leave in about ten minutes. How do you check out?"

"Oh, I don't really care. I'll just check out when I leave. It's no business of theirs why I had it for only six hours."

"Oh. All right then. You're brave."

I'm in love, Jim almost said, but he didn't dare. Instead, he teased, "*You're* skittish."

"Oh, honestly! Good night, Jim. I'll see you tomorrow."

"Good night, Colin."

Tuesday night's dinner was sublime. They agreed to meet again for lunch on Wednesday. This time after lunch they took a walk in Central Park, finding wintry, isolated stretches where they could hold hands or sit on a bench and talk affectionately. Colin told Jim everything about Jeffrey, Henry, his family, his religion, and London. He left out his sexual past though, fearing it would eclipse everything else. Jim found Colin fascinating, and loved hearing him talk. "You've such a brain in you!" he wondered as they walked. "It's amazing that you're as handsome as you are, with an intellect like that." They decided that day to forgo their regular after-work attendance at their respective clubs (for Colin had also joined a businessmen's club), and they met up again to take a walk, have dinner, and then go back to Colin's house.

On Thursday, Jim had a lunch meeting and decided he should also visit one of his clubs that evening. In truth, although he realized it seemed childish, he also wanted to test Colin's feelings for him by being made unavailable. By 5:30 that afternoon, he was cursing himself for such a stupid idea. But it was too late; he was at the club and restlessly tried to carry on conversations with his fellow members. At 7:00 p.m. he thought about stopping by Colin's house to see if he'd eaten dinner yet, but he held back. When they met for lunch on Friday, Jim waited for Colin's reaction to their break the day before. But Colin said nothing. They bantered for a bit and then Jim couldn't stand it. "Colin, didn't you miss me at all yesterday?"

Colin looked up, surprised. "Of course I did. But I... I thought perhaps you were losing interest, and so I didn't want to say anything."

"Losing interest! Why would you think that?"

Colin shrugged. "Well, the way we've been going about things, and I told you so much about myself on Wednesday. Then you decided for us not to meet at all yesterday... but it's all right."

"It's not all right! Colin, it was a stupid experiment on my part to see if you'd miss me. But I was the one going mad! I was about to come by your house after the club but how desperate would I have looked?"

Colin's voice was wistful. "I wish you would have."

"You do? Really, you do?"

Colin looked down shyly. "Yes, I do. I've never been very good at being alone, and the fact that you're willing to spend so much time with me, well, it's been decadent."

"It's been heaven! I don't quite understand what it is about you, and yet I have dozens of reasons. But one thing's for certain: I *am* enjoying your company."

Colin exhaled. "Oh, I'm glad. I'm enjoying yours too."

"And I'm sorry about yesterday. I could kick myself."

"It's all right," Colin shook his head. "I don't think it's realistic for us to expect to spend every day together, anyway. Your wife might get suspicious."

"As long as I'm keeping away from her the time I normally keep away from her, she'll be none the wiser," Jim reassured.

"Well, I hate to say this," Colin began, "but I do have to work late tonight. You could come by my house around 9:00, but I suppose that's not possible."

Jim mulled it over. "Well, let me see..."

Colin frowned. "I don't want you to have to think your way around things, Jim. It makes me nervous."

"Leave the worrying to me."

"I can't. I was in London when Wilde got convicted, you know."

"So you were," Jim replied. "But that wasn't because Wilde got found out. He brought it upon himself."

"It doesn't matter! The point is, you've got to keep evidence to a minimum. You can't possibly understand what happened, Jim. It was horrible! We were all in fear for our lives! I *knew* Wilde!" Colin became quite fretful, and Jim tried to soothe him.

"Colin, it's all right. Calm down. I promise you, I'm not putting us at risk. I was only thinking about my schedule this evening. You may be happy to know I can't make it at nine after all, so it's settled."

Colin's face fell. "Oh. I'm sorry. I wish you could, but I understand if you can't. I didn't expect you to, after all. That's too bad. But I'll be fine."

Jim looked at him, amused. "You're terribly complicated." Colin looked hurt, but Jim smiled at him. "*That's* what I like about you. You're complicated, but in a sweet way. You're too very smart for your own good, the way you think too much. Look at you."

"Oh, stop it."

"But affable," Jim decided. "You're affable. I shall call you Affie!"

Colin looked disgusted. "Affie!"

"Oh yes, Affie! It's perfect!"

"God, that's awful."

Jim laughed. "You'll learn to like it soon enough. It'll just be between us. I promise not to call you that at the club. But I like having a term of endearment for you—stop rolling your eyes, it's no use!"

Colin tried to suppress his smile, but he couldn't. "Affie," he muttered, but then he let out a giggle.

Jim stood up. "Yes. Well, Affie-Taffie, back to work. God, this is wretched; I won't see you until tomorrow night!"

"I know. I'm sorry, Jim. I wish I could see you earlier."

"You're sure you can't?"

Now Colin mulled it over, and finally, he said, "Oh, why not? I'll just go into work on Saturday instead. Come over at six."

"Sharp. What a love! I'll see you then."

"Yes. Goodbye!"

Saturday evening, Colin stopped by his own table first before seeing Jim. "Meredith, how'd you like to go head to head in billiards later on?"

Adam gave him a suspicious look. "What's the bet?"

"No bet. I told Jim last night that I'd teach him how to play, and so we need you and Mike to be the other team."

"We'll kill you!"

"Fine, then. Winner buys a round!"

"Oh, all right. Say... um... did you ever send off that letter to Howard?"

"Yes, on Monday."

"Things seem to be getting pretty serious between you and Pullman."

"Don't start, Adam. Anyway, I've been preparing for him to quit me."

"Why?"

"I dunno. I think this is just a novelty for him. After all, it's not exactly the norm for him, is it? And once the novelty wears off..."

"He's introduced you to his friends, Sewell. What does that tell you?"

"Well, I don't mean it'll happen tonight. In a week or so, perhaps."

"And you want him to?"

"Well, I like him quite a lot, but there's Howard, remember? If Howard comes through, I'll have to end it with Jim."

"And if Howard doesn't?"

Colin paused, and then bowed his head. "I suppose I'd like to still be with Jim," he admitted.

"Well, I was the one who told you to enjoy things as they are until something changes," Adam proclaimed. "So be it."

Colin laughed. "Bless you, Saint Adam. Well, I'm going to go see him. I'll come back to get you later."

Again, Jim's eyes shone when he saw Colin come toward him. Without thinking, he took Colin's hand and drew him close, causing them both to put their hands around each other's waists. To Jim, the new move felt thrilling. To Colin, it felt strange, yet wonderfully familiar. One of the men boomed, "Sewell, what's the big idea, making an honest man out of Pullman?" Jim's friends guffawed and Colin laughed with them.

"I intend to make a sporting one out of him, too."

"Forget it!" Mike said. "He's lucky you're such a good player. I'd say you almost have a chance!"

"Yes, well, I got Meredith to agree that the winner has to buy a round."

"Pah! The devil! For that, I say we go to the table now!"

"Fine with me." Colin turned to Jim. "Are you ready?"

"How can I be ready for something I can't even prepare for?"

"And you say I'm complicated."

The three of them walked over to the billiards room, where Colin motioned Adam over. "Gentlemen, choose your sticks," he announced.

Jim pulled Colin aside. "Here. I was going to give you these later, but perhaps you can use them as good luck. You'll need it with me as your partner." He withdrew his hand from his pocket and held out two ornate silver cufflinks. "They're my father's. And they were his father's..."

"They're heirloom," Colin stared.

Jim nodded. "Yes. I'd like you to have them, Affie."

Colin burst into a grin when he heard his pet name. But then he shook his head. "I couldn't possibly. They're beautiful, but your sons should have them."

"They'll inherit plenty." Jim placed them in Colin's palm and closed his hand around Colin's.

Colin smiled up at him. "Thank you, Jim." He leaned in and gave him a kiss. "I'll put them on now!" He took off the cufflinks he was wearing. "Here, you wear mine. Then we should both have decent luck."

Adam broke, and Colin followed. When it came to be Jim's turn, Colin showed him how to hold the cue stick. "That's good. Now, you'll want to hit that ball over there. Lean over like this..." He half-draped himself over Jim. Then they were cheek to cheek, lining up the ball. "See?"

"Colin?"

"Mm?"

"You smell delicious."

Colin laughed and kissed Jim's cheek. "Isn't billiards fun?"

Watching Adam and Colin bend over the table without their suit jackets caused Mike to turn to Jim and quip, "Lovely game, isn't it?"

Jim sunk the correct ball on his next turn, and Colin was ecstatic. "Fantastic, Jim!" He put his arm around Jim's waist and hugged him. Jim was almost dizzy from the amount of physical contact, as he'd never experienced any while inside the club, in front of everyone. Still, when Colin's turn came up again, Jim sent him off with an encouraging pat on the bottom. Colin hardly noticed, but when he finished, Jim asked in trepidation, "Er... did you mind that?"

Colin grinned. "What, your swat of good luck? I rather liked it." He held his arms out in front of himself. "And I love these cufflinks, Jim! They make me feel like I'm in an old royal court."

"You look like a prince," Jim mused.

Colin's eyes sparkled. "Come on, then, your turn!"

Adam and Mike did win the game. Mike bought the round and Colin kissed his cufflinks. "I still love them," he declared.

An hour and many more drinks later, Colin and Jim bade their group adieu and left. As they stumbled outside, Jim nudged Colin. "Wait until I get you home."

"I may not make it out of the cab," giggled Colin, who had drunk too much champagne.

"Oh? If we have do it in the cab, then *you* have to..." Jim whispered the rest into Colin's ear, and Colin squealed.

"All right! All right!" Colin hailed a cab. "Seventy-first and Fifth Avenue!" he commanded. "Drive slow!"

After ten minutes in the dark coach, Jim pulled Colin up to kiss him and whispered, "I love you, Collie-Aff. So much." He started to cry.

"Oh, Jim..." Colin was too drunk to say any much else.

"I mean it! I love you. I *love* you!" Jim was sobbing now. "What am I going to do?"

"Jim, Jim..." Colin halfway sobered up. He carefully zippered Jim's trousers and put his arm on Jim's shoulder. "It'll be all right." Then he tried to be humorous. "Look! We're two businessmen, remember?" But Jim only wailed. Colin took out his handkerchief. "Please don't cry, Jim. Shh. Shh. Look, now let's not talk anymore. Only hold each other. All right?"

Jim nodded. He blew his nose, wiped his face, and rested his head on Colin, dozing off in his arms.

He loves me, Colin wondered dizzily, as the carriage pitched them along in the darkness. *Goddamn it.*

CHAPTER FORTY

Despite a small feeling of guilt, Colin continued to see Jim every day the following week. They began to talk about going away together, but Jim couldn't think of any excuse to be gone so long. "What about just one day?" Colin asked.

"One day? Where could we go in one day?"

Colin looked pleased with himself. "My house! We could hole ourselves up for the day! You could bring a book to read, or some work to do, and I shall lavish attention upon you as my guest."

"Brilliant!" Jim cried. "I'd love that!" He frowned in thought. "Perhaps we could both take a day off from work... Call in sick, you know. I don't honestly know how I'd get away with a Saturday or Sunday."

"I'll call in sick, but you can't do that—won't Neddy know?"

"That's right. Oh! I'll tell him I'm going Christmas shopping for Laurie!"

"Oh, that's even better! Then *we* can go shopping together! We ought to—you'll need to come home with something, anyway."

"That's wonderful! But we shouldn't be out all day. I'd like to be home with you most of the time."

"Me too," Colin smiled warmly. "It's too bad you still won't be able to spend the night."

"I know, Collie-Aff. I'm sorry. I know how much you'd like that. I would, too."

Colin nodded. He wondered if Jim thought his marriage would become an obstacle that Colin would tire of dodging. In fact, Colin was minding it less than he thought. Two weeks ago, when he spent Thanksgiving with Adam's family, Colin was the most popular grownup with all of the children. By the time he left, his heart was aching to have a child of his own, and he began to wonder: *Maybe I should marry. I could have children, and still be with Jim. In fact, our families could do things together! My wife and Jim's wife could have their tea while the baby's in the nursery. Jim and I could be off in the den...* Colin began to panic over his letter to Howard. *I rushed it! I spoke too soon! If I have Howard, I'll never be able to have children!* But just as quickly, he thought about the idea of having someone to come home to every day. A man he loved, not a woman he tolerated. *Howard would be with me forever and always. Always.* And so Colin was wracked with indecision. *God, just decide for me*, he prayed. *I can't do this on my own.*

Colin also regretted telling Adam about Howard, as Adam had become increasingly disapproving of Colin's relationship with Jim. "You're playing hooky to play house!" he had exclaimed when he found out about their impending day together. "Well now, you're either in love with him or you're not, Sewell."

"Who asked you?" Colin replied sulkily. It was a Sunday, and Adam sat in his usual chair at Colin's home.

"Well, I think you *are* in love with Jim, and I'll bet you haven't even told him, have you? You're too scared."

"Scared of...?"

"Of admitting it! You've already written to Howard, after all."

Colin sighed and sat on the edge of his chair, face in hands. "I know. I keep thinking of how nice it would be to *always* have someone around, like Howard. I mean, do I really want to relegate myself to a life of stolen moments with Jim? We've never even had breakfast together, and we probably never will! It's not as if he's going to divorce his wife and leave her for me. I'm not like a regular mistress."

Adam sighed. "Colin, that's exactly what you are. And men never divorce their wives for their mistresses. Why would they?"

"But then, when I was at Thanksgiving with you, and all of the children, I just... I still want them, Adam. And I can't have children if I have Howard. So I have this ideal vision of me marrying and having a family, and I'd still see Jim. It'd be the best of both worlds."

"Yes, except you're forgetting a very important person."

"Who?"

"Your wife! Colin, marriage isn't a light matter. You know that; it's why you haven't done it all this time. You can't assume that the woman you marry is going to put up with your philandering, and you'll have new responsibilities: a wife, a child, and spent money on both."

"But loads of men do it."

"Loads of men have one-night flings, is all. When they get involved with someone, everyone suffers, somehow. How would you feel if you were married to Jim and you find out he's having an affair with Laurie?"

"Adam..."

"Colin, the point is, even if Laurie never finds out about you and Jim, the potential is always there. And all the while, the time, money, and attention Jim should be spending on his wife, he's spending on you. That's bad enough, from a moral standpoint. But if Laurie ever does find out, she'll be devastated. You told me how shabbily Oscar Wilde treated his wife once he went with Bosie. No woman deserves that, least of all when the mistress is another man!"

Colin shook his head. "That never would have happened if Wilde had just gotten divorced."

Adam was stunned. "You're *Catholic*; how can you say that? And what a thing to do to the children, as well! What do you suppose Wilde's boys think of him?"

"Jim's children are already grown, Adam," Colin argued. "And Jim can't help who he is. He didn't have a choice and now it's just a matter of circumstance. And I certainly don't think his wife is that badly off. She gets anything she wants."

Adam stood up and paced. "Well, let's imagine Jim divorced, or say that you got married, and once you had children, you got divorced. You'd still have to pay your ex-wife alimony, she'll take your children from you, whether your past is found out or not, and then you won't be able to live with them anymore! Of course, there's the scandal of the divorce itself, and you'd be the crux of it, putting a poor woman through a false marriage and then a bitter divorce. All because you wanted everything your way!"

Colin stared at Adam. "My God, I didn't realize you were so against this sort of thing. Don't you think you're taking this all a bit personally?"

Adam crossed his arms. "I *am* taking it personally... because I recently thought about getting divorced myself."

"You?" Colin gasped. "But you've got the perfect life! Tressa's so beautiful, and wonderful! And my God, your children! Adam, your life is the whole reason I've considered marriage!"

"Funny. Your life is the whole reason I've considered divorce."

Adam let the words hang in the air. Then, fearing Colin would get the wrong idea, he said hastily, "Colin, I didn't know how I would ever have gone about life if I didn't get married. Then I met you and heard your story, and I see you going through life just fine. A bit heartsore, but you're true to yourself!" He looked down and sighed. "I'm stuck. I am happy, and I feel very lucky that things didn't turn out too badly, but I know that I can't go back, and here you are, your whole life ahead of you!" Adam shrugged. "I never had the chance to love anyone, and you've loved two men deeply, and now maybe a third, one you could actually spend the rest of your life with.

Whereas men like me may never know love fully at all." He looked at Colin gravely. "You need to appreciate that." Then he paused, a weak smile on his face. "I'm living vicariously through you, if you haven't guessed. So, I'd hate for you to let me down by getting married, Sewell."

Colin turned toward Adam in wonderment. "I can't believe you're saying that. After I gave up so much. I gave up a normal life, Adam. A normal life! God, I wish I could have one."

Adam shrugged. "A life of lies isn't normal, Colin. I don't feel normal. I'm just playing it. But yes, I suppose it's had its rewards. I'm not saying either life is better; that's a matter of personal opinion."

"But then, you *are* saying I should end things with Jim."

"No, not really. That's none of my business and I'm sorry I got into it with you." Adam sighed. "God knows Jim's happier than he's probably ever been, thanks to you. And who's to say his wife isn't benefiting from his improved personality? I'm only saying that, while I understand your desire to have children, Colin, marriage isn't a very good give for the take."

Colin nodded. "You'll be amused to know I prayed for God to sort things out. A pretty cowardly way of going about things, but I'm at my wit's end."

Adam looked at him and smiled. "Well, if He can't figure it out, nobody can. Let's just wait and see."

Colin grinned back. "I'm glad *we're* still friends. That way, if things don't work out with Jim or with Howard, at least I'll still have old Meredith."

Adam rolled his eyes. "Ah yes. Jolly old, good old, decent old Meredith. Pah!" But he smiled at Colin and got up. "I suppose I'd better leave. Enjoy your day of hedonism tomorrow!"

To Colin's delight, snow began to fall on Monday. Jim had arrived early that morning, and Colin brought him to the sitting room, where the fire snapped and crackled and Charlie brought them hot cocoa.

Later on, in the bedroom, Colin lay on the bed in his robe, reading a book and eating chocolates that Jim had brought him, while Jim sat in a chair reading the paper. The snow fell steadily outside. The hearth glowed. *I've never been so happy in all my life,* Jim thought, gazing at Colin and his surroundings. "This is the best vacation I've ever taken!" he declared aloud.

Colin looked up and smiled, and then lolled onto his side. "Isn't it wonderful? Although I think I may have eaten too many chocolates."

Jim got up and went over to the bed. "You've eaten half the box!"

"I can't help it! They're outstanding! Here..." He popped one into Jim's mouth.

"Mm," Jim chewed, looking at Colin. He brought his hand down to stroke Colin's face. "I can't wait to go shopping. I want to see how the snowflakes look on your eyelashes."

"Yes, but here, let's play a bit of cards before I have to get dressed. I'll teach you a game I made up. Oh, wait, not cards. I need a die." He went to retrieve one from his desk and then flopped back onto the bed. "All right, then. Every dot on the die stands for a letter of the alphabet, excluding vowels. So you assign the dots starting with the single dot, which is 'B', then the two dots are 'C' and 'D' and so forth. You first roll the die to determine which side to use, and then you roll it again to choose the letter. For example, if I roll a '3', my letter choices are 'F', 'G', and 'H'. So I roll once more... I got a '6', so I have to roll until I get a '1', '2', or '3'. All right, '3'. So our letter is 'H'. When I say go, we have to take turns saying words beginning with 'H'. The first one who runs out of words has to do what the other person tells them to do." He paused, and then explained, "Obviously, this is a drinking game, done in a group. If you lost, you'd have to take a drink and then the man who went before you gets to pick something you have to do."

"What kinds of things?"

"Oh, small things, mostly involving kissing and the like."

"Colin Sewell! I had no idea!"

Colin grinned. "Oh, it was lots of fun! Of course, half the time, we argued over what letter we were supposed to use, since over the course of the evening our math would turn to slop." He gave the die to Jim. "You roll."

Jim rolled a '5'. "'N', 'P', 'Q', 'R', or 'S,'" Colin announced. "Roll again... A '2'. The letter 'P' it is. Ready? You go first... Go!"

"Peach."

"Pie."

"Piano."

"Pear."

"Pickle."

"Pot."

"Pope."

"Pan."

"Pen."

"Petunia!"

"Pop."

"Pepper."

"Pipe."

"Pitch."

"Pitcher."

"Picture."

"Pan... no, wait, poodle."

"Pine."

"Peter."

"Puh... puh... um..."

"You lose!" Jim crowed.

"Damn."

"Open your robe."

"I'll freeze!"

"Oh, stop whining. Just open the top, then."

Colin sat up and let his robe fall to his waist, and Jim leaned over to kiss his shoulder. "Hmph," Colin disdained. "I'd better win the next round." He took the die and they played again, Colin starting with the letter 'D'.

"Dice."

"Die."

"Dot."

"Door."

"Dim."

"Damn."

"Dip."

"Dab."

"Drum."

"Dance."

"Daub."

"Daub! Diamond."

"Dog."

"Di... da..."

"*Ha!*" Colin shouted. "I would like one long, deep kiss, please."

Jim leaned over on the bed and obliged. Of course, the kiss lasted a long time indeed, and soon Jim ran a hand down Colin's chest and murmured, "I don't want to play anymore, Affie."

Colin leaned back on the bed. "You've got the patience of a gnat," he teased.

"Yes, it's one of my stronger points."

Afterwards the two got dressed and they went out shopping. It was glorious. Jim loved having Colin's companionship, and Colin remembered the old days of when he and Henry would shop together. Colin helped Jim pick out some things for Laurie, for Colin recalled Adam's words, and he told Jim, "We really ought to buy something nice for her." Jim was touched, and he was even happier when Colin told him to leave the store so he could buy a Christmas present for Jim. Jim did the same thing later, eyes shining as he watched the salesman wrap the gift while Colin wandered about in the shop next door.

They walked part of the way back home, regaling in each other's conversation. When they got in a cab for the rest of the trip back, Jim looked at Colin, amused. "Your spectacles have fogged up again."

Colin took them off and sighed irritably. "I know. I hate these things."

"I love them on you."

"Oh, honestly."

"No! It's... well, they're part of what drew me to you, if you must know."

"You're joking."

"I'm not! I've not yet been with a fellow with spectacles. You don't see them too often on young men. And the gold goes with your hair."

"Oh, for heaven's sake!"

"Really! You look so studious. Like a pretty schoolboy."

"Hmph." But Colin smiled, clearly pleased that his glasses weren't a strike against him.

"Have you always worn them?"

"Oh, no. I only needed them several years back." Colin's voice grew bitter. "I strained my eyes working."

"Oh, that's romantic!"

Colin laughed. "Jim, everything is romantic to you!"

"I suppose so." Jim gazed at Colin, whose blond hair brushed his pink cheeks and whose brown eyes looked out brightly at him from under damp lashes. Jim frowned as he struggled to keep his words inside of him. Colin noticed, and a great sadness came over him. Adam was right: he hadn't told Jim that he loved him, and Jim knew it. But for Colin, it still felt too strange to say. And it would mean a total commitment. But there was no doubt about one thing...

"I'm falling in love with this." Colin's voice was low, and he wasn't smiling anymore, nor looking at Jim. Jim glanced up at him and was struck by the young man's troubled expression. He moved to sit next to Colin and put an arm around him.

"I'm sorry," he said in quiet anguish. "I'm sorry you have to put up with me being married, Collie-Aff. I wish I wasn't. I wish I could give you the world."

Colin's eyes watered in spite of himself. "It's all right," he sniffled, embarrassed to be so upset. *Why does it have to be so damn hard? I'm so tired of having to try...*

"Oh God, don't cry, Colin. Please. I love you." Jim brought up his gloved hand to stroke Colin's hair.

Colin turned and buried his face into Jim's coat. "I know," he mourned. "And I'm sorry about that."

"Shh. Why are you sorry? It's not your fault. Well, I guess maybe it is, but 'fault' isn't really the right word, now, is it?"

Colin half-laughed. After a few moments of silence, he whispered, "What are we going to do?"

Jim filled with dread. He had been worried that Colin was going to ask this. "I don't think we can do anything, Affie," he said lightly. "We just have to take things one day at a time, all right?"

Colin nodded. He didn't have any answer, either. "All right."

"Now, we're going back to your house and I'm going to show you how much I love you, hmm?"

"Um-hmm."

And so for the rest of the afternoon the routine was simple: make love, drowse, lounge about, repeat. At six o'clock, Jim said, "The honeymoon is over, alas."

"Alas. But I'll see you tomorrow at lunch?"

"Of course." He kissed Colin goodbye. "We'll do this again soon. It's been one of the best days in my life, Colin."

Colin smiled up at him affectionately. "I loved it too, Jim. I'll see you tomorrow."

As Jim rode in his cab home, he began to feel guilty. *What am I doing? I can't give him what he wants. He's too afraid to even tell me he cares for me, but I know he does. I don't understand. Surely he's not going to ask me to divorce Laurie! I should tell him that I can't, just in case he's thinking about it. Oh, Colin, I hope you're not thinking that. God, but I adore him! And I don't want to lose him either. Pullman! Don't think about it anymore. Take your own advice: one day at a time.*

Four days before Christmas, Jim was in his office when his secretary came in. "Mr. Pullman, there's a Mr. Whittaker here who says he has important personal business to discuss with you."

Jim frowned. The name was unfamiliar. "All right. Send him in." A few moments later, a tall man, not much younger than Jim, entered and closed the door behind him. Jim stood up. "Mr. Whittaker?"

The man came forward and shook his hand, unsmiling. "Yes, Mr. Pullman. How do you do?"

"Fine, I think. Is everything all right?"

"Well... do you mind if we sit down?"

"No, no, of course not."

They sat, and Mr. Whittaker said in a low voice, "Mr. Pullman, I'm a private detective, hired by your wife. She suspected you were having an affair."

"What?"

"Over the past month, I've collected evidence that points to a relationship with one Mr. Colin Sewell."

"A relationship!"

"A physically and emotionally intimate one, yes."

Jim's face burned crimson, and he felt nauseous. "Would you...?" He got up shakily. "I... I need a drink."

"Yes, of course."

Jim poured himself a glass, offering another to Mr. Whittaker, who declined. Jim sat back down. "Umm, how... What kind of evidence are you talking about?"

"Well, rest assured your wife knows nothing about this yet, but I have notes detailing your walks in Central Park, holding hands, kissing, your daily lunches and afternoon outings, the evenings you've spent at his house, your comings and goings together at the Carlisle, displays of affection with each other at the Carlisle—"

"You were at the Carlisle?"

"No, Mr. Pullman. Being a professional investigator, I know how to get this information. Your visits to the Brigand Hotel, and lastly, your spending Monday together at his house and the shopping you did together that day."

"And this is what you'd be telling my wife?"

"I would be obligated to share my findings with her. But in cases like these, I see no point in disrupting the family home, so for a fee I can drop the case and tell your wife I found nothing."

"What's the fee?"

"Five hundred dollars."

"Five hundred dollars! That's outrageous! My God, first my wife uses *my* hard-earned money to hire you, and now I have to spend even more of it to keep you from giving her what she paid for?"

Mr. Whittaker blinked. "I suppose it's your choice, Mr. Pullman."

"But how can I even trust you not to tell her anyway after I pay you?"

"You'll just have to, I'm afraid. I have no personal or financial gain in telling her the truth, and I hardly think I'd still be in business if I'd ever gone back on my word."

"Oh God." Jim opened the drawer of his desk. "I suppose you'd take a bank check."

"Sorry. Cash only."

"What? Well, I haven't got five hundred dollars in my pocket!"

"I understand, Mr. Pullman. I'll come back tomorrow, same time."

Jim rubbed his face. "Did my wife mention why she thought I was having an affair?"

"Yes. She said you'd been unusually happy the past month. Giddy, even. Yet with her you were detached, distracted, and you were coming home at odd hours, whereas apparently when you were attending your clubs, you were always home at nine on the dot." He paused. "She also noticed a pair of diamond and sapphire cufflinks you suddenly had, which she had never seen before, and she didn't think you bought them yourself. She said they weren't your style."

Colin's cufflinks.

"And that's all it took for her to suspect?"

"Yes. If it's any help, Mr. Pullman, you weren't the first case like this, and you won't be the last."

Jim was too humiliated to even respond. *This complete stranger knows that I've been living a deviant lifestyle! Oh God, help me.* He looked at his desk in misery. "So, what *are* you going to tell my wife?"

"I'll tell her that you definitely don't have a mistress, and that you've just been spending more time with your friends. I'll tell her she needs to talk to you, and then *you* should tell her you've been having problems dealing with getting older, that you want to make the most out of life and recapture those old glory days when you were a bachelor. That sort of thing. Then promise you'll spend more time with her, and do so."

Jim nodded. "And the cufflinks?"

"If she brings them up, say you won them in a poker game. You could even offer to reset the stones into jewelry for her."

"All right. But... what about Mr. Sewell? Will he be safe?"

"Yes. He knows nothing and I have no intention of seeing him. But I'm afraid *you* must stop seeing him, Mr. Pullman. No more lunches, afternoon visits, and certainly no more tête-à-têtes at the hotel, his home, or the Carlisle. You mustn't be seen together at all. Otherwise, your wife may continue to have her suspicions and hire another investigator. One who may be less inclined to come to you first, as I'm doing."

"But I love him!" The words burst out before Jim could stop himself.

"That may be, Mr. Pullman. And if so, you must protect him as well as yourself. You understand that."

Jim nodded miserably. "Yes. Yes, of course."

"Good. Then I'll be going. I'll see you here tomorrow." Another nod. "Good day, Mr. Pullman."

Jim sat in his office for the next twenty minutes, struggling to think, but his mind reduced itself to buzzing. Suddenly, he jumped up, grabbed his coat, hat, and gloves, and strode out the door. "I'll be gone the rest of the afternoon," he called out to his secretary. "I have to deliver something."

As soon as he was a block from the office, he began to run. God, he was sprinting! *Path, path, find the path.* He wove in and out, down one street, down another. Left. Right. Two more blocks. Two more... *Thank God.* He flung open the door at McKim, Mead, & White and looked around. "I'm sorry," he panted. "Is Mr. Sewell in?"

One of the draftsmen began walking to the back of the office, "Yes, sir, I'll get him for you."

"Thank you. It's Jim Pullman. I must see him!"

Colin emerged from his office and stopped when he saw Jim, his own expression mirroring Jim's horrified one. He grabbed his coat and hat, telling the men in the office, "I'll be back later."

Jim said nothing until they had turned the corner. Then he took Colin's hand and began to run. "Jim!" Colin panicked. "What's going on?"

"Please," Jim urged. "Please, Colin!" They ran all the way to the Brigand Hotel, and then they ran inside. "A room," Jim gasped to the front desk clerk. "First floor. Please."

The clerk uncertainly handed over a key. "There you are, sir."

"Thank you." Jim pulled Colin along, down the hall, unlocked the door, swept Colin inside, shut and locked the door, and embraced a breathless Colin tightly, almost swinging him off the floor. "I can't see you anymore!" He sobbed, hugging the young man in front of him.

"What?" Colin tried to pull away.

Jim sank onto the bed and told Colin what had just happened at the office. Colin grew hysterical. "Who the hell ratted on us at the Carlisle?"

"I don't know!"

"Oh my God, this man knew everything! He fucking spied on us!"

"I know, Colin!" It took Jim several minutes to calm Colin down somewhat and reassure him that nobody else knew.

"So, what are we supposed to do?" Colin asked, wringing his hands.

"We have to stop seeing each other," Jim said sadly. "If we don't, the detective thinks my wife may hire another one, and we may not be so lucky next time."

"*Lucky!* How much is his extortion fee?"

"Never mind that."

Colin burst into tears. "But you can't pay it alone, Jim! I won't let you! It's my fault that this happened as much as it is yours!" He fumbled in his coat pocket for his billfold and then took out all of his money.

"Colin, stop it..."

"Here... here, I've got... damn it, ten dollars. That's nowhere near enough; oh my God, how much is it? I'll write a check..." He feverishly pulled out his pocketbook.

"Affie, stop." Jim grabbed him gently and looked up at him. "Honey, you can't write a check. It'll be evidence." Colin looked down at him, dazed. Jim stood up and held him again. "It'll be all right, darling. It will."

"But... but..."

"Shh." Jim withdrew himself slightly and dried Colin's face with his handkerchief. "We're going to be fine. I'd never let anything happen to you, you know that."

Colin relaxed and sighed. "I know."

"Now look: I know this isn't the best of moods, but I figure we've got one last time. Right here. To hell with all of them, all right?"

Colin nodded, resigned, "God, I just can't believe it." Then he gave a sniffly laugh. "I liked how you came into the hotel, though."

Jim chuckled. "Can you imagine if it had been the same clerk?" They both laughed, and Jim began undressing Colin tenderly. "If I was ten years younger, I'd run off to France with you," Jim murmured.

"If I was ten years younger, I'd have gone with," Colin replied warmly. Then he stopped unbuttoning Jim's shirt and smiled at him. "But I'm glad we aren't. It's better this way."

He put his arms around Jim's neck and kissed him deeply, while Jim let Colin's trousers slide to the floor. He felt Colin's shirttails brush his hands. "I'll always love you anyway, Affie."

"And I, you," Colin's voice was muffled, but insistent. And he meant it. Now, he meant it.

CHAPTER FORTY-ONE

Christmas arrived. At the last minute, Colin declined the invitation from Adam to spend the day with his family. Now that Jim was gone, only Howard remained, and so Colin didn't dare spend any time with children. As he sat looking out his window that afternoon, he remembered why he had latched onto Jim so eagerly: he had been lonely. Now he would be lonely again, more so because he had decided to refrain from going to the Carlisle. He couldn't stand the thought of being there, since every man he saw could be the mysterious informant who helped to end it all. And he would have to ignore Jim. But as difficult as it would be to give up the Carlisle, Colin knew his weekdays would be even worse. Now he would have to eat lunch alone. Now he would have to go straight home after work or, on occasion, to his businessmen's club, where the sight of so many men living their happy, normal lives would depress him further.

And here it was, Christmas Day. Colin sat staring at his present for Jim. *I can't even give it to him, ever.* Colin wondered if today would be easier for his former lover, with his family festivities to keep him preoccupied.

Jim was miserable. Normally, Christmas was his favorite holiday, but today he had to struggle to put on a good show to the extended family gathered at his house. His wife hadn't said a word about anything pertaining to his suspected affair, and he hoped to God she was just waiting until the guests had left, and not because the detective hadn't yet spoken to her. Meanwhile, he couldn't let on that *he* knew anything, and therefore he was unsure if he should continue to act like his former, unusually happy self or if it was all right to resume his somber "before-the-affair" appearance. He wished he were Colin, who didn't have to act for anybody's sake today. He wondered how things were going at the Meredith estate. The gift box in his drawer came to mind. *I have to get rid of it. But how? I wish he could have it today.* Then, out of the blue, Jim realized he could do it. *Of course! It's a man's gift! Laurie couldn't suspect a thing! I'll send it to Meredith and write a letter directing him to give it to Colin!* Grinning, he excused himself to go upstairs.

"What's the ecstasy all about?" his brother Sam joked.

"Oh!" Jim laughed. "I felt I was forgetting something all day, and I finally remembered what it was!" He was careful not to leap up the staircase.

He quickly sat at his desk, wrote two quick notes, and then retrieved the box from a drawer in his armoire. He looked for Laurie before finding the delivery boy. "Lor, I almost forgot to send this off to Adam Meredith. I'll be right back."

"Adam Meredith?"

"Yes, he's the son of Robert Meredith, the factory owner, remember? He had expressed an interest in a large advertisement campaign using us, and I don't want him to forget it."

He could tell Laurie was studying the box, wanting desperately to ask after its contents. Jim proudly lifted the box. "See? A silk scarf, a key ring, and a pair of gloves."

Laurie's eyes widened, but she sighed with a laugh. "Goodness, he must be a very big fish to land!"

"Unfortunately, yes. We'll see what happens."

"All right, dear."

Jim hurriedly sent it off and wanted to shout his victory. *He'll get it! He'll get it today! The one diamond moment in this filthy coal mine of days!*

When Adam was summoned to the delivery boy, he opened the letter addressed to him.

Please give this to Mr. Sewell. Much thanks. –J.P.

Adam's face fell. "Oh, Mr. Sewell was unable to make it today. But here, let me give you a reply, and I'll have my delivery boy take it to his home." So Jim's delivery boy was sent back with a note.

Recipient not here. At home. Forwarded gift with delivery boy. V. decent of you.

–M.

Colin jumped at the sound of the doorbell. He almost beat Charlie to the door. "Package for Mr. Sewell," the boy said.

Colin's eyes lit up. "Please, come inside for a few minutes. I'm sure I'll have a reply. Charlie, take the boy into the kitchen until I return."

Colin clutched the box to his chest as he went to his bedroom. He sat in the very chair Jim had sat in just two weeks ago. There was an envelope inside. It had been folded three times, as if it previously had been in someone's pocket.

To Mr. C.S.

He opened it.

Merry Christmas, Colin! I haven't stopped thinking of you. I miss you terribly. It's miserable here. I'm so glad to give these to you today. I'll think of how you look with them. That will help. Love, Jim

Colin unfolded the blue velvet cloth and lifted each gift out. The first was a beautiful forest-green silk scarf. The next, an 18-k gold Tiffany key chain. And last were a pair of dark brown lambskin gloves, buttery soft and lined with red fox. *Oh, they're lovely, Jim!* He thought of his own present and had an idea. *I'll send it to Meredith, and tell him to send it to Jim, but pretend it to be from Meredith. A business gift of sorts!* He went to his desk and scribed a letter:

Adam,

Please send this on. It's to look like a gift to J.P. from you. "Business." Thank you.

Indebted,
C.S.

Then the other:

Jim,

Thank you for the gifts. They are of supreme quality. I hope to see you soon to properly thank you.

"A.M."

He prayed Jim would understand the ruse, and he wished he could have written more. He took the letters downstairs and carefully tucked one letter in his gift and gave the other to the messenger boy. "Thank you so much for waiting. These are to be given to Mr. Meredith."

When Adam saw the boy return with a gift, he muttered, "Oh boy..." He read the letter and couldn't help smiling. "*I'll* say you're indebted, Sewell. OK Nicky, take this on to Mr. Pullman."

Jim, who was content enough to learn earlier that his present would be sent on, was still saddened to think of Colin spending the day by himself. When he was told there was a message for him at the door, he felt euphoric again.

A box! Gift-wrapped! Colin, you're playing the game! Good boy!

The messenger bowed. "Mr. Meredith wishes to thank you for your generosity. He'd like you to have this in return."

"Thank you," Jim scrupulously took the gift upstairs and hid it in a drawer in his bedroom. He wanted desperately to open it, but he forced himself to go back downstairs.

The next day, while Laurie was in her room preparing for breakfast, Jim closed the door to his bedchamber and took out his presents. From the box, he lifted a crisp, white sateen dress shirt. Then an Italian silk tie, dark blue, and finally, a silver bar tie clip from Tiffany's, with a sapphire at its end.

Underneath was Colin's letter, and when Jim picked it up, tears welled in his eyes: the letter was scented with Colin's cologne. Jim held it up against his face, kissing it and inhaling its lavender fragrance. When he was able, he opened the letter and read it. *Oh, Colin.* "A.M." *indeed. Thank God you're so clever. I miss you. So much.*

Jim held the letter to his lips again, then stood up to get dressed. *I could wear the shirt and tie—I'll tell Laurie I bought them especially for today. But the tie clip...* Jim had forgotten to tell Colin about his giveaway cufflinks: Jim never wore gemstones. *I'll put the clip away as a keepsake.* He carefully folded it up in its velvet cloth case. Then he dressed rapturously and, in a moment of inspiration, pressed Colin's letter to his wrists. Any time he wanted to remember, he'd need only to run his hand through his hair or rest his head on his chin. He would make it through today.

The day after Christmas was a Saturday, so Jim went to the Carlisle. He was worried when he didn't see Colin anywhere, so he looked for Adam.

"Jim!" Adam exclaimed. "You're back!"

"Well, I've come here every Saturday for the past ten years, so I thought it'd appear even stranger if I didn't keep the same hours. But Colin's not here, is he?"

Adam shook his head. "No. He's still too upset. That one holds a grudge the likes I've never seen, although I can't really blame him. He knows he's not supposed to be seen with you, though, and keeping his distance from you would be too hard for him."

"Is that what he said?"

"Yes. He said he wasn't brought up to ignore people like that, and he can't do it."

Jim nodded sadly. "The poor thing. Oh, and thank you, by the way, for acting as our go-between on Christmas."

Adam smiled. "It's nothing. I'm glad you both got to exchange gifts after all."

Jim sat down next to him. "Well, do you have any suggestions? I'm having a hard time facing this myself."

Adam sighed. "Well, Colin said he's not coming back to this place for as long as he can tolerate it, but that's the stupidest thing I've ever heard, and I told him so. For everyone's benefit, the sooner he comes back, the better. And I think you two need to meet one more time—for lunch only—to decide how you can both proceed without hurting each other."

Jim stared at him. "Quite a voice of reason coming from one so detached from the sensual world!"

Adam laughed. "And that's why." He looked at Jim. "You're a strong man, Pullman. Sewell's quite a magnet."

"Which means you must be even stronger," Jim quipped. "Blessed are the married men!"

Adam raised his glass. "Cursed!" He laughed. "But I'll drink to that!"

On Monday, Colin received a post at work.

Please be at Dolci at 12 sharp. I'll be bringing my son. Trust me.

--J.P.

At twelve noon, Colin was seated at a table inside the restaurant. To play it safe, he looked at the menu and ordered. At 12:15 p.m., a voice came from behind. "Mr. Sewell! Fancy seeing you here!"

Colin turned. "Why, Mr. Pullman!" He stood up and shook Jim's hand.

"This is my son, Neddy."

"How do you do, Neddy?" Colin shook Neddy's hand.

Jim smiled. "Won't you join us at our table?"

Colin demurred. "Oh, I don't want to trouble you."

"Mr. Sewell, it would be an honor," Neddy insisted.

Colin regarded the eager, kind face of Neddy Pullman and thanked God for making the decision He did. "Well then, I would love to join you. I'm alone today, and some company would be most welcome."

Neddy looked as though he would burst. Colin supposed he was a bit in awe of Colin's pedigree, as well as his haberdashery, which probably was more decadent than what a printing firm would allow. They all sat down, and after Jim and Neddy ordered, they had a pleasant conversation. At the end of the meal, Jim told his son, "Someone needs to be back at the firm. I'd like to discuss something with Mr. Sewell. Would you mind, Neddy?"

"No, of course not," Neddy stood up. "Again, it was an honor to have met you, Mr. Sewell."

Colin stood too, enamored of Jim's favorite son. "The honor was mine. You've done right by your father, Neddy. He must be very proud to have such a fine son by his side."

Neddy blushed and stammered a "Thank you." He left, and Colin sat back down.

"I could kiss you, you know," Jim said gratefully.

Colin sighed, shaking his head. "You're brilliant, Jim. A brilliant idea."

"It was Mr. Meredith's idea, remember." Adam had told Colin the plan during yesterday's Sunday visit.

Colin nodded. "I suppose we'll just have to go back to how things were before we met each other."

Jim looked at him searchingly. "Is that all right with you?"

Colin looked up in surprise. "Well, that's very kind of you to ask for permission, when we really haven't any other choice."

Jim looked sad. "No, we don't." Then his voice was quiet. "I want you to know that it's been difficult, Colin. I miss you."

Colin couldn't look at him. "I miss you too, Jim." He took a breath. "But, the sooner we get past this, the better. In fact, I insist you take up with the first boy you lay your eyes on this coming Saturday!"

"Colin…"

"Well, they say the best way to get over a man is to get under one."

"I don't know. I'm certainly not in the mood for that, any time soon."

"I know," Colin admitted. "I'm not, either. To be honest, there are two friends of mine from London who will be visiting next June. I've decided to just re-direct myself toward one of them."

The comment stung Jim. "Oh."

Colin mentally kicked himself. He leaned across the table. "Jim, I don't know how else I'm to get over you. Half of me prepared for you to quit me; the other half prepared to spend my life with you. Well, it was decided for us, and you can't say you didn't think it would be. At least, a part of you. But I'm not going to spend one minute regretting our affair, and neither should you. You're always saying 'To hell with them', and now I'm saying it: to hell with them! We had a wonderful affair, and we had it in its prime. Perhaps it couldn't have lasted, but we'll never know that. As far as we're concerned, it could have. It was 'The Grand Affair.'"

"'The Grand Affair,'" Jim murmured. "I had a Grand Affair." He smiled at Colin. "I'd like to send a drink over to you, from time to time."

"I would love that. You see, that's perfect. I may do the same, if you don't mind."

Jim chuckled. "Not at all. By the way, I wore your gifts the day after Christmas, including the cologne on your letter."

"Really? I went for a walk Christmas Day with your gloves and scarf! And I put my keys on your key ring!" Childishly, Colin produced his keys as proof.

Jim gazed at them. "I'm glad you liked the gifts."

"You have excellent taste," Colin remarked.

Jim stood up, smiling. "That flatters us both. As it should."

It was only five days later that Colin decided to go back to the Carlisle. This night, however, Jim wasn't there, and neither was Adam. It was New Year's Eve, and no married men were present. Instead of sitting at his usual table, Colin sat with Jonathan at the bar. "It's so different, isn't it?" he wondered, looking around the half-empty, yet still noisy club.

Jonathan nodded. "But it's still so much the same."

Colin noticed that the absence of married men made him one of the oldest ones in the club. *Damned twenty-year-olds.* Although Colin had to grudgingly admit they were nice to look at. Before long, one of them sat down next to Colin. "Buy you a drink, Mr. Sewell?"

Colin was surprised. "Oh, I'm fine, thank you." Then he smiled. "If anything, I should be buying you a drink, shouldn't I? What are you having?"

"Gin and bitters."

Colin eyed him. "You're joking."

"I *like* gin!"

"Hmph. A little lowbrow for you. You look more the Grand Marnier type."

"Well, what are *you* drinking? No wait, let me guess." Colin passed him his drink. The boy sniffed it. "Gin!" He took a sip and grinned. "And bitters!"

"Hmm." Colin turned to the bartender. "Chambord and champagne, please." Then he turned to the boy. "What's your story, then?"

"I'm a bartender at the Hudson Club."

"Really? No college for you?"

"Oh, yes. I'm finishing my final year."

"Studying...?"

"Business. I can't wait to be done. How long have you been an architect, Mr. Sewell?"

"Almost ten years. It seems hardly long at all, though. And yet, it feels like half my life."

"Would you mind if I made you a drink?"

Colin regarded the boy. He had a smart look about him. It was clear he intended to stay as long as Colin wanted him to, but he also wouldn't care if he was asked to leave. Jonathan had found someone to talk to as well, so Colin smiled. "I should very much like to see what you come up with."

"All right, then!" The boy jumped up and went to go behind the bar. Colin watched him busy himself showing off, and soon he proudly placed a drink before him.

Colin peered into the glass. "What is it?"

"Just a brandy cocktail."

"Will it kill me?"

"Oh, I don't think so. Go on!"

Colin took a cautious sip. "Well! This is really quite good!"

"Isn't it? There's maraschino, bitters, brandy, and, because you so wisely mentioned earlier, curacao, in the form of our dearly beloved Grand Marnier."

Colin crossed his arms on the bar. "Impressive. All right then, let's see you make a drink for yourself." He gazed at the boy's slender body as he turned away and reached for two bottles. He came from behind the bar and sat next to Colin again.

"This is called a Port and Starboard. This is crème de menthe. It floats on top of the grenadine. Try it."

Colin did. It was delicious. "So, I know the brandy cocktail and the Port and Starboard. What do you call yourself?"

The boy laughed. "My name is Will. Sorry."

"Oh, it doesn't matter. I mean...!"

But Will thought this was even funnier. "No, you're right, I suppose! It doesn't really matter." He batted an eye at Colin, who decided he'd better drink damn fast if he was going to keep up this charade until midnight. He took a cigarette from his case and offered one to Will, who took it graciously. "I'm glad to see you're back, Mr. Sewell."

"It's Colin. And thank you. I can't say I'm all too thrilled about it."

Will looked pleased. "It's a very symbolic gesture."

Colin was puzzled. "Letting you call me by my first name?"

"No," Will laughed. "Your being here on New Year's Eve! 'Start a new year and leave behind your fears.'"

"You *are* a bartender."

"And *you* are reportedly a very successful architect." Will tilted his head back. "I hear you're very rich."

"Is that so?" Colin smiled. "And what do you think?" *I cannot believe it! I am now Henry! And Howard!*

"Oh, I think you must be. I think you're so rich, you don't have to pay for your company."

"And if I agree, what happens to you?"

"Why, I stay on! *I'm* enjoying myself thoroughly! In fact, I think I shall make you another surprise drink."

Colin exhaled. *Since when do the boys get the men drunk?* When he tried the second drink, he made a face. "Ugh. This is strong!"

"It's peppermint schnapps, with a bit of brandy."

"A bit indeed! How many shots of schnapps are in this glass?"

"Never you mind." But only two minutes later, he looked at Colin's drink and giggled. "You've already finished it! You'll regret that."

Colin felt as if he suddenly stepped off a train platform. "Regret is not the foremost feeling right now, I'm afraid." The noise in the room increased fivefold. He tilted his head woozily at Will. "So, what *are* you doing here, by the way?"

"Trying to pair up with you!"

"Tonight?"

"Mm. New Year's Eve, midnight kiss and all that."

"If we don't pass out by then."

"We won't. Get some seltzer."

"You get it!" Colin giggled. He could hardly see straight.

"Very well!" Cigarette dangling from his mouth, Will hopped over the bar and retrieved two glasses.

Colin didn't remember the next forty-five minutes, but then it was one minute to midnight, and Will stood up. "Put out your cigarette. And stand up!"

Colin swayed off the barstool. "Bossy little bartender, aren't you?"

Everyone counted down, and at the stroke of twelve, it was "Happy New Year!" Candles were snuffed, and Colin felt Will's mouth on his own, Will's hands on his hips, behind his hips, in front of his hips. Colin's hands on Will's chest. Will graphically urgent in Colin's ear. Colin whispering back a fierce "Yes!" The two men fumbling to get a cab. The two men fumbling in the cab. Colin stumbling out later at his house, going inside, throwing up, and eventually falling asleep on the floor.

It was 1901.

Adam visited at four o'clock on New Year's Day. Colin, still in pajamas, almost didn't see him.

"Christ, Sewell! Are you dead?"

"Please..." Colin winced. "Too loud." He gingerly sat on the couch.

"You're not even wearing your spectacles."

"They hurt too much. God, your voice..."

"Sorry. So what did you do? Drink to forget?"

"I did forget, mostly..." Colin's voice was hoarse. "I met a boy there."

"You did? Who?"

"Will... William... Wuh... I don't know."

Adam began to laugh, and then clamped his hand over his mouth. "Will, that lovely bartender boy? The business student? Dark hair, blue eyes?"

"Yes, right."

"Oh Colin, you didn't! Did you kiss him at midnight?"

"Mm."

Adam was gleeful. "Did he go home with you?"

Colin laid a hand over his eyes. "We took a cab."

"You screwed him in a cab?" Adam was hopping about.

"Adam..."

"Oh, this is too much!"

"Yes, well, then I came home, got sick all night long, and finally fell asleep sometime this morning."

"Oh." Adam's shoulders slumped and he said sadly, "You had ever so much more fun than I did." Then he paused. "Do you think Jim will be mad?"

"Jim? Well, I don't plan to tell him, for heaven's sake!"

"But he'll find out, Sewell."

Colin shrugged tiredly. "Well then, so what if he does? He shouldn't care. It was nothing. It was worth nothing."

"Well, he might get awfully jealous. He might think it's awfully soon after your parting ways."

"Oh God, it wasn't anything like that," Colin grimaced. "I barely remember it. It was New Year's Eve, after all. Just a stupid one-night thing that I already regret. We're supposed to get over each other, anyway."

"Yes, but sometimes that's easier said than done. Anyway, you may be right. Hope so."

They found out the next Saturday. Colin entered the club, a bit embarrassed to have to acknowledge Will, but it was only proper. As a gesture of kindness, he took over the boy's tab that evening and then went to sit with Adam. He hadn't yet looked in Jim's direction. "How does Jim look?" he asked Adam in a low voice.

"Er... he looks pretty upset," Adam admitted. "Maybe you should go talk to him."

"I can't do that! We're not supposed to! God, why can't he just let go?" But the minute he said the words, he felt guilty. *The man told me he loved me. And he did. And in one week I managed to turn around and welcome in the New Year with a complete stranger in a cab. That's low, Sewell.* Colin took a deep breath. "I guess I'll just wait and see if he comes over here. He can take the risk, not me." And so Colin tried to relax and enjoy his table's company. In thirty seconds, he saw Jim approach out of the corner of his eye. He looked up. Jim's mouth was furious, but his eyes showed hurt.

Colin started to stand. "Jim..." he began, but before he knew it, a full glass of brandy was thrown upon him.

"Here's to your 'Grand Affair', Sewell!" Jim hissed as he slammed the glass on the table and stormed out of the club.

Colin was devastated. The club fell to a hush, and he dropped his shoulders in defeat while Adam tried to mop him up with linen napkins. He couldn't run after Jim. That would be all they'd need: a scene outside in the street. "I'm fine," he told Adam as he took off his glasses. "Just leave it. I'll have it cleaned."

"God, Colin..."

"Well, you called it." Colin sighed. "It's probably all very well that he's mad at me; perhaps now he'll be done with it." But Colin's heart was breaking. It wasn't in his nature to ignore Jim's action. He already was planning in his head a letter of apology, or another lunch meeting.

"Don't even think of it," Adam warned, reading his mind.

"But he's distraught," Colin protested. "I can't have the man go on with his life thinking I cared so little, Adam!"

"You most certainly can. Look here, Colin, this is life. It's hard and you know it. There was even a rumor going 'round that Jim was thinking of divorcing his wife and taking up with you! Personally, I don't believe it, but if that's not what you want, you've got to sever yourself from him! There's no saying that we can't spread the word how sorry you were. Now be strong!"

"Right, right," Colin agreed miserably. "I can't believe he'd get divorced, either. And I wouldn't want the scandal, anyway." As he dried himself off and prepared to leave, he muttered, "All I have to say for this night is, that damned Howard better come through."

After that dreadful evening, Colin stopped going to the Carlisle entirely. "I'm done with it," he said irritably to Adam. "The dramatics in that place make me ill. Maybe I'll go back in a few months, but to be honest, I just don't care for that scene anymore."

"Well, you'll be doing Jim a favor," Adam sighed, after trying to change Colin's mind.

"Then that's the least I can do."

But unfortunately, later that afternoon, Colin remembered something: the heirloom cufflinks. *I can't possibly keep those anymore; it wouldn't be right. I should offer them to him, but how?* In the end, he gave the cufflinks to Adam, who agreed to take them to the club that week.

Jim, Colin learned, took them back without question and with a derogatory word. And it was then that Colin couldn't help it. He stormed off a letter.

I can't believe you think I cared so little for you that I would purposely do something that would hurt you! And so I am deeply sorry that I did. But if you plan to allow anger to be the end result of what things were, then we lost, Jim. And I am sorry for that, too. However, your actions have spoken, and for that, I am most sorry of all.

He gave the letter to Adam. Shortly thereafter, a post arrived at Colin's house. It was a small package. Colin opened it and drew in his breath. It was the tie bar he had given Jim. And a note.

Since we are giving back gifts... I haven't any use for this either. I too am sorry, Colin. I am sorry that you are capable of such unfeeling. I am sorry you took us so lightly. You didn't understand and I thought you did. I don't think either of us should speak to each other anymore, and that goes for writing as well. You can *understand that, can't you?*

Thankfully, two days later Howard's response finally arrived. At five o'clock in the evening Colin was staring at the large package on his desk. *This is it.* The label on the box was addressed plainly enough and gave no indication of the contents. Colin began to knife through the string. He opened the flaps and saw a purple-wrapped box inside, tied with a gauze ribbon. He checked to make sure nothing else was in the box and untied the bow. Inside was a smaller, wrapped package and a cream-colored envelope.

Normally Colin never opened a gift before reading the card, but this was an exception. He carefully tore open the wrapping.

It was a book—*Leaves of Grass*. Colin smiled and opened to the inside cover.

W. Whitman, 1879

Colin gasped. *How did Howard find this?* He stared at the signed book and ran his thumb over the embossed leather cover. He gently put it on the desk and proceeded to the letter.

25 December 1900

Dear Colin,

Your guess was correct. I could not believe your words meant what they did. Today is the Merriest Christmas of my entire life! While I intended to wait until June to tell you of my feelings, I feared someone would sweep you off your feet before that, as someone has, and so I tried to make my intentions a bit more obvious. I just didn't know how to say such a thing in a letter, and once again, you have succeeded where most men could not.

Colin, I absolutely rue the day I said what I did to you in my office. You must understand that I felt I had to preserve my dignity. It is interesting though that if I hadn't felt so guilty about that incident, I may have never written that first letter to you! That first letter was meant to make up for my transgression.

Colin, read To You. Read Quicksand Years. Read A Noiseless, Patient Spider. Read O Me! O Life! Read as I Lay With My Head in Your Lap, Song of the Open Road, Sometimes With the One I Love. Read Of the Terrible Doubt, I Heard You, and One Hour to Madness and Joy. They are all about us! You are all I can think about when I read those poems. You, and Whitman, and how on earth he knew he wrote for us.

You said all of your memories of us are burned into your mind. That you remember our first stroll through Hyde Park! The day I officially fell for the handsome young architect beside me. It was 3rd May 1891, and I'm ashamed to admit that I have never fully recovered since. In any case, our shared history is something few men are ever so fortunate to have, and I too do not take it lightly.

I know anything can happen between now and June, and even then there will be obstacles to overcome. And perhaps we should agree that if things don't work out, that we will be gentlemen about it. However, if your offer to wait still stands, I will take it with all of my heart.

This is clearly the most frightfully melodramatic thing I've ever written, and rest assured, this entire situation is far more embarrassing to me than it is to you, given that I have just admitted to having a ten-year infatuation! While I have a feeling this is not really a surprise to you, I don't envy you having to respond to such a revelation, and I envy myself even less for having to read your reply. What will it say?

Well, as I have told you, "Nothing ventured, nothing gained." Giddy fatalism indeed! I hope you had a most wonderful Christmas and New Year's. If you can't bring yourself to address the contents of this letter, then you may tell me what you did over the holidays. And Colin, thank you so much for the amazing framed rendering of my bank! I have it hanging in my office, and people have been exclaiming over it, for it is a true work of art. Still, your letter was the best gift I have ever received. I wish I could frame it and hang it in my office! Happy 1901, Fearless! I hope the next century proves to be even more fortuitous than the last.

Fondly,
Howard

January 12, 1901

Dear Howard,

It is a long way to June, so I am going to go slow with this letter, but know that it is difficult.

Yes, I will wait! I am so glad that we are of like minds after all, although that shouldn't surprise me. You always understood me better than anyone, even Y.K.W. I am still coming to terms with the fact that you've felt that way about a certain someone *for so long*—it saddens me to think you had to suffer so. And that you felt that a certain someone *was worth it*. For you must understand Howard that the reality may not match the fantasy. Given the span of ten years now, it is unlikely to do so, I'm afraid. But never mind that for now—I like your proposal to agree that we will be civilized toward each other if things do not turn out as planned, although I think that will be more your decision than mine. Remember, you know me well. But let us not show much more than this in our letters. If not for our safety, then for our meeting to not be quite so awkward. You are right—there are matters of practicality we will have to discuss, but I, for one, look forward to finally speaking to you in plain English rather than this doublespeak we must write.

 Howard, wherever did you find a signed copy of Leaves of Grass? It is a treasure, my most favorite! I never would have imagined you to see so much of yourself in Whitman as I do me. And perhaps you felt the connection even more strongly. I was so taken with your poetry selections. I read each one of them right after I read your letter. I read them with your eyes, your voice. It is perhaps the most romantic thing that has ever happened to me. Thank you very much. I am glad you liked my gift, too.

 My holidays were all right. Did you see your family? Did London get any snow? We have about five inches presently. Let me go back to your second-to-last letter... My goodness! Given the current turn of events, many of the points you made in your letter are now moot! (Allow me to momentarily indulge in the pleasure of knowing why...) Well, I do certainly anticipate teaming up with you at billiards! In honor of your (and Kenneth's) visit, I've decided to finally turn my attention to decorating my own house. I suppose this will be the only reason to be thankful that I've six months before seeing you. Do you have a favorite color, Howard? I have an idea, you see, so I'd like to know. I'll bet that it is brown. Now, I've never met anyone whose favorite color is brown, but if there ever was such a person, it'd be you! When I think of you, all I see is brown. Your bank desk. The leather chair you sit in when you work. Your pipe. Your tobacco. Your suits. Your beard, your eyes, the color of your hair. Even the whiskey you drink! Everything is a symphony of mahogany and maple, oak and walnut.

My own favorite color is blue, the deep royal-blue kind. Blue so deep you can dive into it; it will swallow you up. It doesn't really make any sense because I don't use it much at all in my designs, nor is it the best color on me. It just seems to be the most infinite of all the colors.

In other news, I have been made partner at my firm! You can imagine their befuddlement when my only request was for my last name to not be added to theirs. Given what some parties think happened to me once I arrived here, I can't risk such an obvious giveaway. It is a bit difficult, admittedly, having to recede into the shadows as it were, but eventually I'll be able to come forth again, and likely by then, on my own.

I have picked up another project! Actually, it is a collaborative effort. The partners have asked for my input on the department store they're designing. I told them, "Put me in charge of designing the lobby. That's what I want to do." So I'm working on that. It's a damn shame that things like fire codes and tornadoes have to get in the way of creativity! Still, I feel I acquired victory—the lobby is the first thing people see upon entering, after all, and I am going to make this one spectacular! I must admit I have gotten a lot of inspiration lately from several groups: Art Nouveau (mainly a young man named Charles Rennie Macintosh), Secessionists (out of Vienna), and this Frank Lloyd Wright fellow in Chicago.

Wouldn't you know, I've run out of steam. Dull lives lead to dull letters. Won't you please visit an opium den, or how about Montmartre in general? I will always regret not going there when I had the chance, at least once, just to see it for myself. It was funny how Y.K.W. could be so lurid in some ways yet so priggish in others. By the way, it was kind of you to tell me what he said about me that evening when the three of you reminisced. But I am well aware that the Colin he remembered with such fondness is a Colin who no longer exists, and you would do well to remind yourself the same. I am sure he has told you the realities about me, and I myself must warn you that I don't play that clever bit anymore. It's odd how it was so much an act on my part, and yet I find myself falling back on it so frequently. I suppose some part of it is natural, but I always believed you saw through it. No, I know you saw through it, because whenever it was just you and I, things were different, weren't they?

Yours Ever in Patience,
Colin

Several weeks after sending Howard's letter out, Colin went to lunch at a restaurant called Troika. He checked his coat and was being led to his table when he stopped cold. Across the room sat Jim Pullman with what appeared to be several other businessmen. "Um... sir?" Colin said to the maître d'. "I... I changed my mind. I have to leave. Sorry." But as he turned he caught Jim's eye, and he hurried to get his coat.

Jim stared, and then said to his fellow diners, "Gentlemen, would you excuse me a moment? There's someone I have to catch." He rose up and tried to make his way through the tables. Colin was just being handed his coat. "Mr. Sewell!" Jim called.

Colin jumped. He glanced at Jim. "I didn't know you were here," he explained shakily as he began walking away.

Jim followed. "Colin, it's a public restaurant. You don't have to leave."

"I believe I'm not supposed to speak to you anymore." Colin pulled his coat around him and kept walking. They were outside now.

"Colin," Jim protested. "Please stop. Please! I can't keep walking with you—I'm in the middle of lunch with some clients."

"What, then?" Colin turned to him, and Jim saw that he could hardly breathe.

"Colin, I didn't mean for us to be on unpleasant terms forever." Colin just looked at the ground, so Jim tried again. "Everyone thinks you're avoiding the Carlisle because of me."

"You threw brandy on me!" Colin choked.

"I'm sorry."

"I gave you back those cufflinks because they're heirloom, Jim, not because I didn't 'have any use' for them! I didn't want your damned tie bar back!" Now Colin's breaths were in short gasps and he grew angry with himself. "Oh, forget it!" He tried to get away again before he became more upset.

"Colin!" Jim cried, but Colin broke into a jog and ran off. Jim's shoulders sagged. "Damn it," he muttered. He turned around and went back to finish his business lunch.

Colin turned into an alley and leaned against a wall, panting. Even though Howard had now taken Jim's place, Colin still felt wounded by the loss. He composed himself and, having lost any appetite, decided to return to the office.

At two-thirty that afternoon, a clerk approached him. "Mr. Sewell, Mr. Pullman is here to see you."

Colin looked up from his drafts. "He is?"

"Yes, sir. Shall I send him in?"

"No! I'm..." He gave an exaggerated sigh and nodded. "I'm supposed to meet with him. That's right. Yes, I skipped lunch, so I'll be gone for a bit, all right?"

"Certainly sir."

Colin went to get his hat, coat, and gloves. *For someone who's not supposed to be seen with me, he's certainly being careless.* But when he saw Jim, he had to fight from biting his lip. "Mr. Pullman," he acknowledged quietly.

"Mr. Sewell." Jim's carriage was still outside and he motioned for Colin to get inside. Once they were off, Jim began. "Colin, please don't be upset anymore."

Colin sighed. "I'm not upset."

"So you were running away from me for the exercise?" Jim quipped. Colin looked away, and Jim frowned. "Colin, I feel horrible about throwing the brandy on you. Of all the people I could have ever done that to, it kills me to know I did it to you." They both silently relived the moment, and then Jim said, "But I was upset! You have to understand, Colin! I had just lost you and then you went and... and did that on New Year's Eve? How could I have thought anything else?"

Colin was incredulous. "Anything else? It was a stupid one-nighter! I don't even want to call it that! I hardly even remember it! I had too much to drink! I was alone on New Year's Eve, Jim. You weren't the only one who had lost someone, you know. And I'd already been through Christmas alone and I'd be damned if I was going to go through that again. So I just went there and... and after that, all I did was sick myself all night long and lay near death all the next day, and you've got the gall to think *that* was done with some kind of planned intent? You've got the gall to think *that* forgettable experience trumped any single one I had with you?" Colin's voice broke. "You and I were *discovered*, Jim! I didn't have any choice in that!"

"Colin," Jim soothed, and instinctively went over to him and put his arm around Colin's shoulders.

"And the worst of it was your letter!" Colin cried. "I wasn't unfeeling! I didn't take us lightly! I understood everything! I took as much risk as you did! Because I wanted to!"

"I know," Jim gently rocked him, feeling gladder than he had in weeks. "I'm sorry too, Collie-Aff. It was just hard, that's all."

"I know," Colin replied miserably, breaking under the spell of Jim's familiar scent. "I put myself in your place and I think I would have died if I'd found you'd done the same with some boy. But it just wasn't that at all, Jim. It was a stupid mistake."

"It wasn't a mistake. We were officially separated. I know, those things can happen." He squeezed Colin. "I really gave you back that tie bar because I truly can't wear it. My wife knows I don't wear gem-studded attire. I'm sorry I couched that in the form of rejection."

Colin exhaled. "Oh. I didn't know."

"I know you didn't. And it was lovely. I wish I could have worn it." He patted Colin's back. "But we're fine now, all right?"

Colin nodded. "Yes." He sat up and tried to smile. "Are you doing well, then?"

Jim smiled back. "I am. As well as can be, as they say. I promoted Neddy yesterday."

"Did you? That's wonderful. He's a fine boy."

"He is. How is your work going?"

"All right. I was made partner."

"Really? That's outstanding, Colin!"

Colin smiled gratefully. "Thank you."

Jim took a deep breath. "Well, I still miss you. I know we'll have to keep our respective distances, to an extent. But please come back to the Carlisle sometime. I'd feel a lot better if you would."

"All right," Colin agreed slowly. "But it wasn't just you—I'm rather tired of the place in general. All the drama and such."

Jim chuckled. "I understand. Still, I think Meredith misses having you there, too. So do us both a favor."

Colin smiled at him. "Perhaps I will, then." Then he looked at Jim shyly. "I'm glad you came to see me. So I could set things straight with you and all."

"And I with you. All right, then." He pulled the cord to stop. "I'm getting out, but I'll tell the driver to take you back to work, all right?"

"Thank you, Jim." When Jim had stepped out, Colin's face suddenly twisted with emotion. He leaned out and said bravely, "We still had it, you know."

Jim looked up at him and smiled. "I know we did, Colin. I know."

CHAPTER FORTY-TWO

28 January 1901

Dear Colin,

Your letter was a masterpiece! If you can manage a few more of those, I'm sure we'll be at June before we know it. The anticipation for me is already building, I confess. It will just be wonderful to see you again. You and your beard!

I'm glad you liked your belated Christmas gift. Never mind how I procured it; it is enough that it is in your own hands. How else to thank you for the introduction to Whitman? The vision of you reading those poems is a nice picture to keep in my head. Speaking of pictures, I have asked Y.K.W. for yours, since he still has quite a few. I will bring them to you in June; I'm surprised you didn't ask for them. It may please you to know that Y.K.W. kept a particular framed one of you to remember you by, in addition to the Singer Sargent painting. I was told you'd know which one it was? In the meantime, I'm enjoying harboring the rest of the collection.

I actually have never had a favourite color—how about that? If I had, I would have gladly given it up for brown, after you waxed so poetic about it. I liked your definition of blue. Blue is forever. It is the colour of the only two endless things in this world: the sky and the ocean. In any case, I look forward to seeing how your "bachelor quarters," turn out.

And you have made partner! Bravo! Those men would have been fools to decide anything otherwise and they must be relieved you accepted. Well done, Colin! I understand perfectly your decision to leave off your name, though it saddens me as well.

I know the designs for the Bank of Manhattan are secret, but please share some of your ideas for this department store lobby you are designing. Have you settled on one design, or do you present several and they choose? All I can say is, when I do get there in June, we're going to do a bit of financial planning, you and I. I'm worried already about all of this money you are making and where it is going. We'll be long past due for you to receive one of my infamous lectures, don't you think?

Christmas was nice, as usual, for seeing family members. We never did get any snow, though I suppose we've got a month of chances. For New Year's Eve, I stayed home for the first time in five years, opened an 1801 bottle of brandy, and toasted 1901, since it appears to be an auspicious year. You and your "dull life"! You aren't fooling me, Fearless! After all, you're still a young bachelor. However, I am not asking you for details on your New Year's Eve, I assure you!

What a laugh—me in an opium den! Can't you just picture it? I'd be completely befuddled. As for Montmartre, I told you already you're not missing anything. Everything you've done makes for far better tales than the depressing events there. It wasn't the safest of places, either, and I firmly believe that Y.K.W. was fearful for your protection, with good reason.

Speaking of which, you make yourself sound like Jekyll and Hyde, Colin. Don't be silly. I feel you were one and the same all along. Nobody can be charming every hour of every day, and everyone is acting during social occasions anyway. I know what you meant, though, and I appreciate your warning for whatever it's worth. I am confident that you will be the Colin I have always known. The one who has been writing these letters with his own hand and heart.

And yes, you are right. Whenever it was just you and I, I suppose things were different. But it is a moot point about whether or not you're still "so very clever," you see, because it was when you and I were alone that I remember you best. And you impressed me on every occasion.

Yours Fondly,
Howard

The last day of January was bitterly cold in London, and few men ventured out to Porter's that night. Kenneth and Howard had a rare evening there without Henry, who decided to stay home and work on change orders from the Helios House. Shortly after they arrived, Jack Colton appeared at their table. "Gentlemen, may I sit?" The two men looked up, surprised.

"Of course!" Kenneth exclaimed, and Jack slid into Henry's spot.

"I know you two will visit Colin in June," Jack started. "Are you going to try to convince him to come back?"

Kenneth and Howard glanced at each other. "I don't..." Kenneth began.

"No, I don't think..." Howard joined in. "He's not going to come back, Jack."

Jack looked crestfallen. "Really?" Howard and Kenneth shook their heads.

"He's quite established now, Jack," Kenneth smiled. "And he's happy there, too! Your friend has helped him immensely, I think."

Jack nodded. "I'm glad for that, I suppose. Well then Howard, I hope you are going to finally get him for yourself."

Howard's jaw dropped. "God, am I that obvious?"

Jack rolled his eyes. "The entire club has always thought you two were a better match. We're all hoping that there's going to be a bit of romance on this trip of yours, though we thought you'd be bringing him back with you."

Howard turned scarlet. "My humiliation has known no greater depths until now," he muttered. But he felt a renewed optimism with

Jack's revelation. "Yes, we've been exchanging letters, and that is the plan, old friend."

Jack nodded again. "That's wonderful. If you were to say anything otherwise, I'd have asked you to put in a good word for me."

Howard gasped. "You! But... you're joking!"

Jack smiled weakly. "Now, why would I joke about something like that?"

"But... but..." Howard stammered. "You've never shown an interest in him!"

Jack shrugged. "Because he was Henry's. I knew my place. I even told Colin, 'If you were mine, I'd never share you', and his response was, 'Well, it's a good thing we're not together then, isn't it?'"

"Jack, I... I had no idea," Howard said uneasily. "Surely isn't he... well, isn't he rather too old for you now?"

Jack shook his head. "Colin's the exception, isn't he? We were all bewitched by him. And I knew if he came back here, everyone would be trying to get a piece, if he wasn't with you, that is. So I thought I should handicap my odds."

Howard's confidence dissolved. "Well I... I don't even know if things will work out with us. I don't think he knows your feelings, Jack."

Jack chuckled. "It won't matter one bit if you're after him, Durham. You two should be together. It was only if you weren't interested. I wanted to make sure he knew... some of us will never feel the way Henry does."

"Myself included," Howard agreed firmly.

Jack leaned in. "Look here, who is going to run this club when I can't? When I'm gone? I suppose I was hoping Colin could. He's just the most trustworthy soul you've ever met."

"Jack, can I tell him about this conversation?" Howard suddenly asked. "It will mean the world to him. And if for any reason it doesn't work out with us... he's yours."

Jack regarded Howard's earnest expression and laughed, motioning for Georgie to bring champagne. "Let us toast that boy for all of the tomorrows, and to remember the joy he brought to all of us in the yesteryears."

Later, as the club closed and Kenneth and Howard left, they silently agreed to head to Kenneth's house together.

"Oh my God, Kenneth!" Howard panicked, once they were inside Kenneth's smoking room. "Jack Colton! Jack!"

Kenneth paced the floor. "I know! I know, Howard! It's simply amazing!"

"But! Colin has no idea! What if he'd rather have Jack than me? I have to tell him!"

Kenneth stopped abruptly, hands on his hips. "Why didn't you tell Jack how serious things are with you and Colin?"

"I don't know... I was just too shocked, I suppose."

"Colin's not going to choose Jack over you," Kenneth insisted. "And for all of Jack's confessions, *he's* the example of wanting to 'obtain the fantasy', as Henry put it, and after the novelty wore off, out Colin would go, again!"

"Not Jack," Howard disagreed. "He is first-rate and you know it, Kenneth."

"He tried to steal Colin from Henry!"

Howard threw his hands up. "So did I! So did we all!" He took over Kenneth's pacing. "My God, this means Jack's been harboring feelings for Colin all this time as well!" He stopped. "Colin has to be given a choice. I don't want him choosing me because he thinks I'm the only one left who wants him."

"You're the only one left who truly *loves* him," Kenneth said darkly. "Are you telling me that you're going to sabotage all of this because of Jack? Why aren't you fighting for him, Howard?"

Howard glared at his friend. "I will fight for him, Kenneth. But I want to know that even with every other competitor he has here, he still chooses *me*."

"Fine," Kenneth shrugged tiredly. "I don't know why I'm arguing with you, really, Howard. Colin will not choose anyone but you and I would bet my life on that."

Howard grinned. "I think you're right, Fairchild. And I can't wait to prove it."

When Howard finally lay his head on his pillow that night, he was happier than he had been for some time. *This must be what Henry felt,* he mused. *Knowing everyone wanted Colin but he* belonged *to Henry. And now he will belong to me.*

1 February 1901

Dear Colin,

You will hopefully get this letter the day after my last one. Something happened in that one day between that I must share with you. I need to be forthright with you and I trust you will be equally forthright with me when you respond.

People at the club were hoping Kenneth and I would bring you back with us, as you may have guessed. I discovered that while the popular vote goes to you and me, if that were not to be the case, there are apparently a number of fellows who would like it to be them, including—are you prepared for this, because I wasn't—Jack. Yes, our Jack. He is rooting for us, Colin, but I thought you should know that it's not as if I'm the only one left. You should be made aware so you can make a fully conscious choice. I won't allow any alternative.

Now, admittedly, I was quite pleased to know that my suspicion was correct: you are still a very precious commodity, Fearless! And I wouldn't believe you would choose anyone else after all of our letters to each other, but Jack... Well, Jack is in that rarefied circle you and I dwell in, so I'd understand if there's a pull. I will fight for you Colin, but I need to know that if you do choose me, it's because you considered the competition in full.

I can't bring myself to reread this! I'm putting it in the envelope right now and sending it off.

Cautiously Optimistic,
Howard

February 14, 1901

Dear Howard,

Happy Valentine's Day! While I regret you won't be opening this on the day itself, the sentiment remains, regardless. I hope you enjoy the card. I know England doesn't seem to recognize Valentine's Day much anymore, but here in America it's still a very popular holiday. Imagine that!

Howard Durham! That second letter you sent was the most Howard Durham letter I have received yet. That was written like the banker *Howard Durham. The one who wastes no time and says what needs to be said.*

I loved it.

No one even comes close to you, Howard. Not even Jack, not by a mile, but all right, yes, I suppose he'd be the next in line if you were to reject. I too am surprised and flattered, and I know why you said what you did. Permit me, please, to just indulge for a night the fantasy of running that bar. Oh the power I would have! And exert! I'm laughing as I write. But it all ends when I see you there, Howard. Unless you were the one who chose otherwise, I could never work for Jack. And now I am beginning to fantasize about returning there with you. You deserve that so much, Howard, for us to make a final appearance together. But then I also see Y.K.W. sitting there, and I know that I can never go back, and I am so extremely sorry for that. Well, we can discuss all of that further when you are here.

Speaking of which, it is so much nicer going to work every day knowing I will be seeing you in just a few months. You asked after the department store lobby. I drew just one basic design to show the partners. They approved it and then I went to the client to show it to them. They also endorsed the design, so while the store is being built (they break ground in May), I will be finishing out all the details down to the last square foot. I will be ready to design a home again after this, I think. I would love to get a commission to design something in the Adirondacks, which is a mountain range in upstate New York. I will actually be taking you and Kenneth there when you visit! Apparently, the upper crust has chosen the location as the place to escape the "rough and tumble" of city life during the summer by building what they call "great camps." The Vanderbilt and JP Morgan families are already established there, and I hear it's supposed to be supremely scenic. I hope it reminds me of your estate! I think of that *miraculous place often*. Almost as much as I have been thinking of you. Did I make you blush just then? Well so be it. My work has lately suffered for thoughts of our reunion, Howard. It is just that I cannot believe our luck. You may think me premature to say such things, but I want to say them; you deserve to hear them. You are as much a connection to my life in England as Henry ever was. When I think of your quiet pursuit of me all these years... well, it causes me to blush. And this romantic can hardly believe he is living out the story of unrequited love finding its home. I promise to make it worth your while, Howard—I do. I cannot wait to see you. It has become horribly difficult, this waiting. But oh! When I see you, I keep hoping with all my heart that you will feel the same. And so I close this letter with a truly direct answer to your question, since you were so forthright *with me, as you said:*

 Yes! Stay the course, Howard. I beg you!

Yours Deeply,

Colin

After finishing the letter, Howard read his first Valentine card in forty years. Its border was of lace paper, and in the middle was a colorful scene of a little nymph in floral garb, flitting around flowers. Beneath her feet, the poem read:

Never forget our loves, but always cling
To the fixed hope that there will be a time
When we can meet unfettered, and be blest
With the full happiness of certain love.
On the back, Colin wrote:
Will you be my Valentine?
Love, Fearless

Howard held the card to his heart and thought only one thing. *How could Henry have ever given him away?*

1 March 1901

Dear Colin,

My first Valentine in forty years! Only you, Fearless. I absolutely loved it and I have placed it under my pillow. And what a letter! I have never even heard such beautiful words in my entire life, much less seen them in print. I don't know what Y.K.W. was thinking but his loss is definitely my gain. And too bad for the rest of the lot! If you're going to be brave enough to write such things to me then I shall be brave enough to tell you that you, Colin, are the most extraordinary person I have ever known. I knew all those years I never would find someone else like you. You were so damned singular, so special, that it was better just being near you than choosing the company of a lesser man who would keep us further separated! It is easy to say this pathetic declaration now, because of your own heartfelt declarations. But know that I think everything has turned out well. I often wondered if, had I reached you before Henry, we would have stayed together. Could we have appreciated each other as much? I confess most of the time I thought we would. But there is something remarkable about being able to know someone (almost) purely as a friend for many, many years. I don't pretend to be as close to you as Henry was, but I look forward to becoming so. I am so glad the wait is nearing its end. I will see you soon and will tell you everything you want and deserve to hear.

With that thought in mind, let me give you the details about our impending voyage:

Ship: Kaiser Wilhelm der Grosse

Date of Departure: 2 June 1901, 13:00

Date of Arrival: 9 June 1901, 15:00

Passenger Numbers: 130642 (mine)

130643 (Kenneth's)

Also, Colin, I was thinking—perhaps the first week or so we should all remain a threesome and not discuss anything just yet, if that is all right with you. I like the idea of just enjoying your company for a while without worrying what the outcome will be of all this. I am planning for the best but I know I cannot speak for you, and you can't make a decision until we are together.

Thank you again for giving me my very first love letter, Fearless. You still manage to amaze me; I think you always will.

Love,
Howard

P.S. I hope you don't mind your birthday present being belated. I already have it but I'd rather give it to you in person. Look out for a card in the mail, though!

Soon the time came for Colin to worry daily about seeing Howard, while Adam was so excited about the impending visit, one would think he was the one receiving visitors. "It's damn darling how nervous you've become!" he quipped one day during lunch.

"I think I ought to shave my beard," Colin fretted.

"Why on earth would you do that?"

"Howard's only seen me clean-shaven. I don't think he'll like it."

"Clean-shaven! You don't say!" Adam put his hands up to his eyes, trying to picture Colin without his beard.

"Oh, stop it," Colin said irritably.

"Well, Howard shouldn't care whether or not you've got a beard."

"Actually, he told me to keep it, just to see it himself. But I can't stand it!"

"Then shave it off."

"You're a lot of help, you are."

Adam shrugged. "I think that if he sees you on the dock without a beard, he'll smell fear before the plank drops."

"Why?"

"Because you'll look obsessive, Sewell. As if the only way he'll like you is if you both go back to the past. He wants a *future* with you, doesn't he?"

"I don't know. Maybe he thinks he does."

"What's that supposed to mean?"

"It's just that... I can see him, approaching on the ship. He'll look for me, and when he sees me, his heart will sink. 'Oh... he's changed. That's not *my* Colin.'"

Adam nearly choked. "Because you've got a *beard*? Colin, the man is in *love* with you! This is going to be his dream come true! You've got a year's worth of letters to back that up. Really, I suppose if he hates the beard, he'll ask you to get rid of it, but I'm sure that he could give a damn about it!"

Colin laughed. "All right, I'll keep it."

Adam chewed thoughtfully. "I'd be happy to come with you, if it will help."

Colin's brow furrowed. "Well... I don't want to trouble you. But perhaps it *would* be good to have someone to steady me..."

"Oh, please let me come with you! I've got to see them before anyone else does!"

"Fine, then," Colin grinned. "But you'd better keep your thoughts to yourself! I'll be positively wrung out as it is."

"Deal."

On Friday, at 1:30 p.m., the two men stood on the dock. Colin fidgeted from the start. "Do I look all right?"

Adam glanced at him. "You must be joking."

"But I mean, is everything in place?" Colin tugged down his suit coat.

Adam smiled. "You look fine. Very nice." In fact, his friend looked stunning. Colin was wearing a light blue seersucker suit, with a vest two shades darker. Underneath was a fine white cotton shirt with pearl buttons and cufflinks. His blond beard stood out on his lightly tanned face, and under a straw boater his hair shone, neatly combed and lightly pomaded. The look was capped off by Colin's anxious posturing, wringing his gloved hands, tucking his hair behind his ears, and looking about with wide-open eyes.

Finally, they spotted the ship. "Here she comes!" Adam shouted. He held his hand to his forehead. "Oh, my, Mr. Sewell! I think I shall faint! However will I stand it?"

"Very funny," Colin laughed. He looked back at the ship. After forty-five more nerve-wracking minutes, the vessel docked. Colin looked for Howard and Kenneth, trying not to appear frantic. "Adam, do you see them?"

"Well, Sewell, I could be looking straight at them, for all I know."

"Right. Sorry."

And then they appeared! They were emerging from the bottom of the ship, walking the plank to the dock. Colin burst into a grin and grabbed Adam's arm, making his way through the crowd. Howard and Kenneth had already seen Colin from the ship, and both were beaming before he even approached. Suddenly, Kenneth saw a blur of blue and found himself in an embrace. "Kenneth! You made it!"

"Oh, Colin! I can't believe it's you!"

Colin withdrew and held Kenneth's arms. "It's so wonderful to see you!" Then he took a breath and stood, exultant, before Howard. Before he could say anything, Howard chucked Colin under the chin, grinning.

"Look at you! You kept the beard!" He winked. "It looks superb on you."

At Howard's first touch, Colin turned scarlet and a visible shiver raced through him, causing Adam to fall into hysterics. Colin rolled his eyes and sighed. "This is my supposedly supportive friend, Mr. Adam Meredith."

"I'm sorry," Adam gasped. "I've never seen Colin in such a state as today! He's so been looking forward to this!"

"As have we!" Kenneth exclaimed. "Goodness, I'd forgotten how awfully long that trip is! If we'd gone one more day at sea, I'd have thrown myself off the boat!" The four men walked over to the luggage area. Colin asked after their trip, and they had a porter take their things to Colin's carriage.

"I'll pick up a cab, Colin," Adam reminded.

"Are you sure you won't let us take you back?" Colin inquired.

"Oh, no, thank you. You must catch up! Mr. Fairchild, Mr. Durham, it was a pleasure meeting you. I'll see you again later on."

"Thank you, Adam!" Colin called, and the three men left settled in for the ride to Howard and Kenneth's hotel.

"Who was that little treat?" Kenneth asked.

"*That* was Adam Meredith, my best friend here. But calm yourself, Kenneth; he is not available." Colin told them the story and Kenneth sighed.

"What a shame."

"What a *relief*," Howard muttered, and then he smiled at Colin, who laughed and shook his head. They all compared notes about the transatlantic voyage until they reached the hotel. Colin stood with them in the lobby until they received their keys.

"I'll be back to pick you up for dinner at seven," he told them. He shyly lingered his smile on Howard and then bade them farewell.

The two men briefly entered their own suites to pay the porters, and then Kenneth ran over to Howard's room. "Well?" he said excitedly.

Howard sighed. "Oh, he looks beautiful Kenneth, don't you think?"

"Oh, Howard, he does! He definitely looks healthier."

"And the beard is dashing," Howard smiled.

"Agreed! And he couldn't stop beaming!" Kenneth squeezed his friend's arm. "Why, that's the happiest I've seen him in years! Every time he looked at you he was just ecstatic! And it was positively darling how he blushed when you touched his face! I think those are all wonderful signs, don't you?"

Howard nodded. "I hope so." He had seen Colin's eyes himself. *You're here! You're really here!* That was what his eyes had said. And Howard had wished they were in Italy or France, so he could have at least kissed Colin's cheeks. Fortunately, Colin did seem to like Howard's teasing of him. But he really did appear overwhelmed that they had come to see him after all, and Howard decided it would be up to him to bring them closer together. As he began to unpack his clothes, he thought how he would go about it. *Hell, I've traveled over five thousand kilometers already to get closer.* He stopped unpacking and smiled. *Black pawn to white, one move.*

Meanwhile, Colin sent a post to Adam's estate, and within an hour, Adam was ringing at Colin's house. He laughed when he saw Colin jumping around. "Well, what did you think?" Colin asked nervously.

"Oh, he's so very handsome!" Adam grinned. "I don't know why I'm surprised. But you certainly do go for the older set, don't you, what with Henry, Jim, and now Howard?"

Colin blushed. "I suppose so..."

"Well, he has the confidence you need. Oh, and his accent! He's got a lovely deep voice!"

"Yes, doesn't he?"

"And the way you burned up and... and that very definition of a *frisson* when he touched your face!" Adam began laughing again. "Oh, that was funny!"

"Stop it!"

Adam smiled. "Well, it was romantic, Sewell. You really like him, that's for sure. And I don't blame you; he's positively seductive!"

"Really?" Colin had never quite thought of Howard in that way.

"Well goodness, isn't he? He's tall, handsome, and strong looking. He looked as if he could sweep you into his arms and carry you off!"

Colin's eyes widened at the comment. "Yes, I suppose so," he wondered, thinking of the very thing in the past.

"You two have quite a bond," Adam noted warmly. "And I can't wait to hear how things go tonight! Good luck!"

When Colin met his two friends in the lobby four hours later, he was in high spirits and dressed beautifully, albeit more conservatively than in London. He chatted amiably with the two men all the way to dinner. For his part, Colin was pleased to find out that Howard had kept Kenneth abreast of his own activities, as he had worried that he and Howard would make Kenneth feel left out. During dessert, Colin cheerily cut into his cake with the side of his fork. "So, we may as well get it over with. Tell me what Henry is doing these days." The purpose was twofold: Colin wanted Howard to know straight away that he was no longer shackled to his memories of Henry, and of course, he really was curious what Henry had done with his life since Colin had left.

"Well," Kenneth began, "nothing out of the ordinary, really. He's pretty much carrying on as he always has."

Colin nodded. "Is he working longer hours?"

"He was, at first," Howard replied. "Because he had to finish those projects. But he's planning to retire once the Helios House is finished."

"Retire!" Colin exclaimed. Then he shrugged. "Well, I suppose he already was semi-retired after he hired me."

"Exactly," Howard smiled. "He said perhaps he would do some consulting work."

"But he'd still close the office, and all of those poor fellows would be out of a job," Colin said sadly.

"They should easily find work elsewhere, coming from Henry's firm," Kenneth reminded him.

"True enough." Colin's voice became teasing. "And so is James back gracing your presence?"

Kenneth and Howard looked at each other. "Oh..." Kenneth stammered. "Henry's just... being Henry."

Colin hmphed. "Well for heaven's sake, I should *hope* he's enjoying himself, since that was the entire reason he got rid of me!" Then he shook his head and smiled gently. "It's all right. I was just curious." Then his eyes sparkled. "Do you want to hear the itinerary I've planned for the three of us?" And so Colin detailed their plans, beginning with a trip to the theatre district tomorrow and a visit to the Carlisle tomorrow evening. "Oh, I must tell you all about the Carlisle and some of the people there!" Colin said gleefully. He told them about Harold, Adam, and the rest of his circle, and he also warned Howard and Kenneth that nobody there knew of his "notoriety" and that he preferred to keep it that way.

Finally, Howard raised an eyebrow. "What about that fellow you were attracted to not so long ago?"

Colin's eyes widened, and then he admonished his friend. "Oh, Howard, don't be ridiculous! There's not a chance on earth I'd point him out to you."

"Oh, he's that attractive!" Howard teased.

"He's that unimportant," Colin sniffed. "Now, as far as Sunday's plans go..."

The next day went by quickly, and soon Colin was introducing his old friends to his new ones at the Carlisle that evening.

"You must tell us some stories about Colin!" Philip urged Howard and Kenneth. "He won't tell us anything!"

Howard was surprised. "He hasn't told you a single thing about his past?"

"He's told us plenty, but he's left out all the scandalous parts!" Alex agreed. "He's very mean like that. Now go on, Mr. Durham, or Mr. Fairchild."

"Well," Howard chuckled. "Back in London, Henry Sewell was the envy of every man in the club, for having Colin."

"Really?" Adam leaned in, delighted. "Do tell!" Colin fell back on his seat, already embarrassed. He trusted Howard and Kenneth to be careful, but he still wasn't sure what was going to be said.

"Oh, yes," Howard replied. "Colin was the quintessential *boy* when he came into our world. All the other young fellows took their cues from him, didn't they, Kenneth?"

"Yes, they certainly tried to copy him, but he was a true natural."

"Kenneth, really," Colin waved a hand.

"It's true," Howard agreed. "He was never frivolous or spoilt-acting. He was actually made to do real work, which he did, to great acclaim. But his looks and flawless manners were what the men at the club saw. He was a master." Howard laughed. "In fact, we called him a Master in the Dark Arts!"

"You're gushing," Colin warned, cheeks flaming.

"*You're* blushing," Kenneth teased. He looked at Colin's friends. "He *was* a Master in the Dark Arts, because he seduced Henry Sewell, who was never with any boy for more than a few weeks. And yet in just one week, Henry declared he was in love with Colin, in front of the entire club! He asked Colin to move in with him, *and then* he took the outrageous step of adopting him!"

Adam turned to Colin. "That's right—you were adopted! Sewell, what was that all about? You must tell us!" Colin sighed, and explained the story. He couldn't help smiling at the end. "I have to admit it was one of the most brilliant things I've ever heard."

Suddenly, a brief look of anxiety flashed across Colin's face, but he recovered and looked on as Kenneth continued. "Yes, so they spent every waking moment together, and the non-waking ones, of course!" He winked, and the men roared. "Henry bought entire wardrobes for him. Henry bought *everything* for him, as a way of showing everyone how much

Colin was really worth, both as a companion and as an architect." Colin looked at his friends and nodded. "I never got a paycheck." Then he made a face. "Until the end. Then I got severance pay."

Kenneth shrugged. "Well all told, you can imagine it was really the most exciting thing any of us had seen!"

Colin shook his head and laughed while Adam turned to him. "Sewell, you're an absolute rake!"

At the end of the evening, Colin asked to share a cab with Kenneth and Howard. As soon as they started to move, Colin looked at them desperately. "Did Henry ever say anything to either of you about annulling my adoption?"

The men looked surprised. "No!" Kenneth exclaimed. "I thought he would have told you! Why, he said he wasn't going to bother, that he still felt you were the one best trusted to take care of his inheritance if he dies."

"*What?*" Colin was stunned.

Howard was shocked as well. "Didn't he tell you?" Colin furiously shook his head. Howard and Kenneth looked at each other.

"Well..." Kenneth stammered. "I'm quite sure that's the way it stands..."

"Yes. Colin," Howard began gently, "Henry still thinks highly of you. He knew you couldn't possibly change your name yet again. After all, you're famous now, professionally speaking. And he also believed you wouldn't take advantage of him by being his legal heir." He paused. "Your father disowning you made his decision final. He said once was enough."

And Colin couldn't help it; he burst into tears. "Oh God, forgive me," he managed, horrified that Howard was witnessing the outburst. "I just... I'm just so relieved! You see, I didn't realize until tonight that he could have undone the thing! It's just... Once *was* enough and I couldn't stand the symbolism and bad luck of it all if Henry had done it to me too."

Howard and Kenneth exhaled. Howard tried not to make much of it, but it put a damper on the evening. And he couldn't help wondering if

Colin was really ready for him after all. *Steady Durham. Allow the boy some time. You'll see soon enough.*

Fortunately, over the next two days the three friends had a wonderful time together. Howard even got the chance to show off his newfound billiard skills.

"You're quite good!" Colin exclaimed as Howard sunk his sixth ball.

Howard smiled. *I'd better damn well be, after practicing every night for the past four months!* Both men were relaxed in each other's presence, but each night they parted, Howard sat alone in his hotel room, thinking about Whitman and his and Colin's as-yet-unexpressed feelings for each other. It was only Monday, and Howard didn't think he could stand another four days of affectionate glances and friendly nudges. He went next door to talk to Kenneth. "It's not too late," Kenneth said. "Why don't you send a post to him asking if just you and he could spend the day tomorrow?"

"But daylight isn't very conducive to romance," Howard explained. "I was thinking more in terms of perhaps dinner and drinks."

Kenneth grinned. "Were you, then? Well I can't say I blame you! I think Colin's relying on you to take the first step, anyway."

"Yes, I think so too," Howard agreed. "It's ironic, isn't it? How he's come to be so shy?"

Kenneth grew solemn. "I believe he cares quite deeply for you, Howard. And it frightens him. After all, think of his father, and Henry. They loved him so very much... and then they cut him off."

"But I won't," Howard swore.

Kenneth nodded. "*I* know that, and *you* know that, but Colin..." Kenneth shook his head. "Colin may not believe it yet. After all, he was little more than a fantasy to you all those years."

Howard stared at Kenneth, his heart sinking. "That's rather harsh. Do you think that's what he feels?"

"I think it's an explanation for his hesitancy," Kenneth shrugged. Then he brightened, patting Howard's arm. "But you'll be perfect, Howard! He just needs someone like you to be kind to him. Think of how at the end of things Henry kept nagging him about his weight and his age and such."

"I'd rather not, thank you. But no matter; I'll be happy to boost his ego." So Howard dashed off a note.

Dear Colin,

How about that—I'm here in America and you still get a letter from me! I believe I miscalculated on this one-week idea. Would you be willing to have dinner with me tomorrow night? Kenneth will see Harold, and I will make the restaurant arrangements. We would still go ahead with your daytime plans, of course. Please let me know if I'm being too forward.

Regards,
Howard

He sent it off with the hotel's messenger and waited excitedly. In time, he was brought Colin's response:

Dear Howard,

I would love to have dinner with you tomorrow! I have been a little anxious myself, and you have probably noticed. If so, I apologize. I look forward to seeing you tomorrow, more so, tomorrow night.

Sincerely,
Colin

CHAPTER FORTY-THREE

Then next day passed as the ones before, but when the three returned to the hotel, Kenneth winked. "I'm jumping out. You two make your plans."

Howard smiled at Colin. "Would you be able to meet me in the lobby at 6:30?"

"Yes," Colin nodded. "And I thought that perhaps after dinner, I could bring you back to my house? I haven't shown it to you yet."

"That's a wonderful idea! Yes, let's do that," Howard agreed. "I'll see you in a few hours, then."

"Yes." Colin watched Howard exit the cab and waved to him as he rode off.

At 6:30 p.m., Colin was in the hotel lobby, studying the leaded glass windows flanking the entrance. He knew he was supposed to stand toward the center of the room so Howard could see him, but he was distracted by the windows' sparkle when he came in. His nose was practically touching the beveled cuts when he heard the familiar voice over his shoulder. "Why is it that whenever I catch you unawares, you're always absorbed in some architectural feature?"

Colin turned toward Howard with a laugh. "I can't help it!" He regarded the hotel. "The money they must have spent on this place. I can't imagine it."

"It is beautiful, isn't it?"

Colin smiled at Howard. "Yes. And just like your bank, you fit right in." And Howard did. He was wearing the usual black formal dinner attire, but it was obvious his suit was Italian and of a finer quality than most men could afford.

Howard shook his head. "I can't remember the last time I saw *you* in black evening dress! You look absolutely wonderful."

"Thank you," Colin replied modestly. "I thought I should mark the occasion." For a moment he became self-conscious of his glasses and wished he'd left them at home. Taking them off, he said, "Do you think I ought not to wear my spectacles?"

Howard, with his gloved hands, gently but firmly put the glasses back on Colin's face. "I wouldn't have you any other way. Do they bother you?"

Colin shook his head. "I just... I feel like they detract from everything else, in a time like this."

Howard smiled. "Colin, I'm so used to seeing you with them on, I don't even notice them." He chuckled. "Scratch that; I do notice them. I have a story about them, from a long time ago."

Colin frowned. "A story?"

"I'll tell you later. Come along."

Upon arriving at the restaurant, they were seated and Howard ordered a bottle of wine. Colin exhaled. "Well then! Would you like to go first, with that 'running list of questions' you've got in your head?"

"Oh, that's quite all right," Howard demurred. "I want to hear yours first."

Colin laughed. "Fine then. Tell me what happened with Mark."

Howard sighed, and told him the story. Then he decided to add on to it. "Of course, when I showed up at Porter's without him, I had to tell Kenneth and Henry the reason."

"And did Henry know you were writing to me?"

"Yes, remember? But admittedly, he didn't know you and I were corresponding so... intimately, for lack of a better word. When I told them that I had to read your letter in private because it was so personal, Henry inquired further into our correspondence. I had actually brought the next letter to show them, because I was at my wit's end by that point."

"About what?"

"About you! I realized by then that I still cared about what happened to you, and I thought if Henry and Kenneth could read one of your letters, they could decipher whether or not..." and for the first time, Colin saw Howard blush, "I had any sort of chance with you."

"Oh, Howard," Colin smiled. Then his expression froze. "So Henry knows why you came here! What does he think?"

"I was petrified to tell him! It's such a strange turn of events, you know. But as it turned out, Henry practically gave us his blessing. He felt he'd moved on in his life so why shouldn't you in yours? Or me in mine?"

"Well, good," Colin muttered. He struggled to keep his disappointment hidden. *The bastard isn't even jealous!* He glanced at Howard. "I have to say I'm surprised that he didn't tell you that you could do better."

"That's because I can't." Howard folded his arms. "Now Colin, I won't have any of this self-pitying from you. If anyone should be worried about his attractiveness it should be me, and yet for some odd reason, I'm not worried at all. Should I be?"

Colin was chastened. "No, of course not."

"Good." Howard's voice softened. "I know Henry was hard towards you at times, but I never agreed with any of those opinions."

Colin smiled gratefully. "I know. I often thought about how much nicer you were to me. It got to where I began thinking, 'I'll bet Howard wouldn't say that', or 'I'll bet Howard wouldn't do that'." His expression became serious. "It's going to take some time for me to get used to having you around instead of Henry. You've got to make some allowances."

"Fair enough." Howard nodded, proud that Colin had noticed his kindness.

Colin looked down at his plate. "You know Howard, not long after I met Henry I began to feel that I had to prove myself. I felt I had to prove to everyone that I wasn't just a boy with a pretty face, or... or some sort of whore. I was an architect before I met Henry and I became one of the best while I was with him. And even though I didn't convince anyone else until the end, Henry knew." Colin shrugged. "So... I really thought he would always value that above everything. But he didn't."

"He did," Howard insisted. "It's why he kept you on, why he made a commitment for the first time in his life."

Colin shook his head. "It wasn't enough. I really was just a pretty, young whore to him. And then my time ran out." He paused, and then said bitterly, "He was just like the rest after all."

"Don't call yourself that," Howard said angrily. "I told you I won't have it. And mind you, he wasn't like *all* the rest."

Colin smiled. "No, I suppose not. He wasn't like you, was he?" He took Howard's hand and squeezed it. "Nobody's like you, Howard. I'm so glad you're here."

They ended up having a wonderful dinner, and afterwards, they went to Colin's house as planned. Colin took Howard's hand at the door. "Are you ready?" He swept Howard inside and Howard gazed about him. "Oh! It's the Helios House in miniature!"

Colin burst out laughing. He realized Howard hadn't seen the inside of the Lyon Steel Building, the Walton Street Tea Rooms, nor Mrs. Dashworth's home. For this wasn't the Helios House; this was simply Colin's style: white walls, no baseboards, no crown molding, and most of the furnishings designed by him. But he had done it all with the vision of

Howard's visit in mind. That said, the Monet took center stage. Colin had installed a wall eight feet from the door, so that the first thing visitors saw upon entering was the artwork Kenneth and Howard had given him.

But Howard was already in the sitting room. "This lamp was in the Helios House as well!"

Colin regarded it. "Oh, yes. I need to apply for a patent for that. Well, everything here, actually. The stuff in the Helios House was one of a kind, but I printed copies of everything and so some of my things here are reproductions." He winked. "Don't tell Rademaker!"

Howard looked around the room. It was beautiful. Simple. Elegant. Colin. A small picture on one wall drew his eye. "What's this?"

"Oh!" Colin ran over to him. "*That* is an actual photograph of lightning! It is among the very first, taken by William Jennings. Isn't it amazing?"

Howard stared. "However did you find it?"

"Oh, I had read about it and went to his studio, of course. I persuaded him to sell me one of his images."

"A photograph? Surely you didn't have to pay much."

"Howard," Colin said gravely. "Think of how difficult it must be to capture lightning with a camera. Photography is really as much of an art as painting. Now I know it's very unorthodox thinking, but there it is."

Howard grinned. "You know a little about unorthodox thinking. I'll trust you." He looked over to his left. "And is that your study, then?"

"Yes." Colin stepped aside and let Howard approach the room.

"Oh," Howard's voice caught on emotion. Colin stood next to him worriedly.

"What is it?

Howard sighed, shaking his head. "It reminds me of the first time I saw you in Henry's office..." He rubbed his chin in wonder, thinking how long ago that day had been. He spotted papers on the giant drafting table by the window and walked toward them. "Are these prints of the bank?"

"No, no! They're... well, go on then. Have a look at them." There was a hint of nervousness in Colin's voice.

Howard bent his head and regarded the topmost sheet. "Awfully high ceilings..." He peeked at the more finished picture underneath, and the first object his eyes saw was an exquisitely rendered cross. A closer look revealed its surroundings. He gasped and turned to Colin. "Is this your cathedral?"

Colin burst into smiles. "Yes! You remembered!"

Howard turned back to the drawings. "Oh, Colin!" Then he faced the young man. "Then, that means you've done it! You've achieved what you wanted to, if you're designing your cathedral!" He tilted his head and gave Colin a quizzical look. Colin read it immediately and gave a laugh.

"Well, not necessarily. I just..." He returned Howard's smile. "I was so happy when I saw you on the dock, Howard. Everything inside of me just soared. The joy was... immeasurable. That was the joy I had to feel to create something like that." He regarded the drafts warmly. "The beginnings of my cathedral."

Howard fell silent, and he too looked at the papers. Finally he murmured, "What God has brought together, let no man put asunder."

He glanced at Colin, who bit his lip. "That's lovely."

Howard smiled. "Thank you. Well then, let us see the rest of your beautiful bachelor quarters."

When they reached the library, there was a wheeking sound. Howard spotted a cage and shrunk back. "Whatever is in there?"

"That is my guinea pig, Victoria!" Colin walked over and scooped a tumbly black ball of fur into his arms and returned to Howard, who wrinkled his nose.

"Ugh. What on earth is a guinea pig?"

"Oh, they're darling little animals from South America that have been domesticated to use as pets. I was too busy to bother with a dog, and I sneeze around cats. Victoria is exotic, and her size is perfect." He stroked her and she began purring.

"I didn't realize you loved our fair queen so much to memorialize her," Howard quipped.

"I don't. I thought she was a pig."

Howard laughed. "I see. Well, I'll hand you credit for keeping your originality intact."

Colin returned Victoria to her cage, and they moved toward a room with closed doors. "And this," Colin announced, "is what I call 'The Howard Durham Room'!" He pushed open the pocket doors and stepped aside.

"Oh!" Howard breathed. It *was* his room. The walls were covered in honey-hued leather. Maple-stained bookshelves lined one wall. A mahogany desk, inlaid with maple-stained squares, stood next to one of the windows. A large flokati rug lay on the wood floor that gleamed with a walnut finish. Wood-slatted blinds closed against the windows. The fireplaces on opposite walls were white marble, inlaid with burnished walnut. On one mantle was an aged pipe stand and a stuffed peregrine falcon. Above the other mantle was an original painting of a bay thoroughbred by George Stubbs. There was a globe in one corner and a palm tree in another. A mahogany bar with a Baccarat crystal decanter set off the third corner. But it was what stood in the fourth corner that made Howard cry out. There, on a pedestal, in a glass case, was an architectural model Howard had never before seen but one he guessed at immediately.

"It's the Bank of Manhattan," Colin confirmed, smiling. "You're being given a preview."

Howard rushed to it, and Colin followed, giving a brief explanation of all he had planned. He had actually made two models so that this one could stay with him. Howard was stunned. He turned to Colin. "*This* is amazing. And this room! It's a symphony of brown! This was your surprise!"

Colin nodded, beaming. "You should see it in the daytime." Howard walked over to the desk, running his fingers over the smooth surface and shaking his head. "I can't believe it. It's the perfect room."

"It's everything Howard," Colin laughed.

"It's absolutely beautiful!"

"I'm glad you like it."

"But this space is so large!"

"I knocked down a wall. It was actually two rooms. Hence the two fireplaces."

Howard stood in shock. "You knocked down a wall?"

"Yes, why not?"

"You, yourself?"

"Yes, Howard! I did everything myself! It was fun."

Howard took a moment to picture Colin in shirtsleeves wielding a sledgehammer, covered in white dust. He laughed. "Fearless has done it again! You are simply remarkable." He paused. "But, I thought your study was across the way."

Colin took a deep breath. He wasn't sure how to say it. "I know…" Then he lost his nerve. " I just wanted to see if I could do this, was all."

"Hmm. If I move to America, can I rent out this room for an office?" Howard teased.

"If you move to America, you can have it," Colin replied softly, his heart thudding against his chest. "It was meant for you, Howard."

Howard stood, astonished. "What? Do you really mean that?"

Colin nodded and then gave a self-deprecating laugh. "That is to say, if you wanted to. You wouldn't have to, of course. We don't have to discuss that right now."

Howard smiled. "I'd like to discuss it. Why don't you fix us a drink?"

Colin shyly obliged, using the decanter of brandy in the room. He handed over Howard's glass and sighed. "It's just… I can't move back to London, Howard."

Howard looked warmly at him. "I figured as much, Colin. And I'd never ask you to do that if you didn't want to. That's why I've decided that I could move to America, if you'll have me."

Now Colin was taken aback. "You really would move to America? Are you sure?"

"Well, now that I've seen this room, it's not even a question," Howard quipped.

"But what about your job?"

"I'm sure I could manage to find something here, what with my experience. The other partners will be sure to give me an excellent recommendation."

"You'd be willing to do that?"

"Colin, I'd be happy to. I'd be ecstatic! I've already thought it all through."

Colin couldn't hide his elation. "You have? I can't believe it! You're so generous to do such a thing!"

At this, Howard had to laugh. "Generous. Ah, yes. That's my primary motive, certainly."

"But that's... that was the only obstacle!" Colin exclaimed.

Howard almost burst with happiness. "Was it?"

Colin stood, eyes shining exactly like they had on the dock. "Well, yes!" Then he composed himself. "Well, that is, for *me* that was. I um... I can't speak for you, I suppose."

Howard took his hand. "You can. Now come along." He led Colin to the library. "Bring over your *Leaves of Grass*. I'd like to read to you."

Colin blushed. "Oh, it's... it's in the bedroom. I'll get it."

"In the bedroom!" Howard was pleased.

When Colin returned, he was bashful. "Well, I like to read it in bed, sometimes. It helps me fall asleep." He gave Howard the book and sat down next to him, leaning against his shoulder. Howard turned to "O Me! O Life!"

"O me! O life... of the questions of these recurring;

Of the endless trains of the faithless—of cities fill'd with the foolish;

Of myself forever reproaching myself, (for who more foolish than I, and who more faithless?)

Of eyes that vainly crave the light—of the objects mean—of the struggle ever renewed;

Of the poor results of all—of the plodding and sordid crowds I see around me;

Of the empty and useless years of the rest—with the rest me intertwined;

The question, O me! So sad recurring—What good amid these, O me, O life!"

Colin answered:

"That you are here—that life exists, and identity;

That the powerful play goes on, and you will contribute a verse."

He looked fondly at Howard. "Lots of verses, hopefully." Then he nestled against him and sighed apologetically. "Mm, I'm all drowsy."

Howard kissed his head and put an arm around him. "We have all the time in the world. You see, this way, it's like we're courting." He gave him a squeeze. "You ought to go to bed. It's been quite a day."

Colin tiredly stood up and laughed. "Courting!" But then he tilted his head. "It is rather like that, isn't it?"

"Yes. You don't do everything in one night."

Colin shook his head, smiling. He showed Howard to the door. "Thank you, Howard. I cannot wait to see you tomorrow." He bravely leaned in and gave Howard a demure kiss.

Howard smiled and tucked a lock of Colin's hair behind his ear. He kissed him once more. "And I, you, Fearless. Good night."

The next morning, Colin met Howard in the hotel lobby again. "Where's Kenneth?" he asked.

Howard looked sheepish. "He thought just you and I should spend the day together. I tried to persuade him to come but he refused. He insisted that he had plenty to do."

Colin chuckled. "Well, his loss will be our gain. It's a beautiful day for hunting."

Howard stopped outside the door. "In Central Park? Are you joking?"

Colin laughed. "Come along. You'll see."

When Howard entered the cab, he sighed and shook his head. "Butterfly hunting. Very clever, Fearless." There were three nets on the seat and a box of other items on the floor.

"Have you ever been, Howard?"

"I can't say that I have."

"Really? Well, I wasn't so interested in them myself until I saw the collection Mr. Rademaker had. Absolutely amazing!" He smiled excitedly. "There's quite a lot in the park. You can help me start a collection."

"You mean you haven't any at all, yet?"

"Well, no. I haven't made the time. That's why I thought this would be the perfect outing. I even had Katie make us a picnic lunch! Oh, Kenneth... Well, we'll give him his share when we come back." As they rode through the park, Colin watched for the place he wanted the driver to stop. "Here! This is it!" They climbed out and Colin handed over a net. "All right, Howard, good luck!"

Howard eyed the net. "I'll look a bit silly running around with this thing."

"Howard, you don't run with it like a child. You must walk and look around, and when you see a butterfly, you have to sneak up on it and gently net it." Howard looked dubious, so Colin took his arm. "Just come with me." Within minutes, they spotted one. "I think it's a Red-Spotted Purple," Colin whispered.

"Need one whisper around butterflies?" Howard asked, amused. He received an elbow to his side.

"There! Got it!" Colin proclaimed. They walked back to the box of supplies. "Now, Howard, I'll need you to make the killing jar."

"The what?"

"The killing jar. You know, soak a bit of cotton with the ether and put it in the jar. I'll put the butterfly in."

Howard's shoulders sagged. "That sounds horrible."

"Howard, it's completely humane. How did you think I was going to make a collection if I didn't kill them?"

"Well..."

"You've gone on hunting parties!"

"I try not to. Man versus dumb beast isn't sporting to *me*."

"What? Oh, for heaven's sake. Look here, if he keeps beating his wings like this, he won't make a good specimen at all. Fine, you hold him, I'll make the jar."

"Oh Colin, please let him go. I... Well, think about it..." Howard gazed at the butterfly. "You know, he's like *us*, you see? He was going along, minding his own business, doing harm to nobody... and yet helping society by pollinating the flowers! He's going along, doing what's natural to him, when he gets caught. And now, to atone for sins he didn't commit, he has to pay the ultimate price of death!"

Colin frowned. "You're equating us with a butterfly?"

"Yes, I am. Don't you see? You've always wanted to be free to live your own life, and yet you're going to happily snuff out this one's life without a second thought. Exercise your humanity!"

Colin gave a look of disgust, but he acquiesced. "Fine. Let him go." As he watched the butterfly escape, he grumbled, "He'll die in a few days, anyway."

"If the next few days are as glorious as this one, wouldn't you be grateful to see them?"

Colin looked forlorn. "Well, what about my collection?"

"I'll buy you something else instead. The more I think about it, the more horrid it seems to have entire cases full of dead creatures in one's home."

"*Beautiful* creatures," Colin insisted. "We admire them. Haven't you seen those gorgeous hummingbird cases?"

"Blech. More like slaughter cases. Maybe we won't get along after all," Howard teased.

"Very funny. Well, what are we going to do now, if we're not going to catch any?"

"We can still catch them. Half the fun is identifying them anyway, I think. Catch one, put it in a jar to look at, and then we'll set it free."

Colin held up his butterfly book. "Well, how do you think this man wrote his book if he couldn't kill the butterflies for close inspection and proper identification?"

"He's a scientist. We're merely hobbyists."

"Oh, bah." But Colin smiled at Howard. "What a pacifist you are! Some banker!"

"Yes, I reserve all of my aggressive instincts for the office. There's no need to let them spill over into my personal life. Oh, look at that one!"

Colin turned. "Oh, it's a Swallowtail! A Tiger Swallowtail."

"Well, catch it!"

"Oh, I already know what it is."

"*I* should like to see it."

"Howard…" Colin sighed, walking over to net the butterfly. He brought it back, and they put it in the largest jar they had.

"Oh, she's beautiful!" Howard exclaimed.

"How do you know it's a she?"

"I don't. But who cares?"

Suddenly, a little girl ran up. "Miss Beatrice! Miss Beatrice! They caught a butterfly!" The dark-haired child of five years stood in front of the two men. "Ooh, she's pretty!"

Colin smiled and gave her the jar. "Yes, she is. Almost as pretty as you. Have a look."

"What kind is she?"

"She's a Tiger Swallowtail. You see how she's yellow and black, rather like a tiger?"

The girl's nanny came over. "What a fine day for butterflies," she said, smiling.

"Yes, it is," Colin agreed.

"Are you going to keep her?" the little girl asked.

"Oh, no," Colin replied. "She's a wild thing, so we must let her go. She may still need to lay eggs."

"Eggs!"

"Yes, she lays dozens of teeny-tiny eggs, and they turn into caterpillars. And what do you think the caterpillars turn into?"

"Butterflies!"

"That's right! Would you like to let her go?"

"Oh, yes!" The little girl carefully unscrewed the lid and gave a delighted cry when the butterfly flew out and away. "Oh, Miss Beatrice, can we catch one?"

"Some other time, Marie. I'll have your father buy you a net."

Colin held out his. "Here, please take this one. I bought three and a friend wasn't able to join us."

"Oh, we couldn't!"

"I insist! I don't know what I'm going to do with three nets."

Miss Beatrice regarded the two well-dressed gentlemen. "Well, at least let us send you payment."

"I wouldn't hear of it," Colin replied. He crouched down in front of the girl and gave her the jar. "Now Marie, remember, when you catch one, always handle it gently and let it go when you are done looking at it."

"I will. Thank you, sirs! Thank you! Let's catch some, Miss Beatrice! Please?"

Miss Beatrice laughed. "All right." She looked at Colin and Howard. "Thank you ever so much for your kindness. This will be a nice addition to our daily walk."

"Wonderful! Have a good day, then." Colin watched them go. "Well, I hope you're proud of me, Howard. I've become a pacifist just like you!" But when he turned around, Howard was gazing at him sadly. Colin frowned. "What's wrong?"

"You're such a natural with children," Howard said quietly. "Colin, I hope you have really thought things through. I don't want you to have regrets."

"You mean by not having children?"

"Yes."

Colin sighed and stepped closer to Howard. "One can't have everything, can one? I told you in my letter that I'd rather have this than be married." He brightened. "And besides, I've got four nephews, and Adam's children to boot. If I ever want to be around children, I've plenty of options."

Howard nodded. "It's a shame, all the same."

"Hmph. Come along. Let's find another butterfly to 'exercise our humanity' with."

They passed the morning pleasantly. "Do you know," Colin announced happily, "we haven't spent this much time alone since the day you took me to Ellison's!"

"Is that so?" Howard smiled, thinking of their two nights together. "I suppose we haven't. And your company is still as enjoyable."

"Imagine that!" Colin laughed. And so they talked until it was lunchtime. Colin asked Howard to pick a spot, and they sat in the shade of a maple tree. After they had eaten for a bit, Colin asked, "Howard, who was your first?"

"My first? My first love or... the other?"

"They're not one and the same?"

"Well, no. What was the name of that boy you left behind when you came to England?"

"Jeffrey."

"Was he your first love too?"

"Yes. We were each other's first, of both. But I suppose it wasn't the same as what I had with Henry. We were quite green. And scared. And practical." He smiled at Howard. "I'm guessing then, that the love of your life was Luca."

Howard was shocked. "Henry told you about him?"

"Do forgive me, Howard. I asked Henry to tell me more about you... the morning after my first time with you! And it was such a romantic story. I'm so sorry that it went the way it did."

"Oh, no matter. That was so long ago. I can't believe I actually thought things would have worked out, anyway."

"Oh, but he was the one, Howard!"

Howard laughed. "When I look back now, he wasn't anything of the sort. It really wasn't as important as you've been told. I was in a mad crush, that's all." He looked warmly at Colin. "It was nothing like this."

Colin smiled. "I suppose it couldn't be. You knew him for only a month." He looked down shyly. "So then, when was your first experience?"

"Colin, that really isn't a topic for a sunny day in the park."

"Why not? You can't leave everything for when you're drunk or in bed." He laughed. "It's nothing to be ashamed of. *I* ought to know."

But he saw Howard's face darken. "Well, if you don't mind, I'd rather not talk about it. It's a long story."

"Oh." Colin was taken aback. A brief hurt look was on his face, quickly replaced by an expression of nonchalance. "Very well, then. I was just trying to get to know you better, Howard. I suppose that's going to be harder rather than easier at times."

Howard smiled. "Nothing worth having comes easy, don't you think?"

Colin considered this, and then decided, "But being with you is easy."

"Yes, well, getting to this point has been rather difficult."

Colin laughed. "So it has! You're positively Herculean, Howard!"

After lunch, they took a walk through the park. "I can't believe this weather," Howard praised. "However did you find the strength to leave it?"

"I'd forgotten how nice it can be," Colin replied. "Although come August, you won't think it's so lovely." He looked up. "Oh, you won't be here then." He squinted toward the pond. "Howard, how long do you think it will take you to leave England?"

"I don't know. There's the matter of quitting my job, and I may have to stay on a bit to help the new fellow with the transition. I'll have to sell my house and most everything in it. Then I'll have to pack what's left. With some luck, perhaps I can be back by the end of the year."

Colin jerked his head around. "The end of the year! That's six months away!"

"Well, I know. So I was thinking... I know it's not realistic Colin, but I was wondering if you would come back with me, just for that time."

Colin shook his head. "I can't, Howard. I just started working at that office. I couldn't leave for six months!"

"I understand. I'm sorry; I didn't mean to presume you could, but it's going to be hard to leave you."

"No, that's all right. I understand too. I'm just disappointed." Colin stared out ahead of him, trying to think.

"Well, at least we'll have each others' letters to look forward to again," Howard offered cheerfully. Colin shrugged. "And we still have three and a half weeks left!" But Colin looked away. Howard stopped. "Colin, please don't be upset. We'll manage."

Colin stopped too and looked downwards. His voice was strained. "But I... I've become all this fond of you, and now you're going to leave. And then anything might happen once you get back there."

"Such as?"

"You may decide it's not worth the trouble. It'd be easy to just stay there, Howard. I'm not sure you understand what a sacrifice you're offering to make."

"I understand perfectly well. The devil's advocate toured my mind before I got on the ship. I wouldn't have come here if I couldn't leave London for good." He put his hand on Colin's arm. "Colin, I'm quite fond of you, too, remember. And I've nothing back there to be so fond of. The rest of my life is here, next to me." He smiled. "At the risk of using a cliché and being overly romantic, you had my heart from the beginning, and then you took it away with you, so I had to come here to get it. And you'll still have it when I leave, damn you. So I'll have to come back again."

Colin gave a small laugh. "You *are* romantic! All right, I'm sorry. I'm sure I can muster the strength to wait for you if you're promising to come back."

"I am."

"Good. Here, we'll walk back this way." They turned to head back to the entrance to Colin's carriage. As they approached the hotel, Colin gave Howard Kenneth's portion of lunch. "I'll be here at seven sharp for dinner," he reminded him. Howard nodded, and Colin came over to sit by him. He took Howard's hands into his own. "I'm sorry I doubted you. Thank you for setting me straight."

Howard smiled and held Colin's face in his hands. He kissed him deeply, and then drew back. "Thank you for letting the butterflies go, Fearless." The door opened, and Colin caught his breath in time to bid Howard goodbye.

Thursday and Friday Colin spent at the office, working. Both nights, however, he met up with Howard and Kenneth for dinner. And both nights ended the same way: Kenneth would exit their cab and leave his friends alone. Colin and Howard would exchange a few words and then give each other a kiss good night. Kenneth couldn't believe the chastity. "Remember, Kenneth, we're courting," Howard teased.

"Yes, but how much longer do you two plan to keep this up?"

"Well, the opera is tomorrow night. I think we both expect something nice to happen then."

"You're sure he'll be willing?"

"I think so. I know I certainly am, so either way, I'll find out."

Colin, Howard, and Kenneth met up with Adam, Jonathan, and Philip several hours later for a pre-opera dinner at the premium restaurant in town, Delmonico's. The men were served champagne straight away, and Colin raised his glass. "Gentlemen, a toast, if you will. Two, actually." The men held up their glasses. "First, to the six of us. My old friends. My new friends. To all of us being here together. To friendship and to loyalty!"

"Hear, hear!" the men cried, clinking their glasses.

"Second... a certain man at this table—*exceptionally* handsome—mentioned that he fully intended to start depleting his 'incredible amount of wealth' and that this very visit to America would be 'a good start.'" Colin raised his drink to Howard and winked. "To 'a good start.'"

"To a good start!" the men chorused.

Howard met Colin's eyes and smiled. "To an excellent start," he murmured.

As the opera ended and the houselights came on, Colin put his hand on Howard's arm.

"Howard, would you mind if we skipped the Carlisle? I'd rather take a walk."

Howard was pleased. "Not at all. It's a beautiful night." The rest of the group protested their separation, but they winked and grinned until, finally, Colin had to look away, laughing.

They walked for almost an hour amid the city lights and the warm June night, talking and laughing. Finally Howard stopped. "Colin, I have no idea where we are but I have somewhere special I'd like to take you."

"Where?" Colin asked, curious.

"Well, to sound crude, my hotel, but there's a bit more to it than that."

Colin laughed. "Really! Let's get a cab, then."

Before long they were back at the Waldorf-Astoria. But this time, Colin accompanied Howard to the reception desk. "Ah, Mr. Durham!" the clerk said. "I'll fetch the bellhop."

"Thank you," Howard nodded.

"Mr. Durham, follow me, please!"

The three men walked down a hallway and came to a small, gated door. The bellhop said, "Your key, sir?" Howard handed over the key and the bellhop unlocked the door. It was an elevator! Colin beamed at Howard and then quickly regained his nonchalance as they rode to the top, even though he was sure the bellhop was well aware of their intentions. "Penthouse, sir."

"Thank you." Howard tipped him, and he and Colin exited the elevator to enter the room.

Colin watched the elevator glide down its shaft and then turned to Howard. "The penthouse! But you haven't been staying *here* the entire time, have you?"

Howard laughed. "No. I..." he took a deep breath, "I wanted to give you a special evening."

Colin nodded, touched. "*Us*," he corrected. "You wanted to give *us* a special evening." He gazed about. "I've never been in a penthouse before, have you?"

Howard moved toward the bar. "No, I haven't either. Have a look around."

Colin wandered and eventually reached the windows. "Howard! Look at the view!"

Howard approached the window and gave Colin his drink. "Oh!" he exclaimed. "We *are* high up, aren't we?"

Colin pointed to the distance. "Look at the lighthouse over there." He sighed. "I've always thought they were the most intriguing structures, what with the masonry blocks dovetailed into one another to create a profile like a turret, and the invention of the Fresnel lens." Colin's voice grew wistful. "It's extraordinary. I wish I could invent something like that."

Howard regarded Colin's solemn face and said warmly, "You're still so young. You've got all the time in the world."

Colin smiled at Howard. "To spend it with you."

Howard raised his glass. "I'll drink to that."

As they sipped their port, Colin pointed out the various buildings around them. He was identifying the last one he knew when he felt Howard's lips graze his neck. Colin closed his eyes and sighed. "That's nice."

Howard's mouth moved to Colin's ear and then his temple. Colin turned and met Howard's lips with his own. When they drew back, Howard stroked Colin's cheek, suffused with tenderness.

"I love you, Colin. So very much."

Colin could scarcely dare to believe the words. "Really?" he whispered.

Howard kissed him once more and laughed. "Haven't I always?" Then he sighed, holding Colin's head to his chest and murmuring into his hair, "Don't you know what you did to me all those years?" He felt a nod.

"Yes, and I'm so sorry, Howard." Colin pulled back and looked up. "I'm sorry to have tortured you so, because you knew that I loved you, too. I just couldn't... completely."

Howard shook his head. "You were loyal."

Colin smiled. "To the end. But the end came, and so now," he straightened, "I give it all to you, if you'll have it."

"I will. Every ounce. Come along," he beckoned.

Colin faced him. "I can spend the night, then?"

"I locked us in," Howard winked. "You haven't a key."

He put Colin's arms around his neck, and before Colin realized his intentions, Howard scooped him up to head for the bedroom. "Howard!" he protested. "No, I'm heavier since you've last done this! Stop!" But he was laughing, his hand on Howard's chest. Howard stopped and kissed Colin's hand, gazing at his face.

"You're beautiful."

Colin fell silent. He leaned in and kissed Howard deeply. "Let me show you beautiful, Howard."

And they stepped over the threshold once more.

CHAPTER FORTY-FOUR

The slightly humid air lay on Howard's cheek the next morning; it smelled of a hotel room. Howard's eyes opened and he slowly turned on his side. Colin lay facing him, breathing deeply. The bedsheet was draped over most of his body. Still, Howard thrilled at the sight of Colin's bare shoulders and arms, the blond stubble on his cheek, and the rumpled mess of his hair.

I have waited ten years to see what you look like in the morning.

And last night! Howard could scarcely believe it had happened. It was the best night of his entire life, and Colin knew better than to tease when Howard had told him so as they lay together in the dark. Instead he murmured, "Then I shall make it even better." He receded under the sheets, happy to finally share his singular skill with Howard, the skill he had shared with so many less-deserving men before. And this time, he allowed Howard to return the favor, causing them to argue at the end whose experience was better. Then they laughed until they fell asleep.

Howard smiled thinking about it and ran his hand down Colin's side in wonder.

Colin nestled deeper into his pillow and then stirred, opening his eyes. His smile widened. "Good morning, Howard."

"Say that again," Howard whispered.

Colin laughed and nuzzled into Howard's chest. "I'll say it as often as you like. Good morning, Mr. Durham."

"Lift up your head, Fearless."

Colin obeyed and rested in the crook of Howard's arm. He sighed, rubbing his eyes. "Getting to this point *has* been rather difficult."

"I should say so. But it's well worth it."

"Mm."

Howard drank in the warm silence, speaking only after a while. "Colin, do you happen to remember when you said you can't leave everything for when you're drunk and in bed?"

"Yes?"

"Well, I suppose I haven't learnt yet, on the half." He smiled. "How did you decide upon the name 'Colin Edwards'?"

Colin raised his head and slightly sat up. "My God, I've not told you my real name yet, have I?"

Howard gave him a guilty glance. "Well… I'm afraid Henry told me. By accident. I'm so sorry."

Colin sat straight up. "How do you mean, 'by accident'?"

"I was telling him about how you had told me in your letter the story of how you actually came to England, and Henry assumed that you must also have told me your real name. I was impressed that you and he were able to keep it secret so long, and he said, 'Oh, who would have known who Michael Callahan was anyway, in these circles?'"

Colin drew in his breath hearing Howard speak it. "Why didn't you tell me you knew?"

"I didn't want to tell you in a letter. I'm sorry. If it's of any comfort, I was so upset when Henry said your name that I had to leave the club to collect myself, and that was the dead giveaway of how much you meant to me."

Colin bit his lip, then laughed as he lay back down. "You left the club?"

"I'd had the wind knocked out of me with that news!" Howard grew quiet. "So, that is your real name? Michael Callahan?"

Colin shuddered upon hearing it again and buried his head in Howard's chest. "Yes."

"What's the matter?"

"It's just..." Colin pulled his head up and sighed. "I'm sorry that I lost it. Sometimes."

"What do you mean?"

"Well, you can't really get it back, Howard. Once you've changed your name."

"But it's still your legal name, isn't it?"

Colin's tone was resigned. "Not after I took Henry's name. And anyway, I'd never own up to it. It's the name I had when I hid who I was. It's the name my father disinherited."

"But then, why do you miss it?"

"Because it's the name I was baptized with, Howard, you see? And I don't know what I'm to do about that part of things." Howard puzzled over this, and finally Colin said quietly, "You see, I worry sometimes that I won't get into heaven because I'm not living by my baptized name." He blushed. "Sometimes I think my name is the only falsehood left."

They lay in the bed, pondering the matter. Howard sighed. "But you don't want to go back to 'Michael Callahan'?"

"Oh, no, I can't!"

"You're complicated, Fearless."

"So I've heard."

They lay in silence for several moments more. Finally, Howard said gently, "Well, it's a beautiful name and you're right to cherish it. And nobody can really take it from you, Colin; if you have been baptized under it that means you'll always have it. Why, I think your *soul* will always possess it and God will recognize that, even when it is unused."

Colin gazed at Howard. "You're wonderful! You see? You always manage to put things right." He put his head by Howard's chest again. Howard stroked his hair, proud of himself for cheering Colin up. "So Fearless, how *did* you come up with 'Colin Edwards'?"

Colin gave a rueful laugh. "I thought I'd at least do my father the favor of keeping my first name Irish, and I liked the flippant sound of 'Colin'. But I figured in England, I'd do better with an English last name." Then he tilted his head. "Do you know, Henry never asked me how I came up with my name." He sighed. "I suppose that was part of my past too and, ergo, he wanted nothing to do with it." He squeezed Howard's arm. "I'm glad you do. I can't believe all of the things you've listened to me say!"

"Why not?" Howard demanded. "Colin, I told you I'm not like Henry. I want you to talk about your past. I love it! You're so brave to be able to do it."

Colin smiled at him. "You let me be brave."

Howard let his words sink in. Then he said quietly, "Do you remember when you asked about my first time?"

"Yes?"

"Well, I didn't want to tell you because it wasn't a very pleasant experience." He watched Colin's expression change from languid to concerned.

"Howard, why not?"

Howard sighed. "Well... because it occurred when I was fourteen. With my uncle."

Colin bolted upright. "What?"

Howard didn't look at him but stared off into space. "Yes. It was awful."

"But how did that happen?"

Howard's brow furrowed. Then he sighed again and began. "Well, I had grown up with him; he was my father's younger brother. I adored him. He would spend so much time with me. He'd take me to the museums, the theater, the carnival. He lived just two streets away, and he felt more like a big brother than an uncle. At the time, he must have been in his twenties and I was ten. I had only a little brother whom I thought was a pest, and a baby sister, who wasn't much use to me. Uncle Edward figured I didn't get much attention at home, being the oldest, and he was right. So he would only take *me* to all of those places. I overheard my parents joke that I was like a surrogate son for him. I was very proud to hear that. Then, one day, when I was fourteen, I spent the night at his house. I was thrilled! My uncle said we'd have a 'Man's Night'. My parents allowed me, thinking it amusing." Howard couldn't look at Colin, but he continued. "Uncle Ed and I played games, he taught me poker... He poured me a glass of beer and told me to just drink it slowly. But of course, I had to show off and drink it very fast. So he served me another. I grew woozy and giggly. Then my uncle got up and brought back a box. He sat down next to me and opened it. 'Now Howard,' he said, 'you aren't to tell your mum and dad about this, because it's strictly for adults and they still don't consider you one. However, I do.' I remember agreeing fiercely with him. So I peered into the box."

Howard shook his head. "There were dozens of photographs inside. Of nude women and men. They were eroticized, and some of the people were doing obscene acts. As I stared, my uncle put his hand on my leg and said, 'When you're old enough, pictures like these will make you stiff.' Then he took my hand and put it on himself. 'See?' he said, and I quickly withdrew my hand. He laughed. 'It's supposed to do that, so you know you're old enough to lay with a woman and have children.' I believe I said, 'Well, I'm not that old yet.' My uncle smiled and teased me by saying, 'You mean you haven't ever had a stiffie yet, Howard?' 'Of course I have!' I said defiantly. 'But you don't have one now, do you?' he challenged. And unfortunately, I did. I was really quite drunk by now, and the photos hadn't helped at all. I actually giggled about it. I said, 'Yes, I do!' And I fumbled with my trousers and showed him! But you have to remember, my uncle was my best friend, my big brother. I felt perfectly safe with him, even then."

Howard stopped. He was breathing rapidly and had begun to shake. Colin pulled him down next to him and put his hand on Howard's fast-beating heart. "It's all right, Howard. You're all right." He gave him a reassuring kiss, but Howard began to cry.

"I've never told anyone this! I shouldn't go on, Colin. You oughtn't hear it."

Colin himself was trying to stay calm. He'd never heard anything so horrid in his life. *This is what he never told Henry and Kenneth.* He retrieved some handkerchiefs and gave them to Howard. "I think you had better tell me the rest," he urged softly. "It'll do you good to let it out."

Howard swallowed and nodded, collecting himself. "Well, so... there I was, proudly displaying myself." He gave a harsh laugh. "And my uncle whistled. 'Not bad! Have you measured it, then?' And the thought had made me laugh, until he took his out of his trousers and said, 'Well, *I'm* fifteen centimeters. It looks like you're almost the same.' 'Almost?' I said. 'We're a match!' And he laughed and said, 'You may be right... so then, how do you get rid of your stiffie, Howard?' I know I turned red and was extremely flustered. When I didn't answer him, he just sighed and said, 'Howard, your parents are sort of trusting me to help you become a man. So that means even with the awkward things.' God, was I naïve. But how was I to know? I'd talked a bit of that sort of thing with my friends, but Uncle Ed had to be more of the expert. So I just shrugged and said, 'The usual way.' And he asked, 'With your hand?' I mumbled a 'Yes' and then he said, 'Well here: this is the great thing. When men get together like this, we often trade these pictures. And sometimes a fellow gets aroused like you and I are. So he uses the pictures to help him go down.' I was confused by that, and so of course, he decided to demonstrate. I remember him saying 'Now don't take offense. I'm not doing this for my own personal benefit. It's a manly act.' And he took me in his hand and began... working me. He told me to look at the pictures..." Howard's voice became desperate. "Oh God, I'm so ashamed of this! I let him do that, all the way to the end! And I suppose that's bad enough, but then it led to worse things. He told me that I had to do the same to him, because it was only fair, after all. Except he didn't look at the pictures. He said, 'Just let me pretend you're a woman.' And then... while I was doing that to him, he began kissing me and his hands were on me. I should have told him to stop but I was too embarrassed. I worried that he'd tease me and get angry. Call me a baby. It was so repulsive—thank God it lasted just a few minutes. When it was over, I remember him getting up and throwing a handkerchief at me in disgust. I hadn't even realized I was crying! Then he sat back down and apologized and said I should go to bed. I was too frightened to sleep. I felt utterly lost. I remember acting very dull to my parents the next day. My uncle told them that I woke up feeling ill and should be kept quiet. As you can imagine, he told me before we left, 'Now Howard, your parents would hang me if they knew. I thought you were old enough. Please don't tell them anything.' I agreed to it—as if I could speak of such a thing to my parents and, furthermore, that they'd believe it! Besides, I was convinced it was all my fault, what with me drinking the beer and stripping my trousers off.

"The next several times I saw him, it was like old times and I began to relax, thinking that it had just been a misguided ritual. I wanted so badly to have the same friendship with my uncle that I had before. Losing him was unthinkable at the time. Then, one evening we were taking a walk after a picture show, when he brought it up. He said my parents had asked him if he had 'shown me the ways of the world' yet, and he said he hadn't. He said they wanted him to start, that I was old enough to know everything. I remember starting to shake violently, and he admonished me. 'Howard, when you go to university, you'll read about the Greeks. They did this too, you know. An older man shows the younger one what to do, to prepare him for marriage and adult life.' I said, 'What if I don't want to ever marry?' He laughed. 'You have to marry, to have children!' I pointed out that he wasn't married, and he said that he was actually courting a girl and that I'd meet her soon. He said she was wonderful and that women were well worth the odd things we men must do to take them into our lives. He promised me we'd do something different this time, and maybe I'd like it better.

"So..." Howard trailed off. When he found his voice, it was much smaller. "He took me in his mouth. He said it would feel similar to what a woman's privates felt like. Another evening, he lay down on the bed and I had to... do that, because it was similar to when I'd be on top of a woman. And of course, I had to do the same to him, or let him do the same to me, every time. The fact that I always managed to be aroused convinced me that it must be all right and normal, even though it confused me no end. What *was* I to Uncle Ed, after all?

"I began to despise women because I believed that if they didn't exist, I could have just done fun things with Uncle Ed. Now every time we met, we had to 'practice our lessons' first before going anywhere. So I began to hate the art galleries, the museums, the theatre, the zoo. Because they all reminded me of visiting them with him after we had 'practiced'. And how I had to walk or stand around afterwards, sore and feeling sick. The taste of him lingering...

"This went on for perhaps six months. Then it stopped. My uncle got married. But I remember that even on his wedding day, he took me aside and said he was very proud of me but that we may have to 'review' things from time to time because he didn't think I had really grown to enjoy it yet, that I was still 'green'. Can you believe it?"

Colin was gaping. "What happened then?"

"Fortunately, they moved to live near her parents, quite faraway. I didn't care if I never saw him again. I was sent to boarding school shortly after that. As you know, most men like us found this period of their lives to be pure heaven, but not me. I was repelled by all of the boy sex-play there. To me, they were all a bunch of Uncle Eds. So you can imagine my horror when I first fell in love, because of course, it was with another boy! I was at Oxford. I denied it for a while, because I didn't want to be like Uncle Ed. I thought he turned me into what he was. I was terrified and ashamed. To top it off, the boy was 'normal'. I had to finally break off our friendship because I couldn't stand it.

"So I became a banker, and one day I met Kenneth. He was starting to make a name for himself in the theatre, and he needed a loan. We became friends. I liked him a lot—who doesn't like Kenneth? But I was quite a sullen, bitter young man by that time, and Kenneth somehow figured out I was like him. One day, shortly after we had become friends, he asked me if I was heartbroken over a girl. I said no, and he said, 'A fellow, then?' I looked so shocked that he laughed and said, 'Yes, that must be it!' I'm sure if I had acted greatly offended and vigorously denied such a thing, he may have left it. But instead I turned red and said nothing. So Kenneth leaned in and said sympathetically, 'I know what that's like, Durham.' It was all he said, and I just looked at him. 'What do you know about it?' It didn't take long for Kenneth to find out how completely naïve I was, so he decided to take me under his wing and introduce me to his world. I'm sorry to say I didn't embrace it straight away like you did. Not when I saw so many older men with younger ones. But the boys were my age, nineteen or twenty, not fourteen, and they all seemed perfectly happy." Howard paused, smiling. "Just like you were, when you met Henry." He continued. "Nonetheless, I hung back. This was just before Porter's had opened and we were meeting at the homes of various bachelors. Kenneth sensed that I needed time and he was very protective of me. So, everyone was just extremely friendly towards me and I came to see that most of these men were good and honorable. Men who wouldn't do anything of the sort like Uncle Ed. That they really were different from him, and therefore, perhaps I might be, too. What a wonderful relief!

"Then Henry came along and—oh Colin, he never found out, but I actually fell for him at the start! He was so confident and dashing. He dared me one night to go home with a particular boy, although we were boys ourselves at the time. And so I did." Howard exhaled. "Thank God my paramour knew what to do. I was scared half to death when we went to the hotel. He was a few years older, and I wouldn't be surprised if Henry specifically picked him because he was so self-assured and patient and spoke not a word of it afterwards. He remained kind to me to the end. Can you guess who he was?"

Colin knew instantly. "Jack Colton."

"Yes. After that, I was happy for the first time since that first night with Uncle Ed. That had been… eight years of misery!" He turned to Colin. "But you're right—my first love was the one who actually broke my heart. Luca." He looked down and squeezed Colin's arm. "Who would have guessed that the *true* love of my life wouldn't come to me until all these years later?"

He smiled at Colin, who kissed him, and then said sadly, "But you had to suffer yet again for it."

"Never mind that. You're here with me now. It's as if I've finally been rewarded for all of that hell."

"I can't believe you said I was the bravest person you knew, Howard," Colin murmured. "Your story is the most tragic thing I've ever heard." He hugged Howard tightly. "Thank you for telling me. I won't ever leave you, I promise. We'll be strong together."

Howard hugged him back. "Thank you," he whispered, kissing his cheek. "Thank God, and thank you."

Later, when they were at breakfast, Colin looked warmly at Howard, who had been rather quiet, embarrassed by his earlier revelation. "Howard, I was thinking… I wondered if you'd like to move out of the hotel and stay with me for the rest of the time. We could pay for half of Kenneth's room, to be fair."

Howard set down his cup. "You mean, live with you for the next two and a half weeks?"

Colin grinned. "Well, why not? I thought it would be a good way for you to get used to it." He laughed. "You ought to know what you're getting into."

Howard stared. "Are you sure? You'd really want to do that?"

"I'm positive." Colin looked at him affectionately. "We're quite close now after all, aren't we?"

Howard looked into his lap, slightly troubled. "I suppose we are."

"It's wonderful, Howard," Colin insisted. "I want you to wake up with me forever like that! Well, not with tragic stories forever, but next to each other."

Howard laughed. "It was wonderful." He sighed wistfully. "I would love to stay with you."

"Good," Colin smiled. "I'm assuming we'd still have to find an apartment for you eventually, for your 'official residence.'"

Howard tsked. "That seems like such a waste of money. I say, forget the official residence and damn the consequences. If anyone questions us, we'll say I'm renting a room."

"Oh Howard, that's too risky. Who's going to believe that?"

"People believe what they want to believe, and believe me, they'll want to believe that. And I know a little something about risk, being a banker."

"Yes, well people love to gossip, too, and believe me, they'll love to gossip about that."

"Well, we can worry about it later. For now, we can keep my things in your guest bedroom, if that makes you feel better."

"Grand idea."

The next two weeks were rapture, up until the morning of Howard and Kenneth's departure. Howard lay in bed with Colin as long as he could, and then they both rose. When Howard had dressed, Colin peered into the room. "Do you need any help with your packing?"

Howard turned and whistled. "You're giving me quite a sendoff!" Colin was dressed rather extravagantly for standing on a dock. All the same, he had bought the suit just for the occasion. It was of ivory linen, and he wore it with a grey silk vest embroidered with ivory thread. A grey ascot was at his neck, and grey pearl cufflinks finished him out. Suddenly,

Howard's jaw dropped. "You've shaved your beard!" He walked toward Colin. "Why?"

Colin bit his lip and looked at the floor. "I... I don't know." His voice was anguished, his eyes confused.

Howard smiled. "Colin, you silly boy." He kissed Colin's cheek. Then he traced his finger on a line. "You've a scar," he said softly.

"I've a few," Colin replied, morose. "Damned glass."

Howard tenderly examined him, and then declared, "You look lovely. I love you any way you look. Which isn't saying much, since you always look lovely."

"But now I won't even match the picture we had taken of us!"

"Now I'll have two pictures in my head to remember you by," Howard quipped. "Two out of hundreds."

"I'll grow it back if you like."

"Colin." Howard was firm. "Sit down." Colin obeyed, and Howard smiled. "Now, you haven't ever mentioned your birthday present. Have you forgotten about it?"

Colin blushed. "No. But I can't very well ask for my own present."

"Well, no matter. I wouldn't have given it to you until now, anyway."

"Howard!"

Howard grinned. Then he took a small box from inside his coat pocket. Colin smiled at it, and then the color drained from his face.

Howard was down before him on bended knee. In the box was a ring. "Colin, ever since those horrendous, dark days of my childhood, all I have ever wanted was a happy ending. When I heard you say it was your goal in life, I knew that you could be the one to grant it." He beamed. "And here we are! I can't believe you're finally mine! And I want you to know I will love you forever." He looked at the ring. "I know you've always cherished the idea of marriage, too. Well, I don't see why I can't marry you, even if it's in secret. So, Michael Callahan-Colin Sewell... will you be only mine, for the rest of my days on earth?"

Colin looked at Howard, speechless. The words sounded authentic enough, and Howard's expression of joy mixed with nervousness made the moment seem very real indeed. And now Howard took the ring from its case and gently picked up Colin's right hand, smiling. "This way nobody will ask." He checked Colin's face and, seeing that it was euphoric, slid the ring onto Colin's third finger. Colin clasped his hands and gazed at the platinum wedding band. It was intricately carved on the sides and inlaid with a large diamond flanked by sapphires. Howard regarded the two blue stones. "The color of forever," he smiled.

Tears sprang in Colin's eyes. He nodded his head and looked at Howard in apology. "Thank you for saving me from the fire, Howard. I owe my life... I owe this very moment, to you. I love you."

Howard stood and tightly embraced Colin. "I could have never let you do it, Colin. I couldn't."

Colin kissed Howard and regarded him determinedly. "Then I promise you this: There will be a happy ending, Howard. And it will be us."

EPILOGUE

On December 3rd of that year, Colin stood on the dock in New York once more. Although it was a bright, sunny day, he had his black wool coat buttoned to the top and its tawny mink collar turned up. He held onto his hat with a calfskin-gloved hand, peering excitedly at the ship in the distance. A woman stood nearby, with her husband and fifteen-year old son. She noticed the anxious, well-dressed man beside her and said in a friendly tone, "You must be waiting for someone very special."

Colin smiled at her and nodded. "Yes." He looked off toward the sea again. "I am."

"Oh! How nice," the lady responded pleasantly. But the young man said no more. In time, the ship docked, and the woman lost sight of Colin in the crowd. She saw him a half hour later.

He was embracing a man... an older man. *His father?* And then the older man held the young man's face in his hands, looking at him tenderly. He spoke to him, and the young man blushed. She watched as the older man took the younger man's glove off his right hand. They were gazing at... at a ring. She could see its flash from here. The older man raised the young man's hand up and kissed the ring. And the look between them was clearly not one exchanged between father and son.

The woman gaped, but her arm was suddenly jerked away. "This way, Nance! I see your sister!" Her husband dragged her off, but not before she noticed her son gawking at the men as well. She gripped his elbow.

"Come along, Thomas!"

Thomas stared as he was being led away, until the crowd closed behind him and he could see the two men no more. When he finally turned forward, his shocked expression changed. In its place was one of elation. In fact, one could almost call it... triumphant.